WINTERLANDS

By Barbara Hambly

The Darwath Trilogy
THE TIME OF THE DARK
THE WALLS OF AIR
THE ARMIES OF DAYLIGHT

MOTHER OF WINTER
ICEFALCON'S QUEST

Sun Wolf and Starhawk
THE LADIES OF MANDRIGYN
THE WITCHES OF WENSHAR
THE DARK HAND OF MAGIC

The Windrose Chronicles
THE SILENT TOWER
THE SILICON MAGE
DOG WIZARD

STRANGER AT THE WEDDING

Sun-Cross
RAINBOW ABYSS
THE MAGICIANS OF NIGHT

THOSE WHO HUNT THE NIGHT
TRAVELING WITH THE DEAD

SEARCH THE SEVEN HILLS

BRIDE OF THE RAT GOD

DRAGONSBANE

DRAGONSHADOW

THE MINES OF TRALCHET

R. ELVE

FAR WEST RIDING

FROST FELL

ALYN HOLT

ELDSBOUGH

GREATER TODY

THE WINTERLANDS

LANDS OF THE KEDRIDERS

MOUNTAINS

LAKE OF WEIR

DEEP OF WYLDOOM

WOODS OF

EMBER

MIRKHANDS

BARK

NAST WOOD

EASTERN PLAINS

WINDRACHET

WILDSPAE

CITADEL OF HALNATH

DEEP OF YLFERDUN

BELMARIE

BEL

GREENHYTHE

the REALM of the KING

SHELLY SHAPIRO

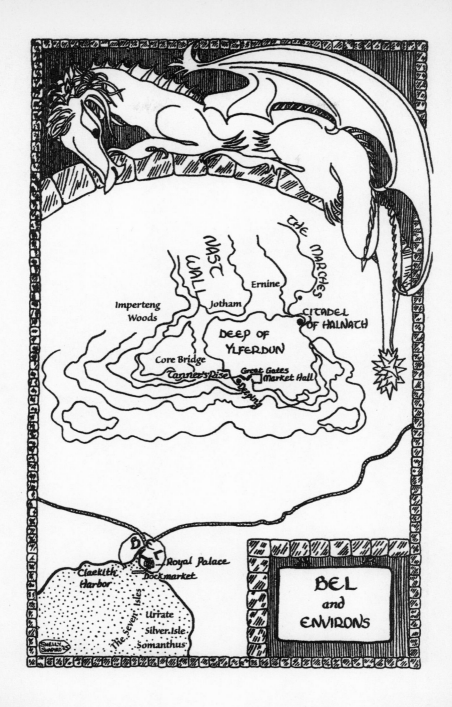

THE MARCHES

NAST WALL

Ernine

Jotham

Imperteng
Woods

CITADEL
OF HALNATH

DEEP OF
YLFERDUN

Core Bridge

Tanner's Rise

Great Gates
Market Hall

Shipping

BEL

Royal Palace

Claekith
Harbor

Dockmarket

The Seven Isles

Urrate

Silver Isle

Somanthus

SHELLY SHAPIRO '15

BEL
and
ENVIRONS

WINTERLANDS

Dragonsbane
Dragonshadow

BARBARA HAMBLY

FANTASY

Published by arrangement with
Del Rey Books
a Division of Random House, Inc.
201 East 50th Street
New York, NY 10022

Visit our website at www.sfbc.com
Visit Del Rey's website at www.randomhouse.com/delrey/

First Science Fiction Book Club printing April 1999

ISBN 0-7394-0278-1

PRINTED IN THE UNITED STATES OF AMERICA

Contents

Dragonsbane

For Allan

1

Bandits often lay in wait in the ruins of the old town at the four-ways—Jenny Waynest thought there were three of them this morning.

She was not sure any more whether it was magic which told her this, or simply the woodcraftiness and instinct for the presence of danger that anyone developed who had survived to adulthood in the Winterlands. But as she drew rein short of the first broken walls, where she knew she would still be concealed by the combination of autumn fog and early morning gloom beneath the thicker trees of the forest, she noted automatically that the horse droppings in the sunken clay of the roadbed were fresh, untouched by the frost that edged the leaves around them. She noted, too, the silence in the ruins ahead; no coney's foot rustled the yellow spill of broomsedge cloaking the hill slope where the old church had been, the church sacred to the Twelve Gods beloved of the old Kings. She thought she smelled the smoke of a concealed fire near the remains of what had been a crossroads inn, but honest men would have gone there straight and left a track in the nets of dew that covered the weeds all around. Jenny's white mare Moon Horse pricked her long ears at the scent of other beasts, and Jenny wind-whispered to her for silence, smoothing the raggedy mane against the long neck. But she had been looking for all those signs before she saw them.

She settled into stillness in the protective cloak of fog and shadow, like a partridge blending with the brown of the woods. She was a little like a partridge herself, dark and small and nearly invisible in the dull, random plaids of the northlands; a thin, compactly built woman, tough as the roots of moorland heather. After a moment of silence, she wove her magic into a rope of mist and cast it along the road toward the nameless ruins of the town.

It was something she had done even as a child, before the old wander-mage Caerdinn had taught her the ways of power. All her thirty-seven
years, she had lived in the Winterlands—she knew the smells of danger.
The late-lingering birds of autumn, thrushes and blackbirds, should have
been waking in the twisted brown mats of ivy that half-hid the old inn's
walls—they were silent. After a moment, she caught the scent of horses,
and the ranker, dirtier stench of men.

One bandit would be in the stumpy ruin of the old tower that commanded the south and eastward roads, part of the defenses of the ruined
town left from when the prosperity of the King's law had given it anything to defend. They always hid there. A second, she guessed, was
behind the walls of the old inn. After a moment she sensed the third,
watching the crossroads from a yellow thicket of seedy tamarack. Her
magic brought the stink of their souls to her, old greeds and the carrion-
bone memories of some cherished rape or murder that had given a
momentary glow of power to lives largely divided between the giving and
receiving of physical pain. Having lived all her life in the Winterlands,
she knew that these men could scarcely help being what they were; she
had to put aside both her hatred of them, and her pity for them, before she
could braid the spells that she laid upon their minds.

Her concentration deepened further. She stirred judiciously at that
compost of memories, whispering to their blunted minds of the bored
sleepiness of men who have watched too long. Unless every illusion and
Limitation was wrought correctly, they would see her when she moved.
Then she loosened her halberd in its holster upon her saddle-tree, settled
her sheepskin jacket a little more closely about her shoulders and, with
scarcely breath or movement, urged Moon Horse forward toward the
ruins.

The man in the tower she never saw at all, from first to last. Through
the browning red leaves of a screen of hawthorn, she glimpsed two horses
tethered behind a ruined wall near the inn, their breath making plumes of
white in the dawn cold; a moment later she saw the bandit crouching
behind the crumbling wall, a husky man in greasy old leathers. He had
been watching the road, but started suddenly and cursed; looking down,
he began scratching his crotch with vigor and annoyance but no particular surprise. He did not see Jenny as she ghosted past. The third bandit,
sitting his rawboned black horse between a broken corner of a wall and a
spinney of raggedy birches, simply stared out ahead of him, lost in the
daydreams she had sent.

She was directly in front of him when a boy's voice shouted from
down the southward road, "LOOK OUT!"

Jenny whipped her halberd clear of its rest as the bandit woke with a start. He saw her and roared a curse. Peripherally Jenny was aware of hooves pounding up the road toward her; the other traveler, she thought with grim annoyance, whose well-meant warning had snapped the man from his trance. As the bandit bore down upon her, she got a glimpse of a young man riding out of the mist full-pelt, clearly intent upon rescue.

The bandit was armed with a short sword, but swung at her with the flat of it, intending to unhorse her without damaging her too badly to rape later. She feinted with the halberd to bring his weapon up, then dipped the long blade on the pole's end down under his guard. Her legs clinched to Moon Horse's sides to take the shock as the weapon knifed through the man's belly. The leather was tough, but there was no metal underneath. She ripped the blade clear as the man doubled up around it, screaming and clawing; both horses danced and veered with the smell of the hot, spraying blood. Before the man hit the muddy bed of the road, Jenny had wheeled her horse and was riding to the aid of her prospective knight-errant, who was engaged in a sloppy, desperate battle with the bandit who had been concealed behind the ruined outer wall.

Her rescuer was hampered by his long cloak of ruby red velvet, which had got entangled with the basketwork hilt of his jeweled longsword. His horse was evidently better trained and more used to battle than he was: the maneuverings of the big liver-bay gelding were the only reason the boy hadn't been killed outright. The bandit, who had gotten himself mounted at the boy's first cry of warning, had driven them back into the hazel thickets that grew along the tumbled stones of the inn wall, and, as Jenny kicked Moon Horse into the fray, the boy's trailing cloak hung itself up on the low branches and jerked its wearer ignominiously out of the saddle with the horse's next swerve.

Using her right hand as the fulcrum of a swing, Jenny swept the halberd's blade at the bandit's sword arm. The man veered his horse to face her; she got a glimpse of piggy, close-set eyes under the rim of a dirty iron cap. Behind her she could hear her previous assailant still screaming. Evidently her current opponent could as well, for he ducked the first slash and swiped at Moon Horse's face to cause the mare to shy, then spurred past Jenny and away up the road, willing neither to face a weapon that so outreached his own, nor to stop for his comrade who had done so.

There was a brief crashing in the thickets of briar as the man who had been concealed in the tower fled into the raw mists, then silence, save for the dying bandit's hoarse, bubbling sobs.

Jenny dropped lightly from Moon Horse's back. Her young rescuer was still thrashing in the bushes like a stoat in a sack, half-strangled on his bejeweled cloak strap. She used the hook on the back of the halberd's blade to twist the long court-sword from his hand, then stepped in to pull the muffling folds of velvet aside. He struck at her with his hands, like a man swatting at wasps. Then he seemed to see her for the first time and stopped, staring up at her with wide, myopic gray eyes.

After a long moment of surprised stillness, he cleared his throat and unfastened the chain of gold and rubies that held the cloak under his chin. "Er—thank you, my lady," he gasped in a slightly winded voice, and got to his feet. Though Jenny was used to people being taller than she, this young man was even more so than most. "I—uh—" His skin was as fine-textured and fair as his hair, which was already, despite his youth, beginning to thin away toward early baldness. He couldn't have been more than eighteen, with a natural awkwardness increased tenfold by the difficult task of thanking the intended object of a gallant defense for saving his life.

"My profoundest gratitude," he said, and performed a supremely graceful Dying Swan, the like of which had not been seen in the Winterlands since the nobles of the Kings had departed in the wake of the retreating royal armies. "I am Gareth of Magloshaldon, a traveler upon errantry in these lands, and I wish to extend my humblest expressions of . . ."

Jenny shook her head and stilled him with an upraised hand. "Wait here," she said, and turned away.

Puzzled, the boy followed her.

The first bandit who had attacked her still lay in the clay muck of the roadbed. The soaking blood had turned it into a mess of heel gouges, strewn with severed entrails; the stink was appalling. The man was still groaning weakly. Against the matte pallor of the foggy morning, the scarlet of the blood stood out shockingly bright.

Jenny sighed, feeling suddenly cold and weary and unclean, looking upon what she had done and knowing what it was up to her yet to do. She knelt beside the dying man, drawing the stillness of her magic around her again. She was aware of Gareth's approach, his boots threshing through the dew-soaked bindweed in a hurried rhythm that broke when he tripped on his sword. She felt a tired stirring of anger at him for having made this necessary. Had he not cried out, both she and this poor, vicious, dying brute would each have gone their ways . . .

. . . And he would doubtless have killed Gareth after she passed. And other travelers besides.

She had long since given up trying to unpick wrong from right, present *should* from future *if*. If there was a pattern to all things, she had given up thinking that it was simple enough to lie within her comprehension. Still, her soul felt filthy within her as she put her hands to the dying man's clammy, greasy temples, tracing the proper runes while she whispered the death-spells. She felt the life go out of him and tasted the bile of self-loathing in her mouth.

Behind her, Gareth whispered, "You—he's—he's dead."

She got to her feet, shaking the bloody dirt from her skirts. "I could not leave him for the weasels and foxes," she replied, starting to walk away. She could hear the small carrion-beasts already, gathering at the top of the bank above the misty slot of the road, drawn to the blood-smell and waiting impatiently for the killer to abandon her prey. Her voice was brusque—she had always hated the death-spells. Having grown up in a land without law, she had killed her first man when she was fourteen, and six since, not counting the dying she had helped from life as the only midwife and healer from the Gray Mountains to the sea. It never got easier.

She wanted to be gone from the place, but the boy Gareth put a staying hand on her arm, looking from her to the corpse in a kind of nauseated fascination. He had never seen death, she thought. At least, not in its raw form. The pea green velvet of his travel-stained doublet, the gold stampwork of his boots, the tucked embroidery of his ruffled lawn shirt, and the elaborate, feathered crestings of his green-tipped hair all proclaimed him for a courtier. All things, even death, were doubtless done with a certain amount of style where he came from.

He gulped. "You're—you're a witch!"

One corner of her mouth moved slightly; she said, "So I am."

He stepped back from her in fear, then staggered, clutching at a nearby sapling for support. She saw then that among the decorative slashings of his doublet sleeve was an uglier opening, the shirt visible through it dark and wet. "I'll be fine," he protested faintly, as she moved to support him. "I just need . . ." He made a fumbling effort to shake free of her hand and walk, his myopic gray eyes peering at the ankle-deep drifts of moldering leaves that lined the road.

"What you need is to sit down." She led him away to a broken boundary stone and forced him to do so and unbuttoned the diamond studs that held the sleeve to the body of the doublet. The wound did not look deep, but it was bleeding badly. She pulled loose the leather thongs that bound the wood-black knots of her hair and used them as a tourniquet above the wound. He winced and gasped and tried to loosen it as she tore a strip from the hem of her shift for a bandage, so that she slapped at his fingers like a child's. Then, a moment later, he tried to get up again. "I have to find . . ."

"I'll find them," Jenny said firmly, knowing what it was that he sought. She finished binding his wound and walked back to the tangle of

hazel bushes where Gareth and the bandit had struggled. The frosty daylight glinted on a sharp reflection among the leaves. The spectacles she
found there were bent and twisted out of shape, the bottom of one round
lens decorated by a star-fracture. Flicking the dirt and wetness from them,
she carried them back.

"Now," she said, as Gareth fumbled them on with hands shaking from
weakness and shock. "You need that arm looked to. I can take you . . ."

"My lady, I've no time." He looked up at her, squinting a little against
the increasing brightness of the sky behind her head. "I'm on a quest, a
quest of terrible importance."

"Important enough to risk losing your arm if the wound turns rot-
ten?"

As if such things could not happen to him, did she only have the wits
to realize it, he went on earnestly, "I'll be all right, I tell you. I am seeking Lord Aversin the Dragonsbane, Thane of Alyn Hold and Lord of Wyr,
the greatest knight ever to have ridden the Winterlands. Have you heard
of him hereabouts? Tall as an angel, handsome as song . . . His fame has
spread through the southlands the way the floodwaters spread in the
spring, the noblest of chevaliers . . . I must find Alyn Hold, before it is too
late."

Jenny sighed, exasperated. "So you must," she said. "It is to Alyn
Hold that I am going to take you."

The squinting eyes got round as the boy's mouth fell open. "To—to
Alyn Hold? Really? It's near here?"

"It's the nearest place where we can get your arm seen to," she said.
"Can you ride?"

Had he been dying, she thought, amused, he would still have sprung
to his feet as he did. "Yes, of course. I—do you know Lord Aversin,
then?"

Jenny was silent for a moment. Then, softly, she said, "Yes. Yes, I
know him."

She whistled up the horses, the tall white Moon Horse and the big
liver-bay gelding, whose name, Gareth said, was Battlehammer. In spite of
his exhaustion and the pain of his roughly bound wound, Gareth made a
move to offer her totally unnecessary assistance in mounting. As they
reined up over the ragged stone slopes to avoid the corpse in its rank-
smelling puddles of mud, Gareth asked, "If—if you're a witch, my lady,
why couldn't you have fought them with magic instead of with a weapon?
Thrown fire at them, or turned them into frogs, or struck them blind . . ."

She had struck them blind, in a sense, she thought wryly—at least
until he shouted.

But she only said, "Because I cannot."

"For reasons of honor?" he asked dubiously. "Because there are some situations in which honor cannot apply . . ."

"No." She glanced sidelong at him through the astonishing curtains of her loosened hair. "It is just that my magic is not that strong."

And she nudged her horse into a quicker walk, passing into the vaporous shadows of the forest's bare, over-hanging boughs.

Even after all these years of knowing it, she found the admission still stuck in her throat. She had come to terms with her lack of beauty, but never with her lack of genius in the single thing she had ever wanted. The most she had ever been able to do was to pretend that she accepted it, as she pretended now.

Ground fog curled around the feet of the horses; through the clammy vapors, tree roots thrust from the roadbanks like the arms of half-buried corpses. The air here felt dense and smelled of mold, and now and then, from the woods above them, came the furtive crackle of dead leaves, as if the trees plotted among themselves in the fog.

"Did you—did you see him slay the dragon?" Gareth asked, after they had ridden in silence for some minutes. "Would you tell me about it? Aversin is the only living Dragonsbane—the only man who has slain a dragon. There are ballads about him everywhere, about his courage and his noble deeds . . . That's my hobby. Ballads, I mean, the ballads of Dragonsbanes, like Selkythar the White back in the reign of Ennyta the Good and Antara Warlady and her brother, during the Kinwars. They say her brother slew . . ." By the way he caught himself up Jenny guessed he could have gone on about the great Dragonsbanes of the past for hours, only someone had told him not to bore people with the subject. "I've always wanted to see such a thing—a true Dragonsbane—a glorious combat. His renown must cover him like a golden mantle."

And, rather to her surprise, he broke into a light, wavery tenor:

> Riding up the hillside gleaming,
> Like flame in the golden sunlight streaming;
> Sword of steel strong in hand,
> Wind-swift hooves spurning land,
> Tall as an angel, stallion-strong,
> Stern as a god, bright as song . . .
>
> In the dragon's shadow the maidens wept,
> Fair as lilies in darkness kept.
> 'I know him afar, so tall is he,
> His plumes as bright as the rage of the sea,'
> Spake she to her sister, 'fear no ill . . .'

Jenny looked away, feeling something twist inside inside her at the memory of the Golden Dragon of Wyr.

She remembered as if it were yesterday instead of ten years ago the high-up flash of gold in the wan northern sky, the plunge of fire and shadow, the boys and girls screaming on the dancing floor at Great Toby. They were memories she knew should have been tinted only with horror; she was aware that she should have felt only gladness at the dragon's death. But stronger than the horror, the taste of nameless grief and desolation came back to her from those times, with the metallic stench of the dragon's blood and the singing that seemed to shiver the searing air . . .

Her heart felt sick within her. Coolly, she said, "For one thing, of the two children who were taken by the dragon, John only managed to get the boy out alive. I think the girl had been killed by the fumes in the dragon's lair. It was hard to tell from the state of the body. And if she hadn't been dead, I still doubt they'd have been in much condition to make speeches about how John looked, even if he had come riding straight up the hill— which of course he didn't."

"He didn't?" She could almost hear the shattering of some image, nursed in the boy's mind.

"Of course not. If he had, he would have been killed immediately."

"Then how . . ."

"The only way he could think of to deal with something that big and that heavily armored. He had me brew the most powerful poison that I knew of, and he dipped his harpoons in that."

"*Poison?*" Such foulness clearly pierced him to the heart. "*Harpoons?* Not a sword at all?"

Jenny shook her head, not knowing whether to feel amusement at the boy's disappointed expression, exasperation at the way he spoke of what had been for her and hundreds of others a time of sleepless, nightmare horror, or only a kind of elder-sisterly compassion for the naïveté that would consider taking a three-foot steel blade against twenty-five feet of spiked and flaming death. "No," she only said, "John came at it from the overhang of the gully in which it was laired—it wasn't a cave, by the way; there are no caves that large in these hills. He slashed its wings first, so that it couldn't take to the air and fall on him from above. He used poisoned harpoons to slow it down, but he finished it off with an ax."

"An *ax*?!" Gareth cried, utterly aghast. "That's—that's the most horrible thing I've ever heard! Where is the glory in that? Where is the honor? It's like hamstringing your opponent in a duel! It's cheating!"

"He wasn't fighting a duel," Jenny pointed out. "If a dragon gets into the air, the man fighting it is lost."

"But it's dishonorable!" the boy insisted passionately, as if that were some kind of clinching argument.

"It might have been, had he been fighting a man who had honorably challenged him—something John has never been known to do in his life. Even fighting bandits, it pays to strike from behind when one is outnumbered. As the only representative of the King's law in these lands, John generally *is* outnumbered. A dragon is upward of twenty feet long and can kill a man with a single blow of its tail. You said yourself," she added with a smile, "that there are situations in which honor does not apply."

"But that's different!" the boy said miserably and lapsed into disillusioned silence.

The ground beneath the horses' feet was rising; the vague walls of the misty tunnel through which they rode were ending. Beyond, the silvery shapes of the round-backed hills could be dimly seen. As they came clear of the trees, the winds fell upon them, clearing the mists and nipping their clothes and faces like ill-trained dogs. Shaking the blowing handfuls of her hair out of her eyes, Jenny got a look at Gareth's face as he gazed about him at the moors. It wore a look of shock, disappointment, and puzzlement, as if he had never thought to find his hero in this bleak and trackless world of moss, water, and stone.

As for Jenny, this barren world stirred her strangely. The moors stretched nearly a hundred miles, north to the ice-locked shores of the ocean; she knew every break in the granite landscape, every black peat-beck and every hollow where the heather grew thick in the short highlands summers; she had traced the tracks of hare and fox and kitmouse in three decades of winter snows. Old Caerdinn, half-mad through poring over books and legends of the days of the Kings, could remember the time when the Kings had withdrawn their troops and their protection from the Winterlands to fight the wars for the lordship of the south; he had grown angry with her when she had spoken of the beauty she found in those wild, silvery fastnesses of rock and wind. But sometimes his bitterness stirred in Jenny, when she worked to save the life of an ailing village child whose illness lay beyond her small skills and there was nothing in any book she had read that might tell her how to save that life; or when the Iceriders came raiding down over the floe-ice in the brutal winters, burning the barns that cost such labor to raise, and slaughtering the cattle that could only be bred up from such meager stock. However, her own lack of power had taught her a curious appreciation for small joys and hard beauties and for the simple, changeless patterns of life and death. It was nothing she could have explained; not to Caerdinn, nor to this boy, nor to anyone else.

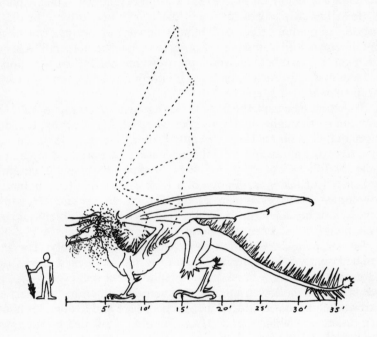

Scale and Structure of a Dragon
(From John Aversin's notes)

1) Mane structure and spikes at joints are thicker than shown. A bone "shield" extends from the back of the skull beneath the mane to protect the nape of the neck.
2) Golden Dragon of Wyr measured approx. 27' of which 12' was tail; there are rumors of dragons longer than 50'.

At length she said softly, "John would never have gone after the dragon, Gareth, had he not been forced to it. But as Thane of Alyn Hold, as Lord of Wyr, he is the only man in the Winterlands trained to and living by the arts of war. It is for this that he is the lord. He fought the dragon as he would have fought a wolf, as a vermin which was harming his people. He had no choice."

"But a dragon isn't vermin!" Gareth protested. "It is the most honorable and greatest of challenges to the manhood of a true knight. You must be wrong! He *couldn't* have fought it simply—simply out of *duty*. He *can't* have!"

There was a desperation to believe in his voice that made Jenny glance over at him curiously. "No," she agreed. "A dragon isn't vermin. And this one was truly beautiful." Her voice softened at the recollection, even through the horror-haze of death and fear, of its angular, alien splendor. "Not golden, as your song calls it, but a sort of amber, grading to brownish smoke along its back and ivory upon its belly. The patterns of the scales on its sides were like the beadwork on a pair of slippers, like woven irises, all shades of purple and blue. Its head was like a flower, too; its eyes and maw were surrounded with scales like colored ribbons, with purple horns and tufts of white and black fur, and with antennae like a crayfish's tipped with bobs of gems. It was butcher's work to slay it."

They rounded the shoulder of a tor. Below them, like a break in the cold granite landscape, spread a broken line of brown fields where the mists lay like stringers of dirty wool among the stubble of harvest. A little further along the track lay a hamlet, disordered and trashy under a bluish smear of woodsmoke, and the stench of the place rose on the whipping ice-winds: the lye-sting of soap being boiled; an almost-visible murk of human and animal waste; the rotted, nauseating sweetness of brewing beer. The barking of dogs rose to them like churchbells in the air. In the midst of it all a stumpy tower stood, the tumble-down remnant of some larger fortification.

"No," said Jenny softly, "the dragon was a beautiful creature, Gareth. But so was the girl it carried away to its lair and killed. She was fifteen— John wouldn't let her parents see the remains."

She touched her heels to Moon Horse's sides and led the way down the damp clay of the track.

"Is this village where you live?" Gareth asked, as they drew near the walls.

Jenny shook her head, drawing her mind back from the bitter and confusing tangle of the memories of the slaying of the dragon. "I have my own house about six miles from here, on Frost Fell—I live there alone.

My magic is not great; it needs silence and solitude for its study." She added wryly, "Though I don't have much of either. I am midwife and healer for all of Lord Aversin's lands."

"Will—will we reach his lands soon?"

His voice sounded unsteady, and Jenny, regarding him worriedly, saw how white he looked and how, in spite of the cold, sweat ran down his hollow cheeks with their faint fuzz of gold. A little surprised at his question, she said, "These are Lord Aversin's lands."

He raised his head to look at her, shocked. *"These?"* He stared around him at the muddy fields, the peasants shouting to one another as they shocked up the last of the corn, the ice-scummed waters of the moat that girdled the rubble fill and fieldstone patches of the shabby wall. "Then—that is one of Lord Aversin's villages?"

"That," Jenny said matter-of-factly as the hooves of their horses rumbled hollowly on the wood of the drawbridge, "is Alyn Hold."

The town huddled within the curtain wall—a wall built by the present lord's grandfather, old James Standfast, as a temporary measure and now hoary with fifty winters—was squalid beyond description. Through the archway beneath the squat gatehouse untidy houses were visible, clustered around the wall of the Hold itself as if the larger building had seeded them, low-built of stone and rubble upon the foundations of older walls, thatched with river reed-straw and grubby with age. From the window-turret of the gatehouse old Peg the gatekeeper stuck her head out, her long, gray-streaked brown braids hanging down like bights of half-unraveled rope, and she called out to Jenny, "You're in luck," in the glottal lilt of the north-country speech. "Me lord got in last night from ridin' the bounds. He'll be about."

"She wasn't—was she talking about *Lord Aversin*?" Gareth whispered, scandalized.

Jenny's crescent-shaped eyebrows quirked upward. "He's the only lord we have."

"Oh." He blinked, making another mental readjustment. " 'Riding the bounds'?"

"The bounds of his lands. He patrols them, most days of the month, he and militia volunteers." Seeing Gareth's face fall, she added gently, "That is what it is to be a lord."

"It isn't, you know," Gareth said. "It is chivalry, and honor, and . . ." But she had already ridden past him, out of the slaty darkness of the gatehouse passage and into the heatless sunlight of the square.

With all its noise and gossipy squalor, Jenny had always liked the village of Alyn. It had been the home of her childhood; the stone cottage in which she had been born and in which her sister and brother-in-law still lived—though her sister's husband discouraged mention of the relationship—still stood down the lane, against the curtain wall. They might regard her with awe, these hard-working people with their small lives circumscribed by the work of the seasons, but she knew their lives only a little less intimately than she knew her own. There was not a house in the village where she had not delivered a child, or tended the sick, or fought death in one of the myriad forms that it took in the Winterlands; she was familiar with them, and with the long-spun, intricate patterns of their griefs and joys. As the horses sloshed through mud and standing water to the center of the square, she saw Gareth looking about him with carefully concealed dismay at the pigs and chickens that shared the fetid lanes so amicably with flocks of shrieking children. A gust of wind blew the smoke of the forge over them, and with it a faint wash of heat and a snatch of Muffle the smith's bawdy song; in one lane laundry flapped, and in another, Deshy Werville, whose baby Jenny had delivered three months ago, was milking one of her beloved cows half-in, half-out of her cottage door. Jenny saw how Gareth's disapproving gaze lingered upon the shabby Temple, with its lumpish, crudely carved images of the Twelve Gods, barely distinguishable from one another in the gloom, and then went to the circled cross of Earth and Sky that was wrought into the stones of so many village chimneys. His back got a little stiffer at this evidence of paganism, and his upper lip appeared to lengthen as he regarded the pigpen built out from the Temple's side and the pair of yokels in scruffy leather and plaids who leaned against the railings, gossiping.

"Course, pigs see the weather," one of them was saying, reaching with a stick across the low palings to scratch the back of the enormous black sow who reposed within. "That's in Clivy's *On Farming*, but I've seen them do it. And they're gie clever, cleverer than dogs. My aunt Mary—you remember Aunt Mary?—used to train them as piglets and she had one, a white one, who'd fetch her shoes for her."

"Aye?" the second yokel said, scratching his head as Jenny drew rein near them, with Gareth fidgeting impatiently at her side.

"Aye." The taller man made kissing sounds to the sow, who raised her head in response with a slurping grunt of deepest affection. "It says in Polyborus' *Analects* that the Old Cults used to worship the pig, and not as a devil, either, as Father Hiero would have it, but as the Moon Goddess." He pushed his steel-rimmed spectacles a little higher on the bridge of his long nose, a curiously professorial gesture for a man ankle-deep in pig-muck.

"That a fact, now?" the second yokel said with interest. "Now you come to speak on it, this old girl—when she were young and flighty, that is—had it figured to a *T* how to get the pen gate open, and would be after . . . Oh!" He bowed hastily, seeing Jenny and the fuming Gareth sitting their horses quietly.

The taller of the two men turned. As the brown eyes behind the thick spectacle lenses met Jenny's, they lost their habitual guarded expression and melted abruptly into an impish brightness. Middle-sized, unprepossessing, shaggy and unshaven in his scruffy dark leather clothing, his old wolfskin doublet patched with bits of metal and scraps of chain mail to protect his joints—after ten years, she wondered, what was there about him that still filled her with such absurd joy?

"Jen." He smiled and held out his hands to her.

Taking them, she slid from the white mare's saddle into his arms, while Gareth looked on in disapproving impatience to get on with his quest. "John," she said, and turned back to the boy. "Gareth of Magloshaldon—this is Lord John Aversin, the Dragonsbane of Alyn Hold."

For one instant, Gareth was shocked absolutely speechless. He sat for a moment, staring, stunned as if struck over the head; then he dismounted so hastily that he clutched his hurt arm with a gasp. It was as if, Jenny thought, in all his ballad-fed fantasies of meeting the Dragonsbane, it had never occurred to him that his hero would be afoot, not to say ankle-deep in mud beside the local pigsty. In his face was plain evidence that, though he himself was over six-foot-three, and must be taller than anyone else he knew, he had never connected this with the fact that, unless his hero was a giant, he would perforce be shorter also. Neither, she supposed, had any ballad mentioned spectacles.

Still Gareth had not spoken. Aversin, interpreting his silence and the look on his face with his usual fiendish accuracy, said, "I'd show you my dragon-slaying scars to prove it, but they're placed where I can't exhibit 'em in public."

It said worlds for Gareth's courtly breeding—and, Jenny supposed, the peculiar stoicism of courtiers—that, even laboring under the shock of his life and the pain of a wounded arm, he swept into a very creditable salaam of greeting. When he straightened up again, he adjusted the set of his cloak with a kind of sorry hauteur, pushed his bent spectacles a little more firmly up onto the bridge of his nose, and said in a voice that was shaky but oddly determined, "My lord Dragonsbane, I have ridden here on errantry from the south, with a message for you from the King, Uriens of Belmarie." He seemed to gather strength from these words, settling into the heraldic sonority of his ballad-snatch of golden swords and bright plumes in spite of the smell of the pigsty and the thin, cold rain that had begun to patter down.

"My lord Aversin, I have been sent to bring you south. A dragon has come and laid waste the city of the gnomes in the Deep of Ylferdun; it lairs there now, fifteen miles from the King's city of Bel. The King begs that you come to slay it ere the whole countryside is destroyed."

The boy drew himself up, having delivered himself of his quest, a look of noble and martyred serenity on his face, very like, Jenny thought, someone out of a ballad himself. Then, like all good messengers in ballads, he collapsed and slid to the soupy mud and cowpies in a dead faint.

2

Rain drummed steadily, drearily, on the walls of Alyn Hold's broken-down tower. The Hold's single guest room was never very bright; and, though it was only mid-afternoon, Jenny had summoned a dim ball of bluish witchfire to illuminate the table on which she had spread the contents of her medicine satchel; the rest of the little cubbyhole was curtained in shadow.

In the bed, Gareth dozed restlessly. The air was sweet with the ghosts of the long-dried fragrances of crushed herbs; the witchlight threw fine, close-grained shadows around the dessicated mummies of root and pod where they lay in the circles Jenny had traced. Slowly, rune by rune, she worked the healing spells over them, each with its own Limitation to prevent a too-quick healing that might harm the body as a whole, her fingers patiently tracing the signs, her mind calling down the qualities of the universe particular to each, like separate threads of the unheard music. It was said that the great mages could see the power of the runes they wrought glowing like cold fire in the air above the healing powders and sense the touch of it like plasmic light drawn from the fingertips. After long years of solitary meditation, Jenny had come to accept that, for her, magic was a depth and a stillness rather than the moving brilliance that it was for the great. It was something she would never quite become reconciled to, but at least it kept her from the resentment that would block what powers she did have. Within her narrow bounds, she knew she worked well.

The key to magic is magic, Caerdinn had said. To be a mage, you must be a mage. There is no time for anything else, if you will come to the fullness of your power.

So she had remained in the stone house on Frost Fell after Caerdinn had died, studying his books and measuring the stars, meditating in the crumbling circle of ancient standing stones that stood on the hillcrest above. Through the slow years her powers had grown with meditation and study, though never to what his had been. It was a life that had contented her. She had looked no further than the patient striving to increase her powers, while she healed others where she could and observed the turning of the seasons.

Then John had come.

The spells circled to their conclusion. For a time silence hung on the air, as if every hearth brick and rafter shadow, the fragrance of the apple-wood fire and the guttural trickle of the rain, had been preserved in amber for a thousand years. Jenny swept the spelled powders together into a bowl and raised her eyes. Gareth was watching her fearfully from the darkness of the curtained bed.

She got to her feet. As she moved toward him, he recoiled, his white face drawn with accusation and loathing. "You are his mistress!"

Jenny stopped, hearing the hatred in that weak voice. She said, "Yes. But it has nothing to do with you."

He turned his face away, fretful and still half-dreaming. "You are just like her," he muttered faintly. "Just like Zyerne . . ."

She stepped forward again, not certain she had heard clearly. "Who?"

"You've snared him with your spells—brought him down into the mud," the boy whispered and broke off with a feverish sob. Disregarding his repulsion, she came worriedly to his side, feeling his face and hands; after a moment, he ceased his feeble resistance, already sinking back to sleep. His flesh felt neither hot nor overly chilled; his pulse was steady and strong. But still he tossed and murmured, "Never—I never will. Spells—you have laid spells on him—made him love you with your witcheries . . ." His eyelids slipped closed.

Jenny sighed and straightened up, looking down into the flushed, troubled face. "If only I had laid spells on him," she murmured. "Then I could release us both—had I the courage."

She dusted her hands on her skirt and descended the narrow darkness of the turret stair.

She found John in his study—what would have been a fair-sized room, had it not been jammed to overflowing with books. For the most part, these were ancient volumes, left at the Hold by the departing armies or scavenged from the cellars of the burned-out garrison towns of the south; rat-chewed, black with mildew, unreadable with waterstains, they crammed every shelf of the labyrinth of planks that filled two walls and they spilled off to litter the long oak table and heaped the floor in the corners. Sheets of notes were interleaved among their pages and between their covers, copied out by John in the winter evenings. Among and between them were jumbled at random the tools of a scribe—prickers and quills, knives and inkpots, pumice stones—and stranger things besides: metal tubes and tongs, plumb-bobs and levels, burning-glasses and pendulums, magnets, the blown shells of eggs, chips of rock, dried flowers, and a half-disassembled clock. A vast spiderweb of hoists and pulleys occupied the rafters in one corner, and battalions of guttered and decaying candles angled along the edges of every shelf and sill. The room was a magpie-nest of picked-at knowledge, the lair of a tinkerer to whom the universe was one vast toyshop of intriguing side issues. Above the hearth, like a giant iron pinecone, hung the tail-knob of the dragon of Wyr—fifteen inches long and nine through, covered with stumpy, broken spikes.

John himself stood beside the window, gazing through the thick glass of its much-mended casement out over the barren lands to the north, where they merged with the bruised and tumbled sky. His hand was pressed to his side, where the rain throbbed in the ribs that the tail-knob had cracked.

Though the soft buckskin of her boots made no sound on the rutted stone of the floor, he looked up as she came in. His eyes smiled greeting into hers, but she only leaned her shoulder against the stone of the doorpost and asked, "Well?"

He glanced ceilingward where Gareth would be lying. "What, our little hero and his dragon?" A smile flicked the corners of his thin, sensitive mouth, then vanished like the swift sunlight of a cloudy day. "I've slain one dragon, Jen, and it bloody near finished me. Tempting as the promise is of getting more fine ballads written of my deeds, I think I'll pass this chance."

Relief and the sudden recollection of Gareth's ballad made Jenny giggle as she came into the room. The whitish light of the windows caught in every crease of John's leather sleeves as he stepped forward to meet her and bent to kiss her lips.

"Our hero never rode all the way north by himself, surely?"

Jenny shook her head. "He told me he took a ship from the south to Eldsbouch and rode east from there."

"He's gie lucky he made it that far," John remarked, and kissed her again, his hands warm against her sides. "The pigs have been restless all day, carrying bits of straw about in their mouths—I turned back yesterday even from riding the bounds because of the way the crows were acting out on the Whin Hills. It's two weeks early for them, but it's in my mind this'll be the first of the winter storms. The rocks at Eldsbouch are shipeaters. You know, Dotys says in Volume Three of his *Histories*—or is it in that part of Volume Five we found at Ember?—or is it in Clivy?—that there used to be a mole or breakwater across the harbor there, back in the days of the Kings. It was one of the Wonders of the World, Dotys—or Clivy—says, but nowhere can I find any mention of the engineering of it. One of these days I'm minded to take a boat out there and see what I can find underwater at the harbor mouth . . ."

Jenny shuddered, knowing John to be perfectly capable of undertaking such an investigation. She had still not forgotten the stone house he had blown up, after reading in some moldering account about the gnomes using blasting powder to tunnel in their Deeps, nor his experiments with water pipes.

Sudden commotion sounded in the dark of the turret stair, treble voices arguing, "She is, too!" and "Let go!" A muted scuffle ensued, and a moment later a red-haired, sturdy urchin of four or so exploded into the room in a swirl of grubby sheepskin and plaids, followed immediately by a slender, dark-haired boy of eight. Jenny smiled and held out her arms to them both. They flung themselves against her; small, filthy hands clutched delightedly at her hair, her skirt, and the sleeves of her shift, and she felt again the surge of ridiculous and illogical delight at being in their presence.

"And how are my little barbarians?" she asked in her coolest voice, which fooled neither of them.

"Good—we been good, Mama," the older boy said, clinging to the faded blue cloth of her skirt. "*I* been good—Adric hasn't."

"Have, too," retorted the younger one, whom John had lifted into his arms. "Papa had to whip Ian."

"Did he, now?" She smiled down into her older son's eyes, heavy-lidded and tip-tilted like John's, but as summer blue as her own. "He doubtless deserved it."

"With a big whip," Adric amplified, carried away with his tale. "A hundred cuts."

"Really?" She looked over at John with matter-of-fact inquiry in her expression. "All at one session, or did you rest in between?"

"One session," John replied serenely. "And he never begged for mercy even once."

"Good boy." She ruffled Ian's coarse black hair, and he twisted and giggled with pleasure at the solemn make-believe.

The boys had long ago accepted the fact that Jenny did not live at the Hold, as other boys' mothers lived with their fathers; the Lord of the Hold and the Witch of Frost Fell did not have to behave like other adults. Like puppies who tolerate a kennelkeeper's superintendence, the boys displayed a dutiful affection toward John's stout Aunt Jane, who cared for them and, she believed, kept them out of trouble while John was away looking after the lands in his charge and Jenny lived apart in her own

house on the Fell, pursuing the solitudes of her art. But it was their father
they recognized as their master, and their mother as their love.

They started to tell her, in an excited and not very coherent duet,
about a fox they had trapped, when a sound in the doorway made them
turn. Gareth stood there, looking pale and tired, but dressed in his own
clothes again, bandages making an ungainly lump under the sleeve of his
spare shirt. He'd dug an unbroken pair of spectacles from his baggage as
well; behind the thick lenses, his eyes were filled with sour distaste and
bitter disillusion as he looked at her and her sons. It was as if the fact that
John and she had become lovers—that she had borne John's sons—had
not only cheapened his erstwhile hero in his eyes, but had made her
responsible for all those other disappointments that he had encountered in
the Winterlands as well.

The boys sensed at once his disapprobation. Adric's pugnacious little
jaw began to come forward in a miniature version of John's. But Ian,
more sensitive, only signaled to his brother with his eyes, and the two
took their silent leave. John watched them go; then his gaze returned,
speculative, to Gareth. But all he said was, "So you lived, then?"

Rather shakily, Gareth replied, "Yes. Thank you—" He turned to
Jenny, with a forced politeness that no amount of animosity could uproot
from his courtier's soul. "Thank you for helping me." He took a step into
the room and stopped again, staring blankly about him as he saw the
place for the first time. Not something from a ballad, Jenny thought,
amused in spite of herself. But then, no ballad could ever prepare anyone
for John.

"Bit crowded," John confessed. "My dad used to keep the books that
had been left at the Hold in the storeroom with the corn, and the rats had
accounted for most of 'em before I'd learned to read. I thought they'd be
safer here."

"Er . . ." Gareth said, at a loss. "I—I suppose . . ."

"He was a stiff-necked old villain, my dad," John went on conversa-
tionally, coming to stand beside the hearth and extend his hands to the
fire. "If it hadn't been for old Caerdinn, who was about the Hold on and
off when I was a lad, I'd never have got past the alphabet. Dad hadn't
much use for written things—I found half an act of Luciard's *Firegiver*
pasted over the cracks in the walls of the cupboard my granddad used to
store winter clothes in. I could have gone out and thrown rocks at his
grave, I was that furious, because of course there's none of the play to be
found now. God knows what they did with the rest of it—kindled the
kitchen stoves, I expect. What we've managed to save isn't much—Volumes Three and Four of Dotys' *Histories;* most of Polyborus' *Analects*
and his *Jurisprudence;* the *Elucidus Lapidarus*; Clivy's *On Farming*—in

its entirety, for all that's worth, though it's pretty useless. I don't think Clivy was much of a farmer, or even bothered to talk to farmers. He says that you can tell the coming of storms by taking measurements of the clouds and their shadows, but the grannies round the villages say you can tell just watching the bees. And when he talks about the mating habits of pigs . . ."

"I warn you, Gareth," Jenny said with a smile, "that John is a walking encyclopedia of old wives' tales, granny-rhymes, snippets of every classical writer he can lay hands upon, and trivia gleaned from the far corners of the hollow earth—encourage him at your peril. He also can't cook."

"I can, though," John shot back at her with a grin.

Gareth, still gazing around him in mystification at the cluttered room, said nothing, but his narrow face was a study of mental gymnastics as he strove to adjust the ballads' conventionalized catalog of perfections with the reality of a bespectacled amateur engineer who collected lore about pigs.

"So, then," John went on in a friendly voice, "tell us of this dragon of yours, Gareth of Magloshaldon, and why the King sent a boy of your years to carry his message when he's got warriors and knights that could do the job as well."

"Er . . ." Gareth looked completely taken aback for a moment—messengers in ballads never being asked for their credentials. "That is—but that's just it. He hasn't got warriors and knights, not that can be spared. And I came because I knew where to look for you, from the ballads."

He fished from the pouch at his belt a gold signet ring, whose bezel flashed in a spurt of yellow hearthlight—Jenny glimpsed a crowned king upon it, seated beneath twelve stars. John looked in silence at it for a moment, then bent his head and drew the ring to his lips with archaic reverence.

Jenny watched his action in silence. The King was the King, she thought. It was nearly a hundred years since he withdrew his troops from the north, leaving that to the barbarians and the chaos of lands without law. Yet John still regarded himself as the subject of the King.

It was something she herself had never understood—either John's loyalty to the King whose laws he still fought to uphold, or Caerdinn's sense of bitter and personal betrayal by those same Kings. To Jenny, the King was the ruler of another land, another time—she herself was a citizen only of the Winterlands.

Bright and small, the gold oval of the ring flashed as Gareth laid it upon the table, like a witness to all that was said. "He gave that to me when he sent me to seek you," he told them. "The King's champions all rode out against the dragon, and none of them returned. No one in the

Realm has ever slain a dragon—nor even seen one up close to know how
to attack it, really. And there is nothing to tell us. I know, I've looked,
because it was the one useful thing that I *could* do. I know I'm not a
knight, or a champion . . ." His voice stammered a little on the admission,
breaking the armor of his formality. "I know I'm no good at sports. But
I've studied all the ballads and all their variants, and no ballad really tells
that much about the actual how-to of killing a dragon. We need a Dragonsbane," he concluded helplessly. "We need someone who knows what
he's doing. We need your help."

"And we need yours." The light timbre of Aversin's smoky voice suddenly hardened to flint. "We've needed your help for a hundred years,
while this part of the Realm, from the River Wildspae north, was being
laid waste by bandits and Iceriders and wolves and worse things, things
we haven't the knowledge anymore to deal with: marsh-devils and Whisperers and the evils that haunt the night woods, evils that steal the blood
and souls of the living. Has your King thought of that? It's a bit late in the
day for him to be asking favors of us."

The boy stared at him, stunned. "But the dragon . . ."

"Pox blister your dragon! Your King has a hundred knights and my
people have only me." The light slid across the lenses of his specs in a
flash of gold as he leaned his broad shoulders against the blackened
stones of the chimney-breast, the spikes of the dragon's tail-knob gleaming evilly beside his head. "Gnomes never have just one entrance to their
Deeps. Couldn't your King's knights have gotten the surviving gnomes to
guide them through a secondary entrance to take the thing from behind?"

"Uh . . ." Visibly nonplussed by the unheroic practicality of the suggestion, Gareth floundered. "I don't think they could have. The rear
entrance of the Deep is in the fortress of Halnath. The Master of Halnath—Polycarp, the King's nephew—rose in revolt against the King not
long before the dragon's coming. The Citadel is under siege."

Silent in the corner of the hearth to which she had retreated, Jenny
heard the sudden shift in the boy's voice, like the sound of a weakened
foundation giving under strain. Looking up, she saw his too-prominent
Adam's apple bob as he swallowed.

There was some wound there, she guessed to herself, some memory
still tender to the touch.

"That's—that's one reason so few of the King's champions could be
spared. It isn't only the dragon, you see." He leaned forward pleadingly.
"The whole Realm is in danger from the rebels as well as the dragon. The
Deep tunnels into the face of Nast Wall, the great mountain ridge that
divides the lowlands of Belmarie from the northeastern Marches. The
Citadel of Halnath stands on a cliff on the other side of the mountain from

the main gates of the Deep, with the town and the University below it. The gnomes of Ylferdun were our allies against the rebels, but now most of them have gone over to the Halnath side. The whole Realm is split. You must come! As long as the dragon is in Ylferdun we can't keep the roads from the mountains properly guarded against the rebels, or send supplies to the besiegers of the Citadel. The King's champions went out . . ." He swallowed again, his voice tightening with the memory. "The men who brought back the bodies said that most of them never even got a chance to draw their swords."

"Gah!" Aversin looked away, anger and pity twisting his sensitive mouth. "Any fool who'd take a sword after a dragon in the first place . . ."

"But they didn't know! All they had to go on were the songs!"

Aversin said nothing to this; but, judging by his compressed lips and the flare of his nostrils, his thoughts were not pleasant ones. Gazing into the fire, Jenny heard his silence, and something like the chill shadow of a wind-driven cloud passed across her heart.

Half against her will, she saw images form in the molten amber of the fire's heart. She recognized the winter-colored sky above the gully, the charred and brittle spears of poisoned grass fine as needle-scratches against it, John standing poised on the gully's rim, the barbed steel rod of a harpoon in one gloved hand, an ax gleaming in his belt. Something rippled in the gully, a living carpet of golden knives.

Clearer than the sharp, small ghosts of the past that she saw was the shiv-twist memory of fear as she saw him jump.

They had been lovers then for less than a year, still burningly conscious of one another's bodies. When he had sought the dragon's lair, more than anything else Jenny had been aware of the fragility of flesh and bone when it was pitted against steel and fire.

She shut her eyes; when she opened them again, the silken pictures were gone from the flame. She pressed her lips taut, forcing herself to listen without speaking, knowing it was and could be none of her affair. She could no more have told him not to go—not then, not now—than he could have told her to leave the stone house on Frost Fell and give up her seeking, to come to the Hold to cook his meals and raise his sons.

John was saying, "Tell me about this drake."

"You mean you'll come?" The forlorn eagerness in Gareth's voice made Jenny want to get up and box his ears.

"I mean I want to hear about it." The Dragonsbane came around the table and slouched into one of the room's big carved chairs, sliding the other in Gareth's direction with a shove of his booted foot. "How long ago did it strike?"

"It came by night, two weeks ago. I took ship three days later, from

Claekith Harbor below the city of Bel. The ship is waiting for us at Elds-bouch."

"I doubt that." John scratched the side of his long nose with one scarred forefinger. "If your mariners were smart they'll have turned and run for a safe port two days ago. The storms are coming. Eldsbouch will be no protection to them."

"But they said they'd stay!" Gareth protested indignantly. "I paid them!"

"Gold will do them no good weighting their bones to the bottom of the cove," John pointed out.

Gareth sank back into his chair, shocked and cut to the heart by this final betrayal. "They can't have gone . . ."

There was a moment's silence, while John looked down at his hands. Without lifting her eyes from the heart of the fire, Jenny said softly, "They are not there, Gareth. I see the sea, and it is black with storms; I see the old harbor at Eldsbouch, the gray river running through the broken houses there; I see the fisher-folk making fast their little boats to the ruins of the old piers and all the stones shining under the rain. There is no ship there, Gareth."

"You're wrong," he said hopelessly. "You have to be wrong." He turned back to John. "It'll take us weeks to get back, traveling overland . . ."

"*Us?*" John said softly, and Gareth blushed and looked as frightened as if he had uttered mortal insult. After a moment John went on, "How big is this dragon of yours?"

Gareth swallowed again and drew his breath in a shaky sigh. "Huge," he said dully.

"How huge?"

Gareth hesitated. Like most people, he had no eye for relative size. "It must have been a hundred feet long. They say the shadow of its wings covered the whole of Deeping Vale."

"Who says?" John inquired, shifting his weight sideways in the chair and hooking a knee over the fornicating sea-lions that made up the left-hand arm. "I thought it came at night, and munched up anyone close enough to see it by day."

"Well . . ." He floundered in a sea of third-hand rumor.

"Ever see it on the ground?"

Gareth blushed and shook his head.

"It's gie hard to judge things in the air," John said kindly, pushing up his specs again. "The drake I slew here looked about a hundred feet long in the air, when I first saw it descending on the village of Great Toby. Turned out to be twenty-seven feet from beak to tail." Again his quick grin illuminated his usually expressionless face. "It comes of being a naturalist. The first thing we did, Jenny and I, when I was on my feet again after killing it, was to go out there with cleavers and see how the thing was put together, what there was left of it."

"It could be bigger, though, couldn't it?" Gareth asked. He sounded a little worried, as if, Jenny thought dryly, he considered a twenty-seven foot dragon somewhat paltry. "I mean, in the Greenhythe variant of the Lay of Selkythar Dragonsbane and the Worm of the Imperteng Wood, they say that the Worm was sixty feet long, with wings that would cover a battalion."

"Anybody measure it?"

"Well, they must have. Except—now that I come to think of it, according to that variant, when Selkythar had wounded it unto death the dragon fell into the River Wildspae; and in a later Belmarie version it says it fell into the sea. So I don't see how anyone could have."

"So a sixty-foot dragon is just somebody's measure of how great Selkythar was." He leaned back in his chair, his hands absentmindedly tracing over the lunatic carvings—the mingled shapes of all the creatures of the Book of Beasts. The worn gilding still caught in the chinks flickered with a dull sheen in the stray glints of the fire. "Twenty-seven feet doesn't sound like a lot, 'til it's there spitting fire at you. You know their flesh will decompose almost as soon as they die? It's as if their own fire consumes them, as it does everything else."

"Spitting fire?" Gareth frowned. "All the songs say they breathe it."

Aversin shook his head. "They sort of spit it—it's liquid fire, and nearly anything it touches'll catch. That's the trick in fighting a dragon, you see—to stay close enough to its body that it won't spit fire at you for fear of burning itself, and not get rolled on or cut to pieces with its scales whilst you're about it. They can raise the scales along their sides like a blowfish bristling, and they're edged like razors."

"I never knew that," Gareth breathed. Wonder and curiosity lessened, for a moment, the shell of his offended dignity and pride.

"Well, the pity of it is, probably the King's champions didn't either. God knows, I didn't when I went after the dragon in the gorge. There was nothing about it in any book I could find—Dotys and Clivy and them. Only a few old granny-rhymes that mention dragons—or drakes or worms, they're called—and they weren't much help. Things like:

"Cock by its feet, horse by its hame,
  Snake by its head, drake by its name.

"Or what Polyborus had in his *Analects* about certain villages believing that if you plant loveseed—those creeper-things with the purple trumpet-flowers on them—around your house, dragons won't come near. Jen and I used bits of that kind of lore—Jen brewed a poison from the loveseed to put on my harpoons, because it was obvious on the face of it that no fiddling little sword was going to cut through those scales. And the poison did slow the thing down. But I don't know near as much about them as I'd like."

"No." Jenny turned her eyes at last from the fire's throbbing core and, resting her cheek upon her hand where it lay on her up-drawn knees, regarded the two men on either side of the book-cluttered table. She spoke softly, half to herself. "We know not where they come from, nor where they breed; why of all the beasts of the earth they have six limbs instead of four . . ."

" 'Maggots from meat,' " quoted John, " 'weevils from rye, dragons from stars in an empty sky.' That's in Terens' *Of Ghosts*. Or Caerdinn's 'Save a dragon, slave a dragon.' Or why they say you should never look into a dragon's eyes—and I'll tell you, Gar, I was gie careful not to do that. We don't even know simple things, like why magic and illusion won't work on them; why Jen couldn't call the dragon's image in that jewel of hers, or use a cloaking-spell against his notice—nothing."

"Nothing," Jenny said softly, "save how they died, slain by men as ignorant of them as we."

John must have heard the strange sorrow that underlay her voice, for she felt his glance, worried and questioning. But she turned her eyes away, not knowing the answer to what he asked.

After a moment, John sighed and said to Gareth, "It's all knowledge that's been lost over the years, like Luciard's *Firegiver* and how they managed to build a breakwater across the harbor mouth at Eldsbouch— knowledge that's been lost and may never be recovered."

He got to his feet and began to pace restlessly, the flat, whitish gray reflections from the window winking on spike and mail-scrap and the brass of dagger-hilt and buckle. "We're living in a decaying world, Gar; things slipping away day by day. Even you, down south in Bel—you're losing the Realm a piece at a time, with the Winterlands tearing off in one direction and the rebels pulling away the Marches in another. You're losing what you had and don't even know it, and all that while knowledge is leaking out the seams, like meal from a ripped bag, because there isn't time or leisure to save it.

"I would never have slain the dragon, Gar—slay it, when we know nothing about it? And it was beautiful in itself, maybe the most beautiful thing I've ever laid eyes on, every color of it perfect as sunset, like a barley field in certain lights you get on summer evenings."

"But you must—you have to slay ours!" There was sudden agony in Gareth's voice.

"Fighting it and slaying it are two different things." John turned back from the window, his head tipped slightly to one side, regarding the boy's anxious face. "And I haven't yet said I'd undertake the one, let alone accomplish the other."

"But you have to." The boy's voice was a forlorn whisper of despair. "You're our only hope."

"Am I?" the Dragonsbane asked gently. "I'm the only hope of all these villagers, through the coming winter, against wolves and bandits. It was because I was their only hope that I slew the most perfect creature I'd ever seen, slew it dirtily, filthily, chopping it to pieces with an ax—it was because I was their only hope that I fought it at all and near had my flesh shredded from my bones by it. I'm only a man, Gareth."

"No!" the boy insisted desperately. "You're the Dragonsbane—the only Dragonsbane!" He rose to his feet, some inner struggle plain upon his thin features, his breathing fast as if forcing himself to some exertion. "The King . . ." He swallowed hard. "The King told me to make whatever terms I could, to bring you south. If you come . . ." With an effort he made his voice steady. "If you come, we will send troops again to protect the northlands, to defend them against the Iceriders; we will send books, and scholars, to bring knowledge to the people again. I swear it." He took up the King's seal and held it out in his trembling palm, and the cold daylight flashed palely across its face. "In the King's name I swear it."

But Jenny, watching the boy's white face as he spoke, saw that he did not meet John's eyes.

As night came on the rain increased, the wind throwing it like seabreakers against the walls of the Hold. John's Aunt Jane brought up a cold supper of meat, cheese, and beer, which Gareth picked at with the air of one doing his duty. Jenny, sitting cross-legged in the corner of the hearth, unwrapped her harp and experimented with its tuning pegs while the men spoke of the roads that led south, and of the slaying of the Golden Dragon of Wyr.

"That's another thing that wasn't like the songs," Gareth said, resting his bony elbows amid the careless scatter of John's notes on the table. "In the songs the dragons are all gay-colored, gaudy. But this one is black, dead-black all over save for the silver lamps of its eyes."

"Black," repeated John quietly, and looked over at Jenny. "You had an old list, didn't you, love?"

She nodded, her hands resting in the delicate maneuverings of the harp pegs. "Caerdinn had me memorize many old lists," she explained to Gareth. "Some of them he told me the meaning of—this one he never did. Perhaps he didn't know himself. It was names, and colors . . ." She closed her eyes and repeated the list, her voice falling into the old man's singsong chant, the echo of dozens of voices, back through the length of years. "Teltrevir heliotrope; Centhwevir is blue knotted with gold; Astirith is primrose and black; Morkeleb alone, black as night . . . The list goes on—there were dozens of names, if names they are." She shrugged and linked her fingers over the curve of the harp's back. "But John tells me that the old dragon that was supposed to haunt the shores of the lake of Wevir in the east was said to have been blue as the waters, marked all over his back with patterns of gold so that he could lie beneath the surface of the lake in summer and steal sheep from the banks."

"Yes!" Gareth almost bounced out of his chair with enthusiasm as he recognized the familiar tale. "And the Worm of Wevir was slain by Antara Warlady and her brother Darthis Dragonsbane in the last part of the reign of Yvain the Well-Beloved, who was . . ." He caught himself up again, suddenly embarrassed. "It's a popular tale," he concluded, red-faced.

Jenny hid her smile at the abrupt checking of his ebullience. "There were notes for the harp as well—not tunes, really. He whistled them to me, over and over, until I got them right."

She put her harp to her shoulder, a small instrument that had also been Caerdinn's, though he had not played it; the wood was darkened almost black with age. By daylight it appeared perfectly unadorned, but when firelight glanced across it, as it did now, the circles of the air and sea were sometimes visible, traced upon it in faded gold. Carefully, she picked out those strange, sweet knots of sound, sometimes two or three notes only, sometimes a string of them like a truncated air. They were individual in the turns of their timing, hauntingly half-familiar, like things remembered from childhood; and as she played she repeated the names: Teltrevir heliotrope, Centhwevir is blue knotted with gold . . . It was part of the lost knowledge, like that from John's scatterbrained, jackdaw quest in the small portion of his time not taken up with the brutal demands of the Winterlands. Notes and words were meaningless now, like a line from a lost ballad, or a few torn pages from the tragedy of an exiled god, pasted to keep wind from a crack—the echoes of songs that would not be heard again.

From them her hands moved on, random as her passing thoughts. She sketched vagrant airs, or snatches of jigs and reels, slowed and touched with the shadow of an inevitable grief that waited in the hidden darkness of future time. Through them she moved to the ancient tunes that held the timeless pull of the ocean in their cadences; sorrows that drew the heart from the body, or joys that called the soul like the distant glitter of stardust banners in the summer night. In time John took from its place in a hole by the hearth a tin pennywhistle, such as children played in the streets, and joined its thin, bright music to hers, dancing around the shadowed beauty of the harp like a thousand-year-old child.

Music answered music, joining into a spell-circle that banished, for a time, the strange tangle of fear and grief and dragonfire in Jenny's heart. Whatever would come to pass, this was what they were and had now. She tossed back the cloudy streams of her hair and caught the bright flicker of Aversin's eyes behind his thick spectacles, the pennywhistle luring the harp out of its sadness and into dance airs wild as hay-harvest winds. As the evening deepened, the Hold folk drifted up to the study to join them, sitting where they could on the floor or the hearth or in the deep embrasures of the windows: John's Aunt Jane and Cousin Dilly and others of the vast tribe of his female relatives who lived at the Hold; Ian and Adric; the fat, jovial smith Muffle; all part of the pattern of the life of the Winterlands that was so dull-seeming at first, but was in truth close-woven and complex as its random plaids. And among them Gareth sat, ill at ease as a bright southern parrot in a rookery. He kept looking about him with puzzled distaste in the leaping restlessness of the red firelight that threw into momentary brightness the moldery rummage of decaying books, of rocks and chemical experiments, and that glowed in the children's eyes and made amber mirrors of the dogs'—wondering, Jenny thought, how a quest as glorious as his could possibly have ended in such a place.

And every now and then, she noticed, his eyes returned to John. There was in them not only anxiety, but a kind of nervous dread, as if he were haunted by a gnawing guilt for something he had done, or something he knew he must yet do.

"Will you go?" Jenny asked softly, much later in the night, lying in the warm nest of bearskins and patchwork with her dark hair scattered like sea-wrack over John's breast and arm.

"If I slay his dragon for him, the King will have to listen to me," John said reasonably. "If I come at his calling, I must be his subject, and if I am—we are—his subjects, as King he owes us the protection of his troops. If I'm not his subject . . ." He paused, as he thought over what his next words would mean about the Law of the Realm for which he had so long fought. He sighed and let the thought go.

For a time the silence was broken only by the groan of wind in the tower overhead and the drumming of the rain on the walls. But even had she not been able to see, catlike, in the dark, Jenny knew John did not sleep. There was a tension in all his muscles, and the uneasy knowledge of how narrow had been the margin between living and dying, when he had fought the Golden Dragon of Wyr. Her hand under his back could still feel the rucked, hard ridges of scar.

"Jenny," he said at last, "my father told me that his dad used to be able to raise four and five hundred of militia when the Iceriders came. They fought pitched battles on the edge of the northern ocean and marched in force to break the strongholds of the bandit-kings that used to cover the eastward roads. When that band of brigands attacked Far West Riding the year before last, do you remember how many men we could come up with, the mayor of Riding, the mayor of Toby, and myself among us? Less than a hundred, and twelve of those we lost in that fight."

As he moved his head, the banked glow of the hearth on the other side of the small sanctum of their bedchamber caught a thread of carnelian from the shoulder-length mop of his hair. "Jen, we can't go on like this. You know we can't. We're weakening all the time. The lands of the King's law, the law that keeps the stronger from enslaving the weaker, are shrinking away. Every time a farm is wiped out by wolves or brigands or Iceriders, it's one less shield in the wall. Every time some family ups and goes south to indenture themselves as serfs there, always provided they make it that far, it weakens those of us that are left. And the law itself is waning, as fewer and fewer people even know why there is law. Do you realize that because I've read a handful of volumes of Dotys and whatever pages of Polyborus' *Jurisprudence* I could find stuck in the cracks of the tower I'm accounted a scholar? We need the help of the King, Jen, if we're not to be feeding on one another within a generation. I can buy them that help."

"With what?" asked Jenny softly. "The flesh off your bones? If you are killed by the dragon, what of your people then?"

Beneath her cheek she felt his shoulder move. "I could be killed by wolves or bandits next week—come to that, I could fall offf old Osprey and break my neck." And when she chuckled, unexpectedly amused at that, he added in an aggrieved voice, "It's exactly what my father did."

"Your father knew no better than to ride drunk." She smiled a little in spite of herself. "I wonder what he would have made of our young hero?"

John laughed in the darkness. "Gaw, he'd have eaten him for breakfast." Seventeen years, ten of which had been spent knowing Jenny, had finally given him a tolerance of the man he had grown up hating. Then he drew her closer and kissed her hair. When he spoke again, his voice was quiet. "I have to do it, Jen. I won't be gone long."

A particularly fierce gust of wind shivered in the tower's ancient bones, and Jenny drew the worn softness of quilts and furs up over her bare shoulders. A month, perhaps, she calculated; maybe a little more. It would give her a chance to catch up on her neglected meditations, to pursue the studies that she too often put aside these days, to come to the Hold to be with him and their sons.

To be a mage you must be a mage, Caerdinn had said. *Magic is the only key to magic.* She knew that she was not the mage that he had been, even when she had known him first, when he was in his eighties and she a skinny, wretched, ugly girl of fourteen. She sometimes wondered whether it was because he had been so old, at the end of his strength, when he came to teach her, the last of his pupils, or because she was simply not very good. Lying awake in the darkness, listening to the wind or to the terrible greatness of the moor silence which was worse, she sometimes admitted the truth to herself—that what she gave to John, what she found herself more and more giving to those two little boys snuggled together like puppies upstairs, she took from the strength of her power.

All that she had, to divide between her magic and her love, was time. In a few years she would be forty. For ten years she had scattered her time, sowing it broadcast like a farmer in summer sunshine, instead of hoarding it and pouring it back into meditation and magic. She moved her head on John's shoulder, and the warmth of their long friendship was in the tightening of his arm around her. Had she forgone this, she wondered, would she be as powerful as Caerdinn had once been? As powerful as she sometimes felt she could be, when she meditated among the stones on her lonely hill?

She would have that time, with her mind undistracted, time to work and strive and study. The snow would be deep by the time John returned.

If he returned.

The shadow of the dragon of Wyr seemed to cover her again, blotting the sky as it swooped down like a hawk over the autumn dance floor at Great Toby. The sickening jam of her heart in her throat came back to her, as John ran forward under that descending shadow, trying to reach the terrified gaggle of children cowering in the center of the floor. The metallic stink of spat fire seemed to burn again in her nostrils, the screams echoing in her ears . . .

Twenty-seven feet, John had said. What it meant was that from the top of the dragon's shoulder to the ground was the height of a man's shoulder, and half again that to the top of its tall haunches, backed by all that weight and strength and speed.

And for no good reason she could think of, she remembered the sudden shift of the boy Gareth's eyes.

After a long time of silence she said, "John?"

"Aye, love?"

"I want to go with you, when you ride south."

She felt the hardening of the muscles of his body. It was nearly a full minute before he answered her, and she could hear in his voice the struggle between what he wanted and what he thought might be best. "You've said yourself it'll be a bad winter, love. I'm thinking one or the other of us should be here."

He was right, and she knew it. Even the coats of her cats were thick this fall. A month ago she had been troubled to see how the birds were departing, early and swiftly, anxious to be gone. The signs pointed to famine and sleet, and on the heels of those would come barbarian raids from across the ice-locked northern sea.

And yet, she thought . . . and yet . . . Was this the weakness of a woman who does not want to be parted from the man she loves, or was it something else? Caerdinn would have said that love clouded the instincts of a mage.

"I think I should go with you."

"You think I can't handle the dragon myself?" His voice was filled with mock indignation.

"Yes," Jenny said bluntly, and felt the ribs vibrate under her hand with his laughter. "I don't know under what circumstances you'll be meeting it," she went on. "And there's more than that."

His voice was thoughtful in the darkness, but not surprised. "It strikes you that way too, does it?"

That was something people tended not to notice about John. Behind his facade of amiable barbarism, behind his frivolous fascination with hog-lore, granny-rhymes, and how clocks were made lurked an agile mind and an almost feminine sensitivity to nuances of situations and relationships. There was not much that he missed.

"Our hero has spoken of rebellion and treachery in the south," she said. "If the dragon has come, it will ruin the harvest, and rising bread-prices will make the situation worse. I think you'll need someone there whom you can trust."

"I've been thinking it, too," he replied softly. "Now, what makes you think I won't be able to trust our Gar? I doubt he'd betray me out of pique that the goods aren't as advertised."

Jenny rolled up onto her elbows, her dark hair hanging in a torrent down over his breast. "No," she said slowly, and tried to put her finger on what it was that troubled her about that thin, earnest boy she had rescued in the ruins of the old town. At length, she said, "My instincts tell me he can be trusted, at heart. But he's lying about something, I don't know what. I think I should go with you to the south."

John smiled and drew her down to him again. "The last time I went against your instincts, I was that sorry," he said. "Myself, I'm torn, for I can smell there's going to be danger here later in the winter. But I think you're right. I don't understand why the King would have given his word and his seal into the keeping of the likes of our young hero, who by the sound of it has never done more than collect ballads in all his life, and not to some proven warrior. But if the King's pledged his word to aid us, then I'd be a fool not to take the chance to pledge mine. Just the fact that there's only the two of us, Jen, shows how close to the edge of darkness all this land lies. Besides," he added, sudden worry in his voice, "you've got to come."

Her thoughts preoccupied by her nameless forebodings, Jenny turned her head quickly. "What is it? Why?"

"We'll need someone to do the cooking."

With a cat-swift move she was on top of him, smothering his face under a pillow, but she was laughing too much to hold him. They tussled, giggling, their struggles blending into lovemaking. Later, as they drifted in the warm aftermath, Jenny murmured, "You make me laugh at the strangest times."

He kissed her then and slept, but Jenny sank no further than the uneasy borderlands of half-dreams. She found herself standing once again on the lip of the gully, the heat from below beating at her face, the poisons scouring her lungs. In the drifting vapors below, the great shape was still writhing, heaving its shredded wings or clawing ineffectually with the stumps of its forelegs at the small figure braced like an exhausted woodcutter over its neck, a dripping ax in his blistered hands. She saw John moving mechanically, half-asphyxiated with the fumes and swaying from the loss of the blood that gleamed stickily on his armor. The small stream in the gully was clotted and red with the dragon's blood; gobbets of flesh choked it; the stones were blackened with the dragon's fire. The dragon kept raising its dripping head, trying to snap at John; even in her dream, Jenny felt the air weighted with the strange sensation of singing, vibrant with a music beyond the grasp of her ears and mind.

The singing grew stronger as she slid deeper into sleep. She saw against the darkness of a velvet sky the burning white disc of the full moon, her private omen of power, and before it the silver-silk flash of membranous wings.

She woke in the deep of the night. Rain thundered against the walls of the Hold, a torrent roaring in darkness. Beside her John slept, and she saw in the darkness what she had noticed that morning in daylight: that for all his thirty-four years, he had a thread or two of silver in his unruly brown hair.

A thought crossed her mind. She put it aside firmly, and just as firmly it reintruded itself. It was not a daylight thought, but the nagging whisper that comes only in the dark hours, after troubled sleep. Don't be a fool, she told herself; the times you have done it, you have always wished you hadn't.

But the thought, the temptation, would not go away.

At length she rose, careful not to wake the man who slept at her side. She wrapped herself in John's worn, quilted robe and padded from the bedchamber, the worn floor like smooth ice beneath her small, bare feet.

The study was even darker than the bedchamber had been, the fire there nothing more than a glowing line of rose-colored heat above a snowbank of ash. Her shadow passed like the hand of a ghost over the slumbering shape of the harp and made the silver of reflected red wink along the pennywhistle's edge. At the far side of the study, she raised a heavy curtain and passed into a tiny room that was little more than a niche in the Hold's thick wall. Barely wider than its window, in daylight it was coolly bright, but now the heavy bull's-eye glass was black as ink, and the witchlight she called into being above her head glittered coldly on the rain streaming down outside.

The phosphorescent glow that illuminated the room outlined the shape of a narrow table and three small shelves. They held things that had belonged to the cold-eyed ice-witch who had been John's mother, or to Caerdinn—simple things, a few bowls, an oddly shaped root, a few crystals like fragments of broken stars sent for mending. Pulling her robe more closely about her, Jenny took from its place a plain pottery bowl, so old that whatever designs had once been painted upon its outer surface had long since been rubbed away by the touch of mages' hands. She dipped it into the stone vessel of water that stood in a corner and set it upon the table, drawing up before it a tall, spindle-legged chair.

For a time she only sat, gazing down into the water. Slips of foxfire danced on its black surface; as she slowed her breathing, she became aware of every sound from the roaring of the rain gusts against the tower's walls to the smallest drip of the eaves. The worn tabletop was like cold glass under her fingertips; her breath was cold against her own lips. For a time she was aware of the small flaws and bubbles in the glaze of the bowl's inner surface; then she sank deeper, watching the colors that seemed to swirl within the endless depths. She seemed to move down toward an absolute darkness, and the water was like ink, opaque, ungiving.

Gray mists rolled in the depths, then cleared as if wind had driven them, and she saw darkness in a vast place, pricked by the starlike points of candleflame. An open space of black stone lay before her, smooth as oily water; around it was a forest, not of trees, but of columns of stone.

Some were thin as silk, others thicker than the most ancient of oaks, and over them swayed the shadows of the dancers on the open floor. Though the picture was silent, she could feel the rhythm to which they danced— gnomes, she saw, their long arms brushing the floor as they bent, the vast, cloudy manes of their pale hair catching rims of firelight like sunset seen through heavy smoke. They danced around a misshapen stone altar, the slow dances that are forbidden to the eyes of the children of men.

The dream changed. She beheld a desolation of charred and broken ruins beneath the dark flank of a tree-covered mountain. Night sky arched overhead, wind-cleared and heart-piercingly beautiful. The waxing moon was like a glowing coin; its light touching with cold, white fingers the broken pavement of the empty square below the hillside upon which she stood, edging the raw bones that moldered in puddles of faintly smoking slime. Something flashed in the velvet shadow of the mountain, and she saw the dragon. Starlight gleamed like oil on the lean, sable sides; the span of those enormous wings stretched for a moment like a skeleton's arms to embrace the moon's stern face. Music seemed to drift upon the night, a string of notes like a truncated air, and for an instant her heart leaped toward that silent, dangerous beauty, lonely and graceful in the secret magic of its gliding flight.

Then she saw another scene by the low light of a dying fire. She thought she was in the same place, on a rise overlooking the desolation of the ruined town before the gates of the Deep. It was the cold hour of the tide's ebbing, some hours before dawn. John lay near the fire, dark blood leaking from the clawed rents in his armor. His face was a mass of blisters beneath a mask of gore and grime; he was alone, and the fire was dying. Its light caught a spangle of red from the twisted links of his torn mail shirt and glimmered stickily on the upturned palm of one blistered hand. The fire died, and for a moment only starlight glittered on the pooling blood and outlined the shape of his nose and lips against the darkness.

She was underground once more, in the place where the gnomes had danced. It was empty now, but the hollow silences beneath the earth seemed filled with the inchoate murmur of formless sound, as if the stone altar whispered to itself in the darkness.

Then she saw only the small flaws in the glaze of the bowl, and the dark, oily surface of the water. The witchlight had long ago failed above her head, which ached as it often did when she had overstretched her power. Her body felt chilled through to the bones, but she was for a time too weary to move from where she sat. She stared before her into the darkness, listening to the steady drum of the rain, hurting in her soul and wishing with all that was in her that she had not done what she had done.

All divination was chancy, she told herself, and water was the most notorious liar of all. There was no reason to believe that what she had seen would come to pass.

So she repeated to herself, over and over, but it did no good. In time she lowered her face to her hands and wept.

3

They set forth two days later and rode south through a maelstrom of wind and water.

In the days of the Kings, the Great North Road had stretched from Bel itself northward like a gray stone serpent, through the valley of the Wildspae River and across the farm and forest lands of Wyr, linking the southern capital with the northern frontier and guarding the great silver mines of Tralchet. But the mines had flagged, and the Kings had begun to squabble with their brothers and cousins over the lordship of the south. The troops who guarded the Winterlands' forts had been withdrawn—temporarily, they said, to shore up the forces of one contender against another. They had never returned. Now the gray stone serpent was disintegrating slowly, like a shed skin; its stones were torn up to strengthen house walls against bandits and barbarians, its ditches choked with decades of detritus, and its very foundations forced apart by the encroaching tree roots of the forest of Wyr. The Winterlands had destroyed it, as they destroyed all things.

Traveling south along what remained of the road was slow, for the autumn storms swelled the icy becks of the moors to white-toothed torrents and reduced the ground in the tree-tangled hollows to sodden, nameless mires. Under the flail of the wind, Gareth could no longer argue that the ship upon which he had come north would still be waiting at Eldsbouch to waft them south in relative comfort and speed, but Jenny suspected he still felt in his heart that it should have been, and, illogically, blamed her that it was not.

They rode for the most part in silence. Sometimes when they halted, as they frequently did for John to scout the tumbled rocks or dense knots of woodland ahead, Jenny looked across at Gareth and saw him gazing

around him in a kind of hurt bewilderment at the desolation through
which they rode: at the barren downs with their weed-grown lines of broken walls; at the old boundary stones, lumpish and melted-looking as
spring snowmen; and at the stinking bogs or the high, bare tors with their
few twisted trees, giant balls of mistletoe snagged weirdly in their naked
branches against a dreary sky. It was a land that no longer remembered
law or the prosperity of ordered living that comes with law, and sometimes she could see him struggling with the understanding of what John
was offering to buy at the stake of his life.

But usually it was plain that Gareth simply found the halts annoying.
"We're never going to get there at this rate," he complained as John
appeared from the smoke-colored tangle of dead heather that cloaked the
lower flanks of a promontory that hid the road. A watchtower had once
crowned it, now reduced to a chewed-looking circle of rubble on the hill's
crest. John had bellied up the slope to investigate it and the road ahead
and now was shaking mud and wet out of his plaid. "It's been twenty days
since the dragon came," Gareth added resentfully. "Anything can have
happened."

"It can have happened the day after you took ship, my hero," John
pointed out, swinging up to the saddle of his spare riding horse, Cow.
"And if we don't look sharp and scout ahead, we *are* never going to get
there."

But the sullen glance the boy shot at John's back as he reined away
told Jenny more clearly than words that, though he could not argue with
this statement, he did not believe it, either.

That evening they camped in the ragged birches of the broken country where the downs gave place to the hoary densities of the Wyrwoods.
When camp was set, and the horses and mules picketed, Jenny moved
quietly along the edge of the clearing, the open ground above the high
bank of a stream whose noisy rushing blended with the sea-sound of the
wind in the trees. She touched the bark of the trees and the soggy mast
of acorns, hazelnuts, and decaying leaves underfoot, tracing them with
the signs that only a mage could see—signs that would conceal the
camp from those who might pass by outside. Looking back toward the
fluttering yellow light of the new fire, she saw Gareth hunkered down
beside it, shivering in his damp cloak, looking wretched and very forlorn.

Her square, full lips pressed together. Since he had learned she was
his erstwhile hero's mistress, he had barely spoken to her. His resentment
at her inclusion in the expedition was still obvious, as was his unspoken
assumption that she had included herself out of a combination of med-
dling and a desire not to let her lover out of her sight. But Gareth was

alone in an alien land, having clearly never been away from the comforts of his home before, lonely, disillusioned, and filled with a gnawing fear of what he would return to find.

Jenny sighed and crossed the clearing to where he sat.

The boy looked up at her suspiciously as she dug into her jacket pocket and drew out a long sliver of smoky crystal on the chain that Caerdinn had used to hang around his neck. "I can't see the dragon in this," she said, "but if you'll tell me the name of your father and something about your home in Bel, at least I should be able to call their images and tell you if they're all right."

Gareth turned his face away from her. "No," he said. Then, after a moment, he added grudgingly, "Thank you all the same."

Jenny folded her arms and regarded him for a moment in the jumpy orange firelight. He huddled a little deeper into his stained crimson cloak and would not meet her eyes.

"Is it because you think I can't?" she asked at last. "Or because you won't take the aid of a witch?"

He didn't answer that, though his full lower lip pinched up a bit in the middle. With a sigh of exasperation, Jenny walked away from him to where John stood near the oil-skin-covered mound of the packs, looking out into the darkening woods.

He glanced back as she came near, the stray gleams of firelight throwing glints of dirty orange on the metal of his patched doublet. "D'you want a bandage for your nose?" he inquired, as if she'd tried to pet a ferret and gotten nipped for her trouble. She laughed ruefully.

"He didn't have any objections to me before," she said, more hurt than she had realized by the boy's enmity.

John put an arm around her and hugged her close. "He feels cheated, is all," he said easily. "And since God forbid he should have cheated himself with his expectations, it must have been one of us that did it, mustn't it?" He leaned down to kiss her, his hand firm against the bare nape of her neck beneath the coiled ridge of her braided hair. Beyond them, among the ghostly birches, the thin underbrush rustled harshly; a moment later a softer, steadier rushing whispered in the bare branches overhead. Jenny smelled the rain almost before she was conscious of its light fingers upon her face.

Behind them, she heard Gareth cursing. He squelched across the clearing to join them a moment later, wiping raindroplets from his spectacles, his hair in lank strings against his temples.

"We seem to have outsmarted ourselves," he said glumly. "Picked a nice place to camp—only there's no shelter. There's a cave down under the cut of the streambank . . ."

"Above the highest rise of the water?" inquired John, a mischievous glint in his eye.

Gareth said defensively, "Yes. At least—it isn't so very far down the bank."

"Big enough to put the horses in, always supposing we could get them down there?"

The boy bristled. "I could go see."

"No," said Jenny. Gareth opened his mouth to protest this arbitrariness, but she cut him off with, "I've laid spells of ward and guard about this camp—I don't think they should be crossed. It's almost full-dark now . . ."

"But we'll get *wet!*"

"You've been wet for days, my hero," John pointed out with cheerful brutality. "Here at least we know we're safe from the side the stream's on—unless, of course, it rises over its bank." He glanced down at Jenny, still in the circle of his arm; she was conscious, too, of Gareth's sulky gaze. "What about the spell-ward, love?"

She shook her head. "I don't know," she said. "Sometimes the spells will hold against the Whisperers, sometimes they don't. I don't know why—whether it's because of something about the Whisperers, or because of something about the spells." Or because, she added to herself, her own powers weren't strong enough to hold even a true spell against them.

"Whisperers?" Gareth demanded incredulously.

"A kind of blood-devil," said John, with an edge of irritation in his voice. "It doesn't matter at the moment, my hero. Just stay inside the camp."

"Can't I even go *look* for shelter? I won't go far."

"If you leave the camp, you'll never find your way back to it," John snapped. "You're so bloody anxious not to lose time on this trip, you wouldn't want to have us spend the next three days looking for your body, would you? Come on, Jen—if you're not after making supper, I'll do it . . ."

"I'll do it, I'll do it," Jenny agreed, with a haste that wasn't entirely jest. As she and John walked back to the smoky, sheltered campfire, she glanced back at Gareth, still standing on the edge of the faintly gleaming spell-circle. His vanity stinging from John's last words, the boy picked up an acorn and hurled it angrily out into the wet darkness. The darkness whispered and rustled, and then fell still again under the ceaseless pattern of the rain.

They left the folded lands of rock hills and leaping streams for good after that and entered the ruinous gloom of the great Forest of Wyr. Here crowded oaks and hawthorn pressed close upon the road, catching the faces of the travelers with warty, overhanging boughs and dirty moss and their horses' hooves with scabrous roots and soggy drifts of dead leaves. The black lattices of bare branches above them admitted only a fraction of the pallid daylight, but rain still leaked through, pattering in an endless, dreary murmur in the dead fern and hazel thickets. The ground was worse here, sodden and unsteady, or flooded in meres of silver water in which the trees stood, knee-deep and rotting; and Aversin remarked that the marshes of the south were spreading again. In many places the road was covered, or blocked with fallen trees, and the labor of clearing it or beating a path through the thickets around these obstacles left them all cold and exhausted. Even for Jenny, used to the hardships of the Winterlands, this was tiring, and the more so because there was no respite; she lay down weary at night and rose weary in the bleak grayness before dawn to travel on once again. What it was to Gareth she could well imagine. As he grew more weary, his temper shortened, and he complained bitterly at every halt.

"What's he looking for now?" he demanded one afternoon, when John ordered their fifth halt in three hours and, armed with his heavy horn hunting-bow, dismounted and vanished into the choking tangle of hazel and blackthorn beside the road.

It had been raining most of the forenoon, and the tall boy drooped miserably on the back of The Stupid Roan, one of the spare horses they'd brought from the Hold. The other spare, Jenny's mount, John had christened The Stupider Roan, a name that was unfortunately apt. Jenny suspected that, in his wearier moments, Gareth even blamed her for the generally poor quality of the Hold's horseflesh. The rain had ceased now, but cold wind still probed through the very weave of their garments; every now and then a gust shook the branches above them and splattered them with leftover rain and an occasional sodden oak leaf that drifted down like a dead bat.

"He's looking for danger." Jenny herself was listening, her nerves queerly on edge, searching the silence that hung like an indrawn breath among the dark, close-crowded trees.

"He didn't find any last time, did he?" Gareth tucked his gloved hands under his cloak for warmth and shivered. Then he looked ostentatiously upward, scanning what sky was visible, calculating the time of day, and from there going on to remember how many days they had been on the road. Under his sarcasm she could hear fear. "Or the time before that, either."

"And lucky for us that he didn't," she replied. "I think you have little understanding of the dangers in the Winterlands . . ."

Gareth gasped, and his gaze fixed. Turning her head quickly, Jenny followed his eyes to the dark shape of Aversin, his plaids making him nearly invisible in the gloom among the trees. With a single slow movement he had raised his bow, the arrow nocked but not yet pulled.

She tracked the trajectory of the arrow's flight to the source of the danger.

Just visible through the trees, a skinny little old man was stooping arthritically to scrape the dry insides from a rotting log for kindling. His wife, an equally lean, equally rag-clad old woman whose thin white hair hung lankly about her narrow shoulders, was holding a reed basket to receive the crumbling chips. Gareth let out a cry of horror. "NO!"

Aversin moved his head. The old woman, alerted also, looked up and gave a thin wail, dropping her basket to shield her face futilely with her arms. The dry, woody punk spilled onto the marshy ground about her feet. The old man caught her by the arm and the two of them began to flee dodderingly into the deeper forest, sobbing and covering their heads with their arms, as if they supposed that the broad-tipped iron war arrow would be stopped by such slack old flesh.

Aversin lowered his bow and let his targets stumble unshot into the wet wilderness of trees.

Gareth gasped, "He was going to kill them! Those poor old people . . ."

Jenny nodded, as John came back to the road. "I know." She understood why; but, as when she had killed the dying robber in the ruins of the old town, she still felt unclean.

"Is that all you can say?" Gareth raged, horrified. "You *know*? He would have shot them in cold blood . . ."

"They were Meewinks, Gar," John said quietly. "Shooting's the only thing you can do with Meewinks."

"I don't care what you call them!" he cried. "They were old and harmless! All they were doing was gathering kindling!"

A small, straight line appeared between John's reddish brows, and he rubbed his eyes. Gareth, Jenny thought, was not the only one upon whom this trip was telling.

"I don't know what you call them in your part of the country," Aversin said tiredly. "Their people used to farm all the valley of the Wildspae. They . . ."

"John." Jenny touched his arm. She had followed this exchange only marginally; her senses and her power were diffused through the damp woods, and in the fading light she scented danger. It seemed to prickle along her skin—a soft plashing movement in the flooded glades to the north, a thin chittering that silenced the small restive noises of fox and weasel. "We should be moving. The light's already going. I don't remember this part of the woods well but I know it's some distance from any kind of camping place."

"What is it?" His voice, like hers, dropped to a whisper.

She shook her head. "Maybe nothing. But I think we should go."

"Why?" Gareth bleated. "What's wrong? For three days you've been running away from your own shadows . . ."

"That's right," John agreed, and there was a dangerous edge to his quiet voice. "You ever think what might happen to you if your own shadow caught you? Now ride—and ride silent."

It was nearly full night when they made camp, for, like Jenny, Aversin was nervous, and it took some time for him to find a camping place that his woodsmanship judged to be even relatively safe. One of them Jenny rejected, not liking the way the dark trees crowded around it; another John passed by because the spring could not be seen from where the fire would be. Jenny was hungry and tired, but the instincts of the Winterlands warned her to keep moving until they found a place that could be defended, though against what she could not tell.

When Aversin ruled against a third place, an almost-circular clearing with a small, fern-choked spring gurgling through one side of it, Gareth's hunger-frayed temper snapped. "What's wrong with it?" he demanded, dismounting and huddling on the lee-side of The Stupid Roan for warmth. "You can take a drink without getting out of sight of the fire, and it's bigger than the other place was."

Annoyance glinted like the blink of drawn steel in John's voice. "I don't like it."

"Well, why in the name of Sarmendes not?"

Aversin looked around him at the clearing and shook his head. The clouds had parted overhead enough to admit watery moonlight to glint on his specs, on the water droplets in his hair when he pushed back his hood, and on the end of his long nose. "I just don't. I can't say why."

"Well, if you can't say why, what would you like?"

"What I'd like," the Dragonsbane retorted with his usual devastating accuracy, "is not to have some snirp of a silk-lined brat telling me a place is safe because he wants his supper."

Because that was obviously Gareth's first concern, the boy exploded, "That isn't the reason! I think you've lived like a wolf for so long you don't trust anything! I'm not going to trek through the woods all night long because . . ."

"Fine," said Aversin grimly. "You can just bloody well stay here, then."

"That's right! Go ahead, abandon me! Are you going to take a shot at me if I try to come after you and you hear the bushes rustle?"

"I might."

"John!" Jenny's cool, slightly gravelly voice cut across his next words. "How much longer can we travel without lights of some kind? Clouds are moving up. It won't rain, but you won't be able to see a foot ahead of you in two hours."

"*You* could," he pointed out. He felt it, too, she thought—that growing sensation that had begun back along the road; the uneasy feeling of being watched.

"I could," she agreed quietly. "But I don't have your woodsmanship. And I know this part of the road—there isn't a better place ahead. I don't like this place either, but I'm not sure that staying here wouldn't be safer than showing up our position by traveling with lights, even a very dim magelight. And even that might not show up signs of danger."

John looked about him at the dark woods, now barely visible in the cold gloom. Wind stirred at the bare boughs interlaced above their heads, and somewhere before them in the clearing Jenny could hear the whisper of the ferns and the rushing voice of the rain-fed stream. No sound of danger, she thought. Why then did she subconsciously watch with her peripheral vision; why this readiness to flee?

Aversin said quietly, "It's too good."

Gareth snapped, "First you don't like it and then you say it's too good . . ."

"They'll know all the camping places anyway," Jenny replied softly across his words.

Furious, Gareth sputtered, "Who'll know?"

"The Meewinks, you stupid oic," snapped John back at him.

Gareth flung up his hands. "Oh, fine! You mean you don't want to camp here because you're afraid of being attacked by a little old man and a little old lady?"

"And about fifty of their friends, yes," John retorted. "And one more word out of you, my hero, and you're going to find yourself slammed up against a tree."

Thoroughly roused now, Gareth retorted, "Good! Prove how clever you are by thrashing someone who disagrees with you! If you're afraid of being attacked by a troop of forty four-foot-tall septuagenarians . . ."

He never even saw Aversin move. The Dragonsbane might not have the appearance of a hero, Jenny thought, but he nevertheless had the physical reflexes of one. Gareth gasped as he was literally lifted off his feet by a double-handful of cloak and doublet, and Jenny strode forward to catch John's spike-studded forearm. With softness as definite as an assassin's footfall, she said, "Be quiet! And drop him."

"Got a cliff handy?" But she felt the momentum of his rage slack.

After a pause he pushed—almost threw—Gareth from him. "Right."
Behind his anger he sounded embarrassed. "Thanks to our hero, it's well
too dark now to be moving on. Jen, can you do anything with this place?
Spell it?"

Jenny thought for a few moments, trying to analyze what it was that
she feared. "Not against the Meewinks, no," she replied at last. She added
acidly, "They'll have tracked you gentlemen by your voices."

"It wasn't me who . . ."

"I didn't ask who it was." She took the reins of the horses and mules
and led them on into the clearing, anxious now to get a camp set and circled with the spells of ward before they were seen from the outside.
Gareth, a little shamefaced at his outburst, followed sulkily, looking at the
layout of the clearing.

In the voice of one who sought to mollify by pretending that the dis-
agreement never happened, he asked, "Does this hollow look all right for
the fire?"

Irritation still crackled in Aversin's voice. "No fire. We're in for a
cold camp tonight—and you'll take the first watch, my hero."

Gareth gasped in protest at this arbitrary switch. Since leaving the
Hold, Gareth had always taken the last watch, the dawn watch, because at
the end of a day's riding he wanted nothing more than to lie down and
sleep; Jenny had always taken second; and John, used to the habits of
wolves who hunted in the early part of the night, took the first. The boy
began, "But I . . ." and Jenny swung around to look at them in the somber
gloom.

"One more word out of either of you and I will lay a spell of dumb-
ness upon you both."

John subsided at once. Gareth started to speak again, then thought
better of it. Jenny pulled the picket rope out of the mule Clivy's pack and
looped it around a sapling. Half to herself, she added, "Though God
knows it couldn't make you any dumber."

Throughout their meager dinner of dried beef, cold cornmeal mush,
and apples, Gareth remained ostentatiously silent. Jenny scarcely noticed,
and John, seeing her preoccupied, said little to her, not wanting to disturb
her concentration. She was not sure how much he felt of the danger she
sensed in the woods all around them—she didn't know how much of it
was only the product of her own weariness. But she wove all her concentration, all her abilities, into the spell-circle that she put around the camp
that night: spells of ward that would make their campsite unnoticeable
from the outside, that would thwart the eye of any who were not actually
within the circle. They would not be much help against the Meewinks,
who would know where the clearing was, but they might provide a delay

that would buy time. To these she added other spells against other dangers, spells that Caerdinn had taught her against the blood-devils and Whisperers that haunted the Woods of Wyr, spells whose efficacy she privately doubted because she knew that they sometimes failed, but the best spells that she—or anyone to whom she had spoken—knew.

She had long suspected that the Lines of magic were thinning and that every generation attenuated the teaching of magic that had been passed down from the old times, the times before the Realm of Belmarie had united all the West under itself and the glittering worship of the Twelve Gods. Caerdinn had been one of the mightiest of the Line of Herne, but, when she had first met him at fourteen, he was already very old, feeble, and a little crazy. He had taught her, trained her in the secrets of the Line passed from master to pupil over a dozen generations. But since his death she had found two instances where his knowledge had been incorrect and had heard of spells from her Line-kindred, the pupils' pupils of Caerdinn's master Spaeth Skywarden, which Caerdinn had either not bothered to teach her, or had not known himself. The spells of guard against the Whisperers that had more and more come to haunt the Wyrwoods were ineffective and sporadic, and she knew of no spell that would drive them or the blood-devils out of an area to render it safe for humans again. Such things might reside somewhere in a book, written down by the mage who discovered them, but neither Jenny, nor any mage she had met, had known of them.

She slept that night uneasily, exhausted in body and troubled by strange shapes that seemed to slide in and out through the cracks in her dreams. She seemed to be able to hear the whistling chitter of the blood-devils as they flitted from tree to tree in the marshy woods across the stream and below them the soft murmurs of the Whisperers in the darkness beyond the barrier of spells. Twice she pulled herself painfully from the sucking darkness of sleep, fearing some danger, but both times she only saw Gareth sitting propped against a pile of packsaddles, nodding in the misty blackness.

The third time she woke up, Gareth was gone.

It had been a dream that woke her; a dream of a woman standing half-hidden among the trees. She was veiled, like all the women of the south; the lace of that veil was like a cloak of flowers scattered over her dark curls. Her soft laughter was like silver bells, but there was a husky note in it, as if she never laughed save with pleasure at something gained. She held out small, slender hands, and whispered Gareth's name.

Leaves and dirt were scuffed where he had crossed the flickering lines of the protective circles.

Jenny sat up, shaking back the coarse mane of her hair, and touched

John awake. She called the witchlight into being, and it illuminated the still, silent camp and glowed in the eyes of the wakened horses. The voice of the spring was loud in the hush.

Like John, she had slept in her clothes. Reaching over to the bundle of her sheepskin jacket, her plaids, her boots and her belt that lay heaped at one side of their blankets, she pulled from its pouch the small scrying-crystal and angled it to the witchlight while John began, without a word, to pull on his boots and wolfskin-lined doublet.

Of the four elements, scrying earth—crystal—was easiest and most accurate, though the crystal itself had to be enchanted beforehand. Scrying fire needed no special preparation, but what it showed was what it would, not always what was sought; water would show both future and past, but was a notorious liar. Only the very greatest of mages could scry the wind.

The heart of Caerdinn's crystal was dark. She stilled her fears for Gareth's safety, calming her mind as she summoned the images; they gleamed on the facets, as if reflected from somewhere else. She saw a stone room, extremely small, with the architecture of some place half-dug into the ground; the only furnishing was a bed and a sort of table formed by a block of stone projecting from the wall itself. A wet cloak was thrown over the table, with a puddle of half-dried water about it—swamp weeds clung to it like dark worms. A much-bejeweled longsword was propped nearby, and on top of the table and cloak lay a pair of spectacles. The round lenses caught a spark of greasy yellow lamplight as the door of the room opened.

Someone in the corridor held a lamp high. Its light showed small, stooped forms crowding in the broad hall beyond. Old and young, men and women, there must have been forty of them, with white, sloped, warty faces and round, fishlike eyes. The first through the doorway were the old man and the old woman, the Meewinks whom John had nearly shot that afternoon.

The old man held a rope; the woman, a cleaver.

The house of the Meewinks stood where the land lay low, on a knoll above a foul soup of mud and water from whose surface rotting trees projected like half-decayed corpses. Squat-built, it was larger than it looked—stone walls behind it showed one wing half-buried underground. In spite of the cold, the air around the place was fetid with the smell of putrefying fish, and Jenny closed her teeth hard against a queasiness that washed over her at the sight of the place. Since first she had known what they were, she had hated the Meewinks.

John slid from his dapple war horse Osprey's back and looped his rein and Battlehammer's over the limb of a sapling. His face, in the rainy darkness, was taut with a mingling of hatred and disgust. Twice households of Meewinks had tried to establish themselves near Alyn Hold; both times, as soon as he had learned of them, he had raised what militia he could and burned them out. A few had been killed each time, but he had lacked the men to pursue them through the wild lands and eradicate them completely. Jenny knew he still had nightmares about what he had found in their cellars.

He whispered, "Listen," and Jenny nodded. From the house she could detect a faint clamor of voices, muffled, as if half-below the ground, thin and yammering like the barking of beasts. Jenny slid her halberd from the holster on Moon Horse's saddle and breathed to all three mounts for stillness and silence. She sketched over them the spells of ward, so that the casual eye would pass them by, or think they were something other than horses—a hazel thicket, or the oddly shaped shadow of a tree. It was these same spells upon the camp, she knew, that had prevented Gareth from finding his way back to it, once what must have been the Whisperer had led him away.

John tucked his spectacles into an inner pocket. "Right," he murmured. "You get Gar—I'll cover you both."

Jenny nodded, feeling cold inside, as she did when she emptied her mind to do some great magic beyond her power, and steeled herself for what she knew was coming. As they crossed the filthy yard and the strange, muffled outcry in the house grew stronger, John kissed her and, turning, smashed his booted foot into the small house's door.

They broke through the door like raiders robbing Hell. A hot, damp fetor smote Jenny in the face as she barged through on John's heels, the putrid stink of the filth the Meewinks lived in and of the decaying fish they ate—above it all was the sharp, copper-bright stench of new-shed blood. The noise was a pandemonium of yammering screams; after the darkness outside, even the smoky glow of the fire in the unnaturally huge hearth seemed blinding. Bodies seethed in a heaving mob around the small door at the opposite side of the room; now and then sharp flashes of light glinted from the knives clutched in moist little hands.

Gareth was backed to the doorpost in the midst of the mob. He had evidently fought his way that far but knew if he descended into the more open space of the big room he would be surrounded. His left arm was wrapped, shieldlike, in a muffling tangle of stained and filthy bedding; in his right hand was his belt, the buckle-end of which he was using to slash at the faces of the Meewinks all around him. His own face was streaming with blood from knife-cuts and bites—mixed with sweat, it ran down and encrimsoned his shirt as if his throat had been cut. His naked gray eyes were wide with a look of sickened, nightmare horror.

The Meewinks around him were gibbering like the souls of the damned. There must have been fifty of them, all armed with their little knives of steel, or of sharpened shell. As John and Jenny broke in, Jenny saw one of them crawl in close to Gareth and slash at the back of his knee. His thighs were already gashed with a dozen such attempts, his boots sticky with runnels of blood; he kicked his attacker in the face, rolling her down a step or two into the mass of her fellows. It was the old woman he had kept John from shooting.

Without a word, John plunged down into the heaving, stinking mob. Jenny sprang after him, guarding his back; blood splattered her from the first swing of his sword, and around them the noise rose like the redoubling of a storm at sea. The Meewinks were a small folk, though some of the men were as tall as she; it made her cringe inside to cut at the slack white faces of people no bigger than children and to slam the weighted butt of the halberd into those pouchy little stomachs and watch them fall, gasping, vomiting, and choking. But there were so many of them. She had kilted her faded plaid skirts up to her knees to fight and she felt hands snatch and drag at them, as one man caught up a cleaver from among the butcher's things lying on the room's big table, trying to cripple her. Her blade caught him high on the cheekbone and opened his face down to the opposite corner of his jaw. His scream ripped the cut wider. The stench of blood was everywhere.

It seemed to take only seconds to cross the room. Jenny yelled, "Gareth!" but he swung at her with the belt—she was short enough to be a Meewink, and he had lost his spectacles. She flung up the halberd; the belt wrapped itself around the shaft, and she wrenched it from his hands. "It's Jenny!" she shouted, as John's sword strokes came down, defending them both as it splattered them with flying droplets of gore. She grabbed the boy's bony wrist, jerking him down the steps into the room. "Now, run!"

"But we can't . . ." he began, looking back at John, and she shoved him violently in the direction of the door. After what appeared to be a momentary struggle with a desire not to seem a coward by abandoning his rescuers, Gareth ran. They passed the table and he caught up a meat hook in passing, swinging at the pallid, puffy faces all around them and at the little hands with their jabbing knives. Three Meewinks were guarding the door, but fell back screaming before the greater length of Jenny's weapon. Behind her, she could hear the squeaky cacophony around John rising to a crescendo; she knew he was outnumbered, and her instincts to rush back to fight at his side dragged at her like wet rope. It was all she could do to force herself to hurl open the door and drag Gareth at a run across the clearing outside.

Gareth balked, panicky. "Where are the horses? How are we . . . ?"

For all her small size, she was strong; her shove nearly toppled him. "Don't ask questions!" Already small, slumped forms were running about the darkness of the woods ahead. The ooze underfoot soaked through her boots as she hauled Gareth toward where she, at least, could see the three horses, and she heard Gareth gulp when they got close enough for the spells to lose their effectiveness.

While the boy scrambled up to Battlehammer's back, Jenny flung herself onto Moon Horse, caught Osprey's lead-rein, and spurred back toward the house in a porridgey spatter of mud. Pitching her voice to cut through the screaming clamor within, she called out, "JOHN!" A moment later a confused tangle of figures erupted through the low doorway, like a pack of dogs trying to bring down a bear. The white glare of the witch-light showed Aversin's sword bloody to the pommel, his face streaked and running with his own blood and that of his attackers, his breath pouring like a ribbon of steam from his mouth. Meewinks clung to his arms and his belt, hacking and chewing at the leather of his boots.

With a screaming battle cry like a gull's, Jenny rode down upon them, swinging her halberd like a scythe. Meewinks scattered, mewing and hissing, and John wrenched himself free of the last of them and flung himself up to Osprey's saddle. A tiny Meewink child hurled up after him, clinging to the stirrup leather and jabbing with its little shell knife at his groin; John swung his arm downward and caught the child across its narrow temple with the spikes of his armband, sweeping it off as he would have swept a rat.

Jenny wheeled her horse sharply, spurring back to where Gareth still clung to Battlehammer's saddle on the edge of the clearing. With the precision of circus riders, she and John split to grab the big gelding's reins, one on either side, and, with Gareth in tow between them, plunged back into the night.

"There." Aversin dipped one finger into a puddle of rainwater and flicked a droplet onto the iron griddle balanced over the fire. Satisfied with the sizzle, he patted cornmeal into a cake and dropped it into place. Then he glanced across at Gareth, who was struggling not to cry out as Jenny poured a scouring concoction of marigold-simple into his wounds. "Now you can say you've seen Aversin the Dragonsbane run like hell from a troop of forty four-foot-tall septuagenarians." His bitten, bandaged hands patted another cake into shape, and the dawn grayness flashed off his specs as he grinned.

"Will they be after us?" Gareth asked faintly.

"I doubt it." He picked a fleck of cornmeal off the spikes of his armbands. "They'll have enough of their own dead to keep them fed awhile."

The boy swallowed queasily, though having seen the instruments laid out on the table in the Meewinks' house, there could be little doubt what they had meant for him.

At Jenny's insistence, after the rescue, they had shifted their camp away from the garnered darkness of the woods. Dawn had found them in relatively open ground on the formless verges of a marsh, where long wastes of ice-scummed, standing water reflected a steely sky among the black pen strokes of a thousand reeds. Jenny had worked, cold and weary, to lay spells about the camp, then had occupied herself with the contents of her medicine satchel, leaving John, somewhat against her better judgment, to make breakfast. Gareth had dug into his packs for the bent and battered spectacles that had survived the fight in the ruins up north, and they perched forlornly askew now on the end of his nose.

"They were always a little folk," John went on, coming over to the packs where the boy sat, letting Jenny finish binding up his slashed knees. "After the King's troops left the Winterlands, their villages were forever being raided by bandits, who'd steal whatever food they raised. They never were a match for an armored man, but a village of 'em could pull one down—or, better still, wait till he was asleep and hack him up as he lay. In the starving times, a bandit's horse could feed a whole village for a week. I expect it started out as only the horses."

Gareth swallowed again and looked as if he were going to be ill.

John put his hands through his metal-plated belt. "They generally strike right before dawn, when sleep is deepest—it's why I switched the watches, so I'd be the one they dealt with, instead of you. It was a Whisperer that got you away from the camp, wasn't it?"

"I—I suppose so." He looked at the ground, a shadow crossing his thin face. "I don't know. It was something . . ." Jenny felt him shudder.

"I've seen them on my watch, once or twice . . . Jen?"

"Once." Jenny spoke shortly, hating the memory of those crying shapes in the darkness.

"They take all forms," John said, sitting on the ground beside her and wrapping his arms about his knees. "One night one even took Jen's, with her lying beside me . . . Polyborus says in his *Analects*—or maybe it's in that half-signature of Terens' *Of Ghosts*—that they read your dreams and take on the forms that they see there. From Terens—or is it Polyborus? Or maybe it's in Clivy, though it's a bit accurate for Clivy—I get the impression they used to be much rarer than they are now, whatever they are."

"I don't know," Gareth said quietly. "They must have been, because I'd never heard of them, or of the Meewinks, either. After it—it lured me into the woods, it attacked me. I ran, but I couldn't seem to find the camp again. I ran and ran . . . and then I saw the light from that house . . ." He fell silent again with a shudder.

Jenny finished wrapping Gareth's knee. The wounds weren't deep, but, like those on John's face and hands, they were vicious, not only the knife cuts, but the small, crescent-shaped tears of human teeth. Her own body bore them, too, and experience had taught her that such wounds were filthier than poisoned arrows. For the rest, she was aching and stiff with pulled muscles and the general fatigue of battle, something she supposed Gareth's ballads neglected to mention as the inevitable result of physical combat. She felt cold inside, too, as she did when she worked the death-spells, something else they never mentioned in ballads, where all killing was done with serene and noble confidence. She had taken the lives of at least four human beings last night, she knew, for all that they had been born and raised into a cannibal tribe; had maimed others who would either die when their wounds turned septic in that atmosphere of festering decay, or would be killed by their brothers.

To survive in the Winterlands, she had become a very competent killer. But the longer she was a healer, the more she learned about magic and about life from which all magic stemmed, the more she loathed what she did. Living in the Winterlands, she had seen what death did to those who dealt it out too casually.

The gray waters of the marsh began to brighten with the remote shine of daybreak beyond the clouds. With a soft winnowing of a thousand wings, the wild geese rose from the black cattail beds, seeking again the roads of the colorless sky. Jenny sighed, weary to her bones and knowing that they could not afford to rest—knowing that she would have no rest until they crossed the great river Wildspae and entered the lands of Belmarie.

Quietly, Gareth said, "Aversin—Lord John—I—I'm sorry. I didn't understand about the Winterlands." He looked up, his gray eyes tired and unhappy behind their cracked specs. "And I didn't understand about you. I—I hated you, for not being what—what I thought you should be."

"Oh, aye, I knew that," John said with a fleet grin. "But what you felt about me was none of my business. My business was to see you safe in a land you had no knowledge of. And as for being what you expected— Well, you can only know what you know, and all you knew were those songs. I mean, it's like Polyborus and Clivy and those others. I know bears aren't born completely shapeless for their mothers to sculpt with their tongues, like Clivy says, because I've seen newborn bear cubs. But for all I know, lions *may* be born dead, although personally I don't think it's likely."

"They aren't," Gareth said. "Father had a lioness once as a pet, when I was very little—her cubs were born live, just like big kittens. They were spotted."

"Really?" Aversin looked genuinely pleased for one more bit of knowledge to add to the lumber room of his mind. "I'm not saying Dragonsbanes aren't heroic, because Selkythar and Antara Warlady and the others might have been, and may have gone about it all with swords in golden armor and plumes. It's just that I know I'm not. If I'd had a choice, I'd never have gone near the bloody dragon, but nobody asked me." He grinned and added, "I'm sorry you were disappointed."

Gareth grinned back. "I suppose it had to rain on my birthday sometime," he said, a little shyly. Then he hesitated, as if struggling against some inner constraint. "Aversin, listen," he stammered. Then he coughed as the wind shifted, and smoke swept over them all.

"God's Grandmother, it's the bloody cakes!" John swore and dashed back to the fire, cursing awesomely. "Jen, it isn't my fault . . ."

"It is." Jenny walked in a more leisurely manner to join him, in time to help him pick the last pitiful black lump from the griddle and toss it into the waters of the marsh with a milky plash. "I should have known better than to trust you with this. Now go tend the horses and let me do what you brought me along to do." She picked up the bowl of meal. Though she kept her face stern, the touch of her eyes upon his was like a kiss.

4

In the days that followed, Jenny was interested to notice the change in Gareth's attitude toward her and toward John. For the most part he seemed to return to the confiding friendliness he had shown her after she had rescued him from the bandits among the ruins, before he had learned that she was his hero's mistress, but it was not quite the same. It alternated with a growing nervousness and with odd, struggling silences in his conversation. If he had lied about something at the Hold, Jenny thought, he was regretting it now—but not regretting it enough yet to confess the truth.

Whatever the truth was, she felt that she came close to learning it the day after the rescue from the Meewinks. John had ridden ahead to scout the ruinous stone bridge that spanned the torrent of the Snake River, leaving them alone with the spare horses and mules in the louring silence of the winter woods. "Are the Whisperers real?" he asked her softly, glancing over his shoulder as if he feared to see last night's vision fading into daytime reality from the mists between the trees.

"Real enough to kill a man," Jenny said, "if they can lure him away from his friends. Since they drink blood, they must be fleshly enough to require sustenance; but, other than that, no one knows much about them. You had a narrow escape."

"I know," he mumbled, looking shamefacedly down at his hands. They were bare, and chapped with cold—as well as his cloak and sword, he had lost his gloves in the house of the Meewinks; Jenny suspected that later in the winter the Meewinks would boil them and eat the leather. One of John's old plaids was draped on over the boy's doublet and borrowed jerkin. With his thin hair dripping with moisture down onto the lenses of his cracked spectacles, he looked very little like the young courtier who had come to the Hold.

"Jenny," he said hesitantly, "thank you—this is the second time—for saving my life. I—I'm sorry I've behaved toward you as I have. It's just that . . ." His voice tailed off uncertainly.

"I suspect," said Jenny kindly, "that you had me mistaken for someone else that you know."

Ready color flooded to the boy's cheeks. Wind moaned through the bare trees—he startled, then turned back to her with a sigh. "The thing is, you saved my life at the risk of your own, and I endangered you both stupidly. I should have known better than to trust the Meewinks; I should never have left the camp. But . . ."

Jenny smiled and shook her head. The rain had ceased, and she had put back her hood, letting the wind stir in her long hair; with a touch of her heels, she urged The Stupider Roan on again, and the whole train of them moved slowly down the trail.

"It is difficult," she said, "not to believe in the illusions of the Whisperers. Even though you know that those whom you see cannot possibly be there outside the spell-circle crying your name, there is a part of you that needs to go to them."

"What—what shapes have you seen them take?" Gareth asked in a hushed voice.

The memory was an evil one, and it was a moment before Jenny answered. Then she said, "My sons. Ian and Adric." The vision had been so real that even calling their images in Caerdinn's scrying-crystal to make sure that they were safe at the Hold had not entirely banished her fears for them from her mind. After a moment's thought she added, "They have an uncanny way of taking the shape that most troubles you; of knowing, not only your love, but your guilt and your longing."

Gareth flinched at that, and looked away. They rode on in silence for a few moments; then he asked, "How do they know?"

She shook her head. "Perhaps they do read your dreams. Perhaps they are themselves only mirrors and, like mirrors, have no knowledge of what they reflect. The spells we lay upon them cannot be binding because we do not know their essence."

He frowned at her, puzzled. "Their what?"

"Their essence—their inner being." She drew rein just above a long, flooded dip in the road where water lay among the trees like a shining snake. "Who are you, Gareth of Magloshaldon?"

He startled at that, and for an instant she saw fright and guilt in his gray eyes. He stammered, "I—I'm Gareth of—of Magloshaldon. It's a province of Belmarie . . ."

Her eyes sought his and held them in the gray shadows of the trees. "And if you were not of that province, would you still be Gareth?"

"Er—yes. Of course. I . . ."

"And if you were not Gareth?" she pressed him, holding his gaze and mind locked with her own. "Would you still be you? If you were crippled, or old—if you became a leper, or lost your manhood—who would you be then?"

"I don't know—"

"You know."

"Stop it!" He tried to look away and could not. Her grip upon him tightened, as she probed at his mind, showing him it through her eyes: a vivid kaleidoscope of the borrowed images of a thousand ballads, burning with the overwhelming physical desires of the adolescent; the raw wounds left by some bitter betrayal, and over all, the shadowing darkness of a scarcely bearable guilt and fear.

She probed at that darkness—the lies he had told her and John at the Hold, and some greater guilt besides. A true crime, she wondered, or only that which seemed one to him? Gareth cried, "Stop it!" again, and she heard the despair and terror in his voice; for a moment, through his eyes, she saw herself—pitiless blue eyes in a face like a white wedge of bone between the cloud-dark streams of her hair. She remembered when Caerdinn had done this same thing to her, and released Gareth quickly. He turned away, covering his face, his whole body shivering with shock and fright.

After a moment Jenny said softly, "I'm sorry. But this is the inner heart of magic, the way all spells work—with the essence, the true name. It is true of the Whisperers and of the greatest of mages as well." She clucked to the horses and they started forward again, their hooves sinking squishily into the tea-colored ooze. She went on, "All you can do is ask yourself if it is reasonable that those you see would be there in the woods, calling to you."

"But that's just it," said Gareth. "It was reasonable. Zyerne . . ." He stopped himself.

"Zyerne?" It was the name he had muttered in his dreams at the Hold, when he had flinched aside from her touch.

"The Lady Zyerne," he said hesitantly. "The—the King's mistress." Under its streaking of rain and mud his face was bright carnation pink. Jenny remembered her strange and cloudy dream of the dark-haired woman and her tinkling laughter.

"And you love her?"

Gareth blushed even redder. In a stifled voice he repeated, "She is the King's mistress."

As I am John's, Jenny thought, suddenly realizing whence his anger at her had stemmed.

"In any case," Gareth went on after a moment, "we're all in love with her. That is—she's the first lady of the Court, the most beautiful . . . We write sonnets to her beauty . . ."

"Does she love you?" inquired Jenny, and Gareth fell silent for a time, concentrating on urging his horse through the mud and up the stony slope beyond.

At length he said, "I—I don't know. Sometimes I think . . ." Then he shook his head. "She frightens me," he admitted. "And yet—she's a witch, you see."

"Yes," said Jenny softly. "I guessed that, from what you said at the Hold. You feared I would be like her."

He looked stricken, as if caught in some horrible social gaffe. "But—but you're not. She's very beautiful . . ." He broke off, blushing in earnest, and Jenny laughed.

"Don't worry. I learned a long time ago what a mirror was for."

"But you *are* beautiful," he insisted. "That is—Beautiful isn't the right word."

"No." Jenny smiled. "I do think 'ugly' *is* the word you're looking for."

Gareth shook his head stubbornly, his honesty forbidding him to call her beautiful and his inexperience making it impossible to express what he did mean. "Beauty—beauty really doesn't have anything to do with it," he said at last. "And she's nothing like you—for all her beauty, she's crafty and hard-hearted and cares for nothing save the pursuit of her powers."

"Then she is like me," said Jenny. "For I am crafty—skilled in my crafts, such as they are—and I have been called hard-hearted since I was a little girl and chose to sit staring at the flame of a candle until the pictures came, rather than play at house with the other little girls. And as for the rest . . ." She sighed. "The key to magic is magic; to be a mage you must be a mage. My old master used to say that. The pursuit of your power takes all that you have, if you will be great—it leaves neither time, nor energy, for anything else. We are born with the seeds of power in us and driven to be what we are by a hunger that knows no slaking. Knowledge—power—to know what songs the stars sing; to center all the forces of creation upon a rune drawn in the air—we can never give over the seeking of it. It is the stuff of loneliness, Gareth."

They rode on in silence for a time. The woods about them were pewter and iron, streaked here and there with the rust of the dying year. In the wan light Gareth looked older than he had when they began, for he had lost flesh on the trip, and lack of sleep had left permanent smudges of bister beneath his eyes. At length he turned to her again and asked, "And do the mageborn love?"

Jenny sighed again. "They say that a wizard's wife is a widow. A woman who bears a wizard's child must know that he will leave her to raise the child alone, should his powers call him elsewhere. It is for this reason that no priest will perform the wedding ceremony for the mageborn, and no flute player will officiate upon the rites. And it would be an act of cruelty for a witch to bear any man's child."

He looked across at her, puzzled both by her words and by the coolness of her voice, as if the matter had nothing to do with her.

She went on, looking ahead at the half-hidden road beneath its foul mire of tangled weeds, "A witch will always care more for the pursuit of her powers than for her child, or for any man. She will either desert her child, or come to hate it for keeping her from the time she needs to meditate, to study, to grow in her arts. Did you know John's mother was a witch?"

Gareth stared at her, shocked.

"She was a shaman of the Iceriders—his father took her in battle. Your ballads said nothing of it?"

He shook his head numbly. "Nothing—in fact, in the Greenhythe variant of the ballad of Aversin and the Golden Worm of Wyr, it talks about him bidding farewell to his mother in her bower, before going off to fight the dragon—but now that I think of it, there is a scene very like it in the Greenhythe ballad of Selkythar Dragonsbane and in one of the late Halnath variants of the Song of Antara Warlady. I just thought it was something Dragonsbanes did."

A smile brushed her lips, then faded. "She was my first teacher in the ways of power, when I was six. They used to say of her what you thought of me—that she had laid spells upon her lord to make him love her, tangling him in her long hair. I thought so, too, as a little child—until I saw how she fought for the freedom that he would not give her. When I knew her, she had already borne his child; but when John was five, she left in the screaming winds of an icestorm, she and the frost-eyed wolf who was her companion. She was never seen in the Winterlands again. And I . . ."

There was long silence, broken only by the soft squish of hooves in the roadbed, the patter of rain, and the occasional pop of the mule Clivy's hooves as he overreached his own stride. When she went on, her voice was low, as if she spoke to herself.

"He asked me to bear his children, for he wanted children, and he

wanted those children to be mine also. He knew I would never live with
him as his wife and devote my time to his comfort and that of his sons. I
knew it, too." She sighed. "The lioness bears her cubs and then goes back
to the hunting trail. I thought I could do the same. All my life I have been
called heartless—would that it were really so. I hadn't thought that I
would love them."

Through the trees, the dilapidated towers of the Snake River bridge
came into view, the water streaming high and yellow beneath the crumbling arches. Before them, a dark figure sat his horse in the gloomy road,
spectacles flashing like rounds of dirty ice in the cold daylight, signaling
that the way was safe.

They made camp that night outside the ruined town of Ember, once
the capital of the province of Wyr. Nothing remained of it now save a
dimpled stone mound, over-grown with birch and seedling maple, and the
decaying remains of the curtain wall. Jenny knew it of old, from the days
when she and Caerdinn had searched for books in the buried cellars. He
had beaten her, she remembered, when she had spoken of the beauty of
the skeleton lines of stone that shimmered through the dark cloak of the
fallow earth.

As dusk came down, they pitched their camp outside the walls. Jenny
gathered the quick-burning bark of the paper birch for kindling and
fetched water from the spring nearby. Gareth saw her coming and broke
purposefully away from his own tasks to join her. "Jenny," he began, and
she looked up at him.

"Yes?"

He paused, like a naked swimmer on the bank of a very cold pool,
then visibly lost his courage. "Er—is there some reason why we didn't
camp in the ruins of the town itself?"

It was patently not what he had been about to say, but she only
glanced back toward the white bones of the town, wrapped in shadow and
vine. "Yes."

His voice dropped. "Is there—is there *something* that haunts the
ruins?"

The corner of her mouth tucked a little. "Not that I know of. But the
entire town is buried under the biggest patch of poison ivy this side of the
Gray Mountains. Even so," she said, kneeling beside the little dry fire-
wood they had been able to find and arranging the birchbark beneath it, "I
have laid spells of ward about the camp, so take care not to leave it."

He ducked his head a little at this gentle teasing and blushed.

A little curiously, she added, "Even if this Lady Zyerne of yours is a
sorceress—even if she is fond of you—she would never have come here

from the south, you know. Mages only transform themselves into birds in ballads, for to change your essence into the essence of some other life form—which is what shapeshifting is—aside from being dangerous, requires an incredible amount of power. It is not something done lightly. When the mageborn go, they go upon their two feet."

"But . . ." His high forehead wrinkled in a frown. Having decided to be her champion, he was unwilling to believe there was anything beyond her powers. "But the Lady Zyerne does it all the time. I've seen her."

Jenny froze in the act of arranging the logs, cut by an unexpected pang of a hot jealousy she had thought that she had long outgrown—the bitter jealousy of her youth toward those who had greater skills than she. All her life she had worked to rid herself of it, knowing it crippled her from learning from those more powerful. It was this that made her tell herself, a moment later, that she ought not to be shocked to learn of another's use of power.

Yet in the back of her mind she could hear old Caerdinn speaking of the dangers of taking on an alien essence, even if one had the enormous power necessary to perform the transformation and of the hold that another form could take on the minds of all but the very greatest.

"She must be a powerful mage indeed," she said, rebuking her own envy. With a touch of her mind, she called fire to the kindling, and it blazed up hotly beneath the logs. Even that small magic pricked her, like a needle carelessly left in a garment, with the bitter reflection of the smallness of her power. "What forms have you seen her take?" She realized as she spoke that she hoped he would say he had seen none himself and that it was, in fact, only rumor.

"Once a cat," he said. "And once a bird, a swallow. And she's taken other shapes in—in dreams I've had. It's odd," he went on rather hastily. "In ballads they don't make much of it. But it's hideous, the most horrible thing I've ever seen—a woman, and a woman I—I—" He stumbled in his words, barely biting back some other verb that he replaced with, "—I know, twisting and withering, changing into a beast. And then the beast will watch you with her eyes."

He folded himself up cross-legged beside the fire as Jenny put the iron skillet over it and began to mix the meal for the cakes. Jenny asked him, "Is she why you asked the King to send you north on this quest? To get away from her?"

Gareth turned his face from her. After a moment he nodded. "I don't want to betray—to betray the King." His words caught oddly as he spoke. "But sometimes I feel I'm destined to do so. And I don't know what to do.

"Polycarp hated her," he went on, after a few moments during which John's voice could be heard, cheerfully cursing the mules Clivy and Melonhead as he unloaded the last of the packs. "The rebel Master of Halnath. He always told me to stay away from her. And he hated her influence over the King."

"Is that why he rebelled?"

"It might have had something to do with it. I don't know." He toyed wretchedly with a scrap of meal left in the bowl. "He—he tried to murder the King and—and the Heir to the throne, the King's son. Polycarp is the next heir, the King's nephew. He was brought up in the palace as a sort of a hostage after his father rebelled. Polycarp stretched a cable over a fence in the hunting field on a foggy morning when he thought no one would see until it was too late." His voice cracked a little as he added, "I was the one who saw him do it."

Jenny glanced across at his face, broken by darkness and the leaping light of the flames into a harsh mosaic of plane and shadows. "You loved him, didn't you?"

He managed to nod. "I think he was a better friend to me than anyone else at Court. People—people our age there—Polycarp is five years older than I am—used to mock at me, because I collect ballads and because I'm clumsy and can't see without my spectacles; they'd mock at him because his father was executed for treason and because he's a philosopher. Many of the Masters have been. It's because of the University at Halnath—they're usually atheists and troublemakers. His father was, who married the King's sister. But Polycarp was always like a son to the King." He pushed back the thin, damp weeds of his hair from his high forehead and finished in a strangled voice, "Even when I saw him do it, I couldn't believe it."

"And you denounced him?"

Gareth's breath escaped in a defeated sigh. "What could I do?"

Had this, Jenny wondered, been what he had hidden from them? The fact that the Realm itself was split by threat of civil war, like the Kinwars that had drawn the King's troops away from the Winterlands to begin with? Had he feared that if John knew that there was a chance the King would refuse to lend him forces needed at home, he would not consent to make the journey?

Or was there something else?

It had grown fully dark now. Jenny picked the crisp mealcakes from the griddle and set them on a wooden plate at her side while she cooked salt pork and beans. While Gareth had been speaking, John had come to join them, half-listening to what was said, half-watching the woods that hemmed them in.

As they ate, Gareth went on, "Anyway, Polycarp managed to get out of the city before they came for him. The King's troops were waiting for him on the road to Halnath, but we think he went to the Deep, and the gnomes took him through to the Citadel that way. Then they—the gnomes—bolted up the doors leading from the Deep to the Citadel and said they would not meddle in the affairs of men. They wouldn't admit the King's troops through the Deep to take the Citadel from the rear, but they wouldn't let the rebels out that way, either, or sell them food. There was some talk of them using blasting powder to close up the tunnels to Halnath completely. But then the dragon came."

"And when the dragon came?" asked John.

"When the dragon came, Polycarp opened the Citadel gates that led into the Deep and let the gnomes take refuge with him. At least, a lot of the gnomes *did* take refuge with him, though Zyerne says they were the ones who were on the Master's side to begin with. And she should know—she was brought up in the Deep."

"Was she, now?" John tossed one of the small pork bones into the fire and wiped his fingers on a piece of corncake. "I thought the name sounded like the tongue of the gnomes."

Gareth nodded. "The gnomes used to take a lot of the children of men as apprentices in the Deep—usually children from Deeping, the town that stands—stood—in the vale before the great gates of the Deep itself, where the smelting of the gold and the trade in foodstuffs went on. They haven't done so in the last year or so—in fact in the last year they forbade men to enter the Deep at all."

"Did they?" asked John, curious. "Why was that?"

Gareth shrugged. "I don't know. They're strange creatures, and tricky. You can't ever tell what they're up to, Zyerne says."

As the night deepened, Jenny left the men by the fire and silently walked the bounds of the camp, checking the spell-circles that defended it against the blood-devils, the Whisperers, and the sad ghosts that haunted the ruins of the old town. She sat on what had been a boundary stone, just beyond the edge of the fire's circle of light, and sank into her meditations, which for some nights now she had neglected.

It was not the first time she had neglected them—she was too well aware of the nights she had let them go by while she was at the Hold with John and her sons. Had she not neglected them—had she not neglected the pursuit of her power—would she be as powerful as this Zyerne, who could deal in shapeshifting at a casual whim? Caerdinn's strictures against it returned to her mind, but she wondered if that was just her own jealousy speaking, her own spite at another's power. Caerdinn had been old, and there had been nowhere in the Winterlands that she could turn for other instruction after he had died. Like John, she was a scholar bereft of the meat of scholarship; like the people of the village of Alyn, she was circumscribed by the fate that had planted her in such stony soil.

Against the twisting yellow ribbons of the flames, she could see John's body swaying as he gestured, telling Gareth some outrageous story from his vast collection of tales about the Winterlands and its folk. The Fattest Bandit in the Winterlands? she wondered. Or one about his incredible Aunt Mattie? It occurred to her for the first time that it was for her, as well as for his people, that he had undertaken the King's command—for the things that she had never gotten, and for their sons.

It's not worth his life! she thought desperately, watching him. *I do well with what I have!* But the silent ruins of Ember mocked at her, their naked bones veiled by darkness, and the calm part of her heart whispered to her that it was his to choose, not hers. She could only do what she was doing—make her choice and abandon her studies to ride with him. The King had sent his command and his promise, and John would obey the King.

Five days south of Ember, the lands opened up once more. The forests gave way to the long, flat, alluvial slopes that led down to the Wildspae, the northern boundary of the lands of Belmarie. It was an empty countryside, but without the haunted desolation of the Winterlands; there were farms here, like little walled fortresses, and the road was at least passably drained. Here for the first time they met other travelers, merchants going north and east, with news and rumor of the capital—of the dread of the dragon that gripped the land, and the unrest in Bel due to the high price of grain.

"Stands to reason, don't it?" said a foxlike little trader, with his cavalcade of laden mules behind him. "What with the dragon ruining the harvest, and the grain rotting in the fields; yes, and the gnomes what took refuge in Bel itself hoarding the stuff, taking it out of the mouths of honest folk with their ill-got gold."

"Ill-got?" asked John curiously. "They mined and smelted it, didn't they?" Jenny, who wanted news without irritating its bearer, kicked him surreptitiously in the shin.

The merchant spat into the brimming ditch by the roadside and wiped his grizzled reddish beard. "That gives them no call to buy grain away from folks that needs it," he said. "And word has it that they're trafficking regular with their brothers up in Halnath—yes, and that they and the Master between them kidnapped the King's Heir, his only child, to hold for ransom."

"Could they have?" John inquired.

"Course they could. The Master's a sorcerer, isn't he? And the gnomes have never been up to any good, causing riot and mayhem in the capital . . ."

"Riot and mayhem?" Gareth protested. "But the gnomes have been our allies for time out of mind! There's never been trouble between us."

The man squinted up at him suspiciously. But he only grumbled, "Just goes to show, doesn't it? Treacherous little buggers." Jerking on his lead mule's bridle, he passed them by.

Not long after this they met a company of the gnomes themselves, traveling banded together, surrounded by guards for protection, with their wealth piled in carts and carriages. They peered up at John with wary, shortsighted eyes of amber or pale blue beneath low, wide brows, and gave him unwilling answers to his questions about the south.

"The dragon? Aye, it lairs yet in Ylferdun, and none of the men the King has sent have dislodged it." The gnome leader toyed with the soft fur trim of his gloves, and the thin winds billowed at the silk of his strangely cut garments. Behind him, the guards of the cavalcade watched the strangers in deepest suspicion, as if fearing an attack from even that few. "As for us, by the heart of the Deep, we have had enough of the charity of the sons of men, who charge us four times the going price for rooms the household servants would scorn and for food retrieved from the rats." His voice, thin and high like that of all the gnomes, was bitter with the verjuice of hate given back for hate. "Without the gold taken from the Deep, their city would never have been built, and yet not a man will speak to us in the streets, save to curse. They say in the city now that we plot with our brethren who fled through the back ways of the Deep into the Citadel of Halnath. By the Stone, it is lies; but such lies are believed now in Bel."

From the carts and carriages and curtained litters, a murmur of anger went up, the rage of those who have never before been helpless. Jenny, sitting quietly on Moon Horse, realized that it was the first time she had ever seen gnomes by daylight. Their eyes, wide and nearly colorless, were ill-attuned for its glare; the hearing that could catch the whispers of the cave bats would be daily tortured by the clamor of the cities of men.

Aversin asked, "And the King?"

"The King?" The gnome's piping voice was vicious, and his whole stooping little body bristled with the raw hurt of humiliation. "The King cares nothing for us. With all our wealth mewed up in the Deep, where the dragon sits hoarding over it, we have little to trade upon but promises, and with each day that passes those promises buy less in a city where bread is dear. And all this, while the King's whore sits with his head in her lap and poisons his mind as she poisons everything she touches—as she poisoned the very heart of the Deep."

Beside her, Jenny heard the hissing of Gareth's indrawn breath and saw the anger that flashed in his eyes, but he said nothing. When her glance questioned him, he looked away in shame.

As the gnomes moved out of sight once again into the mists, John remarked, "Sounds a proper snakes' nest. *Could* this Master really have kidnapped the King's child?"

"No," Gareth said miserably, as the horses resumed their walk toward the ferry, invisible in the foggy bottomlands to the south. "He couldn't have left the Citadel. He isn't a sorcerer—just a philosopher and an atheist. I—don't worry about the King's Heir." He looked down at his hands, and the expression on his face was the one that Jenny had seen in the camp outside Ember that night—a struggle to gather his courage. "Listen," he began shakily. "I have to . . ."

"Gar," said John quietly, and the boy startled as if burned. There was an ironic glint in John's brown eyes and an edge like chipped flint to his voice. "Now—the King wouldn't by any chance have sent for me for some other reason than the dragon, would he?"

"No," Gareth said faintly, not meeting his eyes. "No, he—he didn't."

"Didn't what?"

Gareth swallowed, his pale face suddenly very strained. "He—he didn't send for you—for any other reason. That is . . ."

"Because," John went on in that quiet voice, "if the King happened to send me his signet ring to get me involved in rescuing that child of his, or helping him against this Master of Halnath I hear such tell of, or for his dealings with the gnomes, I do have better things to do. There are real problems, not just money and power, in my own lands, and the winter closing in looks to be a bad one. I'll put my life at risk against the dragon for the sake of the King's protection to the Winterlands, but if there's aught else in it . . ."

"No!" Gareth caught his arm desperately, a terrible fear in his face, as if he thought that with little more provocation the Dragonsbane would turn around then and there and ride back to Wyr.

And perhaps, Jenny thought, remembering her vision in the water bowl, it might be better if they did.

"Aversin, it isn't like that. You are here to slay the dragon—because you're the only Dragonsbane living. That's the only reason I sought you out, I swear it. I swear it! Don't worry about politics and—and all that." His shortsighted gray eyes pleaded with Aversin to believe, but in them there was a desperation that could never have stemmed from innocence.

John's gaze held his for a long moment, gauging him. Then he said, "I'm trusting you, my hero."

In dismal silence, Gareth touched his heels to Battlehammer's sides, and the big horse moved out ahead of them, the boy's borrowed plaids making them fade quickly into no more than a dark, cut-out shape in the colorless fogs. John, riding a little behind, slowed his horse so that he was next to Jenny, who had watched in speculative silence throughout.

"Maybe it's just as well you're with me after all, love."

She glanced from Gareth up to John, and then back. Somewhere a crow called, like the voice of that melancholy land. "I don't think he means us ill," she said softly.

"That doesn't mean he isn't gormless enough to get us killed all the same."

The mists thickened as they approached the river, until they moved through a chill white world where the only sound was the creak of harness leather, the pop of hooves, the faint jingle of bits, and the soughing rattle of the wind in the spiky cattails growing in the flooded ditches. From that watery grayness, each stone or solitary tree emerged, silent and dark, like a portent of strange events. More than all else, Jenny felt the weight of Gareth's silence, his fear and dread and guilt. John felt it, too, she knew; he watched the tall boy from the corner of his eye and listened to the hush of those empty lands like a man waiting for ambush. As evening darkened the air, Jenny called a blue ball of witchfire to light their feet, but the soft, opalescent walls of the mist threw back the light at them and left them nearly as blind as before.

"Jen." John drew rein, his head cocked to listen. "Can you hear it?"

"Hear what?" Gareth whispered, coming up beside them at the top of the slope which dropped away into blankets of moving fog.

Jenny flung her senses wide through the dun-colored clouds, feeling as much as hearing the rushing voice of the river below. There were other sounds, muffled and altered by the fog, but unmistakable. "Yes," she said quietly, her breath a puff of white in the raw air. "Voices—horses—a group of them on the other side."

John glanced sharply sidelong at Gareth. "They could be waiting for the ferry," he said, "if they had business in the empty lands west of the river at the fall of night."

Gareth said nothing, but his face looked white and set. After a moment John clucked softly to Cow, and the big, shaggy sorrel plodded forward again down the slope to the ferry through the clammy wall of vapor.

Jenny let the witchlight ravel away as John pounded on the door of the squat stone ferry house. She and Gareth remained in the background while John and the ferryman negotiated the fare for three people, six horses, and two mules. "Penny a leg," said the ferryman, his squirrel-dark eyes darting from one to the other with the sharp interest of one who sees all the world pass his doorstep. "But there'll be supper here in an hour, and lodging for the night. It's growing mortal dark, and there's chowder fog."

"We can get along a few miles before full dark; and besides," John added, with an odd glint in his eye as he glanced back at the silent Gareth, "we may have someone waiting for us on the far bank."

"Ah." The man's wide mouth shut itself like a trap. "So it's you they're expecting. I heard 'em out there a bit ago, but they didn't ring no bell for me, so I bided by my stove where it's warm."

Holding up the lantern and struggling into his heavy quilted jacket, he led the way down to the slip, while Jenny followed silently behind, digging in the purse at her belt for coin.

The great horse Battlehammer had traveled north with Gareth by ship and, in any case, disdained balking at anything as sheer bad manners; neither Moon Horse nor Osprey nor any of the spares had such scruples, with the exception of Cow, who would have crossed a bridge of flaming knives at his customary phlegmatic plod. It took Jenny much whispered talk and stroking of ears before any of them would consent to set foot upon the big raft. The ferryman made the gate at the raft's tail fast and fixed his lantern on the pole at its head; then he set to turning the winch that drew the wide, flat platform out across the opaque silk of the river. The single lantern made a woolly blur of yellowish light in the leaden smoke of the fog; now and then, on the edge of the gleam, Jenny could see the brown waters parting around a snagged root or branch that projected from the current like a drowned hand.

From somewhere across the water she heard the jingle of metal on metal, the soft blowing of a horse, and men's voices. Gareth still said nothing, but she felt that, if she laid a hand upon him, she would find him quivering, as a rope does before it snaps. John came quietly to her side, his fingers twined warm and strong about hers. His spectacles flashed softly in the lanternlight as he slung an end of his voluminous plaid around her shoulders and drew her to his side.

"John," Gareth said quietly, "I—I have something to tell you."

Dimly through the fog came another sound, a woman's laugh like the tinkling of silver bells. Gareth twitched, and John, a dangerous flicker in his lazy-lidded eyes, said, "I thought you might."

"Aversin," Gareth stammered and stopped. Then he forced himself on with a rush, "Aversin, Jenny, listen. I'm sorry. I lied to you—I betrayed you, but I couldn't help it; I had no other choice. I'm sorry."

"Ah," said John softly. "So there was something you forgot to mention before we left the Hold?"

Unable to meet his eyes, Gareth said, "I meant to tell you earlier, but—but I couldn't. I was afraid you'd turn back and—and I couldn't let you turn back. We need you, we really do."

"For a lad who's always on about honor and courage," Aversin said, and there was an ugly edge to his quiet voice, "you haven't shown very much of either, have you?"

Gareth raised his head, and met his eyes, "No," he said. "I—I've been realizing that. I thought it was all right to deceive you in a good cause—that is—I had to get you to come . . ."

"All right, then," said John. "What is the truth?"

Jenny glanced from the faces of the two men toward the far shore, visible dimly now as a dark blur and a few lights moving like fireflies in the mist. A slightly darker cloud beyond would be the woodlands of Belmarie. She touched John's spiked elbow warningly, and he looked quickly in that direction. Movement stirred there, shapes crowding down to wait for the ferry to put in. The horse Battlehammer flung up his head and whinnied, and an answering whinny trumpeted back across the water. The Dragonsbane's eyes returned to Gareth and he folded his hands over the hilt of his sword.

Gareth drew a deep breath. "The truth is that the King didn't send for you," he said. "In fact, he—he forbade me to come looking for you. He said it was a foolish quest, because you probably didn't exist at all and, even if you did, you'd have been killed by another dragon long ago. He said he didn't want me to risk my life chasing a phantom. But—but I had to find you. He wasn't going to send anyone else. And you're the only Dragonsbane, as it was in all the ballads . . ." He stammered uncertainly. "Except that I didn't know then that it wasn't like the ballads. But I knew you had to exist. And I knew we needed someone. I couldn't stand by and let the dragon go on terrorizing the countryside. I had to come and find you. And once I found you, I had to bring you back . . ."

"Having decided you knew better about the needs of my people and my own choice in the matter than I did?" John's face never showed much expression, but his voice had a sting to it now, like a scorpion's tail.

Gareth shied from it, as from a lash. "I—I thought of that, these last days," he said softly. He looked up again, his face white with an agony of shame. "But I couldn't let you turn back. And you will be rewarded, I swear I'll see that you get the reward somehow."

"And just how'll you manage that?" John's tone was sharp with disgust. The deck jarred beneath their feet as the raft ground against the shoals. Lights like marsh candles bobbed down toward them through the

gloom. "With a mage at the Court, it couldn't have taken them long to figure out who'd pinched the King's seal, nor when he'd be back in Belmarie. I expect the welcoming committee . . ." he gestured toward the
dark forms crowding forward from the mists. ". . . is here to arrest you for
treason."

"No," Gareth said in a defeated voice. "They'll be my friends from
Court."

As if stepping through a door the forms came into visibility; lanternlight danced over the hard gleam of satin, caressed velvet's softer nap,
and touched edges of stiffened lace and the cloudy gauze of women's
veils, salted all over with the leaping fire of jewels. In the forefront of
them all was a slender, dark-haired girl in amber silk, whose eyes, golden
as honey with a touch of gray, sought Gareth's and caused the boy to turn
aside with a blush. One man was holding a cloak for her of ermine-tagged
velvet; another her golden pomander ball. She laughed, a sound at once
silvery and husky, like an echo from a troubled dream.

It could be no one but Zyerne.

John looked inquiringly back at Gareth.

"That seal you showed me was real," he said. "I've seen it on the old
documents, down to the little nicks on its edges. They're taking its theft a
bit casually, aren't they?"

He laid hold of Cow's bridle and led him down the short gangplank,
forcing the others to follow. As they stepped ashore, every courtier on the
bank, led by Zyerne, swept in unison into an elaborate Phoenix Rising
salaam, touching their knees in respect to the clammy, fish-smelling mud.

Crimson-faced, Gareth admitted, "Not really. Technically it wasn't
theft. The King is my father. I'm the missing Heir."

5

"**S**o that's your Dragonsbane, is it?"

At the sound of Zyerne's voice, Jenny paused in the stony blue dimness of the hall of the enchantress's hunting lodge. From the gloom in which she stood, the little antechamber beyond the hall glowed like a lighted stage; the rose-colored gauze of Zyerne's gown, the whites and violets of Gareth's doublet, sleeves, and hose, and the pinks and blacks of the rugs beneath their feet all seemed to burn like the hues of stained glass in the ember-colored lamplight. The instincts of the Winterlands kept Jenny to the shadows. Neither saw her.

Zyerne held her tiny goblet of crystal and glass up to one of the lamps on the mantel, admiring the blood red lights of the liqueur within. She smiled mischievously. "I must say, I prefer the ballad version myself."

Seated in one of the gilt-footed ivory chairs on the opposite side of the low wine table, Gareth only looked unhappy and confused. The dimple on the side of Zyerne's curving, shell pink lips deepened, and she brushed a corner of her lace veils aside from her cheek. Combs of crystal and sardonyx flashed in her dark hair as she tipped her head.

When Gareth didn't speak, her smile widened a little, and she moved with sinuous grace to stand near enough to him to envelop him in the faint aura of her perfume. Like shooting stars, the lamplight jumped from the crystal facets of Gareth's goblet with the involuntary tremor of his hand.

"Aren't you even going to thank me for coming to meet you and offering you the hospitality of my lodge?" Zyerne asked, her voice teasing.

Because she was jealous of Zyerne's greater powers, Jenny had forced herself to feel, upon meeting her at the ferry, nothing but surprise at the enchantress's youth. She looked no more than twenty, though at the lowest computation—which Jenny could not keep herself from making, though the cattiness of her reaction distressed her—her age could not have been much less than twenty-six. Where there was jealousy, there could be no learning, she had told herself; and in any case she owed this girl justice.

But now anger stirred in her. Zyerne's closeness and the hand that she laid with such artless intimacy on Gareth's shoulder, so that less than a half-inch of her fingertip touched the flesh of his neck above his collar-lace could be nothing but calculated temptations. From what he had told her—from every tense line of his face and body now—Jenny knew he was struggling with all that was in him against his desire for his father's mistress. Judging by her expression in the lamplight, Gareth's efforts to resist amused Zyerne very much.

"Lady—Lady Jenny?"

Jenny's head turned quickly at the hesitant voice. The stairway of the lodge was enclosed in an elaborate latticework of pierced stone; in the fretted shadows, she could make out the shape of a girl of sixteen or so. Only a little taller than Jenny herself, she was like an exquisitely dressed doll, her hair done up in an exaggeration of Zyerne's elaborate coiffure and dyed like white-and-purple taffy.

The girl curtseyed. "My name is Trey, Trey Clerlock." She glanced nervously at the two forms framed in the lighted antechamber, then back up the stair, as if fearing that one of Zyerne's other guests would come down and overhear. "Please don't take this wrongly, but I came to offer to lend you a dress for dinner, if you'd like one."

Jenny glanced down at her own gown, russet wool with a hand like silk, banded with embroideries of red and blue. In deference to custom which dictated that no woman in polite society was ever seen with her hair uncovered, she had even donned the white silk veil John had brought back to her from the east. In the Winterlands she would have been accounted royally clad.

"Does it matter so much?"

The girl Trey looked as embarrassed as years of deportment lessons would let her. "It shouldn't," she said frankly. "It doesn't, really, to me, but . . . but some people at Court can be very cruel, especially about things like being properly dressed. I'm sorry," she added quickly, blushing as she stepped out of the checkered darkness of the stair. Jenny could see now that she carried a bundle of black and silver satin and a long, trailing mass of transparent gauze veils, whose random sequins caught stray spangles of light.

Jenny hesitated. Ordinarily the conventions of polite society never had bothered her, and her work left her little time for them in any case.

Knowing she would be coming to the King's court, she had brought the best gown she had—her only formal gown, as a matter of fact—aware that it would be out of date. It had been no concern to her what others thought of her for wearing it.

But from the moment she had stepped from the ferry earlier that evening, she had had the feeling of walking among unmarked pitfalls. Zyerne and her little band of courtiers had been all polite graciousness, but she had sensed the covert mockery in their language of eyebrows and glances. It had angered her and puzzled her, too, reminding her too much of the way the other children in the village had treated her as a child. But the child in her was alive enough to feel a morbid dread of their sport.

Zyerne's sweet laughter drifted out into the hall. "I vow the fellow was looking about him for a bootscraper as he crossed the threshold . . . I didn't know whether to offer him a room with a bed or a pile of nice, comfortable rushes on the floor—you know a good hostess must make her guests feel at home . . ."

For a moment Jenny's natural suspicion made her wonder if the offer of a gown itself might be part of some scheme to make her look ridiculous. But Trey's worried blue eyes held nothing but concern for her—and a little for herself, lest she be spotted in the act of spoiling sport. Jenny considered for a moment defying them, then discarded the idea—whatever gratification it might bring was scarcely worth the fight. She had been raised in the Winterlands, and every instinct she possessed whispered for the concealment of protective coloration.

She held out her hands for the slithery armfuls of satin.

"You can change in the little room beneath the stairs," Trey offered, looking relieved. "It's a long way back to your rooms."

"And a longer one back to your own home," Jenny pointed out, her hand on the latch of the concealed door. "Did you send for this specially, then?"

Trey regarded her with guileless surprise. "Oh, no. When Zyerne knew Gareth was returning, she told us all we'd come here for a welcome dinner: my brother Bond and myself, the Beautiful Isolde, Caspar of Walfrith and Merriwyn of Longcleat, and all the others. I always bring two or three different dinner gowns. I mean, I didn't know two days ago what I might want to wear."

She was perfectly serious, so Jenny repressed her smile.

She went on, "It's a little long, but I thought it looked like your colors. Here in the south, only servants wear brown."

"Ah." Jenny touched the folds of her own gown, which caught a cinnamon edge in the glow from the antechamber's lamps. "Thank you, Trey, very much—and Trey? Could I ask yet another favor?"

"Of course," the girl said generously. "I can help . . ."

"I think I can manage. John—Lord Aversin—will be down in a few moments . . ." She paused, thinking of the somewhat old-fashioned but perfectly decent brown velvet of his doublet and indoor cloak. But it was something about which she could do nothing, and she shook her head. "Ask him to wait, if you would."

The room beneath the stairs was small, but showed evidence of hasty toilettes and even hastier romantic assignations. As she changed clothes, Jenny could hear the courtiers assembling in the hall to await the summons for dinner. Occasionally she could catch some of the muted bustling from the servants in the dining hall beyond the antechamber, laying the six cloths and undercover so necessary, according to Gareth, to the proper conduct of a meal; now and then a maid would laugh and be rebuked by the butler. Nearer, soft voices gossiped and teased: ". . . well, really, what can you say about someone who still wears those awful smocked sleeves—and she's so *proud* of them, too!" . . . "Yes, but in broad daylight? *Outdoors?* And with her *husband?*" . . . "Well, of course it's all a plot by the gnomes . . ." "Did you hear the joke about why gnomes have flat noses?"

Closer, a man's voice laughed, and asked, "Gareth, are you sure you found the right man? I mean, you didn't mistake the address and fetch someone else entirely?"

"Er—well—" Gareth sounded torn between his loyalty to his friends and his dread of mockery. "I suppose you'd call him a bit barbaric, Bond . . ."

"A bit!" The man Bond laughed richly. "That is to say that the dragon has caused 'a bit' of trouble, or that old Polycarp tried to murder you 'a bit.' And you're taking him to Court? Father *will* be pleased."

"Gareth?" There was sudden concern in Zyerne's lilting voice. "You did get his credentials, didn't you? Membership in the Guild of Dragonsbanes, Proof of Slaughter . . ."

"Testimonials from Rescued Maidens," Bond added. "Or is that one of his rescued maidens he has with him?"

Above her head, Jenny felt rather than heard a light descending tread on the steps. It was the tread of a man raised to caution and it stopped, as her own had stopped for a moment, at the point on the stairs just behind where the light fell from the room beyond. As she hastened to pull on the stiffened petticoats, she could feel his silence in the entwining shadows of the latticed staircase.

"Of course!" Bond was saying, in the voice of a man suddenly
enlightened. "He has to carry her about with him because nobody in the
Winterlands can read a written testimonial! It's similar to the barter sys-
tem, you see . . ."

"Well," another woman's voice purred, "if you ask me, she isn't
much of a maiden."

With teasing naughtiness, Zyerne giggled. "Perhaps it wasn't much
of a dragon."

"She must be thirty if she's a day," someone else added.

"Now, my dear," Zyerne chided, "let us not be catty. That rescue was
a long time ago."

In the general laugh, Jenny was not sure, but she thought she heard
the footsteps overhead soundlessly retreat. Zyerne went on, "I do think, if
this Dragonsbane of yours was going to cart a woman along, he might at
least have picked a pretty one, instead of someone who looks like a
gnome—a short little thing with all that hair. She scarcely needs a veil for
modesty."

"That's probably why she doesn't wear one."

"If you're going to be charitable, my dear . . ."

"She isn't . . ." began Gareth's voice indignantly.

"Oh, Gareth, don't take everything so seriously!" Zyerne's laughter
mocked him. "It's such a bore, darling, besides giving you wrinkles.
There. Smile. Really, it's all in jest—a man who can't take a little joking
is only a short step from far more serious sins, like eating his salad with a
fish fork. I say, you don't think . . ."

Her hands shaking with a queerly feelingless anger, Jenny straightened her veils. The mere touch of the stiffened gauze fired a new spurt of
irritation through her, annoyance at them and that same sense of bafflement she had felt before. The patterns of human relationships interested
her, and this one, shot through with a web of artificiality and malice,
explained a good deal about Gareth. But the childishness of it quelled her
anger, and she was able to slip soundlessly from her cubbyhole and stand
among them for several minutes before any of them became aware of her
presence.

Lamps had been kindled in the hall. In the midst of a small crowd of
admiring courtiers, Zyerne seemed to sparkle bewitchingly under a pow-
dering of diamonds and lace. "I'll tell you," she was saying. "However
much gold Gareth was moved to offer the noble Dragonsbane as a
reward, I think we can offer him a greater one. We'll show him a few of
the amenities of civilization. How does that sound? He slays our dragon
and we teach him how to eat with a fork?"

There was a good deal of appreciative laughter at this. Jenny noticed the girl Trey joining in, but without much enthusiasm. The man standing next to her must be her brother Bond, she guessed; he had his sister's fine-boned prettiness, set off by fair hair of which one lovelock, trailing down onto a lace collar, was dyed blue. Beside his graceful slimness, Gareth looked—and no doubt felt—gangly, overgrown, and miserably out of place; his expression was one of profound unhappiness and embarrassment.

It might have been merely because he wasn't wearing his spectacles—they were doubtless hideously unfashionable—but he was looking about him at the exquisite carvings of the rafters, at the familiar glimmer of lamplit silk and stiffened lace, and at the faces of his friends, with a weary confusion, as if they had all become strangers to him.

Even now, Bond was saying, "And is your Dragonsbane as great as Silkydrawers the Magnificent, who slew the Crimson-and-Purple-Striped Dragon in the Golden Woods back in the Reign of Potpourri the Well-Endowed—or was it Kneebiter the Ineffectual? Do enlighten me, Prince."

But before the wretched Gareth could answer, Zyerne said suddenly, "My dears!" and came hurrying to Jenny, her small white hands stretched from the creamy lace of her sleeve ruffles. The smile on her face was as sweet and welcoming as if she greeted a long-lost friend. "My dearest Lady Jenny—forgive me for not seeing you sooner! You look exquisite! Did darling Trey lend you her black-and-silver? How very charitable of her . . ."

A bell rang in the dining room, and the minstrels in the gallery began to play. Zyerne took Jenny's arm to lead in the guests—first women, then men, after the custom of the south—to dinner. Jenny glanced quickly around the hall, looking for John but knowing he would not be there. A qualm crossed her stomach at the thought of sitting through this alone.

Beside her, the light voice danced on. "Oh, yes, you're a mage, too, aren't you? . . . You know I did have some very good training, but it's the sort of thing that has always come to me by instinct. You must tell me about using your powers to make a living. I've never had to do that, you know . . ." Like the prick of knives in her back, she felt the covert smiles of those who walked in procession behind.

Yet because they were deliberate, Jenny found that the younger woman's slights had lost all power to wound her. They stirred in her less anger than Zyerne's temptation of Gareth had. Arrogance she had expected, for it was the besetting sin of the mageborn and Jenny knew herself to be as much prey to it as the others and she sensed the enormous power within Zyerne. But this condescension was a girl's ploy, the trick of one who was herself insecure.

What, she wondered, did Zyerne have to feel insecure about?

As they took their places at the table, Jenny's eyes traveled slowly along its length, seeing it laid like a winter forest with snowy linen and the crystal icicles of candelabra pendant with jewels. Each silver plate was inlaid with traceries of gold and flanked with a dozen little forks and spoons, the complicated armory of etiquette; all these young courtiers in their scented velvet and stiffened lace were clearly her slaves, each more interested in carrying on a dialogue, however brief, with her, than with any of their neighbors. Everything about that delicate hunting lodge was designed to speak her name, from the entwined Zs and Us carved in the corners of the ceiling to the delicate bronze of the horned goddess of love Hartemgarbes, wrought in Zyerne's image, in its niche near the door. Even the delicate music of hautbois and hurdy-gurdy in the gallery was a proclamation, a boast that Zyerne had and would tolerate nothing but the very finest.

Why then the nagging fear that lay behind pettiness?

She turned to look at Zyerne with clinical curiosity, wondering about the pattern of that girl's life. Zyerne's eyes met hers and caught their expression of calm and slightly pitying question. For an instant, the golden orbs narrowed, scorn and spite and anger stirring in their depths. Then the sweet smile returned, and Zyerne asked, "My dear, you haven't touched a bite. Do you use forks in the north?"

There was a sudden commotion in the arched doorway of the hall. One of the minstrels in the gallery, shocked, hit a glaringly wrong squawk out of his recorder; the others stumbled to silence.

"Gaw," Aversin's voice said, and every head along the shimmering board turned, as if at the clatter of a dropped plate. "Late again."

He stepped into the waxlight brightness of the hall with a faint jingle of scraps of chain mail and stood looking about him, his spectacles glinting like steel-rimmed moons. He had changed back into the battered black leather he'd worn on the journey, the wolfhide-lined jerkin with its stray bits of mail and metal plates and spikes and the dark leather breeches and scarred boots. His plaids were slung back over his shoulder like a cloak, cleaned of mud but frayed and scruffy, and there was a world of bright mischief in his eyes.

Gareth, at the other end of the table, went red with mortification to the roots of his thinning hair. Jenny only sighed, momentarily closed her eyes, and thought resignedly, *John*.

He strode cheerily into the room, bowing with impartial goodwill to the courtiers along the board, not one of whom seemed capable of making a sound. They had, for the most part, been looking forward to baiting a country cousin as he tried unsuccessfully to ape his betters; they had scarcely been prepared for an out-and-out barbarian who obviously wasn't even going to bother to try.

With a friendly nod to his hostess, he settled into his place on the opposite side of Zyerne from Jenny. For a moment, he studied the enormous battery of cutlery arrayed on both sides of his plate and then, with perfect neatness and cleanliness, proceeded to eat with his fingers.

Zyerne recovered her composure first. With a silky smile, she picked up a fish fork and offered it to him. "Just as a suggestion, my lord. We *do* do things differently here."

Somewhere down the board, one of the ladies tittered. Aversin regarded Zyerne with undisguised suspicion. She speared a scallop with the fish fork and held it out to him, by way of demonstration, and he broke into his sunniest smile. "Ah, so that's what they're for," he said, relieved. Removing the scallop from the tines with his fingers, he took a neat bite out of it. In a north-country brogue six times worse than anything Jenny had ever heard him use at home, he added, "And here I was thinking I'd been in your lands less than a night, and already challenged to a duel with an unfamiliar weapon, and by the local magewife at that. You had me gie worrit."

On his other side, Bond Clerlock nearly choked on his soup, and John thumped him helpfully on the back.

"You know," he went on, gesturing with the fork in one hand and selecting another scallop with the other, "we did uncover a great box of these things—all different sizes they were, like these here—in the vaults of the Hold the year we looked out the bath for my cousin Kat's wedding. We hadn't a clue what they were for, not even Father Hiero—Father Hiero's our priest—but the next time the bandits came down raiding from the hills, we loaded the lot into the ballistas instead of stone shot and let fly. Killed one of 'em dead on the spot and two others went riding off over the moor with all these little spikey things sticking into their backs . . ."

"I take it," Zyerne said smoothly, as stifled giggles skittered around the table, "that your cousin's wedding was an event of some moment, if it occasioned a bath?"

"Oh, aye." For someone whose usual expression was one of closed watchfulness, Aversin had a dazzling smile. "She was marrying this southern fellow . . ."

It was probably, Jenny thought, the first time that anyone had succeeded in taking an audience away from Zyerne, and, by the glint in the sorceress's eyes, she did not like it. But the courtiers, laughing, were drawn into the circle of Aversin's warm and dotty charm; his exaggerated barbarity disarmed their mockery as his increasingly outrageous tale of his cousin's fictitious nuptials reduced them to undignified whoops. Jenny had enough of a spiteful streak in her to derive a certain amount of enjoyment from Zyerne's discomfiture—it was Zyerne, after all, who had mocked Gareth for not being able to take jests—but confined her attention to her plate. If John was going to the trouble of drawing their fire so that she could finish her meal in peace, the least she could do was not let his efforts go to waste.

On her other side, Trey said softly, "He doesn't look terribly ferocious. From Gareth's ballads, I'd pictured him differently—stern and handsome, like the statues of the god Sarmendes. But then," she added, winkling the meat from an escargot with the special tongs to show Jenny how it was done, "I suppose it would have been a terrific bore for you to ride all the way back from the Winterlands with someone who just spent his time 'scanning th'encircling welkin with his eagle-lidded eyes,' as the song says."

In spite of Zyerne's disapproving glances, her handsome cicisbeo Bond was wiping tears of laughter from his eyes, albeit with great care for his makeup. Even the servants were having a hard time keeping their faces properly expressionless as they carried in peacocks roasted and resplendent in all their feathers and steaming removes of venison in cream.

". . . So the bridegroom looked about for one of those wood things such as you have here in my rooms," John was continuing, "but as he couldn't find one, he hung his clothes over the armor-stand, and damned if Cousin Kat didn't wake in the night and set about it with her sword, taking it for a bandit . . ."

Trust John, Jenny thought, that if he couldn't make an impression on them on their own grounds, he wouldn't try to do it on the grounds of Gareth's ballads, either. They had succumbed to the devil of mischief in him, the devil that had drawn her from the first moment they had met as adults. He had used his outrageousness as a defense against their scorn, but the fact that he had been able to use it successfully made her think a little better of these courtiers of Zyerne's.

She finished her meal in silence, and none of them saw her go.

"Jenny, wait." A tall figure detached itself from the cluster of bright forms in the antechamber and hurried across the hall to catch her, tripping over a footstool halfway.

Jenny paused in the enclosing shadow of the stair lattice. From the anteroom, music was already lilting—not the notes of the hired musicians, this time, but the complex tunes made to show off the skill of the courtiers themselves. To play well, it seemed, was the mark of a true gentleperson; the music of the cwrdth and the double-dulcimer blended into a counterpoint like lace, from which themes would emerge like half-familiar faces glimpsed in a crowd. Over the elaborate harmonies, she heard the blithe, unrepentant air of the pennywhistle, following the melody by ear, and she smiled. If the Twelve Gods of the Cosmos came down, they would be hard put to disconcert John.

"Jenny, I—I'm sorry." Gareth was panting a little from his haste. He had resumed his battered spectacles; the fracture in the bottom of the right-hand lens glinted like a star. "I didn't know it would be like that. I thought—he's a Dragonsbane . . ."

She was standing a few steps up the flight; she put out her hand and touched his face, nearly on level with her own. "Do you remember when you first met him?"

He flushed with embarrassment. In the illuminated antechamber, John's scruffy leather and plaids made him look like a mongrel in a pack of lapdogs. He was examining a lute-shaped hurdy-gurdy with vast interest, while the red-haired, Beautiful Isolde of Greenhythe told the latest of her enormous stock of scatalogical jokes about the gnomes. Everyone guffawed but John, who was far too interested in the musical instrument in his lap to notice; Jenny saw Gareth's mouth tighten with something between anger and confused pain. He went north seeking a dream, she thought; now he had neither that which he had sought nor that to which he had thought he would return.

"I shouldn't have let them bait you like that," he said after a moment. "I didn't think Zyerne . . ."

He broke off, unable to say it. She saw bitterness harden his mouth, and a disillusion worse than the one John had dealt him beside the pigsty at Alyn. He had probably never seen Zyerne being petty before, she thought; or perhaps he had only seen her in the context of the world she had created, never having been outside of it himself. He took a deep breath and went on, "I know I should have taken up for you somehow, but . . . but I didn't know how!" He spread his hands helplessly. With the first rueful humor at himself that Jenny had seen, he added, "You know, in ballads it's so easy to rescue someone. I mean, even if you're defeated, at least you can die gracefully and not have everyone you know laugh at you for the next three weeks."

Jenny laughed and reached out to pat his arm. In the gloom, his features were only an edge of gold along the awkward cheekline, and the twin circles of glass were opaque with the lamplight's reflection that glinted on a few flame-caught strands of hair and formed a spiky illumination along the edges of his lace collar. "Don't worry about it." She smiled. "Like slaying dragons, it's a special art."

"Look," said Gareth, "I—I'm sorry I tricked you. I wouldn't have done it, if I'd known it would be like this. But Zyerne sent a messenger to my father—it's only a day's ride to Bel, and a guest house is being prepared for you in the Palace. I'll be with you when you present yourselves to him, and I know he'll be willing to make terms . . ." He caught himself, as if remembering his earlier lying assurances. "That is, I really *do* know it, this time. Since the coming of the dragon, there's been a huge standing reward for its slaying, more than the pay of a garrison for a year. He has to listen to John."

Jenny leaned one shoulder against the openwork of the newel post, the chips of reflected lamplight filtering through the lattice and dappling her black and silver gown with gold. "Is it so important to you?"

He nodded. Even with the fashionable padding of his white-and-violet doublet, his narrow shoulders looked stooped with tiredness and defeat. "I didn't tell very much truth at the Hold," he said quietly. "But I did tell this: that I know I'm not a warrior, or a knight, and I know I'm not good at games. And I'm not stupid enough to think that the dragon wouldn't kill me in a minute, if I went there. But—I know everyone around here laughs when I talk about chivalry and honor and a knight's duty, and you and John do, too . . . But that's what makes John the Thane of the Winterlands and not just another bandit, doesn't it? He didn't *have* to kill that first dragon." The boy gestured wearily, a half-shrug that sent fragments of luminosity slithering along the white stripes of his slashed sleeves to the diamonds at his cuffs. "I couldn't not do something. Even if I did muff it up."

Jenny felt she had never liked him so well. She said, "If you had truly muffed it up, we wouldn't be here."

She climbed the stairs slowly and crossed the gallery that spanned the hall below. Like the stair, it was enclosed in a stone trellis cut into the shapes of vines and trees, and the shadows flickered in a restless harlequin over her gown and hair. She felt tired and cold from holding herself braced all evening—the sly baiting and lace-trimmed malice of Zyerne's court had stung more than she cared to admit. She pitied them, a little, for what they were, but she did not have John's brass hide.

She and John had been given the smaller of the two rooms at the end of the wing; Gareth, the larger, next door to theirs. Like everything else in Zyerne's lodge, they were beautifully appointed. The red damasked bed hangings and alabaster lamps were designed both as a setting for Zyerne's beauty and a boast of her power to get what she wanted from the King. No wonder, thought Jenny, Gareth distrusted and hated any witch who held sway over a ruler's heart.

As she left the noise of the gallery behind her and turned down the corridor toward her room, she became conscious of the stiff rustling of her borrowed finery upon the inlaid wood of the floor and, with her old instinct for silence, gathered the heavy skirts up in her hands. Lamplight from a half-opened door laid a molten trapezoid of brightness across the darkness before her. Zyerne, Jenny knew, was not downstairs with the others, and she felt uneasy about meeting that beautiful, spoiled, power-ful girl, especially here in her own hunting lodge where she held sole dominion. Thus Jenny passed the open doorway in a drift of illusion; and, though she paused in the shadows at what she saw by the lights within, she remained herself unseen.

It would have been so, she thought later, even had she not been cloaked in the spells that thwart the casual eye. Zyerne sat in an island of brightness, the glow of a night-lamp stroking the gilt-work of her black-wood chair, so still that not even the rose-point shadows of her lace veils stirred upon her gown. Her hands were cupped around the face of Bond Clerlock, who knelt at her feet, and such was his immobility that not even the sapphires pinning his hair glinted, but burned steadily with a single reflection. Though he looked up toward her face, his eyes were closed; his expression was the contorted, intent face of a man in ecstasy so strong that it borders pain.

The room smoked with magic, the weight of it like a glittering lour in the air. As a mage, Jenny could feel it, smell it like an incense; but it was an incense tainted with rot. She stepped back, repelled. Though the touch of Zyerne's hands upon Bond's face was the only contact between their two bodies, she had the sickened sensation of having looked upon that which was obscene. Zyerne's eyes were closed, her childlike brow puck-ered in slight concentration; the smile that curved her lips was one of physical and emotional satisfaction, like a woman's after the act of love.

Not love, thought Jenny, drawing back from the scene and moving soundlessly down the hall once more, but some private satiation.

She sat for a long time in the dark window embrasure of her room and thought about Zyerne. The moon rose, flecking the bare tips of the trees above the white carpet of ground mists; she heard the clocks strike downstairs and the drift of voices and laughter. The moon was in its first quarter, and something about that troubled her, though she could not for the moment think what. After a long time she heard the door open softly behind her and turned to see John silhouetted in the dim lamplight from the hall, its reflection throwing a scatter of metallic glints from his dou-blet and putting a rough halo on the coarse wool of his plaids.

Into the darkness he said softly, "Jen?"

"Here."

Moonlight flashed across his specs. She moved a little—the barring of the casement shadows on her black and silver gown made her nearly invisible. He came cautiously across the unfamiliar terrain of the floor, his hands and face pale blurs against his dark clothing.

"Gaw," he said in disgust as he slung off his plaids. "To come here to risk my bones slaying a dragon and end up playing dancing bear for a pack of children." He sat on the edge of the curtained bed, working at the heavy buckles of his doublet.

"Did Gareth speak to you?"

His spectacles flashed again as he nodded.

"And?"

John shrugged. "Seeing the pack he runs with, I'm not surprised he's a gammy-handed chuff with less sense than my Cousin Dilly's mulberry bushes. And he did take the risk to search for me, I'll give him that." His voice was muffled as he bent over to pull off his boots. "Though I'll wager all the dragon's gold to little green apples he had no idea how dangerous it would be. God knows what I'd have done in his shoes, and him that desperate to help and knowing he hadn't a chance against the dragon himself." He set his boots on the floor and sat up again. "However we came here, I'd be a fool not to speak with the King and see what he'll offer me, though it's in my mind that we'll run up against Zyerne in any dealings we have with him."

Even while playing dancing bear, thought Jenny as she drew the pins from her hair and let her fashionable veils slither to the floor, John didn't miss much. The stiffened silk felt cold under her fingers, from the touch of the window's nearness, even as her hair did when she unwound its thick coil and let it whisper dryly down over her bony, half-bared shoulders.

At length she said, "When Gareth first spoke to me of her, I was jealous, hating her without ever having seen her. She has everything that I wanted, John: genius, time . . . and beauty," she added, realizing that that, too, mattered. "I was afraid it was that, still."

"I don't know, love." He got to his feet, barefoot in breeches and creased shirt, and came to the window where she sat. "It doesn't sound very like you." His hands were warm through the stiff, chilly satins of her borrowed gown as he collected the raven weight of her hair and sorted it into columns that spilled down through his fingers. "I don't know about her magic, for I'm not mageborn myself, but I do know she is cruel for the sport of it—not in the big things that would get her pointed at, but in the little ones—and she leads the others on, teaching them by example and jest to be as cruel as she. Myself, I'd take a whip to Ian, if he treated a guest as she treated you. I see now what that gnome we met on the road meant when he said she poisons what she touches. But she's only a mistress, when all's said. And as for her being beautiful . . ." He shrugged "If I was a bit shapecrafty, I'd be beautiful, too."

In spite of herself Jenny laughed and leaned back into his arms.

But later, in the darkness of the curtained bed, the memory of Zyerne returned once more to her thoughts. She saw again the enchantress and Bond in the rosy aura of the nightlamp and felt the weight and strength of the magic that had filled the room like the silent build of thunder. Was it the magnitude of the power alone that had frightened her, she wondered. Or had it been some sense of filthiness that lay in it, like the back-taste of souring milk? Or had that, in its turn, been only the worm-wood of her own jealousy of the younger woman's greater arts?

John had said that it didn't sound very like her, but she knew he was wrong. It was like her, like the part of herself she fought against, the four-teen-year-old girl still buried in her soul, weeping with exhausted, bitter rage when the rains summoned by her teacher would not disperse at her command. She had hated Caerdinn for being stronger than she. And although the long years of looking after the irascible old man had turned that hatred to affection, she had never forgotten that she was capable of it. Even, she added ironically to herself, as she was capable of working the death-spells on a helpless man, as she had on the dying robber in the ruins of the town; even as she was capable of leaving a man and two children who loved her, because of her love of the quest for power.

Would I have been able to understand what I saw tonight if I had given all my time, all my heart, to the study of magic? Would I have had power like that, mighty as a storm gathered into my two hands?

Through the windows beyond the half-parted bedcurtains, she could see the chill white eye of the moon. Its light, broken by the leading of the casement, lay scattered like the spangles of a fish's mail across the black and silver satin of the gown that she had worn and over the respectable brown velvet suit that John had not. It touched the bed and picked out the scars that crossed John's bare arm, glimmered on the upturned palm of his hand, and outlined the shape of his nose and lips against the darkness. Her vision in the water bowl returned to her again, an icy shadow on her heart.

Would she be able to save him, she wondered, if she were more pow-erful? If she had given her time to her powers wholly, instead of portion-ing it between them and him? Was that, ultimately, what she had cast unknowingly away?

Somewhere in the night a hinge creaked. Still her breathing to listen, she heard the almost soundless pat of bare feet outside her door and the muffled vibration of a shoulder blundering into the wall.

She slid from beneath the silken quilts and pulled on her shift. Over it she wrapped the first garment she laid hands on, John's voluminous plaids, and swiftly crossed the blackness of the room to open the door.

"Gar?"

He was standing a few feet from her, gawky and very boyish-looking in his long nightshirt. His gray eyes stared out straight ahead of him, without benefit of spectacles, and his thin hair was flattened and tangled from the pillow. He gasped at the sound of her voice and almost fell, groping for the wall's support. She realized then that she had waked him.

"Gar, it's me, Jenny. Are you all right?"

His breathing was fast with shock. She put her hand gently on his arm to steady him, and he blinked myopically down at her for a moment. Then he drew a long breath. "Fine," he said shakily. "I'm fine, Jenny. I . . ." He looked around him and ran an unsteady hand through his hair. "I—I must have been walking in my sleep again."

"Do you often?"

He nodded and rubbed his face. "That is . . . I didn't in the north, but I do sometimes here. It's just that I dreamed . . ." He paused, frowning, trying to recall. "Zyerne . . ."

"Zyerne?"

Sudden color flooded his pallid face. "Nothing," he mumbled, and avoided her eyes. "That is—I don't remember."

After she had seen him safely back to the dark doorway of his room, Jenny stood for a moment in the hall, hearing the small sounds of bedcurtains and sheets as he returned to his rest. How late it was, she could not guess. The hunting lodge was deathly silent about her, the smells of long-dead candles, spilled wine, and the frowsty residue of spent passions now flat and stale. All the length of the corridor, every room was dark save one, whose door stood ajar. The dim glow of a single nightlamp shone within, and its light lay across the silky parquet of the floor like a dropped scarf of luminous gold.

6

"**H**e'll have to listen to you." Gareth perched himself in the embrasure of one of the tall windows that ran the length of the southern wall of the King's Gallery, the wan sunlight shimmering with moony radiance in the old-fashioned jewels he wore. "I've just heard that the dragon destroyed the convoy taking supplies out to the siege troops at Halnath last night. Over a thousand pounds of flour and sugar and meat destroyed—horses and oxen dead or scattered—the bodies of the guards burned past recognition."

He nervously adjusted the elaborate folds of his ceremonial mantlings and peered shortsightedly at John and Jenny, who shared a carved bench of ebony inlaid with malachite. Due to the exigencies of court etiquette, formal costume had been petrified into a fashion a hundred and fifty years old out of date, with the result that all the courtiers and petitioners assembled in the long room had the stilted, costumed look of characters in a masquerade. Jenny noticed that John, though he might persist in playing the barbarian in his leather and plaids among the admiring younger courtiers, was not about to do so in the presence of the King. Gareth had draped John's blue-and-cream satin mantlings for him—a valet's job. Bond Clerlock had offered to do it but, Jenny gathered, there were rigid sartorial rules governing such matters; it would have been very like Bond to arrange the elaborate garment in some ridiculous style, knowing the Dragonsbane was unable to tell the difference.

Bond was present among the courtiers who awaited the arrival of the King. Jenny could see him, further down the King's Gallery, standing in one of the slanting bars of pale, platinum light. As usual, his costume outshone every other man's present; his mantlings were a miracle of complex folds and studied elegance, so thick with embroidery that they glittered like a snake's back; his flowing sleeves, six generations out of date, were precise to a quarter-inch in their length and hang. He had even painted his face in the archaic formal fashion, which some of the courtiers did in preference to the modern applications of kohl and rouge—John had flatly refused to have anything to do with either style. The colors accentuated the pallor of young Clerlock's face, though he looked better, Jenny noted, than he had yesterday on the ride from Zyerne's hunting lodge to Bel—less drawn and exhausted.

He was looking about him now with nervous anxiety, searching for someone—probably Zyerne. In spite of how ill he had seemed yesterday, he had been her most faithful attendant, riding at her side and holding her whip, her pomander ball, and the reins of her palfrey when she dismounted. Small thanks, Jenny thought, he had gotten for it. Zyerne had spent the day flirting with the unresponsive Gareth.

It was not that Gareth was immune to her charms. As a nonparticipant, Jenny had an odd sense of unobserved leisure, as if she were watching squirrels from a blind. Unnoticed by the courtiers, she could see that Zyerne was deliberately teasing Gareth's senses with every touch and smile. Do the mageborn love? he had asked her once, back in the bleak Winterlands. Evidently he had come to his own conclusions about whether Zyerne loved him, or he her. But Jenny knew full well that love and desire were two different things, particularly to a boy of eighteen. Under her innocently minxish airs, Zyerne was a woman skilled at manipulating the passions of men.

Why? Jenny wondered, looking up at the boy's awkward profile against the soft cobalt shadows of the gallery. For the amusement of seeing him struggle not to betray his father? Somehow to use his guilt to control him so that one day she could turn the King against him by crying rape?

A stir ran the length of the gallery, like wind in dry wheat. At the far end, voices murmured, "The King! The King!" Gareth scrambled to his feet and hastily checked the folds of his mantlings again. John rose, pushing his anachronistic specs a little more firmly up on the bridge of his nose. Taking Jenny's hand, he followed more slowly, as Gareth hurried toward the line of courtiers that was forming up in the center of the hall.

At the far end, bronze doors swung inward. The Chamberlain Badegamus stepped through, stout, pink, and elderly, emblazoned in a livery of crimson and gold that smote the eye with its splendor. "My lords, my ladies—the King."

Her arm against Gareth's in the press, Jenny was aware of the boy's shudder of nervousness. He had, after all, stolen his father's seal and disobeyed his orders—and he was no longer as blithely unaware of the consequences of his actions as the characters of most ballads seemed to be. She felt him poised, ready to step forward and execute the proper salaam, as others down the rank were already doing, and receive his father's acknowledgement and invitation to a private interview.

The King's head loomed above all others, taller even than his son; Jenny could see that his hair was as fair as Gareth's but much thicker, a warm barely-gold that was beginning to fade to the color of straw. Like the steady murmuring of waves on the shore, voices repeated "My lord . . . my lord . . ."

Her mind returned briefly to the Winterlands. She supposed she should have felt resentment for the Kings who had withdrawn their troops and left the lands to ruin, or awe at finally seeing the source of the King's law that John was ready to die to uphold. But she felt neither, knowing that this man, Uriens of Bel, had had nothing to do with either withdrawing those troops or making the Law, but was merely the heir of the men who had. Like Gareth before he had traveled to the Winterlands, he undoubtedly had no more notion of those things than what he had learned from his tutors and promptly forgotten.

As he approached, nodding to this woman or that man, signing that he would speak to them in private, Jenny felt a vast sense of distance from this tall man in his regal crimson robes. Her only allegiance was to the Winterlands and to the individuals who dwelt there, to people and a land she knew. It was John who felt the ancient bond of fealty; John who had sworn to this man his allegiance, his sword, and his life.

Nevertheless, she felt the tension as the King approached them, tangible as a color in the air. Covert eyes were on them, the younger courtiers watching, waiting to see the reunion between the King and his errant son.

Gareth stepped forward, the oak-leaf-cut end of his mantlings gathered like a cloak between the second and third fingers of his right hand. With surprising grace, he bent his long, gangly frame into a perfect Sarmendes-in-Splendor salaam, such as only the Heir could make, and then only to the monarch. "My lord."

King Uriens 11 of Belmarie, Suzerain of the Marches, High Lord of Wyr, Nast, and the Seven Islands, regarded his son for a moment out of hollow and colorless eyes set deep within a haggard, brittle face. Then, without a word, he turned away to acknowledge the next petitioner.

The silence in the gallery would have blistered the paint from wood. Like black poison dumped into clear water, it spread to the farthest ends of the room. The last few petitioners' voices were audible through it, clearer and clearer, as if they shouted; the closing of the gilded bronze doors as the King passed on into his audience room sounded like the booming of thunder. Jenny was conscious of the eyes of all the room looking anywhere but at them, then sliding back in surreptitious glances, and of Gareth's face, as white as his collar lace.

A soft voice behind them said, "Please don't be angry with him, Gareth."

Zyerne stood there, in plum-colored silk so dark it was nearly black, with knots of pink-tinted cream upon her trailing sleeves. Her mead-colored eyes were troubled. "You did take his seal, you know, and depart without his permission."

John spoke up. "Bit of an expensive slap on the wrist, though, isn't it? I mean, there the dragon is and all, while we're here waiting for leave to go after it."

Zyerne's lips tightened a little, then smoothed. At the near end of the King's Gallery, a small door in the great ones opened, and the Chamberlain Badegamus appeared, quietly summoning the first of the petitioners whom the King had acknowledged.

"There really is no danger to us here, you know. The dragon has been confining his depredations to the farmsteads along the feet of Nast Wall."

"Ah," John said comprehendingly. "That makes it all right, then. And is this what you've told the people of those farmsteads to which, as you say, the dragon's been confining his depredations?"

The flash of anger in her eyes was stronger then, as if no one had ever spoken to her so—or at least, thought Jenny, observing silently from John's side, not for a long time. With visible effort, Zyerne controlled herself and said with an air of one reproving a child, "You must understand. There are many more pressing concerns facing the King . . ."

"More pressing than a dragon sitting on his doorstep?" demanded Gareth, outraged.

She burst into a sweet gurgle of laughter. "There's no need to enact a Dockmarket drama over it, you know. I've told you before, darling, it isn't worth the wrinkles it will give you."

He pulled his head back from her playful touch. "Wrinkles! We're talking about people being killed!"

"Tut, Gareth," Bond Clerlock drawled, strolling languidly over to them. "You're getting as bad as old Polycarp used to be."

Under the paint, his face looked even more washed-out next to Zyerne's sparkling radiance. With a forced effort at his old lightness, he went on, "You shouldn't grudge those poor farmers the only spice in their dull little lives."

"Spice . . ." Gareth began, and Zyerne squeezed his hand chidingly.

"Don't tell me you're going to go all dull and altruistic on us. What a bore that would be." She smiled. "And I will tell you this," she added more soberly. "Don't do anything that would further anger your father. Be patient—and try to understand."

Halfway down the long gallery, the Chamberlain Badegamus was returning, passing the small group of gnomes who sat, an island of isolation, in the shadow of one of the fluted ornamental arches along the east wall. As the Chamberlain walked by, one of them rose in a silken whisper of flowing, alien robes, the cloudy wisps of his milk-white hair floating around his slumped back. Gareth had pointed him out to Jenny earlier—Azwylcartusherands, called Dromar by the folk of men who had little patience with the tongue of gnomes, longtime ambassador from the Lord of the Deep to the Court of Bel. Badegamus saw him and checked his stride, then glanced quickly at Zyerne. She shook her head. Badegamus averted his face and walked past the gnomes without seeing them.

"They grow impudent," the enchantress said softly. "To send envoys here, when they fight on the side of the traitors of Halnath."

"Well, they can hardly help that, can they, if the back way out of the Deep leads into the Citadel," John remarked.

"They could have opened the Citadel gates to let the King's troops in."

John scratched the side of his long nose. "Well, being a barbarian and all, I wouldn't know how things are done in civilized lands," he said. "In the north, we've got a word for someone who'd do that to a man who gave him shelter when he was driven from his home."

For an instant Zyerne was silent, her power and her anger seeming to crackle in the air. Then she burst into another peal of chiming laughter. "I swear, Dragonsbane, you do have a refreshingly naive way of looking at things. You make me feel positively ancient." She brushed a tendril of her hair aside from her cheek as she spoke; she looked as sweet and guileless as a girl of twenty. "Come. Some of us are going to slip away from this silliness and go riding along the sea cliffs. Will you come, Gareth?" Her hand stole into his in such a way that he could not avoid it without rudeness—Jenny could see his face color slightly at the touch. "And you, our barbarian? You know the King won't see you today."

"Be that as it may," John said quietly. "I'll stay here on the off chance."

Bond laughed tinnily. "There's the spirit that won the Realm!"

"Aye," John agreed in a mild voice and returned to the carved bench where he and Jenny had been, secure in his established reputation for barbarous eccentricity.

Gareth drew his hand from Zyerne's and sat down nearby, catching his mantlings in the lion's-head arm of the chair. "I think I'll stay as well," he said, with as much dignity as one could have while disentangling oneself from the furniture.

Bond laughed again. "I think our Prince has been in the north too long!" Zyerne wrinkled her nose, as if at a joke in doubtful taste.

"Run along, Bond." She smiled. "I must speak to the King. I shall join you presently." Gathering up her train, she moved off toward the bronze doors of the King's antechamber, the opals that spangled her veils giving the impression of dew flecking an apple blossom as she passed the pale bands of the windowlight. As she came near the little group of gnomes, old Dromar rose again and walked toward her with the air of one steeling himself for a loathed but necessary encounter. But she turned her glance from him and quickened her step, so that, to intercept her, he would have to run after her on his short, bandy legs. This he would not do, but stood looking after her for a moment, smoldering anger in his pale amber eyes.

"I don't understand it," said Gareth, much later, as the three of them jostled their way along the narrow lanes of the crowded Dockmarket quarter. "She said Father was angry, yes—but he knew whom I'd be bringing with me. And he must have known about the dragon's latest attack." He hopped across the fish-smelling slime of the gutter to avoid a trio of sailors who'd come staggering out of one of the taverns that lined the cobbled street and nearly tripped over his own cloak.

When Badegamus had announced to the nearly empty gallery that the King would see no one else that day, John and Jenny had taken the baffled and fuming Gareth back with them to the guest house they had been assigned in one of the outer courts of the Palace. There they had changed out of their borrowed court dress, and John had announced his intention of spending the remainder of the afternoon in the town, in quest of gnomes.

"Gnomes?" Gareth said, surprised.

"Well, if it hasn't occurred to anyone else, it has occurred to me that, if I'm to fight this drake, I'm going to need to know the layout of the caverns." With surprising deftness, he disentangled himself from the intricate crisscross folds of his mantlings, his head emerging from the double-faced satin like a tousled and unruly weed. "And since it didn't seem the thing to address them at Court . . ."

"But they're plotting!" Gareth protested. He paused in his search for a place to dump the handful of old-fashioned neck-chains and rings among the already-accumulating litter of books, harpoons, and the contents of Jenny's medical pouch on the table. "Speaking to them at Court would have been suicide! And besides, you're not going to fight him in the Deep, are you? I mean . . ." He barely stopped himself from the observation that in all the ballads the Dragonsbanes had slain their foes in front of their lairs, not in them.

"If I fight him outside and he takes to the air, it's all over," John returned, as if he were talking about backgammon strategy. "And though it's crossed my mind we're walking through a morass of plots here, it's to no one's advantage to have the dragon stay in the Deep. The rest of it's all none of my business. Now, are you going to guide us, or do we go about the streets asking folk where the gnomes might be found?"

To Jenny's surprise and probably a little to his own, Gareth offered his services as a guide.

"Tell me about Zyerne, Gar," Jenny said now, thrusting her hands deep into her jacket pockets as she walked. "Who is she? Who was her teacher? What Line was she in?"

"Teacher?" Gareth had obviously never given the matter a thought. "Line?"

"If she is a mage, she must have been taught by someone." Jenny glanced up at the tall boy towering beside her, while they detoured to avoid a gaggle of passersby around a couple of street-corner jugglers. Beyond them, in a fountain square, a fat man with the dark complexion of a southerner had set up a waffle stand, bellowing his wares amid clouds of steam that scented the raw, misty air for yards.

"There are ten or twelve major Lines, named for the mages that founded them. There used to be more, but some have decayed and died. My own master Caerdinn, and therefore I and any other pupils of his, or of his teacher Spaeth, or Spaeth's other students, are all in the Line of Herne. To a mage, knowing that I am of the Line of Herne says—oh, a hundred things about my power and my attitude toward power, about the kinds of spells that I know, and about the kind that I will not use."

"Really?" Gareth was fascinated. "I didn't know it was anything like that. I thought that magic was just something—well, something you were born with."

"So is the talent for art," Jenny said. "But without proper teaching, it never comes to fullest fruition; without sufficient time given to the study of magic, sufficient striving . . ." She broke off, with an ironic smile at herself. "All power has to be paid for," she continued after a moment. "And all power must come from somewhere, have been passed along by someone."

It was difficult for her to speak of her power; aside from the confusion of her heart about her own power, there was much in it that any not mageborn simply did not understand. She had in all her life met only one who did, and he was presently over beside the waffle stand, getting powdered sugar on his plaids.

Jenny sighed and came to a halt to wait for him at the edge of the square. The cobbles were slimy here with sea air and offal; the wind smelled of fish and, as everywhere in the city of Bel, of the intoxicating wildness of the sea. This square was typical of the hundreds that made up the interlocking warrens of Bel's Dockmarket, hemmed in on three-and-a-half sides by the towering, rickety tenements and dominated by the moldering stones of a slate-gray clock tower, at whose foot a neglected shrine housed the battered image of Quis, the enigmatic Lord of Time. In the center of the square bubbled a fountain in a wide basin of chip-edged granite, the stones of its rim worn smooth and white above and clotted beneath with the black-green moss that seemed to grow everywhere in the damp air of the city. Women were dipping water there and gossiping, their skirts hiked up almost to their thighs but their heads modestly covered in clumsy wool veils tied in knots under their hair to keep them out of the way.

In the mazes of stucco and garish color of the Dockmarket, John's outlandishness hadn't drawn much notice. The sloping, cobbled streets were crowded with sojourners from three-fourths of the Realm and all the Southern Lands: sailors with shorn heads and beards like coconut husks; peddlers from the garden province of Istmark in their old-fashioned, bundly clothes, the men as well as the women wearing veils; money-changers in the black gabardine and skullcaps that marked them out as the Wanderer's Children, forbidden to own land; whores painted to within an inch of their lives; and actors, jugglers, scarf sellers, rat killers, pick-pockets, cripples, and tramps. A few women cast looks of dismissive scorn at Jenny's uncovered head, and she was annoyed at the anger she felt at them.

She asked, "How much do you know about Zyerne? What was she apprenticed as in the Deep?"

Gareth shrugged. "I don't know. My guess would be in the Places of Healing. That was where the greatest power of the Deep was supposed to lie—among their healers. People used to journey for days to be tended there, and I know most of the mages were connected with them."

Jenny nodded. Even in the isolated north, among the children of men who knew virtually nothing of the ways of the gnomes, Caerdinn had spoken with awe of the power that dwelled within the Places of Healing in the heart of the Deep of Ylferdun.

Across the square, a religious procession came into view, the priests of Kantirith, Lord of the Sea, walking with their heads muffled in their ceremonial hoods, lest an unclean sight distract them, the ritual wailing of the flutes all but drowning out their murmured chants. Like all the cere-monials of the Twelve Gods, both the words and the music of the flutes had been handed down by rote from ancient days; the words were unintelligible, the music like nothing Jenny had heard at Court or elsewhere.

"And when did Zyerne come to Bel?" she asked Gareth, as the muttering train filed past.

The muscles of the boy's jaw tightened. "After my mother died," he said colorlessly. "I—I suppose I shouldn't have been angry at Father about it. At the time I didn't understand the way Zyerne can draw people, sometimes against their will." He concentrated his attention upon smoothing the ruffles of his sleeve for some moments, then sighed. "I suppose he needed someone. I wasn't particularly good to him about Mother's death."

Jenny said nothing, giving him room to speak or hold his peace. From the other end of the square, another religious procession made its appearance, one of the southern cults that spawned in the Dockmarket like rabbits; dark-complexioned men and women were clapping their hands and singing, while skinny, androgynous priests swung their waist-length hair and danced for the little idol borne in their midst in a carrying shrine of cheap, pink chintz. The priests of Kantirith seemed to huddle a little more closely in their protecting hoods, and the wailing of the flutes increased. Gareth spared the newcomers a disapproving glance, and Jenny remembered that the King of Bel was also Pontifex Maximus of the official cult; Gareth had no doubt been brought up in the most careful orthodoxy.

But the din gave them the illusion of privacy. For all any of the crowd around them cared, they might have been alone; and after a time Gareth spoke again.

"It was a hunting accident," he explained. "Father and I both hunt, although Father hasn't done so lately. Mother hated it, but she loved my father and would go with him when he asked her to. He teased her about it, and made little jokes about her cowardice—but he wasn't really joking. He can't stand cowards. She'd follow him over terrible country, clinging to her sidesaddle and staying up with the hunt; after it was over, he'd hug her and laugh and ask her if it wasn't worth it that she'd plucked up her courage—that sort of thing. She did it for as long as I can remember. She used to lie and tell him she was starting to learn to enjoy it; but when I was about four, I remember her in her hunting habit—it was peach-colored velvet with gray fur, I remember—just before going out, throwing up because she was so frightened."

"She sounds like a brave lady," Jenny said quietly.

Gareth's glance flicked up to her face, then away again. "It wasn't really Father's fault," he went on after a moment. "But when it finally did happen, he felt that it was. The horse came down with her over some rocks—in a sidesaddle you can't fall clear. She died four or five days later. That was five years ago. I—" He hesitated, the words sticking in his throat. "I wasn't very good to him about it."

He adjusted his specs in an awkward and unconvincing cover for wiping his eyes on his sleeve ruffle. "Now that I look back on it, I think, if she'd been braver, she'd probably have had the courage to tell him she didn't want to go—the courage to risk his mockery. Maybe that's where I get it," he added, with the shy flash of a grin. "Maybe I should have seen that I couldn't possibly blame him as much as he blamed himself—that I didn't say anything to him that he hadn't already thought." He shrugged his bony shoulders. "I understand now. But when I was thirteen, I didn't. And by the time I did understand, it had been too long to say anything to him. And by that time, there was Zyerne."

The priests of Kantirith wound their way out of sight up a crooked lane between the drunken lean of crazy buildings. Children who had stopped to gawk after the procession took up their games once more; John resumed his cautious way across the moss-edged, herringbone pattern of the wet cobbles toward them, stopping every few paces to stare at some new marvel—a chair-mender pursuing his trade on the curbstone, or the actors within a cheap theater gesticulating wildly while a crier outside shouted tidbits of the plot to the passersby around the door. He would never, Jenny reflected with rueful amusement, learn to comport himself like the hero of legend that he was.

"It must have been hard for you," she said.

Gareth sighed. "It was easier a few years ago," he admitted. "I could hate her cleanly then. Later, for a while I—I couldn't even do that." He blushed again. "And now . . ."

A commotion in the square flared suddenly, like the noise of a dogfight; a woman's jeering voice yelled, "Whore!" and Jenny's head snapped around.

But it was not she and her lack of veils that was the target. A little gnome woman, her soft mane of hair like an apricot cloud in the wan sunlight, was making her hesitant way toward the fountain. Her black silk trousers were hitched up over her knees to keep them out of the puddles in the broken pavement, and her white tunic, with its flowing embroideries and carefully mended sleeves, proclaimed that she was living in poverty alien to her upbringing. She paused, peering around her with a painful squint in the too-bright daylight; then her steps resumed in the direction of the fountain, her tiny, round hands clutching nervously at the handle of the bucket that she inexpertly bore.

Somebody else shouted, "Come slumming, have we, m'lady? Tired of sitting up there on all that grain you got hid? Too cheap to hire servants?"

The woman stopped again, swinging her head from side to side as if seeking her tormentors, half-blind in the outdoor glare. Someone caught her with a dog turd on the arm. She hopped, startled, and her narrow feet in their soft leather shoes skidded on the wet, uneven stones. She dropped the bucket as she fell, and groped about for it on hands and knees. One of the women by the fountain, with the grinning approbation of her neighbors, sprang down to kick it beyond her reach.

"That'll learn you to hoard the bread you've bought out of honest folks' mouths!"

The gnome made a hasty scrabble around her. A faded, fat woman who'd been holding forth the loudest in the gossip around the fountain kicked the pail a little further from the searching hands.

"And to plot against the King!"

The gnome woman raised herself to her knees, peering about her, and one of the children darted out of the gathering crowd behind her and pulled the long wisps of her hair. She spun around, clutching, but the boy had gone. Another took up the game and sprang nimbly out to do the same, too engrossed in the prospect of fun to notice John.

At the first sign of trouble, the Dragonsbane had turned to the man next to him, a blue-tattooed easterner in a metalsmith's leather apron and not much else, and handed him the three waffles he held stacked in his hands. "Would you ever hold these?" Then he made his way unhurriedly through the press, with a courteous string of "Excuse me . . . pardon . . ." in time to catch the second boy who'd jumped out to take up the baiting where the first had begun it.

Gareth could have told them what to expect—Zyerne's courtiers weren't the only ones deceived by John's appearance of harmless friendliness. The bully, caught completely offguard from behind, didn't even have time to shriek before he hit the waters of the fountain. A huge splash doused every woman on the steps and most of the surrounding idlers. As the boy surfaced, spitting and gasping, Aversin turned from picking up the bucket and said in a friendly tone, "Your manners are as filthy as your clothes—I'm surprised your mother lets you out like that. They'll be a bit cleaner now, won't they?"

He dipped the bucket full and turned back to the man who was holding his waffles. For an instant Jenny thought the smith would throw them into the fountain, but John only smiled at him, bright as the sun on a knifeblade, and sullenly the man put the waffles into his free hand. In the back of the crowd a woman sneered, "Gnome lover!"

"Thanks." John smiled, still at his brass-faced friendliest. "Sorry I threw offal in the fountain and all." Balancing the waffles in his hand, he descended the few steps and walked beside the little gnome woman across the square toward the mouth of the alley whence she had come. Jenny, hurrying after him with Gareth at her heels, noticed that none followed them too closely.

"John, you are incorrigible," she said severely. "Are you all right?" This last was addressed to the gnome, who was hastening along on her short, bowed legs, clinging to the Dragonsbane's shadow for protection.

She peered up at Jenny with feeble, colorless eyes. "Oh, yes. My thanks. I had never—always we went out to the fountain at night, or sent the girl who worked for us, if we needed water during the day. Only she left." The wide mouth pinched up on the words, at the taste of some unpleasant memory.

"I bet she did, if she was like that lot," John remarked, jerking his thumb back toward the square. Behind them, the crowd trailed menacingly, yelling, "Traitors! Hoarders! Ingrates!" and fouler things besides. Somebody threw a fish head that flicked off Jenny's skirts and shouted something about an old whore and her two pretty-boys; Jenny felt the bristles of rage rise along her spine. Others took up this theme. She felt angry enough to curse them, but in her heart she knew that she could lay no greater curse upon them than to be what they already were.

"Have a waffle?" John offered disarmingly, and the gnome lady took the proferred confection with hands that shook.

Gareth, carmine with embarrassment, said nothing.

Around a mouthful of sugar, John said, "Gie lucky for us fruit and vegies are a bit too dear these days to fling, isn't it? Here?"

The gnome ducked her head quickly as she entered the shadows of a doorway to a huge, crumbling house wedged between two five-storey tenements, its rear wall dropping straight to the dank brown waters of a stagnant canal. The windows were tightly shuttered, and the crumbling stucco was written over with illiterate and filthy scrawls, splattered with mud and dung. From every shutter Jenny could sense small, weak eyes peering down in apprehension.

The door was opened from within, the gnome taking her bucket and popping through like a frightened mole into its hill. John put a quick hand on the rotting panels to keep them from being shut in his face, then braced with all his strength. The doorkeeper was determined and had the prodigious muscles of the gnomes.

"Wait!" John pleaded, as his feet skidded on the wet marble of the step. "Listen! I need your help! My name's John Aversin—I've come from the north to see about this dragon of yours, but I can't do it without your aid." He wedged his shoulder into the narrow slit that was all that was left. "Please."

The pressure on the other side of the door was released so suddenly that he staggered inward under his own momentum. From the darkness beyond a soft, high voice like a child's said in the archaic High Speech that the gnomes used at Court, "Come in, thou others. It does thee no good to be thus seen at the door of the house of the gnomes."

As they stepped inside, John and Gareth blinked against the dimness, but Jenny, with her wizard's sight, saw at once that the gnome who had admitted them was old Dromar, ambassador to the court of the King.

Beyond him, the lower hall of the house stretched in dense shadow. It had once been grand in the severe style of a hundred years ago—the old manor, she guessed, upon whose walled grounds the crowded, stinking tenements of the neighborhood had later been erected. In places, rotting frescoes were still dimly visible on the stained walls; and the vastness of the hall spoke of gracious furniture now long since chopped up for fire-wood and of an aristocratic carelessness about the cost of heating fuel. The place was like a cave now, tenebrous and damp, its boarded windows letting in only a few chinks of watery light to outline stumpy pillars and the dry mosaics of the impluvium. Above the sweeping curve of the old-fashioned, open stair she saw movement in the gallery. It was crowded with gnomes, watching warily these intruders from the hostile world of men.

In the gloom, the soft, childlike voice said, "Thy name is not unknown among us, John Aversin."

"Well, that makes it easier," John admitted, dusting off his hands and looking down at the round head of the gnome who stood before him and into sharp, pale eyes under the flowing mane of snowy hair. "Be a bit awkward if I had to explain it all, though I imagine Gar here could sing you the ballads."

A slight smile tugged at the gnome's mouth—the first, Jenny suspected, in a long time—as he studied the incongruous, bespectacled reality behind the glitter of the legends. "Thou art the first," he remarked, ushering them into the huge, chilly cavern of the room, his mended silk robes whispering as he moved. "How many hast thy father sent out, Prince Gareth? Fifteen? Twenty? And none of them came here, nor asked any of the gnomes what they might know of the dragon's coming—we, who saw it best."

Gareth looked disconcerted. "Er—that is—the wrath of the King . . ."

"And whose fault was that, Heir of Uriens, when rumor had been noised abroad that we had made an end of thee?"

There was an uncomfortable silence as Gareth reddened under that cool, haughty gaze. Then he bent his head and said in a stifled voice, "I am sorry, Dromar. I never thought of—of what might be said, or who would take the blame for it, if I disappeared. Truly I didn't know. I behaved rashly—I seem to have behaved rashly all the way around."

The old gnome sniffed. "So." He folded his small hands before the complicated knot of his sash, his gold eyes studying Gareth in silence for a time. Then he nodded, and said, "Well, better it is that thou fall over thine own feet in the doing of good than sit upon thy hands and let it go undone, Gareth of Magloshaldon. Another time thou shalt do better." He turned away, gesturing toward the inner end of the shadowed room, where a blackwood table could be distinguished in the gloom, no more than a foot high, surrounded by burst and patched cushions set on the floor in the fashion of the gnomes. "Come. Sit. What is it that thou wish to know, Dragonsbane, of the coming of the dragon to the Deep?"

"The size of the thing," John said promptly, as they all settled on their knees around the table. "I've only heard rumor and story—has anybody got a good, concrete measurement?"

From beside Jenny, the high, soft voice of the gnome woman piped, "The top of his haunch lies level with the frieze carved above the pillars on either side of the doorway arch, which leads from the Market Hall into the Grand Passage into the Deep itself. That is twelve feet, by the measurements of men."

There was a moment's silence, as Jenny digested the meaning of that piece of information. Then she said, "If the proportions are the same, that makes it nearly forty feet."

"Aye," Dromar said. "The Market Hall—the first cavern of the Deep, that lies just behind the Great Gates that lead into the outer world—is one hundred and fifty feet from the Gates to the inner doors of the Grand Passage at the rear. The dragon was nearly a third of that length."

John folded his hands on the table before him. Though his face remained expressionless, Jenny detected the slight quickening of his breath. Forty feet was half again the size of the dragon that had come so close to killing him in Wyr, with all the dark windings of the Deep in which to hide.

"D'you have a map of the Deep?"

The old gnome looked affronted, as if he had inquired about the cost of a night with his daughter. Then his face darkened with stubborn anger. "That knowledge is forbidden to the children of men."

Patiently, John said, "After all that's been done you here, I don't blame you for not wanting to give out the secrets of the Deep; but I need to know. I can't take the thing from the front. I can't fight something that big head-on. I need to have some idea where it will be lairing."

"It will be lairing in the Temple of Sarmendes, on the first level of the Deep." Dromar spoke grudgingly, his pale eyes narrow with the age-old suspicion of a smaller, weaker race that had been driven underground millennia ago by its long-legged and bloodthirsty cousins. "It lies just off the Grand Passage that runs back from the Gates. The Lord of Light was beloved by the men who dwelt within the Deep—the King's ambassadors and their households, and those who had been apprenticed among our people. His Temple is close to the surface, for the folk of men do not like to penetrate too far into the bones of the Earth. The weight of the stone unnerves them; they find the darkness disquieting. The dragon will lie there. There he will bring his gold."

"Is there a back way into it?" John asked. "Through the priests' quarters or the treasuries?"

Dromar said, "No," but the little gnome woman said, "Yes, but thou would never find it, Dragonsbane."

"By the Stone!" The old gnome whirled upon her, smoldering rage in his eyes. "Be silent, Mab! The secrets of the Deep are not for his kind!" He looked viciously at Jenny and added, "Nor for hers."

John held up his hand for silence. "Why wouldn't I find it?"

Mab shook her head. From beneath a heavy brow, her round, almost colorless blue eyes peered up at him, kindly and a little sad. "The ways lead through the warrens," she said simply. "The caverns and tunnels there are a maze that we who dwell there can learn, in twelve or fourteen years of childhood. But even were we to tell thee the turnings thou must take, one false step would condemn thee to a death by starvation and to the madness that falls upon men in the darkness under the earth. We filled the mazes with lamps, but those lamps are quenched now."

"Can you draw me a map, then?" And, when the two gnomes only looked at him with stubborn secrets in their eyes, he said, "Dammit, I can't do it without your help! I'm sorry it has to be this way, but it's trust me or lose the Deep forever; and those are your only choices!"

Dromar's long, outward-curling eyebrows sank lower over the stub of his nose. "So be it, then," he said.

But Miss Mab turned resignedly and began to rise. The ambassador's eyes blazed. "No! By the Stone, is it not enough that the children of men seek to steal the secrets of the Deep? Must thou give them up freely?"

"Tut," Mab said with a wrinkled smile. "This Dragonsbane will have problems enow from the dragon, without going seeking in the darkness for others."

"A map that is drawn may be stolen!" Dromar insisted. "By the Stone that lies in the heart of the Deep . . ."

Mab got comfortably to her feet, shaking out her patched silken garments, and pottered over to the scroll-rack that filled one corner of the dim hall. She returned with a reed pen and several sheets of tattered papyrus paper in her hand. "Those whom you fear would steal it know the way to the heart of the Deep already," she pointed out gently. "If this barbarian knight has ridden all the way from the Winterlands to be our champion, it would be paltry not to offer him a shield."

"And her?" Dromar jabbed one stumpy finger, laden with old-fashioned, smooth-polished gems, at Jenny. "She is a witch. What surety have we that *she* will not go snooping and spying, delving out our secrets, turning them against us, defiling them, poisoning them, as others have done?"

The gnome woman frowned down at Jenny for a moment, her wide mouth pursed up with thought. Then she knelt beside her again and pushed the writing things across the table at Dromar. "There," she said. "Thou may draw the maps, and put upon them what thou will, and leave from them what thou will."

"And the witch?" There was suspicion and hatred in his voice, and Jenny reflected that she was getting very tired of being mistaken for Zyerne.

"Ah," said Miss Mab, and reaching out, took Jenny's small, scratched, boyish brown hands in her own. For a long moment she looked into her eyes. As if the small, cold fingers clasping hers stirred at the jewel heap of her dreams, Jenny felt the gnome woman's mind probing at her thoughts, as she had probed at Gareth's, seeking to see the shape of her essence. She realized that Miss Mab was a mage, like herself.

Reflex made her stiffen. But Mab smiled gently and held out to her the depths of her own mind and soul—gentle and clear as water, and stubborn as water, too, containing none of the bitterness, resentments, and doubts that Jenny knew clotted the corners of her own heart. She relaxed, feeling as ashamed as if she had struck out at an inquiry kindly made, and felt some of her own angers dissolving under that wise scrutiny. She felt the other woman's power, much greater than her own, but gentle and warm as sunlight.

When Miss Mab spoke, it was not to Dromar, but to her. "Thou art afraid for him," she said softly. "And perhaps thou should be." She put out one round little hand, to pat Jenny's hair. "But remember that the dragon is not the greatest of evils in this land, nor is death the worst that can befall; neither for him, nor for thee."

7

In the week that followed, Jenny returned many times to the crumbling house in the Dockmarket. Twice John accompanied her, but John, for the most part, spent his days in the King's Gallery with Gareth, waiting for a sign from the King. His evenings he spent with the wild young courtiers who surrounded Zyerne, playing dancing bear, as he called it, and dealing as best as he could with the slow torture of waiting for a combat that could cost his life. Being John, he did not speak of it, but Jenny felt it when they made love and in his silences when they were alone together, this gradual twisting of the nerves that was driving him nearly mad.

She herself avoided the Court for the most part and spent her days in the city or in the house of the gnomes. She went there quietly, wrapped in spells to conceal her from the folk in the streets, for, as the days ground by, she could feel the ugly miasma of hate and fear spreading through the streets like poisoned fog. On her way through the Dockmarket quarter, she would pass the big taverns—the Lame Ox, the Gallant Rat, the Sheep in the Mire—where the unemployed men and women who had come in off the ruined farms gathered daily, hoping for a few hours' hire. Those in need of cheap labor knew to go there to find people who would move furniture or clean out stables for a few coppers; but with the winter storms making the shipping scarce and the high price of bread taking all the spare funds to be had, there were few enough who could afford to pay even that. None of the gnomes still living in the city—and there were many of them, in spite of the hardships—dared go by the Sheep in the Mire after noontime, for by that hour those within would have given up hope of work that day and would be concentrating what little energy they had on getting drunk.

So Jenny moved in her shadowy secrets, as she had moved through the lawless Winterlands, to visit the Lady Taseldwyn, who was called Miss Mab in the language of men.

From the first, she had been aware that the gnome woman was a more powerful mage than she. But, rather than jealousy and resentment, she felt only gladness that she had found someone to teach her after all those years.

In most things, Mab was a willing teacher, though the shape of the gnomes' wizardry was strange to Jenny, alien, as their minds were alien. They had no Lines, but seemed to transmit their power and knowledge whole from generation to generation of mages in some fashion that Jenny did not understand. Mab told her of the healing spells for which the Deep was famous, of the drugs now sequestered there, lost to them as surely as the dragon's gold was lost, of the spells that could hold the soul, the essence of life, to the flesh, or of the more dangerous spells by which the life-essence of one person could be drawn to strengthen the crumbling life of another. The gnome woman taught her other spells of the magic underground—spells of crystal and stone and spiraling darkness, whose meaning Jenny could only dimly comprehend. These she could only memorize by rote, hoping that with later meditation, skill and under-standing would come. Mab spoke also to her of the secrets of the earth, the movement of water, and how stones thought; and she spoke of the dark realms of the Deep itself, cavern beneath cavern in endless succession of hidden glories that had never seen light.

Once, she spoke of Zyerne.

"Aye, she was apprenticed among us Healers." She sighed, putting aside the three-stringed dulcimer upon which she had been outlining to Jenny the song-spells of their craft. "She was a vain little girl, vain and spoiled. She had her talent for mockery even then—she would listen to the Old Ones among us, the great Healers, who had more power at their command than she could ever dream of, nodding that sleek little head of hers in respect, and then go and imitate their voices to her friends in Deeping."

Jenny remembered the silvery chime of the sorceress's laughter at dinner and the way she had hurried her steps to make Dromar run after her if he would speak.

It was early evening. For all its cold, the great hall of the gnomes' house was stuffy, the air stagnant beneath its massive arches and along the faded pavement of its checkered corridors. The noises of the streets had fallen to their dinnertime lull, save for the chiming of the clock towers all over the city and one lone kindling-peddler crying his wares.

Mab shook her head, her voice low with remembrance of times past. "She was greedy for secrets, as some girls are greedy for sweets—covetous for the power they could give her. She studied out the hidden ways around the Places of Healing so that she could sneak and spy, hiding to listen in darkness. All power must be paid for, but she took the secrets of those greater than she and defiled them, tainted them—poisoned them as she poisoned the very heart of the Deep—yes, she did poison it!—and turned all our strength against us."

Jenny shook her head, puzzled. "Dromar said something of the kind," she said. "But how can you taint spells? You can spoil your own magic, for it colors your soul as you wield it, but you cannot spoil another's. I don't understand."

Mab glanced sharply at her, as if remembering her presence and remembering also that she was not one of the folk of the gnomes. "Nor should thou," she said in her soft, high voice. "These are things that concern the magic of gnomes only. They are not human things."

"Zyerne seems to have made them human things." Jenny moved her weight on her heels, easing her knees on the hardness of the stone floor through the shabby cushion. "If it is, indeed, from the Places of Healing that she learned the arts that have made her the most powerful mage in the land."

"Pah!" the gnome mage said in disgust. "The Healers of the Deep were more powerful than she—by the Stone, *I* was more powerful!"

"Was?" Jenny said, perplexed. "I know that most of the Healers in the Deep were killed with the coming of the dragon; I had thought none of sufficient strength survived to defy her. The magic of gnomes is different from the spells of men, but power is power. How could Zyerne have lessened yours?"

Mab only shook her head furiously, so that her pale, web-colored hair whipped back and forth, and said, "These are the things of the gnomes."

In those days Jenny did not see much of Zyerne, but the enchantress was often on her mind. Zyerne's influence pervaded the court like the faint waft of her cinnamon perfume; when Jenny was in the Palace confines, she was always conscious of her. However Zyerne had acquired her power and whatever she had done with it since, Jenny never forgot that it was so much greater than hers. When she neglected what tomes of magic John was able to pilfer from the Palace library to sit with her scrying-stone, watching the tiny, soundless images of her sons skylarking perilously along the snow-covered battlements of the Hold, she felt a pang of guilt. Zyerne was young, at least ten years younger than she; her power shone from her like the sun. Jenny no longer felt jealousy and she could not, in all honesty, feel anger at Zyerne for having what she herself did not, as long as she was not willing to do what was needful to obtain that power. But she did feel envy, the envy of a traveler on a cold night who saw into the warmth of a lighted room.

But when she asked Mab about Zyerne—about the powers that had once been less than Mab's, but now were greater; about why the gnomes had forbidden her to enter the Deep—the little mage would only say stubbornly, "These are the things of the gnomes. They have naught to do with men."

In the meantime John went his own way, a favorite of the younger courtiers who laughed at his extravagant barbarism and called him their tame savage, while he held forth about engineering and the mating customs of pigs, or quoted classical authors in his execrable north-country drawl. And still, every morning, the King passed them by in the gallery, turning his dull eyes aside from them, and the etiquette of the Court forbade Gareth to speak.

"What's his delay?" John demanded as he and Gareth emerged from the arched porticoes of the gallery into the chill, fleet sunlight of the deserted terrace after yet another futile day's waiting. Jenny joined them quietly, coming up the steps from the deserted garden below, carrying her harp. She had been playing it on the rocks above the sea wall, waiting for them and watching the rainclouds scud far out over the sea. It was the season of winds and sudden gales, and in the north the weather would be sleety and cold, but here days of high, heatless sunlight alternated with fogs and blowing rains. The matte, white day-moon was visible, sinking into the cloud wrack over the sea; Jenny wondered what it was that troubled her about its steady waxing toward its half. Against the loamy colors of the fallow earth, the clothes of Zyerne and her court stood out brightly as they passed on down into the garden, and Jenny could hear the enchantress's voice lifted in a wickedly accurate imitation of the gnomes' shrill speech.

John went on, "Is he hoping the dragon will fall on the Citadel and spare him the trouble of the siege?"

Gareth shook his head. "I don't think so. I'm told Polycarp has catapults for slinging naphtha set up on the highest turrets. The dragon keeps his distance." In spite of the Master's treason, Jenny could hear in the Prince's voice a trace of pride in his former friend.

Unlike John, who had rented a Court costume from a shop outside the palace gates which specialized in such things for petitioners to the King, Gareth owned at least a dozen of them—like all Court costumes, criminally expensive. The one he wore today was parakeet green and primrose and, in the uncertain light of the afternoon, it turned his rather sallow complexion yellow.

John pushed his specs a little further up on the bridge of his nose. "Well, I tell you, I'm not exactly ettling to go on kicking my heels here like a rat catcher waiting for the King to decide he wants my services. I came here to protect my lands and my people, and right now they're getting nothing from the King who's supposed to guard them, nor from me."

Gareth had been gazing down into the garden at the little group around the leaf-stained marble statue of the god Kantirith absently, as if not aware of where he looked; now he turned his head quickly. "You can't go," he said, worry and fear in his voice.

"And why not?"

The boy bit his lip and did not answer, but his glance darted nervously back down to the garden. As if she felt the touch of it, Zyerne turned and blew him a playful kiss, and Gareth looked away. He looked tired and hagridden, and Jenny suddenly wondered if he still dreamed of Zyerne.

The uncomfortable silence was broken, not by him, but by the high voice of Dromar.

"My lord Aversin . . ." The gnome stepped out onto the terrace and blinked painfully in the wan, overcast light. His words came haltingly, as if they were unfamiliar in his mouth. "Please—do not go."

John glanced down at him sharply. "You haven't precisely extended your all in welcome and help, either, have you?"

The old ambassador's gaze challenged him. "I drew thee the maps of the Deep. By the Stone, what more canst thou want?"

"Maps that don't lie," John said coolly. "You know as well as I do the maps you drew have sections of 'em left blank. And when I put them together, the maps of the various levels and the up-and-down map, damned if it wasn't the same place on all of them. I'm not interested in the secrets of your bloody Deep, but I can't know what's going to happen, nor where I may end up playing catch-me in the dark with the dragon, and I'd just as soon have an accurate map to do it with."

There was an edge of anger on his level voice, and an edge of fear. Dromar must have heard both, for the answering blaze died out of his own countenance, and he looked down at his hands, clasped over the knots of his sash. "This is a matter that has nothing to do with the dragon, nothing to do with thee," he said quietly. "The maps are accurate—I swear it by the Stone in the heart of the Deep. What is left off is the affair of the gnomes, and the gnomes only—the very secret of the heart of the Deep. Once, one of the children of men spied out that heart, and since then we have had cause to regret it bitterly."

He lifted his head again, pale eyes somber under the long shelf of snowy brow. "I beg that thou trust me, Dragonsbane. It goes against our ways to ask the aid of the children of men. But thou must help us. We are miners and traders; we are not warriors, and it is a warrior that we need. Day by day, more of our folk are forced to leave this city. If the Citadel falls, many of the people of the Deep will be slaughtered with the rebels who have given them not only the shelter of their walls, but the very bread of their rations. The King's troops will not let them leave the Citadel, even if they would—and believe me, many have tried. Here in Bel, the cost of bread rises, and soon we shall be starved out, if we are not murdered by the mobs from the taverns. In a short time we shall be too few to hold the Deep, even should we be able to pass its gates."

He held out his hands, small as a child's and grotesquely knotted with age, pallidly white against the soft black layerings of his strangely cut sleeves. "If thou dost not help us, who among the children of men will?"

"Oh, run along, Dromar, do." Clean and sweet as a silver knife, Zyerne's voice cut across his last words. She came mounting the steps from the garden, light as an almond blossom floating on the breeze, her pink-edged veils blown back over the dark and intricate cascades of her hair. "Isn't it enough that you try to foist your way into the King's presence day after day, without troubling these poor people with politics out of season? Gnomes may be vulgar enough to talk business and buttonhole their betters in the evening, but here we feel that once the day is done, it should be a time for enjoyment." She made shooting gestures with her well-kept hands and pouted in impatience. "Now run along," she added in a teasing tone, "or I shall call the guards."

The old gnome stood for a moment, his eyes upon hers, his cloudy white hair drifting like cobwebs around his wrinkled face in the stir of the sea winds. Zyerne wore an expression of childlike pertness, like a well-loved little girl demanding her own way. But Jenny, standing behind her, saw the delighted arrogance of her triumph in every line and muscle of her slim back. She had no doubt that Zyerne would, in fact, call the guards.

Evidently Dromar hadn't, either. Ambassador from the court of one monarch to another for thirty years, he turned and departed at the behest of the King's leman. Jenny watched him stump away down the gray and lavender stonework of the path across the garden, with Bond Clerlock, pale and brittle-looking, imitating his walk behind his back.

Ignoring Jenny as she generally did, Zyerne slid one hand through Gareth's arm and smiled up at him. "Backbiting old plotter," she remarked. "I must present myself to your father at supper in an hour, but there's time for a stroll along the sea wall, surely? The rains won't start until then."

She could say it with surety, thought Jenny; at the touch of her spells, the clouds would come and depart like lapdogs waiting to be fed.

Still holding Gareth's arm and leaning her suppleness against his height, she drew him toward the steps leading down into the garden; the courtiers there were already dispersing, and its walks were empty under the wind-driven scurry of fugitive leaves. Gareth cast a despairing glance back at John and Jenny, standing together on the terrace, she in the plaids and sheepskin jacket of the north, and he in the ornate blue-and-cream satins of the Court, his schoolboy spectacles balanced on his nose.

Jenny nudged John gently. "Go after them."

He looked down at her with a half-grin. "So from a dancing bear I'm being promoted to a chaperon for our hero's virtue?"

"No," Jenny said, her voice low. "A bodyguard for his safety. I don't know what it is about Zyerne, but he feels it, too. Go after them."

John sighed and bent to kiss her lips. "The King had better pay me extra for this." His hug was like being embraced by a satin lion. Then he was off, trotting down the steps and calling to them in horrible north-country brogue, the wind billowing his mantlings and giving him the appearance of a huge orchid in the gray garden.

In all, it was just over a week, before the King finally sent for his son.

"He asked me where I'd been," Gareth said quietly. "He asked me why I hadn't presented myself to him before." Turning, he struck the side of his fist against the bedpost, his teeth gritted to fight tears of rage and confusion. "Jenny, in all these days he hasn't even *seen* me!"

He swung angrily around. The faded evening light, falling through the diamond-shaped panes of the window where Jenny sat, brushed softly across the citron-and-white satins of his Court mantlings and flickered eerily in the round, facetless old jewels on his hands. His hair had been carefully curled for the audience with his father and, as was the nature of fine hair, hung perfectly straight around his face again, except for a stray lock or two. He'd put on his spectacles after the audience, cracked and bent and unlikely-looking with his finery; the lenses were speckled with the fine blowing rain that chilled the windowglass.

"I don't know what to do," he said in a strangulated voice. "He said— he said we'd talk about the dragon the next time he saw me. I don't under-stand what's going on . . ."

"Was Zyerne there?" John inquired. He was sitting at the spindly desk, which, like the rest of the upper floor of his and Jenny's guest house, was heaped with books. The whole room, after eight days, had the appearance of a ransacked library; volumes were propped against one another, places marked by pages of John's notes or odd articles of cloth-ing or other books—and in one case a dagger—slipped between the leaves.

Gareth nodded miserably. "Half the time when I asked him things, she'd answer. Jenny, could she be holding him under some kind of spell?"

Jenny started to say, "Possibly . . ."

"Well, of course she is," John said, tipping back his high stool to lean the small of his back against the desk. "And if you hadn't been so bloody determined to do that slick little baggage justice, Jen, you'd have seen it a week ago. Come!" he added, as a soft tapping sounded at the door.

It opened wide enough for Trey Clerlock to put her head around the doorframe. She hesitated a moment; then, when John gestured, she came in, carrying a pearwood hurdy-gurdy with ivory stars scattered at random over its stubby neck box and playing pegs. John beamed with delight as he took it, and Jenny groaned.

"You're not going to play that thing, are you? You'll frighten the cattle for miles around, you know."

"I'll not," John retorted. "And besides, there's a trick to making it louder or softer . . ."

"Do you know it?"

"I can learn. Thank you, Trey, love—some people just haven't any appreciation for the sound of fine music."

"Some people haven't any appreciation for the sound of a cat being run through a mangle," Jenny replied. She turned back to Gareth. "Zyerne could be holding him under a spell, yes—but from what you've told me of your father's stubbornness and strength of will, I'm a little surprised that her influence is that great."

Gareth shook his head. "It isn't only that," he said. "I—I don't know how to put this, and I can't be sure, because I wasn't wearing my spectacles during the interview, but it almost seems that he's *faded* since I've been gone. That's a stupid idea," he recanted at once, seeing Jenny's puzzled frown.

"No," said Trey unexpectedly. The other three looked at her, and she blushed a little, like a flustered doll. "I don't think it's stupid. I think it's true, and *faded* is a good word for it. Because I—I think the same thing is happening to Bond."

"Bond?" Jenny said, and the memory of the King's face flashed across her mind; how hollow and brittle he had looked, and how, like Bond, the paint on his face had seemed to stand out from the waxiness beneath.

Trey appeared to concentrate for a moment on carefully straightening the lace on her left cuff. An opal flickered softly in the particolored coils of her hair as she looked up. "I thought it was just me," she said in a small voice. "I know he's gotten heavier-handed, and less funny about his jests, the way he is when his mind is on something else. Except that his mind doesn't seem to *be* on anything else; it just isn't on what he's doing, these days. He's so absentminded, the way your father's gotten." Her gaze went to Jenny's, imploring. "But why would Zyerne put a spell on my brother? She's never needed to hold him to her. He's always squired her around. He was one of the first friends she had at Court. He—he loved her. He used to dream about her . . ."

"Dream about her how?" Gareth demanded sharply.

Trey shook her head. "He wouldn't tell me."

"Did he sleepwalk?"

The surprise in the girl's eyes answered the question before she spoke. "How did you know?"

The fitful rain outside had ceased; in the long silence, the voices of the palace guards in the court below the guest house windows could be heard clearly, telling a story about a gnome and a whore in town. Even the hazy light of the afternoon was failing, and the room was cold and slate gray. Jenny asked, "Do you dream about her still, Gareth?"

The boy turned red as if scalded. He stammered, shook his head, and finally said, "I—I don't love her. I truly don't. I try—I don't want to be alone with her. But . . ." He gestured helplessly, unable to fight the traitor dreams.

Jenny said softly, "But she is calling you. She called you that first night we were in her hunting lodge. Had she done so before?"

"I—I don't know." He looked shaken and ill and very frightened, as he had when Jenny had probed at his mind, as if looking at things that he did not want to see. Trey, who had gone to take a spill from the fire and was lighting the small ivory lamps on the edge of John's desk, shook out her taper, went quietly over to him, and got him to sit down beside her on the edge of the curtained bed.

At length Gareth said, "She might have. A few months ago she asked me to dine with her and my father in her wing of the palace. I didn't go. I was afraid Father would be angry at me for slighting her, but later on he said something that made me wonder whether he'd even known about it. I wondered then. I thought . . ." He blushed still more hotly. "That was when I thought she might have been in love with me."

"I've seen loves like that between wolves and sheep, but the romance tends to be a bit one-sided," John remarked, scratching his nose. "What prevented you from going?"

"Polycarp." He toyed with the folds of his mantlings, which caught a soft edge of brightness where the angle of the lamplight came down past the curtains of the bed. "He was always telling me to beware of her. He found out about the dinner and talked me out of going."

"Well, I don't know much about magic and all that, but just offhand, lad, I'd say he might have saved your life." John braced his back against the desk's edge and fingered a silent run of melody up the hurdy-gurdy's keys.

Gareth shook his head, puzzled. "But why? It wasn't a week before he tried to kill us—me and my father both."

"If that was him."

The boy stared at him, slowly-growing horror and realization in his face. He whispered, "But I saw him."

"If she could take the shape of a cat or a bird, putting on the form of the Master of Halnath wouldn't be beyond her—Jen?" He glanced across the room to where she sat silent, her arm resting across one up-drawn knee, her chin upon her wrist.

"She wouldn't have taken on his actual being," she said quietly. "An illusion would have served. Shapeshifting requires enormous power—but then, Zyerne *has* enormous power. However she did it, the act itself is logical. If Polycarp had begun to suspect her intentions toward Gareth, it would dispose of and discredit him at once. By making you the witness, Gar, she removed all chance of your helping him. She must have known how bitter a betrayal it would be."

Numbly, Gareth whispered, "No!" struck by the horror of what he had done.

Trey's voice was soft in the stillness. "But what does she want with Gareth? I can understand her holding the King, because without his support she'd—she wouldn't exactly be nothing, but she certainly wouldn't be able to live as she does now. But why entrap Gareth as well? And what does she want with Bond? He's no good to her . . . We're really only a very minor family, you know. I mean, we haven't any political power, and not that much money." A rueful smile touched one corner of her lips as she fingered the rose-point lace of her cuff. "All this . . . One must keep up appearances, of course, and Bond is trying to marry me off well. But we really haven't anything Zyerne would want."

"And why destroy them?" Gareth asked, desperate concern for his father in his voice. "Do all spells do that?"

"No," Jenny said. "That's what surprises me about this—I've never heard of a spell of influence that would waste the body of the victim as it holds the mind. But neither have I heard of one holding as close as the one which she has upon your father, Gareth; nor of one that lasts so long. But her magic is the magic of the gnomes and unlike the spells of men. It may be that among their secrets is one that will hold the very essence of another, twining around it like the tendrils of a morning-glory vine, which can tear the foundations of a stone house asunder. But then," she went on, her voice low, "it is almost certain that to have that kind of control over him, at the first, she had to obtain his consent."

"His consent?" Trey cried, horrified. "But how could he? How could anyone?"

Gareth, Jenny was interested to note, said nothing to this. He had seen, however briefly, on the road in the north, the mirror of his own soul—and he also knew Zyerne.

Jenny explained, "To tamper that deeply with another's essence always requires the consent of the victim. Zyerne is a shapeshifter—the principle is the same."

Trey shook her head. "I don't understand."

Jenny sighed and, rising to her feet, crossed to where the two young people sat side-by-side. She put her hand on the girl's shoulder. "A shapeshifter can change someone else's essence, even as she can change her own. It requires enormous power—and first she must in some fashion obtain the victim's consent. The victim can resist, unless the shapeshifter can find some chink of consenting, some hidden demon within—some part of the essence that wills to be changed."

The deepening darkness outside made the lamplight even more golden, like honey where it lay over the girl's face. Under the shadows of the long, thick lashes, Jenny could read both fear and fascination, that half-understanding that is the first whisper of consent.

"I think you would resist me if I tried to transform you into a lapdog, had I the power to do so. There is very little of the lapdog in your soul, Trey Clerlock. But if I were to transform you into a horse—a yearling filly, smoke-gray and sister to the sea winds—I think I could obtain your consent to that."

Trey jerked her eyes away, hiding them against Gareth's shoulder, and the young man put a protective arm around her as well as he could, considering that he was sitting on the trailing ends of his extravagant sleeves.

"It is the power of shapeshifting and the danger," Jenny said, her voice low in the silence of the room. "If I transformed you into a filly, Trey, your essence would be the essence of a horse. Your thoughts would be a horse's thoughts, your body a mare's body; your loves and desires would be those of a young, swift beast. You might remember for a time what you were, but you could not find your way back to be it once again. I think you would be happy as a filly."

"Stop it," Trey whispered, and covered her ears. Gareth's hold about her tightened. Jenny was silent. After a moment the girl looked up again, her eyes dark with the stirred depths of her dreams. "I'm sorry," she said, her voice small. "It's not you I'm afraid of. It's me."

"I know," Jenny replied softly. "But do you understand now? Do you understand what she might have done to your father, Gareth? It is some-times less painful to give over striving and let another mind rule yours. When Zyerne first came to power she couldn't have acquired that kind of hold over you, because you would not come near enough for her to do it. You hated her, and you were only a boy—she could not draw you as she draws men. But when you became a man . . ."

"I think that's loathsome." It was Trey's turn to put a protective arm around Gareth's satin shoulders.

"But a damn good way to keep her power," John pointed out, leaning one arm across the hurdy-gurdy resting upon his knees.

"I still can't be sure that this is what she did," Jenny said. "And it still wouldn't explain why she did the same thing to Bond. I would not know for certain until I could see the King, speak to him . . ."

"God's Grandmother, he'll scarcely speak to his own son, love, let alone me or thee." John paused, listening to his own words. "Which might be a good reason for not speaking to me or thee, come to that." His eyes flickered to Gareth. "You know, Gar, the more I see of this, the more I think I'd like to have a few words with your dad."

8

In the deathly hush that hung over the gardens, Gareth's descent from the wall sounded like the mating of oxen in dry brush. Jenny winced as the boy crashed down the last few feet into the shrubbery; from the shadows of the ivy on the wall top at her side she saw the dim flash of spectacle lenses and heard a voice breathe, "You forgot to shout 'Eleven o'clock and all's well,' my hero!"

A faint slur of ivy followed. She felt John land on the ground below more than she heard him. After a last check of the dark garden half-visible through the woven branches of the bare trees, she slipped down to join them. In the darkness, Gareth was a gawky shadow in rust-colored velvet, John barely to be seen at all, the random pattern of his plaids blending into the colors of the night.

"Over there," Gareth whispered, nodding toward the far side of the garden where a light burned in a niche between two trefoil arches. Its brightness spangled the wet grass like pennies thrown by a careless hand.

He started to lead the way, but John touched his arm and breathed, "I think we'd better send a scout, if it's burglary and all we're after. I'll work round the three sides through the shadows of the wall; when I get there, I'll whistle once like a nightjar. Right?"

Gareth caught his sleeve as he started to move off. "But what if a real nightjar whistles?"

"What, at this time of the year?" And he melted like a cat into the darkness. Jenny could see him, shifting his way through the checkered shadows of the bare topiary that decorated the three sides of the King's private court; by the way Gareth moved his head, she could tell he had lost sight of him almost at once.

Near the archways there was a slither of rosy lamplight on a spectacle frame, the glint of spikes, and the brief outline of brightness on the end of a long nose. Gareth, seeing him safe, started to move, and Jenny drew him soundlessly back again. John had not yet whistled.

An instant later, Zyerne appeared in the doorway arch.

Though John stood less than six feet from her, she did not at first see him, for he settled into stillness like a snake in leaves. The enchantress's face, illuminated in the warm apricot light, wore that same sated look Jenny had seen in the upstairs room at the hunting lodge near the Wildspae—the look of deep content with some wholly private pleasure. Now, as then, it raised the hackles on Jenny's neck, and at the same time she felt a cold shudder of fear.

Then Zyerne turned her head. She startled, seeing John motionless so near to her; then she smiled. "Well. An enterprising barbarian." She shook out her unbound, unveiled hair, straying tendrils of it lying against the hollow of her cheek, like an invitation to a caress. "A little late, surely, to be paying calls on the King."

"A few weeks late, by all I've heard." Aversin scratched his nose self-consciously. "But better late than never, as Dad said at Granddad's wedding."

Zyerne giggled, a sweet and throaty sound. Beside her, Jenny felt Gareth shiver, as if the seductive laughter brought memories of evil dreams.

"And impudent as well. Did your mistress send you along to see if Uriens had been entangled in spells other than his own stupidity and lust?"

Jenny heard the hiss of Gareth's breath and sensed his anger and his shock at hearing the guttersnipe words fall so casually from those pink lips. Jenny wondered why she herself was not surprised.

John only shrugged and said mildly, "No. It's just I'm no dab hand at waiting."

"Ah." Her smile widened, lazy and alluring. She seemed half-drunk, but not sleepy as drunkards are; she glowed, as she had on that first morning in the King's Gallery, bursting with life and filled with the casual arrogance of utter well-being. The lamp in its tiled niche edged her profile in amber as she stepped toward John, and Jenny felt again the grip of fear, as if John stood unknowingly in deadly danger. "The barbarian who eats with his hands—and doubtless makes love in his boots."

Her hands touched his shoulders caressingly, shaping themselves to the muscle and bone beneath the leather and plaid. But Aversin stepped back a pace, putting distance between them, rather as she had done in the gallery to Dromar. Like Dromar, she would not relax her self-consequence enough to pursue.

In a deliberately deepened north-country drawl, he said, "Aye, my lack of manners does give me sleepless nights. But it weren't to eat prettily nor yet to make love that I came south. I was told you had this dragon eating folks hereabouts."

She giggled again, an evil trickle of sound in the night. "You shall have your chance to slay it when all is ready. Timing is a civilized art, my barbarian."

"Aye," John's voice agreed, from the dark cutout of his silhouette against the golden light. "And I've had buckets of time to study it here, along with all them other civilized arts, like courtesy and kindness to suppliants, not to speak of honor, and keeping one's faith with one's lover, instead of rubbing up against his son."

There were perhaps three heartbeats of silence before she spoke. Jenny saw her back stiffen; when she spoke again, her voice, though still sweet, had a note to it like a harp string taken a half-turn above its true note. "What is it to you, John Aversin? It is how things are done here in the south. None of it shall interfere with your chance of glory. That is all that should concern you. I shall tell you when it is right for you to go.

"Listen to me, Aversin, and believe me. I know this dragon. You have slain one worm—you have not met Morkeleb the Black, the Dragon of Nast Wall. He is mightier than the worm you slew before, mightier than you can ever know."

"I'd guessed that." John pushed up his specs, the rosy light glancing off the spikes of his armbands as from spear-points. "I'll just have to slay him how I can, seemingly."

"No." Acid burned through the sweetness of her voice like poisoned candy. "You can not. I know it, if you and that slut of yours don't. Do you think I don't know that those stinking offal-eaters, the gnomes, have lied to you? That they refused to give you true maps of the Deep? I know the Deep, John Aversin—I know every tunnel and passage. I know the heart of the Deep. Likewise I know every spell of illusion and protection, and believe me, you will need them against the dragon's wrath. You will need my aid, if you are to have victory—you will need my aid if you are to come out of that combat with your life. Wait, I say, and you shall have that aid; and afterward, from the spoils of the Deep, I shall reward you beyond the dreams of any man's avarice."

John tilted his head a little to one side. "*You'll* reward me?"

In the silence of the sea-scented night, Jenny heard the other woman's breath catch.

"How is it you'll be the one to divvy up the gnomes' treasure?" John asked. "Are you anticipating taking over the Deep, once the dragon's out of the way?"

"No," she said, too quickly. "That is—surely you know that the insolence of the gnomes has led them to plot against his Majesty? They are no longer the strong folk they were before the coming of Morkeleb. Those that were not slain are divided and weak. Many have left this town, forfeiting all their rights, and good riddance to them."

"Were I treated as I've seen them treated," John remarked, leaning one shoulder against the blue-and-yellow tiles of the archway, "I'd leave, myself."

"They deserved it." Her words stung with sudden venom. "They kept me from . . ." She stopped herself, then added, more reasonably, "You know they are openly in league with the rebels of Halnath—or you should know it. It would be foolish to dispose of the dragon before their plots are uncovered. It would only give them a strong place and a treasure to return to, to engage in plotting further treason."

"I know the King and the people have heard nothing but how the gnomes are plotting," Aversin replied in a matter-of-fact voice. "And from what I hear, the gnomes up at the Citadel haven't much choice about whose side they're on. Gar's being gone must have been a real boon to you there; with the King half-distracted, he'd have been about ready to believe anything. And I suppose it would be foolish to get rid of the dragon before so many of the gnomes have left the Realm—or some reason can be found for getting rid of the rest of 'em—that they can't reoccupy their stronghold, if so be it happened someone else wanted the place, that is."

There was a moment's silence. Jenny could see the light slither quickly along the silk facing of Zyerne's sleeve, where her small hand clenched it in anger, leaving a print of wrinkles like the track of invisible thoughts. "These are matters of high polity, Dragonsbane. It is nothing to you, after all. I tell you, be patient and wait until I tell you it is time for us to ride together to the Deep, you and I. I promise that you shall not be cheated of this slaying."

She stepped close to him again, and the diamonds on her hands threw little spits of fire against the dullness of leather and plaid.

"No," Aversin said, his voice low. "Nor shall you be cheated of the Deep, after I've done your butchering for you. You summoned the dragon, didn't you?"

"No." The word was brittle as the snap of a frost-killed twig. "Of course not."

"Didn't you, love? Then it's gie lucky for you that it came along just when it did, when you were wanting a power base free of the King, in case he tired of you or died; not to speak of all that gold."

Jenny felt the scorch of her wrath like an invisible explosion across the garden, even as Zyerne raised her hand. Jenny's throat closed on a cry of fear and warning, knowing she could never have moved in time to help and could not have stood against the younger woman's magic, if she did; Aversin, his back to the stone of the arch, could only throw his arm before his eyes as the white fire snaked from Zyerne's hand. The hissing crackle of it in the air was like lightning; the blaze of it, so white it seemed edged in violet, seared over every stone chink and moss tuft in the pavement and outlined each separate, waxy petal of the winter roses in colorless glare. In its aftermath, the air burned with the smell of ozone and scorched leaves.

After a long moment, John raised his face from his protecting arms. Even across the garden, Jenny could see he was shaking; her own knees were so weak from shock and fear she felt she could have collapsed, except forer greater fear of Zyerne; and she cursed her own lack of power. John, standing before Zyerne, did not move.

It was Zyerne who spoke, her voice dripping with triumph. "You get above yourself, Dragonsbane. I'm not that snaggle-haired trollop of yours, that you can speak to me with impunity. I am a true sorceress."

Aversin said nothing, but carefully removed his spectacles and wiped his eyes. Then he replaced them and regarded her silently in the dim light of the garden lamp.

"I am a true sorceress,"she repeated softly. She held out her hands to him, the small fingers plucking at his sleeves, and a husky note crept into her sweet voice. "And who says our alliance must be so truculent, Dragonsbane? You need not spend your time here tugging with impatience to be gone. I can make the wait pleasant."

As her delicate hands touched his face, however, Aversin caught the fragile wrists, forcing her away at arm's length. For an instant they stood so, facing one another, the silence absolute but for the racing draw of their breath. Her eyes were fixed upon his, probing at his mind, Jenny knew, the same way she had probed at Gareth's earlier, seeking some key of consent.

With a curse she twisted free of his grip. "So," she whispered. "That raddled bitch can at least get her rutting-spells right, can she? With her looks, she'd have to. But let me tell you this, Dragonsbane. When you ride to meet the dragon, like it or not, it will be me who rides with you, not her. You shall need my aid, and you shall ride forth when I say so, when I tell the King to give you leave, and not before. So learn a little of the civilized art of patience, my barbarian—for without my aid against Morkeleb, you shall surely die."

She stepped away from him and passed under the lamp-lit arch, reaching out to take the light with her as she went. In its honeyed bright-ness her face looked as gentle and guileless as that of a girl of seventeen, unmarked by rage or perversion, pettiness or spite. John remained where he was, watching her go, sweat beading his face like a mist of diamonds, motionless save where he rubbed the thin, sharp flashburns on his hands.

A moment later, the window behind him glowed into soft life. Through the fretted screen of scented shrubs and vine that twined its fili-greed lattice, Jenny got a glimpse of the room beyond. She had an impression of half-seen frescoes on the walls, of expensive vessels of gold and silver, and of the glint of bullion embroidery thickly edging the hangings of the bed. A man lay in the bed, moving feebly in some restless dream, his gold hair faded and colorless where it lay in disorder over the embroidered pillows. His face was sunken and devoid of life, like the face of the man whom a vampire has kissed.

"It would serve her right if you left tonight!" Gareth stormed. "Rode back north and left her to deal with her own miserable worm, if she wanted it so badly!"

He swung around to pace the big chamber of the guest house again, so furious he could barely splutter. In his anger, he seemed to have for-gotten his own fear of Zyerne and his desire for protection against her, forgotten his long quest to the Winterlands and his desperation to have it succeed. From her seat in the window, Jenny watched him fulminate, her own face outwardly calm but her mind racing.

John looked up from tinkering with the keys of the hurdy-gurdy. "It wouldn't do, my hero," he said quietly. "However and whyever it got here, the dragon's here now. As Zyerne said, the people hereabouts are no concern of mine, but I can't be riding off and leaving them to the dragon. Leaving out the gnomes, there's the spring planting to be thought of."

The boy stopped in his pacing, staring at him. "Hunh?"

John shrugged, his fingers stilling on the pegs. "The harvest's gone," he pointed out. "If the dragon's still abroad in the land in the spring, there'll be no crop, and then, my hero, you'll see real starvation in this town."

Gareth was silent. It was something he had never thought of, Jenny guessed. He had clearly never gone short of food in his life.

"Besides," John went on, "unless the gnomes can reoccupy the Deep pretty quick, Zyerne will destroy them here, as Dromar said, and your friend Polycarp in the Citadel as well. For all Dromar's hedging about keeping us out of the heart of the Deep, the gnomes have done for us what they can; and the way I see it, Polycarp saved your life, or at least kept you from ending up like your father, so deep under Zyerne's spells he can't tell one week from the next. No, the dragon's got to be killed."

"But that's just it," Gareth argued. "If you kill the dragon, she'll be free to take over the Deep, and then the Citadel will fall because they'll be able to attack it from the rear." He looked worriedly over at Jenny. "*Could* she have summoned the dragon?"

Jenny was silent, thinking about that terrible power she had felt in the garden, and the dreadful, perverted lour of it in the lamplit room at Zyerne's hunting lodge. She said, "I don't know. It's the first time I've heard of human magic being able to touch a dragon—but then, Zyerne derives her magic from the gnomes. I have never heard of such a thing . . ."

"*Cock by its feet, horse by its hame* . . ." repeated John. "Could she be holding the dragon by his name? She knows it, right enough."

Jenny shook her head. "Morkeleb is only the name men give it, the way they call Azwylcartusherands Dromar, and Taseldwyn Mab. If she'd had his true name, his essence, she could send him away again; and she obviously can't, or she would have killed you in the garden tonight."

She hitched her shawl up over her shoulders, a thin and glittering spiderweb of South Islands silk, the thick masses of her hair lying over it like a second shawl. Cold seemed to breathe through the window at her back.

Gareth went back to pacing, his hands shoved in the pockets of the old leather hunting breeches he'd put on to go burgling.

"But she didn't know its name, did she?"

"No," replied Jenny. "And in that case . . ." She paused, then frowned, dismissing the thought.

"What?" John wanted to know, catching the doubt in her voice.

"No," she repeated. "It's inconceivable that at her level of power she wouldn't have been taught Limitations. It's the first thing anyone learns." And seeing Gareth's incomprehension, she explained. "It's one of the things that takes me so long when I weave spells. You have to limit the effect of any spell. If you call rain, you must specify a certain heaviness, so as not to flood the countryside. If you call a curse of destruction upon someone or something, you have to set Limitations so that their destruction doesn't come in a generalized catastrophe that wipes out your own house and goods. Magic is very prodigal in its effects. Limitations are among the earliest things a mage is taught."

"Even among the gnomes?" Gareth asked. "You said their magic is different."

"It is taught differently—transmitted differently. There are things Mab has said that I do not understand and things that she refuses to tell me about how their power is formed. But it is still magic. Mab knows the Limitations—from what she has told me, I gather they are more important in the night below the ground. If she studied among the gnomes, Zyerne would *have* to have learned about them."

John threw back his head and laughed in genuine amusement. "Gaw, it must be rotting her!" He chuckled. "Think of it, Jen. She wants to get rid of the gnomes, so she calls down a generalized every-worst-curse she can think of upon them—and gets a dragon she can't get rid of! It's gie beautiful!"

"It's 'gie' frivolous," Jenny retorted.

"No wonder she threw fire at me! She must be that furious just thinking about it!" His eyes were dancing under his singed brows.

"It just isn't possible," Jenny insisted, in the cool voice she used to call their sons back from skylarking. Then, more seriously, "She can't have gotten to that degree of power untaught, John. It's impossible. All power must be paid for, somehow."

"But it's the sort of thing that would happen if it hadn't been, isn't it?"

Jenny didn't reply. For a long time she stared out the window at the dark shape of the battlements, visible beneath the chilly autumn stars. "I don't know," she said at last, stroking the spiderweb fringes of her gauze shawl. "She has so much power. It's inconceivable that she hasn't paid for it in some fashion. The key to magic is magic. She has had all time and all power to study it fully. And yet . . ." She paused, identifying at last her own feelings toward what Zyerne was and did. "I thought that someone who had achieved that level of power would be different."

"Ah," John said softly. Across the room, their eyes met. "But don't think that what she's done with her achievement has betrayed your striving, love. For it hasn't. It's only betrayed her own."

Jenny sighed, reflecting once again on John's uncanny ability to touch the heart of any problem, then smiled a little at herself; and they traded a kiss in a glance.

Gareth said quietly, "But what are we going to do? The dragon has to be destroyed; and, if you destroy it, you'll be playing right into her hands."

A smile flicked across John's face, a glimpse of the bespectacled schoolboy peeking out from behind the complex barricades raised by the hardships of the Winterlands and his father's embittered domination. Jenny felt his eyes on her again—the tip of one thick reddish brow and the question in the bright glance. After ten years, they had grown used to speaking without words.

A qualm of fear passed over her, though she knew he was right. After a moment, she drew her breath in another sigh and nodded.

"Good." John's impish smile widened, like that of a boy intent on doing mischief, and he rubbed his hands briskly. He turned to Gareth. "Get your socks packed, my hero. We leave for the Deep tonight."

9

"**S**top."

Puzzled, Gareth and John drew rein on either side of Jenny, who sat Moon Horse where she had halted her in the middle of the leaf-drifted track. All around them the foothills of Nast Wall were deathly silent, save for the trickle of wind through the charred trunks of what had once been woods to either side of the road and the faint jingle of brass as Osprey tugged at his leading-rein and Clivy began foraging prosaically in the sedges of the ditch-side. Lower down the hills, the woods were still whole, denuded by coming winter rather than fire; under the pewter-gray trunks of the beeches, the rust-colored underbrush lay thick. Here it was only a tangle of brittle stems, ready to crumble at a touch. Half-hidden in the weeds near the scorched paving stones of the road were the blackened bones of fugitives from the dragon's first attack, mixed with shattered cooking vessels and the silver coins that had been dropped in flight. The coins lay in the mud still. No one had ventured this close to the ruined town to retrieve them.

Up ahead in the weak sunlight of winter, the remains of the first houses of Deeping could be seen. According to Gareth the place had never been walled. The road ran into the town under the archway below the broken clock tower.

For a long while Jenny sat listening in silence, turning her head this way and that. Neither of the men spoke—indeed, ever since they had slipped out of the Palace in the small hours before dawn, Jenny had been acutely conscious of John's growing silence. She glanced across at him now, where he sat withdrawn into himself on his riding horse Cow, and remembered for the dozenth time that day Zyerne's words—that without her assistance, neither he nor Jenny would be capable of meeting the dragon Morkeleb.

Beyond a doubt John was remembering them, too.

"Gareth," Jenny said at last, her voice little more than a whisper, "is there another way into the town? Some place in the town that is farther from the Gates of the Deep than we are now?"

Gareth frowned. "Why?"

Jenny shook her head, not certain herself why she had spoken. But something whispered across her nerves, as it had all those weeks ago by the ruins of the nameless town in the Winterlands—a sense of danger that caused her to look for the signs of it. Under Mab's tutelage she had become more certain of trusting her instincts, and something in her hated to go closer than the ruined clock tower into the sunlight that fell across Deeping Vale.

After a moment's consideration Gareth said, "The farthest point in Deeping from the Great Gates would be the Tanner's Rise. It's at the bottom of that spur over there that bounds the town to the west. I think it's about a half-mile from the Gates. The whole town isn't—wasn't—much more than a quarter-mile across."

"Will we have a clear view of the Gates from there?"

Confused by this bizarre stipulation, he nodded. "The ground's high, and most of the buildings were flattened in the attack. But if we wanted a lookout on the gates, you can see there's enough of the clock tower left for a . . ."

"No," Jenny murmured. "I don't think we can go that near."

John's head came sharply around at that. Gareth faltered, "It can't—it can't *hear* us, can it?"

"Yes," Jenny said, not knowing why she said it. "No—it isn't hearing, exactly. I don't know. But I feel something, on the fringes of my mind. I don't think it knows we're here—not yet. But if we rode closer, it might. It is an old dragon, Gareth; it must be, for its name to be in the Lines. In one of the old books from the Palace library, it says that dragons change their skins with their souls, that the young are simply colored and bright; the mature are complex of pattern and the old become simpler and simpler again, as their power deepens and grows. Morkeleb is black. I don't know what that means, but I don't like what I think it implies—great age, great power—his senses must fill the Vale of Deeping like still water, sensitive to the slightest ripple."

"He pox-sure heard your father's knights coming, didn't he?" John added cynically.

Gareth looked unhappy. Jenny nudged her mare gently and took a step or two closer to the clock tower, casting her senses wide over all the

Vale. Through the broken webs of branches overhead, the massive darkness of the westward-facing cliffs of Nast Wall could be seen. Their dizzy heights towered like rusted metal, streaked with purple where shadows hit; boulders flashed white upon it like outcroppings of broken bone. Above the line of the dragon's burning, the timber grew on the flanks of the mountain around the cliffs, up toward the mossed rocks of the cirques and snowfields above. The ice-gouged horns of the Wall's bare and ragged crest were veiled in cloud now, but beyond its hunched shoulder to the east a thin track of smoke could be seen, marking the Citadel of Halnath and the siege camps beneath it.

Below that wall of stone and trees, the open spaces of the Vale lay, a huge well of air, a gulf filled with pale, sparkly sunlight—and with something else. Jenny's mind touched it briefly and shrank from that living consciousness that she sensed, coiled like a snake in its dark lair.

Behind her, she heard Gareth argue, "But the dragon you killed up in the gully in Wyr didn't know you were coming." The very loudness of his voice scraped her nerves and made her want to cuff him into silence. "You were able to get around behind it and take it by surprise. I don't see how . . ."

"Neither do I, my hero," John cut in softly, collecting Cow's reins in one hand and the charger Osprey's lead in the other. "But if you're willing to bet your life Jen's wrong, I'm not. Lead us on to the famous Rise."

On the night of the dragon, many had taken refuge in the buildings on Tanner's Rise; their bones lay everywhere among the blackened ruin of crumbled stone. From the open space in front of what had been the warehouses, it had once been possible to overlook the whole thriving little town of Deeping, under its perpetual haze of smoke from the smelters and forges down below. That haze was gone now, burned off in the dragon's greater fire; the whole town lay open to the mild, heatless glitter of the winter sunlight, a checkerwork of rubble and bones.

Looking about her at the buildings of the Rise, Jenny felt cold with shock, as if she had been struck in the pit of the stomach; then, as she realized why she recognized the place, the shock was replaced by horror and despair.

It was the place where she had seen John dying, in her vision in the water bowl.

She had done divination before, but never so accurately as this. The precision of it appalled her—every stone and puddle and broken wall was the same; she remembered the way the looming line of the dark cliffs looked against the sky and the very patterns of the bones of the town below. She felt overwhelmed by a despairing urge to change something— to shatter a wall, to dig a hole, to clear away the brush at the gravelly lip of the Rise where it sloped down to the town—anything to make it not as it had been. Yet in her soul she knew doing so would change nothing and she feared lest whatever she did would make the picture she had seen more, rather than less, exact.

Her lips felt stiff as she spoke. "Is this the only point in the town this far from the Gates?" She knew already what Gareth would reply.

"It had to be, because of the smell of the tanneries. You see how nothing was built near it. Even the water tanks and reservoirs were put up in those rocks to the north, rather than here where the better springs were."

Jenny nodded dully, looking out toward the high rocks to the north of the town where he was pointing. Her whole soul was crying *No! No . . .*

She felt suddenly hopeless and stupid, overmatched and unprepared and incredibly naïve. We were fools, she thought bitterly. The slaying of the first worm was a fluke. We should never have been so stupid as to presume upon it, never have thought we could do it again. Zyerne was right. Zyerne was right.

She looked over at John, who had dismounted from Cow and was standing on the rocky lip of the Rise where the ground fell sharply to the dale below, looking across toward the opposite rise of the Gates. Cold seemed to cover her bones like a vast, winged shadow blocking the sun, and she heeled Moon Horse gently over beside him.

Without looking up at her, he said, "I figure I can just make it. The Temple of Sarmendes is about a quarter-mile along the Grand Passage, if Dromar was telling the truth. If Osprey and I go full-pelt, we should just about be able to catch the dragon in the Market Hall, just within the Gates. Saying he's able to hear me the minute I start down the Rise, I should still be able to catch him before he can get out into the air. I'll have room to fight him in the Market Hall. That will be my only chance."

"No," Jenny said quietly. He looked up at her, eyebrows quirking. "You have another chance, if we ride back now to Bel. Zyerne can help you take the thing from behind, deeper in the caves. Her spells will protect you, too, as mine can not."

"Jen." The closed wariness of his expression split suddenly into the white flash of teeth. He held up his hands to help her down, shaking his head reprovingly.

She made no move. "At least it is to her advantage to preserve you safe, if she wants the dragon slain. The rest is none of your affair."

His smile widened still further. "You have a point, love," he assented. "But she doesn't look to me like she can cook worth a row of beans." And he helped her down from her horse.

The foreboding that weighed on Jenny's heart did not decrease; rather, it grew upon her through the short afternoon. She told herself, again and again, as she paced out the magic circles and set up her fire in their midst to brew her poisons, that water was a liar; that it divined the future as crystal could not, but that its divinations were less reliable even than fire's. But a sense of impending doom weighed upon her heart, and, as the daylight dimmed, in the fire under her simmering kettle she seemed to see again the same picture: John's shirt of chain mail rent open by claws in a dozen places, the broken links all glittering with dark blood.

Jenny had set up her fire at the far end of the Rise, where the wind would carry the smoke and the vapors away from both the camp and the Vale, and worked throughout the afternoon spelling the ingredients and the steel of the harpoons themselves. Miss Mab had advised her about the more virulent poisons that would work upon dragons, and such ingredients as the gnome wizard had not had among her slender stocks Jenny had purchased in the Street of the Apothecaries in the Dockmarket in Bel. While she worked, the two men prowled the Rise, fetching water for the horses from the little well some distance into the woods, since the fountain house that had served the tanneries had been crushed like an eggshell, and setting up a camp. John had very little to say since she had spoken to him on the edge of the Rise; Gareth seemed to shiver all over with a mingling of excitement and terror.

Jenny had been a little surprised at John's invitation that Gareth join them, though she had planned to ask John to extend it. She had her own reasons for wanting the boy with them, which had little to do with his expressed desire—though he had not expressed it lately—to see a dragonslaying close at hand. She—and undoubtedly John as well—knew that their departure would have left Gareth unprotected in Bel.

Perhaps Mab had been right, she thought, as she turned her face from the ghastly choke of the steam and wiped it with one gloved hand. There were worse evils than the dragon in the land—to be slain by it might, under certain circumstances, be construed as a lesser fate.

The voices of the men came to her from the other side of the camp as they moved about preparing supper; she had noticed that neither spoke very loudly when they were anywhere near the edge of the Rise. John said, "I'll get this right yet," as he dropped a mealcake onto the griddle and looked up at Gareth. "What's the Market Hall like? Anything I'll be likely to trip over?"

"I don't think so, if the dragon's been in and out," Gareth said after a moment. "It's a huge hall, as Dromar said; over a hundred feet deep and even wider side to side. The ceiling's very high, with fangs of rock hanging down from it—chains, too, that used to support hundreds of lamps. The floor was leveled, and used to be covered with all kinds of booths, awnings, and vegetable stands; all the produce from the Realm was traded to the Deep there. I don't think there was anything there solid enough to resist dragon fire."

Aversin dropped a final mealcake on the griddle and straightened up, wiping his fingers on the end of his plaid. Blue darkness was settling over Tanner's Rise. From her small fire, Jenny could see the two of them outlined in gold against a background of azure and black. They did not come near her, partly because of the stench of the poisons, partly because of the spell-circles glimmering faintly in the sandy earth about her. The key to magic is magic—Jenny felt that she looked out at them from an isolated enclave of another world, alone with the oven-heat of the fire, the biting stench of the poison fumes, and the grinding weight of the death-spells in her heart.

John walked to the edge of the Rise for perhaps the tenth time that evening. Across the shattered bones of Deeping, the black skull-eye of the Gates looked back at him. Slabs of steel and splintered shards of burned wood lay scattered over the broad, shallow flight of granite steps below them, faintly visible in the watery light of the waxing moon. The town itself lay in a pool of impenetrable dark.

"It isn't so far," said Gareth hopefully. "Even if he hears you coming the minute you ride into the Vale, you should reach the Market Hall in plenty of time."

John sighed. "I'm not so sure of that, my hero. Dragons move fast, even afoot. And the ground down there's bad. Even full-tilt, Osprey won't be making much speed of it, when all's said. I would have liked to scout for the clearest route, but that isn't possible, either. The most I can hope for is that there's no uncovered cellar doors or privy pits between here and the Gates."

Gareth laughed softly. "It's funny, but I never thought about that. In the ballads, the hero's horse never trips on the way to do battle with the dragon, though they do it from time to time even in tourneys, where the ground of the lists has been smoothed beforehand. I thought it would be—oh, like a ballad. Very straight. I thought you'd ride out of Bel, straight up here and on into the Deep . . ."

"Without resting my horse after the journey, even on a lead-rein, nor scouting the lay of the land?" John's eyes danced behind his specs. "No wonder the King's knights were killed at it." He sighed. "My only worry is that if I miss my timing by even a little, I'm going to be spot under the thing when it comes out of the Gates . . ."

Then he coughed, fanning at the air, and said, "Pox blister it!" as he dashed back to pick the flaming mealcakes off the griddle. Around burned fingers, he said, "And the damn thing is, even Adric cooks better than I do . . ."

Jenny turned away from their voices and the sweetness of the night beyond the blazing heat of her fire. As she dipped the harpoons into the thickening seethe of brew in her kettle, the sweat plastered her long hair to her cheeks, running down her bare arms from the turned-up sleeves of her shift to the cuffs of the gloves she wore; the heat lay like a red film over her toes and the tops of her feet, bare as they often were when she worked magic.

Like John, she felt withdrawn into herself, curiously separated from what she did. The death-spells hung like a stench in the air all around her, and her head and bones were beginning to ache from the heat and the effort of the magic she had wrought. Even when the powers she called were for good, they tired her; she felt weighed down by them now, exhausted and knowing that she had wrought nothing good from that weariness.

The Golden Dragon came to her mind again, the first heartstopping instant she had seen it dropping from the sky like amber lightning and had thought, This is beauty. She remembered, also, the butchered ruin left in the gorge, the stinking puddles of acid and poison and blood, and the faint, silvery singing dying out of the shivering air. It might have been only the fumes she inhaled, but she felt herself turn suddenly sick at the thought.

She had slaughtered Meewinks, or mutilated them and left them to be eaten by their brothers; she remembered the crawling greasiness of the bandit's hair under her fingers as she had touched his temples. But they were not like the dragon. They had chosen to be what they were.

Even as I have.

And what are you, Jenny Waynest?

But she could find no answer that fitted.

Gareth's voice drifted over to her from the other fire. "That's another thing they never mention in the ballads that I've been meaning to ask you. I know this sounds silly, but—how do you keep your spectacles from getting broken in battle?"

"Don't wear 'em," John's voice replied promptly. "If you can see it coming, it's too late anyway. And then, I had Jen lay a spell on them, so they wouldn't get knocked off or broken by chance when I *do* wear them."

She looked over at the two of them, out of the condensing aura of death-spells and the slaughter of beauty that surrounded her and her kettle of poison. Firelight caught in the metal of John's jerkin; against the blueness of the night it gleamed like a maker's mark stamped in gold upon a bolt of velvet. She could almost hear the cheerful grin in his voice,

"I figured if I was going to break my heart loving a magewife, I might as well get some good from it."

Over the shoulder of Nast Wall the moon hung, a half-open white eye, waxing toward its third quarter. With a stab like a shard of metal embedded somewhere in her heart, Jenny remembered then that it had been so, in her vision in the water.

Silently, she pulled herself back into her private circle of death, closing out that outer world of friendship and love and silliness, closing herself in with spells of ruin and despair and the cold failing of strength. It was her power to deal death in this way, and she hated herself for it; though, like John, she knew she had no choice.

"Do you think you'll make it?" Gareth nattered. Before them, the ruins of the broken town were purple and slate with shadow in the early light. The war horse Osprey's breath was warm over Jenny's hand where she held the reins.

"I'll have to, won't I?" John checked the girths and swung up into the saddle. The cool reflection of the morning sky gleamed slimily on the grease Jenny had made for him late last night to smear on his face against the worst scorching of the dragon's fire. Frost crackled in the weeds as Osprey fidgeted his feet. The last thing Jenny had done, shortly before dawn, had been to send away the mists that seeped up from the woods to cloak the Vale, and all around them the air was brilliantly clear, the fallow winter colors warming to life. Jenny herself felt cold, empty, and overstretched; she had poured all her powers into the poisons. Her head ached violently and she felt unclean, strange, and divided in her mind, as if she were two separate people. She had felt so, she recalled, when John had ridden against the first dragon, though then she had not known why. Then she had not known what the slaughter of that beauty would be like. She feared for him and felt despair like a stain on her heart; she only wanted the day to be over, one way or the other.

The mail rings on the back of John's gloves rattled sharply as he reached down, and she handed him up his harpoons. There were six of them, in a quiver on his back; the steel of their barbed shafts caught a slither of the early light, save for the ugly black that covered their points. The leather of the grips was firm and tough under her palms. Over his metal-patched doublet, John had pulled a chain mail shirt, and his face was framed in a coif of the same stuff. Without his spectacles and with his shaggy hair hidden beneath it, the bones of his face were suddenly prominent, showing what his features could look like in an old age he might never reach.

Jenny felt she wanted to speak to him, but there was nothing she could think of to say.

He gathered the reins in hand. "If the dragon comes out of the Gate before I reach it, I want the pair of you to leg it," he said, his voice calm. "Get into cover as deep as you can, the higher up the ridge the better. Let the horses go if you can—there's a chance the dragon will go after them first." He did not add that by that time he would already be dead.

There was a momentary silence. Then he bent from the saddle and touched Jenny's lips with his own. His felt, as they always did, surprisingly soft. They had spoken little, even last night; each had already been drawn into an armor of silence. It was something they both understood.

He reined away, looking across the Vale to the black eye of the Deep, and to the black thing waiting within. Osprey fiddle-footed again, catching John's battle nerves; the open ground of Deeping seemed suddenly to stretch away into miles of enormous, broken plain. To Jenny's eye, every tumbled wall looked as tall as the house it had once been, every uncovered cellar a gaping chasm. He would never cross in time, she thought.

Beside her, John leaned down again, this time to pat Osprey's dappled neck encouragingly. "Osprey, old friend," he said softly, "don't spook on me now."

He drove in his spurs, and the sharp crack of ironshod hooves as they shot forward was like the chip of distant lightning on a summer noon. Jenny took two steps down the loose, rocky slope after him, watching the gray horse and the pewter-dark shape of the man as they plunged through the labyrinth of gaping foundations, broken beams, standing water who knew how deep, slipping down drifts of charred wood chips and racing toward the open black mouth of the Gates. Her heart hammering achingly in her chest, Jenny stretched her mageborn senses toward the Gate, straining to hear. The cold, tingling air seemed to breathe with the dragon's mind. Somewhere in that darkness was the slithery drag of metallic scales on stone . . .

There was no way to call the image of the dragon in her scrying-stone, but she sat down suddenly where she was on the loose, charred rubble of the slope and pulled the slip of dirty-white crystal upon its chain from her jacket pocket. She heard Gareth call her name from the top of the slope, but she vouchsafed neither answer nor glance. Across the Vale, Osprey leaped the split ruin of the demolished Gates on the granite steps, cool blue shadows falling over him and his rider like a cloak as the Gate swallowed them up.

There was a flick and a gleam, as the wan sunlight caught in the facets of the jewel. Then Jenny caught a confused impression of hewn stone walls that could have encompassed the entire palace of Bel, a cavern-ceiling bristling with stone teeth from which old lamp-chains hung down into vast, cobalt spaces of air . . . black doorways piercing the walls, and the greatest of them opening opposite. . . .

Jenny cupped her hands around the jewel, trying to see into its depths, straining past the curtains of illusion that covered the dragon from her sight. She thought she saw the flash of diffuse sunlight on chain mail and saw Osprey trip on the charred debris of blackened bones and spilled coins and half-burned poles that littered the floor. She saw John pull him out of the stumble and saw the gleam of the harpoon in his hand . . . Then something spurted from the inner doors, like a drench of thrown bathwater, splattering viscously into the dry ash of the floor, searing upward in a curtain of fire.

There was a darkness in the crystal and in that darkness, two burning silver lamps.

Nothing existed around her, not the cool shift of the morning air, nor the sunlight warming her ankles in her buckskin boots where her heels rested on the chopped-up slope of gravel and weeds, not the wintry smell of water and stone from below, nor the small noises of the restless horses above. Cupped in her hands, the edges of the crystal seemed to burn in white light, but its heart was dark; through that darkness only fragmentary images came—a sense of something moving that was vast and dark, the swinging curve of John's body as he flung a harpoon, and the cloudy swirls of blinding fumes.

In some way she knew Osprey had gone down, smitten by the stroke of the dragon's tail. She had a brief impression of John on his knees, his eyes red and swollen from the acrid vapors that filled the hall, aiming for another throw. Something like a wing of darkness covered him. She saw flame again and, as a queer, detached image, three harpoons lying like scattered jackstraws in the middle of a puddle of blackened and steaming slime. Something within her turned to ice; there was only darkness and movement in the darkness, and then John again, blood pouring through the rips in his mail shirt, staring up at a towering shape of glittering shadow, his sword in his hand.

Blackness swallowed the crystal. Jenny was aware that her hands were shaking, her whole body hurting with a pain that radiated from a seed of cold under her breast-bone, her throat a bundle of twisted wires. She thought blindly, *John*, remembering him striding with graceful insouciance into Zyerne's dining room, his armor of outrageousness protecting him from Zyerne's claws; she remembered the flash of autumn daylight on his specs as he stood ankle-deep in pig muck at the Hold, reaching up his hands to help her dismount.

She could not conceive of what life would be like without that fleeting, triangular grin.

Then somewhere in her mind she heard him call out to her: *Jenny* . . .

She found him lying just beyond the edge of the trapezoid of light that fell through the vast square of the Gates. She had left Moon Horse outside, tossing her head in fear at the acrid reek of the dragon that pervaded all that end of the Vale. Jenny's own heart was pounding, so that it almost turned her sick; all the way across the ruins of Deeping she had been waiting for the dark shape of the dragon to emerge from the Gates.

But nothing had come forth. The silence within the darkness was worse than any sound could have been.

After the brightness of the Vale, the blue vaults of the Market Hall seemed almost black. The air was murky with vapors that diffused what little light there was. The trapped fumes burned her eyes and turned her dizzy, mixed with the smoke of burning and the heavy reek of poisoned slag. Even with a wizard's sight, it took Jenny's eyes a moment to accustom themselves. Then sickness came over her, as if the blood that lay spread everywhere had come from her body, rather than John's.

He lay with his face hidden by his outflung arm, the mail coif dragged back and the hair beneath it matted with blood where it had not been singed away. Blood lay in a long, inky trail behind him, showing where he had crawled after the fight was over, past the carcass of the horse Osprey, leading like a sticky path to the vast, dark bulk of the dragon.

The dragon lay still, like a shining mound of obsidian knives. Supine, it was a little higher than her waist, a glittering blacksnake nearly forty feet long, veiled in the white smoke of its poisons and the darkness of its magic, harpoons sticking from it like darts. One foreleg lay stretched out toward John, as if with its last strength it had reached to tear him, and the great talon lay like a skeleton hand in a pool of leaked black blood. The atmosphere all about it seemed heavy, filled with a sweet, clear singing that Jenny thought was as much within her skull as outside of it. It was a song with words she could not understand; a song about stars and cold and the long, ecstatic plunge through darkness. The tune was half-familiar, as if she had heard a phrase of it once, long ago, and had carried it since in her dreams.

Then the dragon Morkeleb raised his head, and for a time she looked into his eyes.

They were like lamps, a crystalline white kaleidoscope, cold and sweet and burning as the core of a flame. It struck her with a sense of overwhelming shock that she looked into the eyes of a mage like herself.

It was an alien intelligence, clean and cutting as a silver of black glass. There was something terrible and fascinating about those eyes; the singing in her mind was like a voice speaking to her in words she almost understood. She felt a calling within her to the hungers that had all of her life consumed her.

With a desperate wrench, she pulled her thoughts from it and turned her eyes aside.

She knew then why the legends warned never to look into a dragon's eyes. It was not only because the dragon could snag some part of your soul and paralyze you with indecision while it struck.

It was because, in pulling away, you left some shred of yourself behind, snared in those ice-crystal depths.

She turned to flee, to leave that place and those too-knowing eyes, to run from the singing that whispered to the harmonics of her bones. She would have run, but her booted foot brushed something as she turned. Looking down to the man who lay at her feet, she saw for the first time that his wounds still bled.

10

"**H**e can't be dying!" Gareth finished laying a heap of fresh-cut branches beside the low fire and turned to Jenny, his eyes pleading with her. As if, Jenny thought, with what power was left in her numbed mind, his saying could make it so.

Without speaking, she leaned across to touch the ice-cold face of the man who lay covered with plaids and bearskins, so close to the flickering blaze.

Her mind felt blunted, like a traveler lost in the woods who returned again and again to the same place, unable to struggle clear.

She had known that it would come to this, when first she had taken him into her life. She should never have yielded to the mischief in those brown eyes. She should have sent him away and not given in to that weak part of herself that whispered: I want a friend.

She stood up and shook out her skirts, pulling her plaid more tightly around her sheepskin jacket. Gareth was watching her with frightened dog eyes, hurt and pleading; he followed her over to the heap of the packs on the other side of the fire.

She could have had her fill of lovers. There were always those who would lie with a witch for the novelty of it or for the luck it was said to bring. Why had she let him stay until morning and talked to him as if he were not a man and an enemy whom she knew even then would fetter her soul? Why had she let him touch her heart as well as her body?

The night was dead-still, the sky dark save for the white disc of the waxing moon. Its ghostly light barely outlined the broken bones of the empty town below. A log settled in the dying fire; the spurt of light touched a spangle of red on the twisted links of John's mail shirt and glimmered stickily on the upturned palm of one blistered hand. Jenny felt her whole body one open wound of grief.

We change what we touch, she thought. Why had she let him change her? She had been happy, alone with her magic. The key to magic is magic—she should have held to that from the start. She had known even then that he was a man who would give his life to help others, even others not his own.

If he had waited for Zyerne . . .

She pushed the thought away with bitter violence, knowing Zyerne's magic could have saved him. All day she had wanted to weep, not only with grief, but with anger at herself for all the choices of the past.

Thin and plaintive as a child's, Gareth's voice broke into her circle of stumbling self-hate. "Isn't there anything that you can do?"

"I have done what I can," she replied wearily. "I have washed his wounds and stitched them shut, laid spells of healing upon them. The dragon's blood is a poison in his veins, and he has lost too much blood of his own."

"But surely there's *something* . . ." In the brief gleam of the fire, she could see that he had been weeping. Her own soul felt cold now and drained as John's flesh.

"You have asked me that seven times since it grew dark," she said. "This is beyond my skills—beyond the medicines that I have—beyond my magic."

She tried to tell herself that, even had she not loved him, even had she not given up the time she could have spent studying, it would still have been so.

Would she have been able to save him, if she had not given him all those hours; if she had spent all those early mornings meditating among the stones in the solitude of the hilltop instead of lying talking in his bed?

Or would she only have been a little bleaker, a little madder—a little more like the worst side of herself—a little more like Caerdinn?

She did not know, and the hurt of that was almost as bad as the hurt of suspecting that she did know.

But she had only her own small powers—spells worked one rune at a time, patiently, in the smallest increments of thought. She slowed and calmed her mind, as she did when she worked magic, and realized she could not cure him. What then could she do for him? What had Mab said, when she had spoken of healing?

She ran her hands through her long hair, shifting the weight of it from her face and neck. Her shoulders hurt with cramp; she had not slept in two nights, and her body ached.

"The most we can do now is keep heating stones in the fire to put around him," she said at last. "We must keep him warm."

Gareth swallowed and wiped his nose. "Just that?"

"For now, yes. If he seems a little stronger in the morning, we may be able to move him." But she knew in her heart that he would not live until morning. Like a whispering echo, the vision in the water bowl returned to her, a bitter nightmare of failed hope.

Hesitantly, Gareth offered, "There are physicians up at Halnath. Polycarp, for one."

"And an army around its walls." Her voice sounded very cold to her own ears. "If he's still alive in the morning . . . I didn't want you to risk putting yourself once again where Zyerne might reach you, but in the morning, I think you should take Battlehammer and ride back to Bel."

Gareth looked frightened at the mention of Zyerne's name and at the thought of possibly facing her alone, but he nodded. Jenny was interested to note, in some detached portion of her tired soul, that, having sought all his life for heroism, while Gareth might now flinch from it, he did not flee.

She went on, "Go to the house of the gnomes and fetch Miss Mab here. The medicines of the gnomes may be locked away in the Deep, but . . ." Her voice trailed off. Then she repeated softly, "The medicines of the gnomes."

Like pins and needles in a numbed limb, the hurt of hope renewed as a sudden wash of agony. She whispered, "Gareth, where are John's maps?"

Gareth blinked at her uncomprehendingly, too preoccupied for the moment with his own fears of Zyerne to realize what she was getting at. Then he gave a start, and hope flooded into his face, and he let out a whoop that could have been heard in Bel. "The Places of Healing!" he cried, and threw his arms around her, sweeping her off her feet. "I knew it!" he shouted, with all his old forlorn cockiness. "I knew you could think of something! You can . . ."

"You don't know anything of the kind." She fought free of him, angry at him for expressing what was already surging through her veins like a swig of cheap brandy. She brushed past him and almost ran to John's side, while Gareth, gamboling like a large puppy, began to ransack the camp for the maps.

If there was anything worse than the pain of despair, she thought, it was the pain of hope. At least despair is restful. Her own heart was hammering as she brushed aside the russet hair from John's forehead, almost black-looking now against the bloodless flesh. Her mind was racing ahead, ticking off the remedies Mab had spoken of: distillations to slow and strengthen the thready heartbeat; slaves to promote the healing of the flesh; and philters to counteract poison and give him back the blood he had lost. There would be spell-books, too, she thought, hidden in the Places of Healing, words with which to bind the soul to the flesh, until the flesh itself could recover. She could find them, she told herself desperately, she must. But the knowledge of what was at stake lay on her heart like stones. For a moment she felt so tired that she almost wished for his death, because it would require no further striving from her and threaten her with no further failure.

Holding his icy hands, she slid for a moment into the outer fringes of the healing trance and whispered to him by his inner name. But it was as if she called at the head of a descending trail along which he had long since passed—there was no answer.

But there was something else. In her trance she heard it, a soft touch of sound that twisted her heart with fright—the slur of scales on rock, the shiver of alien music.

Her eyes opened; she found herself shaking and cold.

The dragon was alive.

"Jenny?" Gareth came nattering over to her side, his hands full of creased bits of dirty papyrus. "I found them, but—but the Places of Healing aren't on them." His eyes were filled with worry behind the cracked, crazy specs. "I've looked . . ."

Jenny took them from his hand with fingers that shook. In the firelight she could make out passages, caverns, rivers, all marked in Dromar's strong, runic hand, and the blank spots, unmarked and unlabeled. *The affair of the gnomes.*

Anger wrenched at her, and she threw the maps from her. "Damn Dromar and his secrets," she whispered viciously. "Of course the Places of Healing are the heart of the Deep that they all swear by!"

"But—" Gareth stammered weakly. "Can you—can you find them anyway?"

Fury welled up in her, of hope thwarted, first by fear and now by one gnome's stubbornness, like molten rock pouring through the cracks of exhaustion in her soul. "In those warrens?" she demanded. For a moment anger, weariness, and the knowledge of the dragon claimed her, tearing at her so that she could have screamed and called down the lightning to rive apart the earth.

As Zyerne did, she told herself, fighting for calm. She closed her fists, one around the other, and pressed her lips against them, willing the rage and the fear to pass; and when they passed, there was nothing left. It was as if the unvoiced scream had burned everything out of her and left only a well of dark and unnatural calm, a universe deep.

Gareth was still looking at her, his eyes pleading. She said quietly,

"Maybe. Mab spoke of the way. I may be able to reason it out." Mab had also said that one false step would condemn her to a death by starvation, wandering in darkness.

Like an answer, she knew at once what John would have said to that—*God's Grandmother, Jen, the dragon'll eat you before you get a chance to starve.*

Trust John, she thought, to make me laugh at a time like this.

She got to her feet, chilled to the bone and feeling a hundred years old, and walked to the packs once more. Gareth trailed along after her, hugging his crimson cloak about himself for warmth and chattering on about one thing and another; locked in that strange stasis of calm, Jenny scarcely heard.

It was only as she slung her big satchel about her shoulder and picked up her halberd that he seemed to feel her silence. "Jenny," he said doubtfully, catching the edge of her plaid. "Jenny—the dragon is dead, isn't it? I mean, the poison did work, didn't it? It must have, if you were able to get John out of there . . ."

"No," Jenny said quietly. She wondered a little at the weird silence within her; she had felt more fear listening for the Whisperers in the Woods of Wyr than she did now. She started to move off toward the darkness of the shadow-drowned ruins. Gareth ran around in front of her and caught her by the arms.

"But—that is—how long . . ."

She shook her head. "Too long, almost certainly." She put her hand on his wrist to move him aside. Having made up her mind what she must do, she wanted it over with, though she knew she would never succeed.

Gareth swallowed hard, his thin face working in the low ruby light of the fire. "I—I'll go," he volunteered shakily. "Tell me what I should look for, and I . . ."

For an instant, laughter threatened to crack all her hard-won resolve —not laughter at him, but at the wan gallantry that impelled him, like the hero of a ballad, to take her place. But he would not have understood how she loved him for the offer, absurd as it was; and if she began to laugh she would cry, and that weakness she knew she could not now afford. So she only stood on her toes and pulled his shoulders down so that she could kiss his soft, thin cheek. "Thank you, Gareth," she murmured. "But I can see in the darkness, and you cannot, and I know what I seek."

"Really," he persisted, torn visibly between relief at her refusal, awareness that she was in fact far better suited than he for the task, a lifetime of chivalric precept, and a very real desire to protect her from harm.

"No," she said gently. "Just see that John stays warm. If I don't come back . . ." Her voice faltered at the knowledge of what lay before her—the death by the dragon, or the death within the maze. She forced strength into her words. "Do what seems best to you, but don't try to move him too soon."

The admonition was futile, and she knew it. She tried to remember Mab's words regarding the lightless labyrinths of the Deep and they slid from her mind like a fistful of water, leaving only the recollection of the shining wheels of diamond that were the dragon's watching eyes. But she had to reassure Gareth; and while John breathed, she knew she could never have remained in camp.

She squeezed Gareth's hand and withdrew from him. Hitching her plaids higher on her shoulder, she turned toward the shadowy trails through the Vale and the dark bulk of Nast Wall that loomed against a sullen and pitchy sky. Her final glimpse of John was of the last glow of the dying fire that outlined the shape of his nose and lips against the darkness.

Long before she reached the Great Gates of the Deep, Jenny was aware of the singing. As she crossed the frost-skimmed stones of the ruins, bled of all their daytime color by the feeble wash of the moonlight, she felt it—a hunger, a yearning, and a terrifying beauty, far beyond her comprehension. It intruded into her careful piecing-together of those fragmentary memories of Mab's remarks about the Places of Healing, broke even into her fears for John. It seemed to float around her in the air, and yet she knew that it could only be heard by her; it shivered in her bones, down to her very finger ends. When she stood in the Gates with the blackness of the Market Hall lying before her and her own shadow a diffuse smudge on the scuffed and blood-gummed refuse of the floor, it was almost overwhelming.

There was no sound to it, but its rhythm called her blood. Braided images that she could neither completely sense nor wholly understand twisted through her consciousness—knots of memory, of starry darkness that sunlight had never seen, of the joyous exhaustion of physical love whose modes and motives were strange to her, and of mathematics and curious relationships between things that she had never known were akin. It was stronger and very different from the singing that had filled the gully when the Golden Dragon of Wyr lay gasping its last. There was a piled strength in it of years lived fully and of patterns comprehended across unknowable gulfs of time.

The dragon was invisible in the darkness. She heard the soft scrape of his scales and guessed him to be lying across the inner doors of the Market Hall, that led to the Grand Passage and so into the Deep. Then the silver lamps of his eyes opened and seemed to glow softly in the reflected moonlight, and in her mind the singing flowed and intensified its colors into the vortex of a white core. In that core words formed.

Have you come seeking medicines, wizard woman? Or is that weapon you carry simply what you have deluded yourself into thinking sufficient to finish what your poisons do too slowly for your convenience?

The words were almost pictures, music and patterns shaped as much by her own soul as by his. They would hurt, she thought, if allowed to sink too deeply.

"I have come seeking medicines," she replied, her voice reverberating against the fluted dripstone of the toothed ceiling. "The power of the Places of Healing was everywhere renowned."

This I knew. There was a knot of gnomes that held out in the place where they took all the wounded. The door was low, but I could reach through it like a wolf raiding a bury of rabbits. I fed upon them for many days, until they were all gone. They had the wherewithal to make poisons there, too. They poisoned the carrion, as if they did not think that I could see the death that tainted the meat. This will be the place that you seek.

Because he spoke partially in pictures, she glimpsed also the dark ways into the place, like a half-remembered dream in her mind. Her hope stirred, and she fixed the pictures in her thoughts—tiny fragments, but perhaps enough to serve.

With her wizard's sight she could distinguish him now, stretched before her across the doors in the darkness. He had dislodged the harpoons from his throat and belly, and they lay blackened with his blood in the muck of slime and ash on the floor. The thorny scales of his back and sides lay sleek now, their edges shining faintly in the dim reflection of the moon. The heavy ridges of spikes that guarded his backbone and the joints of his legs still bristled like weapons. The enormous wings lay folded neatly along his sides, and their joints, too, she saw, were armored and spined. His head fascinated her most, long and narrow and birdlike, its shape concealed under a mask of bony plates. From those plates grew a vast mane of ribbonlike scales, mingled with tufts of fur and what looked like growths of ferns and feathers; his long, delicate antennae with their glittering bobs of jet lay limp upon the ground around his head. He lay like a dog, his chin between his forepaws; but the eyes that burned into hers were the eyes of a mage who is also a beast.

I will bargain with you, wizard woman.

She knew, with chill premonition but no surprise what his bargain would be, and her heart quickened, though whether with dread or some strange hope she did not know. She said, "No," but within herself she felt, like a forbidden longing, the unwillingness to let something this beautiful, this powerful, die. He was evil, she told herself, knowing and believing it in her heart. Yet there was something in those silver eyes that drew her, some song of black and latent fire whose music she understood.

The dragon moved his head a little on the powerful curve of his neck. Blood dripped down from the tattered ribbons of his mane.

Do you think that even you, a wizard who sees in darkness, can search out the ways of the gnomes?

The pictures that filled her mind were of the darkness, of clammy and endless mazes of the world underground. Her heart sank with dread at the awareness of them; those few small images of the way to the Places of Healing, those fragmentary words of Mab's, turned in her hands to the pebbles with which a child thinks it can slaughter lions.

Still she said, "I have spoken to one of them of these ways."

And did she tell the truth? The gnomes are not famed for it in matters concerning the heart of the Deep.

Jenny remembered the empty places on Dromar's maps. But she retorted, "Nor are dragons."

Beneath the exhaustion and pain, she felt in the dragon's mind amusement at her reply, like a thin spurt of cold water in hot.

What is truth, wizard woman? The truth that dragons see is not pleasant to the human eyes, however uncomfortably comprehensible it may be to their hearts. You know this.

She saw that he had felt her fascination. The silver eyes drew her; his mind touched hers, as a seducer would have touched her hand. She saw, also, that he understood that she would not draw back from that touch. She forced her thoughts away from him, holding to the memories of John and of their sons, against the power that called to her like a whisper of amorphous night.

With effort, she tore her eyes from his and turned to leave.

Wizard woman, do you think this man for whom you risk the bones of your body will live longer than I?

She stopped, the toes of her boots touching the hem of the carpet of moonlight which lay upon the flagstoned floor. Then she turned back to face him, despairing and torn. The wan light showed her the pools of acrid blood drying over so much of the floor, the sunken look to the dragon's flesh; and she realized that his question had struck at her weakness and despair to cover his own.

She said calmly, "There is the chance that he will."

She felt the anger in the movement of his head, and the pain that sliced through him with it. *And will you wager on that? Will you wager that, even did the gnomes speak the truth, you will be able to sort your way through their warrens, spiral within spiral, dark within dark, to find what you need in time? Heal me, wizard woman, and I will guide you with my mind and show you the place that you seek.*

For a time she only gazed up at that long bulk of shining blackness, the dark mane of bloody ribbons, and the eyes like oiled metal ringing eternal darkness. He was a wonder such as she had never seen, a spined and supple shadow from the thorned tips of his backswept wings to the horned beak of his nose. The Golden Dragon John had slain on the windswept hills of Wyr had been a being of sun and fire, but this was a smoke-wraith of night, black and strong and old as time. The spines of his head grew into fantastic twisted horns, icy-smooth as steel; his forepaws had the shape of hands, save that they had two thumbs instead of one. The voice that spoke in her mind was steady, but she could see the weakness dragging at every line of that great body and feel the faint shiver of the last taut strength that fought to continue the bluff against her.

Unwillingly, she said, "I know nothing of the healing of dragons."

The silver eyes narrowed, as if she had asked him for something he had not thought to give. For a moment they faced one another, cloaked in the cave's darkness. She was aware of John and of time—distantly, like something urgent in a dream. But she kept her thoughts concentrated upon the creature that lay before her and the diamond-prickled darkness of that alien mind that struggled with hers.

Then suddenly the gleaming body convulsed. She felt, through the silver eyes, the pain like a scream through the steel ropes of his muscles. The wings stretched out uncontrollably, the claws extending in a terrible spasm as the poison shifted in his veins. The voice in her mind whispered, *Go.*

At the same moment memories flooded her thoughts of a place she had never been before. Vague images crowded to her mind of blackness as vast as the night outdoors, columned with a forest of stone trees that whispered back the echo of every breath, of rock seams a few yards across whose ceilings were lost in distant darkness, and of the murmuring of endless water under stone. She felt a vertigo of terror as in a nightmare, but also a queer sense of *déjà vu*, as if she had passed that way before.

It came to her that it was Morkeleb and not she who had passed that way; the images were the way to the Places of Healing, the very heart of the Deep.

The spined black body before her twisted with another paroxysm of anguish, the huge tail slashing like a whip against the rock of the wall. The pain was visible now in the silver eyes as the poison ate into the dragon's blood. Then his body dropped slack, a dry clatter of horns and spines like a skeleton falling on a stone floor, and from a great distance off she heard again, *Go.*

His scales had all risen in a blanket of razors at his agony; quiveringly, they smoothed themselves flat along the sunken sides. Jenny gathered her courage and strode forward; without giving herself time to think of what she was doing, she scrambled over the waist-high hill of the ebony flank that blocked the doorway of the Grand Tunnel. The backbone ridge was like a hedge of spears, thrusting stiffly from the unsteady footing of the hide. Kilting up her skirt, she put a hand to steady herself on the carved stone pillar of the doorjamb and leaped over the spines awkwardly, fearing to the last that some renewed convulsion would thrust them into her thighs.

But the dragon lay quiet. Jenny could sense only the echoes of his mind within hers, like a faint gleam of faroff light. Before her stretched the darkness of the Deep.

If she thought about them, the visions she had seen retreated from her. But she found that if she simply walked forward, as if she had trodden this way before, her feet would lead her. Dream memories whispered through her mind of things she had seen, but sometimes the angle of sight was different, as if she had looked down upon them from above.

The upper levels of the Deep were dry, wrought by the gnomes after the fashion of the tastes of men. The Grand Passage, thirty feet broad and paved in black granite, worn and runnelled with the track of uncounted generations of feet, had been walled with blocks of cut stone to hide the irregularities of its shape; broken statues lying like scattered bones in the dark attested the classical appearance of the place in its heyday. Among the fragmented whiteness of the marble limbs lay real bones, and with them the twisted bronze frames and shattered glass of the huge lamps that had once depended from the high ceiling, all scraped together along the walls, like leaves in a gutter, by the passage of the dragon's body. Even in the darkness, Jenny's wizard's sight showed her the fire-blackening where the spilled oil had been ignited by the dragon's breath.

Deeper down, the place had the look of the gnomes. Stalagmites and columns ceased to be carved into the straight pillars favored by the children of men, and were wrought into the semblance of trees in leaf, or beasts, or grotesque things that could have been either; more and more frequently they had simply been left to keep the original shape of pouring water which had been their own. The straight, handsomely finished water courses of the higher levels gave place to tumbling streams in the lower deeps; in some places the water fell straight, fifty or a hundred feet from distant ceilings, like a living pillar, or gushed away into darkness through conduits shaped like the skulls of gargoyles. Jenny passed through caverns and systems of caves that had been transformed into the vast, interconnected dwelling places of the great clans and families of the gnomes, but elsewhere she found halls and rooms large enough to contain all the village of Deeping, where houses and palaces had been built freestanding, their bizarre spires and catwalks indistinguishable from the groves of stalagmites that clustered in strange forests on the banks of pools and rivers like polished onyx.

And through these silent realms of wonder she saw nothing but the evidences of ruin and decay and the scraping track of the dragon. White ur-toads were everywhere, squabbling with rats over the rotting remains of stored food or month-old carrion; in some places, the putrescent fetor of what had been hoards of cheese, meat, or vegetables was nearly unbreathable. The white, eyeless vermin of the deeper pits, whose names she could only guess at from Mab's accounts, slipped away at her approach, or hid themselves behind the fire-marked skulls and dropped vessels of chased silver that everywhere scattered the halls.

As she went deeper, the air became cold and very damp, the stone increasingly slimy beneath her boots; the weight of the darkness was crushing. As she walked the lightless mazes, she understood that Mab had been right; without guidance, even she, whose eyes could pierce that utter darkness, would never have found her way to the heart of the Deep.

But find it she did. The echo of it was in the dragon's mind, setting up queer resonances in her soul, a lamination of feelings and awareness whose alien nature she shrank from, uncomprehending. Beside its doors, she felt the aura of healing that lingered still in the air, and the faint breath of ancient power.

All through that series of caverns, the air was warm, smelling of dried camphor and spices; the putrid stench of decay and the crawling vermin were absent. Stepping through the doors into the domed central cavern, where ghost-pale stalactites regarded themselves in the oiled blackness of a central pool, she wondered how great a spell it would take to hold that healing warmth, not only against the cold in the abysses of the earth, but for so long after those who had wrought the spell had perished.

The magic here was great indeed.

It pervaded the place; as she passed cautiously through the rooms of meditation, of dreaming, or of rest, Jenny was conscious of it as a living presence, rather than the stasis of dead spells. At times the sensation of it grew so strong that she looked back over her shoulder and called out to the darkness, "Is someone there?" though in her reason she knew there was not. But as with the Whisperers in the north, her feelings argued against her reason, and again and again she extended her senses through that dark place, her heart pounding in hope or fear—she could not tell which. But she touched nothing, nothing but darkness and the drip of water falling eternally from the hanging teeth of the stones.

There was living magic there, whispering to itself in darkness—and like the touch of some foul thing upon her flesh, she felt the sense of evil.

She shivered and glanced around her nervously once more. In a small room, she found the medicines she sought, row after row of glass phials and stoppered jars of the green-and-white marbled ware the gnomes made in such quantity. She read their labels in the darkness and stowed them in her satchel, working quickly, partly from a growing sense of uneasiness and partly because she felt time leaking away and John's life ebbing like the going-out of the tide.

He can't die, she told herself desperately, not after all this—but she had come too late to too many bedsides in her years as a healer to believe that. Still, she knew that the medicines alone might not be enough. Hastily, glancing back over her shoulder as she moved from room to dark and silent room, she began searching for the inner places of power, the libraries where they would store the books and scrolls of magic that, she guessed, made up the true heart of the Deep.

Her boots swished softly on the sleek floors, but even that small noise twisted at her nerves. The floors of the rooms, like all the places inhabited by gnomes, were never at one level, but made like a series of terraces; even the smallest chambers had two or more. And as she searched, the eerie sense of being watched grew upon her, until she feared to pass through new doors, half-expecting to meet some evil thing gloating in the blackness. She felt a power, stronger than any she had encountered—stronger than Zyerne's, stronger than the dragon's. But she found nothing, neither that waiting, silent evil, nor any book of power by which magic would be transmitted down the years among the gnome mages—only herbals, anatomies, or catalogs of diseases and cures. In spite of her uneasy fear, she felt puzzled—Mab had said that the gnomes had no Lines, yet surely the power had to be transmitted somehow. So she forced herself to seek, deeper and deeper, for the books that must contain it.

Exhaustion was beginning to weaken her like slow illness. Last night's watching and the night's before weighed her bones, and she knew she would have to abandon her search. But knowledge of her own inadequacy drove her, questing inward into the forbidden heart of the Deep, desperate to find what she might before she returned to the surface to do what she could with what she had.

She stepped through a door into a dark place that echoed with her breathing.

She had felt cold before, but it seemed nothing now; nothing compared to the dread that congealed around her heart.

She stood in the place she had seen in the water bowl, in the visions of John's death.

It shocked her, for she had come on it unexpectedly. She had thought to find an archive there, a place of teaching, for she guessed this to be the heart and center of the blank places on Dromar's ambiguous maps. But through a knotted forest of stalactites and columns, she glimpsed only empty darkness that smelled faintly of the wax of a thousand candles, which slumped like dead things in the niches of the rock. No living thing was there, but she felt again that sense of evil and she stepped cautiously forward into the open spaces of black toward the misshapen stone altar.

She laid her hands upon the blue-black, soapy-feeling stone. In her vision the place had been filled with muttering whispers, but now there was only silence. For a moment, dark swirlings seemed to stir in her mind, the inchoate whisperings of fragmentary visions, but they passed like a groundswell, leaving no more aftertaste than a dream.

Still, they seemed to take from her the last of her strength and her will; she felt bitterly weary and suddenly very frightened of the place. Though she heard no sound, she whirled, her heart beating so that she could almost hear its thudding echo in the dark. There was evil there, somewhere—she knew it now, felt it close enough to leer over her shoulder. Shifting the bulging satchel upon her shoulder, she hastened like a thief across the slithery darkness of the gnomes' dancing floor, seeking the ways that would lead her out of the darkness, back to the air above.

Morkeleb's mind had guided her down into the abyss, but she could feel no touch of it now. She followed the marks she had made, runes that only she could see, drawn upon the walls with her forefinger. As she ascended through the dark rock seams and stairs of amber flowstone, she wondered if the dragon were dead. A part of her hoped that he was, for the sake of the people of these lands, for the gnomes, and for the Master; a part of her felt the same grief that she had, standing above the dragon's corpse in the gully of Wyr. But there was something about that grief that made her hope still more that the dragon was dead, for reasons she hesitated to examine.

The Grand Passage was as dark as the bowels of the Deep had been, bereft of even the little moonlight that had leaked in to illuminate it before; but even in the utter darkness, the air here was different—cold but dry and moving, unlike the still, brooding watchfulness of the heart of the Deep.

Her wizard's sight showed her the dark, bony shape of the dragon's haunch lying across the doorway, the bristling spears of his backbone pointing inward toward her. As she came nearer she saw how sunken the scaled skin lay on the curve of the bone.

Listen as she would, she heard no murmur of his mind. But, the music that had seemed to fill the Market Hall echoed there still, faint and piercing, with molten shivers of dying sound.

He was unconscious—dying, she thought. *Do you think this man will live longer than I?* he had asked.

Jenny unslung her plaid from her shoulder and laid the thick folds over the cutting knives of the dragon's spine. The edges drove through the cloth; she added the heavy sheepskin of her jacket and, shivering as the outer cold sliced through the thin sleeves of her shift, worked her foot onto the largest of the spines. Catching the doorpost once again for leverage, she swung herself nimbly up and over. For an instant she balanced on the haunch, feeling the slender suppleness of the bones under the steel scales and the soft heat that radiated from the dragon's body; then she sprang down. She stood for a moment, listening with her ears and her mind.

The dragon made no move. The Market Hall lay before her, blue-black and ivory with the feeble trickle of starlight that seemed so bright after the utter night below the ground. Even though the moon had set, every pot sherd and skewed lampframe seemed to Jenny's eyes outlined in brightness, every shadow like spilled ink. The blood was drying though the place stank of it. Osprey still lay in a smeared pool of darkness, surrounded by glinting harpoons. The night felt very old. A twist of wind brought her the smell of woodsmoke from the fire on Tanner's Rise.

Like a ghost Jenny crossed the hall, shivering in the dead cold. It was only when she reached the open night of the steps that she began to run.

11

At Dawn she felt John's hand tighten slightly around her own.

Two nights ago she had worked the death-spells, weaving an aura of poison and ruin—the circles of them still lay scratched in the earth at the far end of the Rise. She had not slept more than an hour or so the night before that, somewhere on the road outside Bel, curled in John's arms. Now the drifting smoke of the low fire was a smudge of gray silk in the pallid morning air, and she felt worn and chilled and strange, as if her skin had been sandpapered and every nerve lay exposed. Yet she felt strangely calm.

She had done everything she could, slowly, meticulously, step by step, following Miss Mab's remembered instructions as if the body she knew so well were a stranger's. She had given him the philters and medicines as the gnomes did, by means of a hollow needle driven into the veins, and had packed poultices on the wounds to draw from them the poison of the dragon's blood. She had traced the runes of healing where the marks of the wounds cut the paths of life throughout his body, touching them with his inner name, the secret of his essence, woven into the spells. She had called him patiently, repeatedly, by the name that his soul knew, holding his spirit to his body by what force of magic she could muster, until the medicines could take hold.

She had not thought that she would succeed. When she did, she was exhausted past grief or joy, able to think no further than the slight lift of his ribcage and the crease of his blackened eyelids with his dreams.

Gareth said softly, "Will he be all right?" and she nodded. Looking at the gawky young prince who hunkered at her side by the fire, she was struck by his silence. Perhaps the closeness of death and the endless weariness of the night had sobered him. He had spent the hours while she was in the Deep patiently heating stones and placing them around John's body as he had been told to do—a dull and necessary task, and one to which, she was almost certain, she owed the fact that John had still been alive when she had returned from the dragon's lair.

Slowly, her every bone hurting her to move, she put off the scuffed scarlet weight of his cloak. She felt scraped and aching, and wanted only to sleep. But she stood up, knowing there was something else she must do, worse than all that had gone before. She stumbled to her medicine bag and brought out the brown tabat leaves she always carried, dried to the consistency of leather. Breaking two of them to pieces, she put them in her mouth and chewed.

Their wringing bitterness was in itself enough to wake her, without their other properties. She had chewed them earlier in the night, against the exhaustion that she had felt catching up with her while she worked. Gareth watched her apprehensively, his long face haggard within the straggly frame of his green-tipped hair, and she reflected that he must be almost as weary as she. Lines that had existed only as brief traces of passing expressions were etched there now, from his nostrils to the corners of his mouth, and others showed around his eyes when he took off his broken spectacles to rub the inner corners of the lids—lines that would deepen and settle into his manhood and his old age. As she ran her hands through the loosened cloud of her hair, she wondered what her own face looked like, or would look like after she did what she knew she must do.

She began collecting medicines into her satchel once more.

"Where are you going?"

She found one of John's plaids and wrapped it about her, all her movements stiff with weariness. She felt threadbare as a piece of worn cloth, but the uneasy strength of the tabat leaves was already coursing through her veins. She knew she would have to be careful, for the tabat was like a usurer; it lent, but it had a way of demanding back with interest when one could least afford to pay. The moist air felt cold in her lungs; her soul was oddly numb.

"To keep a promise," she said.

The boy watched her with trepidation in his earnest gray eyes as she shouldered her satchel once more and set off through the misty silences of the ruined town toward the Gates of the Deep.

"Morkeleb?"

Her voice dissipated like a thread of mist in the stillness of the Market Hall. Vapor and blue morning shadow cloaked the Vale outside, and the light here was gray and sickly. Before her the dragon lay like a dropped garment of black silk, held to shape only by its bonings. One wing stretched out, where it had fallen after the convulsions of the night before; the long antennae trailed limp among the ribbons of the mane. Faint singing still lay upon the air, drawing at Jenny's heart.

He had given her the way through the Deep, she thought; it was John's life that she owed him. She tried to tell herself that it was for this reason only that she did not want that terrible beauty to die.

Her voice echoed among the upended ivory turrets of the roof. "Morkeleb!"

The humming changed within her mind, and she knew he heard. One delicate, crayfish antenna stirred. The lids of silver eyes slipped back a bare inch. For the first time she saw how delicate those lids were, tinted with subtle shades of violet and green within the blackness. Looking into the white depths they partly shielded, she felt fear, but not fear for her body; she felt again the cross-blowing winds of present *should* and future *if*, rising up out of the chasms of doubt. She summoned calm to her, as she summoned clouds or the birds of the hawthorn brakes, and was rather surprised at the steadiness of her voice.

"Give me your name."

Life moved in him then, a gold heat that she felt through the singing of the air. Anger and resistance; bitter resistance to the last.

"I cannot save you without knowing your name," she said. "If you slip beyond the bounds of your flesh, I need something by which to call you back."

Still that molten wrath surged through the weakness and pain. She remembered Caerdinn saying, "Save a dragon, slave a dragon." At that time, she had not known why anyone would wish to save the life of such a creature, nor how doing so would place something so great within your power. Cock by its feet . . .

"Morkeleb!" She walked forward, forgetting her fear of him—perhaps through anger and dread that he would die, perhaps only through the tabat leaves—and laid her small hands on the soft flesh around his eyes. The scales there were tinier than the ends of needles. The skin felt like dry silk beneath her hand, pulsing with warm life. She felt again that sense, half-fright, half-awe, of taking a step down a road which should not be trodden, and wondered if it would be wiser and better to turn away and let him die. She knew what he was. But having touched him, having looked into those diamond eyes, she could more easily have given up her own life.

In the glitter of the singing within her mind, one single air seemed to detach itself, as if the thread that bound together the complex knots of its many harmonies had suddenly taken on another color. She knew it immediately in its wholeness, from the few truncated fragments Caerdinn had whistled for her in a hedgerow one summer day. The music itself was the dragon's name.

It slid through her fingers, soft as silken ribbons; taking it, she began to braid it into her spells, weaving them like a rope of crystal around the dragon's fading soul. Through the turns of the music, she glimpsed the entrance to the dark, starry mazes of his inner mind and heart and, by the flickering light of it, seemed to see the paths that she must take to the healing of his body.

She had brought with her the medicines from the Deep, but she saw now that they were useless. Dragons healed themselves and one another through the mind alone. At times, in the hours that followed, she was terrified of this healing, at others, only exhausted past anything she had ever experienced or imagined, even in the long night before. Her weariness grew, encompassing body and brain in mounting agony; she felt entangled in a net of light and blackness, struggling to draw across some barrier a vast, cloudy force that pulled her toward it over that same frontier. It was not what she had thought to do, for it had nothing to do with the healing of humans or beasts. She summoned the last reserves of her own power, digging forgotten strengths from the marrow of her bones to battle for his life and her own. Holding to the ropes of his life took all this strength and more that she did not have; and in a kind of delirium, she understood that if he died, she would die also, so entangled was her essence in the starry skeins of his soul. Small and clear, she got a glimpse of the future, like an image in her scrying-stone—that if she died, John would die within the day, and Gareth would last slightly less than seven years, as a husk slowly hollowed by Zyerne's perverted powers. Turning from this, she clung to the small, rock-steady strength of what she knew: old Caerdinn's spells and her own long meditations in the solitude among the stones of Frost Fell.

Twice she called Morkeleb by his name, tangling the music of it with the spells she had so laboriously learned rune by rune, holding herself anchored to this life with the memory of familiar things—the shapes of the leaves of plants, gentian and dog's mercury, the tracks of hares upon the snow, and wild, vagrant airs played on the pennywhistle upon summer nights. She felt the dragon's strength stir and the echo of his name return.

She did not remember sleeping afterward. But she woke to the warmth of sunlight on her hair. Through the open Gates of the Deep, she could see the looming rock face of the cliffs outside drenched with cinnabar and gold by the afternoon's slanted light. Turning her head, she saw that the dragon had moved and lay sleeping also, great wings folded once more and his chin upon his foreclaws like a dog. In the shadows, he was nearly invisible. She could not see that he breathed, but wondered if she ever had. Did dragons breathe?

Lassitude flooded her, burying her like silk-fine sand. The last of the tabat leaves had burned out of her veins, and that exhaustion added to the rest. Scraped, drained, wrung, she wanted only to sleep again, hour after hour, for days if possible.

But she knew it was not possible. She had saved Morkeleb, but was under no illusion that this would let her sleep safely in his presence, once he had regained a little of his strength. A detached thread of amusement at herself made her chuckle; Ian and Adric, she thought, would boast to each other and every boy in the village that their mother could go to sleep in a dragon's lair—that is, if she ever made it back to tell them of it. Even rolling over hurt her bones. The weight of her clothes and her hair dragged at her like chain mail as she stood.

She stumbled to the Gates and stood for a moment, leaning against the rough-hewn granite of the vast pillar, the dry, moving freedom of the air fingering her face. Turning her head, she looked back over her shoulder and met the dragon's open eyes. Their depths stared into hers for one instant, crystalline flowers of white and silver, like glittering wells of rage and hate. Then they slid shut again. She walked from the shadows out into the brilliance of the evening.

Her mind as well as her body felt numbed as she walked slowly back through Deeping. Everything seemed queer and changed, the shadow of each pebble and weed a thing of new and unknown significance to her, as if for years she had walked half-blind and now had opened her eyes. At the northern side of the town, she climbed the rocks to the water tanks, deep black pools cut into the bones of the mountain, with sun flashing on their opaque surfaces. She stripped and swam, though the water was very cold. Afterward she lay for a long time upon her spread-out clothing, dreaming she knew not what. Wind tracked across her bare back and legs like tiny footprints, and the sun-dance changed in the pool as shadows crept across the black water. She felt it would have been good to cry, but was too weary even for that.

In time she got up, put on her clothes again, and returned to camp. Gareth was asleep, sitting with his knees drawn up and his face upon them on his crossed arms, near the glowing ashes of the fire.

Jenny knelt beside John, feeling his hands and face. They seemed warmer, though she could detect no surface blood under the thin, fair skin. Still, his eyebrows and the reddish stubble of his beard no longer seemed so dark. She lay down beside him, her body against his beneath the blankets, and fell asleep.

In the drowsy warmth of half-waking, she heard John murmur, "I thought that was you calling me." His breath was no more than a faint touch against her hair. She blinked into waking. The light had changed again. It was dawn.

She said, "What?" and sat up, shaking back the thick weight of her hair from her face. She still felt tired to death, but ravenously hungry. Gareth was kneeling by the campfire, tousled and unshaven with his battered spectacles sliding down the end of his nose, making griddle-cakes. She noted that he was better at it than John had ever been.

"I thought you were never waking up," he said.

"I thought I was never waking up either, my hero," John whispered. His voice was too weak to carry even that short distance, but Jenny heard him and smiled.

She climbed stiffly to her feet, pulled on her skirt again over her creased shift, laced her bodice and put on her boots, while Gareth set water over the coals to boil for coffee, a bitter black drink popular at Court. When Gareth went to fetch more water from the spring in the woods beyond the wrecked well house, Jenny took some of the boiling water to renew John's poultices, welcoming the simplicity of human healing; and the smell of herbs soon filled the little clearing among the ruins, along with the warm, strange smell of the drink. John fell asleep again, even before Jenny had finished with the bandages, but Gareth fetched her some bannocks and honey and sat with her beside the breakfast fire.

"I didn't know what to do, you were gone so long," he said around a mouthful of mealcake. "I thought about following you—that you might need help—but I didn't want to leave John alone. Besides," he added with a rueful grin, "I've never managed to rescue you from anything yet."

Jenny laughed and said, "You did right."

"And the promise you made?"

"I kept it."

He let out his breath with a sigh and bowed his head, as if some great weight that had been pressing down upon him had been lifted. After a while he said shyly, "While I was waiting for you, I made up a song . . . a ballad. About the slaying of Morkeleb, the Black Dragon of Nast Wall. It isn't very good . . ."

"It wouldn't be," Jenny said slowly, and licked the honey from her fingers. "Morkeleb is not dead."

He stared at her, as he once had when she had told him that John had killed the Golden Dragon of Wyr with an ax. "But I thought—wasn't your promise to John to—to slay him if—if John could not?"

She shook her head, the dark cloud of her hair snagging in the grubby fleece of her jacket collar. "My promise was to Morkeleb," she said. "It was to heal him."

Collecting her feet beneath her, she rose and walked over to John once more, leaving Gareth staring after her in appalled and unbelieving bewilderment.

A day passed before Jenny returned to the Deep. She stayed close to the camp, taking care of John and washing clothes—a mundane task, but one that needed to be done. Somewhat to her surprise, Gareth helped her in this, fetching water from the spring in the glade, but without his usual chatter. Knowing she would need her strength, she slept a good deal, but her dreams were disquieting. Her waking hours were plagued with a sense of being watched. She told herself that this was simply because Morkeleb, waking, had extended his awareness across the Vale and knew where they were, but certain understandings she had found within the mazes of the dragon's mind would not allow her to believe this.

She was aware that Gareth was watching her, too, mostly when he thought she wasn't looking.

She was aware of other things, as well. Never had she felt so conscious of the traces and turnings of the wind, and of the insignificant activities of the animals in the surrounding woods. She found herself prey to strange contemplation and odd knowledge of things before unsuspected—how clouds grow, and why the wind walked the way it did, how birds knew their way south, and why, in certain places of the world at certain times, voices could be heard speaking indistinctly in empty air. She would have liked to think these changes frightened her because she did not understand them, but in truth the reason she feared them was because she did.

While she slept in the late afternoon, she heard Gareth speak to John of it, seeing them and understanding through the depths of her altered dreams.

"She healed him," she heard Gareth whisper, and was aware of him squatting beside the tangle of bearskins and plaids where John lay. "I think she promised to do so, in trade for his letting her past him to fetch the medicines."

John sighed and moved one bandaged hand a little where it lay on his chest. "Better, maybe, she had let me die."

"Do you think . . ." Gareth swallowed nervously and cast a glance at her, as if he knew that asleep, she still could hear. "Do you think he's put a spell on her?"

John was silent for a time, looking up at the gulfs of sky above the Vale, thinking. Though the air down here was still, great winds racked the upper atmosphere, herding piled masses of cloud, charcoal gray and blinding white, up against the shaggy flanks of the mountains. At length he said, "I think I'd feel it, if there were another mind controlling hers. Or I'd like to flatter myself to thinking I'd feel it. They say you should never look into a dragon's eyes, lest he put a spell on you. But she's stronger than that."

He turned his head a little and looked at where she lay, squinting to focus his shortsighted brown eyes upon her. The bare flesh on either side of the bandages on his arms and chest was livid with bruises and pitted with tiny scabs where the broken links of the mail shirt had been dragged through it. "When I used to dream of her, she didn't look the same as in waking. When I was delirious, I dreamed of her—it's as if she's grown more herself, not less."

He sighed and looked back at Gareth. "I used to be jealous of her, you know. Not of another man, but jealousy of herself, of that part of her she'd never give me—though God knows, back in those days, what I wanted it for. Who was it who said that jealousy is the only vice that gives no pleasure? But that was the first thing I had to learn about her, and maybe the hardest I've ever learned about anything—that she is her own, and what she gives me is of her choosing, and the more precious because of it. Sometimes a butterfly will come to sit in your open palm, but if you close your hand, one way or the other, it—and its choice to be there—are gone."

From there Jenny slid into deeper dreams of the crushing darkness of Ylferdun and the deep magic she sensed slumbering in the Places of Healing. As if from a great distance, she saw her children, her boys, whom she had never wanted to conceive but had borne and birthed for John's sake, but loved uneasily, unwillingly, and with desperately divided heart. With her wizard's sight she could see them sitting up in their curtained bed in the darkness, while wind drove snow against the tower walls; not sleeping at all, but telling one another tales about how their father and mother would slay the dragon and ride back with pack trains and pack trains of gold.

She woke when the sun lay three-quarters down the sky toward the flinty crest of the ridge. The wind had shifted; the whole Vale smelled of sharp snow and pine needles from the high slopes. The air in the lengthening slaty shadows was cold and damp.

John was asleep, wrapped in every cloak and blanket in the camp. Gareth's voice could be heard in the woods near the little stone fountain, tunelessly singing romantic lyrics of passionate love for the edification of the horses. Moving with her habitual quiet, Jenny laced up her bodice and put on her boots and her sheepskin jacket. She thought about eating something and decided not to. Food would break her concentration, and she felt the need of every fragment of strength and alertness that she could muster.

She paused for a moment, looking around her. The old, uneasy sensation of being watched returned to her, like a hand touching her elbow. But she sensed, also, the faint tingling of Morkeleb's power in the back of her mind and knew that the dragon's strength was returning far more quickly than that of the man he had almost slain.

She would have to act and act now, and the thought of it filled her with fear.

"Save a dragon, slave a dragon," Caerdinn had said. Her awareness of how small her own powers were terrified her, knowing what it was against which she must pit them. So this, in the end, was what she had paid for John's love, she told herself, with a little wry amusement. To go into a battle she could not hope to win. Involuntarily another part of her thought at once that at least it wasn't John's life, but her own, that would be forfeit, and she shook her head in wonderment at the follies of love. No wonder those with the power were warned against it, she thought.

As for the dragon, she had a sense, almost an instinct, of what she must do, alien to her and yet terrifyingly clear. Her heart was hammering as she selected a scruffy plaid from the top of the pile over John. The thin breezes fluttered at its edges as she slung it around her; its colors faded into the muted hues of weed and stone as she made her way silently down the ridge once more and took the track for the Deep.

Morkeleb no longer lay in the Market Hall. She followed the scent of him through the massive inner doors and along the Grand Passage—a smell that was pungent but not unpleasant, unlike the burning, metallic reek of his poisons. The tiny echoes of her footfalls were like far-off water dripping in the silent vaults of the passage—she knew Morkeleb would hear them, lying upon his gold in the darkness. Almost, she thought, he would hear the pounding of her heart.

As Dromar had said, the dragon was laired in the Temple of Sarmendes, some quarter-mile along the passage. The Temple had been built for the use of the children of men and so had been wrought into the likeness of a room rather than a cave. From the chryselephantine doors Jenny looked about, her eyes piercing the absolute darkness there, seeing how the stalagmites that rose from the floor had been cut into pillars, and how walls had been built to conceal the uneven shape of the cavern's native rock. The floor was smoothed all to one level; the statue of the god, with his lyre and his bow, had been sculpted of white marble from the royal quarries of Istmark, as had been his altar with its carved garlands. But none of this could conceal the size of the place, nor the enormous, irregu-

lar grandeur of its proportions. Above those modestly classical walls
arched the ceiling, a maze of sinter and crystal that marked the place as
nature's work timidly home-steaded by man.

The smell of the dragon was thick here, though it was clean of offal
or carrion. Instead the floor was heaped with gold, all the gold of the
Deep, plates, holy vessels, reliquaries of forgotten saints and demigods,
piled between the pillars and around the statues, tiny cosmetic pots
smelling of balsam, candlesticks quivering with pendant pearls like aspen
leaves in spring wind, cups whose rims flashed with the dark fire of jewels, a votive statue of Salernesse, the Lady of Beasts, three feet high and
solid gold . . . All the things that gnomes or men had wrought of that soft
and shining metal had been gathered there from the farthest tunnels of the
Deep. The floor was like a beach with the packed coins that had spilled
from their torn sacks, and through it gleamed the darkness of the floor,
like water collected in hollows of the sand.

Morkeleb lay upon the gold, his vast wings folded along his sides,
their tips crossed over his tail, black as coal and seeming to shine, his
crystal eyes like lamps in the dark. The sweet, terrible singing that Jenny
had felt so strongly had faded, but the air about him was vibrant with the
unheard music.

"Morkeleb," she said softly, and the word whispered back at her from
the forest of glittering spikes overhead. She felt the silver eyes upon her
and reached out, tentatively, to the dark maze of that mind.

Why gold? she asked. *Why do dragons covet the gold of men?*

It was not what she had meant to say to him, and she felt, under his
coiled anger and suspicion, something else move.

What is that to you, wizard woman?

*What was it to me that I returned here to save your life? It would
have served me and mine better to have let you die.*

Why then did you not?

There were two answers. The one she gave him was, *Because it was
understood between us that if you gave me the way into the heart of the
Deep, I should heal you and give you your life. But in that healing you
gave me your name, Morkeleb the Black*—and the name she spoke in her
mind was the ribbon of music that was his true name, his essence; and she
saw him flinch. *They have said, Save a dragon, slave a dragon, and by
your name you shall do as I bid you.*

The surge of his anger against her was like a dark wave, and all along
his sides the knifelike scales lifted a little, like a dog's hackles. Around
them in the blackness of the Temple, the gold seemed to whisper, picking
up the groundswell of his wrath.

I am Morkeleb the Black. I am and will be slave to no one and noth-

*ing, least of all a human woman, mage though she may be. I do no bid-
ding save my own.*

The bitter weight of alien thoughts crushed down upon her, heavier
than the darkness. But her eyes were a mage's eyes, seeing in darkness;
her mind held a kind of glowing illumination that it had not had before.
She felt no fear of him now; a queer strength she had not known she possessed stirred in her. She whispered the magic of his name as she would
have formed its notes upon her harp, in all its knotted complexities, and
saw him shrink back a little. His razor claws stirred faintly in the gold.

By your name, Morkeleb the Black, she repeated, *you shall do my
bidding. And by your name, I tell you that you will do no harm, either to
John Aversin, or to Prince Gareth, or to any other human being while you
remain here in the south. When you are well enough to sustain the journey, you shall leave this place and return to your home.*

Ire radiated from his scales like a heat, reflected back about him by
the thrumming gold. She felt in it the iron pride of dragons, and their contempt for humankind, and also his furious grief at being parted from the
hoard that he had so newly won. For a moment their souls met and
locked, twisting together like snakes striving, fighting for advantage. The
tide of her strength rose in her, surging and sure, as if it drew life from the
combat itself. Terror and exhilaration flooded her, like the tabat leaves,
only far stronger, and she cast aside concern for the limitations of her
flesh and strove against him mind to mind, twisting at the glittering chain
of his name.

She felt the spew of his venomous anger, but would not let go. *If you
kill me, I shall drag you down with me into death,* she thought; *for dying,
I shall not release your name from my mind.*

The strength that was breaking the sinews of her mind drew back, but
his eyes held to hers. Her thoughts were suddenly flooded with images
and half-memories, like the visions of the heart of the Deep; things she
did not understand, distracting and terrifying in their strangeness. She felt
the plunging vertigo of flight in darkness; saw black mountains that cast
double shadows, red deserts unstirred by wind since time began and
inhabited by glass spiders that lived upon salt. They were dragon memories, confusing her, luring her toward the place where his mind could
close around hers like a trap, and she held fast to those things of her own
life that she knew and her memory of the piping of old Caerdinn
whistling the truncated air of Morkeleb's true name. Into that air she
twisted her own spells of breaking and exhaustion, mingling them with
the rhythm of his heart that she had learned so well in the healing, and she
felt once more his mind draw back from hers.

His wrath was like the lour of thunder-sky, building all around her; he loomed before her like a cloud harboring lightning. Then without warning he struck at her like a snake, one thin-boned claw raised to slash.

He would not strike, she told herself as her heart contracted with terror and her every muscle screamed to flee . . . He could not strike her for she had his name and he knew it . . . She had saved him; he must obey . . . Her mind gripped the music of his name even as the claws hissed down. The wind of them slashed at her hair, the saber blades passing less than a foot from her face. White eyes stared down at her, blazing with hate; the rage of him beat against her like a storm.

Then he settled back slowly upon his bed of gold. The tang of his defeat was like wormwood in the air.

You chose to give me your name rather than die, Morkeleb. She played his name like a glissando and felt the surge of her own rising power hum in the gold against his. *You will go from these lands and not return.*

For a moment more she felt his anger, resentment, and the fury of his humbled pride. But there was something else in the hoarfrost glitter of his gaze upon her, the knowledge that she was not contemptible.

He said quietly, *Do you not understand?*

Jenny shook her head. She looked around her once again at the Temple, its dark archways piled high with more gold than she had ever seen before, a treasure more fabulous than any other upon earth. It would have bought all of Bel and the souls of most of the men who dwelled there. But, perhaps because she herself had little use for gold, she felt drawn to ask again, *Why gold, Morkeleb? Was it the gold that brought you here?*

He lowered his head to his paws again, and all around them the gold vibrated with the whisper of the dragon's name. *It was the gold, and the dreams of the gold,* he said. *I had discontent in all things; the longing grew upon me while I slept. Do you not know, wizard woman, the love that dragons have for gold?*

She shook her head again. *Only that they are greedy for it, as men are greedy.*

Rose-red light rimmed the slits of his nostrils as he sniffed. *Men,* he said softly. *They have no understanding of gold; no understanding of what it is and of what it can be. Come here, wizard woman. Put your hand upon me and listen with my mind.*

She hesitated, fearing a trap, but her curiosity as a mage drove her. She picked her way over the cold, uneven heaps of rings, platters, and candlesticks, to rest her hand once more against the soft skin below the dragon's great eye. As before, it felt surprisingly warm, unlike a reptile's skin, and soft as silk. His mind touched hers like a firm hand in the darkness.

In a thousand murmuring voices, she could hear the gold pick up the music of the dragon's name. The blended nuances of thought were magnified and made richer, distinct as subtle perfumes, piercing the heart with beauty. It seemed to Jenny that she could identify every piece of gold within that enormous chamber by its separate sounding, and hear the harmonic curve of a vessel, the melding voices of every single coin and hairpin, and the sweet tingling locked in the crystal heart of every jewel. Her mind, touching the dragon's, flinched in aching wonder from the caress of that unbearable sweetness as the echoes awoke answering resonances within her soul. Memories of dove-colored dusks on the Fell that was her home pulled at her with the deep joy of winter nights lying on the bearskins before the hearth at Alyn Hold, with John and her sons at her side. Happiness she could not name swept over her, breaking down the defenses of her heart as the intensity of the music built, and she knew that for Morkeleb it was the same in the chimeric deeps of his mind.

When the music faded, she realized she had closed her eyes, and her cheeks were wet with tears. Looking about her, though the room was as black as before, she thought that the memory of the dragon's song lingered in the gold, and a faint luminosity clung to it still.

In time she said, *That is why men say that dragon's gold is poisoned. Others say that it is lucky . . . but it is merely charged with yearning and with music, so that even dullards can feel it through their fingers.*

Even so, whispered the voice of the dragon in her mind.

But dragons cannot mine gold, nor work it. Only gnomes and the children of men.

We are like the whales that live in the sea, he said, *civilizations without artifacts, living between stone and sky in our islands in the northern oceans. We lair in rocks that bear gold, but it is impure. Only with pure gold is this music possible. Now do you understand?*

The sharing had broken something between them, and she felt no fear of him now. She went to sit close to the bony curve of his shoulder and picked up a gold cup from the hoard. She felt as she turned it over in her hands that she could have chosen it out from a dozen identical ones. Its resonance was clear and individuated in her mind; the echo of the dragon's music held to it, like a remembrance of perfume. She saw how precisely it was formed, chastened and highly polished, its handles tiny ladies with garlands twined in their hair where it streamed back over the body of the cup; even microscopically fine, the flowers were recognizable as the lilies of hope and the roses of fulfillment. Morkeleb had killed the owner of this cup, she thought to herself, only for the sake of the incredible music which he could call from the gold. Yet his love for the gold had as little to do with its beauty as her love for her sons had to do with their—undeniable, she thought—good looks.

How did you know this was here?

Do you not think that we, who live for hundreds of years, would be aware of the comings and goings of men? Where they build their cities, and with whom they trade, and in what? I am old, Jenny Waynest. Even among the dragons, my magic is accounted great. I was born before we came to this world; I can sniff gold from the bones of the earth and follow its path for miles, as you follow ground water with a hazel twig. The gold-seams of the Wall rise to the surface here like the great salmon of the north country rising to spawn.

The dragon's words were spoken in her mind, and in her mind she had a brief, distant glimpse of the Earth as the dragons saw it, spread out like a mottled carpet of purple and green and brown. She saw the green-black pelt of the forests of Wyr, the infinitely delicate cloud shapes of the crowns of the tall oaks, fragile and thready with winter, and saw how, toward the north, they were more and more replaced by the coarse spiky teeth of pine and fir. She saw the gray and white stones of the bare Winterlands, stained all the colors of the rainbow with lichen and moss in summer, and saw how the huge flashing silver shapes of eight- and ten-foot salmon moved beneath the waters of the rivers, under the blue, gliding shadow of the dragon's wings. For an instant, it was as if she could feel the air all about her, holding her up like water; its currents and countereddies, its changes from warm to cold.

Then she felt his mind closing around hers, like the jaws of a trap. For an instant she was locked into suffocating darkness, the utter darkness that not even the eyes of a wizard could pierce. Panic crushed her. She could neither move nor think, and felt only the acid gloating of the dragon all around her, and, opening beneath her, a bottomless despair.

Then as Caerdinn had taught her, as she had done in healing John— as she had always done within the circumscribed limits of her small magic—she forced her mind to calm and began to work rune by rune, note by note, concentrating singly and simply upon each element with her whole mind. She felt the wrath of the dragon smothering her like a hot sea of night, but she wedged open a crack of light, and into that crack she drove the music of the dragon's name, fashioned by her spells into a spear.

She felt his mind flinch and give. Her sight returned, and she found herself on her feet among the knee-deep piles of gold, the monstrous dark shape backing from her in anger. This time she did not let him go, but flung her own wrath and her will after him, playing upon the music of his name and weaving into it the fires that scorched his essence. All the spells of pain and ruin she had wrought into the poison flooded to her mind; but, like her fury at the bandits at the crossroads these many weeks ago, her anger had no hate in it, offering him no hold upon her mind. He shrank back from it, and the great head lowered so that the ribbons of his mane swept the coins with a slithery tinkle.

Wrapped in a rage of magic and fire, she said, *You shall not dominate me, Morkeleb the Black—either with your power nor with your treachery. I have saved your life, and you shall do as I command you. By your name you shall go, and you shall not return to the south. Do you hear me?*

She felt him resist, and drove her will and the strength of her new-found powers against him. Like a wrestler's body, she felt the dark, sulfurous rage slither from beneath the pressure of her will; she stepped back, almost instinctively, and faced him where he crouched against the wall like a vast, inky cobra, his every scale bristling with glittering wrath.

She heard him whisper, *I hear you, wizard woman*, and heard, in the cold voice, the reasonance not only of furious anger at being humbled, but of surprise that she could have done so.

Turning without a word, she left the Temple and walked back toward the square of diffuse light that marked the outer hall at the end of the Grand Passage and the Great Gates beyond.

12

When Jenny came down the steps of the Deep she was shaking with exhaustion and an aftermath of common sense that told her that she should have been terrified. Yet she felt curiously little fear of Morkeleb, even in the face of his treachery and his wrath. Her body ached—the power she had put forth against him had been far in excess of what her flesh was used to sustaining—but her head felt clear and alert, without the numbed weariness she felt when she had overstretched her powers. She was aware, down to her last finger end, of the depth and greatness of the dragon's magic, but was aware also of her own strength against him.

Evening wind dusted across her face. The sun had sunk beyond the flinty crest of the westward ridge, and though the sky still held light, Deeping lay at the bottom of a lake of shadow. She was aware of many things passing in the Vale, most of them having nothing to do with the affairs of dragons or humankind—the *shreak* of a single cricket under a charred stone, the flirt of a squirrel's tail as it fled from its hopeful mate, and the flutterings of the chaffinches as they sought their nightmare nests. Where the trail turned downward around a broken pile of rubble that had once been a house, she saw a man's skeleton lying in the weeds, the bag of gold he had died clutching split open and the coins singing softly to her where they lay scattered among his ribs.

She was aware, suddenly, that someone else had entered the Vale.

It was analagous to sound, though unheard. The scent of magic came to her like smoke on the shift of the wind. She stopped still in the dry tangle of broomsedge, cold shreds of breeze that frayed down from the timberline stirring in her plaids. There was magic in the Vale, up on the ridge. She could hear the slither and snag of silk on beech mast, the startled splash of spilled water in the dusk by the fountain, and Gareth's voice halting over a name . . .

Catching up her skirts, Jenny began to run.

The smell of Zyerne's perfume seemed everywhere in the woods. Darkness was already beginning to collect beneath the trees. Panting, Jenny sprang up the whitish, flinty rocks to the glade by the fountain. Long experience in the Winterlands had taught her to move in utter silence, even at a dead run; and thus, for the first moment, neither of those who stood near the little well was aware of her arrival.

It took her a moment to see Zyerne. Gareth she saw at once, standing frozen beside the wellhead. Spilled water was soaking into the beech mast around his feet; a half-empty bucket balanced on the edge of the stone trough beside the well itself. He didn't heed it; she wondered how much of his surroundings he was aware of at all.

Zyerne's spells filled the small glade like the music heard in dreams. Even she, a woman, felt the scented warmth of the air that belied the tingly cold lower down in the Vale and sensed the stirring of need in her flesh. In Gareth's eyes was a kind of madness, and his hands were shaking where they were clenched, knotted into fists, before him. His voice was a whisper more desperate than a scream as he said, "No."

"Gareth." Zyerne moved, and Jenny saw her, as she seemed to float like a ghost in the dusk among the birch trees at the glade's edge. "Why pretend? You know your love for me has grown, as mine has for you. It is like fire in your flesh now; the taste of your mouth in my dreams has tormented me day and night . . ."

"While you were lying with my father?"

She shook back her hair, a small, characteristic gesture, brushing the tendrils of it away from her smooth brow. It was difficult to see what she wore in the dusk—something white and fragile that rippled in the stirrings of the wind, pale as the birches themselves. Her hair was loosened down her back like a young girl's; and, like a young girl, she wore no veils. Years seemed to have vanished from her age, young as she had seemed before. She looked like a girl of Gareth's age, unless, like Jenny, one saw her with a wizard's eye.

"Gareth, I never lay with your father," she said softly. "Oh, we agreed to pretend, for the sake of appearances at Court—but even if he had wanted me to, I don't think I could have. He treated me like a daughter. It was you I wanted, you . . ."

"That's a lie!" His mouth sounded dried by fever heat.

She held out her hands, and the wind lifted the thin fabric of her sleeves back from her arms as she moved a step into the glade. "I could bear waiting no longer. I had to come, to learn what had happened to you—to be with you . . ."

He sobbed, "Get away from me!" His face was twisted by something close to pain.

She only whispered, "I want you . . ."

Jenny stepped from the somber shade of the trail and said, "No, Zyerne. What you want is the Deep."

Zyerne swung around, her concentration breaking, as Morkeleb had tried to break Jenny's. The lurid sensuality that had dripped from the air shattered with an almost audible snap. At once, Zyerne seemed older, no longer the virgin girl who could inflame Gareth's passion. The boy dropped to his knees and covered his face, his body racked with dry sobs.

"It's what you've always wanted, isn't it?" Jenny touched Gareth's hair comfortingly, and he threw his arms around her waist, clinging to her like a drowning man to a spar. Oddly enough, she felt no fear of Zyerne now, or of the greater strength of the younger woman's magic. She seemed to see Zyerne differently, even, and felt calm as she faced her— calm and ready.

Zyerne uttered a ribald laugh. "So there's our boy who won't tumble his father's mistress? You had them both to yourself, didn't you, slut, coming down from the north? Enough time and more to tangle him in your hair."

Gareth pulled free of Jenny and scrambled to his feet, shaking all over with anger. Though Jenny could see he was still terrified of the sorceress, he faced her and gasped, "You're lying!"

Zyerne laughed again, foully, as she had in the garden outside the King's rooms. Jenny only said, "She knows it isn't true. What did you come here for, Zyerne? To do to Gareth what you've done to his father? Or to see if it's finally safe for you to enter the Deep?"

The enchantress's mouth moved uncertainly, and her eyes shifted under Jenny's cool gaze. Then she laughed, the mockery in it marred by her uncertainty. "Maybe to get your precious Dragonsbane at the same time?"

A week—even a day—ago, Jenny would have responded to the taunt with fear for John's safety. But she knew Zyerne had not gone anywhere near John. She knew she would have sensed it, if such magic had been worked so near—almost, she thought, she would have heard their voices, no matter how softly they spoke. And in any case, John was unable to flee; one deals with the unwounded enemy first.

She saw Zyerne's hand move and felt the nature of the spell, even as she smelled the singed wool of her skirts beginning to smoke. Her own spell was fast and hard, called with the mind and the minimal gesture of the hand rather than the labor it had once entailed. Zyerne staggered back, her hands over her eyes, taken completely by surprise.

When Zyerne raised her head again, her eyes were livid with rage, yellow as a devil's in a face transformed with fury. "You can't keep me from the Deep," she said in a voice which shook. "It is mine—it will be mine. I've driven the gnomes from it. When I take it, no one, *no one*, will be able to contend against my power!"

Stooping, she seized a handful of old leaves and beechnuts from the mast that lay all about their feet. She flung them at Jenny. In the air, they burst into flame, growing as they burned, a tangled bonfire that Jenny swept aside with a spell she had hardly been aware she'd known. The blazing logs scattered everywhere, throwing streamers of yellow fire into the blue gloom and blazing up in half-a-dozen places where they touched dry weeds. Doubling like a hare upon her tracks, Zyerne darted for the path that led down into the Vale. Jenny leaped at her heels, her soft boots in three strides outdistancing the younger woman's precarious court shoes.

Zyerne twisted in her grip. She was taller than Jenny but not physically as strong, even taking into account Jenny's exhaustion; for an instant their eyes were inches apart, the yellow gaze boring like balefire into the blue.

Like a hammerblow, Jenny felt the impact of a mind upon hers, spells of hurt and terror that gripped and twisted at her muscles, utterly different from the weight and living strength of the dragon's mind. She parried the spell, not so much with a spell as with the strength of her will, throwing it back at Zyerne, and she heard the younger woman curse her in a spate of fury like a burst sewer. Nails tore at her wrists as she sought the yellow eyes with her own again, catching Zyerne's silky curls in a fist like a rock, forcing her to look. It was the first time she had matched strength in anger with another mage, and it surprised her how instinctive it was to probe into the essence—as she had probed into Gareth's, and Mab into hers—not solely to understand, but to dominate by understanding, to give nothing of her own soul in return. She had a glimpse of something sticky and foul as the plants that eat those foolish enough to came near, the eroded remains of a soul, like an animate corpse of the young woman's mind.

Zyerne screamed as she felt the secrets of her being bared, and power exploded in the air between them, a burning fire that surrounded them in a whirlwind of tearing force. Jenny felt a weight falling against her, a blackness like the dragon's mind but greater, the shadow of some crushing power, like an ocean of uncounted years. It drove her to her knees, but she held on, sloughing away the crawling, biting pains that tore at her skin, the rending agony in her muscles, the fire, and the darkness, boring into Zyerne's mind with her own, like a white needle of fire.

The weight of the shadow faded. She felt Zyerne's nerve and will break and got to her feet again, throwing the girl from her with all her strength. Zyerne collapsed on the dirt of the path, her dark hair hanging in a torrent over her white dress, her nails broken from tearing at Jenny's wrists, her nose running and dust plastered to her face with mucus. Jenny stood over her, panting for breath, her every muscle hurting from the twisting impact of Zyerne's spells. "Go," she said, her voice quiet, but with power in her words. "Go back to Bel and never touch Gareth again."

Sobbing with fury, Zyerne picked herself up. Her voice shook. "You stinking gutter-nosed sow! I won't be kept from the Deep! It's mine, I tell you; and when I come there, I'll show you! I swear by the Stone, when I have the Deep, I'll crush you out like the dung-eating cockroach you are! You'll see! They'll all see! They have no right to keep me away!"

"Get out of here," Jenny said softly.

Sobbing, Zyerne obeyed her, gathering up her trailing white gown and stumbling down the path that led toward the clock tower. Jenny stood for a long time watching her go. The power Jenny had summoned to protect her faded slowly, like fire banked under embers until it was needed again.

It was only after Zyerne was out of sight that she realized that she should never have been able to do what she had just done—not here and not in the Deep.

And it came to her then, what had happened to her when she had touched the mind of the dragon.

The dragon's magic was alive in her soul, like streaks of iron in gold. She should have known it before; if she had not been so weary, she thought, perhaps she would have. Her awareness, like Morkeleb's, had widened to fill the Vale, so that, even in sleep, she was conscious of things taking place about her. A shiver passed through her flesh and racked her bones with terror and wonderment, as if she had conceived again, and something alive and alien was growing within her.

Smoke from the woods above stung her nose and eyes, white billows of it telling her that Gareth had succeeded in dousing the flames. Somewhere the horses were whinnying in terror. She felt exhausted and aching, her whole body wrenched by the cramp of those gripping spells, her wrists smarting where Zyerne's nails had torn them. She began to tremble, the newfound strength draining away under the impact of shock and fear.

A countersurge of wind shook the trees around her, as if at the stroke of a giant wing. Her hair blowing about her face, she looked up, but for a moment saw nothing. It was something she'd heard of—that dragons, for all their size and gaudiness, could be harder to see in plain daylight than the voles of the hedgerow. He seemed to blend down out of the dusk, a vast shape of jointed ebony and black silk, silver-crystal eyes like small moons in the dark.

He could feel my power nearing its end, she thought despairingly, remembering how he had turned on her before. The terrible, shadowy weight of Zyerne's spells still lay on her bones; she felt they would break if she tried to summon the power to resist the dragon. Wrung with a weariness close to physical nausea, she looked up to face him and hardened her mind once again to meet his attack.

Even as she did so, she realized that he was beautiful, as he hung for a moment like a black, drifting kite upon the air.

Then his mind touched hers, and the last pain of Zyerne's spells was sponged away.

What is it, wizard woman? he asked. *It is only evil words, such as fishwives throw at one another.*

He settled before her on the path, folding his great wings with a queerly graceful articulation, and regarded her with his silver eyes in the dusk.

He said, *You understand.*

No, she replied. *I think I know what has happened, but I do not understand.*

Bah. In the leaky gray twilight beneath the trees, she saw all the scale-points along his sides ruffle slightly, like the hair of an affronted cat. *I think that you do. When your mind was in mine, my magic called to you, and the dragon within you answered. Know you not your own power, wizard woman? Know you not what you could be?*

With a cold vertigo that was not quite fear she understood him then and willed herself not to understand.

He felt the closing of her mind, and irritation smoked from him like a white spume of mist. *You understand,* he said again. *You have been within my mind; you know what it would be to be a dragon.*

Jenny said, *No,* not to him, but to that trickle of fire in her mind that surged suddenly into a stream.

As in a dream, images surfaced of things she felt she had once known and forgotten, like the soaring freedom of flight. She saw the earth lost beneath her in the clouds, and about her was a vaporous eternity whose absolute silence was broken only by the sheer of her wings. As from great height, she glimpsed the stone circle on Frost Fell, the mere below it like a broken piece of dirty glass, and the little stone house a chrysalis, cracked open to release the butterfly that had slept within.

She said, *I have not the power to change my essence.*

I have, the voice whispered among the visions in her mind. *You have the strength to be a dragon, once you consent to take the form. I sensed that in you when we struggled. I was angry then, to be defeated by a human; but you can be more than human.*

Gazing up at the dark splendor of the dragon's angular form, she shook her head. *I will not put myself thus in your power, Morkeleb. I cannot leave my own form without your aid, nor could I return to it. Do not tempt me.*

Tempt? Morkeleb's voice said. *There is no temptation from outside the heart. And as for returning—what are you as a human, Jenny Waynest? Pitiful, puling, like all your kin the slave of time that rots the body before the mind has seen more than a single flower in all the meadows of the Cosmos. To be a mage you must be a mage, and I see in your mind that you fight for the time to do even that. To be a dragon . . .*

"To be a dragon," she said aloud, to force her own mind upon it, "I have only to give over my control of you. I will not lose myself thus in the dragon mind and the dragon magic. You will not thus get me to release you."

She felt the strength press against the closed doors in her mind, then ease, and heard the steely rustle of his scales as his long tail lashed through the dry grasses with annoyance. The dark woods came back into focus; the strange visions receded like a shining mist. The light was waning fast about them, all the colors bled from straggly briar and fern. As if his blackness took on the softer hues of the evening, the dragon was nearly invisible, his shape blending with the milky stringers of fog that had begun to veil the woods and with the black, abrupt outlines of dead branch and charred trunk. Somewhere on the ridge above her, Jenny could hear Gareth calling her name.

She found she was trembling, not solely from weariness or the piercing cold. The need within her was terrifying—to be what she had always wished to be, to have what she had wanted since she had been fourteen, ugly, and cursed with a terrible need. She had tasted the strength of the dragon's fire, and the taste lingered sweet in her mouth.

I can give you this, the voice in her mind said.

She shook her head, more violently this time. *No. I will not betray my friends.*

Friends? Those who would bind you to littleness for their own passing convenience? The man who grudges you the essence of your soul out of mourning for his dinner? Do you cling to all these little joys because you are afraid to taste the great ones, Jenny Waynest?

He had been right when he had said that there is no temptation from outside the heart. She flung back her long hair over her shoulders and called to herself all the strength remaining in her, against the star-prickled darkness that seemed to draw upon the very marrow of her bones.

Get away from me, she told him. *Go now and return to the islands in the northern sea that are your home. Sing your songs to the rock-gold and the whales, and let be forever the sons of men and the sons of gnomes.*

As if she had struck a black log that, breaking, had revealed the living fire smoldering within, she felt the surge of his anger again. He reared back, his body arched against the dimming sky. The dark wire and silk of his wings rattled as he said, *Be it so then, wizard woman. I leave to you the gold of the Deep—take of it what you will. My song is in it. When old age comes, whose mortal frost you have already begun to feel upon your bones, press it to your heart and remember that which you have let pass you by.*

He gathered himself upon his haunches, his compact, snakelike shape rising above her as he gathered about him the glitter of magic in the air. Black wings unfurled against the sky, looming over her so that she could see the obsidian gleam of his sides, the baby-skin softness of the velvet belly, still puckered with the crimped, ugly mouths of harpoon wounds. Then he flung himself skyward. The great stroke of his wings caught him up. She felt the magic that swirled about him, a spindrift of enchantment, the star trail of an invisible comet. The last rays of sinking light tipped his wings as he rose beyond the blue shadow of the ridge. Then he was gone.

Jenny watched him go with desolation in her heart. All the woods seemed laden now with the smell of wet burning, and the murky earthiness of dead smoke. She became slowly aware that the hem of her skirt was sodden from kneeling in the wet path; her boots were damp and her feet cold. Listless weariness dragged upon her, from muscles pulled by exertion and Zyerne's spells and also from the words the dragon had spoken to her when she had turned away from what he had offered.

As a dragon, she would have no more hold upon him, nor would she wish any longer to drive him from the Deep. Was that, she wondered, why he had offered her the splendid and terrifying freedom of that form? They said that dragons did not entrap with lies but with truth, and she knew he had read accurately the desires of her soul.

"Jenny?" A smudged, dirty Gareth came hurrying toward her down the path. To her ears, used to the voice of the dragon, he sounded tinny and false. "Are you all right? What happened? I saw the dragon . . ." He had removed his specs and was seeking a sufficiently clean patch of his sooty, spark-holed shirt to wipe them on, without much success. Against the grime on his face the lenses had left two white circles, like a mask, in which his gray eyes blinked nakedly.

Jenny shook her head. She felt weary to the point of tears, almost incapable of speech. He fell into step with her as she began slowly climbing the path up the Rise once more.

"Did Zyerne get away?"

She looked at him, startled. After what had passed between herself and Morkeleb, she had nearly forgotten Zyerne. "She—she left. I sent her away." It seemed like days ago.

"You *sent her away*?" Gareth gasped, dumfounded.

Jenny nodded, too tired to explain. Thinking about it, she frowned, as something snagged at her mind. But she only asked, "And you?"

He looked away from her and reddened with shame. Part of Jenny sighed in exasperation at this foolishness, so petty after the force of the dragon's greater seduction; but part of her remembered what it was like to be eighteen, and prey to the uncontrollable yearnings of the body. Comfortingly, she touched the skinny arm under the ripped lawn of his shirtsleeve.

"It is a spell she had on you," she said. "Nothing more. We are all tempted . . ." She pushed aside the echoing memory of the dragon's words. ". . . And what is in our deepest hearts is still not what we are judged on, but rather what we ultimately do. She only uses such spells to draw you to her, to control you as she controls your father."

They reached the clearing, soggy and dirty-looking, like a garment upon which acid had been spilled, with charred spots and little puddles of gleaming water which still steamed faintly from the smolder they had quenched.

"I know." Gareth sighed and picked up the bucket from the sodden ground to dip it once more into the well. He moved stiffly from pulled muscles and exertion but didn't complain of them as he once might have done. On the edge of the well trough, he found his tin cup and dipped water from the bucket to hand to her, the wetness icy against her fingers. She realized with a little start that she had neither eaten nor drunk since breakfast. There had been no time, and now she felt old and exhausted as she took the cup from his hand.

"You just sent her away?" Gareth asked again. "And she went? She didn't turn herself into a falcon . . . ?"

"No." Jenny looked up, as it came to her what it was that had bothered her about the events of the evening. "Morkeleb . . ." She stopped, not wanting to speak of what Morkeleb had offered to her.

But even so, she thought, she could not have taken on a dragon's form without his help. His powers had broken through to the powers within her, but her powers were still raw and small. And Zyerne . . .

"I defeated her," she said slowly. "But if she's as shape-crafty as you have said—if she has that kind of strength—I shouldn't have been able to defeat her, even though my powers have grown."

She almost said, "Even with the dragon's powers in me," but the words stuck on her lips. She felt the powers stir in her, like an alien child in the womb of fate, and tried to put aside the thought of them and of what they might mean. She raised the cup to her lips, but stopped, the water untasted, and looked up at Gareth again.

"Have you drunk any of the water from this well?" she asked.

He looked at her in surprise. "We've all been drinking it for days," he said.

"This evening, I mean."

He looked ruefully around at the clearing and his own soaked sleeves. "I was too busy throwing it about to drink any," he said. "Why?"

She passed her hand across the mouth of the cup. As things were visible to a wizard in darkness, she saw the viscid sparkle of green luminosity in the water.

"Has it gone bad?" he asked worriedly. "How can you tell?"

She upended the cup, dumping the contents to the ground. "Where was Zyerne when you came into the clearing?"

He shook his head, puzzled. "I don't remember. It was like a dream . . ." He looked around him, though Jenny knew that the clearing, soggy and trampled in the dismal gloom, was very different from the soft place of twilight enchantment if had appeared an hour or so ago.

At last he said, "I think she was sitting where you are now, on the edge of the wellhead."

Morkeleb had said, *They did not think that I could see the death that tainted the meat.* Was it Dromar who had remarked that dragons were impossible to poison?

She twisted her body and moved her hands across the surface of the bucket that Gareth had drawn up. The reek of death rose from it, and she recoiled in disgust and horror, as if the water had turned to blood beneath her fingers.

13

"**B**ut why?" Squatting before the fire on his hunker-bones, Gareth turned to look at John, who lay in his nest of bearskin blankets and ratty plaids a few feet away. "As far as she was concerned, you'd slain her dragon for her." He unraveled the screw of paper in which they'd brought the coffee up from Bel, decided there wasn't enough to bother with measuring, and dumped it into the pot of water that bubbled over the fire. "She didn't know then that Jenny was any threat to her. Why poison us?"

"At a guess," John said, propping himself with great care up on one elbow and fitting his spectacles to his dirty, unshaven face, "to keep us from riding back to Bel with the news that the dragon was dead before she could get your dad to round up the remaining gnomes on some trumped-up charge. As far as she knew, the dragon was dead—I mean, she couldn't have seen him in a crystal or a water bowl, but she could see us all alive and chipper, and the inference is a pretty obvious one."

"I suppose." Gareth unrolled his turned-up sleeves and slung his cloak around his shoulders once more. The morning was foggy and cold, and the sweat he'd worked up clearing out the well house close to their camp in the ruined tanneries was drying.

"I doubt she'd have poisoned you," John went on. "If she'd wanted you dead, she'd never have waited for you."

Gareth blushed hotly. "That isn't why she waited," he mumbled.

"Of course not," John said. "Dead, you're not only no good to her— if you die, she loses everything."

The boy frowned. "Why? I mean, I can see her wanting me under her power so I'd no longer be a threat to her, the same reason she put Polycarp out of the way. And if she killed the two of you, she'd need me to back up her story about the dragon still being in the Deep, at least until she could get rid of the gnomes." He sniffed bitterly and held out his blistered hands to the fire. "She'd probably use Bond and me as witnesses to say eventually that *she* slew the dragon. Then she'd be able to justify having my father give her the Deep."

He sighed, his mouth tight with disillusionment. "And I thought Polycarp stretching a bit of cable over a fence sounded like the depths of perfidy." He settled the griddle over the fire, his thin face looking much older than it had in the jonquil pallor of the daytime flames.

"Well," John said gently, "it isn't only that, Gar." He glanced over at Jenny, who sat in the shadows of the newly cleared doorway of the well house, but she said nothing. Then he looked back to Gareth. "How long do you think your father's going to last with Zyerne alive? I don't know what her spells are doing to him, and I know a dying man when I see one. As it is, for all her power, she's only a mistress. She needs the Deep for a power base and fortress independent of the King, and she needs the Deep's gold."

"My father would give it to her," Gareth said softly. "And I—I suppose I'm just the contingency plan, in case he should die?" He poked at the softly sizzling cakes on the griddle. "Then she had to destroy Polycarp, whether or not he tried to warn me of her. The Citadel guards the back way into the Deep."

"Well, not even that." John lay back down again and folded his hands on his breast. "She wanted to be rid of Polycarp because he's an alternative heir."

"Alternative to whom?" Gareth asked, puzzled. "To me?"

John shook his head. "Alternative to Zyerne's child."

The horror that crossed the boy's face was deeper than fear of death—deeper, Jenny thought with the strange dispassion that had lain upon her all that morning and through the previous night, than fear of being subjugated to the enchantress's spells. He looked nauseated by the thought, as if at the violation of some dark taboo. It was a long time before he could speak. "You mean—my father's child?"

"Or yours. It would scarcely matter which, as long as it had the family looks." Bandaged hands folded, John looked shortsightedly up at the boy as, half-numbed, Gareth went through the automatic motions of forking griddlecakes from the skillet. Still in that gentle, matter-of-fact voice, he went on, "But you see, after this long under Zyerne's spells, your father may not be capable of fathering a child. And Zyerne needs a child, if she's to go on ruling."

Jenny looked away from them, thinking about what it would be, to be that child. The same wave of sickness Gareth had felt passed over her at the knowledge of what Zyerne would do to any child of hers. She would not feed upon it, as she fed upon the King and Bond; but she would raise it deliberately as an emotional cripple, forever dependent upon her and her love. Jenny had seen it done, by women or by men, and knew what manner of man or woman emerged from that smothered childhood. But even then, the twisting had been from some need of the parent's heart, and not something done merely to keep power.

She thought of her own sons and the absurd love she bore them. She might have abandoned them, she thought with sudden fury at Zyerne, but even had she not loved them, even were they got on her by rape, she would never have done that to them. It was a thing she would have liked to think she herself could scarcely conceive of anyone doing to an innocent child—except that in her heart she knew exactly how it could be done.

Anger and sickness stirred in her, as if she had looked upon torture.

"Jenny?"

Gareth's voice broke her from her thoughts. He stood a few paces from her, looking pleadingly down at her. "He will get better, won't he?" he asked hesitantly. "My father, I mean? When Zyerne is banished, or— or is killed—he will be the way he was before?"

Jenny sighed. "I don't know," she replied in a low voice. She shook her mind free of the lethargy that gripped her, a weariness of the spirit as much as the ache of her body left by the battering of Zyerne's spells. It was not only that she had badly overstretched her own newfound powers, not only that her body was unused to sustaining the terrible demands of the dragon's magic. She was aware now that her very perceptions were changing, that it was not only her magic that had been changed by the touch of the dragon's mind. *The dragon in you answered,* he had said— she was starting to see things as a dragon saw.

She got stiffly to her feet, staggering a little against the shored-up doorpost of the well house, feeling physically drained and very weak. She had watched through the night, telling herself it was for Zyerne that she watched, though in her heart she knew the enchantress would not be back, and it was not, in fact, for her that she waited. She said, "It isn't the spells that she holds him under that are harming him. Zyerne is a vampire, Gareth—not of the blood, like the Whisperers, but of the life-essence itself. In her eyes last night I saw her essence, her soul; a sticky and devouring thing, yes, but a thing that must feed to go on living. Miss Mab told me of the spells of the Places of Healing that can shore up the life of a dying man by taking a little of the life-energy of those who consent to give it. It is done seldom, and only in cases of great need. I am certain this is what she has done to your father and to Bond. What I don't understand is why she would need to. Her powers are such that . . ."

"You know," John broke in, "it says in Dotys' *Histories* . . . or maybe it's in Terens . . . or is it the *Elucidus Lapidarus* . . . ?"

"But what can we *do*?" Gareth pleaded. "There must be something! I could ride back to Bel and let Dromar know it's safe for the gnomes to reoccupy the Deep. It would give them a strong base to . . ."

"No," Jenny said. "Zyerne's hold on the city is too strong. After this, she'll be watching for you, scrying the roads. She'd intercept you long before you came near Bel."

"But we have to do something!" Panic and desperation lurked at bay in his voice. "Where can we go? Polycarp would give us shelter in the Citadel . . ."

"You going to tell the siege troops around the walls you want a private word with him?" John asked, forgetting all about his speculations upon the classics.

"There are ways through the Deep into Halnath."

"And a nice locked door at the end of 'em, I bet, or the tunnels sealed shut with blasting powder to keep the dragon out—even if old Dromar *had* put them on his maps, which he didn't. I had a look for that back in Bel."

"Damn him . . ." Gareth began angrily, and John waved him silent with a mealcake in hand.

"I can't blame him," he said. Against the random browns and heathers of the bloodstained plaid folded beneath his head his face still looked pale but had lost its dreadful chalkiness. Behind his specs, his brown eyes were bright and alert. "He's a canny old bird, and he knows Zyerne. If she didn't know where the ways through to the Citadel hooked up into the main Deep, he wasn't going to have that information down on paper that she could steal. Still, Jen might be able to lead us."

"No." Jenny glanced over at him from where she sat cross-legged beside the fire, dipping the last bite of her griddlecake into the honey. "Even being able to see in darkness, I could not scout them out unaided. As for you going through them, if you try to get up in under a week, I'll put a spell of lameness on you."

"Cheat."

"Watch me." She wiped her fingers on the end of her plaid. "Morkeleb guided me through to the heart of the Deep; I could never have found it, else."

"What was it like?" Gareth asked after a moment. "The heart of the Deep? The gnomes swear by it . . ."

Jenny frowned, remembering the whispering darkness and the soapy feel of the stone altar beneath her fingertips. "I'm not sure," she said softly. "I dreamed about it . . ."

As one, the horses suddenly flung up their heads from the stiff, frosted grass. Battlehammer nickered softly and was answered, thin and clear, from the mists that floated on the fringes of the woods that surrounded Deeping Vale. Hooves struck the stone, and a girl's voice called out, "Gar? Gar, where are you?"

"It's Trey." He raised his voice to shout. "Here!"

There was a frenzied scrambling of sliding gravel, and the whitish mists solidified into the dark shapes of a horse and rider and a fluttering of dampened veils. Gareth strode to the edge of the high ground of the Rise to catch the bridle of Trey's dappled palfrey as it came stumbling up the last slope, head-down with exhaustion and matted with sweat in spite of the day's cold. Trey, clinging to the saddlebow, looked scarcely better off, her faced scratched as if she had ridden into low-hanging branches in the wood and long streamers clawed loose from her purple-and-white coiffure.

"Gar, I knew you had to be all right." She slid from the saddle into his arms. "They said they saw the dragon—that Lady Jenny had put spells upon him—I knew you had to be all right."

"We're fine, Trey," Gareth said doubtfully, frowning at the terror and desperation of the girl's voice. "You look as if you've ridden here without a break."

"I had to!" she gasped. Under the torn rags of her white Court dress, her knees were trembling, and she clung to Gareth's arm for support; her face was colorless beneath what was left of its paint. "They're coming for you! I don't understand what's happening, but you've got to get out of here! Bond . . ." She stumbled on her brother's name.

"What about Bond? Trey, what's going on?"

"I don't know!" she cried. Tears of wretchedness and exhaustion overflowed her eyes, and she wiped them impatiently, leaving faint streaks of blue-black kohl on her round cheeks. "There's a mob on its way, Bond's leading it . . ."

"Bond?" The idea of the lazy and elegant Bond troubling himself to lead anyone anywhere was absurd.

"They're going to kill you, Gar! I heard them say so! You, and Lady Jenny, and Lord John."

"What? Why?" Gareth was growing more and more confused.

"More to the point, who?" John asked, propping himself up among his blankets once again.

"These—these people, laborers mostly—smelters and artisans from Deeping out of work, the ones who hang around the Sheep in the Mire all day. There are Palace guards with them, too, and I think more are coming—I don't know why! I tried to get some sense out of Bond, but it's as if he didn't hear me, didn't know me! He slapped me—and he's never hit me, Gar, not since I was a child . . ."

"Tell us," Jenny said quietly, taking the girl's hand, cold as a dead bird in her warm rough one. "Start from the beginning."

Trey gulped and wiped her eyes again, her hands shaking with weariness and the exertion of a fifteen-mile ride. The ornamental cloak about her shoulders was an indoor garment of white silk and milky fur, designed to ward off the chance drafts of a ballroom, not the bitter chill of a foggy night such as the previous one had been. Her long fingers were chapped and red among their diamonds.

"We'd all been dancing," she began hesitantly. "It was past midnight when Zyerne came in. She looked strange—I thought she'd been sick, but I'd seen her in the morning and she'd been fine then. She called Bond to her, into an alcove by the window. I—" Some color returned to her too-white cheeks. "I crept after them to eavesdrop. I know it's a terribly rude and catty thing to do, but after what we'd talked of before you left I—I couldn't help doing it. It wasn't to learn gossip," she added earnestly. "I was afraid for him—and I was so scared because I'd never done it before and I'm not nearly as good at it as someone like Isolde or Merriwyn would be."

Gareth looked a little shocked at this frankness, but John laughed and patted the toe of the girl's pearl-beaded slipper in commiseration. "We'll forgive you this time, love, but don't neglect your education like that again. You see where it leads you?" Jenny kicked him, not hard, in his unwounded shoulder.

"And then?" she asked.

"I heard her say, 'I must have the Deep. They must be destroyed, and it must be now, before the gnomes hear. They mustn't be allowed to reach it.' I followed them down to that little postern gate that leads to the Dock-market; they went to the Sheep in the Mire. The place was still full of men and women; all drunk and quarreling with each other. Bond went rushing in and told them he'd heard you'd betrayed them, sold them out to Polycarp; that you had the dragon under Lady Jenny's spells and were going to turn it against Bel; that you were going to keep the gold of the Deep for yourselves and not give it to them, its rightful owners. But they weren't *ever* its rightful owners—it always belonged to the gnomes, or to the rich merchants in Deeping. I tried to tell that to Bond . . ." Her cold-reddened hand stole to her cheek, as if to wipe away the memory of a handprint.

"But they were all shouting how they had to kill you and regain their gold. They were all drunk—Zyerne got the innkeeper to broach some more kegs. She said she was going to re-enforce them with the Palace guards. They were yelling and making torches and getting weapons. I ran back to the Palace stables and got Prettyfeet, here . . ." She stroked the exhausted pony's dappled neck, and her voice grew suddenly small. "And then I came here. I rode as fast as I dared—I was afraid of what might happen if they caught me. I'd never been out riding alone at night . . ."

Gareth pulled off his grubby crimson cloak and slung it around her shoulders as her trembling increased.

She concluded, "So you have to get out of here . . ."

"That we do." John flung back the bearskins from over his body. "We can defend the Deep."

"Can you ride that far?" Gareth asked worriedly, handing him his patched, iron-plated leather jerkin.

"I'll be gie in trouble if I can't, my hero."

"Trey?"

The girl looked up from gathering camp things as Jenny spoke her name.

Jenny crossed quietly to where she stood and took her by the shoulders, looking into her eyes for a long moment. The probing went deep, and Trey pulled back with a thin cry of alarm that brought Gareth running. But to the bottom, her mind was a young girl's—not always truthful, anxious to please, eager to love and to be loved. There was no taint on it, and its innocence twisted at Jenny's own heart.

Then Gareth was there, indignantly gathering Trey to him.

Jenny's smile was crooked but kind. "I'm sorry," she said. "I had to be sure."

By their shocked faces she saw that it had not occurred to either of them that Zyerne might have made use of Trey's form—or of Trey.

"Come," she said. "We probably don't have much time. Gar, get John on a horse. Trey, help him."

"I'm perfectly capable . . ." John began, irritated.

But Jenny scarcely heard. Somewhere in the mists of the half-burned woods below the town, she felt sudden movement, the intrusion of angry voices among the frost-rimmed silence of the blackened trees. They were coming and they were coming fast—she could almost see them at the turning of the road below the crumbling ruin of the clock tower.

She turned swiftly back to the others. "Go!" she said. "Quickly, they're almost on us!"

"How . . ." began Gareth.

She caught up her medicine bag and her halberd and vaulted to Moon Horse's bare back. "Now! Gar, take Trey with you. John, RIDE, damn you!" For he had wheeled back, barely able to keep upright in Cow's saddle, to remain at her side. Gareth flung Trey up to Battlehammer's back in a flurry of torn skirts; Jenny could hear the echo of hooves on the trail below.

Her mind reached out, gathering spells together, even the small effort wrenching at her. She set her teeth at the stabbing pain as she gathered the dispersing mists that had been burning off in the sun's pallid brightness— her body was not nearly recovered from yesterday. But there was no time for anything else. She wove the cold and dampness into a cloak to cover all the Vale of Deeping; like a secondary pattern in a plaid, she traced the spells of disorientation, of *jamais vu*. Even as she did so, the hooves and the angry, incoherent voices were very close. They rang in the misty woods around the Rise and near the gatehouse in the Vale as well— Zyerne must have told them where to come. She wheeled Moon Horse and gave her a hard kick in her skinny ribs, and the white mare threw herself down the rocky slope in a gangly sprawl of legs, making for the Gates of the Deep.

She overtook the others in the gauzy boil of the mists in the Vale. They had slowed down as visibility lessened; she led them at a canter over the paths that she knew so well through the town. Curses and shouts, muffled by the fog, came from the Rise behind them. Cold mists shredded past her face and stroked back the black coils of her hair. She could feel the spells that held the brume in place fretting away as she left the Rise behind, but dared not try to put forth the strength of will it would take to hold them after she was gone. Her very bones ached from even the small exertion of summoning them; she knew already that she would need all the strength she could summon for the final battle.

The three horses clattered up the shallow granite steps. From the great darkness of the gate arch, Jenny turned to see the mob still milling about in the thinning fog, some fifty or sixty of them, of all stations and classes but mostly poor laborers. The uniforms of the handful of Palace guards stood out as gaudy splotches in the grayness. She heard their shouts and swearing as they became lost within plain sight of one another in territory they had all known well of old. That won't last long, she thought.

Moon Horse shied and fidgeted at the smell of the dragon and of the old blood within the vast gloom of the Market Hall. The carcass of the horse Osprey had disappeared, but the place still smelled of death, and all the horses felt it. Jenny slid from her mare's tall back and stroked her neck, then whispered to her to stay close to the place in case of need and let her go back down the steps.

Hooves clopped behind her on the charred and broken flagstones. She looked back and saw John, ashen under the stubble of beard, still somehow upright in Cow's saddle. He studied the Vale below them with his usual cool expressionlessness. "Zyerne out there?" he asked, and Jenny shook her head.

"Perhaps I hurt her too badly. Perhaps she's only remaining at the Palace to gather other forces to send against us."

"She always did like her killing to be done by others. How long will your spells hold them?"

"Not long," Jenny said doubtfully. "We have to hold this gate here, John. If they're from Deeping, many of them will know the first levels of the Deep. There are four or five ways out of the Market Hall. If we retreat further in, we'll be flanked."

"Aye." He scratched the side of his nose thoughtfully. "What's wrong with just letting them in? We could hide up somewhere—once they got to the Temple of Sarmendes with all that gold, I doubt they'd waste much energy looking for us."

Jenny hesitated for a moment, then shook her head. "No," she said. "If they were an ordinary mob, I'd say yes, but—Zyerne wants us dead. If she cannot break and overwhelm my mind with her magic, she's not going to give up before she has destroyed my body. There are enough of them that would keep hunting us, and we can't take a horse into the deeper tunnels to carry you; without one, we'd never be able to move swiftly enough to avoid them. We'd be trapped in a cul-de-sac and slaughtered. No, if we're to hold them, it has to be here."

"Right." He nodded. "Can we help you?"

She had returned her attention to the angry snarl of moving figures out in the pale ruins. Over her shoulder, she said, "You can't even help yourself."

"I know *that*," he agreed equably. "But that wasn't my question, love. Look . . ." He pointed. "That bloke there's figured out the way. Here they come. Gaw, they're like ants."

Jenny said nothing, but felt a shiver pass through her as she saw the trickle of attackers widen into a stream.

Gareth came up beside them, leading Battlehammer; Jenny whispered to the big horse and turned him loose down the steps. Her mind was already turning inward upon itself, digging at the strength in the exhausted depths of her spirit and body. John, Gareth, and the slender girl in the white rags of a Court gown, clinging to Gareth's arm, were becoming mere wraiths to her as her soul spiraled down into a single inner vortex, like the single-minded madness that comes before childbearing —nothing else existed but herself, her power, and what she must do.

Her hands pressed to the cold rock of the gate pillar, and she felt that she drew fire and strength from the stone itself and from the mountain beneath her feet and above her head—drew it from the air and the darkness that surrounded her. She felt the magic surge into her veins like a reined whirlwind of compressed lightning. Its power frightened her, for she knew it was greater than her body would bear, yet she could afford no Limitation upon these spells. It was thus, she knew, with dragons, but her body was not a dragon's.

She was aware of John reining Cow sharply back away from her, as if frightened; Gareth and Trey had retreated already. But her mind was out in the pale light of the steps, looking down over Deeping, contemplating in leisurely timelessness the men and women running through the crumbled walls of the ruins. She saw each one of them with the cool exactness of a dragon's eyes, not only how they were dressed, but the composition of their souls through the flesh they wore. Bond she saw distinctly, urging them on with a sword in his hand, his soul eaten through with abcesses like termite-riddled wood.

The forerunners hit the cracked pavement and dust of the square before the gates. Like the chirp of an insect in a wall, she heard Gareth nattering, "What can we do? We have to help her!" as she dispassionately gathered the lightning in her hands.

"Put that down," John's voice said, suddenly weak and bleached. "Get ready to run for it—you can hide in the warrens for a time if they get through. Here's the maps . . ."

The mob was on the steps. Incoherent hate rose around her like a storm tide. Jenny lifted her hands, the whole strength of rock and darkness funneling into her body, her mind relaxing into the shock instead of bracing against it.

The key to magic is magic, she thought. Her life began and ended in each isolate crystal second of impacted time.

The fire went up from the third step, a red wall of it, whole and all-consuming. She heard those trapped in the first rush screaming and smelled smoke, charring meat, and burning cloth. Like a dragon, she killed without hate, striking hard and cruel, knowing that the first strike must kill or her small group would all be dead.

Then she slammed shut before her the illusion of the doors that had long ago been broken from the gateway arch. They appeared like faded glass from within, but every nail and beam and brace of them was wrought perfectly from enchanted air. Through them she saw men and women milling about the base of the steps, pointing up at what they saw as the renewed Gates of the Deep and crying out in wonder and alarm. Others lay on the ground, or crawled helplessly here and there, beating out the flames from their clothes with frenzied hands. Those who had not been trapped in the fire made no move to help them, but stood along the bottom of the step, looking up at the gates and shouting with drunken rage. With the cacophony of the screams and groans of the wounded, the noise was terrible, and worse than the noise was the stench of sizzling flesh. Among it all, Bond Clerlock stood, staring up at the phantom gates with his hunger-eaten eyes.

Jenny stepped back, feeling suddenly sick as the human in her looked upon what the dragon in her had done. She had killed before to protect her own life and the lives of those she loved. But she had never killed on this scale, and the power she wielded shocked her even as it drained her of strength.

The dragon in you answered, Morkeleb had said. She felt sick with horror at how true his knowledge of her had been.

She staggered back, and someone caught her—John and Gareth, looking like a couple of not-very-successful brigands, filthy and battered and incongruous in their spectacles. Trey, with Gareth's tattered cloak still draped over her mud-stained white silks and her purple-and-white hair hanging in asymmetrical coils about her chalky face, wordlessly took a collapsible tin cup from her pearl-beaded reticule, filled it from the water bottle on Cow's saddle, and handed it to her.

John said, "It hasn't stopped them for long." A mist of sweat covered his face, and the nostrils of his long nose were marked by dints of pain from the mere effort of standing. "Look, there's Bond drumming up support for a second go. Silly bleater." He glanced across at Trey and added, "Sorry." She only shook her head.

Jenny freed herself and walked unsteadily to the edge of the shadow gate. Her head throbbed with exhaustion that bordered nausea. The voices of the men and her own voice, when she spoke, sounded flat and unreal. "He'll get it, too."

In the square below the gates, Bond was running here and there among the men, stepping over the charred bodies of the dying, gesticulating and pointing up at the phantom doors. The Palace guards looked uncertain, but the laborers from the Dockmarket were gathered about him, listening and passing wineskins among themselves. They shook their fists up at the Deep, and Jenny remarked, "Like the gnomes, they've had their taste of poverty."

"Yes, but how can they blame us for it?" Gareth objected indignantly. "How can they blame the gnomes? The gnomes were even more victims of it than they."

"Whether or no," John said, leaning against the stone pillar of the Gate, "I bet they're telling themselves the treasures of the Deep are theirs by right. It's what Zyerne will have told 'em, and they obviously believe it enough to kill for them."

"But it's silly!"

"Not as silly as falling in love with a witch, and we've both done that," John replied cheerfully. In spite of her exhaustion, Jenny chuckled. "How long can you hold them, love?"

Something in the sound of his voice made her look back quickly at him. Though he had dismounted from Cow to help her, it was obvious he could not stand alone; his flesh looked gray as ash. Shouting from below drew her attention a moment later; past the smoke still curling from the steps, she could see men forming up into a ragged line, the madness of unreasoning hate in their eyes.

"I don't know," she said softly. "All power must be paid for. Maintaining the illusion of the Gates draws still more of my strength. But it buys us a little time, breaking the thrust of their will if they think they'll have to break them."

"I doubt that lot has the brains to think that far." Still leaning heavily on the pillar, John looked out into the slanted sun of the square outside. "Look, here they come."

"Get back," Jenny said. Her bones hurt with the thought of drawing forth power from them and from the stone and air around her one more time. "I don't know what will happen without Limitations."

"I can't get back, love; if I let go of this wall, I'll fall down."

Through the ghost shape of the Gates, she saw them coming, running across the square toward the steps. The magic came more slowly, dredged and scraped from the seared core of her being—her soul felt bleached by the effort. The voices below rose in a mad crescendo, in which the words "gold" and "kill" were flung up like spars of driftwood on the rage of an incoming wave. She glimpsed Bond Clerlock, or what was left of Bond Clerlock, somewhere in their midst, his Court suit pink as a shell among the blood-and-buttercup hues of the Palace guards. Her mind locked into focus, like a dragon's mind; all things were clear to her and distant, impersonal as images in a divining crystal. She called the white dragon rage like a thunderclap and smote the steps with fire, not before them now, but beneath their feet.

As the fire exploded from the bare stone, a wave of sickness consumed her, as if in that second all her veins had been opened. The shrieking of men, caught in the agony of the fire, struck her ears like a slapping hand, as grayness threatened to drown her senses and heat rose through her, then sank away, leaving behind it a cold like death.

She saw them reeling and staggering, ripping flaming garments from charred flesh. Tears of grief and weakness ran down her face at what she had done, though she knew that the mob would have torn the four of them apart and had known, that time, that she could summon fire. The illusion of the Gates felt as tenuous as a soap-bubble around her—like her own body, light and drifting. John stumbled to catch her as she swayed and pulled her back to the pillar against which he had stood; for a moment they both held to it, neither strong enough to stand.

Her eyes cleared a little. She saw men running about the square in panic, rage, and pain; and Bond, oblivious to burns which covered his hand and arm, was chasing after them, shouting.

"What do we do now, love?"

She shook her head. "I don't know," she whispered. "I feel as if I'm going to faint."

His arm tightened around her waist. "Oh, do," he encouraged enthusiastically. "I've always wanted to carry you to safety in my arms."

Her laughter revived her, as he had no doubt meant it to. She pushed herself clear of his support as Gareth and Trey came up, both looking ill and frightened.

"Could we run for it through the Deep?" Gareth asked, fumbling the maps from an inner pocket and dropping two of them. "To the Citadel, I mean?"

"No," Jenny said. "I told John—if we left the Market Hall, they'd flank us; and carrying John, we couldn't outdistance them."

"I could stay here, love," John said quietly. "I could buy you time."

Sarcastically, she replied, "The time it would take them to pick themselves up after tripping over your body in the archway would scarcely suffice."

"*One* of us could try to get through," Trey suggested timidly. "Polycarp and the gnomes at the Citadel would know the way through from that side. They could come for the rest of you. I have some candles in my reticule, and some chalk to mark the way, and I'm no good to you here . . ."

"No," Gareth objected, valiantly fighting his terror of the dark warrens. "I'll go."

"You'd never find it," Jenny said. "I've been down in the Deep, Gareth, and believe me, it is not something that can be reasoned out with chalk and candles. And, as John has said, the door at the end will be locked in any case, even if they didn't blast it shut."

Down below them, Bond's voice could be heard dimly, shouting that the Gate wasn't real, that it was just a witch's trick, and that all the gold that had been lost was theirs by right. People were yelling, "Death to the thieves! Death to the gnome-lovers!" Jenny leaned her head against the stone of the pillar, a bar of sunlight falling through the Gate around her and lying like a pale carpet on the fire-black rubble of the Market Hall. She wondered if Zyerne had ever felt like this, when she had called upon the deep reserves of her powers, without Limitations—helpless before the anger of men.

She doubted it. It did something to you to be helpless.

All power must be paid for. Zyerne had never paid.

She wondered, just for a moment, how the enchantress had managed that.

"What's that?"

At the sound of Trey's voice, she opened her eyes again and looked out to where the girl was pointing. The light filling the Vale glinted harshly on something up near the ruined clock tower. Listening, she could pick out the sound of hooves and voices and feel the distant clamor of anger and unthinking hate. Against the dull slate color of the tower's stones, the weeds of the hillside looked pale as yellow wine; between them the uniforms of half a company of Palace guards glowed like a tumble of hothouse poppies. The sun threw fire upon their weapons.

"Gaw," John said. "Reinforcements."

Bond and a small group of men were running up through the rubble and sedge toward the new company, flies swarming thick on the young courtier's untended wounds. Small with distance, Jenny saw more and more men under the shadow of the tower, the brass of pike and cuirass flashing, the red of helmet crests like spilled blood against the muted hues of the stone. Exhaustion ate like poison into her bones. Her skin felt like a single open, throbbing wound; through it, she could feel the illusion of the Gate fading to nothingness as her power drained and died.

She said quietly, "You three get back to the doors into the Grand Passage. Gar, Trey—carry John. Bolt the doors from the inside—there are winches and pulleys there."

"Don't be stupid." John was clinging to the gatepost beside her to stay upright.

"Don't *you* be stupid." She would not take her eyes from the swarming men in the square below.

"We're not leaving you," Gareth stated. "At least, I'm not. Trey, you take John . . ."

"No," Trey and the Dragonsbane insisted in approximate unison. They looked at one another and managed the ghost of a mutual grin.

"It's all of us or none of us, love."

She swung around on them, her eyes blazing palely with the crystalline coldness of the dragon's eyes. "None of you can be of the slightest use to me here against so many. John and Trey, all you'll be is killed immediately. Gareth . . ." Her eyes pinned his like a lance of frost. "You may not be. They may have other instructions concerning you, from Zyerne. I may have the strength for one more spell. That can buy you some time. John's wits may keep you alive for a while more in the Deep; you'll need Trey's willingness as well. Now go."

There was a short silence, in which she could feel John's eyes upon her face. She was conscious of the men approaching in the Vale; her soul screamed at her to get rid of these three whom she loved while there was yet time.

It was Gareth who spoke. "Will you really be able to hold the Gate against another charge? Even of—of my father's men?"

"I think so," Jenny lied, knowing she hadn't the strength left to light a candle.

"Aye, then, love," said John softly. "We'd best go." He took her halberd to use as a crutch; holding himself upright with it, he put a hand on her nape and kissed her. His mouth felt cold against hers, his lips soft even through the hard scratchiness of five days' beard. As their lips parted, their eyes met, and, through the dragon armor of hardness, she saw he knew she'd lied.

"Let's go, children," he said. "We won't shoot the bolts till we have to, Jen."

The line of soldiers was descending through the labyrinth of shattered foundations and charred stone. They were joined by the men and women of Deeping, those, Jenny noted, who had thrown garbage at Miss Mab in the fountain square of Bel. Makeshift weapons jostled pikes and swords. In the brilliance of daylight everything seemed hard and sharp. Every house beam and brick stood out to Jenny's raw perceptions like filigree work, every tangle of weed and stand of grass clear and individuated. The amber air held the stench of sulfur and burned flesh. Like a dim background to angry ranting and exhortation rose the keening of the wounded and, now and again, voices crying, "Gold . . . gold . . ."

They scarcely even know what it is for, Morkeleb had said.

Jenny thought about Ian and Adric, and wondered briefly who would raise them, or if, without her and John's protection of the Winterlands, they would live to grow up at all. Then she sighed and stepped forth from the shadows into the light. The pale sun drenched her, a small, skinny, black-haired woman alone in the vast arch of the shattered Gate. Men pointed, shouting. A rock clattered against the steps, yards away. The sunlight felt warm and pleasant upon her face.

Bond was screaming hysterically, "Attack! Attack now! Kill the witch-bitch! It's our gold! We'll get the slut this time—get her . . ."

Men began to run forward up the steps. She watched them coming with a curious feeling of absolute detachment. The fires of dragon-magic had drained her utterly—one last trap, she thought ironically, from Morkeleb, a final vengeance for humiliating him. The mob curled like a breaking wave over the ruined beams and panels of the shattered gates, the sunlight flashing on the steel of the weapons in their hands.

Then a shadow crossed the sunlight—like a hawk's, but immeasurably more huge.

One man looked up, pointed at the sky, and screamed.

Again the sunlight was darkened by circling shade. Jenny raised her head. The aureate light streamed translucently through the black spread of bones and the dark veins of sable wings, sparkled from the spikes that tipped the seventy-foot span of that silent silk, and gilded every horn and ribbon of the gleaming mane.

She watched the dragon circling, riding the thermals like a vast eagle, only peripherally conscious of the terrified shouting of the men and the frenzied squeals of the guards' horses. Yelling and crashing in the rubble, the attackers of the Deep turned and fled, trampling upon their dead and dropping their weapons in their headlong flight.

The Vale was quite empty by the time Morkeleb lighted upon the heat-cracked steps of the Deep.

14

Why did you return?

The sun had set. Echoes of its brightness lingered on the cinnamon edges of the cliff above. After the firelight and blackness of the Market Hall, where Gareth and Trey could be heard talking softly beside the small blaze they had kindled, the windy coolness of the steps was deeply refreshing. Jenny ran tired hands through her hair, the cold of her fingers welcome against her aching skull.

The great, gleaming black shape that lay like a sphinx along the top step turned its head. In the reflected glow from the fire in the hall she saw the long edges of that birdlike skull, the turn and flutter of the ribboned mane and the glint of the bobs of jet that quivered on long antennae.

His voice was soft in her mind. *I need your help, wizard woman.*

What? It was the last thing she would have expected from the dragon. She wondered illogically if she had heard rightly, though with dragons there was never a question of that. *My HELP? MY help?*

Bitter anger curled from the dragon like an acrid smoke, anger at having to ask the help of any human, anger at needing help, anger at admitting it, even to himself. But in the close-shielded mind, she felt other things—exhaustion approaching her own and the chill thread of fear.

By my name you drove me forth from this place, he said. *But something else, something beyond my name, draws me back.* Like a jewel, one jet-bobbed antenna flicked in the wind. *Like the discontented dreams that first brought me to this place, it will not let me rest; it is a yearning like the craving for gold, but worse. It tormented me as I flew north, mounting to pain, and the only ease I had was when I turned south again. Now all the torments of my soul and my dreams center upon this mountain. Before you entered my mind, it was not so—I came and went as I pleased, and naught but my own desire for the gold made me return. But this pain, this longing of the heart, is something I never felt before, in all my years; it is something I never knew of, until your healing touched me. It is not of you, for you commanded me to go. It is a magic that I do not understand, unlike the magic of dragons. It gives me no rest, no peace. I think of this place constantly, though, by my name, wizard woman, it is against my will that I return.*

He shifted upon his haunches, so that he lay as a cat will sometimes lie, his forelimbs and shoulders sphinx-like, but his hinder legs stretched out along the uppermost step. The spiked club of his tail lashed slightly at its clawed tip.

It is not the gold, he said. *Gold calls to me, but never with a madness like this. It is alien to my understanding, as if the soul were being rooted from me. I hate this place, for it is a place of defeat and disgrace to me now, but the craving to be here consumes me. I have never felt this before and I do not know what it is. Has it come from you, wizard woman? Do you know what is it?*

Jenny was silent for a time. Her strength was slowly returning, and she felt already less weak and brittle than she had. Sitting on the steps between the dragon's claws, his head rose above hers, the thin, satiny ribbons of his mane brushing against her face. Now he cocked his head down; looking up, she met one crystalline silver eye.

She said, *It is a longing such as humans feel. I do not know why it should possess you, Morkeleb—but I think it is time that we found out. You are not the only one drawn to the Deep as if possessed. Like you, I do not think it is the gold. There is something within the Deep. I sense it, feel it within my bones.*

The dragon shook his great head. *I know the Deep*, he said. *It was my hold and dominion. I know every dropped coin and every soda-straw crystal; I heard the tread of every foot passing in the Citadel overhead and the slipping of the blind white fish through the waters deep below. I tell you, there is nothing in the Deep but water, stone, and the gold of the gnomes, sleeping in the darkness. There is nothing there that should draw me so.*

Perhaps, Jenny said. Then, aloud, she called into the echoing cavern behind her, "Gareth? John? Trey?"

The dragon lifted his head with indignation as soft footfalls scuffled within. Like speech without words, Jenny felt the sharp flash of his pride and his annoyance at her for bringing other humans into their counsels and she longed to slap his nose as she slapped her cat's when he tried to steal food from her fingers.

He must have felt the returning glint of her exasperation, for he subsided, his narrow chin sinking to rest upon the long-boned hooks of one black foreclaw. Beyond the spears of his backbone she saw the great tail lash.

The others came out, Gareth and Trey supporting John between them. He had slept a little and rested and looked better than he had. The spells of healing she had laid upon him were having their effect. He gazed up at the dark shape of the dragon, and Jenny felt their eyes meet and knew that Morkeleb spoke to him, thought she heard not what he said.

John replied in words. "Well, it was just as well, wasn't it? Thank you."

Their eyes held for a moment more. Then the dragon raised his head and turned it away irritably, transferring his cold silver gaze to Gareth. Jenny saw the young man flush with shame and confusion; whatever the dragon said to him, he made no reply at all.

They laid John down with his back to the granite door pillar, his plaid folded beneath his shoulders. His spectacles caught the starlight, rather like the silvery glow of the dragon's eyes. Jenny seated herself on the steps between him and the dragon's talons; Gareth and Trey, as if for mutual protection, sat opposite and close together, staring up in wonder at the thin, serpentine form of the Black Dragon of Nast Wall.

In time, Jenny's flawed, silver-shot voice broke the silence. "What is in the Deep?" she asked. "What is it that Zyerne wants so badly there? All her actions have been aimed toward having it—her hold over the King, her attempts to seduce Gareth, her desire for a child, the siege of Halnath, and the summoning of the dragon."

She did not summon me, retorted Morkeleb angrily. *She could not have done that. She has no hold upon my mind.*

"You're here, ain't you?" John drawled, and the dragon's metallic claws scraped upon the stone as his head swung round.

Jenny said sharply, "John! Morkeleb!"

The dragon subsided with a faint hiss, but the bobs of his antennae twitched with annoyance.

She went on, "Might it be that she is herself summoned?"

I tell you there is nothing there, the dragon said. *Nothing save stone and gold, water and darkness.*

"Let's back up a bit, then," John said. "Not what does Zyerne want in the Deep, but just what does she want?"

Gareth shrugged. "It can't be gold. You've seen how she lives. She could have all the gold in the Realm for the asking. She has the King . . ." He hesitated, and then went on calmly, "If I hadn't left for the north when I did, she would certainly have had me, and very probably a son to rule through for the rest of her life."

"She used to live in the Deep," Trey pointed out. "It seems that, ever since she left it, she's been trying to get control of it. Why did she leave? Did the gnomes expel her?"

"Not really," Gareth said. "That is, they didn't formally forbid her to enter the Deep at all until this year. Up until then she could come and go in the upper levels, just like any other person from Bel."

"Well if she's shapestrong, that's to say she had the run of the place, so long as she stayed clear of the mageborn," John reasoned, propping his specs with one forefinger. "And what happened a year ago?"

"I don't know," Gareth said. "Dromar petitioned my father in the name of the Lord of the Deep not to let her—or any of the children of men, for that matter . . ."

"Again, that's a logical precaution against a shape-shifter."

"Maybe." Gareth shrugged. "I didn't think of it then—a lot of the unpopularity of the gnomes started then, because of that stipulation. But they said Zyerne specifically, because she had . . ." He fished in his compendious, ballad-trained memory for the exact wording. ". . . 'defiled a holy thing.' "

"No idea what it was?"

The prince shook his head. Like John, he looked drawn and tired, his shirt a fluttering ruin of dirt and spark holes, his face sparkling faintly with an almost-invisible adolescent stubble. Trey, sitting beside him, looked little better. With her typical practicality, she had carried a comb in her reticule and had combed out her hair, so that it hung past her hips in crinkled swaths, the smooth sheen of its fantastic colors softened to a stippling of snow white and violet, like the pelt of some fabulous beast against the matted nap of Gareth's cloak.

"Defiled a holy *thing*." Jenny repeated thoughtfully. "It isn't how Mab put it. She said that she had poisoned the heart of the Deep—but the heart of the Deep is a place, rather than an object."

"Is it?" said John curiously.

"Of course. I've been there." The silence of it whispered along her memory. "But as for what Zyerne wants . . ."

"You're a witch, Jen," said John. "What do you want?"

Gareth looked shocked at the comparison, but Jenny only thought for a moment, then said, "Power. Magic. The key to magic is magic. My greatest desire, to which I would sacrifice all things else, is to increase my skills."

"But she's already the strongest sorceress in the land," Trey protested.

"Not according to Mab."

"I suppose there were gnome wizards in the Deep stronger," John said interestedly. "If there hadn't been, she wouldn't have been needed to summon Morkeleb."

She did not summon me! The dragon's tail lashed again, like a great cat's. *She could not. Her power is not that great.*

"Somebody's is," John remarked. "Before you wiped out the Deep and the mages in it, the gnomes were strong enough to keep Zyerne out. But they all perished, or at least all the strong ones did . . ."

"No," Jenny said. "That's what has puzzled me. Mab said that she herself was stronger than Zyerne at some time in the past. That means that either Mab grew weaker, or Zyerne stronger."

"Could Mab's power have been weakened in some way when Morkeleb showed up?" John glanced up at the dragon. "Would that be possible? That your magic would lessen someone else's?"

I know nothing of the magic of humans, nor yet of the magic of gnomes, the dragon replied. *Yet among us, there is no taking away of another's magic. It is like taking away another's thoughts from him, and leaving him with none.*

"That's another thing," Jenny said, folding her arms about her drawn-up knees. "When I met Zyerne yesterday . . . My powers have grown, but I should not have been able to defeat her as I did. She is shapestrong—she should have far more strength than I did." She glanced over at Gareth. "But she didn't shift shape."

"But she can," the boy protested. "I've *seen* her."

"Lately?" asked John suddenly.

Gareth and Trey looked at one another.

"Since the coming of the dragon? Or, to put it another way, since she hasn't been able to enter the Deep?"

"But either way, it's inconceivable," Jenny insisted. "Power isn't something that's contingent upon any place or thing, any more than knowledge is. Zyerne's power couldn't have weakened any more than Mab's could. Power is within you—here, or in Bel, or in the Winterlands, or wherever you are. It is something you learn, something you develop. All power must be paid for . . ."

"Except that it's never looked as if Zyerne had paid for hers," John said. His glance went from Jenny to the dragon and back. "You said the magic of the gnomes is different. Is there a way she could have stolen power, Jen? That she could be using something she's no right to? I'm thinking how you said she doesn't know about Limitations—obviously, since she summoned a dragon she can't get rid of . . ."

She did not summon me!

"She seems to think she did," John pointed out. "At least she's kept saying how she was the one who kicked the gnomes out of the Deep. But mostly I'm thinking about the wrinkles on her face."

"But she doesn't have any wrinkles," Trey objected, disconcerted at this lightning change of topic.

"Exactly. Why doesn't she? Every mage I've known—Mab, who isn't that old as gnomes go, old Caerdinn, that crazy little wander-mage who used to come through the Winterlands, and you, Jen—the marks of power are printed on their faces. Though it hasn't aged you," he added quickly, with a concern for her vanity that made Jenny smile.

"You are right," she said slowly. "Now that you speak of it, I don't think I've ever encountered a mage that—that sweet-looking. Maybe that's what first troubled me. And Mab said something about Zyerne stealing secrets. Zyerne herself said that when she is able to get into the Deep, she'll have the power to destroy us all." She frowned, some other thought tugging at her mind. "But it doesn't make sense. If you think she could have gained her powers by studying arts possessed by the gnomes—by breaking into and reading the books of their deeper magic—you're wrong. I searched through the Places of Healing in quest of just such books, and found none."

"That's a bit odd in itself, isn't it?" John mused. "But when you said power isn't contingent on any thing, any more than knowledge is—knowledge can be stored in a book. Is there any way power can be stored? *Can* a mage use another mage's power?"

Jenny shrugged. "Oh, yes. Power can be accumulated by breadth as well as by depth; several mages can focus their power together and direct it toward a single spell that lies beyond their separate strengths. It can be done by chanting, meditating, dancing . . ." She broke off, as the vision rose once more to her mind—the vision of the heart of the Deep. "Dancing . . ." she repeated softly, then shook her head. "But in any case, the power is controlled by those who raise it."

"Is it?" asked John. "Because in Polyborus it says . . ."

Morkeleb cut him off. *But if she were forbidden the Deep, Zyerne could have been nowhere near it when the power was raised that sent this yearning unto me and called me back. Nor, indeed, could she have been near the Deep to conjure the dreams that first brought me here. And no other mages would have combined to raise that power.*

"That's what I'm trying to tell you!" John broke in. "In Dotys—or Polyborus' *Analects*—or maybe it's the *Elucidus Lapidarus* . . ."

"What?" demanded Jenny, well aware that John was perfectly capable of fishing for the source of reference for ten minutes in the jackdaw-nest of his memory.

"Dotys—or Polyborus—says that it used to be rumored that mages

could use a certain type of stone for a power-sink. They could call power
into it, generation after generation, sometimes, or they could combine—
and I think he mentioned dancing—and when they needed great power,
for the defense of their realm or defeat of a dragon or a really powerful
devil, they could call power out of it."

They looked at one another in silence—witch and prince, maiden and
warrior and dragon.

John went on, "I think what the gnomes were guarding—what lies in
the heart of the Deep—is a power sink."

"The Stone," Jenny said, knowing it for truth. "They swear 'by the
Stone' or 'by the Stone in the heart of the Deep.' Even Zyerne does. In my
vision, they were dancing around it."

John's voice was soft in the velvety darkness. "And in that case, all
Zyerne would have needed to steal was the key to unlock it. If she was
apprenticed in the Places of Healing near there, that wouldn't have been
hard."

"If she's mentally in contact with it, she could use it somewhat, even
at a distance," Jenny said. "I felt it, when I struggled with her—some
power I have never felt. Not living, like Morkeleb—but strong because it
is dead and does not care what it does. It must be the source of all her
strength, for shapechanging and for the curse she sent to the gnomes, the
curse that brought you here from the north, Morkeleb."

"A curse that's still holding good whether she wants it to or not."
John's spectacles flashed in the starlight as he grinned. "But she must not
be able to wield it accurately at a distance, even as Miss Mab can't use it
against her. It would explain why she's so wild not to let them get even a
chance of going back."

So what then? demanded Morkeleb grimly. *Did your estimable
Dotys, your wise Polyborus, speak of a way to combat the magic of these
stones?*

"Well," John said, a faint grin of genuine amusement touching the
corners of his mouth, "that was the whole point of my coming south, you
see. My copy of the *Elucidus Lapidarus* isn't complete. Almost nothing
in my library is. It's why I agreed to become a Dragonsbane for the
King's hire in the first place—because we need books, we need knowledge. I'm as much a scholar as I can be, but it isn't easy."

With the size of a human brain, it would not be! Morkeleb snapped,
irrationally losing his temper. *You are no more scholar than you are
Dragonsbane!*

"But I never claimed to be," John protested. "It's just there's all these
ballads, see . . ."

The jet claws rattled again on the pavement. Jenny, exasperated with them both, began, "I really am going to let him eat you this time . . ."

Trey put in hastily, "Could you use the Stone yourself, Lady Jenny? Use it against Zyerne?"

"Of course!" Gareth bounced like a schoolboy on the hard step. "That's it! Fight fire with fire."

Jenny was silent. She felt their eyes upon her—Trey's, Gareth's, John's, the crystal gaze of the dragon turned down at her from above. The thought of the power stirred in her mind like lust—Zyerne's power. The key to magic is magic . . .

She saw the worry in John's eyes and knew what her own expression must look like. It sobered her. "What are you thinking?"

He shook his head. "I don't know, love."

He meant that he would not stand in the way of any decision she made. Correctly interpreting his look, she said gently, "I would not misuse the power, John. I would not become like Zyerne."

His voice was pitched to her ears alone. "Can you know that?"

She started to reply, then stilled herself. Shrill and clear she heard Miss Mab's voice saying, *She took the secrets of those greater than she, defiled them, tainted them, poisoned the very heart of the Deep* . . . She remembered, too, that sense of perverted power that had sparkled in the lamplight around Zyerne and the luckless Bond, and how the touch of the dragon's mind had changed her.

"No," she said at last. "I cannot know. And it would be stupid of me to meddle with something so powerful without knowing its dangers, even if I could figure out the key by myself."

"But," Gareth protested, "it's our only chance of defeating Zyerne! They'll be back—you know they will! We can't stay holed up here forever."

"Could we learn enough about the Stone for you to circumvent its powers somehow?" Trey suggested. "Would there be a copy of the Whatsus Howeverus you talked about in the Palace library?"

Gareth shrugged. His scholarship might extend to seven minor variants of the ballad of the Warlady and the Red Worm of Weldervale, but it was a broken reed insofar as obscure encyclopedists went.

"There would be one at Halnath, though, wouldn't there?" Jenny said. "And if it didn't contain the information, there are gnomes there who might know."

"If they'd tell." John propped himself gingerly a little higher against the granite of the gate pillar, the few portions of his shirt not darkened with bloodstains very white in the rising moonlight against the metallic glints of his doublet. "Dromar's lot wouldn't even admit it existed. They've had enough of humans controlling the Stone, and I can't say as I blame them. But whatever happens," he added, as the others subsided from their enthusiasm into dismal reflection once more, "our next move had better be to get out of here. As our hero says, you know Bond and the King's troops will be back. The only place we *can* go is Halnath, and maybe not there. How tight are the siege lines, Gar?"

"Tight," Gareth said gloomily. "Halnath is built on a series of cliffs— the lower town, the upper town, the University, and the Citadel above that, and the only way in is through the lower town. Spies have tried to sneak in over the cliffs on the mountain side of the city and have fallen to their deaths." He readjusted his cracked spectacles. "And besides," he went on, "Zyerne knows as well as we do that Halnath is the only place we can go."

"Pox." John glanced over at Jenny, where she sat against the alien curves of the dragon's complicated shoulder bones. "For something that was never any of our business to begin with, this is looking worse and worse."

"I could go," Trey ventured. "The troops would be least likely to recognize me. I could tell Polycarp . . ."

"They'd never let you through," John said. "Don't think Zyerne doesn't know you're here, Trey; and don't think she'd let you off because you're Bond's sister or that Bond would risk Zyerne so much as pouting at him to get you off. Zyerne can't afford even one of us returning to the gnomes with word the dragon's left the Deep."

That, Morkeleb said thinly, *is precisely our problem. The dragon has NOT left the Deep. Nor will he, until this Zyerne is destroyed. And I will not remain here docile, to watch the gnomes carrying on their petty trafficking with my gold.*

"*Your* gold?" John raised an eyebrow. With a swift gesture of her mind Jenny stilled Morkeleb again.

Nor would they allow it, she said, *for the dragon alone. It would only be a matter of time until their distrust of you mastered them, and they tried to slay you. No—you must be freed.*

Freed! The voice within her mind was acrid as the stench of vinegar. *Freed to be turned like a beggar onto the roads?* The dragon swung his head away, the long scales of his mane clashing softly, like the searingly thin notes of a wind chime. *You have done this to me, wizard woman! Before your mind touched mine I was not bound to this place . . .*

"You were bound," Aversin said quietly. "It's just that, before Jenny's mind touched yours, you weren't aware of it. Had you tried to leave before?"

I remained because it was my will to remain.

"And it's the old King's will to remain with Zyerne, though she's killing him. No, Morkeleb—she got you through your greed, as she got poor Gar's dad through his grief and Bond through his love. If we hadn't come, you'd have stayed here, bound with spells to brood over your hoard till you died. It's just that now you know it."

That is not true!

True or not, Jenny said, *it is my bidding, Morkeleb, that as soon as the sky grows light, you shall carry me over the mountain to the Citadel of Halnath, so that I can send Polycarp the Master to bring these others to safety there through the Deep.*

The dragon reared himself up, bristling all over with rage. His voice lashed her mind like a silver whip. *I am not your pigeon nor your servant!*

Jenny was on her feet now, too, looking up into the blazing white deeps of his eyes. No, she said, holding to the crystal chain of his inner name. *You are my slave, by that which you gave me when I saved your life. And by that which you gave me, I tell you this is what you shall do.*

Their eyes held. The others, not hearing what passed between their two minds, saw and felt only the dragon's scorching wrath. Gareth caught up Trey and drew her back toward the shelter of the gateway; Aversin made a move to rise and sank back with a gasp. He angrily shook off Gareth's attempt to draw him to safety, his eyes never leaving the small, thin form of the woman who stood before the smoking rage of the beast.

All this Jenny was aware of, but peripherally, like the weave of a tapestry upon which other colors are painted. Her whole mind focused in crystal exactness against the mind that surged like a dark wave against hers. The power born in her from the touch of the dragon's mind strengthened and burned, forcing him back. Her understanding of his name was a many-pointed weapon in her hands. In time Morkeleb sank to his haunches again, and back to his sphinx position.

In her mind his voice said softly, *You know you do not need me, Jenny Waynest, to fly over the mountains. You know the form of the dragons and their magic. One of them you have put on already.*

The other I might put on, she replied, *for you would help me in that, to be free of my will. But you would not help me put it off again.*

The deeps of his eyes were like falling into the heart of a star. *If you wished it, I would.*

The need in her for power, to separate herself from all that had separated her from its pursuit, shuddered through her like the racking heat of fever. "To be a mage you must be a mage," Caerdinn had said.

He had also said, "Dragons do not deceive with lies, but with truth." Jenny turned her eyes from those cosmic depths. *You say it only because in becoming a dragon, I will cease to want to hold power over you, Morkeleb the Black.*

He replied, *Not 'only,' Jenny Waynest.*

Like a wraith he faded into the darkness.

Though still exhausted from the battle at the Gates, Jenny did not sleep that night. She sat upon the steps, as she had sat awake most of the night before, watching and listening—for the King's men, she told herself, though she knew they would not come. She was aware of the night with a physical intensity, the moonlight like a rime of molten silver on every chink and crack of the scarred steps upon which she sat, turning to slips of white each knotted weed-stem in the scuffed dust of the square below. Earlier, while she had been tending to John by the fire in the Market Hall, the bodies of the slain rioters had vanished from the steps, though whether this was due to fastidiousness on Morkeleb's part or hunger, she wasn't sure.

Sitting in the cold stillness of the night, she meditated, seeking an answer within herself. But her own soul was unclear, torn between the great magic that had always lain beyond her grasp and the small joys she had cherished in its stead—the silence of the house on Frost Fell, the memory of small hands that seemed to be printed on her palms, and John.

John, she thought, and looked back through the wide arch of the Gate to where he lay, wrapped in bearskins beside the small glow of the fire.

In the darkness she made out his shape, the broad-shouldered compactness that went so oddly with the whippet litheness of his movements. She remembered the fears that had driven her to the Deep to seek medicines—that had driven her first to look into the dragon's silver eyes. Now, as then, she could scarcely contemplate years of her life that did not—or would not—include that fleeting, triangular smile.

Adric had it already, along with the blithe and sunny half of John's quirky personality. Ian had his sensitivity, his maddening, insatiable curiosity, and his intentness. His sons, she thought. My sons.

Yet the memory of the power she had called to stop the lynch mob on these very steps returned to her, sweetness and terror and exultation. Its results had horrified her, and the weariness of it still clung to her bones, but the taste that lingered was one of triumph at having wielded it. How could she, she wondered, have wasted all those years before this beginning? The touch of Morkeleb's mind had half-opened a thousand doors within her. If she turned away from him now, how many of the rooms behind those doors would she be able to explore? The promise of the magic was something only a mageborn could have felt; the need, like lust or hunger, something only the mageborn would have understood. There was a magic she had never dreamed of that could be wrought from the light of certain stars, knowledge unplumbed in the dark, eternal minds of dragons and in the singing of the whales in the sea. The stone house on the Fell that she loved came back to her like the memory of a narrow prison; the clutch of small hands on her skirts, of an infant's mouth at her breast, seemed for a time nothing more than bonds holding her back from walking through its doors to the moving air outside.

Was this some spell of Morkeleb's? she wondered, wrapping the soft weight of a bearskin more tightly around her shoulders and gazing at the royal blue darkness of the sky above the western ridge. Was it something he had sung up out of the depths of her soul, so that she would leave the concerns of humans and free him of his bondage to her?

Why did you say, "Not" 'only,' " Morkeleb the Black?

You know that as well as I, Jenny Waynest.

He had been invisible in the darkness. Now the moonlight sprinkling his back was like a carpet of diamonds and his silver eyes were like small, half-shut moons. How long he had been there she did not know—the moon had sunk, the stars moved. His coming had been like the floating of a feather on the still night.

What you give to them you have taken from yourself. When our minds were within one another, I saw the struggle that has tortured you all your life. I do not understand the souls of humans, but they have a brightness to them, like soft gold. You are strong and beautiful, Jenny Waynest. I would like it if you would become one of us and live among us in the rock islands of the northern seas.

She shook her head. *I will not turn against those that I love.*

Turn against? The sinking moonlight striped his mane with frost as he moved his head. *No. That I know you would never do, though, for what their love has done to you, they would well deserve it if you did. And as to this love you speak of, I do not know what it is—it is not a thing of dragons. But when I am freed of the spells that bind me here, when I fly to the north again, fly with me. This is something also that I have never felt— this wanting of you to be a dragon that you can be with me. And tell me, what is it to you if this boy Gareth becomes the slave of his father's woman or to one of his own choosing? What is it to you who rules the Deep, or how long this woman Zyerne can go on polluting her mind and her body until she dies because she no longer recalls enough about her own magic to continue living? What is it to you if the Winterlands are ruled and defended by one set of men or another, or if they have books to read about the deeds of yet a third? It is nothing, Jenny Waynest. Your powers are beyond that.*

To leave them now would be to turn against them. They need me.

They do not need you, the dragon replied. *Had the King's troops killed you upon these steps, it would have been the same for them.*

Jenny looked up at him, that dark shape of power—infinitely more vast than the dragon John had slain in Wyr and infinitely more beautiful. The singing of his soul reechoed in her heart, magnified by the beauty of the gold. Clinging to the daylight that she knew against the calling of the dark, she shook her head again and said, *It would not have been the same.*

She gathered the furs about her, rose, and went back into the Deep.

After the sharpness of the night air, the huge cavern felt stuffy and stank of smoke. The dying fire threw weird flickers of amber against the ivory labyrinth of inverted turrets above and glinted faintly on the ends of the broken lamp chains that hung down from the vaulted blackness. It was always so, going from free night air to the frowsty stillness of indoors, but her heart ached suddenly, as if she had given up free air for a prison forever.

She folded the bearskin, laid it by the campfire, and found where her halberd had been leaned against the few packs they had brought with them from the camp. Somewhere in the darkness, she heard movement, the sound of someone tripping over a plaid. A moment later Gareth's voice said softly, "Jenny?"

"Over here." She straightened up, her pale face and the metal buckles of her sheepskin jacket catching the low firelight. Gareth looked tired and bedraggled in his shirt, breeches, and a stained and scruffy plaid, as unlike as possible to the self-conscious young dandy in primrose-and-white Court mantlings of less than a week ago. But then, she noted, there was less in him now than there had been, even then, of the gawky and earnest young man who had ridden to the Winterlands in quest of his hero.

"I must be going," she said softly. "It's beginning to turn light. Gather what kindling you can, in case the King's men return and you have to barricade yourselves behind the inner doors in the Grand Passage. There are foul things in the darkness. They may come at you when the light is gone."

Gareth shuddered wholeheartedly and nodded.

"I'll tell Polycarp how things stand. He should come back here to get you, if they didn't blast shut the ways into the Deep. If I don't make it to Halnath . . ."

The boy looked at her, the heroically simple conclusions of a dozen ballads reverberant in his shocked features.

She smiled, the pull of the dragon in her fading. She reached up the long distance to lay a hand on his bristly cheek. "Look after John for me."

Then she knelt and kissed John's lips and his shut eyelids. Rising, she collected a plaid and her halberd and walked toward the clear slate-gray air that lay like water outside the darker arch of the Gate.

As she passed through it, she heard a faint north-country voice behind her protest, "Look after John, indeed!"

15

Light watered the darkness, changing the air from velvet to silk. Cold cut into Jenny's hands and face, imbuing her with a sense of strange and soaring joy. The high cirques and hanging valleys of the Wall's toothy summits were stained blue and lavender against the charcoal gray of the sky; below her mist clung like raveled wool to the bones of the shadowy town. For a time she was alone and complete, torn by neither power nor love, only breathing the sharp air of dawn.

Like a shift in perception, she became aware of the dragon, lying along the bottom step. Seeing her, he rose and stretched like a cat, from nose to tail knob to the tips of the quivering wings, every spine and horn blinking in the gray-white gloom.

Wrap yourself well, wizard woman. The upper airs are cold.

He sat back upon his haunches and, reaching delicately down, closed around her one gripping talon, like a hand twelve inches across the back and consisting of nothing but bone wrapped in muscle and studded with spike and horn. The claws lapped easily around her waist. She felt no fear of him; though she knew he was treacherous, she had been within his mind and knew he would not kill her. Still, a shivery qualm passed through her as he lifted her up against his breast, where she would be out of the airstream.

The vast shadow of his wings spread against the mauve gloom of the cliff behind them, and she cast one quick glance down at the ground, fifteen feet below. Then she looked up at the mountains surrounding the Vale and at the white, watching eye of the moon on the flinty crest of the ridge, a few days from full and bright in the western air as the lamps of the dragon's eyes.

Then he flung himself upward, and all the world dropped away.

Cold sheered past her face, its bony fingers clawing through her hair. Through the plaids wrapped around her, she felt the throbbing heat of the dragon's scales. From the sky she looked to the earth again, the Vale like a well of blue shadow, the mountain slopes starting to take on the colors of dawn as the sun brushed them, rust and purple and all shades of brown from the whitest dun to the deep hue of coffee, all edged and trimmed with the dark lace of trees. The rain tanks north of Deeping caught the new day like chips of mirror; as the dragon passed over the flanks of the mountain, circling higher, she saw the bright leap of springs among the pine trees, and the white spines of thrusting rock.

The dragon tilted, turning upon the air, the vast wings searing faintly at the wind. Occasional eddies of it whistled around the spikes that defended the dragon's backbone—some of them no longer than a finger, others almost a cubit, dagger-sharp. In flight the dragon seemed to be a thing made of silk and wire, lighter than his size would lead one to think, as if the flesh and muscle, like the mind and the shape of his bones, were different in composition from all things else upon the Earth.

This is the realm of the dragons, Morkeleb's voice said within her mind. *The roads of the air. It is yours, for the stretching out of your hand.*

In the slant of the light they laid no shadow upon the ground, but it seemed to Jenny that she could almost see the track of their passage written like a ship's wake upon the wind. Her mind half-within the dragon's, she could sense the variations of the air, updraft and thermal, as if the wind itself were of different colors. With the dragon's awareness, she saw other things in the air as well—the paths of energy across the face of the world, the tracks that traveled from star to star, like the lines of force that were repeated in the body, smaller and smaller, in the spreads of dealt cards or thrown runes or the lie of leaves in water. She was aware of life everywhere, of the winter-white foxes and hares in the patchy snowlines beneath the thin scrum of cloud below, and of the King's troops, camped far down upon the road, who pointed and cried out as the dragon's dark shape passed overhead.

They crossed the flank of the mountain to its daylight side. Before and below her, she saw the cliff and hill and Citadel of Halnath, a spiky conglomerate of thrusting gray ramparts clinging like a mud-built swallow's nest to the massive shoulder of a granite cliff. From its feet, the land lay crisscrossed with wooded ravines to the silver curve of a river; mist blended with the blue of woodsmoke to veil the straggling lines of tents and guard posts, horse lines and trenches raw with yellow mud, that made up the siege camps. An open ring of battered ground lay between the walls and the camp, ravaged by battle and bristling with the burned-out shells of the small truck farms that nestled around the walls of any town.

Beyond, to the north, the green stretches of the Marches vanished away under a gauze of mists, the horse-and-cattle-lands that were the Master's fief and strength. From the river marshes where pewter waters spread themselves, a skein of danglefoot herons rose through the milky vapors, tiny and clear as a pen sketch.

There. Jenny pointed with her mind toward the battlements of the high Citadel. *The central court there. It's narrow, but long enough for us to land.*

Wind and her long hair lashed her eyes as the dragon wheeled.

They have armored their wall, the dragon said. *Look.*

Men were running about the ramparts, pointing and waving at the enormous wings flashing in the air. Jenny glimpsed catapults mounted on the highest turrets, counterweighted slings bearing buckets that burst suddenly into red flame and massive crossbows whose bolts could point nowhere but at the sky.

We'll have to go in, Jenny said. *I'll protect you.*

By catching the bolts in your teeth, wizard woman? Morkeleb asked sarcastically, circling away as some overeager slinger slipped his ropes and a bucketful of naphtha described a curving trajectory, flames streaming like faded orange pennants against the brightness of the new day. *What protection can you, a human, offer me?*

Jenny smiled to herself, watching the naphtha as it broke into blazing lumps in falling. None of them landed in the town on the slopes below— they knew their mathematics, these defenders of Halnath, and how to apply them to ballistics. For herself, she supposed she should have been terrified, to be carried this high above the reeling earth—if she fell, she would fall for a long time before she died. But whether it was her trust in Morkeleb, or the dragon's mind that enveloped hers in the thoughts of those who lived in the airstream, she felt no fear of it. Indeed, she almost believed that, if she were to drop, she had only to spread out her own wings, as she did in dreams of flight.

Small as toys on the walls of the Citadel, the machines of defense were being cranked around to bear upon them. They looked, at this distance, like nothing so much as John's little models. *And to think I grew impatient when he insisted upon showing me how every one of them fired.* She smiled, half to Morkeleb and half to herself. *Swing north, Morkeleb, and come at them from along that ridge. The problem with machines has always been that it requires only the touch of a wizard's mind to fox their balance.*

There were two engines guarding the approach she had set, a bolt-firing catapult and a spring-driven sling. She had thrown her magic before, conjuring images within her mind, to foul the bowstrings of bandits in the north and to cause their feet to find roots as they ran, or their swords to stick in their sheaths. Having seen the mechanisms of these weapons in John's models, she found this no harder. Ropes twisted in the catapult, jamming the knots when the triggering cord was jerked. With a dragon's awareness, she saw a man running in panic along the battlements; he knocked over a bucket into the mechanism of the sling so that it could not be turned to aim. The dragon swung lazily from the weapon's possible path, guided by the touch of Jenny's mind within his; and she felt, like a chuckle of dark laughter, his appreciation for the ease with which she thwarted the mechanical devices.

You are small, wizard woman, he said, amused, *but a mighty defender of dragons, nevertheless.*

Throwing her streaming hair back from her eyes, Jenny could see men on the battlements below them clearly now. They were clothed in makeshift uniforms, the black, billowing gowns of scholars covered with battered bits of armor, some of it stamped with the royal arms and obviously taken from prisoners or the slain. They fled in all directions as the dragon drew near, save for one man, tall, red-haired, and thin as a scarecrow in his ragged black gown, who was swinging something to bear upon them that looked for a moment like a telescope—a metal tube braced upon stakes. The walls swooped closer. At the last moment Jenny saw harpoons stacked beside him and, instead of glass in the tube's mouth, the glint of a metal point.

The lone defender had a burning spill in one hand, lighted from one of the naphtha buckets. He was watching them come in, taking aim— *Blasting powder*, thought Jenny; *the gnomes will have brought plenty up from the mines.* She remembered John's abortive experiments with rockets.

The scene rushed to meet them, until every chipped stone of the wall and every patch on the scholar's ragged gown seemed within reach of Jenny's hand. As he brought the spill down to the touch-hole, Jenny used her mind to extinguish the flame, as she would have doused a candle.

Then she spread out her arms and cried, "STOP!" at the top of her voice.

He froze in mid-motion, the harpoon he had snatched from the pile beside him cocked back already over his shoulder, though Jenny could tell by the way he held it that he had never thrown one before and could not have hit them. Even at that distance, she saw wonder, curiosity, and delight on his thin face. Like John, she thought, he was a true scholar, fascinated with any wonder, though it carried his death upon its wings.

Morkeleb braked in the air, the shift of his muscles rippling against Jenny's back. All men had fled the long, narrow court of the Citadel and the walls around it, save that single defender. The dragon hung for a moment like a hovering hawk, then settled, delicate as a dandelion seed, to perch on the wall above the shadowy well of the court. The great hind-talons gripped the stone as the long neck and tail counterbalanced, and he stooped like a vast bird to set Jenny on her feet upon the rampart.

She staggered, her knees weak from shock, her whole body trembling with exhilaration and cold. The tall, red-haired young man, harpoon still in one hand, moved forward along the walkway, black robe billowing beneath an outsize hauberk of chain mail. Though he was clearly cautious, Jenny thought from the way he looked at Morkeleb that he could have stood and studied the dragon for hours; but there was a court-bred politeness in the way he offered Jenny his hand.

It took her a moment to remember to speak in words.

"Polycarp of Halnath?"

He looked surprised and disconcerted at hearing his name. "I am he." Like Gareth, it took more than dragons or bandits to shake his early training; he executed a very creditable Dying Swan in spite of the harpoon.

Jenny smiled and held out her hands to him. "I am Jenny Waynest, Gareth's friend."

"Yes, there is a power sink in the heart of the Deep." Polycarp, Master of the Citadel of Halnath and Doctor of Natural Philosophy, folded long, narrow hands behind his back and turned from the pointed arches of the window to look at his rescued, oddly assorted guests. "It is what Zyerne wants; what she has always wanted, since first she knew what it was."

Gareth looked up from the ruins of the simple meal which strewed the plain waxed boards of the workroom table. "Why didn't you tell me?"

The bright blue eyes flickered to him. "What could I have said?" he asked. "Up until a year ago I wasn't even sure. And when I was . . ." His glance moved to the gnome who sat at the table's head, tiny and stooped and very old, his eyes like pale green glass beneath the long mane of milk-white hair. "Sevacandrozardus—Balgub, in the tongue of men; brother of the Lord of the Deep who was slain by the dragon—forbade me to speak of it. I could not break his confidence."

Beyond the tall windows, the turrets of the lower Citadel, the University, and the town beneath could be glimpsed, the sunlight on them yellow as summer butter, though the buildings below were already cloaked in the shadows of the mountain as the sun sank behind its shoulder. Sitting on the end of the couch where John lay, Jenny listened in quiet to the debating voices. Her body ached for sleep and her mind for stillness, but she knew that both would be denied her. Neither the words of the impromptu

council nor the recollection of the trip back through the Deep with Polycarp and the gnomes to fetch the others had eradicated from her thoughts
the soaring memory of the dragon's flight.

She knew she ought not to let it hold her so. She ought to be more
conscious of her own gladness that they were, at least for the moment,
relatively safe and more preoccupied with their exchange of information
with the Master and with plans for how to deal with the Stone and its mistress. Yet the flight and the memory of the dragon's mind had shaken her
to the bones. She could not put that wild intoxication from her heart.

The old gnome was saying, "It has always been forbidden to speak of
the Stone to outsiders. After it became clear that the girl Zyerne had heard
of it somehow and had spied upon those who used it and learned its key,
my brother, the Lord of the Deep, redoubled the anathema. It has from the
darkness of time been the heart of the Deep, the source of power for our
Healers and mages, and has made our magic so great that none dared to
assault the Deep of Ylferdun. But always we knew its danger as well—
that the greedy could use such a thing for their own ends. And so it was."

Jenny roused herself from her thoughts to ask, "How did you know
she had used it?" Like the others, she had bathed and was now dressed
like them all in the frayed black gown of a scholar of the University, too
large for her and belted tight about her waist. Her hair, still damp from
washing, hung about her shoulders.

The gnome's light eyes shifted. Grudgingly, he said, "To take power
from the Stone, there must be a return. It gives to those who draw upon it,
but later it asks back from them. Those who were used to wielding its
power—myself, Taseldwyn whom you know as Miss Mab, and others—
could feel the imbalance. Then it corrected itself, or seemed to. I was content." He shook his head, the opals that pinned his white hair flashing in
the diffuse light of the long room. "Mab was not."

"What return does it ask?"

For a moment his glance touched her, reading in her, as Mab had
done, the degree of her power. Then he said, "Power for power. All power
must be paid for, whether it is taken from your own spirit, or from the
holding-sink of others. We, the Healers, of whom I was chief, used to
dance for it, to concentrate our magic and feed it into the Stone, that others might take of its strength and not have their very life-essences drawn
from them by it—the woman Zyerne did not know how to make the
return of magic to it, did not even learn that she should. She was never
taught its use, but had only sneaked and spied until she learned what she
thought was its secret. When she did not give back to it, the Stone began
to eat at her essence."

"And to feed it," said Jenny softly, suddenly understanding what she had seen in the lamplight of Zyerne's room, "she perverted the healing spells that can draw upon the essences of others for strength. She drank, like a vampire, to replace what was being drunk from her."

In the pale light of the window, Polycarp said, "Yes," and Gareth buried his face in his hands. "Even as she can draw upon the Stone's magic at a distance, it draws upon her. I am glad," he added, the tone of his light voice changing, "to see you're still all right, Gar."

Gareth raised his head despairingly. "Did she try to use you?"

The Master nodded, his thin, foxy face grim. "And when I kept my distance and made you keep yours, she turned to Bond, who was the nearest one she could prey upon. Your father . . ." He fished for the kindest words to use. "Your father was of little more use to her by that time."

The prince's fist struck the table with a violence that startled them all—and most of all Gareth himself. But he said nothing, and indeed, there was little he could say, or that any could say to him. After a moment, Trey Clerlock rose from the couch in the corner, where she had been lying like a child playing dress-up in her flapping black robe, and came over to rest her hands upon his shoulders.

"Is there any way of destroying her?" the girl asked, looking across the table to the tiny gnome and the tall Master who had come to stand at his side.

Gareth turned to stare up at her in shock, having, manlike, never suspected the ruthless practicality of women.

"Not with the power she holds through the King and through the Stone," Polycarp said. "Believe me, I thought about it, though I knew I truly would face a charge of murder for it." A brief grin flickered across his face. "But as I ended up facing one anyway . . ."

"What about destroying the Stone, then?" John asked, turning his head from where he lay flat on his back on a tall-legged sleeping couch. Even the little he had been able to eat seemed to have done him good. In his black robe, he looked like the corpse at a wake, washed and tended and cheerful with his specs perched on the end of his long nose. "I'm sure you could find a good Stonebane someplace . . ."

"Never!" Balgub's wrinkled walnut face grew livid. "It is the source of the healing arts of the gnomes! The source of the strength of the Deep! It is ours . . ."

"It will do you precious little good if Zyerne gets her hands on it," John pointed out. "I doubt she could break through all the doors and gates you locked behind us on our way up here through the Deep, but if the King's troops manage to breach the Citadel wall, that won't make much difference."

"If Jenny could be given the key to the use of the Stone . . ." suggested Gareth.

"No!" Balgub and Jenny spoke at once. All those in the Master's long, scrubbed stone workroom, John included, looked curiously at the witch of Wyr.

"No human shall touch it!" insisted the gnome with shrill fury. "We saw the evil it did. It is for the gnomes, and only for us."

"And I would not touch it if I could." Jenny drew her knees up close to her chest and folded her arms around them; Balgub, in spite of his protest, looked affronted that the greatest treasure of the Deep should be refused. Jenny said, "According to Mab, the Stone itself has been defiled. Its powers, and the spells of those that use it, are polluted by what Zyerne has done."

"That is not true." Balgub's tight little face set in an expression of obstinancy. "Mab insisted that the Stone's powers were becoming unpredictable and its influence evil on the minds of those who used it. By the heart of the Deep, this is not so, and so I told her, again and again. I do not see how . . ."

"After being fed chewed-up human essences instead of controlled spells, it would be a wonder if it didn't become unpredictable," John said, with his usual good-natured affability.

The gnome's high voice was scornful. "What can a warrior know of such things? A warrior hired to slay the dragon, who has," he added, with heavy sarcasm, "signally failed in even that task."

"I suppose you'd rather he'd signally succeeded?" Gareth demanded hotly. "You'd have had the King's troops coming at you through the Deep by this time."

"Lad," John reached patiently out to touch the angry prince's shoulder. "Let's don't fratch. His opinion does me no harm and shouting at him isn't going to change it."

"The King's troops would never have found their way through the Deep, even with the gates unbolted," Balgub growled. "And now the gates are locked; if necessary we will seal them with blasting powder—it is there and ready, within yards of the last gate."

"If Zyerne was leading them, they would have found the way," Polycarp returned. The links of the too-large mail shirt he wore over his gown rattled faintly as he folded his arms. "She knows the way to the heart of the Deep well enough from the Deeping side. As you all saw, from there to the underground gates of the Citadel it's an almost straight path. And as for the Stone not having been affected by what she has put into it . . ." He glanced down at the stooped back and round white head of the gnome perched in the carved chair beside him. "You are the only Healer who escaped the dragon to come here, Balgub," he said. "Now that the dragon is no longer in the Deep, will you go in and use the Stone?"

The wide mouth tightened, and the green eyes did not meet the blue.

"So," said the Master softly.

"I do not believe that Mab was right," Balgub insisted stubbornly. "Nevertheless, until she, I, and the remaining Healers in Bel can examine the thing, I will not have it tampered with for good or ill. If it came to saving the Citadel, or keeping Zyerne from the Deep, yes, I would risk using it, rather than let her have it." Little and white as two colorless cave shrimp, his hands with their smooth moonstone rings closed upon each other on the inkstained tabletop. "We have sworn that Zyerne shall never again have the use of the Stone. Every gnome—and every man . . ." He cast a glance that was half-commanding, half-questioning up at the Master, and Polycarp inclined his head slightly, "—in this place will die before she lays a hand upon what she seeks."

"And considering what her powers will be like if she does," Polycarp added, with the detached speculation of a scholar, "that would probably be just as well."

"Jen?"

Jenny paused in the doorway of the makeshift guest room to which she and John had been assigned. After the windy ramparts, the place smelled close and stuffy, as the Market Hall had last night. The mingled scents of dusty paper and leather bindings of the books stored there compounded with the moldery ordors of straw ticks that had gone too long without having the straw changed; after the grass-and-water scents of the east wind, they made the closeness worse. The lumpish shapes of piles of books heaped along two walls and the ghostly scaffolding of scroll racks lining the third made her think of John's overcrowded study in the north; several of the volumes that had been put here to make room for refugees trapped by the siege had been taken from their places and already bore signs of John's reading. John himself stood between the tall lights of two of the pointed windows, visible only as a white fold of shirt sleeve and a flash of round glass in the gloom.

She said, "You shouldn't be out of bed."

"I can't be on the broad of my back forever." Through his fatigue, he sounded cheerful. "I have the feeling we're all going to be put to it again in the near future, and I'd rather do it on my feet this time."

He was silent for a moment, watching her silhouette in the slightly lighter doorway.

He went on, "And for a woman who hasn't slept more than an hour or so for three nights now, you've no room to speak. What is it, Jen?"

Like a dragon, she thought, he has a way of not being lied to. So she did not say, "What is what?" but ran her hands tiredly through her hair and crossed to where he stood.

"You've avoided speaking to me of it—not that we've had time to do so, mind. I don't feel you're angry with me, but I do feel your silence. It's to do with your power, isn't it?"

His arm was around her shoulder, her head resting against the rock-hardness of his pectoral, half-uncovered by the thin muslin shirt. She should have known, she told herself, that John would guess.

So she nodded, unable to voice the turmoil that had been all day in her mind, since the dragon's flight and all the night before. Since sunset she had been walking the ramparts, as if it were possible to outwalk the choice that had stalked her now for ten years.

Morkeleb had offered her the realms of the dragons, the woven roads of the air. All the powers of earth and sky, she thought, and all the years of time. The key to magic is magic; the offer was the answer to all the thwarted longings of her life.

"Jen," John said softly, "I've never wanted you to be torn. I know you've never been complete and I didn't want to do that to you. I tried not to."

"It wasn't you." She had told herself, a hundred years ago it seemed, that it was her choice, and so it had been—the choice of doing nothing and letting things go on as they were, or of doing something. And, as always, her mind shrank from the choice.

"Your magic has changed," he said. "I've felt it and I've seen what it's doing to you."

"It is calling me," she replied. "If I embrace it, I don't think I would want to let go, even if I could. It is everything that I have wanted and worth to me, I think, everything that I have."

She had said something similar to him long ago, when they had both been very young. In his jealous possessiveness, he had screamed at her, "But you are everything that I have or want to have!" Now his arms only tightened around her, as much, she sensed, against her grief as his own, though she knew the words he had spoken then were no less true tonight.

"It's your choice, love," he said. "As it's always been your choice. Everything you've given me, you've given freely. I won't hold you back." Her cheek was pressed to his chest, so that she only felt the quick glint of his smile as he added, "As if I ever could, anyway."

They went to the straw mattress and huddle of blankets, the only accommodation the besieged Citadel had been able to offer. Beyond the windows, moisture glinted on the black slates of the crowded stone houses below; a gutter's thread was like a string of diamonds in the moonlight. In the siege camps, bells were ringing for the midnight rites of Sarmendes, lord of the wiser thoughts of day.

Under the warmth of the covers, John's body was familiar against hers, as familiar as the old temptation to let the chances of pure power go by for yet another day. Jenny was aware, as she had always been, that it was less easy to think about her choices when she lay in his arms. But she was still there when sleep finally took her, and she drifted into ambiguous and unresolved dreams.

16

When Jenny wakened, John was gone.

Like a dragon, in her dreams she was aware of many things; she had sensed him walking and lying for a long while propped on one elbow beside her, watching her as she slept; she had been aware, too, of him rising and dressing, and of the slow painfulness of donning his shirt, breeches, and boots and of how the bandages pulled painfully over the half-healed mess of slashes and abrasions on his back and sides. He had taken her halberd for support, kissed her gently, and gone.

Still weary, she lay in the tangle of blankets and strawticks, wondering where he had gone, and why she felt afraid.

Dread seemed to hang in the air with the stormclouds that reared dark anvil heads above the green distances north of Nast Wall. There was a queer lividness to the light that streamed through the narrow windows, a breathless sense of coming evil, a sense that had pervaded her dreams . . .

Her dreams, she thought confusedly. What had she dreamed?

She seemed to remember Gareth and the Master Polycarp walking on the high battlements of the Citadel, both in the billowing black robes of students, talking with the old ease of their interrupted friendship. "You must admit it was a singularly convincing calumny," Polycarp was saying.

Gareth replied bitterly, "I didn't have to believe it as readily as I did."

Polycarp grinned and drew from some pocket in his too-ample garments a brass spyglass, unfolding its jointed sections to scan the fevered sky. "You're going to be Pontifex Maximus one day, Cousin—you need practice in believing ridiculous things," And looking out toward the road that led south he had stared, as if he could not believe what he saw.

Jenny frowned, remembering the cloudy tangles of the dream.

The King, she thought—it had been the King, riding up the road toward the siege camps that surrounded the Citadel. But there had been something wrong with that tall, stiff form and its masklike face, riding through the sulfurous storm light. An effect of the dream? she wondered. Or had the eyes really been yellow—Zyerne's eyes?

Troubled, she sat up and pulled on her shift. There was a wash bowl in a corner of the room near the window, the surface of the water reflecting the sky like a piece of smoked steel. Her hand brushed across it; at her bidding, she saw Morkeleb, lying in the small upper courtyard of the Citadel, a small square of stone which contained nothing save a few withered apple trees, a wooden lean-to that had once held gardening equipment and now, like every other shelter in the Citadel, housed displaced books. The dragon lay stretched out like a cat in the pallid sunlight, the jeweled bobs of his antennae flicking here and there as if scenting the welter of the air, and beside him, on the court's single granite bench, sat John.

The dragon was saying, *Why this curiosity, Dragonsbane? That you may know us better, the next time you choose to kill one of us?*

"No," John said. "Only that I may know dragons better. I'm more circumscribed than you, Morkeleb—by a body that wears out and dies before the mind has seen half what it wants to, by a mind that spends half its time doing what it would really rather not, for the sake of the people who're in my care. I'm as greedy about knowledge as Jenny is—as you are for gold, maybe more so—for I know I have to snatch it where I can."

The dragon sniffed in disdain, the velvet-rimmed nostril flaring to show a surface ripple of deeper currents of thought; then he turned his head away. Jenny knew she ought to feel surprise at being able to call Morkeleb's image in the water bowl, but did not; though she could not have phrased it in words, but only in the half-pictured understandings of dragon-speech, she knew why it had formerly been impossible, but was possible to her now. Almost, she thought, she could have summoned his image and surroundings without the water.

For a time they were silent, man and dragon, and the shadows of the black-bellied thunderheads moved across them, gathering above the Citadel's heights. Morkeleb did not look the same in the water as he did face to face, but it was a difference, again, that could not be expressed by any but a dragon. A stray wind shook the boughs of the cronelike trees, and a few spits of rain speckled the pavement of the long court below them. At its far end, Jenny could see the small and inconspicuous—and easily defensible—door that led into the antechambers of the Deep. It was not wide, for the trade between the Citadel and the Deep had never been in anything bulkier than books and gold, and for the most part their traffic had been in knowledge alone.

Why? Morkeleb asked at length. *If, as you say, yours is a life limited by the constraints of the body and the narrow perimeters of time, if you are greedy for knowledge as we are for gold, why do you give what you have, half of all that you own, to others?*

The question had risen like a whale from unguessed depths, and John was silent for a moment before answering. "Because it's part of being human, Morkeleb. Having so little, we share among ourselves to make any of it worth having. We do what we do because the consequences of not caring enough to do it would be worse."

His answer must have touched some chord in the dragon's soul, for Jenny felt, even through the distant vision, the radiant surge of Morkeleb's annoyance. But the dragon's thoughts sounded down to their depths again, and he became still, almost invisible against the colors of the stone. Only his antennae continued to move, restless, as if troubled by the turmoil in the air.

A thunderstorm? Jenny thought, suddenly troubled. In winter?

"Jenny?" She looked up quickly and saw the Master Polycarp standing in the tall slit of the doorway. She did not know why at first, but she shuddered when she saw hanging at his belt the brass spyglass he had used in her dream. "I didn't want to wake you—I know you've been without sleep . . ."

"What is it?" she asked, hearing the trouble in his voice.

"It's the King."

Her stomach jolted, as if she had missed one step of a stairway in darkness, the dread of her dream coalescing in her, suddenly hideously real.

"He said he's escaped from Zyerne—he wanted sanctuary here, and wanted above all to talk to Gar. They went off together . . ."

"No!" Jenny cried, horrified, and the young philosopher looked at her in surprise. She snatched up and flung on the black robe she had been wearing earlier, dragging its belt tight. "It's a trick!"

"What . . . ?"

She pushed her way past him, shoving up the robe's too-long sleeves over her forearms; cold air and the smell of thunder smote her as she came into the open and began to run down the long, narrow stairs. She could hear Morkeleb calling to her, faint and confused with distance; he was waiting for her in the upper court, his half-risen scales glittering uneasily in the sickly storm light.

Zyerne, she said.

Yes. I saw her just now, walking with your little prince to the door that leads down into the Deep. She was in the guise of the old King—they had already passed through the door when I spoke of it to Aversin. Is it possible that the prince did not know it, as Aversin said to me? I know that humans can fool one another with the illusions of their magic, but are even his own son and his nephew whom he raised so stupid that they could not have told the difference between what they saw and what they knew?

As always, his words came as pictures in her mind—the old King leaning, whispering, on Gareth's shoulder for support as they walked the length of the narrow court toward the door to the Deep, the look of pity, involuntary repulsion, and wretched guilt on the boy's face—feeling repelled, and not knowing why.

Jenny's heart began to pound. *They know the King has been ill,* she said. *No doubt she counted upon their forgiveness of any lapses. She will go to the Stone, to draw power from it, and use Gareth's life to replace it. Where's John now? He has to . . .*

He has gone after them.

WHAT? Like a dragon, the word emerged only as a blazing surge of incredulous wrath. *He'll kill himself!*

He will likely be forestalled, Morkeleb replied cynically. But Jenny did not stay to listen. She was already running down the steep twist of steps to the lower court. The cobbles of the pavement there were uneven and badly worn, with tiny spangles of vagrant rain glittering among them like silver beads on some complex trapunto; the harshness of the stone tore at her feet as she ran toward that small, unprepossessing door.

She flung back to the dragon the words, *Wait for her here. If she reaches the Stone, she will have all power at her command—I will never be able to defeat her, as I did before. You must take her when she emerges . . .*

It is the Stone that binds me, the dragon's bitter voice replied in her mind. *If she reaches it, what makes you think I shall be able to do anything but her will?*

Without answering Jenny flung open the door and plunged through into the shadowy antechambers of the earth.

She had seen them the previous morning, when she had passed through with the gnomes who had gone to fetch John, Gareth, and Trey from the other side of the Deep. There were several rooms used for trade and business, and then a guardroom, whose walls were carved to three-quarters of their height from the living bone of the mountain. The windows, far up under the vaulted ceilings, let in a shadowy blue light by which she could just see the wide doors of the Deep itself, faced and backed with bronze and fitted with massive bars and bolts of iron.

These gates were still locked, but the man-sized postern door stood ajar. Beyond it lay darkness and the cold scent of rock, water, and old decay. Gathering up her robes, Jenny stepped over the thick sill and hurried on, her senses probing ahead of her, dragonlike, her eyes seeking the silvery runes she had written on the walls yesterday to mark her path.

The first passage was wide and had once been pleasant, with basins and fountains lining its walls. Now some were broken, others clogged in the months of utter neglect; moss clotted them and water ran shining down the walls and along the stone underfoot, wetting the hem of Jenny's robe and slapping coldly at her ankles. As she walked, her mind tested the darkness before her; retracing yesterday's route, she paused again and again to listen. The way through the Deep ran near the Places of Healing, but not through them; somewhere, she would have to turn aside and seek the unmarked ways.

So she felt at the air, seeking the living tingle of magic that marked the heart of the Deep. It should lie lower than her own route, she thought, and to her left. Her mind returned uncomfortably to Miss Mab's words about a false step leaving her to die of starvation in the labyrinthine darkness. If she became lost, she told herself, Morkeleb could still hear her, and guide her forth . . .

But not, she realized, if Zyerne reached the Stone. The power and longing of the Stone were lodged in the dragon's mind. If she got lost, and Zyerne reached the Stone and gained control of Morkeleb, there would be no daylight for her again.

She hurried her steps, passing the doors that had been raised for the defense of the Citadel from the Deep, all unlocked now by Gareth and the one he supposed to be the King. By the last of them, she glimpsed the sacks of blasting powder that Balgub had spoken of, that final defense in which he had placed such faith. Beyond was a branching of the ways, and she stopped again under an arch carved to look like a monstrous mouth, with stalactites of ivory grimacing in a wrinkled gum of salmon-pink stone. Her instincts whispered to her that this was the place—two tunnels diverged from the main one, both going downwards, both to the left. A little way down the nearer one, beside the trickle of water from a broken gutter, a wet footprint marked the downward-sloping stone.

John's, she guessed, for the print was dragged and slurred. Further along that way, she saw the mark of a drier boot, narrower and differently shaped. She saw the tracks again, dried to barely a sparkle of dampness on the first steps of a narrow stair which wound like a path up a hillslope of gigantic stone mushrooms in an echoing cavern, past the dark alabaster mansions of the gnomes, to a narrow doorway in a cavern wall. She scribbled a rune beside the door and followed, through a rock seam whose walls she could touch with her outstretched hands, downward, into the bowels of the earth.

In the crushing weight of the darkness, she saw the faint flicker of yellow light.

She dared not call out, but fled soundlessly toward it. The air was warmer here, unnatural in those clammy abysses; she felt the subtle vibrations of the living magic that surrounded the Stone. But there was an unwholesomeness in the air now, like the first smell of rot in decaying meat or like the livid greenness that her dragon eyes had seen in the poisoned water. She understood that Miss Mab had been right and Balgub wrong. The Stone had been defiled. The spells that had been wrought with its strength were slowly deteriorating, perverted by the poisons drawn from Zyerne's mind.

At the end of a triangular room the size of a dozen barns, she found a torch, guttering itself out near the foot of a flight of shallow steps. The iron door at the top stood unbolted and ajar, and across its threshold John lay unconscious, scavenger-slugs already sniffing inquiringly at his face and hands.

Beyond, in the darkness, Jenny heard Gareth's voice cry, "Stop!" and the sweet, evil whisper of Zyerne's laughter.

"Gareth," the soft voice breathed. "Did you ever think it was possible that you could stop me?"

Shaken now with a cold that seemed to crystallize at the marrow of her bones, Jenny ran forward into the heart of the Deep.

Through the forest of alabaster pillars she saw them, the nervous shadows of Gareth's torch jerking over the white stone lace that surrounded the open floor. His face looked dead white against the black, baggy student gown he wore; his eyes held the nightmare terror of every dream, every encounter with his father's mistress, and the knowledge of his own terrifying weakness. In his right hand he held the halberd John had been using for a crutch. John must have warned him that it was Zyerne, Jenny thought, before he collapsed. At least Gareth has a weapon. But whether he would be capable of using it was another matter.

The Stone in the center of the onyx dancing floor seemed to glow in the vibrating dark with a sickly corpse light of its own. The woman before it was radiant, beautiful as the Death-lady who is said to walk on the sea in times of storm. She looked younger than Jenny had ever seen her, with the virgin fragility of a child that was both an armor against Gareth's desperation and a weapon to pierce his flesh if not his heart. But even at her most delicate, there was something nauseating about her, like poisoned marzipan—an overwhelming, polluted sensuality. Wind that Jenny could not feel seemed to lift the soft darkness of Zyerne's hair and the sleeves of the frail white shift that was all that she wore. Stopping on the edge of the flow-stone glades, Jenny realized that she was seeing Zyerne as she had once been, when she first had come to this place—a mageborn girl-child who had run through these lightless corridors seeking power, as she herself had sought it in the rainy north; trying, as she herself had tried, to overcome the handicap of its lack in whatever way she could.

Zyerne laughed, her sweet mouth parting to show pearls of teeth. "It is my destiny," she whispered, her small hands caressing the blue-black shine of the Stone. "The gnomes had no right to keep it all to themselves. It is mine now. It was meant to be mine from the founding of the world. As you were."

She held out her hands, and Gareth whispered, "No." His voice was thin and desperate as the wanting of her clutched at his flesh.

"What is this *No*? You were made for me, Gareth. Made to be King. Made to be my love. Made to father my son."

Like a phantom in a dream, she drifted toward him over the oily blackness of the great floor. Gareth slashed at her with the torch, but she only laughed again and did not even draw back. She knew he hadn't the courage to touch her with the flame. He edged toward her, the halberd in his hand, but Jenny could see his face rolling with streams of sweat. His whole body shook as he summoned the last of his strength to cut at her when she came near enough—fighting for the resolution to do that and not to fling down the weapon and crush her in his arms.

Jenny strode forward from the alabaster glades in a blaze of blue witchlight, and her voice cut the palpitant air like a knife tearing cloth. She cried, "ZYERNE!" and the enchantress spun, her eyes yellow as a cat-devil's in the white blaze of the light, as they had been in the woods. The spell over Gareth snapped, and at that instant he swung the halberd at her with all the will he had left.

She flung the spell of deflection at him almost contemptuously; the weapon rang and clattered on the stone floor. Swinging back toward him, she raised her hand, but Jenny stepped forward, her wrath swirling about her like woodsmoke and phosphorous, and flung at Zyerne a rope of white fire that streamed coldly from the palm of her hand.

Zyerne hurled it aside, and it splattered, sizzling, on the black pavement. Her yellow eyes burned with unholy light. "You," she whispered. "I told you I'd get the Stone—and I told you what I'd do to you when I did, you ignorant bitch. I'll rot the stinking bones of your body for what you did!"

A spell of crippling and ruin beat like lightning in the close air of the cavern, and Jenny flinched from it, feeling all her defenses buckle and twist. The power Zyerne wielded was like a weight, the vast shadow she had only sensed before turned now to the weight of the earth where it smote against her. Jenny threw it aside and writhed from beneath it; but for a moment, she hadn't the strength to do more. A second spell struck her, and a third, cramping and biting at the muscles and organs of her body, smoking at the hem of her gown. She felt something break within her and tasted blood in her mouth; her head throbbed, her brain seemed to blaze, all the oxygen in the world was insufficient to her lungs. Under the ruthless battering she could do no more than defend herself; no counter-spell would come, no way to make it stop. And through it all, she felt the weaving of the death-spells, swollen and hideous perversions of what she herself had woven, returning like a vengeance to crush her beneath them. She felt Zyerne's mind, powered by the force of the Stone, driving like a black needle of pain into hers; felt the grappling of a poisoned and vicious essence seeking her consent.

And why not? she thought. Like the black slime of bursting pustules, all her self-hatreds flowed into the light. She had murdered those weaker than herself; she had hated her master; she had used a man who loved her for her own pleasure and had abandoned the sons of her body; she had abandoned her birthright of power out of sloth and fear. Her body screamed, and her will to resist all the mounting agonies weakened before the scorching onslaught of the mind. How could she presume to fight the evil of Zyerne, when she herself was evil without even the excuse of Zyerne's grandeur?

Anger struck her then, like the icy rains of the Winterlands, and she recognized what was happening to her as a spell. Like a dragon, Zyerne deceived with the truth, but it was deception all the same. Looking up she saw that perfect, evil face bending over her, the golden eyes filled with gloating fire. Reaching out, Jenny seized the fragile wrists, the very bones of her hands hurting like an old woman's on a winter night; but she forced her hands to close.

Grandeur? her mind cried, slicing up once more through the fog of pain and enchantment. *It is only you who see yourself as grand, Zyerne. Yes, I am evil, and weak, and cowardly, but, like a dragon, I know what it is that I am. You are a creature of lies, of poisons, of small and petty fears—it is that which will kill you. Whether I die or not, Zyerne, it is you who will bring your own death upon yourself, not for what you do, but for what you are.*

She felt Zyerne's mind flinch at that. With a twist of fury Jenny broke the brutal grip it held upon hers. At the same moment her hands were struck aside. From her knees, she looked up through the tangle of her hair, to see the enchantress's face grow livid. Zyerne screamed "You! You . . ."

With a piercing obscenity, the sorceress's whole body was wrapped in the rags of heat and fire and power. Jenny, realizing the danger was now to her body rather than to her mind, threw herself to the floor and rolled out of the way. In the swirling haze of heat and power stood a creature she had never seen before, hideous and deformed, as if a giant cave roach had mated with a tiger. With a hoarse scream, the thing threw itself upon her.

Jenny rolled aside from the rip of the razor-combed feet. She heard Gareth cry her name, not in terror as he would once have done, and from the corner of her eye she saw him slide the halberd across the glass-slick floor to her waiting hand. She caught the weapon just in time to parry a second attack. The metal of the blade shrieked on the tearing mandibles as the huge weight of the thing bore her back against the blue-black Stone. Then the thing turned, doubling on its tracks as Zyerne had done that evening in the glade, and in her mind Jenny seemed to hear Zyerne's distant voice howling, "I'll show you! I'll show you all!"

It scuttled into the forest of alabaster, making for the dark tunnels that led to the surface.

Jenny started to get to her feet to follow and collapsed at the foot of the Stone. Her body hurt her in every limb and muscle; her mind felt pulped from the ripping cruelty of Zyerne's spells, bleeding still from her own acceptance of what she was. Her hand, which she could see lying over the halberd's shaft, seemed no longer part of her, though, rather to her surprise, she saw it was still on the end of her arm and attached to her body; the brown fingers were covered with blisters, from some attack she had not even felt at the time. Gareth was bending over her, holding the guttering torch.

"Jenny—Jenny, wake up—Jenny *please*! Don't make me go after it alone!"

"No," she managed to whisper and swallowed blood. Some instinct told her the lesion within her had healed, but she felt sick and drained. She tried to rise again and collapsed, vomiting; she felt the boy's hands hold her steady even though they shook with fear. Afterward, empty and chilled, she wondered if she would faint and told herself not to be silly.

"She's going to get Morkeleb," she whispered, and propped herself up again, her black hair hanging down in her face. "The power of the Stone rules him. She will be able to hold his mind, as she could not hold mine."

She managed to get to her feet, Gareth helping her as gently as he could, and picked up the halberd. "I have to stop her before she gets clear of the caverns. I defeated her mind—while the tunnels limit her size, I may be able to defeat her body. Stay here and help John."

"But . . ." Gareth began. She shrugged free of his hold and made for the dark doorway at a stumbling run.

Beyond it, spells of loss and confusion tangled the darkness. The runes that she had traced as she'd followed John were gone, and for a few moments the subtle obscurity of Zyerne's magic smothered her mind and made all those shrouded ways look the same. Panic knotted around her throat as she thought of wandering forever in the darkness; then the part of her that had found her way through the woods of the Winterlands said, *Think. Think and listen.* She released magic from her mind and looked about her in the dark; with instinctive woodcraftiness, she had taken back-bearings of her route while making her rune-markings, seeing what the landmarks looked like coming the other way. She spread her senses through the phantasmagoric domain of fluted stone, listening for the echoes that crossed and recrossed in the blackness. She heard the muted murmur of John's voice speaking to Gareth about doors the gnomes had meant to bar and the clawed scrape of unclean chitin somewhere up ahead. She deepened her awareness and heard the skitter of the vermin of the caves as they fled, shocked, from a greater vermin. Swiftly, she set off in pursuit.

She had told Morkeleb to stand guard over the outer door. She prayed now that he had had the sense not to, but it scarcely mattered whether he did or not. The power of the Stone was in Zyerne—from it she had drawn the deepest reserves of its strength, knowing that, when the time came to pay it back, she would have lives aplenty at her disposal to do it. The power of the Stone was lodged in Morkeleb's mind, tighter now that his mind and hers had touched. With the dragon her slave, the Citadel would fall, and the Stone be Zyerne's forever.

Jenny quickened once more to a jog that felt ready to break her bones. Her bare feet splashed in the trickling water, making a faint, sticky pattering among the looming shapes of the limestone darkness; her hands felt frozen around the halberd shaft. How long a start Zyerne had she didn't know, or how fast the abomination she had become could travel. Zyerne had no more power over her, but she feared to meet her now and pit her body against that body. A part of her mind thought wryly: John should have been doing this, not she—it was his end of the bargain to deal with monsters. She smiled bitterly. Mab had been right; there were other evils besides dragons in the land.

She passed a hillslope of stone mushrooms, an archway of teeth like grotesque daggers. Her heart pounded and her chilled body ached with the ruin Zyerne had wrought on her. She ran, passing the locks and bars the gnomes had set such faith in, knowing already that she would be too late.

In the blue dimness of the vaults below the Citadel, she found the furniture toppled and scattered, and she forced herself desperately to greater speed. Through a doorway, she glimpsed a reflection of the fevered daylight outside; the stench of blood struck her nostrils even as she tripped and, looking down, saw the decapitated body of a gnome lying in a pool of warm blood at her feet. The last room of the Citadel vaults was a slaughterhouse, men and gnomes lying in it and in the doorway to the outside, their makeshift black livery sodden with blood, the close air of the room stinking with the gore that splattered the walls and even the ceiling. From beyond the doorway, shouting and the stench of burning came to her; and, stumbling through the carnage, Jenny cried out *Morkeleb*! She hurled the music of his name like a rope into the sightless void. His mind touched hers, and the hideous weight of the Stone pressed upon them both.

Light glared in her eyes. She scrambled over the bodies in the doorway and stood, blinking for an instant in the lower court, seeing all around the door the paving stones charred with a crisped muck of blood. Before her the creature crouched, larger and infinitely more hideous in the befouled and stormy daylight, metamorphosed into something like a winged ant, but without an ant's compact grace. Squid, serpent, scorpion, wasp—it was everything hideous, but no one thing in itself. The screaming laughter that filled her mind was Zyerne's laughter. It was Zyerne's voice that she heard, calling to Morkeleb as she had called to Gareth, the power of the Stone a tightening noose upon his mind.

The dragon crouched immobile against the far rampart of the court. His every spike and scale were raised for battle, yet to Jenny's mind came nothing from him but grating agony. The awful, shadowy weight of the Stone was tearing at his mind, a power built generation after generation, fermenting in upon itself and directed by Zyerne upon him now, summoning him to her bidding, demanding that he yield. Jenny felt his mind a knot of iron against that imperious command, and she felt it when the knot fissured.

She cried again, *Morkeleb*! and flung herself, mind and body, toward him. Their minds gripped and locked. Through his eyes, she saw the horrible shape of the creature and recognized how he had known Zyerne through her disguise—the patterning of her soul was unmistakable. Peripherally, she was aware that this was true for every man and gnome who cowered within the doorways and behind the protection of each turret; she saw things as a dragon sees. The force of the Stone hammered again at her mind, and yet it had no power over her, no hold upon her. Through Morkeleb's eyes, she saw herself still running toward him— toward, in a sense, herself—and saw the creature turn to strike at that small, flying rag of black-wrapped bones and hair that she knew in a detached way for her own body.

Her mind was within the dragon's, shielding him from the burning grip of the Stone. Like a cat, the dragon struck, and the creature that had been Zyerne wheeled to meet the unexpected threat. Half within her own body, half within Morkeleb's, Jenny stepped in under the sagging, bloated belly of the monster that loomed so hugely near her and thrust upward with her halberd. As the blade slashed at the stinking flesh, she heard Zyerne's voice in her mind, screaming at her the back-street obscenities of a spoiled little slut whom the gnomes had taken in on account of the promise of her power. Then the creature gathered its mismated limbs beneath it and hurled itself skyward out of their way. From overhead, Jenny felt the hot rumble of thunder.

Her counterspell blocked the bolt of lightning that would have come hurling down on the court an instant later; she used a dragon-spell, such as those who walked the roads of the air used to allow them to fly in storms. Morkeleb was beside her then, her mind shielding his from the Stone as his body shielded hers from Zyerne's greater strength. Minds interlinked, there was no need of words between them. Jenny seized the knife-tipped spikes of his foreleg as he raised her to his back, and she wedged herself uncomfortably between the spearpoints that guarded his spine. More thunder came, and the searing breathlessness of ozone. She flung a spell to turn aside that bolt, and the lightning—channeled, she saw, through the creature that hovered in the livid air above the Citadel like a floating sack of pus—struck the tubular harpoon gun on the rampart. It exploded in a bursting star of flame and shattered iron, and the two men who were cranking another catapult to bear on the monster turned and fled.

Jenny understood then that the storm had been summoned by Zyerne, called by her powers through the Stone from afar, and the Stone's magic gave her the power to direct the lightning when and where she would. It had been her weapon to destroy the Citadel—the Stone, the storm, and the dragon.

She pulled off her belt and used it to lash herself to the two-foot spike before her. It would be little use if the dragon turned over in flight, but would keep her from being thrown off laterally, and that was all she could hope for now. She knew her body was exhausted and hurt, but the dragon's mind lifted her out of herself; and in any case, she had no choice. She sealed herself off from the pain and ripped the Limitations from mind and flesh.

The dragon hurtled skyward to the thing waiting above.

Winds tore at them, buffeting Morkeleb's wings so that he had to veer sharply to miss being thrown into the highest turret of the Citadel. From above them, the creature spat a rain of acid mucus. Green and stinking, it seared Jenny's face and hands like poison and made smoking tracks of corrosion on the steel of the dragon's scales. Furiously keeping her mind concentrated against the searing agony, Jenny cast her will at the clouds, and rain began to sluice down, washing the stuff away and half-blinding her with its fury. Long black hair hung stickily down over her shoulders as the dragon swung on the wind, and she felt lightning channeling again into the hovering creature before them. Seizing it with her mind, she flung it back. It burst somewhere between them, the shock of it striking her bones like a blow. She had forgotten she was not a dragon, and that her flesh was mortal.

Then the creature fell upon them, its stumpy wings whirring like a foul bug's. The weight of it rolled the dragon in the air so that Jenny had to grasp the spikes on either side of her, below the blades and yet still cutting her fingers. The earth rolled and swung below them, but her eyes and mind locked on the thing above. Its stink was overpowering, and from the pullulant mass of its flesh, a sharklike head struck, biting at the massive joints of the dragon's wings, while the whirlwind of evil spells sucked and ripped around them, tearing at their linked minds.

Ichorous yellow fluid burst from the creature's mouth as it bit at the spikes of the wing-joints. Jenny slashed at the eyes, human and as big as her two fists, gray-gold as mead—Zyerne's eyes. The halberd blade clove through the flesh—and from among the half-severed flaps of the wound, other heads burst like a knot of snakes among spraying gore, tearing at her robe and her flesh with suckerlike mouths. Grimly, fighting a sense of nightmare horror, she chopped again, her blistered hands clotted and running with slime. Half her mind called from the depths of the dragon's soul the healing-spells against the poisons she knew were harbored in those filthy jaws.

When she slashed at the other eye, the creature broke away from them. The pain of Morkeleb's wounds as well as her own tore at her as he swung and circled skyward, and she knew he felt the burning of her ripped flesh. The Citadel dropped away below them; rain poured over them like water from a pail. Looking up, she could see the deadly purplish glow of stored lightning rimming the black pillows of cloud so close above their heads. The battering of Zyerne's mind upon theirs lessened as the sorceress rallied her own spells, spells of wreckage and ruin against the Citadel and its defenders below.

Mists veiled the thrusting folds of the land beneath them, the toy fortress and the wet, slate-and-emerald of the meadows beside the white stream of the river. Morkeleb circled, Jenny's eyes within his seeing all things with clear, incredible calm. Lightning streaked down by her and she saw, as if it had been drawn in fine lines before her eyes, another catapult explode on the ramparts, and the man who had been winding it flung backward over the parapet, whirling limply down the side of the cliff.

Then the dragon folded his wings and dropped. Her mind in Morkeleb's, Jenny felt no fear, clinging to the spikes while the wind tore her sopping hair back and her bloody, rain-wet robes plastered to her body and arms. Her mind was the mind of a stooping falcon. She saw, with precise pleasure, the sacklike, threshing body that was their target, felt the joy of impending impact as the dragon fisted his claws . . .

The jar all but threw her from her precarious perch on the dragon's backbone. The creature twisted and sagged in the air, then writhed under them, grabbing with a dozen mouths at Morkeleb's belly and sides, heedless of the spikes and the monstrous slashing of the dragon's tail. Something tore at Jenny's back; turning, she hacked the head off a serpentine tentacle that had ripped at her, but she felt the blood flowing from the wound. Her efforts to close it were fogged and slow. They seemed to have fallen into a vortex of spells, and the weight of the Stone's strength dragged upon them, trying to rend apart the locked knot of their minds.

What was human magic and what dragon she no longer knew, only that they sparkled together, iron and gold, in a welded weapon that attacked both body and mind. She could feel Morkeleb's growing exhaustion and her own dizziness as the Citadel walls and the stone-toothed cliffs of Nast Wall wheeled crazily beneath them. The more they hacked and cut at the awful, stinking thing, the more mouths and gripping tentacles it sprouted and the tighter its clutch upon them became. She felt no more fear than a beast might feel in combat with its own kind, but she did feel the growing weight of the thing as it multiplied, getting larger and more powerful as the two entwined bodies thrashed in the sea of streaming rain.

The end, when it came, was a shock, like the impact of a club. She was aware of a booming roar somewhere in the earth beneath them, dull and shaking through her exhausted singlemindedness; then, more clearly, she heard a voice like Zyerne's screaming, multiplied a thousandfold through the spells that suffocated her until it axed through her skull with the rending echo of indescribable pain.

Like the passage from one segment of a dream to another, she felt the melting of the spells that surrounded them and the falling-away of the clinging, flaccid flesh and muscle. Something flashed beneath them, falling through the rainy air toward the wet roof crests of the Citadel below, and she realized that the plunging flutter of streaming brown hair and white gauze was Zyerne.

The instantaneous *Get her* and Morkeleb's *Let her fall* passed between them like a spark. Then he was plunging again, as he had plunged before, falconlike, tracking the falling body with his precise crystal eyes and plucking it from the air with the neatness of a child playing jacks.

Charcoal-gray with rain, the walls of the Citadel court rose up around them. Men, women, and gnomes were everywhere on the ramparts, hair slicked down with the pouring cloudburst to which nobody was paying the slightest attention. White smoke poured from the narrow door that led into the Deep, but all eyes were raised skyward to that black, plummeting form.

The dragon balanced for a moment upon the seventy-foot span of his wings, then extended three of his delicate legs to touch the ground. With the fourth, he laid Zyerne on the puddled stone pavement, her dark hair spreading out around her under the driving rain.

Sliding from the dragon's back, Jenny knew at once that Zyerne was dead. Her mouth and eyes were open. Distorted with rage and terror, her face could be seen to be pointy and shrewish with constant worry and the cancerous addiction to petty angers.

Trembling with weariness, Jenny leaned against the dragon's curving shoulder. Slowly, the scintillant helix of their minds unlinked. The rim of brightness and color that had seemed to edge everything vanished from her vision. Living things had solid bodies once more, instead of incorporeal ghosts of flesh through which shone the shapes of souls.

A thousand pains came back to her—of her body and of the stripped, hurting ruin of her mind. She became aware of the blood that stuck her torn robe to her back and ran down her legs to her bare feet—became aware of all the darkness in her own heart, which she had accepted in her battle with Zyerne.

Holding to the thorned scales for support, she looked down at the sharp, white face staring upward at her from the rain-hammered puddles. A human hand steadied her elbow, and turning, she saw Trey beside her, her frivolously tinted hair plastered with wet around her pale face. It was the closest, she realized, that she had seen any human besides herself come to Morkeleb. A moment later Polycarp joined them, one arm wrapped in makeshift dressings and half his red hair burned away by the creature's first attack upon the door.

White smoke still billowed from the door of the Deep. Jenny coughed, her lungs hurting, in the acrid fumes. Everyone in the court was coughing—it was as if the Deep itself were in flames.

More coughing came from within. In the shadowy slot, two forms materialized, the shorter leaning upon the taller. From soot-blackened faces, two pairs of spectacle lenses flashed whitely in the pallid light.

A moment later they emerged from the smoke and shadow into the stunned silence of the watching crowd in the court.

"Miscalculated the blasting powder," John explained apologetically.

17

It was not for several days after John and Gareth blew up the Stone that Jenny began to recover from the battle beneath and above the Citadel.

She had cloudy recollections of them telling Polycarp how they had backtracked to the room by the gates where the blasting powder had been left, while her own consciousness darkened, and a vague memory of Morkeleb catching her in his talons as she fell and carrying her, catlike, to the small shelter in the upper court. More clear was the remembrance of John's voice, forbidding the others to go after them. "She needs a healing we can't give her," she heard him say to Gareth. "Just let her be."

She wondered how he had known that. But then, John knew her very well.

Morkeleb healed her as dragons heal, leading the body with the mind. Her body healed fairly quickly, the poisons burning themselves out of her veins, the slashed, puckered wounds left by the creature's mouths closing to leave round, vicious-looking scabs the size of her palm. Like John's dragon-slaying scars, she thought, they would stay with her for what remained of her life.

Her mind healed more slowly. Open wounds left by her battle with Zyerne remained open. Worst was the knowledge that she had abandoned the birthright of her power, not through the fate that had denied her the ability or the circumstances that had kept her from its proper teaching, but through her own fear.

They are yours for the stretching-out of your hand, Morkeleb had said.

She knew they always had been.

Turning her head from the shadows of the crowded lean-to, she could see the dragon lying in the heatless sun of the court, a black cobra with his tasseled head raised, his antennae flicking to listen to the wind. She felt her soul streaked and mottled with the mind and soul of the dragon and her life entangled with the crystal ropes of his being.

She asked him once why he had remained at the Citadel to heal her. *The Stone is broken—the ties that bind you to this place are gone.*

She felt the anger coiled within him stir. *I do not know, wizard woman. You cannot have healed yourself—I did not wish to see you broken forever.* The words in her mind were tinted, not only with anger, but with the memory of fear and with a kind of shame.

Why? she asked. *You have often said that the affairs of humankind are nothing to dragons.*

His scales rattled faintly as they hackled, then, with a dry whisper, settled again. Dragons did not lie, but she felt the mazes of his mind close against her.

Nor are they. But I have felt stirring in me things that I do not understand, since you healed me and shared with me the song of the gold in the Deep. My power has waked power in you, but what it is in you that has waked its reflection in me I do not know, for it is not a thing of dragons. It let me feel the grip of the Stone, as I flew north—a longing and a hurt, which before was only my own will. Now because of it, I do not want to see you hurt—I do not want to see you die, as humans die. I want you to come with me to the north, Jenny; to be one of the dragons, with the power for which you have always sought. I want this, as much as I have ever wanted the gold of the earth. I do not know why. And is it not what you want?

But to that, Jenny had no reply.

Long before he should have been on his feet, John dragged himself up the steps to the high court to see her, sitting behind her on the narrow makeshift cot in her little shelter, brushing her hair as he used to at the Hold on those nights when she would come there to be with him and their sons. He spoke of commonplaces, of the dismantling of the siege troops around the Citadel and of the return of the gnomes to the Deep, of Gareth's doings, and of the assembling of the books they would take back to the north, demanding nothing of her, neither speech, decision, nor thought. But it seemed to her that the touch of his hands brought more bitter pain to her than all Zyerne's spells of ruin.

She had made her choice, she thought, ten years ago when first they had met; and had remade it every day since then. But there was, and always had been, another choice. Without turning her head, she was aware of the thoughts that moved behind the diamond depths of Morkeleb's watching eyes.

When he rose to go, she laid a hand on the sleeve of his frayed black robe. "John," she said quietly. "Will you do something for me? Send a message to Miss Mab, asking her to choose out the best volumes of magic that she knows of, both of the gnomes and of humankind, to go north also?"

He regarded her for a moment, where she lay on the rough paillasse on her narrow cot which for four nights now had been her solitary bed, her coarse dark hair hanging over the whiteness of her shift. "Wouldn't you rather look them out for yourself, love? You're the one who's to be using them, after all."

She shook her head. His back was to the light of the open court, his features indistinct against the glare; she wanted to reach out her hand to touch him, but somehow could not bring herself to do so. In a cool voice like silver she explained, "The magic of the dragon is in me, John; it is not a thing of books. The books are for Ian, when he comes into his power."

John said nothing for a moment. She wondered if he, too, had realized this about their older son. When he did speak, his voice was small. "Won't you be there to teach him?"

She shook her head. "I don't know, John," she whispered. "I don't know."

He made a move to lay his hand on her shoulder, and she said, "No. Don't touch me. Don't make it harder for me than it already is."

He remained standing for a moment longer before her, looking down into her face. Then, obedient, he silently turned and left the shed.

She had come to no further conclusion by the day of their departure from the Citadel, to take the road back to the north. She was conscious of John watching her, when he thought she wasn't looking; conscious of her own gladness that he never used the one weapon that he must have known would make her stay with him—he never spoke to her of their sons. But in the nights, she was conscious also of the dark cobra shape of the dragon, glittering in the moonlight of the high court, or wheeling down from the black sky with the cold stars of winter prickling upon his spines, as if he had flown through the heart of the galaxy and come back powdered with its light.

The morning of their departure was a clear one, though bitterly cold. The King rode up from Bel to see them off, surrounded by a flowerbed of courtiers, who regarded John with awe and fear, as if wondering how they had dared to mock him, and why he had not slain them all. With him, also, were Polycarp and Gareth and Trey, handfast like schoolchildren. Trey had had her hair redyed, burgundy and gold, which would have looked impressive had it been done in the elaborate styles of the Court instead of in two plaits like a child's down her back.

They had brought with them a long line of horses and mules, laden with supplies for the journey and also with the books for which John had so cheerfully been prepared to risk his life. John knelt before the tall, vague, faded old man, thanking him and swearing fealty; while Jenny, clothed in her colorless northlands plaids, stood to one side, feeling queerly distant from them all and watching how the King kept scanning the faces of the courtiers around him with the air of one who seeks someone, but no longer remembers quite who.

To John the King said, "Not leaving already? Surely it was only yesterday you presented yourself?"

"It will be a long way home, my lord." John did not mention the week he had spent waiting the King's leave to ride forth against the dragon—it was clear the old man recalled little, if anything, of the preceding weeks. "It's best I start before the snows come on heavy."

"Ah." The King nodded vaguely and turned away, leaning on the arms of his tall son and his nephew Polycarp. After a pace or two, he halted, frowning as something surfaced from the murk of his memory, and turned to Gareth. "This Dragonsbane—he did kill the dragon, after all?"

There was no way to explain all that had passed, or how rightness had been restored to the kingdom, save by the appropriate channels, so Gareth said simply, "Yes."

"Good," said the old man, nodding dim approval. "Good."

Gareth released his arm; Polycarp, as Master of the Citadel and his host, led the King away to rest, the courtiers trailing after like a school of brightly colored, ornamental fish. From among them stepped three small, stout forms, their silken robes stirring in the ice winds that played from the soft new sky.

Balgub, the new Lord of the Deep of Ylferdun, inclined his head; with the stiff unfamiliarity of one who has seldom spoken the words, he thanked Lord Aversin the Dragonsbane, though he did not specify for what.

"Well, he hardly could, now, could he?" John remarked, as the three gnomes left the court in the wake of the King's party. Only Miss Mab had caught Jenny's eye and winked at her. John went on, "If he came out and said, 'Thank you for blowing up the Stone,' that would be admitting that he was wrong about Zyerne not poisoning it."

Gareth, who was still standing hand-in-hand with Trey beside them, laughed. "You know, I think he does admit it in his heart, though I don't think he'll ever completely forgive us for doing it. At least, he's civil to me in Council—which is fortunate, since I'm going to have to be dealing with him for a long time."

"Are you?" A flicker of intense interest danced in John's eye.

Gareth was silent for a long moment, fingering the stiff lace of his cuff and not meeting John's gaze. When he looked up again, his face was weary and sad.

"I thought it would be different," he said quietly. "I thought once Zyerne was dead, he would be all right. And he's better, he really is." He spoke like a man trying to convince himself that a mended statue is as beautiful as it was before it broke. "But he's—he's so absentminded. Badegamus says he can't be trusted to remember edicts he's made from one day to the next. When I was in Bel, we made up a Council—Badegamus, Balgub, Polycarp, Dromar, and I—to sort out what we ought to do; then I tell Father to do it—or remind him it's what he was going to do, and he'll pretend he remembers. He knows he's gotten forgetful, though he doesn't quite remember why. Sometimes he'll wake in the night, crying Zyerne's name or my mother's." The young man's voice turned momentarily unsteady. "But what if he never recovers?"

"What if he never does?" John returned softly. "The Realm will be yours in any case one day, my hero." He turned away and began tightening the cinches of the mules, readying them for the trek down through the city to the northward road.

"But not now!" Gareth followed him, his words making soft puffs of steam in the morning cold. "I mean—I never have time for myself anymore! It's been months since I worked on my poetry, or tried to complete that southern variant of the ballad of Antara Warlady . . ."

"There'll be time, by and by." The Dragonsbane paused, resting his hand on the arched neck of Battlehammer, Gareth's parting gift to him. "It will get easier, when men know to come to you directly instead of to your father."

Gareth shook his head. "But it won't be the same."

"Is it ever?" John moved down the line, tightening cinches, checking straps on the parcels of books—volumes of healing, Anacetus' works on greater and lesser demons, Luciard's *Firegiver*, books on engineering and law, by gnomes and men. Gareth followed him silently, digesting the fact that he was now, for all intents and purposes, the Lord of Bel, with the responsibilities of the kingdom—for which he had been academically prepared under the mental heading of "some day"—thrust suddenly upon his unwilling shoulders. Like John, Jenny thought pityingly, he would have to put aside the pursuit of his love of knowledge for what he owed his people and return to it only when he could. The only difference was that his realm was at peace and that John had been a year younger than Gareth was when the burden had fallen to him.

"And Bond?" John asked gently, looking over at Trey.

She sighed and managed to smile. "He still asks about Zyerne," she said softly. "He really did love her, you know. He knows she's dead and he tries to pretend he remembers it happening the way I told him, about her falling off a horse . . . But it's odd. He's kinder than he was. He'll never be considerate, of course, but he's not so quick or so clever, and I think he hurts people less. He dropped a cup at luncheon yesterday—he's gotten very clumsy—and he even apologized to me." There was a slight wryness to her smile, perhaps to cover tears. "I remember when he would not only have blamed me for it, but gotten me to blame myself."

She and Gareth had been following John down the line, still hand in hand, the girl's rose-colored skirts bright against the pewter grayness of the frosted morning. Jenny, standing apart, listened to their voices, but felt as if she saw them through glass, part of a life from which she was half-separated, to which she did not have to go back unless she chose. And all the while, her mind listened to the sky, hearing with strange clarity the voices of the wind around the Citadel towers, seeking something . . .

She caught John's eye on her and saw the worry crease between his brows; something wrung and wrenched in her heart.

"Must you go?" Gareth asked hesitantly, and Jenny, feeling as if her thoughts had been read, looked up; but it was to John that he had spoken. "Could you stay with me, even for a little while? It will take nearly a month for the troops to be ready—you could have a seat on the Council. I—I can't do this alone."

John shook his head, leaning on the mule Clivy's withers. "You are doing it alone, my hero. And as for me, I've my own realm to look after. I've been gone long as it is." He glanced questioningly at Jenny as he spoke, but she looked away.

Wind surged down around them, crosswise currents swirling her plaids and her hair like the stroke of a giant wing. She looked up and saw the shape of the dragon melting down from the gray and cobalt of the morning sky.

She turned from the assembled caravan in the court without a word and ran to the narrow stair that led up to the walls. The dark shape hung like a black kite on the wind, the soft voice a song in her mind.

By my name you have bidden me go, Jenny Waynest, he said. *Now that you are going, I too shall depart. But by your name, I ask that you follow. Come with me, to the islands of the dragons in the northern seas. Come with me, to be of us, now and forever.*

She knew in her heart that it would be the last time of his asking; that if she denied him now, that door would never open again. She stood poised for a moment, between silver ramparts and silver sky. She was aware of

John climbing the steps behind her, his face emptied of life and his spectacle lenses reflecting the pearly colors of the morning light; was aware, through him, of the two little boys waiting for them in the crumbling tower of Alyn Hold—boys she had borne without intention of raising, boys she should have loved, she thought, either more or less than she had.

But more than them, she was aware of the dragon, drifting like a ribbon against the remote white eye of the day moon. The music of his name shivered in her bones; the iron and fire of his power streaked her soul.

To be a mage you must be a mage, she thought. The key to magic is magic.

She turned and looked back, to see John standing on the root-buckled pavement between the barren apple trees behind her. Past him, she glimpsed the caravan of horses in the court below, Trey and Gareth holding the horses' heads as they snorted and fidgeted at the scent of the dragon. For a moment, the memory of John's body and John's voice overwhelmed her—the crushing strength of his muscles and the curious softness of his lips, the cold slickness of a leather sleeve, and the fragrance of his body mixed with the more prosaic pungence of woodsmoke and horses that permeated his scruffy plaids.

She was aware, too, of the desperation and hope in his eyes.

She saw the hope fade, and he smiled. "Go if you must, love," he said softly. "I said I wouldn't hold you, and I won't. I've known it for days."

She shook her head, wanting to speak, but unable to make a sound, her dark hair swirled by the wind of the dragon's wings. Then she turned from him, suddenly, and ran to the battlements, beyond which the dragon lay waiting in the air.

Her soul made the leap first, drawing power from the wind and from the rope of crystal thought that Morkeleb flung her, showing her the way. The elements around the nucleus of her essence changed, as she shed the shape that she had known since her conception and called to her another, different shape. She was half-conscious of spreading her arms against the wind as she strode forward over the edge of the battlement, of the wind in her dark hair as she sprang outward over the long drop of stone and cliff and emptiness. But her mind was already speeding toward the distant cloud peaks, the moon, the dragon.

On the walls behind her, she was aware of Trey whispering, "She's beautiful . . ."

Against the fading day moon, the morning's strengthening light caught in the milk-white silk of her spreading wings and flashed like a spiked carpet of diamonds along the ghost-pale armor of the white dragon's back and sides.

But more than of that, she was conscious of John, Dragonsbane of ballad and legend, watching her with silent tears running down his still face as she circled into the waiting sky, like a butterfly released from his hand. Then he turned from the battlements, to the court where the horses waited. Taking the rein from the stunned Gareth, he mounted Battlehammer and rode through the gateway, to take the road back to the north.

18

They flew north together, treading the woven roads of the sky.

The whole Earth lay below her, marked with the long indigo shadows of morning, the bright flash of springing water, and the icy knives of the glaciers. She saw the patterns of the sea, with its currents of green and violet, its great, gray depths, and the scrum of white lace upon its surface, and those of the moving air. All things were to her as a dragon sees them, a net of magic and years, covering the Earth and holding it to all the singing universe in a crystal web of time.

They nested among the high peaks of Nast Wall, among the broken bone ends of the world, looking eastward over the gorges where the bighorn sheep sprang like fleas from rock to rock, past dizzying drops of green meltwater and woods where the dampness coated each tree in pillows of emerald moss, and down to the woods on the foothills of the Marches, where those who swore fealty to the Master dwelt. Westward, she could look past the glacier that lay like a stilled river of green and white through the gouged gray breakers of the cliffs, past cold and barren rocks, to see the Wildspae gleaming like a sheet of brown silk beneath the steam of its mists and, in the glimmering bare woods along its banks, make out the lacework turrets of Zyerne's hunting lodge among the trees.

Like a dragon, she saw backward and forward in time; and like a dragon, she felt no passion at what she saw.

She was free, to have what she had always sought—not only the power, which the touch of Morkeleb's mind had kindled in her soul, but freedom to pursue that power, released from the petty grind of the work of days.

Her mind touched and fingered that knowledge, wondering at its beauty and its complexity. It was hers now, as it had always been hers for the taking. No more would she be asked to put aside her meditations, to trek ten miles on foot over the wintry moors to deliver a child; no more would she spend the hours needed for the study of her power ankle-deep in a half-frozen marsh, looking for frogwort for Muffle the smith's rheumatism.

No more would her time—and her mind—be divided between love and power.

Far off, her dragon's sight could descry the caravan of horses, making their antlike way along the foothills and into the woods. So clear was her crystal sight that she could identify each beast within that train—the white Moon Horse, the balky roans, the stupid sorrel Cow, and the big liver-bay Battlehammer—she saw, too, the flash of spectacle lenses and the glint of metal spikes on a patched old doublet.

He was no more to her now than the first few inches upon the endless ribbon of dragon years. Like the bandits and the wretched Meewinks—like his and her sons—he had his own path to follow through the labyrinth patterns of darkening time. He would go on with his fights for his people and with his dogged experiments with rock salts and hot-air balloons, his model ballistas and his quest for lore about pigs. One day, she thought, he would take a boat out to the rough waters of Eldsbouch Cove to search for the ruins of the drowned breakwater, and she would not be waiting for him on the round pebbles of the gravel beach . . . He would ride out to the house beneath the standing stones on Frost Fell, and she would not be standing in its doorway.

In time, she knew, even these memories would fade. She saw within herself, as she had probed at the souls of others. Trey's, she recalled, had been like a clear pool, with bright shallows and unsuspected depths. Zyerne's had been a poisoned flower. Her own soul she saw also as a flower whose petals were turning to steel at their outer edges but whose heart was still soft and silky flesh. In time, it would be all steel, she saw, breathtakingly beautiful and enduring forever—but it would cease to be a flower.

She lay for a long time in the rocks, motionless save for the flick of her jeweled antennae as she scried the colors of the wind.

It was thus to be a dragon, she told herself, to see the patterns of all things from the silence of the sky. It was thus to be free. But pain still poured from some broken place inside her—the pain of choice, of loss, and of stillborn dreams. She would have wept, but there was nothing within dragons that could weep. She told herself that this was the last time she would have to feel this pain or the love that was its source. It was for this immunity that she had sought the roads of the sky.

The key to magic is magic, she thought. And all magic, all power, was now hers.

But within her some other voice asked, For what purpose? Afar off she was aware of Morkeleb, hunting the great-horned sheep in the rocks. Like a black bat of steel lace, he passed as soundlessly as his own shadow over the snowfields, wrapping himself in the colors of the air to drop down the gorges, the deceptive glitter of his magic hiding him from the nervous, stupid eyes of his prey. Magic was the bone of dragon bones, the blood of their blood; the magic of the cosmos tinted everything they perceived and everything they were.

And yet, in the end, their magic was sterile, seeking nothing but its own—as Zyerne's had been.

Zyerne, Jenny thought. The key to magic is magic. For it Zyerne had sacrificed the men who loved her, the son she would have borne, and, in the end, her very humanity—even as she herself had done!

Caerdinn had been wrong. For all his striving to perfect his arts, in the end he had been nothing but a selfish, embittered old man, the end of a Line that was failing because it sought magic for magic's sake. The key to magic was not magic, but the use of magic; it lay not in having, but in giving and doing—in loving, and in being loved.

And to her mind there rose the image of John, sitting beside Morkeleb in the high court of the Citadel. Having so little, we shared among ourselves to make any of it worth having . . . the consequences of not caring enough to do it would have been worse . . .

It had been John all along, she thought. Not the problem, but the solution.

Shadow circled her, and Morkeleb sank glittering to the rocks at her side. The sun was half-down the west and threw the shimmer of the blue glacier light over him like a sparkling cloak of flame.

What is it, wizard woman?

She said, *Morkeleb, return me to being what I was.*

His scales bristled, flashing, and she felt the throb of his anger deep in her mind. *Nothing can ever return to being what it was, wizard woman. You know that. My power will be within you forever, nor can the knowledge of what it is to be a dragon even be erased from your mind.*

Even so, she said. *Yet I would rather live as a woman who was once a dragon than a dragon who was once a woman. On the steps of the Deep, I killed with fire, as a dragon kills; and like a dragon, I felt nothing. I do not want to become that, Morkeleb.*

Bah, Morkeleb said. Heat smoked from the thousand razor edges of his scales, from the long spikes and the folded silk of his wings. *Do not be a fool, Jenny Waynest. All the knowledge of the dragons, all their power, is yours, and all the years of time. You will forget the loves of the earth soon and be healed. The diamond cannot love the flower, for the flower lives only a day, then fades and dies. You are a diamond now.*

The flower dies, Jenny said softly, *having lived. The diamond will never do either. I do not want to forget, and the healing will make me what I never wanted to be. Dragons have all the years of time, Morkeleb, but even dragons cannot roll back the flow of days, nor return along them to find again time that they have lost. Let me go.*

No! His head swung around, his white eyes blazing, his long mane bristling around the base of his many horns.

I want you, wizard woman, more than I have ever wanted any gold. It is something that was born in me when your mind touched mine, as my magic was born in you. Having you, I will not give you up.

She gathered her haunches beneath her and threw herself out into the void of the air, white wings cleaving the wind. He flung himself after, swinging down the gray cliffs and waterfalls of Nast Wall, their shadows chasing one another over snow clefts dyed blue with the coming evening and rippling like gray hawks over the darkness of stone and chasm. Beyond, the world lay carpeted by autumn haze, red and ochre and brown; and from the unleaved trees of the woods near the river, Jenny could see a single thread of smoke rising, far off on the evening wind.

The whiteness of the full moon stroked her wings; the stars, through whose secret paths the dragons had once come to the earth and along which they would one day depart, swung like a web of light in their unfolding patterns above. Her dragon sight descried the camp in the woods and a lone, small figure patiently scraping burned bannocks off the griddle, books from a half-unpacked box stacked around him.

She circled the smoke, invisible in the colors of the air, and felt the darkness of a shadow circling above her.

Wizard woman, said the voice of the dragon in her mind, *is this truly what you want?*

She did not reply, but she knew that, dragon-wise, he felt the surge and patterns of her mind. She felt his bafflement at them, and his anger, both at her and at something within himself.

At length he said, *I want you, Jenny Waynest. But more that you, I want your happiness, and this I do not understand—I do not want you in grief.* And then, his anger lashing at her like a many-tailed whip, *You have done this to me!*

I am sorry, Morkeleb, she said softly. *What you feel is the love of humans, and a poor trade for the power that the touch of your mind gave me. It is what I learned first, from loving John—both the pain and the fact that to feel it is better than not to be able to feel.*

Is this the pain that drives you? he demanded.

She said, *Yes.*

Bitter anger sounded in his mind, like the far-off echo of the gold that he had lost. *Go, then*, he said, and she circled down from the air, a thing of glass and lace and bone, invisible in the soft, smoky darkness. She felt the dragon's power surround her with heat and magic, the pain shimmering along her bones. She leaned into the fear that melted her body, as she had leaned into the winds of flight.

Then there was only weariness and grief. She felt alone in the darkness of the autumn woods, the night chill biting into all the newly healed wounds of her back and arms. Through the warty gray and white of the tree boles, she could see the red glow of fire and smell the familiar odors of woodsmoke and horses; the plaintive strains of a pennywhistle keened thinly in the air. The bright edge of color had vanished from all things; the evening was raw and misty, colorless, and very cold. She shivered and drew her sheepskin jacket more closely about her. The earth felt damp where her knees pressed it through her faded skirts.

She brushed aside the dark, coarse mane of her hair and looked up. Beyond the bare lace of the trees, she could see the black dragon still circling, alone in the sounding hollow of the empty sky.

Her mind touched his, with thanks deeper than words. Grief came down to her, grief and hurt, and rage that he could feel hurt.

It is a cruel gift you have given me, wizard woman, he said. *For you have set me apart from my own and destroyed the pleasure of my old joys; my soul is marked with this love, though I do not understand what it is and, like you, I shall never be able to return to what I have been.*

I am sorry, Morkeleb, she said to him. *We change what we touch, be it magic, or power, or another life. Ten years ago I would have gone with you, had I not touched John, and been touched by him.*

Like an echo in her mind she heard his voice. *Be happy, then, wizard woman, with this choice that you have made. I do not understand the reasons for it, for it is not a thing of dragons—but then neither, any longer, am I.*

She felt rather than saw him vanish, flying back in the darkness toward the empty north. For a moment he passed before the white disk of the moon, skeletal silk over its stern face—then he was gone. Grief closed her throat, the grief of roads untaken, of doors not opened, of songs unsung—the human grief of choice. In freeing her, the dragon, too, had made his choice, of what he was and would be.

We change what we touch, she thought. And in that, she supposed,

John—and the capacity to love and to care that John had given her—was, and forever would be, Morkeleb's bane.

She sighed and got stiffly to her feet, dusting the twigs and leaves from her skirts. The shrill, sweet notes of the pennywhistle still threaded the evening breeze, but with them was the smell of smoke, and of bannocks starting to burn. She hitched her plaid up over her shoulder and started up the path for the clearing.

Dragonshadow

For J.W.L.

BOOK ONE
The Skerries of Light

1

Dragonsbane, they called him.

Slayer of dragons.

Or *a* dragon, anyway. And, he'd later found out, not such a very big one at that.

Lord John Aversin, Thane of the Winterlands, leaned back in the mended oak chair in his library as the messenger's footfalls retreated down the tower stairs, and looked across at Jenny Waynest, who was curled up on the windowsill with a cat dozing in her lap.

"Bugger," he said.

The night's first appreciable breeze—warm and sticky as such things were in the Winterlands in summer—brought the grit of woodsmoke through the open window and made the candle flames shudder among the heaped books.

"A hundred feet long," Jenny murmured.

John shook his head. "Gaw, any dragon looks a hundred feet long if you're under it." He pushed his round-lensed spectacles more firmly onto the bridge of his long nose. "Or in a position where you have to think about bein' under it in the near future. I doubt it's over fifty. That one we slew over by Far West Riding wasn't quite thirty . . ." He nodded to the cold fireplace, where the black spiked mace of the golden dragon's tail-tip hung. "And Morkeleb the Black was forty-two, though I thought he'd whack me over the back of the head when I asked could I measure him." He grinned at the memory, but behind the spectacles Jenny could see the fear in his eyes.

Almost as an afterthought he added, "We'll have to go after it."

Jenny stroked the cat's head. "Yes." Her voice was inaudible. The cat purred and made bread on her knee.

"Funny, that." John got to his feet and stretched to get the crick out of his back. "I've put together every account I can find of past Dragonsbanes—all them old ballads and tales—and matched 'em up as well as I could with the King-lists." He gestured to the vast rummage that covered desk and floor and every shelf of the low-vaulted study: bound bundles of notes, parchments half copied from waterstained books found in the ruins south of Wrynde. Curillius on *The Deeds of the Ancient Heroes,* Gorgonimir's *Creatures and Phenomena.* A fair copy of a fragment of the old *Liever Draiken* sent by the Regent of Bel, a connoisseur of both ancient manuscripts and the tales of Dragonsbanes. Notes yet to be copied—he'd jotted them down two years ago—of a dragon-slaying song sung by one of the garrison at Cair Corflyn, all mixed up with wax note tablets, candles, inkwells, scrapers, prickers, pumice, candle scissors, and dismantled clocks. For the fourteen years they'd been together, Jenny had heard John swear every year or two he'd put the place in order, and she knew that the phrase "put together" must not be taken too literally.

Magpie gleanings of learning by a man whose curiosity was an unfilled well; accretions of useful, interesting, or merely frivolous lore spewed back at random by circumstance and the mad God of Time.

"Some Dragonsbanes slay one dragon and that's that, they're in the ballads for good," mused John. "Others slay two or three, and two of those, as far as I can figure 'em, are within ten years of the singletons. Then you'll get generations, fifty, sixty, seventy years, when the dragons mind their own business, whatever that is, and nobody slays anybody. This is three for me. How'd I get so lucky?"

"The North is being settled again." Jenny set Skinny Kitty aside and went to stand behind John, her arms around his waist. Through his rough red wool doublet and patched linen shirt she felt the ribs under the hard sheath of muscle, the warmth of his flesh. "It was the cattle herd at Skep Dhû garrison that the dragon hit. There probably hasn't been this much livestock in the North since the Kings left. It may have drawn this one."

"Gaw," he said again, and set his hand over the folded knot of hers. An oddly deft hand for a warrior's, inkstained and blistered in two places from a chemical experiment that took an unexpected turn. But thick, like his forearm, with the muscle of a lifetime of wielding a sword. In profile his was the face of a scholar. In his reddish-brown hair, hanging loose to his shoulders, the candlelight gilded the first flecks of gray.

He'd been twenty-four when he'd gone against the gold Dragon of Wyr, and his side still hurt like a knife-thrust from the damaged ribs whenever the weather turned. Jenny's fingers could detect the ridge of the biggest scar he'd taken when he fought Morkeleb the Black in the burned-out Deep beneath Nast Wall. *Life is fragile,* she thought. *Life is precious, and life is short.* "How many is the most any Dragonsbane has been able to slay?" she asked, and John half-turned his head to grin down over his shoulder at her.

"Three. That was Alkmar the Godborn. His third dragon killed him."

In the hour or so that separated them from moonrise, John and Jenny mustered all they would need for the slaying of the Dragon of Skep Dhû, such of them as were stored at the Hold. John's battle armor, almost as battered and sorry as the doublet of black leather and iron in which he was wont to patrol his lands. Two axes, one a short, single-grip weapon that could be wielded from the back of a horse, the other longer and heavier, a two-handed thing for finishing a creature dying on the ground. Eight harpoons, like boar spears but larger, barbed and massive and written over with spells of death and ruin.

John's half-brother Muffle, sergeant of the local militia and smith of the village of Alyn, had forged the first two in a hurry, when the Dragon of Wyr had descended on the herds of Great Toby fourteen years ago, and the others had been made a few weeks after that. Jenny had put spells of death on them all. In those days her powers had been small, hedge-witch magics taught her by old Caerdinn, who had once been tutor at Alyn Hold, and she had known little of dragons, only scraps and snippets culled from John's books. Killing the golden dragon had taught her something of a dragon's nature, so when Prince Gareth of Magloshaldon, later Regent for the King of Belmarie, had come begging John's help against the Dragon of Nast Wall, she had been able to weave more accurate spells. Her magic was still, at that time, small.

Now she sat on the wooden platform that John and Muffle had built at the top of the tower for John's telescope. The eight harpoons lay before her on the planks. Far below she heard John's voice, and Muffle's, distant as birdsong but far more profane, as they dragged out cauldrons and wood. She heard Adric's voice, too, a gay treble—her second son, at eight burly and red-haired and every inch the descendant of John's formidable, bearlike father: *He should be in bed!* Beyond a doubt three-year-old Mag was trailing, silent as a marsh fey, at his heels.

For a moment she felt annoyed at John's Cousin Dilly, who was supposed to be looking after the children, and then let all thought of them slip away with the releasing of her breath. *You cannot be a mage,* old Caerdinn had said to her, *if your thoughts are ever straying: to your supper, to your child, to whether you will have the next breath of air after this one is gone from under your ribs. The key to magic is magic. Never forget that.*

And though she had found that magic's key was something else, in many ways the old man had been correct. Her thought circled, like the power circle she had drawn on the platform around herself and the harpoons, and like the power that came down to her in silver threads from the shape of the stars, her thought took shape.

Cruelty. Uncaring. The quenching of life. The weary welcoming of the final dark.

Death-spells. And behind the death-spells, the gold fierce fire of dragon-magic.

For four years, now, that dragon-blaze had burned in her blood.

Morkeleb, she thought, *forgive me.*

Or was it not a thing of dragons to forgive?

Morkeleb the Black. The Dragon of Nast Wall.

She summoned the magic down from the stars, out of the air, called it from the core of fire within her that had burned into life when, by Morkeleb's power, she had been transformed to dragon-kind. Though she had returned to human form, abandoning the immortality of the star-drakes, part of her essence, her inner heart, had remained the essence of a dragon, and she understood power as dragons understood it. Since it was not a thing of dragons to think or care, she did not, as she wove her death-spells, think or care about Morkeleb, who had loved her.

Loved her enough to let her return to human form.

Loved her enough to return her to John.

But after the death-spells were wrought and bound into the harpoons, she sat on the rickety platform above the Hold, her arms clasped round her knees, listening to the far-off voices of her husband and her son and remembering the skeletal black shape in the darkness, the silver labyrinthine eyes.

Morkeleb.

"Mother?"

Starlight showed the trapdoor that opened among the slates of the turret roof, but it did not penetrate the shadow underneath. Mageborn, Jenny was able to see her elder son, Ian, a weedy twelve-year-old, her own night-black hair and blue eyes in John's beaky face. He stepped onto the steeply slanting roof and made to come down the stairs, and she said, "No, wait there." The weariness of working the death-songs dragged at her bones. "Let me gather these up and send them on their way."

Ian, she knew, would understand what she said. Only this year his own powers had started to manifest: small, as any teenager's were—the ability to call fire and find lost objects, to sometimes see in fire things far away. Ian sat on the trapdoor's sill and watched in fascination as she drew the glimmer from out of the circles, collecting it like cold spider-silk in her hands. All magic, Caerdinn had taught her, depended on Limitations.

Before even beginning to lay down the circles of power, let alone summon the death-spells, she had cleansed the platform with rainwater and
hyssop and laid on each separate rough-hewn plank such Words as would
keep the vile magics from attaching to the place itself. Spells, too, were
required to hold the wicked ferocity of what she had done within a small
space, so it would not disperse over the countryside and cause ruin and
death to everyone in the Hold, in the village, in the farms that nestled
close to the walls. Like a miser picking up pinhead-sized crumbs of gold
dust with his fingernails, so Jenny gathered into her palms each whisper
and shudder of the death-spells' residue, named them and neutralized
them and released them into the turning starlight.

"Can I help?"

"No, not this time. You see what I'm doing, though?" He nodded. As
she worked, she felt, rising through her—as it always rose, it seemed to
her, at the most inopportune of times—the miserable flush of heat, the
reminder that the change of a woman's life was coming upon her.
Patiently, wearily, she called upon other spells, little silvery cantrips of
blood and time, to put that heat aside. "With spells of cursing you must be
absolutely thorough, absolutely clean, particularly with spells worked in
a high place," she said.

Ian's eyes went to John's telescope, mounted at the far side of the
platform; she saw he read her thought. It would not take much, they both
knew, for the rail to give way, or John to lose his balance. A fragment of
curse, a stray shadow of ill will, would be enough to cause John or Ian or
anyone else to forget to latch the trapdoor, or for the latch to stick, so that
Adric or Mag, or one of Cousin Rowanberry's ever-multiplying brood,
could come up here . . .

And even so, the platform was the safest place in all the Hold to work
such spells.

As she and Ian bore the harpoons down the twisting stair, Jenny
remembered what it had been, to be a dragon. To be a creature of diamond heart and limitless power. A creature to whom magic was not
something that one *did*—well or less well—but the thing that one *was*:
will and magic, flesh and bone, all one.

And not caring if a child fell from the platform.

With the moon's rising John and Jenny and Ian rode out from Alyn
Hold to the stone house on Frost Fell, where Jenny had for so many years
lived alone. It had been Caerdinn's house, and Jenny had lived as the old
wizard's pupil from the time she was thirteen and the buds of power she'd
had as a child began to blossom. A single big room and a loft, book-
shelves, a table of pickled pine, a vast hearth, and a big bed. It was to this
house that John had first come to her, twenty-two and needing help

against one of the bandit hordes that had been the scourge of the Winter-lands in the days before the King sent his protecting armies to them again. He'd been challenged, Jenny recalled, to single combat by some bandit chief—maybe the one who had slain his father—and had heard that no weapon could harm a man who'd lain with a witch.

But she'd remembered him from her own childhood and his. His mother had been Jenny's first teacher in the arts of power, a captive woman, an Icerider witch: The scandal when Lord Aver married her had been a nine days' wonder through the Winterlands. When her son was four and Jenny seven, Kahiera Nightraven had vanished, gone back to the Iceriders, leaving Jenny with no better instructor than Caerdinn, who had hated all Iceriders and Kahiera above the rest. From that time until his arrival at Frost Fell, she had seen Kahiera's son barely a score of times.

Riding up the fell now, she saw him in her mind as she had seen him then—cocky, quirky, aggressive, the scourge of maidens in five villages . . . And angry. It was his anger she remembered most, and the shy fleeting sweetness of his smile.

"Place needs thatching," he remarked now, standing in Battleham-mer's stirrups to pull a straw from the overhang of the roof. "According to Dotys' *Catalogues*, villagers on the Silver Isles used to braid straw into solid tiles and peg 'em to the rafterwork, which must have been gie heavy. Cowan"—the head stableman at the Hold—"says it can't be done, but I've a mind to try this summer, if I can find how they did the braiding. If we're all still alive by haying, that is." Chewing the straw, he dropped from the warhorse's back, looped the rein around the gate, and trailed Jenny and Ian into the house. "Garn," he added, sniffing. "Why is it no matter what kind of Weirds you lay around the house, Jen, to keep wan-derers from even seein' the place, mice always seem to get in just fine?"

Jenny flashed him a quick glance by the soft blue radiance of the witchlight she called and bent to pull from under the bed the box of herbs she kept there. Hellebore, yellow jessamine, and the bright red caps of panther-mushroom, carefully potted in wax-stoppered jars. Jars and box were written around with spells, as the house walls were written, to keep intruders away, but there were two mice dead under the bed nevertheless.

Jenny traced the box with her blunt brown fingertips, automatically undoing the wards she had woven. Calabash gourds from the south con-tained the heads of water-vipers and the dried bodies of certain jellyfish. Nameless leaves were tied in ensorcelled thread, and waxed-parchment packets held deadly earths and salts. On the other side of the room Ian hunted among the few books still on the shelf; John caught Jenny around the waist, tripped her and tossed her onto the old flattened mattress, grinning impishly as she flung a spell across the room to keep Ian unaware of his parents' misbehavior . . .

"Behave yourself." She wriggled from his grasp, giggling like a village girl.

"It's been too long since we've come here." He let her up, but held her with one arm on either side of her, hands grasping the rough bedpost behind her back. Though only a little over medium height himself, John was easily a foot taller than she; the witchlight flashed silvery in his spectacles and in the twinkle of his eyes.

"And whose fault is that?" She kept her voice low—Ian was still preoccupied with his search. "*I* wasn't the one who made stinks and messes and explosions in quest of self-igniting kindling all spring. *I* wasn't the one who had to try to make a flying machine from drawings he'd found in some old book . . ."

"That was Heronax of Ernine," protested John. "He flew from Ernine to the Silver Isles in it—wherever Ernine was—and I've gie near got the thing working properly now. You'll see."

He gathered her hair up in his hands, an overflowing double handful of oceanic night, and bent to kiss her lips. His body pressed hers to the tall, smooth-hewn post, and her hand explored the leather of his doublet, the rough wool of the dull-colored plaid wrapped over his shoulder, the hard muscle beneath the linen sleeve. Ian apparently bethought himself of some ingredient hidden inexplicably in the garden, for he wandered unseeing outside; the scents of the old house wrapped them around, moldy thatch and mice and the wild whisper of summer night in the Winterlands.

The heat of her body's changing whispered to her, and she whispered back, *Go away.* It was not just the little cantrips, the knots of warding and change, that turned aside those migraines, those flashes of moodiness, those alien angers. It was this knowledge, this man, the lips that sought hers and the warmth of his flesh against her. The joy of a girl who had been ugly, who had been scorned and stoned in the village streets, who had been told, *You're a witch and will grow old alone.*

The knowledge that this was not true.

Later she breathed, "*And* your dragon-slaying machine."

"Aye, well." He straightened from hunting her fallen hairpins, and the hard line returned to crease the corner of his mouth. "That's near done, too. More's the pity I spent this past winter tryin' to learn to fly instead."

Early in the morning Jenny kindled fire under the cauldrons that Sergeant Muffle had set up in the Hold's old barracks court. She fetched water from the well in the corner and spent the day brewing poisons to put on the ensorcelled harpoons. In this she accepted Ian's help, and John's, too, and it was all John's various aunts could do to keep Adric and Mag from stealing into the court and poisoning themselves in the process of lending a hand. By the late-gathering summer twilight they were dipping the harpoons into the thickened black mess, and the messenger from Skep Dhû joined them in the court.

"It isn't just the garrison that relies on that herd," the young man said, glancing, a little uncertainly, from the unprepossessing, bespectacled form of the Dragonsbane, stripped to a rather sooty singlet, doeskin britches, and boots, to that of the Witch of Frost Fell. His name was Borin, and he was a lieutenant of cavalry at the garrison, and like most southerners had to work very hard not to bite his thumb against evil in Jenny's presence. "The manors the Regent is trying to establish to feed all the new garrisons depend on those cattle as well, for breeding and restocking. And we lost six, maybe eight bulls and as many cows, as far as we can gather—the carcasses stripped and gouged, the whole pasture swept with fire."

John glanced at Jenny, who could almost read his thoughts. Fifteen cattle was a lot.

"And you got a good look at it?"

Borin nodded. "I saw it flying away toward the other side of the Skepping Hills. Green, as I said to you last night. The spines and horns down its back, and the barb on its tail, were crimson as blood."

There was a moment's silence. Ian, on the other side of the court, carefully propped two of the harpoons against the long shed that served John as a workroom; Sergeant Muffle leaned against the side of the bee-hive-shaped clay furnace in the center of the yard and wiped the sweat from his face. John said softly, "Green with crimson horns," and Jenny knew why that small upright line appeared between his brows. He was fishing through his memory for the name of a star-drake of those colors in the old dragon-lists. *Teltrevir, heliotrope,* the old list said, the list handed down rote from centuries ago, compiled by none knew whom. *Centhwevir blue, knotted with gold.*

"Only a dozen or so are on the list," said Jenny quietly. "There must be dozens—hundreds—that are not."

"Aye." He moved two of the harpoons, a restless gesture, not meeting her eyes. "We don't even know how many dragons there are in the world, or where they live—or what they eat, for that matter, when they're not makin' free with our herds." His voice was deep, like scuffed brown velvet; Jenny could sense him drawing in on himself, gathering himself for the fight. "In Gantering Pellus' *The Encyclopedia of Everything in the*

Material World it says they live in volcanoes that are crowned with ice, but then again Gantering Pellus also says bears are born shapeless like dough and licked into shape by their fathers. I near got meself killed when I was fifteen, findin' out how much he didn't know about bears. The *Liever Draiken* has it that dragons come down from the north . . ."

"Will you want a troop of men to help you?" asked Borin. In the short time he'd been at the Hold he'd already learned that when the Thane of the Winterlands started on ancient writings it was better to simply interrupt if one wanted anything done. "Commander Rocklys said she could dispatch one to meet you at Skep Dhû."

John hesitated, then said, "Better not. Or at least, have 'em come, but no nearer than Wormwood Ford. There's a reason them old heroes are always riding up on the dragon's lair by themselves, son. Dragons listen, even in their sleep. Just three or four men, they'll hear 'em coming, miles off, and be in the air by the time company arrives. If a dragon gets in the air, the man going after it is dead. You *have* to take 'em on the ground."

"Oh." Borin tried hard to look unconcerned about this piece of news. "I see."

"At a guess," John added thoughtfully, "the thing's laired up in the ravines on the northwest side of the Skepping Hills, near where the herd was pastured. There's only one or two ravines large enough to take a dragon. It shouldn't be hard to figure out which. And then," he said grimly, "then we'll see who gets slain."

2

It was a ride of almost two days, east to the Skepping Hills. John and Jenny took with them, in addition to Borin and the two southern soldiers who'd ridden with him—a not-unreasonable precaution in the Winterlands—Skaff Gradely, who acted as militia captain for the farms around Alyn Hold, and two of Jenny's cousins from the Darrow Bottoms, all of whom were unwilling to leave their farms this close to haying-time but equally unwilling to have the dragon move west. Sergeant Muffle was left in command of the Hold.

"There's no reason for it," argued Borin, who appeared to have gotten the Hold servants to launder and press his red military tunic and polish his boots. "There's been no sign of bandits this spring. Commander Rocklys has put this entire land under law again, so there's really no call for a man to walk armed wherever he goes." He almost, but not quite, looked pointedly at Gradely and the Darrow boys, who, as usual for those born and bred in the Winterlands, bristled with knives, spiked clubs, axes, and the long slim savage northern bows. Jenny knew that in the King's southern lands, farmers did not even carry swords—most of the colonists who had come in the wake of the new garrisons were, in fact, serfs, transplanted by royal fiat to these manors and forbidden to carry weapons at all.

"There's never any sign of bandits that're good at their jobs." John signaled a halt for the dozenth time and dismounted to scout, though by order of the Commander of the Winterlands, roads in this part of the country had been cleared for a bow shot's distance on either side. In Jenny's opinion, whoever had done the clearing had no idea how far a northern longbow could shoot.

Borin said, "Really!" as John disappeared into the trees, his green and brown plaid mingling with the colors of the thick-matted brush. "Every one of these stops loses us time, and . . ."

Jenny lifted her hand for silence, listening ahead, around, among the trees. Stretching out her senses, as wizards did. Smelling for horses. Listening for birds and rabbits that would fall silent at the presence of man. Feeling the air as a wealthy southern lady would feel silk with fingers white and sensitive, seeking a flaw, a thickened thread . . .

Arts that all of Jenny's life, of all the lives of her parents and grandparents, had meant the difference between life and death in the Winterlands.

In time she said, quietly, "I apologize if this seems to discount Commander Rocklys' defenses of the Realm, Lieutenant. But Skep Dhû is the boundary garrison in these parts, and beyond it, the bandit troops might still be at large. The great bands, Balgodorus Black-Knife's, or that of Gorgax the Red, number in hundreds. If I know them, they've been waiting all spring for a disruption such as a dragon would cause to raid the new manors while your captain's attention is elsewhere."

The lieutenant looked as if he would protest, then simply looked away. Jenny didn't know whether this was because she carried her own halberd and bow slung behind Moon Horse's saddle—women in the south did not customarily go armed, though there were some notable exceptions—or because she was a wizard, or for some other reason entirely. Many of the southern garrisons were devout worshipers of the Twelve Gods and regarded the Winterlands as a wilderness of heresy. In any case, disapproving silence reigned for something like half an hour— Gradely and the Darrow boys sitting their scrubby mounts ten or twelve paces away, scratching under their plaids and picking their noses—until John returned.

They camped that night in the ruins of what had been a small village or a large manor farm three centuries ago, when the Winterlands still supported such things. A messenger met them there with word that the dragon was in fact laired in the largest of the ravines east of the Skepping Hills—"The one with the oak wood along the ridge at its head, my lord"—and that Commander Rocklys had personally led a squadron of fifty to meet them at Wormwood Ford.

"Gaw, leavin' who to garrison Cair Corflyn, if they get themselves munched up?" demanded John, horrified. "You get back now, son, and tell the lot of 'em to stay put. Do they think this is a bloody fox-hunt? The thing'll hear 'em coming ten miles off!"

The second night they made camp early, while light was still high in the sky, in a gully just west of the Skepping Hills. Beyond, the northern arm of the Wood of Wyr lay thick, a land of knotted trees and dark, slow-moving streams that flowed down out of the Gray Mountains, a land that had never been brought under the dominion of the Kings. Lying with John under their spread-out plaids, Jenny felt by his breathing that he did not sleep.

"I hate this," he said softly. "I'd hoped, after meeting Morkeleb— after speaking with him, touching him . . . hearing that voice of his speak in me mind—I'd hoped never to have to go after a dragon again in me life."

Jenny remembered the Dragon of Nast Wall. "No."

He sat up, his arms wrapped around his knees, and looked down at her, knowing how her own experience of the dragon-kind had touched her. "Don't hate me for it, Jen."

She shook her head, knowing that she so easily could. If she didn't understand about the Winterlands, and about what it was to be Thane. "No." John loved wolves, too, and studied every legend, every hunter's tale: He'd built a blind for himself so he could sit and watch them for hours at their howlings and their hunts. He'd drive them away sooner than kill them, if they preyed on the cattle. But he'd kill them without compunction if he had to.

He was Thane of the Winterlands, as his father had been. He could no more turn his back on a fight with a dragon than he could turn his back should a bandit chief, handsome and wise as the priests said gods were, start raiding the farms.

Jenny supposed that if a god were to come burning the fields and killing the stock, exposing the people to the perils of these terrible lands, John would read everything he could on the subject, pick up whatever weapon seemed appropriate, and try to take it on.

The fact that he'd never wanted any of this was beside the point.

An hour after midnight he rose for good, ate cold barley bannocks— none of them had been so foolish as to suggest cooking, within a few miles of a dragon's lair—and armed himself in his fighting doublet, his close-fitting helmet, and iron-backed gloves. Jenny knew that dragons were neither strictly nocturnal nor diurnal, but woke and slept like cats; still, she also knew that most dragons were aground and asleep in the hours just before dawn. She flung a little ravel of witchlight close to the ground, just enough for the horses to see the trail, and led the way toward the razor-backed hunch of the Skepping Hills and the oak-fringed ravine.

Mist swirled around the knees of the horses, floated like rags of silk among the heather. They left Borin on the edge of the heath, to watch from afar. Stretching her senses, Jenny felt everywhere the tingle and touch of magic. Had the dragon summoned these unseasonable mists for protection? she wondered. Would it sense her, sense them, if she raised a counterspell to send them away?

For a star-drake's body to be simply of one color, she thought, it must be either very young or very old, and if very old, its senses would fill the lands around, like still water that would carry the slightest ripple to its dreams. But this she did not feel. She had sensed Morkeleb's awareness when she and John had first ridden to do battle with the black dragon under the shadows of the Deep of Ylferdun . . . The red horns and spikes and tail seemed to argue for a young dragon anyway, but would a youngster be large enough to be mistaken for something a hundred feet long?

She touched John's wrist and whispered, though they were close enough now to the head of the ravine to need absolute silence, "John, wait. There's something wrong."

The ravine before them was a drift of gray mist. His spectacles, framed by his helmet, glinted like the eyes of an enormous moth. In a hunter's whisper, he asked, "Can it hear us? Feel us?"

"I don't know. But I don't . . . I don't feel it. At all."

He tilted his head, inquiring.

"I don't know. Get ready to run or to charge."

Then she reached out with her mind, her will, her dragon-heart and dragon-spells, and tore the mists from the ravine in a single fierce swirl of chilling wind.

The slice and flash of early light blinked on metal in the oak woods above the ravine, and a second later something came roaring and flapping up from between the hills: green, red-horned, bat-winged, snake-headed, serpentine tail tipped with something that looked like a gargantuan crimson arrowhead and absolutely unlike any dragon Jenny had ever seen outside the illuminations of John's old books. John said, "Bugger all!" and Jenny yelled, "John, look out, it's an illusion . . . !"

Unnecessarily, for John was turning already, sword drawn, spurring toward the nearest cover. Jenny followed, flinging behind her a blast and hammer of fire-spells, ripping up from the heather between them and the riders that galloped out of the woods.

Bandits. The illusory dragon dissolved in midair the moment it was clear that neither John nor Jenny was distracted by its presence, and the bearded attackers in makeshift panoplies of hunting leathers and stolen mail converged on the cut overhang of a streambank that provided the only defensible ground in sight.

Jenny followed the fire-spells with a sweeping Word of Poor Aim, and to her shock felt counterspells whirl and clutch at her. Beside her, John cursed and staggered as an arrowhead slashed his thigh. She felt fire-spells in the air around them and breathed Words of Limitation and counterspells herself, distracting her mind from her own magics. Behind the spells she felt the mind of the wizard: an impression of untaught power, of crude talent without training, of enormous strength. She felt stunned, as if she'd walked into a wall in darkness.

John cursed again and nocked the arrows he'd pulled down with him when he'd dismounted; at least, thought Jenny, casting her mind to the head of the stream that the outlaws would have to cross to get at them, their attackers could only come at them from two sides. She tried to call back the mists, to make them work for her and John as they'd concealed the bandits before, but again the counterspells of the other wizard twisted and grabbed at her mind. Fire in the heather, at the same time damping the fire-spells that filled the cut under the bank with smoke; spells of breaking and damage to bowstrings and arrows . . .

And then the bandits were on them. Illusion, distraction—Jenny called them into being, worked them on the filthy, scarred, furious men who waded through the rising stream. Swords, pikes, the hammering rain of slung stones, some of which veered aside with her warding-spells, some of which punched through them as if they had not been there. A man would stop, staring about him in confusion and horror—Jenny's spells of flaring lights, of armed warriors around herself and John taking effect . . . John's sword, or Jenny's halberd, would slash into his flesh. But as many times as not the man would spring back with a cry, seeing clearly, and Jenny would feel on her mind the cold grip of the other mage's counterspell. Illusion, too, she felt, for there were bandits who simply dissolved as the illusion of the dragon had dissolved . . .

And through it all she thought, *The bandits have a wizard! The bandits have a wizard with them!*

In John's words: *Bugger, bugger, bugger.*

Jenny didn't know how long they held them off. Certainly not much longer than it would take to hard-boil an egg, though it seemed far longer. Still, the sun had just cleared the Skepping Hills when she and John first saw the bandits, and when the blare of trumpets sliced golden through the ruckus and Commander Rocklys and her troops rode out of the hills in a ragged line, the shadows hadn't shortened by more than a foot. Jenny felt the other wizard's spells reach out toward the crimson troopers and threw her own power to intercept them, shattering whatever illusions the rescuers would have seen and attacked. Rocklys, standing in her stirrups, drew rein and fired into the thick of the outlaw horde; Jenny saw one of the leaders fall. Then a great voice bellowed, "Out of it, men!" and near the head of the ravine a tall man sprang up on a boulder, massive and black-bearded, like a great dirty bear.

John said, "Curse," and Rocklys, whipping another arrow to her short black southern bow, got off a shot at him. But the arrow went wide—Jenny felt the Word that struck it aside—and then battle surged around them, mist and smoke rising out of the ground like dust from a beaten rug. The spells she'd called onto the stream were working now and the water rushed in furious spate, sweeping men off their feet, the water splashing icy on John's boots and soaking the hem of Jenny's skirt. Then the bandits fled; Rocklys and her men in pursuit.

"Curse it," said John. "Balgodorus Black-Knife, damn his tripes, and they had a wizard with 'em, didn't they, love?" He leaned against the clay wall of the bank, panting; Jenny pressed her hand against his thigh, where the first arrowhead had cut, but felt no poison in the wound.

"Somebody who knew enough about dragon-slaying to know we'd have to attack it alone, together."

"Maggots fester it—ow!" he added, as Jenny applied a rough bandage to the wound. "Anybody'd know that who's heard me talk about it, or talked to someone who had. Anyway, it wasn't me they was after, love." He reached down and touched her face. "It was you."

She looked up, filthy with sweat and soot, her dark hair unraveled: a thin small brown woman of forty-five, flushed—she was annoyed to note—with yet another rise of inner heat. She sent it away, exasperated at the untimeliness and the reminder of her age.

"Me?" She got to her feet. The rush of the stream was dying as quickly as it had risen. Bandits slain by John's sword, or her halberd, or by the arrows of Rocklys' men, lay where the water had washed them.

"You're the only mage in the Winterlands." John tucked up a wet straggle of her hair into a half-collapsed braid, broke off a twig from a nearby laurel bush and worked it in like a hairpin to hold it in place. "In the whole of the King's Realm, for all I know. Gar"—that was the Regent—"told me he's been trying to find wizards in Bel and Greenhythe and all around the Realm, and hasn't located a one, bar a couple of gnomes. So if a bandit like Balgodorus Black-Knife's got a wizard in his troop, and we have none . . ."

"We'd have been in a lot of trouble," Jenny said softly, "had this ambush succeeded."

"And it might have," mused John, "if their boy—"

"Girl."

"Eh?"

"Their mage is a woman. I'm almost certain of it."

He sniffed. "Girl, then. If their girl had known the first thing about star-drakes, beyond that they have wings and long tails, you might not have twigged soon enough to keep us out of the jaws of the trap. Which goes to demonstrate the value of a classical education . . ."

Commander Rocklys returned in a clatter of hooves, Borin at her side. "Are you all right?" She sprang down from her tall bronze-bay warhorse, a lanky powerful woman of thirty, gold-stamped boots spattered with mud and gore. "We were saddled and ready to ride to your help with the dragon when Borin charged into camp shouting you were being ambushed."

"The dragon was a hoax," John said briefly. He wiped a gout of blood from his cheekbone and scrubbed his gloved fingers with the end of his plaid. "Better if it had been a real drake than what's really going on."

Rocklys of Galyon listened, arms folded, to his account. It was a rare woman, Jenny knew, who could get men to follow her into combat; on the whole, most soldiers knew of women only what they saw of their victims during the sack of farmsteads or towns, or what they learned from the camp whores. Some, like John, were willing to learn different. Others had to be strenuously taught. Though the women soldiers Jenny had met— mostly bandits—tended to gang together to protect one another in the war camps, a woman commander as a rule had to be large and strong enough to take on and beat a good percentage of the men under her command.

Rocklys of the House of Uwanë was such a woman. The royal house of Bel was a tall one, and she was easily John's nearly six-foot height, with powerful arms and shoulders that could only have been achieved by the most strenuous physical training. As a cousin of the King, Jenny guessed she would have been granted a position as second-in-command or a captaincy of royal guards regardless, but it was clear by the set of her square chin that an honorary post was not what she wanted.

For the rest, she was fair-haired, like her cousin the Regent Gareth— though the last time Jenny had seen Gareth, two years ago, he'd still affected a dandy's habit of dyeing portions of his hair blue or pink or whatever the fashionable shade was that year. Her eyes, like Gareth's, were a light, cold gray. She neither interrupted nor reacted to John's tale, only stood with the slight breezes moving the gold tassels on her swordbelt and on the red wool oversleeves that covered her linen shirt. At the end of his recital she said, "Damn it." Her voice was a sort of husky growl, and Jenny guessed she'd early acquired the habit of deepening it. "If I'd known there was a wizard with them I'd never have called off the men so soon. You're sure?"

"I'm sure." Jenny stepped up beside John. "Completely aside from the green dragon, which was sheer illusion—only created to lure John and me—I could feel this mage's mind, her power, with every spell I tried to cast. There's a wizard with Balgodorus, and a strong one."

"Damn it." Rocklys' mouth hardened, and for a moment Jenny saw a genuine fury in her eyes. Then they shifted, thoughtful, considering the two people before her: the bloodied and shabby Dragonsbane and the Witch of Frost Fell. Jenny knew the look in her eyes, for she'd seen it often in John's. The look of a commander, considering the tools she has and the job that needs to be done.

"Lady Jenny," she said. "Lord John."

"Now we're in trouble." John looked up from polishing his spectacles on his shirt. "Anytime anyone comes to me and says . . ." He shifted into an imitation of that of the Mayor of Far West Riding, or one of the councilmen of Wrynde, when those worthies would come to the Hold asking him to kill wolves or deal with bandits, " 'Lord John'—or worse, 'Your lordship.' "

Commander Rocklys, who didn't have much of a sense of humor, frowned. "But we are in trouble," she said. "And we shall be in far worse trouble should Balgodorus Black-Knife continue at large, with a witch . . ." She hesitated—she'd used a southern word for the mageborn that had pejorative connotations of evil and slyness—and politely changed it. ". . . with a wizard in his band. Surely you agree."

"And you want our Jen to go after 'em."

Rocklys looked a little surprised to find her logic so readily followed. As if, thought Jenny, the necessity for her to pursue the renegade mage was not obvious to all. "For the good of all the Winterlands, you must agree."

John glanced at Jenny, who nodded slightly. He sighed and said, "Aye." The good of all the Winterlands had ruled his life for twenty-two years, since his father's death. Even before that, when as his father's only son he had been torn from his books and his music and his tinkerings with pulleys and steam, and had a sword thrust into his hand.

Four years ago it had been the good of all the Winterlands that took him south, to barter his body and bones in the fight against Morkeleb the Black, so the King would in return send troops to garrison those lost territories and bring them again under the rule of law.

"Aye, love, you'd best go. God knows if you don't we'll only have 'em besiegin' the Hold in the end."

"Good." Rocklys nodded briskly, though she still looked vexed. "I've already sent one of the men back to Skep Dhû, with orders to outfit a pack-train, Lady Jenny; you'll ride with twenty-five of my men here."

"Twenty-five?" said John. "There were at least twenty in the band that attacked us, and rumor has it Balgodorus commands hundreds these days."

Rocklys shook her head. "My scouts report no more than forty.

Untrained men at that, scum and outlaws, no match for disciplined troops."

"If at all possible," she went on, "bring the woman back alive. The Realm needs mages, Lady Jenny. You know that, you and I have talked of this before. It is only the most appalling prejudice that has caused wizardry to fall into disrepute, so that the Lines of teaching died out or went underground. I am told the gnomes have wizards: That alone should have convinced my uncle and his predecessors to foster, rather than forbid, the study of those arts. Instead, what did they do? Simply crippled themselves, so that four years ago when an evil mage like the Lady Zyerne rose up, no one was prepared to deal with her. That situation cannot be allowed to repeat itself. Yes, Geryon?"

She turned as an orderly spoke to her; John put his hands on Jenny's shoulders.

"Will you be all right?" she asked him, and he bent to kiss her lips. She tasted blood on his, and sweat and dirt; he must have tasted the same.

"Who, me? With Muffle and Ian and me aunties to defend the Hold if we're attacked? Nothing to it." Deadpan, he propped his spectacles more firmly onto the bridge of his long nose. "Shall I send a messenger after you with your good shoes and a couple of silk dresses just in case you want a change?"

"I'll manage with what I have," said Jenny gravely. "Borin was right, you know, " she added. "The garrisons may be a nuisance, and the farmers may grumble about the extra taxes, but there hasn't been a major bandit attack since their coming. I'll scry you, and the Hold, in my crystal every night—a pity Ian's powers haven't grown strong enough yet for him to learn to speak with me through a crystal or through fire. But he's a fair healer already. And if there's trouble . . ." She raised her hand, touched the long hair where it straggled, pointy with sweat, over his bruised face. "Braid a red ribbon into your hair. I'll see it when I call your image. If I can, I'll return to you."

John caught her hand as she would have lowered it and kissed her dirty fingers; and she drew down his in return, pressed her lips to the scruffy leather, the battered chain-mail of his glove. Skaff Gradely and the Darrow boys had come up by this time, arguing all the way with Borin's fellow messengers, with the spare horses and the baggage, so there was little to stay for.

"Borin will ride with you," Commander Rocklys said, "and his fellows. Send one of them to me when you've come up with these bandits and their wizard. Let us know where you are and if you need troops. I'll dispatch as many as I can, as swiftly as I can. And bring the woman alive, at whatever the cost. We'll make it worth her while to pledge her services to the Realm."

"Even so." Jenny swung to Moon Horse's saddle again and adjusted her halberd and bow. She wondered what reward she herself would consider "worth her while" to betray John, to turn against him, to ride with his foes . . .

Or, she thought, as the twenty-five picked pursuers formed up around her, *to leave him and our children and the folk of Alyn Hold to their own devices, when I know there's a bandit wizard abroad in the lands?*

The good of all the Winterlands, maybe.

The good of the Realm, which John considered his first and greatest loyalty.

She lifted her hand to him as she and the men rode off. A little later, as they crested the rise above the ravine and approached the oak woods into which the bandits had fled, she looked back to see Commander Rocklys marshaling her forces to ride back to Cair Corflyn, the garrison on the banks of the Black River, which was the headquarters for the whole network of new manors and forts. John's doing, those garrisons, she thought. The protection he had bought with the blood he'd shed, dragon-fighting four years ago. His reward.

As the dragon-magic in her veins was hers.

John himself stood, a small tatty black figure on the high ground above the stream, watching her. She lifted her hand again to him, and his spectacles flashed like mirrors as he waved good-bye. The wasting moon still stood above the moors to the west, a pale crescent like a slice of cheese.

Less than three weeks later, before that moon waxed again to its full, a real dragon descended on the farms near Alyn Hold.

3

"**A** hundred feet long it was, my lord." Deke Brown from the Lone Steadings, a man John had known all his life, folded his hands together before his knees and leaned forward from the library chair in the flicker of the candlelight. His face was bruised, and there was a running burn on his forehead, the kind John knew was made by a droplet of the flaming acid that dragons spit. "Blue it was, but like as if it had gold flowers spread all over it, and golden wings, and the horns of it all black and white stripes, and maned like a lion. It had three of the cows, and I bare got April and the babies out'n the house and in the root cellar in time."

In the silence John was very conscious of the hoarseness of the man's breathing, and of the thumping of his own heart.

No illusion this time. Or a damn good one if it was.

Jenny, wherever you are, I need you. I can't handle this alone.

"I heard down in the village that Ned Wooley was up here yesterday, from Great Toby." Brown spoke diffidently, trying to word it without sounding accusing. "They said this thing killed his horse and his mule on the road to the Bottom Farms, and near as check killed him."

John said, "Aye." He swallowed hard, feeling very cold inside. "We've been makin' up the poisons and gettin' ready to go all day. You didn't happen to see which way it went?"

"I didn't, no, my lord. I was that done up about the cows. They're all we've got. But April says it went off northwest. She says to tell you she saw it circling above Cair Dhû."

"You give April a kiss for me." He knew the ruins of the old watch-tower, every ditch, bank, and clump of broken masonry; he'd played there as a child, risking life and soul because blood-devils haunted them at certain times of the year. He'd hunted rabbits there, too, and hidden from his father. *At least I'll be fighting it on familiar ground.* "Get Cousin Dilly to give you something from the kitchen, you look fagged out. I'll be going there in the morning."

He drew a deep breath, trying to put the thought of the dragon from his mind. "We'll see about getting you another cow. One of the Red Shaggies is heavy with calf; I could probably let you have the both of them. Clivy writes that red cows give more wholesome milk that's higher in butter, but I've never measured—still, it's the best I can do. We'll talk about it when I get back."

If I get back.

Brown disappeared down the tower stair.

Jenny, I need you.

Behind him a clock chimed the hour, amid a great parade of mechanical lions, elephants, trumpeters, and flying swans. The moon turned its phases, and an allegorical representation of Good thumped Evil repeatedly over the head with a golden mallet. John watched the show with his usual grave delight, then got up and consulted the water-clock that gurgled quietly in a corner of the study.

Not even close.

Shaking his head regretfully, he descended the tower stair.

He passed the kitchen, where Dilly, Rowan, and Jane clustered around Deke Brown, exclaiming over his few bruises and filling him in on what had befallen Ned Wooley—"A hundred feet long, it was, and breathed green fire . . ."

Ian was in the old barracks court, the firelight under the cauldrons gleaming on the sweat that sheathed his bare arms. Tawny light tongued Jenny's red and black poison pots, carefully stoppered and arranged along a wall out of all possible chance of being tripped over, broken, or gotten into by anything or anyone. The fumes burned John's eyes. It was all a repeat of the scene three weeks ago.

He hoped to hell the stuff would work.

"Father." The boy laid his stirring stick down and crossed the broken and weedy pavement toward him. Muffle and Adric put down their loads of wood and followed, stripped, like Ian, to their breeches, boots, and knitted singlets in the heat; clothed like Ian in sweat. "That messenger wasn't . . . ?"

"Deke Brown. It hit his farm."

"Devils bugger it," Muffle said. He hitched his belt under the muscled roll of his huge belly. "April and the children . . . ?"

"Are fine. April saw the thing to ground at Cair Dhû."

"Good for April." John's half-brother regarded him for a moment, his

thick, red-stubbled face eerily like their father's, trying to read his
thoughts. "No word from Jenny?"

John shook his head, his own face ungiving: a holdover, he supposed,
from growing up with his father's notions about what a man and the Lord
of Alyn Hold must and must not feel. It would never have occurred to him
to beat Adric for showing fear—not that Adric had the slightest concept
of what the word meant. And Ian . . .

Mageborn children feared different things.

"Wherever she is, she can't come." The bloody light darkened the red
ribbon he'd braided yesterday into his hair. *I'll scry every evening in my
crystal* . . . "Or she can't come in time."

"I could go to the house on Frost Fell." Ian wiped his face with the
back of his arm. "Mother's books—old Caerdinn has to have written
down how to do . . ." he hesitated, "how to do death-spells."

"No." John had thought of that yesterday.

"I don't think these poisons are going to work against a dragon unless
there are fresh death-spells put into their making." Returning from the
false alarm and ambush, John had cleansed the harpoons with water and
with fire, as Jenny had instructed him to do: a necessary precaution given
little Mag's eerie facility with locks, bolts, and anything else she was particularly not supposed to get into. Jenny, he knew, was conscientious
about the Limitations she put on the death-spells. It had never occurred to
either of them that they'd be needed again so soon. "We need to put
death-spells on the harpoons as well."

"No." John had thought of that, too. "I don't want you touching such
stuff."

"But *we* don't want *you* to die!" protested Adric reasonably.

Muffle raised his brows and looked away in a fashion that said, *The
boy's got a point.*

"Mother uses them."

"You're twelve years old, Ian." John swallowed hard, hoping by all
the gods that his own fear didn't show. "Leavin' out the fact that certain
spells can be too strong for an inexperienced mage to wield—"

"I'm not inexperienced."

"—you haven't learned near all there is to know about Limitations,
and I for one don't want to end up havin' one of me feet fall off from lep-
rosy in the middle of the fight because you got a word wrong."

Surprised into laughter, Ian looked quickly aside, mouth pursed to
prevent it. Like many boys he had the disapproving air of one who feels
that laughter is not the appropriate response to facing death, especially
not for one's father. John had suspected for some time that both his sons
regarded him as frivolous.

"Now, get back to stirring," he ordered. "Is that stuff settin' up at all like it's supposed to? Adric, as long as you're down here you might as well stir that other cauldron, but for God's sake put gloves on . . . We've got a long night." He stripped off his old red doublet and his shirt and hung both on pegs on the work shed wall. The smell of summer hay from the fields beyond the Hold filled the night. Though midnight lay only a few hours off, the sky still glowed with light. As he pulled on his gloves, John watched them all in the firelit court: his sons, his brother—his aunts, Jane and Rowe and Hol, and Cousin Dilly, coming down with gingerwater and trying to tell Adric it was time for him to go to bed. Seeing them as Jenny would be seeing them, wherever the hell she was, gazing into her crystal. Rowe with her long untidy braids of graying red and Dilly peering shortsightedly at Muffle, and all of them chatting like a nest of magpies—the real rulers, if the truth be told, of Alyn Hold.

She has to know what all this means. He closed his eyes, desperately willing that Jenny be on her way. *I'm sorry. I waited as long as I could.*

Teltrevir, heliotrope . . . His mind echoed the fragments of the old dragon-list. *Centhwevir is blue knotted with gold. Nymr blue violet-crowned, Glammring Gold-Horns bright as emeralds* . . . Scraps of information and old learning:

Maggots from meat, weevils from rye,
Dragons from stars in an empty sky.

And, *Save a dragon, slave a dragon.*

Secondhand accounts, most of them a mash of broken half-volumes; notes of legends and granny rhymes; jumbled ballads that Gareth collected and sent copies of. Everything left of learning in the Winterlands, after the King's armies had abandoned them to bandits, Iceriders, cold, and plague. He'd gathered them painfully from ruins, collated them in those few moments between fighting for his own life and the lives of those who depended on him . . . Secondhand accounts and the speculations of scholars who'd never come closer to a dragon than the sites of old slayings, or a nervously cursory inspection of torn-up, blood-soaked, acid-burned ground.

Something in there might save his life, but he didn't know what.

Antara Warlady was supposed to have gotten right up next to the Worm of Wevir by wrapping herself in a fresh-flayed pig hide, according to the oldest Drymarch version of her tale; Grimonious Grimblade had supposedly put out live lambs as bait.

Alkmar the Godborn had been killed by the third dragon he fought.

Selkythar of golden curls and sword of sunlight flashing,
Seeking meed of glory through the dragon's talons lashing.
Cried he, "Strike again, foul worm, my bloody blade is slashing . . ."

John shook his head. He'd never sought a meed of glory in his life, and if he ever decided to start, it wouldn't be by riding smack up a long hill in open daylight as Selkythar had reportedly done, armed with only a sword—well, a shield, too, as if a shield ever did any good against a thirty-foot hellstorm of spitting acid and whirling spikes.

"The boy may be right." Muffle's voice pulled him out of his memories of the Dragon of Wyr, of Morkeleb's black talons sweeping down at him from darkness . . .

John dipped the harpoon he held into the cauldron and watched the liquid drip off the iron, thin as water.

"Stuff ain't thickenin' up," he sighed. "Maybe I should get Auntie Jane back here. Her gravies always set."

Muffle caught his arm. "Be serious, son."

"Why?" John rested the harpoon's spines on the vat's edge and coughed in the smoke. "I may be dead twenty-four hours from now."

"So you may," replied the blacksmith softly, and glanced across at Ian in the amber glare. "And what then? Four years ago you bargained with the King to send garrisons. Well, they've been gie helpful, but you know there's a price. If you die, d'you think your boys are going to be let to inherit? In the south they've laws against wizards holding property or power, and Adric's but eight. You think the King's council's going to let a witch be Regent of Wyr? Especially if they think they can get tax money by ruling here themselves?"

"I'm the King's subject." John stepped back from the fire, hellmouth hot on his bare arms. "And the King's servant, and the Regent's me friend. What're you askin'? That I not fight this drake?"

"I'm asking that you let Ian do what he's asked to do."

"No."

Muffle pursed his lips, which made him look astoundingly like their father. Except, thought John, that their father had never let things stop with pursed lips, nor would he have reacted to *No* with that simple grimace. The last time John had said a flat-out *No* to old Lord Aver, at the age of twelve, he'd been lucky his collarbone had set straight.

"In the village they say the boy's good. He goes over those magic-books in your library like you go over the ones on steam and smokes and old machines. He knows enough . . ."

"No," said John. And then, seeing the doubt, the fear for him in the fat man's small brown eyes, he said, "There's things a boy his years shouldn't know about. Not so soon."

"Things you'd put your life at risk—your people at risk—to spare him?"

John thought about them, those things Jenny had told him lay in old

Caerdinn's crumbling books. Things he'd read in the books that had been part of his bargain with Prince Gareth to fight the Dragon of Nast Wall. Things he read in Jenny's silence when he surprised her sometimes in her own small study, studying in the deep of night.

He said, "Aye." And saw the shift in Muffle's eyes.

"People hereabouts know the magic Jen does for them." John picked up the harpoon and turned the shaft in his hands. "Or what old Caerdinn did. Birthin' babies, and keepin' the mice out of the barns in a bad year, or maybe buyin' an hour on the harvest when a storm's coming in. Those that remember me mother are mostly dead." He glanced up at Muffle over the rims of his spectacles. "And anyway, by what I hear from our aunties, me mother never did the worst she could have done."

Except maybe only once or twice, he thought, and pushed those barely coherent recollections from his mind.

"People here don't know what magic really is," John went on. "They haven't seen what it can do, and they haven't seen what it can do to those that do it. You always pay for it somehow, and sometimes other people besides you do the payin'. Gaw," he added, turning back to the cauldron and dipping the harpoon once more, "this's blashier than Cousin Rowanberry's tea. Let's put some flour in it, see if we can get it thick enough to do us some good."

Ian's heart beat hard as he kicked his scrubby pony to a gallop up Toadback Hill.

Death-spells.

And the dragon.

He'd always hated the harpoons with which his father had killed the Dragon of Wyr, two years before he was born. He had instinctively avoided the cupboard in his father's cluttered study in which they were locked. If he touched the wood he could feel them, even before he realized that he had magic in him. Sometimes he dreamed about them, each barbed and pronged shaft of iron its own ugly entity, whispering in the darkness about pain and cold and giving up.

His mother had wrought well.

Ian shivered.

For the first eight years of Ian's life he had only seen her now and then, for she'd lived alone with her cats on the Fell, coming to be with his father at the Hold for a few days together. She had told him later—when his own powers had crossed through that wall from dreaming to daytime reality—that in those days her powers were small. She had kept herself apart to study and meditate, to work on what little she had. There was only so much time in her life to give.

And then had come the Dragon of Nast Wall.

His parents had gone away to the south together to fight it, along with the messenger who'd fetched them, a gawky nearsighted boy in spectacles. That boy had turned out to be Prince Gareth, later Regent for the ailing King Uriens of Belmarie. At that time Ian had accepted without question that his father could easily slay a dragon and hadn't been particularly concerned. As if to confirm him in this opinion, his parents had returned more or less unharmed, and he didn't learn until much later how close both had come to not returning at all.

After that, Jenny had lived at the Hold. But she still went sometimes to meditate in the stone house on Frost Fell, and it was there that she'd begun to teach Ian, away from the Hold's distractions. In that quiet house he did not need to be a brother or a nephew or a father's firstborn son.

Even had Ian not been mageborn and able to see easily in the clear blue darkness, he could have followed the path that led away from the village fields over Toadback Hill. Ruins dotted the far slope, one of the many vanished towns that spoke of what the Winterlands had been and had become. Shattered walls, slumped puddles where wells had been, all were nearly drowned now in the mists that rose from the cranberry bog.

From the hill crest he looked back and saw his father and his uncle by the village gates, talking with Peg the Gatekeeper. The gates were squat and solid, built up of rubble filched from the broken town. Lanterns burned over them, but Ian did not need those dim yellow smudges to see how his father turned in Battlehammer's saddle, searching the formless swell of the hills, gesturing as he spoke.

He knows I'm gone. Ian felt a stab of guilt. He'd laid a word on Peg, causing her to rise from her bed in the turret and lower the drawbridge to let him pass. This cantrip wasn't something his mother had taught him, but he'd learned it from one of Caerdinn's books and had experimented, mostly on the unsuspecting Adric. He knew perfectly well that such magic was an act of betrayal, of violation, and he squirmed with shame every time he did it, but as a wizard, he felt driven to learn.

He was glad he'd practiced it, now.

It was still too dark to distinguish his pony's hoofprints in the mud. In any case, he guessed his father had no time to search. Nor had he, Ian, any to linger. He shrugged his old jacket closer around him and put his pony to a fast trot through the battered walls, and the rags of bog mist swallowed them.

Death-spells. His palms grew clammy at the thought. In a corner of his mind he knew perfectly well that he might not have the strength to wield them, certainly not to wield the dreadful power he sensed whenever he touched the harpoons. But he could think of no other way to help.

Since the coming of that first word of the dragon yesterday, he'd tried desperately to make contact with his mother in the ways she'd told him wizards could, by looking into fire or water or chips of ensorcelled crystal or glass. But he had seen only confusing images of trees, and once a moss-covered standing stone, and water glimmering in the moon's waxing light.

Remember the Limitations, he told himself, ticking over his mother's instructions in his mind. *And gather up the power circles afterward and disperse them. Don't work in a house. Don't work near water* . . .

There had to be something in the house at Frost Fell that he could use to save his father's life.

Frost Fell was a hard gray skull of granite, rising nearly two hundred feet above waterlogged bottomlands—enough to be free of the mosquitoes that made the summers of Winterlands such a horror. In spring, huge poppies grew there, and in fall, yellow daisies. Most of the other fells were barren of anything but heather and gorse, but Frost Fell boasted a modest pocket of soil at its top, where centuries ago some hardy crofter had cultivated oats. These days it was his mother's garden, circled like the house in wardings and wyrd-lines. Ian reviewed these in his mind, hoping he'd be able to get past the gate, hoping he could open the doors. *Triangle, triangle, rune of the Eye* . . . The last two times he'd been there she'd simply stood back and let him do it, so there was a chance . . .

Light burned in the house.

She's back! Exultation, and blinding relief. A dim glow of candle flame, like a stain on the blue bulk of shadow. The rosy flicker of hearthfire glimpsed through half-open doors. He wrapped the pony's rein hastily around the gate, ran up the path. *She's back, she'll be able to help!*

It wasn't until his foot was on the step that he thought, *If it was Mother, she'd have ridden at once to the Hold.*

And at that moment, he saw something bright on the step.

He stopped and knelt to look at it. Like a seashell wrought of glass, thin as a bubble, broken at one end. A little beyond the broken end lay what appeared to be a blob of quicksilver, glistening on the wet stone in the reflected candle-glow.

"Go ahead." A deep, friendly voice spoke from within the house. "It's all right to touch it. It's perfectly safe."

Looking up Ian saw a man sitting by his mother's hearth, a man he'd never seen before. Big and square and pleasant-faced, he was clothed like the southerners who came from the King's court, in a short close coat of quilted violet silk lined with fur, and a fur-lined silk cap embroidered with violets. Expensive boots sheathed his calves and a pair of black kid gloves lay across his knee, and in his pale fingers he turned a jewel over and over, a sapphire dark as the sea. Ian knew he had to be a wizard, because he was in the house, but he asked, "Are you a mage, sir?"

"I am that." The man smiled again and gestured with his finger to the frail glass shell, the bead of quicksilver on the step. "And I'm here to help you, Ian. Bring that to me, if you would, my boy."

Ian reached toward it and hesitated, for he thought the quicksilver moved a little on the stone of the step. For an instant he had the impression that there were eyes within it, looking up at him. Bright small eyes, like a lizard or a crab. That it had its own name, and moreover that it knew his. But a moment later he thought, *It has to be just the light.* He carefully scooped the thing up in his hand.

4

Alkmar the Godborn, greatest of the heroes of antiquity (it was said), slew two dragons while serving the King of Ernine—though according to Prince Gareth there was a late Imperteng version of the legend that said four—using a lasso made of chain and an iron spear heated red-hot, which he threw down each dragon's throat. *Must have been on a cable,* thought John, though of course Alkmar had been seven and a half feet tall, thewed like an ox, and presumably had a lot of time to spend at throwing practice.

For someone a thumb's breadth under six feet and thewed like a thirty-eight-year-old man who's spent most of his life riding boundary in cold weather, other strategies would probably be required.

John Aversin flexed his shoulders and listened, hoping to hell Sergeant Muffle and the spare horses were keeping absolutely quiet in the base camp at Deep Beck. Was three and a half miles far enough?

Morning stillness lay on the folded world of heather and stone, broken only by the hum of mosquitoes and bees. Even the creak of his stirrup leather seemed deafening, and the dry swish of Battlehammer's tail.

Interesting that the greatest hero of legend was described as throwing something at the dragon, rather than nobly slicing its head off with a single blow of his mighty sword and to hell with Selkythar and Antara Warlady and Grimonious Grimblade, thank you very much.

Battlehammer snuffled and flattened his ears. Though the wind blew south off the ruins of Cair Dhû, if the stallion could smell the dragon from here, could the dragon smell them?

Or hear them, in the utter absence of the raucous dawn chitter of birds?

Dragonsbane. He was the one who was supposed to know all this.

John flexed his hands. The walls of the gorge still protected him, and the purl of the stream might conceivably cover the clack of Battlehammer's hooves. The problem with dragons was that, mostly, nobody knew what worked.

He slid from the saddle, checked the girths, checked the harpoons in their holsters. Lifted each of the warhorse's four feet to make sure he hadn't picked up a stone. *That's all I'd need.* While he did this, in his mind he reviewed the ruins. He'd checked them a few months ago; there couldn't have been much change. The dragon would be lairing in the crypt.

He'd have to catch it there, before it got into the air.

Stair, hall, doorway, doorway . . . How fast did dragons move? Morkeleb had come out of the dark of Ylferdun Deep's great market-hall like a snake striking. Broken walls, the drop of a slope, everything tangled with heather and fallen masonry. Ditches invisible where weeds grew across them . . . *What a place for a gallop.* At least he knew the ground.

He settled his iron cap tighter on his head, the red ribbon still fluttering in his hair. *Jen, I'm in trouble, I need you, come at once.*

Though he supposed if she scried him now she'd get the idea without the ribbon.

He propped his spectacles again, dropped his hand back to touch the first of the harpoons in their holsters, and took a deep breath.

"Strike again, foul worm," he whispered, and drove in his heels.

At five hundred yards, they knew you were coming, upwind, downwind, dark or storm. That seemed to be the consensus of the ballads. Maybe more than five hundred. Maybe a lot more.

Battlehammer hit open ground at a dead gallop and John watched the walls pour toward him: broken stone, stringers of outwalls, craggy pine and dwarf willow spreading around the ground. Everything broken now and burned with dragon-acid and the poisons of its breath. He saw it in his mind, slithering up those shattered stairways. A hundred feet long . . . *God of the Earth, let them be wrong about that . . .*

It was there in the riven gate. *Centhwevir is blue knotted with gold.* Fifty feet in front of him, rising on long hind legs to swing that birdlike head. Blue as gentian, blue as lapis and morning glories, iridescent blue as the summer sea all stitched and patched and flourished with buttercup yellow, and eyes like twin molten opals, gold as ancient glass. The beauty of it stopped his breath as his hand went back, closed around the nearest harpoon, knowing he was too far yet for a throw and thinking, *Sixty feet if it's an inch . . .*

Centhwevir is blue knotted with gold.

The thing came under the gate and the wings opened and John threw:

arm, back, thighs, every muscle he possessed. The harpoon struck in the pink hollow beneath the right wing where the skin was delicate as velvet, and he was reining Battlehammer hard away and angling for distance, catching up another weapon, swinging to throw for the mouth.

Alkmar, if you're there among the gods, I could use the help . . .

That one missed as the snakelike neck struck at him, huge narrow head framed in its protective mane of black and white, primrose and cyan. Battlehammer screamed and fell and rolled, lifted from his feet by the hard counterswipe of the dragon's tail, and John kicked free of the stirrups and tumbled almost by instinct. Yellow-green acid slapped the heather at his feet, the stiff brush bursting into flame.

Battlehammer. He could hear the horse scream again in pain but didn't dare turn to look, only scooped up four harpoons from the ground—as many as he could reach—and ran in.

Keep it under the gate. Keep it under the gate. If it stays on the ground, you've a chance.

The star-drake struck at him again, head and tail, spitting acid that ignited in the air. John flung himself under the shelter of a broken wall, then rolled clear, coming in close, fast, striking up at the rippling wall of blue-and-golden spikes. The heather around them blazed, smoke searing his eyes. The dragon snapped, slashed, drove him back, slithered free of the confining walls. He struck with the harpoon, trying to hold it; talons like gold-bladed daggers snagged his leg, hurling him off balance. He struck up with the harpoon again as the head came down at him, teeth like dripping chisels, the spattering sear of blood.

Blind hacking, heat, fighting to get free. Once he fell and rolled into an old defensive ditch only seconds before the spiked knob at the end of the dragon's tail smote the earth. He was aware he was hurt and bleeding badly and didn't know when or how it had happened. Only pain and the fact that he couldn't breathe. He drove in a second harpoon, and a third, and then there was that great terrible leathery crack of wings, and he saw sunlight through the golden membranes, shining crimson veins, as the dragon lifted, lifted weightless as a blown leaf. Desperate, John flung himself for the shelter of a fallen wall and rather to his surprise found he couldn't stand up.

Buggery damn.

He threw himself under the stone a second before the acid drench of fire poured on top of him: smoke and suffocation, poison. Mind clouded, he fought and wriggled farther into the crack, tallying where he could go from here, how he could get away and wait for the poison to work. Would the flour he'd used to thicken it keep it from doing its job? Pain in his calf and thigh and dizzying weakness told him where he'd been slashed. He

fumbled from his pocket one of Jenny's silk scarves, twisted the tourniquet around his leg, and then fire, acid, poison streamed down again on
the stone above him. Smoke. Heat.

It'll tear the stone away from the top . . .

He had a belt-ax and pulled it free, cut at the claws that ripped down
through the stone and roots above his head. A huge five-fingered hand,
eighteen inches across, and he struck at it with all his strength, the blood
that exploded out scorching his face. Above him, above the protecting
stones, he heard Centhwevir scream, and the stones caved on top of him,
struck by that monstrous tail.

*Damn it, with all that poison in you, you should at least be feeling
poorly by now!*

The wall above him gave way. Darkness, pain, fire devouring his
bleeding flesh.

Stillness.

His hold on consciousness slipped, as if he clung to rock above an
abyss. He knew what lay in that abyss and didn't want to look down.

Ian's face, wreathed in woodsmoke and poison fumes, glistening
with tears. He couldn't imagine shedding tears for his own father, not at
twelve, nor at sixteen when that brawling, angry, red-faced man had died,
nor indeed at any other time. The dreams shifted and for a time the smoke
that burned his eyes was that of parchment curling and blackening in the
hearth of Alyn Hold. The pain was the pain of cracked ribs that kept him
from breathing, as he watched that big bear-shape black against the hall
fireplace where his books burned: an old copy of Polybius he'd begged a
trader to sell him, two volumes of the plays of Darygambe he'd ridden a
week out to Eldsbouch to buy . . .

His father's brawling voice. "The people of the Hold don't need a
bloody schoolmaster! They don't want some prig who can tell them about
how steam can turn wheels or what kind of rocks you find at the bottom
of the maggot-festerin' sea! What the hell good is that when the Iceriders
come down from the north or the black wolves raid in winter's dead
heart? This is the Winterlands, you fool! They need someone who'll
defend 'em, body and bones! Who'll die defendin' 'em!"

Beyond him in a wall of blurred fire—all things were blurred in that
chiaroscuro of hearthlight and myopia—John's books burned.

In the fire he saw still other things.

A distant vision of a tall thin woman, black-haired, frost-eyed, standing on the Hold's battlement with a gray wolf at her side. Wind frayed at
the fur of her collar, and she gazed over the moors and streams of that
stony thankless desolation that had been the frontier of the King's realm.
His mother, though he could not remember her voice, nor her touch, nor

anything about her save that for years he had dreamed of seeking her, never finding her again. One of the village girls had been her apprentice, skinny, tiny, with a thin brown face half-hid in an oceanic night of hair and a quirky triangular smile.

He seemed to hear her voice speaking his name.

"The poison won't keep him down for long," she seemed to be saying. "We have to finish him."

It wasn't the blue and gold dragon she was talking about. It was the first dragon, the golden dragon, the beautiful creature of sunlight and jewel-bright patterns of purple and red and black.

And she was right. He'd been hurt in that first fight, too, in the gully on the other side of Great Toby. She'd brought him to with those words. There was no way of knowing whether the poisons would kill a dragon or only numb it temporarily. He still didn't know. Now as then, he had to finish the matter with an ax.

It took everything he had to drag himself back to consciousness. The mortar that had held together the wall above him had perished with time. Acrid slime leaked through, staining the granite; bits of scrub and weed smoldered fitfully. His body hurt as if every bone were broken, and he felt weak and giddy, but he knew he'd better get the matter done with if he didn't want to go through all this again.

Body and bones, his father had said. *Body and bones.*

Maggot-festering old bastard.

He brought up his hand and fumbled at his spectacles. The slab of stone that had knocked him out had driven the steel frame into the side of his face, but the glass hadn't broken. The spell Jenny had put on them worked so far. He drew breath and cold agony sliced from toes to crown by way of the belly and groin.

No sound from outside. Then a dragging rasp, a thick scratching, metal on stone.

The dragon was still moving. But it was down.

No time. No time.

It took all his strength to shift the stone. Acid burned his hands through the charred remains of his gloves. Broken boulders, knobs of earth rained in his eyes. He got an elbow over the granite foundation, inched himself clear, like pulling his bones out of his flesh in splinters.

The ax, he thought, fighting nausea, fighting the gray buzzing warmth that closed around his vision. *The ax. Jenny, I can't do this without you.*

The sunlight was like having a burning brand rammed through his eyes into his brain. He waited for his head to clear.

Centhwevir lay before him, fallen among the ruins, a gorgeous tesselation of blue and gold. Striped wings spread, patterned like a butterfly's: black blood leaked from beneath one of them. A wonderment of black and white fur pillowed the birdlike head: long scales like sheet-gold ribbons, horns striped lengthwise and crosswise, antennae tipped in glowing, jeweled bobs. Spikes and corkscrews and razor-edged ridges of scales rose through it along the spine, glistened on the joints of those thin deadly forepaws, on the enormous narrow hindquarters, down the length of the deadly tail. It was, John estimated, some sixty-five feet in length, with a wingspan close to twice that, the biggest star-drake he had ever seen.

Music returned to his mind through a haze of exhaustion and smoke. Delicate airs and snippets of tunes that Jenny played on her harp, fragments of the forgotten songs that were the true names of the dragons. With them the memory of Jenny's ancient lists: *Teltrevir heliotrope; Centhwevir is blue knotted with gold . . .*

Ancient beings, more ancient than men could conceive, the foci of a thousand strange legends and broken glints of song.

Wings first. He forced his mind from his own sickened horror, his disgust at himself for butchering such beauty. A dragon could in a few short weeks destroy the fragile economy of the Winterlands, and there was no way of driving a dragon away as one could drive away bandits or wolves. Jenny was right. The dragons would seek to feed on the garrison herds. Bandits and Iceriders would be watching for any slackening in the garrison's strength. To drive the King's men, and the King's law, out; to have the lands as their own to prey on once more.

Moving as in a dream he found his ax, worked it painfully from beneath the rocks that had protected him. The stench of burned earth and acid numbed him. He could feel his hands and feet grow cold, his body sinking into shock. *Not now,* he thought. *Damn it, not now!*

Centhwevir moved his head, regarded him with those molten aureate eyes.

John felt his consciousness waver and begin to break up, like a raft coming to pieces in high seas.

Rock scraped. A slither of falling fragments on the other side of the old curtain wall.

Muffle! John's heart leaped. *You disobeyed and came after me! I could kiss you, you great chowderheaded lout!*

But it was not the blacksmith who stood framed, a moment later, against the pallid morning sky.

A man John had not seen before, a stranger to the Winterlands. He seemed in his middle fifties, big and broad-shouldered, with a calmly smiling face. John thought, through a haze of crimson agony that came and went, that he was wealthy. Though he did not move with a courtier's trained grace, neither had he the gait of a man who fought for his living, or worked. The violet silk of his coat was a color impossible without the dye-trade of the south. The curly black fur of his collar a southerner's bid for warmth. His hair was gray under an embroidered cap, and he bore a staff carved with a goblin's head, a white moonstone glowing in its mouth.

If this was a hallucination, thought John giddily, trying to breathe against the sinking cold that seemed to spread through his body, it was a bloody precise one. Had the fellow fallen out of the air? Did he have a horse cached somewhere out of sight? He carried a saddlebag at any rate, brass buckles clinking faintly as he picked his way down the slope. Halfway down the jumble of the broken wall he paused and turned his head in John's direction. He did not appear to be surprised, either by the dragon, dying, or by the broken form of the man.

Though the distance between them was probably a dozen yards, John could see in the set of his shoulders, in the tilt of that sleek-groomed head, the moment when the stranger dismissed him. Not important. Dying, and to be disregarded.

The stranger walked past him to the dragon.

Centhwevir lashed his tail feebly, hissed and moved his head. The man stepped back. Then, cautiously, he worked his way around to the other side—*Yes,* thought John, irritated despite the fact that he was only half-conscious. *That ball of spikes on the end of the tail isn't just to impress the she-dragons, you stupid oic.* Was this a dream?

He couldn't be sure. Pain grew and then seemed to diminish as images fragmented through the smoke. He saw his father again, belting him with a heavy wooden training-sword, yelling, "Use the shield! Use the shield, damn you!" A shield the child could barely lift . . . Probably a dream. He wasn't sure what to make of the image of that prim gentleman in the violet silk coat sliding a spike from the saddlebag, holding it up to the sun. Not a spike, but an icicle with a core of quicksilver . . . Now where would he have gotten an icicle in June?

John's mind scouted the trail of something he'd read in Honoribus Eppulis about the manufacture of ice from salt, trying to track down the reference, and for a time he wandered in smoky hallucinations of vats and straw and cold. So cold. He came out with the music of Jenny's harp in his mind again and saw he hadn't been unconscious for more than a moment, for the gentleman in purple was standing on the dragon's neck, straddling its backbone. Wan moorland sunlight caught in the frost-white icicle as the man drove it into the back of the dragon's skull.

Centhwevir opened his mouth and hissed again—*Missed the spinal cord, you silly bugger.* John wanted to go over and take it from him and do it right. *It's right there in front of you. Hope you've got another one of those.*

But the stranger stepped away, tucked his staff beneath his arm, and took from his bag things John recognized: vials of silver and blood, wands of gold and amethyst. The paraphernalia of wizardry. *I thought Jen said you were a girl.* Of healing. Centhwevir lay still, but his long spiked tail moved independently, like a cat's—*Dammit, the poison would have worked!*—as the man spread a green silk sheet upon the ground and began to lay out on it a circle of power. Despairing, feeling his own life seeping away, John watched him make the spells that would call back life from the frontiers of darkness.

No! John tried to move, tried to gather his strength to move, before he realized what a stupid thing that would have been. *Dammit, no!* It was a moot point anyway, since he couldn't summon the strength to so much as lift his hand. He felt the hopeless urge to weep. *Don't make me do all this again!*

Was this hell? Father Anmos, the priest at Cair Corflyn, would say so. Some infernal punishment for his sins, that he had to go on slaying the same dragon over and over? And would the gent in the violet coat come over and heal him next, and hand him his ax and a couple of harpoons and say, *Sorry, lad, up and at 'em.* Was he going to resurrect Battlehammer? What had poor Battlehammer done to deserve getting killed over and over again in the same fight with the same dragon through eternity?

This ridiculous vision occupied his mind for a time, coming and going with the braided golden threads of that remembered music—or was the mage in the heather playing a flute?—and with the thought of darkness and of stars that did not twinkle but blazed with a distant, steady light.

Then from a great distance he seemed to see Ian, standing where the unknown wizard had stood at the top of the broken wall.

Can't be a hallucination, John found himself thinking. *That's his old jacket he's wearing*—the sleeve was stained with poisons from last night.

At the dragon's side, the wizard held out his hand.

Ian jumped lightly down from the wall, strode across the scorched and smoking ground without a blink, without a hesitation, grimy plaid fluttering in the morning breeze. The dragon raised its head, and the mage smiled, and John thought suddenly, *Ian, run!* Panic filled him, for no good reason, only that he knew this man in his embroidered cap was evil and that he was saving the dragon's life with ill in mind.

The dragon sat up like a dog on its haunches: its brilliant, blood-stained wings folded. Its injured foot it held a little off the ground. John could see where the slash had been stitched together again. The wizard who had saved its life set aside the flute of bone and ivory.

It was said that if you saved a dragon's life it was your slave. It was true that when Jenny had saved the life of Morkeleb the Black, the Dragon of Nast Wall, she had done so by means of the dragon's name. That music, salvaged from ancient lore, had given her power. *Save a dragon, slave a dragon . . .*

Ian, go back!

He tried to scream the words, and his breath would not come.

Ian, no!

John raised himself on his elbows, then his hands. It was as if every cord and muscle of his flesh tore loose. *Ian . . . !*

The boy paused, as if he'd heard his voice. Turning, he walked over to where John lay and stood looking down at him, and his bright sapphire eyes were no longer his own eyes, no longer Jenny's. No longer anything human.

With a smile on his face that was almost friendly, he kicked John in the side as a man would kick a dying dog that had bitten him.

Then he walked away.

When John's eyes cleared, he saw the dragon Centhwevir lowering himself to the earth, saw the strange wizard settling himself a little uneasily among the bristling ridges of the dragon's back. He stretched down a hand and helped Ian up behind him. Like a dream of cornflowers and daffodils, like lapis and golden music, the star-drake spread his wings.

"Ian . . ." It was like falling onto a harrow, but John tried to make himself crawl, as if he could somehow reach them, somehow snatch his son back.

The moonstone flashed in the wizard's staff. The dragon loosed its hold on the world, like the wind taking a kite. Weightless and perfect in its beauty it rose, and John tried and failed to call his son's name, though what he thought that would accomplish he knew not.

He only knew that the dragon was taking his son.

A dream, he thought, seeing again Ian's face and the flame of hell in those blue eyes. *It has to be a dream.*

Darkness took him.

5

"**D**amn you, John." Jenny Waynest sank back on the straw tick and covered her mouth with her hands. She was trembling. "*Damn* you." For a moment more the images glowed in the fire's core: the blue and gold dragon stretched dying in its blood, the crumpled form of the man in his battered doublet of black leather and iron plate. Then they faded.

Ian, she thought. *Ian must have come.* Mages cannot see mages, in fire, water, stone, unless they consent to be seen. *Goddess of Earth, let it be that I can't see now because Ian has come.*

Ian was already a good enough healer that it might be just possible for him to save a man's life. To stop bleeding, anyway; to keep the lungs drawing air. To keep the cold of shock from reaching the heart. John would have forbidden him to follow, but knowing Ian there was a good chance that he had.

She closed her eyes, trying to breathe, trying to abate the shaking that racked her flesh. *God of the Earth, help him . . .*

Voices came to her through the window behind her head. Soldiers in the courtyard. "By the gods, I thought he had us last night." "Not a chance." A southerner's voice, one of the surviving dozen of the twenty-five who'd ridden with her from the Skepping Hills. "He's just a robber, when all's said."

But he wasn't. Or more properly, someone in his band was more than just a robber's follower. And it was abundantly clear that John's information concerning the band's numbers—and capabilities—was far more accurate than Rocklys'. Well, the southerners would learn—if they lived long enough.

Smoke from breakfast fires stung Jenny's nostrils, reminding her of her hunger. They had been at Palmorgin, the largest of the new fortified manors in the deeps of the Wyrwoods, when Balgodorus turned and attacked. Fortunately there had been surplus grain in the storerooms. That probably had a good deal to do with the bandit's choice of target, though Jenny wasn't sure. They'd have to have known she was following them, and their goal, it was clear, was to eliminate her; to knock magic from John's—and Rocklys'—armory of resources. Then, too, the fine southern swordblades, arrowheads, and spears stored at Palmorgin made it a target. Early summer—before the harvest was in—was a hard time for bandits as for everyone else. The families from the outlying farms had managed to bring in the remnants of last year's oats and barley, and a handful had res-cued pigs, cows, and chickens, but Palmorgin's lord Pellanor had never-theless confiscated the lot and put everything under armed guard. After a week of siege, and no help in sight, Jenny was glad the elderly baron had taken this precaution.

Things were bad enough without starvation.

With her mind she walked from the storeroom where she slept down the corridor, past the guard and out onto the parapet that ran around the whole of the manor's outer wall. Testing and listening, smelling at every mark of ward and guard she had put on the place, to see if counterspells had probed them in her few hours of sleep since last night's attack. She'd have to make the walk in person as soon as she got up, but this probing had on a dozen occasions alerted her to trouble spots that she might not have reached for an hour or more: fires starting in the stables or under the kitchen roof, spells of sleep or inattention muttering to the guards.

Balgodorus' witch was good.

And under her mental probes, Jenny heard other voices. Women in the kitchen, chatting of commonplaces or gossiping of those not present—"She's been carrying on with Eamon like a common whore . . ." "Well, what do you suppose her mother was? And Eamon's wife with child!" None of them dared to speak of what filled all their minds: *What if Balgodorus breaks the gate?*

There were women in the eastern villages, women who had been through Balgodorus' raids, who still wore masks and would do so until they died. Those were the ones who had been deemed not pretty enough or strong enough to be sold as slaves in the far southeast.

Somewhere a child laughed, and a small girl patiently explained to a playmate the only correct rules for Hide-the-Bacon. Many bandit troops killed children as a matter of course: too expensive to feed. Balgodorus' was one of these.

Ian . . .

Jenny forced herself to concentrate.

Walls, kitchen, barracks. "Three years sweating it out in this godsforsaken wilderness, build this wall and clear that field and drink that cow-piss they call wine hereabouts." A man's voice, almost certainly one of the conscripts sent north from the King's lands in Greenhythe or Bel-marie. "And for what? If the folk here had the sense Sister Illis gave to goats they'd have moved out a hundred years ago . . ."

Jenny sighed. Sister Illis was the southern name they gave to the Many-Colored Goddess. As for the sentiment, it was a common one among serfs who'd been uprooted from their villages and forcibly relocated. There were things that ending happily ever after did not address, and one of them was how everything got paid for.

"One of them's got to have gotten through." Very clearly she heard the Baron Pellanor's scratchy voice. At the same time she saw him in her mind, a tall, stringy, graying man of about her own age wearing service-able back and breast-plate armor and a cloak of red wool, the color of the House of Uwanë.

So Grand John Alyn must have been, she thought, once upon a long-ago time. Another king had sent that ten-times removed ancestor north to govern and protect those who dwelled between the Gray Mountains and the bitter river Eld. A prosperous land it had been in those days. Caerdinn had told her of a land of rich barley and oats, of sheep and shaggy-coated cattle; a land of endlessly argumentative scholars, of strange heresies that sprang up among the silver miners in the Gray Mountains and the Skep-ping Hills; of ingenious weavers and bards and workers in silver and steel. That ancient king had told Grand John Alyn, *Hold the land, defend the law, protect my people with your life.*

And King Uriens—or rather Prince Gareth, who ruled in his father's mental absence—had given charge of these lands in the southeastern Wyrwoods to Pellanor, a minor cadet of the Lords of Grampyn, after twenty-seven years' service in arms.

"I don't know, m'lord," said a man-at-arms. "The bandits got men all through the forest. They got Kannid and Borin . . ."

Jenny saw Pellanor lift a hand and turn his face away. Borin had been sent for help four days ago. Yesterday his burned and emasculated body had been dumped in the open ground sixty feet from the gates. It was a difficult shot with an arrow, but after ten or twelve tries one of the men-at-arms had finally been able to kill him.

"Can't that witch-lady get a word to the Commander at Corflyn?" another soldier asked the baron. "With a talking bird, like in the stories?"

The Baron sighed. "Well, Ront, I'm sure if Mistress Jenny could do such a thing she would have, days ago. Wizards can get word to one another, but as far as I know there aren't any other wizards at Corflyn now."

There aren't any other wizards, Jenny thought wearily, *in the whole of the Winterlands. Nor have there been for many years.* Only herself. And Ian, not yet sufficiently versed in power to speak through crystal or fire.

And this woman in Balgodorus' band.

It was time to get up.

She opened her eyes. The fire had burned down low in the brazier, a jewel-box huddle of ember and coal. The heat seemed suddenly unbearable—she whispered the rush of it aside, dissolved with a Word that mimicked the echoes of youth.

John, she thought, staring again into the blaze's blue-glowing core. *John.*

The ruined walls of Cair Dhû formed themselves once more before her, sharp and tiny as the reflections in a diamond. Fumes of smoldering heather veiled her sight. John lay close to the broken mess of acid-scorched wall. The warhorse Battlehammer, bleeding from flanks and sides, stood over him, head down, favoring his right hind leg when he moved.

No dragon remained. Nor was there any sign of what had happened to it, neither bones nor tracks of dragging. *But John wounded it,* she thought, baffled. *Wounded it unto death.*

Somehow it had prevailed. It had won.

Then she saw Battlehammer raise his head, and from smoke and ruin Sergeant Muffle appeared, glancing warily about him, ax at his belt and his big hammer in hand, his own mount and a packhorse led by the reins.

Four years ago Cair Corflyn had been only a circle of broken walls, a stronghold for whatever bandit troop was powerful enough to hold it. In the twenty-two years he'd been Thane of the Winterlands, John Aversin had led three attacks against it, and it was there that his father had been killed.

The inhabitants of the current gaggle of thatch-roofed taverns, bordellos, shops, and shacks that circled Corflyn's new gates didn't take much notice of John and Muffle. Having left Battlehammer at Alyn Hold to recuperate ("You're the one who should be recuperating!" Muffle had scolded), he was mounted on his second-string warhorse, Jughead, a skillful animal in battle or ambush but hairy-footed, bony as a withy fence, and of a color unfashionable in the ballads. John's scuffed and mended gear, iron-plated here and there and with jangling bits of chain-mail protecting his joints, was stained and old, and the plaids over it frayed. And Sergeant Muffle looked exactly what he was: a fat backcountry blacksmith.

The guards at the gate recognized them, though. "You did it, didn't you?" asked a hard-faced boy of not too many more than Ian's years. John had heard they recruited them as young as sixteen off the docks and taverns of Claekith, and drunk out of the slums. "Killed the dragon that cut up the Beck post so bad? Killed it by yourself? They say you did."

"They're lyin', though." John slid painfully from Jughead's back and clung for a moment to the saddle-bow until the grayness retreated from his vision. "God knows where the thing is now."

Commander Rocklys was waiting for him; he was shown directly in.

"Thunder of Heaven, man, you shouldn't even be on your feet!" She crossed from the window and caught his arm in her heavy grip, to get him to a chair. "They say you slew the dragon of Cair Dhû . . ."

"So everybody's tellin' me." He sank into the carved seat, annoyed with the way his legs shook and how his ribs stabbed him under the plaster dressing every time he so much as turned his head. His breath was shallow from the pain. "But it's a filthy lie. I don't know where the beast is, nor if it'll be back."

A middle-aged chamberlain brought them watered southern wine in painted cups. With her back to the window that overlooked the camp parade ground it was hard to read Rocklys' expression, but when John was finished she said, "A wizard. *Damn.* Another wizard. A man . . . You're sure?"

"No," said John. "No, I'm not sure. I was far gone, and the very earth around me smoking, and some of what I saw I know wasn't real. Or if it was, then me dad sure fooled the lot of us at his funeral." Rocklys frowned. Like his sons, she disapproved on principle of frivolity under duress. "But Muffle tells me he saw no dragon when he reached the place an hour later and found me out colder than a sailor after a spree."

"And your son?"

John's jaw tightened. "Well," he said, and said nothing more. The Commander shoved away from the wall with her shoulders and went to a cupboard: She took out a silver flask and poured a quantity of brandy into his empty wine cup. John drank and looked out past her for a time, at two soldiers in the blue cloaks of auxiliaries arguing in the parade ground. Father Anmos and the cult flute player emerged from the shrine of the Lord of War, heads shrouded in the all-covering crimson hoods designed to blot out any sight or sound detrimental to the god's worship. Raised in the heresy of the Old God, John wondered who the god of dragons would be, and if he prayed for the return of his son whether it would do any good. He felt as if barbed iron was lodged somewhere inside him.

"Muffle doesn't know. *I* don't know. Ian . . ."

He took a deep breath and raised his head again to meet her eyes. "Adric—me other boy, you know—tells me Ian set off just after midnight for Jenny's house to get death-spells to lay on the dragon; somethin' I'd forbade him to do." He forced himself to sound matter-of-fact. "By the tracks next mornin'—or so says Jen's second cousin Gniffy, and he's a hunter—there'd been someone at the house, a man in new boots that looked like city work, who went off with Ian. Gniffy lost the tracks over the moors, but it's pretty clear where they ended up."

His jaw tightened, and he looked down into the cup, trying not to remember the look in Ian's eyes.

"Ian's powers aren't great. At least that's what Jen tells me. For me, anybody who can light a candle by just lookin' at the wick is far and away a marvel, and I wish I could do it. She says he'll never be one of the great ones, never one of those that can scry the wind or shift his shape or call down the magic of the stars. Which is no reason, she says, why he can't be a truly fine middlin'-strong wizard."

"Of course not." Rocklys set down the flask. "And by the Twelve, the world has more use for a well-trained and competent mediocrity than for half a cohort of brilliant fools. Which is why," she added gently, "I wish you had left your boy here."

"Well, be that as it may," sighed John. "Even if he'd been here, Ian would have stolen a horse and run away home at first word of the dragon, so it would all have come out the same." He ran his fingers through his hair. The red ribbon was still braided in it, faded and stained with blood. "But who this is, or if he's in league with Balgodorus as well . . . I take it you've no word from Jen?"

The Commander shook her head. Her eyes were troubled, resting on John's face. He must, he thought, look worse than he supposed.

"I got one message two weeks ago: Balgodorus seemed to be heading for the mountains. He has a stronghold there. I've sent search parties in that direction but they've found nothing, and frankly, in the Wyrwoods, unless you know what you're looking for you're not going to find it. You know those woods. Thickets that have been growing in on themselves since before the founding of the Realm; ranges of hills we've never heard of, swallowed in trees. They may be untrained scum, but they know the land, and they're rebellious, tricky, stopping at nothing . . ."

Her face suddenly set, grim anger in her eyes. "And some of the southern lords are as bad, or nearly so. Barons, they call themselves, or nobles—wolves tearing at the fabric of the Realm for their own purposes. Well"—she shook her head—"at least the likes of Balgodorus don't pretend allegiance and then make deals behind the Regent's back."

"Two weeks." John gazed into the dab of amber fluid at the bottom of his goblet. Two days' ride from Alyn, with Muffle scolding all the way. Ian had been gone for five days.

Old Caerdinn returned to his mind, as he had on and off since the strange mage's appearance. A vile old man, John remembered, dirty and obsessed. He had been John's tutor as well, and a quarter of the books at Alyn Hold had been dug from ruins by that muttering, bearded old bundle of rags, or bargained from any who had even the blackest scraps of paper to sell. He—and John's mother—were the only other wizards John had ever heard of north of the Wildspae, and they had hated one another cordially.

Had Caerdinn had other pupils? Pupils whose wizardry was stronger than Jenny's, maybe even stronger than Jenny's human magic alloyed with the alien powers of dragons? This woman of Balgodorus', or the person who had taught her. The man with the moonstone in his staff?

Somehow he couldn't see the gentleman in the purple coat taking instruction from a toothless dribbling old beggar, much less meekly letting Caerdinn beat him, as Jenny had done.

But there were other Lines of magic. Other provenances of teaching handed down in the south, in Belmarie or the Seven Isles. And as Rocklys had said, though their magic was very different from human magic, there were wizards also among the gnomes.

He sighed again and raised his head, to meet Rocklys' worried gaze. "I have to believe that I saw at least some of what I think I saw," he said simply. "I was flat on my back for three days after the fight, and it rained during that time. Gniffy had a look round but he said the tracks were so torn up, he couldn't be sure of anything. But Centhwevir's gone. And Ian's gone."

"Of this Centhwevir I've heard nothing." Rocklys walked to the niche in the wall, where in former centuries commandants had put the closed shrines of the gods. She had a shrine there to the Lord of War, and another to the Lord of Law, but where in the south he'd seen little charred basins of incense, and the stains of proffered wine and blood, was only clean-scrubbed marble. The rest of the niche held books, and his eye ran over the titles: Tenantius' *Theory of Laws*, Gurgustus' *Essays*, *The Liever Regulae*, and Caecilius' *The Righteous Monarch*. On the table before these books was a strongbox of silver pieces, and beside it a small casket containing half a handful of gems. He remembered the complaints that had come to him from the mayors of Far West Riding and Great Toby, how the King's commissioners demanded more to pay for the garrison than even the greediest thane ever had.

"Of this new wizard . . ." She shook her head. "Can Jenny have been mistaken? Or might the man you saw have been some kind of . . . of illusion, as the dragon was?"

"And be really this woman?" John shook his head. "But why? Why go to the trouble to fool me?"

"In any case," said the Commander, "all of this convinces me—well, I was convinced before—that we *must* establish this school I've spoken of, this academy of wizards, here in Corflyn. I hope now that when she returns, Jenny will agree to come here and teach others. We can't go on like this."

"No."

Save a dragon, slave a dragon . . . The old granny-rhyme drifted back through his mind, and the bodies he'd found the last time Balgodorus had raided a village.

And as he heard the words again he saw the wizard in his violet coat and embroidered cap mounting Centhwevir's back, holding out his hand to Ian.

His ribs ached where the boy's boot toe had driven in.

The Commander turned from the neglected shrines, the books of the Legalist scholars, very real distress on her face. "It isn't just bandit mages who are the danger. You know that! Look at the gnomes, operating what amount to independent kingdoms at the very heart of the King's Realm! Buying slaves, too, clean against the King's Law, no matter what they swear and claim! They have wizards among them, and who knows what or who they teach. Look at lords like the Master of Halnath, and the Prince of Greenhythe, and the merchant princes of the Seven Isles! Look at Tinán of Imperteng, claiming that his ancient title to the lands at the base of the mountains is equal in rank to that of the King himself!"

John propped his spectacles on his nose. "Well, accordin' to Dotys' *Histories*, it is."

"What kind of argument is that?!" Rocklys demanded angrily. "The revolt of the Prince of Wyr, four hundred years ago, broke the Realm in two! That should never have been permitted. And Prince Gareth—though I have nothing but respect for him as a scholar and an administrator—is letting it happen all over again!"

"Our boy Gar's not done so very ill," John pointed out quietly. "For one coming new to the game and untaught, he's doing gie well."

He smiled a little, remembering the gangly boy with the fashionable green streaks in his fair hair, broken glasses perched on the end of his long nose, delivering himself of an oratorical message from the King before collapsing in a faint in the Alyn Hold pigyard. Comic, maybe, thought John. But it had taken genuine courage to sail north to an unknown land; genuine courage to ride overland from the harbor at Eldsbouch to Alyn Hold. The boy was lucky he hadn't had his throat slit for his boots on the way.

Maybe luckier still that he'd set out on his journey when he had. In those days the witch Zyerne had been tightening her grip on the old King's mind and soul, draining his energy and looking about her for a new victim.

"That's exactly my point!" Rocklys drove her fist into her palm, her face hard. "His Highness the Prince is untaught. And inexperienced. And he's making mistakes that will cost the Realm dear. It will take years— decades—to repair them, if they can be repaired at all. His . . ." She stopped herself with an effort.

"I'm sorry," she said. "He's your friend, as he is my cousin. I suppose I can't get over my memories of him prancing along with his friends, wearing those silly shoulder-banners that were all the rage, and toe-points so long they had to be chained to his garters. You're not going to go seeking Jenny?" She came over to him and rested a big hand on his shoulder. John realized he was so tired it would cost him great effort to stand, and his hands were growing colder and colder around the painted rim of the cup.

"I'll ride on back to the Hold," he said. "Jenny'll know Ian's gone, and something's gie wrong. She'll be on her way back to the Hold as fast as she can."

"I thought mages couldn't scry other mages."

"Nor can they. So she'll know I haven't been next or nigh Ian in five days, and that I've got meself out of bed and down here before my cuts have fair scabbed. She'll put two and two together—she's good at that kind of addition, is Jenny. And it's as well," he added, setting the cup aside and rising cautiously from his chair. "For in truth, she can't return too soon for comfort."

"And if she doesn't return?" asked Rocklys. "If this bandit chief and his tame mage have found a way to imprison or destroy her?"

"Ah, well." John scratched the side of his long nose. "Then just us standin' off a couple of wizards, and a dragon, and all . . . I'd say we're in real trouble." He took three steps toward the door and fainted, as if struck over the head with a house beam.

6

Wait for me, you idiot! thought Jenny furiously, and let the images in the fire fade. *WAIT FOR ME!* She wondered why the Goddess of Women had seen fit to cause her to fall in love with a blockhead.

Moonlight streamed through the window, just tinged now with the smoke of far-off fires. Somewhere beyond the walls a whippoorwill cried. Jenny drew her plaid around her shoulders and wished with all that was in her that she could slip over the palisade, summon Moon Horse from her patient foraging in the woods, and ride for Alyn Hold as fast as she could go.

Or if all that were not possible—and it was not, not without leaving close to three hundred people to die—she wished that at least she knew what was going on.

Silence cupped Palmorgin manor in its invisible hand. Even the guards had nothing to say, focused through their exhaustion on the open ground beyond the moat. This was the dead hour of night that Balgodorus favored for his attacks. Mosquitoes whined in the darkness, but worn down as she was even the spells of "Go bite someone else" scraped at her, like a rough spot on the inside of a shoe after the tenth or twelfth mile.

No sign of Centhwevir. Under the best of circumstances it wasn't always possible to scry dragons, for their flesh, their very essence, was woven of magic. But over the past seven days, she had scried the outposts along the fell country, scried the towns of Great Toby and Far West Riding, scried Alyn itself.

No burned ground. No tangles of stripped and acid-charred bones.

And at the Hold, no mourning. But she saw Aunt Jane and Aunt Rowan and Cousin Dilly weeping; saw Adric sitting alone on the battlements, looking out to the south. And John, after his brief interview with

Rocklys, had refused to remain in bed, had instead dragged himself next morning back onto his horse and taken the road for home, Muffle behind him scolding all the way.

Ian.

Something had happened to Ian.

Wait till I get there, John. This can't last.

She slipped from the room.

Women and children slept rolled in blankets along the corridor outside her door. She picked her way among them, drawing her skirts aside. Pale blue light glowed around the door handles of other storerooms, warding away touch with spells of dread. Warding away, too, every spell of rats and mold and insects, leaks and fire, anything and everything Jenny could think of.

In the archway that led onto the palisade she nodded to the guard, and the night breeze lifted the dark hair from her face. Balgodorus' tame mage hadn't stopped with illusion. As she passed the roofs of the buildings around the court, Jenny checked the faint-glowing threads of ward-signs, of wyrds and counterspells. In some places the fire-spells still lingered, the wood or plaster hot beneath her fingers. She scribbled additional marks, and in one place opened one of the several pouches at her belt and dipped her finger into the spelled mix of powdered silver and dried fox-blood, to strengthen the ward. She didn't like the untaught craziness of those wild spells, without Limitations to keep them from devouring and spreading where their sender had no intention of letting them go.

There had been other spells besides fire. Spells to summon bees from their hives and hornets from their nests in furious unseasonal swarms. Spells of sickness, of fleas, of unreasoning panic and rage. Anything to break the concentration of the defenders. The palisade and the block-houses were a tangle of counterspells and amulets; the smelly air a lour of magic.

How could anyone, she wondered, born with the raw gold of magic in them, use it in the service of a beast like Balgodorus: slave trader, killer, rapist, and thief?

"Mistress Waynest?" Lord Pellanor appeared at the top of the ladder from the court below. He carried his helm under his arm, and the gold inlay that was its sole decoration caught the fire's reflection in a frivolous curlicue of light. Without it his balding, close-cropped head above gorget and collar looked silly and small. "Is all well?"

"As of sunset. I'm just starting another round."

"Can she see in?" asked the Baron. "I mean, look with a mirror or a crystal or with fire the way you do, to see where to plant those spells of hers?"

"I don't think so." Jenny folded her arms under her plaid. "She might be able to see in a room where I'm not, despite scry-wards I've put on everything I can think of. She's strong enough to keep me from looking into their camp. She's laying down spells at random, the way I've done: sickness on a horse or a man, fire in hay or wood, foulness in water. And she wouldn't know any more than I do how much effect those spells are having."

The Baron puffed his breath, making his long mustaches jump. "Where would she have learned, eh?" He started to bite his thumb against evil, then glanced at her and changed the gesture to simply scratching his chin. "I . . . er . . . don't suppose the man who taught you might still be about?"

Jenny shook her head.

"You're sure?"

She looked aside. "I buried him. Twenty-five years ago."

"Ah."

"I was the last of his students." Jenny scanned the formless yards of open ground below. They had fought, daily, over that ground, and daily, nightly, those ragged filthy foul-mouthed men had come back, with ladders, with axes, with brush to try to burn the gates or rams to try to break them. There were, she guessed, nearly twice as many bandits as there were defenders of fighting strength. They attacked in shifts.

Even now she could see the twinkle of lights from their camp and smell its stink on the breeze. Eating, drinking, resting up for another attack. Her bones ached with fatigue.

"He was very old," she went on, "and very bitter, I suppose through no fault of his own." She remembered the way his stick would whine as it slashed through the air, and the bite of the leather strap on her flesh. The better, he said, for her to remember her lessons. But she'd felt his satisfaction in the act of punishment alone, the relief of a frustration that ate him alive. She had wept for days, at the old man's lonely death. She still did not know why.

"He remembered the last of the King's troops, marching away to the south. That must have been the final garrison from Great Toby, because the others had gone centuries before that. He said his own teacher left with them, and after that he could only work at the books his teacher left. There was no one else in the north who could teach properly—not healing, not magic, not music. Nothing. Caerdinn was too young to follow the legions south, he said. Then the Iceriders came, and everything changed."

Pellanor cleared his throat apologetically, as if it were up to him to defend the decision of the man whom history knew as the Primrose King. "Well, Hudibras II was faced with a very difficult situation during the Kin-Wars. And the plague struck hardest among the armies. Your teacher seems to have learned enough on his own to have taught you well."

Jenny thought of all those things she'd learned in the south that Caerdinn hadn't known, the holes in his knowledge she'd struggled with all her life. Spells that could have saved lives, had she known them. But Pellanor had done her no harm, and didn't understand, so she only said, "So he did."

Had the old man's anger stemmed from that ancient desertion? she wondered, as she moved on into the corner turret. Under her touch the rough-dressed stone walls, the heavily plastered timbers, felt normal—no new spells embedded like embers within. Or had his rage at her been because she was herself untalented, born with only mediocre powers, when he considered himself fit to have instructed the great?

Had the masters of those ancient Lines truly had some method of raising small powers such as hers—and his—to primacy? Or was that just some fantasy of his own?

The fact remained that her greater powers had come from contact with the Dragon of Nast Wall. That dragon-magic she sent out now, flowing like thin blue lightning through rock and wood, thatch and tile, listening as dragons listened, sniffing and tasting for that other wizard's spells.

There. Summonings of rats, and fleas—good God, did that mageborn imbecile know nothing about the spread of plague? Another fire-spell . . . No, two. One under the rafters of the main hall. Another in the air in the courtyard, a stickiness waiting for someone to walk by. She probed at them, encysted them in Limits, pinched them dead.

Irresponsible. Foolish, insane. Bandit-magic. Like Balgodorus himself, uncaring what ill he caused as long as he got what he wanted.

Jenny renewed the Weirds on the turret and hastened, her soft sheepskin boots soundless on the rough dirty plank floors, to the places where the flea-spells had taken hold.

They were badly wrought, drifting patches of them scattered like seeds through the stable, through the kitchen corridor used as a barrack for Rocklys' men, and the dormitory set up among the arches under the main tower. It took Jenny weary hours to trace them down, to neutralize the knots and quirks of hunger and circumstance that would draw vermin to those places in swarms. They weren't strong enough to do any real damage under most circumstances, but still too strong to neglect. The foul, pissy smell of rodents was in any case stronger everywhere in the manor than she liked. A dangerous smell, with so many people crowded so close.

Did Balgodorus think he was immune? Did he think his tame mage's unhoned powers were up to combating full-scale plague?

As she traced the Runes and Circles and Summonings over and over, on walls and floors and furniture; as she called forth the power of the stars, of the earth, of water and moon-tide and air; as she wrought magic from her own flesh and bones and concentration, Jenny wanted to slap that ignorant, selfish, arrogant bandit-witch until her ears rang. Whatever Caerdinn's failings, he had started his teaching with Limitations. The old man's tales had been filled with well-meaning adepts whose cantrips to draw wealth to the deserving had resulted in the deaths of moneyed but otherwise innocent relatives, and whose fever-cures slew their patients from shock or chill.

The short summer night was nearing its end when she finished. The warriors who'd watched around the courtyard fire had sought their rest. Somewhere in the dormitory a child cried out in her sleep, and Jenny heard a second child's whispering voice start a story about a wandering prince in exile, to beguile her sister back to sleep. The quarter moon stood high above the parapets: the Gray God, the mages' God of the High Faith. Jenny leaned her back against the stone arch and looked up at that neat white semi-circle, glowing so brightly that she could see the thin edge of light around the remainder of the velvety disc.

Listening as dragons listened, she felt the souls of Balgodorus' camp, a mile or so distant in the rock-girt clearing by Gan's Brook. Spirits like filthy laundry, grease-slick and reeking from short lifetimes of brutality, rape, and greed. She could scent the very blood of the camp horses and dogs.

So the star-drake had smelled John's blood as he'd ridden to meet it.

Had Ian ridden out after John?

He must have. She'd scried John and Muffle, at least until the bandits had attacked the manor again and she'd had to abandon her vision of the battle and turn to her own battle. Stumbling with exhaustion, she'd returned in time to see the confused vision of fire and blood that was the actual combat. Had Ian been there, she would have seen nothing. But had he followed? The wonder was that Adric hadn't found a way to get himself into trouble as well.

So what had happened?

Her mind returned, troubled, to the vision she'd had of John, only a few hours ago. John in that patched red robe of threadbare velvet he wore after a bath, sitting in his study once again, with every book on dragons and dragon-slaying that he owned heaped around him, his silly clocks chiming and whirling soundlessly in the dark at his back. He read, it seemed to her, with a concentrated, desperate energy, as she'd seen him read when he was trying to course out some half-remembered clue tossed to the surface of the magpie-nest of his memory.

Trying to find something before it was too late.

And at last, just as she let the vision fade, he took off his spectacles and sat with head bowed: weariness, desperation, and terrible knowledge in his immobile face.

He had found what he sought, whatever it was.

Wait for me.

She opened her eyes. Her head throbbed, but there was one more thing yet to do tonight.

She heard the breathing of Balgodorus Black-Knife's men, unseen in the misty eaves of the woods. Like a dragon, she smelled their blood. But in this dead hour of night, it was a good guess that the bandit-mage, whoever it was, slept.

Jenny hitched her plaids up over her shoulder and climbed the stair to the parapet again.

Pellanor was returning from his own rounds, craggy face drawn with strain. Jenny didn't know when the man slept last. He helped her fetch a rope and wrapped it around a post while she drew the signs of power in the air and on the stonework and wove about herself and the rope the signs of Look-Over-There. Even another wizard might easily miss her. Her mind still weaving those silvery webs about herself, she girdled up her faded blue skirts and let herself down over the wall.

She carried a long dagger and a short dagger, and her halberd slung over her back: slung also, awkward beside the weapon, was the small harp she'd borrowed from Pellanor. "Be careful," Pellanor whispered, when she knew he wanted to say *Come back soon.* In her absence anything could befall.

But this was something that had to be done.

Crossing the moat was easy. The bandits had been heaving rocks and dirt, broken trees and beams into it for weeks to provide their scaling ladders with footing. As she came under the trees of the woods that drew close to the wall at this point, she passed between two watchers, a woman and a man, ugly leathery brutes crouched like wolves waiting beside water for prey. Even if she had not been mageborn, she thought she would have been able to smell them in the dark. She'd walked one night to the edge of Balgodorus' camp, perhaps a mile and a half down the rough-sloping ground. Seen the shimmer of ward-sigils and elf-light that fenced the place, guarding it as her own guarded Palmorgin's walls.

The clearing she sought tonight was half a mile from the bandit camp and long known to her. An ash tree stood in it, ruinously old, the sole survivor of some long-ago fire. The rock by which it grew could have been a natural one, unless you looked at it from a certain angle and realized it had been hewn into the shape of a crouching pig. There was a hollow in the top that collected dew. Around this hollow Jenny traced a circle with her fingers, her eyes slipping half-closed.

She formed in her heart the power of the moon, when it should lie one day closer to its dying than it lay tonight. The turning stars, white and cold and ancient. With her fingers she braided the moonlight, slippery-cold as heavy silk, and with a little spoon of crystal and silver drawn from her pocket she dipped up dew from the grass. Spiderweb and milkweed she bound into the spells and brushed them with the spoon-back into the air again: a whispering of longing and of pain. With the shadows of her hair she painted runes into the darkness, and from the pale starflash made sigils of pallid light.

Her knee braced on the rock, she slipped the harp free of its casing: balanced it in her arm as she had balanced her children when they were babies. There were barely strings for her two hands. The spells she wove she had learned from the Dragon of Nast Wall, and scarcely knew what emotion she wove into tomorrow's moonlight, tomorrow's stars, as she had woven it last night into the slant of tonight's milky shadows.

Hunger for what was gone forever. Heart-tearing sweetness glowing in the core of a bitter fruit. A hand curved around the illusion of fire or a jewel; books hidden long in the earth.

For two weeks she had come, while the silver coin of the moon swelled to fullness, then was clipped away bit by bit: the Gray God covering over with his sleeve the white paper he wrote on, they said, that men could not read what would work their ruin. For two weeks she had made this song of dreams of grief. Then in the silence that followed the song she waited.

Far off to her right one of the watchers around the manor swatted a gnat and cursed.

The stars moved. The moon rode high, singing its triumph. Bones and body ached. Moreover, the grief of the spell, as is the way of spells without words, was her own. Thin mists no higher than Jenny's knees stirred among the trees, and in time she smelled the change in the air that spoke of dawn.

She drew a mist about herself, and the changeable illusion of dreams. Like a deer wrought of glass, she picked her way back through thickets and dew-soaked ferns, through the dell where fey-lights danced among the mushrooms and the ringed stones. Those who crouched on picket, squinting across open ground to the new stone walls, the trash-filled moat and ruined outbuildings, didn't see her when she paused between them, looking at Pellanor's Hold.

A rough square of stone walls, perhaps sixty yards to the side, floating in a milky drift of mist. Turrets at each corner and a blockhouse on the west. Gate and gatehouse. Stables and granaries. Three hundred and fifty people—men, women, and children . . .

A gift, as Balgodorus would see it, of good southern weaponry and steel, of slaves for the selling and grain to feed his troops. And Jenny herself, a mageborn weapon in the Law's hand.

As this girl, whoever she was, was Black-Knife's weapon.

And against that she saw the burned-out havoc of Cair Dhû; Adric huddled alone among the sheepskins of the big curtained bed he and his brother shared. John in his study with his spectacles in his hand, reading one passage over and over, two times, three times, in the light of the candles, and then slowly leaning his forehead down on his hand.

She closed her eyes. She had only to whistle up Moon Horse and ride.

That fleck of light on the parapet would be Pellanor, waiting for her sign below to let down the rope.

Dawn rinsed the blackness over the walls with the thinnest pallor of gray.

Jenny sighed and wrapped invisibility around her. Like a shred of mist she moved among the ruins of the village, past the bandit watchers, to the beleaguered Hold once more.

7

*"*M*aggots from meat, weevils from rye.*
Dragons from stars in an empty sky."

John Aversin sat for a long time with the second volume of *The Ency-*
clopedia of Everything in the Material World open before him:

"Dragons come down out of the north, being formed in the hearts of
the volcanoes that erupt in the ice. The combination of the heat and the
cold, and the vapors from under the earth, give birth to eggs, and the eggs
so to the dragons themselves. Being born not of flesh, they are invulnera-
ble to all usages of the flesh . . ."

Among the green curlicues, gold-leaf flowers, and carmine berries of
the marginalia could be found enlightening illuminations of perfectly
conical mountains spitting forth orange dragon eggs as if they were
melon seeds, accompanied by drawings of hugely grinning and rather
crocodilian dragons.

"Teltrevir, heliotrope," whispered Jenny's voice in his mind and
behind it the braided threads of music from her harp, the tunes that were
joined to those names. "Centhwevir is blue knotted with gold. Nymr sea-
blue, violet-crowned; Gwedthion ocean-green and Glammring Gold-
Horns bright as emeralds . . ."

And each tune, each air, separate and alien and haunting. John closed
his eyes, exhaustion grinding at his flesh, and remembered a round-dance
he'd seen as a child. Its music had been spun from the twelfth of those
nameless passages. The twelfth name on Jenny's list was Sandroving,
gold and crimson. The girls had called the dance Bloodsnake. He could
still whistle the tune.

Dotys had more to say. "The star-drakes, or dragons as such things
are called, dwelt anciently in the archipelagoes of rock and ice that string

the northern seas westward from the Peninsula of Tralchet, islands called by the gnomes the Skerries of Light. These skerries, or reefs, of rock are utterly barren, and so the dragons must descend to the lands of men to hunt, for they are creatures of voracious appetite, as well as archetypes of greed and lust and all manner of willfulness."

And they live on what between times? thought John.

On the corner of his desk Skinny Kitty woke long enough to scratch her ear and wash, then returned to sleep with her paw over her nose. In the cinder darkness beyond the window a cock crowed.

He touched the sheaf of parchment that the young Regent had sent him. The old ballads had been copied in beautiful bookhand by a court scribe. It was astonishing what coming to power could do for obsessions previously sneered at by the fashionable.

" *'For lo,' she quoth, 'do dragons sing*
More beautifully than birds.' "

Who in their right mind would, or could, make up a detail like that?

"Southward-flying shadows of fire."

"From isles of ice and rock beneath the moon."

A candle guttered, smoking. John looked up in surprise and groped around until he found a pair of candle scissors to trim the wick. The sky in the stone window frame had gone from cinder to mother-of-pearl.

His body hurt, as if he'd been beaten with lengths of chain. Even the effort of sitting up for several hours made his breath short. Most of the candles had burned out, and their smutted light stirred uneasily in the networks of experimental pulleys and tackle that hung from the rafters. It would soon be time to go.

". . . isles of ice and rock . . ."

The other volume lay in front of him also. The partial volume of Juronal he had found in a ghoul's hive, near what had been the Tombs of Ghrai; the volume he had read on his return, two nights ago, as he searched for that half-remembered bit of information that told him what had become of Ian and why he could wait no longer to embark on his quest for help.

North, he thought. He took off his spectacles and leaned his forehead on his hand. *Alone. God help me.*

The key to magic is magic! Jenny flinched away from the hard knobbed hands striking her, the toothless mouth shouting abuse. The dirty, smoky stink of the house on Frost Fell returned to her through the dream's haze. Caerdinn's cats watched from the windowsills and doors, untroubled by the familiar scene. *The key to magic is magic!* The old man's grip like iron, he dragged her from the hearth by her hair, pulled the old harp from her hands, thrust her at the desk where the books lay, black lettering nearly invisible on the tobacco-colored pages.

The more you do, the more you'll be able to do! It's laziness, laziness, laziness that keeps you small!

It isn't true! She wanted to shout back at him, across all those years of life. *It isn't true.*

But at fourteen she hadn't known that. At thirty-nine she hadn't known.

In her dream she saw the summer twilight, the beauty of the nights when the sky held light until nearly midnight and breathed dawn again barely three hours later. In her dream she heard the sad little tunes she'd played on her master's harp, tunes that had nothing to do with the ancient music-spells handed down along the Line of Herne. Like all of Caerdinn's knowledge, those spells of music were maddeningly ambiguous, fragments of airs learned by rote.

In her dream Jenny thought she saw the black skeletal shape of a dragon flying before the ripe summer moon.

The key to magic was not magic.

Out of darkness burned two crystalline silver lamps. Stars that drank in the soul and tangled the mind in mazes of still-deeper dream. A white core of words forming in fathomless darkness.

What is truth, Wizard-woman? The truth that dragons see is not pleasant to the human eyes, however uncomfortably comprehensible it may be to their hearts. You know this.

The knots of colored music that were his true name.

The kaleidoscope of memory that she touched when she touched his mind.

The gold fire of magic that had flowed into her veins.

Plunging herself, dragon form, into the wind . . .

Mistress Waynest . . . !

This love you speak of, I do not know what it is. It is not a thing of dragons . . .

Mistress, wake up!

"Wake up!"

Gasping, she pulled clear of the mind-voice in the shadows. Raw smoke tore her throat; the air was a clamor of men shouting and the frenzied screams of cattle and horses in pain. "What is it?" She scrambled to a sitting position, head aching, eyes thick. Nemus, one of Rocklys' troopers, stood beside her narrow bed.

"Balgodorus . . ."

As if it would or could be anything else. Jenny was already grabbing for her halberd and her slingstones—she slept clothed and booted these days—trying to thrust the leaden exhaustion from her bones. Her mind registered details automatically: mid-morning, noise from all sides, concerted attack . . .

"—fire-arrows," the young man was saying. "Burning the block-house roof, but there's a storeroom in flames . . ."

Fire-spells.

". . . as if the animals have all gone mad . . ."

Curse, thought Jenny. *Curse, curse, curse . . .*

The stables were in flames, too. She had no idea of the nature of the spell that had been put on the animals, but the horses, mules, and cattle were rushing crazily around the central court, charging and slashing at one another, kicking the walls, throwing themselves at the doors. Bellowing, shrieking, madness in their eyes. The smoke that rolled over the whole scene seemed to Jenny to be laden with magic, as if something foul burned and spread with the blaze.

Damn her, she thought, *who taught that bitch such a spell?*

Scaling ladders wavered and jerked beyond the frieze of palisade spikes. Arrows filled the air. On the north wall men were already being stabbed at and hacked by the defenders within. Slingstones cracked against the walls and an arrow splintered close to Jenny's head. Someone was bellowing orders. She got a brief glimpse of Pellanor in his steel-plated armor swaying hand-to-hand at the top of the wall with a robber in dirty leathers, as she sprang down the steps to the court.

"Watch out, m'lady!" yelled another soldier, racing along the cat-walk. "Them horses is insane!"

Curse it, thought Jenny, trying to concentrate through exhaustion and the blurring blindness of a too-familiar migraine, trying to snatch the form and nature of the spell out of the air. There were panic-spells working, too, a new batch of them . . .

She banged on the shutters of the storerooms where the children hid during attacks. "It's me, Jenny Waynest!" she called out. "One of you, any of you . . ."

The shutters cracked. A girl's face showed in the slit.

"The names of the cows," said Jenny. She'd have to do this the hard way, with Limitations, not a counterspell. "Quick."

The girl, thank God, didn't ask her if she was insane, or if she meant what she said. "Uh—Florrie. Goddess. Ginger. You want me to point out which is which? They're moving awful fast."

"Just the names." Jenny already knew the names of the horses. "Give me a minute; I'll be back. Be thinking of all of them." She sprinted across the court, two cows and a mule turning, charging her. She barely reached the stair at the base of the east tower before them, leaped and scrambled up out of their reach, drew a Guardian on the stonework. Smoke poured like a river from under the eaves of the workrooms between the east tower and the north, but it was better than trying to get past the melee in the court. Jenny swung herself up, darted across the roof, forming counterspells to the fire as she ran and thanking the Twelve that the roof beneath her feet was tile. A man's body plunged from above, spraying blood.

Get the danger contained, thought Jenny. *Madness-spells, fire-spells, get those taken care of first.*

And then, by the Moon-Scribe's little white dog, you and I have a reckoning, my ill-instructed friend.

The Limitations quieted the maddened animals, exempting them one by one from the spell. It made Jenny's head ache to concentrate amid the chaos, the smell of smoke and the fear that any moment the bandits would come over the wall.

From the top of the west wall Jenny picked out Balgodorus himself, a tall man, strong enough to dominate any of his men, dark and with a bristling beard. Men were rallying around him now, ready for another attack. They wound their crossbows, milled and shouted among themselves, working up their anger. Balgodorus was saying something to them, gesturing at the walls . . .

"Probably telling them about all the food and wealth we have in here," muttered Pellanor, his voice hollow within his steel helm as he came to Jenny's side. He was panting hard and smelled of sweat and the blood that ran down the steel.

Balgodorus gestured to the woman who stood near him.

Jenny said softly, "That's her."

"What?"

"The witch. She's wearing a skirt, and unarmed. Bandit-women dress as men. Why else would she be at the battle? I'll need a rope." Jenny strode along the palisade, dark hair billowing in a crazy cloud behind her, Pellanor hurrying after. "I don't suppose there's a scaling ladder still standing."

On all the walls the defenders were panting, resting their spears and their swords against the palisade, wiping sweat or blood from their eyes. Children ran along the catwalk with water; a man could be heard telling them sharply to get back indoors and bar themselves in. Below, in the court, the horses stamped, restless at the smell of smoke and blood, and all around could be heard the faint, frenzied squealing of the mice, the cats, the rats still under the influence of the mad-spell.

"Great Heaven, no!"

She felt for her stones and sling, shrugging her shoulder through the halberd's strap. "Go back. They're gathering for another try." She stepped over a dead bandit, kilting up her skirts.

"You can't seriously think of leaving in the middle of an attack! You'll be slaughtered!" Jenny had never used spells of illusion in or near the Hold, for fear of the effects they might have on the watchers on the wall, or on the counterspells against illusion with which she'd so carefully ringed the fortress. Last night she had renewed those counterspells after a scout told her there was untoward movement around the bandit camp. She'd had only time for a quick, disquieting glimpse of John, who should have been flat on his back in bed, loading provisions into that horror of an airship he'd built last spring. Muffle had been with him—*Muffle, for love of the Goddess, knock some sense into his head!*

"An attack is the only time she'll be concentrating on something else." Jenny found the rope down which Pellanor had let her climb two nights ago, still coiled just inside the door of the north turret. She checked the land below, and the ruined and trampled fields that lay to the east. No bandits in sight on that side of the keep. Arrows littered the ground, floated in the moat like straws. A single body, the legacy of an attack three days ago, bobbed obscenely among the half-sunk timbers and boughs.

"Whatever you do, hold them now," she said. "This shouldn't take long."

"What if she uses more spells?" asked the Baron worriedly. "Without you to counter them . . ."

"I'm counting on her to do just that," said Jenny. "It will give me a better chance at her. Hold fast and don't let anyone panic. I can't return until after the attack is driven off, but that shouldn't be long." She slithered under the dripping, charred spikes of the palisade, hanging onto the rope. "I'll be watching."

"May the gods of war and magic go with you, then." Pellanor saluted and snapped his visor down again. "Damn," he added, as the noise rose from the other side of the fortress. "Here they come."

Jenny dropped, playing the rope out fast, thankful that she and John still worked out against one another with halberd and sword. Still, she was forty-one and felt it. No sleep last night and precious little the night before, and when she did sleep, she saw in her mind what John was doing with that monstrosity he'd built . . .

She pushed away the images, her frantic fear and the desire to break her beloved's legs to keep him in bed until she got there, forced her thoughts to return to spells of protection, of concealment, as she ran for the fields. Broken crops offered some concealment from the men she could hear shouting beneath the walls.

"At 'em, men!" Balgodorus' voice clashed like an iron gong. "Make 'em wish they never been born!" He had come around with his forces, sword in hand, and now stood close to where Jenny lay in the broken stubble.

"And you, bitch—" He grabbed the arm of the woman beside him. Girl, Jenny saw now. No more than fifteen. Snarled chestnut hair and the kind of ill-fitting gown common to bandits' whores, expensive silk stamped with gold, black with sweat under the arms, kilted to show no petticoat beneath and quite clearly worn over neither corset nor shift. A thin little face like a shut door, dead eyes long past either tears or joy.

"You do your stuff or you'll feel it tonight, understand."

He thrust her off from him and ran to overtake his men, loping easily, like a big dark lion, sword raising high. A cheer greeted him. Some were already bracing themselves, letting fly arrows toward the walls, and the two or three warriors Balgodorus had left standing around the witch-girl watched, too, cursing and cheering and making jokes.

The girl closed her eyes and made the signs of power with her hands. *No Limitations,* thought Jenny, disgusted. *No amplifications of power either—she must be calling it all out of her own bones and flesh.* The thin face was taut, lost in concentration, expressionless, though Jenny thought she saw the mouth tremble.

No older than she had been herself when Caerdinn had beaten the remnants of his learning into her.

And like her, probably starved for whatever craft she could learn.

It was too easy. Jenny slipped a stone from her purse and into the pocket of the sling, whipped it around her head as she rose to her knees. Timing, timing . . . The first of the scaling ladders went up against the manor wall, and Balgodorus scrambled up. One of the witch-girl's watchers yelled, "Have at 'em, Chief!" and raised his fist. The witch-girl's brows pulled hard together, pain in her face—as spent and battered, Jenny realized, as she was herself.

She felt a deep ache of pity as she let the sling-thong slip.

The girl twisted as if struck by invisible lightning and fell without a sound.

8

"**Y**ou're mad, Johnny!"

Aversin turned from lashing the boxes, crates, and struts to the sides of what appeared to be a long, narrow boat wrought of wicker—curious enough given the distance Alyn Hold lay from any navigable water—and regarded his half-brother a moment in silence. Then he leaped over the boat's gunwale, scooped up a handful of packing straw from a broached barrel nearby, and, scrubbing it into his hair, executed a startling series of jigs and pirouettes without sound or change of expression. Sergeant Muffle stepped back in alarm.

"I'd get on me knees and bark like a dog," said John, catching the boat's railing for balance and panting, suddenly white, "but I've a touch of rheumatism." He was trembling all over, and Muffle strode forward and caught his arm to steady him.

"You've a touch of being torn up by a dragon, and lunacy into the bargain! You can't be serious about what you're going to do."

"Serious as falling over a cliff, son." He tried to draw his arm away. Despite the summer warmth condensed in the court, his bare flesh was cold against the blacksmith's big hand.

"Falling over a cliff would be a damned sight safer than what you're proposing. And more useful, too."

John had turned away, discreetly steadying himself on the half-carved, half-wickerwork figurehead on the boat's stern. He was stripped to his boots, doeskin breeches, and singlet; evening light gleamed on the round lenses of his spectacles as he dragged the boat nearer to the small furnace that had been burning for the past hour. The bandages on his chest and shoulder couldn't completely hide the bruised flesh; under the bruises, the scars taken in an encounter with another dragon shone dark.

Heavily loaded though it was, the boat moved easily. It was mounted on wheels wrought, like the machinery in its midsection, from the lightweight steels and alloys made by the gnomes. When the King's troops had arrived in the Winterlands two years ago, John had taken the occasion to ride to the gnomes' Deep at Wyldoom, having heard they needed a warrior to deal with a nest of cave-grues they'd disturbed in their digging. This machinery, made to John's specifications from designs he'd found in an ancient text of Heronax, had been his pay for two weeks of peril and horror in the dark.

"The year Adric was born, Jen and I were trapped by skelks and holed up for near two months in the Moonwood," he said to Muffle. "Jen'll be all right, wherever she is, but I can't wait for her to return. It's ten days that Ian's been gone."

"Ian'll be okay." Adric stepped close, a kind of bluff warrior's defiance in his stance. Mag toddled silently at his heels and began to examine the wicker boat with her usual careful intentness. The boy caught her hand and drew her back, having had plenty of experience with Mag's investigations. "And Mama can take care of any old crummy mage."

"Yeah." John grinned, and tousled his son's hair. "But it may take her a bit." He looked back at Muffle, eyes wary in his sweat-streaked face.

"There's something you're not telling me, Johnny."

John raised his eyebrows, looking surprised. "I'm not telling you to go take a long walk because none of this is your business, but that's 'cause you're me brother and bigger than me."

"John, you should be in bed!" Aunt Jane, the oldest and stoutest of old Lord Aver's three sisters, bustled down the broken stair from the courtyard above. "Muffle, I'm surprised at you for letting him be up!"

The blacksmith began to protest that he wasn't his brother's nursie, but Aunt Jane went on, "And mucking with all your heathen machinery when you should be resting!" She frowned disapprovingly at John's telescope, mounted on the rear gunwale. "And bringing the children, too! They'll end up as bad as you."

"Papa didn't bring us," Adric declared stoutly. "We snuck." He stepped to his father's side as though to defend him, still keeping a conscientious grip on his sister's hand.

"Honestly!" Aunt Jane paused and looked the boat up and down, though none of the aunts had much interest in their nephew's scholarly and mechanistic pursuits. She turned away with a shrug the next moment, scolding, as if the curious hybrid look of the thing had not struck her at all: boat-shaped, but, save for its bottom planking, made of lacquered wicker; wheeled and mounted with a whole array of sails, yards, booms, and masts as well as its strange clockwork and wires, fan-blades and springs. She did not seem to associate it with the framework of withes that stood above the furnace's stumpy chimney. Crates of folded silk lay open beside it, amid long skeins of gnome-woven cable, steel rings, and leather valves.

"Now you come upstairs," she ordered. "Come on! Gallivanting off all over the countryside when you should be resting . . ."

She reascended the stair, muttering, and Sergeant Muffle, with a worried glance back at John, picked up little Mag as if she'd been a single white poppy and carried her after. As soon as they were out of sight John sat down rather quickly on the pile of wood beside the furnace.

"Are you okay?" Adric came over to him, like John stripped to britches, boots, and singlet, hands folded over the hilt of the little sword that hung at his belt. It was only with difficulty that John persuaded him to take the weapon off when he went to bed.

"Just send me down another dragon," said John cheerily. "I'll wring his neck for him like a chicken."

Adric grinned and hoisted himself onto the woodpile at his father's side. "Are you going to go away and find Ian?"

"I've got to, son."

"Can I come with you? You're going to need help," added the boy, seeing his father draw breath for the inevitable refusal. "Even if you do take along all Mama's poisons and your dragon-slaying machine. You've never tried it out against a real dragon, you know. I can use a sword." He patted his blade confidently. "And I can shoot and rope and throw a javelin. You know I'm better than Ian."

This was true. Since the boys were small John had worked to teach them his skills with weapons, knowing they'd need them in the Winterlands, maybe long before they came to manhood. Where Ian learned intently, the younger boy devoured his lessons with a blithe ferocity that left John in no doubt as to who would take over as protector of the Winterlands when he himself was gone.

And probably do a better job of it, he reflected ruefully, than he ever had.

"You're going to tell me you'd really like to," sighed Adric, "but you can't. Is that right?"

"That's right, son," said John. He plucked a twig from the heap of logs and made mice-scampers for Skinny Kitty, who had come down to investigate the courtyard. The cat merely regarded it incuriously and settled herself to wash. "There'll be folk to supper, and for dancing, but if you could go up to my room while everyone's busy and bring my bundles down to the *Milkweed* here"—he jerked his thumb at the boat—"I'd take it as a favor; if me credit still runs to favors."

Adric's eyes sparkled, and he sprang down from the woodpile and raced up the stairs like a mountain goat. John followed more slowly, limping and holding on to the wall. He slept for a few hours, with Fat Kitty and Skinny Kitty somnolent gray lumps at his side, and waking, pulled on his jerkin and made a small bundle of clothes, spare boots, plaids, and his shaving razor. Beside this he set the satchel containing all the poisonous ingredients he and Ian had gleaned from Jenny's study and the house on Frost Fell, all those pots and packets either deadly or merely soporific; and a long bundle of parchment fragments begged from the scriptorium at Corflyn. Then despite the protests of his aunts he limped down to the noise and torchflame of the hall.

There was always someone from the village at the Hold for supper— Jane's legions of friends, or the brothers and sisters of the Hold servants, sometimes Jenny's sister Sparrow and her children or Muffle and his family or the long-suffering Father Hiero, whose attempts to perform the proper worship of the Gods in the village were met with universal indifference and a deep-seated stubborn faith in the Old God. John was obliged to retail for Sparrow and Aunt Hol and Cousin Rowanberry all that he'd seen and heard of Cair Corflyn, and all that Rocklys had said of the unrest in the south; the height of the corn and the progress of the new stone water mill and the numbers of the cattle ("What do you mean you don't know?" demanded old Cram Grabbitch from Ditch Farm. "Can't you count, boy?") and what the wives of the southern sergeants wore. It exhausted him, but he was loath to leave. He told himself that this was because it would be weeks before he saw them again, and he kept from even thinking, *Never*. After supper he brought out the hurdy-gurdy that had been part of his dragon-slayer's fee four years ago and played the four-hundred-year-old war songs, and children's rounds, and sentimental ballads he'd learned from a blackened book he found in the ruins of Eldsbouch. Muffle and Adric joined in on the hand drums and Aunt Jane on her wooden flutes. Aunt Rowan and Aunt Hol—Muffle's mother and his father's mistress for years—and Peg the gatekeeper danced with surprising lightness in a whirl of plaids and rags and long gray hair.

They were still at music when he said he was going to bed. But as he left the hall, he caught Adric's eye.

The boy joined him in the kitchen court a few minutes later. Together they descended the stair through warm blue darkness, seeing the smoldering amber eye of the furnace in the old barracks court below, laced and lidded with its frame of willow withe. The night was still and brought them the scents of ripening barley all around the Hold, and the great wet green pong of the marshes north and eastward. The music came to them still, faint and gay and wild, and with it the crying of crickets and frogs.

The moon had just lifted clear of the broken horizon, waning but brave and yellow as a pumpkin's heart.

"They'll be after me hammer and tongs the minute they know I'm bound away," said John, as he checked the leather hose that led from the furnace to the great silvery masses of silk, laid out carefully on the broken pavement. During the past few hours they'd begun to lift and move, swelling upward . . .

In the crimson glare the boy's face quirked in his wide grin, "You mean you're afraid Aunt Jane won't let you go."

"I'm the Lord of the Hold, I'll thank you to remember, sir." John chucked a short length of elm into the furnace, glad that he'd had servants bring out the cut wood earlier. "Show a bit of respect for an old, tired man."

But Adric only grinned wider. He knew all about the hammer and tongs. For a time they worked together, stoking the belly of the oven, the heat laving their faces and the gritty white smoke puffing out in the starlight. In time John kicked the door shut and dug in the pouch at his belt for the things he'd gotten from the gnomes of Wyldoom, two or three white stones about as big as crab apples, chalky and soft to the touch. The furnace had a sort of iron basket in the top of its chimney, and into this John put the stones, then checked again the great swelling sheets of gray silk. Ropes, valves, and hose were adjusted as the ancient books had said, and as John had figured out over months of experimentation and trial.

"Is it magic?" Adric whispered in time.

He was hard to impress. John felt a trifle pleased with himself for having done so.

"The balloons aren't, no." He stepped back and leaned unobtrusively against the boat for support. "Heronax of Ernine, twelve hundred years ago, used hot air to fill a silk bag and flew seventy-five miles in it, at least so he claims, all the way from Ernine, wherever that was, to the Silver Island. In Volume Four of Dotys' *Histories*—or is it in Polyborus?—there's talk of men building flying machines with the help of gnomes' magic, though whether they were balloons or like that winged machine I made a few years ago it doesn't say. *And* I'll thank you not to giggle about that machine," he added with dignity. "It nearly worked."

"So did your parachute," pointed out Adric, mispronouncing the archaic word. "And the glass bottle for going underwater. And the rockets. And . . ."

"Now, each and every one of those things worked in the past," retorted John, shedding his rough jerkin in the heat. "It's only me dragon-slayin' machine that's completely new, and all me own invention. If the ancients could do it, I can do it."

The silk billowed and shifted, like some huge version of the mice-feet he performed under the blankets of the bed to interest the torporous Fat Kitty—not that they ever did. Torchlight and moonlight flowed in watery patterns over the fabric. Slowly the silk began to rise, as if some great creature beneath were lifting itself out of the ground. Adric came around beside him, hands thrust casually through his sword-belt, trying to appear nonchalant but his eyes enormous.

"Hot air rises, y'see. That's what Cerduces says in the *Principia Mundis*, and it's true. If you put a bit of paper or a leaf on a fire, you've seen how it swirls up."

Adric nodded. He was generally less than interested in his father's scholarly pursuits, and he'd been hearing all his life about the flying machines without ever witnessing anything more impressive than the debacle of the winged vehicle the summer before last. "What happens when the air gets cool?" he asked.

"You come down. You can delay it a bit by takin' on more than you need and carryin' weights and such—accordin' to Cerduces, anyway—but in the end that's what happens. That's where the hothwais—them little rocks the gnomes gave me—come in. They charge the air to keep the heat. It's part of gnome-magic. Gnomes can charge rocks to hold certain kinds of light, to hold sounds, or even hold air around 'em, the same way your mum uses air-spells to swim underwater. I've heard rumor about other stuff as well, but the gnomes are damn chary about lettin' anybody know much of their magic. Now, in that fragment of Ibikus I found over in Eldsbouch it said . . ."

"And that's how you're going to go find the dragon that carried off Ian?"

John was silent. Aware of his son's eyes on his face; aware, too, that he had never lied to any of his children. Aware that his silence was too long.

Adric said, "You know what happened to Ian, don't you?"

Very quietly, John said, "No."

"But you think you know."

He closed his eyes, wishing he could lie. Wishing he could tell his son anything but what he suspected was the truth. "Yes." The wicker and withy binding of the boat's gunwales bit into his hands as he closed them hard, and his wounds ached—bled again, he thought, or else it was just exhaustion.

He wished it were possible to wait for Jenny.

Wished it were possible to do this any other way.

Wished he knew if what he was undertaking would even succeed.

Adric sounded scared. "Where are you going?"

"To find someone who can help me," said John.

If he doesn't kill me on sight.

In the days of the heroes a band of mages made slaves of dragons . . .

He closed his eyes, and the memory of what he had read in that battered half-volume of Juronal returned to him, as if it lay again before his eyes.

In the days of the heroes a band of mages made slaves of dragons.

He saw the blue-and-gold beauty of Centhwevir, bleeding on the black and smoking ground. The flash of crystal in the wizard's hand. *Save a dragon, slave a dragon . . .*

The southern mage's calm intent face. Ian's alien, hellish smile.

John slung his little bundle of clothes into the *Milkweed,* checked the masts and the rigging, and the machinery that would propel it in calm. He'd flown it before, or its earlier and less efficient brethren, but never so far, nor so heavily laden. The pieces of the dragon-slaying machine that he'd been tinkering with for the past three years, lashed among the food-stuffs and water-skins along the gunwales, narrowed the meagre space almost to nothing.

All those futile, tiny toys, against the glory of a dragon. Against the power of a wizard mighty enough to save one's life and hold it as his slave.

This is stupid, I'm not even mageborn . . .

In the days of the heroes . . . The story had gone on to relate that the mages, with the dragons who were their slaves, had conquered the land of Ernine, triggering a series of wars that had devastated the whole of what, by geographical references, seemed to have been the Bel Marches, and laid waste a dynasty and a civilization. Juronal had written centuries after the events, and much of what he said was clearly fantastic or borrowed from other tales. But thinking it over, as he had thought it over for days, readying his two machines, he was sure the account contained a core of truth.

He looked up at the *Milkweed's* balloons, small moons in the first stain of the high summer dawn. The lights from the hall above were dim. The furnace's roaring heat beat against his body as he tonged the hothwais to the basket under the balloon valves. A hundred tiny tasks and checks, with the light wicker boat jerking on its moorings; with the ache of fatigue in his bones and scars, and the words of Juronal circling over and over in his mind.

The sky was bright. They'd all be waking soon.

He hugged Adric tight, fighting desperately against the desire to take the boy with him. For he would need help, he knew. It was in his mind also that it was very possible he was seeing his son for the last time. *Damn it*, he thought, *damn it, damn it, damn it . . .*

"Wherever she is, your mum'll know where I've gone," he said. His throat ached with the effort of keeping his voice from shaking. "We'll make out all right."

The balloons were dragging hard on the tiny craft. It was time to go.

"You pull that rope." John took a deep breath. "All the moorings'll let go at once." He swung himself up the rope ladder, scrambled over the gunwale and caught his boot on a curved metal segment of the dragon-slayer's steering cage, nearly precipitating himself ten feet to the ground. "You take care of your sister."

Adric raised his hand. "You take care of yourself."

"I'll see you when I'm back."

A cock crowed in the village. All over the moor birds were crying their territories. The dawn bells rang, calling those few who were interested to the worship of the Lord of the Sun. *Sarmendes, golden son of day . . .* But all John saw, as Adric gave a mighty and delighted yank on the mooring rope, was the faded lettering of Juronal's account that was embedded in his mind.

The dragons all died, and the mages also.

The Hold sank away below him. Wind took the sails.

The dragons all died, and the mages also.

John set the sails for the north.

9

Like its namesake, the *Milkweed* rode the silver dawn. Each tree and roof of Alyn Village passed beneath and John felt he could name every thatch and leaf. Fields he knew, walls, sheep and sheepdogs, the Brazen Hussy Inn, laundry, and cats on walls. Later he saw Far West Riding, and in the peat bogs that gleamed like flakes of steel farmers and peat-cutters shouted good-natured greetings: Would he need rescuing this time? Herd-boys pointed and stared, then cursed as their sheep fled. Later still, where the trees failed and only bogs and lichen and rocks rolled mile upon mile below, the great herds of reindeer and elk fled also, and hawks in flight circled near him to see, and then away.

It was a shining time. John felt as if his whole soul and body were permeated in light.

Early in the day, when the wind lay from the east, there was no sound at all save for the throb and crack of the sails, and the groan of the rigging in the gusts. Toward noon the wind came around from the west and the bitter north, and John let out some of his ballast—water from the barracks court well, dangling beneath the craft in rawhide sacks—looking for where the currents of the wind changed higher up, as eighteen months of experimental flights had shown him it did. He found enough of a difference high up that he could shift the sails to tack into it, for he was a good sailor, in water or in air. The beauty of the land below, dizzying and tiny, took his breath away.

Had it been his first flight he knew he'd never have survived. Like a child he'd have stared at the ground or the hills or the wonderments of the birds hanging so close to him in the air, and so have come to grief a thousand times. Heronax's notes about ballast and steering had been less than helpful. For most of the day he was able to pick out and name every stream and tor, every copse and ruined farm, but later he got out his parchments and drew maps with sticks of coarse charcoal and lead: silly and idiosyncratic, as were all his drawings, and he entertained himself by giving them absurd names.

When the winds turned completely against him, he took in sail and dropped the anchor into the trees near Gagney's Pond. He dragged the *Milkweed* down by main strength and a dozen pulleys and gears, for he didn't dare let out any of the heated air. The atmosphere was still closer to earth. He took on as much ballast as he could carry, cranked the engine to life, and the fan-blades made a great clicking and whirring as they pressed the *Milkweed* forward.

He anchored at what had been a watchtower on Cair Corbie, barely a ring of stone now, and climbed down the ladder to build a supper fire. Wrapped in plaids and furs he sat cross-legged on the stumps of old walls and ate burned barley-bannocks, and gazed north across treeless barrens where the King's Law had never run, a million mosquitoes and gnats whining in his ears. According to Dotys' *Histories*, Crow Tower had boasted woodlots around its base, and there was always a pyre standing ready to be kindled in warning, though, maddeningly, the part of the volume that spoke of what the tower watched against was missing. Few trees grew hereabouts anyway, and as far as John could see through the moonstone light, there was no sign there'd ever been a wood about the tower . . . Still, he looked north and wondered.

Iceriders, probably. Or some of their long-forgotten kin. The Kin-Wars and the plague had drawn the King's soldiers south long ago. Something had certainly destroyed this tower and emptied all the lands between it and Far West Riding, which still boasted a formidable wall.

Probably, thought John, slapping for the thousandth time at a whining invisible attacker, the mosquitoes drove them back, or likelier ate them alive.

Weary though he was, he lingered for a long while, watching the lands lose their color. It seemed to him that he could descry their shape, formed of every shade of translucent blue, until the late moon rose and washed all things in frost and magic. He fetched out his hurdy-gurdy and played its great wild wailing voice in a song he'd written for Jenny, wanting her with him, not only because of what he knew he must face but to share this beauty with her, this nightfall and these sights, and the wonder of the day's flight. He touched the red ribbon, still bravely braided into his hair.

From high up, just before dropping anchor, he'd seen the horns of the Tralchet Mountains, white-crusted and cloaked in glaciers whose arms ended abruptly in the green-black sea. It was a desperate distance for the second day of flight, with the heat-spells of the hothwais slowly failing. The gnomes who'd given them to him had said they'd last for three solid days, but he had his doubts.

Still, there was nothing else for it. The gnomes of Tralchet Deep were his only hope of success in his quest, and he could only pray they'd heard his name from their kinfolk. In time he climbed the ladder, and with his telescope sought in the southern heavens the comet he'd calculated from ancient writings should be there but wasn't. Then he put in as much cranking of the engine-machinery as he could manage before rolling himself in his plaids and bearskins to sleep. It seemed to him that he lay awake a long time, watching the seven moon-white balloons jostle in the night breeze and, over the wicker gunwales, the dim-shining glimmer of the northern lights, blue and purple and white, rippling in the opal sky.

By morning the *Milkweed* had sunk a good twenty feet. This wasn't as bad as John had feared, but it wasn't good. Mist had come up in the night, so when he woke before dawn from exhausted slumber he had a moment's panic, unable to see, as if he had been struck blind. But the next moment the comforting icy clamminess told him that it was only one of the killer fogs of the moors. Moon-eaters, they were called, or kidth-fogs, after the three magic sisters—or priestesses, according to the *Elucidus Lapidarius*—who were said to travel in them seeking to devour travelers' souls. In a way it was a comfort. He'd checked the vicinity of Cair Corbie very thoroughly for tracks and had found nothing more sinister than evidence of tundra wolves, but it would be a gie clever foe indeed who could find and climb the *Milkweed's* anchor-rope in fog like this.

He felt along the gunwale to the ropes of the ballast bags. Kidth-fog seldom lay more than thirty feet high—he'd taken measurements against the side of the Alyn Hold tower for many years—so he emptied a little water from two bags on opposite sides of the boat, turn and turn, until the dim gray moons of the air bags slowly materialized overhead. Then, suddenly, as if rising through water, he was above the fog, vapors billowing around the wicker hull, through which gray stone hills rose distantly, islands in a lavender world of fading stars.

The black tusks of the mountains had become cliffs on the far shore of that numinous ocean. He let the ladder overside long enough to climb down and disengage the anchor, the boat drifting a little as he scrambled up again. It meant last night's cold burned bannocks for breakfast instead of something fresh and hot, but the thought of dawn over such a world of brume was worth the exchange, and he gave the engines a few final cranks and set the levers. The fan-blades turned, strangely flashing in the half-light.

If I die in the north, he thought, *at least I will have had this.*

He only wished Jenny were there to share it.

If Jen were here to share it there'd be gie less chance of me dyin' in the north, but there you have it.

Sunrise among the columns of rising vapors. Birds shooting through the surface like flying fish. The day moon glowing like God's shaving mirror. Beauty beyond beauty beyond beauty, as the mists thinned and lifted and then dispersed and all the lands lay untouched and unknown in the morning light below.

During the day John mapped, once the kidth-fog cleared, and set the sails, and assembled the vessel's weapons: five small catapults with crossbows of southern steel and horn, armed with six-foot harpoons. Some were poisoned, with the last of the batch he and Ian had made up. Others contained corrosives, or incendiaries such as he'd cooked up from his ancient recipes to use last year against the Iceriders. How much good they'd do he didn't know. Maybe none. If he encountered the wizard who had taken his son, they'd be useless.

Ian, he thought, *I'm doing the best I can.*

Sometimes he was able not to think about Ian's eyes as he came down the hill toward the dragon; was able not to think about the dragon's terrible gold opal gaze that turned to meet the boy. Sometimes he could think of nothing else.

He played the pennywhistle against the clicketing of the engines and the soft creak of the rigging. The twilight covered the mountains ahead in ghostly shadows, and in those shadows he saw spots of light, torches on the gates of Tralchet Deep.

In the dark that dwelled in the hollows of the hottest fire, Jenny saw him anchor his ridiculous craft and climb the road to Tralchet Deep. *Damn it, not NOW!* she thought. Thrice in ten years rumor had reached them that it was the gnomes of Tralchet who were behind the bandits' slave-raids on the farms, that the Lords of the Deep—Ragskar and Ringchin as they were known to humankind—used humans to work the deepest tunnels of the mines, where the air was foul and earth-skelks and cave-grues dwelled. John had not been reticent about speaking on the subject, even to the gnomes of Wyldoom whom he had served. It was this that had caused him to leave Wyldoom quickly and at night.

So tired that she could barely sit up before the brazier of coals, she saw the gnomes come out of the gates, squat armored forms with their fantastic manes of pale hair drawn through the spikes of their helmets; saw them surround him with their halberds and their spears. John, not the least discomposed, brushed aside the blades with the back of his iron-spiked glove and strode up to the commander of the gate guards, grabbed his hand and shook it; she could almost hear him exclaiming "Muggychin me old wart . . ." or Mouldiwarp or Gundysnatch or whatever it was, "how is it with you? And are Their Majesties in? Would you let 'em know John Aversin's here, there's a good chap."

The gates shut behind him, a black steel maw. She had tried before to scry within Tralchet Deep in search of the slaves and had learned that the Deep was surrounded by scry-wards and gnome-magic. She lowered her forehead to her hand.

John, she thought, *I hope you know what you're doing.*

All the day, and the day before, between bandaging men's wounds and weaving healing magic yet one more time, she had returned to her harp and the spells of music that she channeled through it, through the water in the moss-grown stone in the ash grove, to the witch-girl in Balgodorus' camp. The girl was still unconscious, she knew. Through the day she had glimpsed in her mind the orange smutch of torchlight on a tangle of thatch and poles, or in the midst of snatching a hasty meal of gruel and cheese had tasted in the cavities of her nose the harsh pong of smoke, and on her tongue a rude mix of herbs and cheap liquor. Then the vision would slip away, leaving her with a skull throbbing and a stomach queasy from shock.

Now, with the night's cool stillness whispering over the land, she put the vision of John aside, and with it all thought of him, as dragons did. Her harp slung over her back, she climbed down the rope on the wall and moved like a shadow into the woods.

Beside the moss-grown stone she dipped her fingers into the dew, stroked moonlight into silky filaments, as if she were spinning thread. From those fibers she plaited again her web of power and cast it around her in a shining curtain: moonlight and stillness, starshine and peace. And when that web was woven she took up her harp and sang gently, softly, about hope, about longing; about a sweetness drowned and buried, forgotten for years.

Child, she thought, *it isn't too late.*

Not long before dawn, she heard the whisper of rough wool against hazel branches and the tiny breath of grass beneath soft-booted feet. It was hard for her to bring her mind out of the music's dark-shining depths. She timed the girl's passage across the smaller spring, then the larger, heard when her jacket of pelts brushed the limbs of the birches just beyond the clearing.

The music, funneled through the pool on the stone, drew the girl's eyes to the stone first. Opening her own eyes, or rather adjusting them to common sight and common awareness, Jenny saw that she did not perceive her, thinking her only another tree, or a rock a little taller than the first.

The witch-girl was tall for her age, thin with the thinness of those poor trappers and hunters who eked out livings in the deep woods, barely seeing any but their families from one season to another. These people, though not quite sunk to the level of Meewinks and Grubbies, were often brutish in the extreme. Jenny's long acquaintance with their kind was studded with the knowledge of bestialities, of casual murder and incest, of almost unbelievable ignorance and want. The girl's long, narrow face was marked with such crimes, sullen and dirty, great eyes peering from beneath the coarse tangle of her hair. Her heavy lips were soft and sad. She crossed the clearing to the stone and reached wonderingly to dip her fingers into the hollow with its water, bringing them up to touch the wet tips to her eyes, her mouth, her temples.

Knowing the girl to be still dazed by the blow to her head, Jenny pitched her voice to the voice of dreaming, "What is it you want, child?"

The girl shook her head. "Me ma," she replied, the truth of her heart.

"What is your name?"

"Yseult." She raised her head then, blinking at the dark small shape of Jenny in the darkness under the trees.

As a mage herself the girl could see through illusion, and Jenny used none on her, only a gentleness she used for her own sons. "Is Balgodorus good to you?" She was not, Jenny thought, many years older than Ian.

The girl nodded. Then she said, "No. Not no worse than Pa when he was liquored. Some of 'em's worse."

"But you don't have to let them hurt you," Jenny reasoned softly. "That's what magic's for."

Yseult sniffled and rubbed her head, not the back of the skull where Jenny's slung stone had cracked, but the temples. Jenny saw the girl's days-old blacked eye and a triangular scar on the back of her hand where it looked like a hot knife-blade had been laid. There were older scars the same shape, and a mark on her chin such as a woman's teeth make when a man punches her in the jaw. "I get scared," she said. Her short square-ended fingers picked at the untied points of her shift. "Men starts yellin' at me and knockin' me about, and I can't think. I get angry, like I could call down fire and fling it at 'em by handfuls, but then most times it don't work. And Balgodorus, he says if any of the men, any of 'em, come to grief it'll go the worse for me. I can't make it work all the time."

The bitten nails twitched and pulled at the tapes, and the bruised dark eyelids veiled her eyes.

Improper sourcing, thought Jenny. *No sense of where the power's coming from, or how it changes, with the course of the moon and the movements of the stars. The poor child probably doesn't even know how to track her own moon-cycles to take advantage of her body's aura.*

"Would you like to leave him?"

The lids flicked up, a glance like a deer seen in a thicket for an instant before flight. The girl's body tensed, lifting on her toes.

"What is it? Don't go." She put Power into this last, a gentle touch that could have been shaken off like the touch of a staying hand. The girl's mouth trembled.

"You're from Rocklys."

Jenny shook her head. "I know Commander Rocklys," she said. "I don't work for her."

"You're with her men, them in the fort. You came with her soldiers. You want to take me away. I got to go."

"Please don't."

"You're a witch."

"So are you."

"I ain't! Not really." She'd backed almost to the clearing's edge. There were spells Jenny knew that might have constrained the girl, especially with her concentration shaken by fear and the dizziness of her wound. But Yseult would have felt them and known them for what they were.

"Would you like to be?" she asked instead. And when Yseult's eyes grew thoughtful, "Men don't hurt witches."

Yseult came down off her toes, and her breath went out. One grubby finger explored her nostril.

"You're a witch?" It was a question now, and Jenny had the sense that the girl was looking at her for the first time. Seeing her as she was, not as her fears had painted her.

Above the trees the dark was thinning. Jenny's dragon-senses brought her a tangle of voices, tiny and sharp as images in far-off crystal: "I'll teach the little bitch!" And, "You can't trust 'em, Captain, not a one of 'em!"

She kept her voice steady. "I'm called Jenny. If you like, I'll help you leave Balgodorus."

Sharp little white teeth peeked out, biting the scarred and chapped lip. "He'll catch me."

"He won't."

"He catched me before." She trembled, and Jenny felt a rush of fury at the man.

"You didn't have a true wizard protecting you before."

Crashing in the trees, boots in the stream, on the rocks. Impossible that Yseult didn't hear—hadn't she even learned that much?

"You're trying to trick me." The girl backed again, and the dark pupils of her eyes were ringed in white. "You're a witch for Commander Rocklys, and I heard what she does to witch-girls. I heard it from the Iceriders."

"She doesn't do anything," said Jenny. "She's trying to start a school, to help mages learn."

"It's all lies!" Yseult's voice edged with panic. "She lies to 'em to get 'em to come, so she can feed 'em to demons!"

"That isn't true." Jenny had heard that old tale a dozen times in a dozen different guises. It was a favorite with the Iceriders: John's mother had told Jenny as a child that the kings of old drank the blood of witch-born children, or sacrificed them to demons on the rocks beside the sea, or on the lap of an idol wrought of brass. Other tales said they used a magic spell to transform them into sparrows, or mice, or cats.

"She's never harmed me, nor my son, who is mageborn, too."

"You're lying to me!" Trapped between fear of Balgodorus and terror of the unknown, Yseult's voice shrilled with panic. "You just want me to help you hurt my man."

"He's not *your man*," said Jenny tiredly. "He's . . ."

Yseult's head went up. In the gloom beneath the trees voices cried out: "I'll skin the bitch! Answer me, you little whore, or . . ."

"I'm here!" cried Yseult desperately. "I'm here! She's tryin' to catch me, trying to kill me!" She flung a spell, rough and undisciplined, and Jenny's belly and bones gripped with nausea and pain. At the same moment Jenny heard one of Balgodorus' men cry out and fall retching among the brush. *Limitations.* Furious, Jenny flung off the magic, which had no more holding power than a child's hand, and faded back into the green-black shadows beneath the trees.

"Don't hurt me!" she heard Yseult scream. "She magicked me away! She went there, see her in the trees?"

She was pointing—her mageborn senses were at least that good—and Jenny turned and glided sidelong, wrapping the dark patterns of her plaids around her to break up the shape of her body. Balgodorus struck the girl, sending her to her knees in last year's dead leaves, and Jenny felt in her bones the desperate flutter of unformed magic that Yseult tried to fling at him: make him forget, make him love me, make him not hurt me, make him go away . . .

Nothing to the purpose, even had they not been shattered by the girl's fear: not only fear, but her desperation to be loved by someone, even the man whose boot-toe smashed into her ribs. "It was her that made them spells!" Yseult sobbed. "She put that pain on you just now!"

The men were spreading out, swords drawn, into the woods. Jenny remained still, veiled in mists and darkness, until they passed, while Balgodorus dragged Yseult to her feet by the hair, stripped her bodice from her back and welted her with his belt, new red marks burning on the white skin among the old. Only when he thrust her, shivering with her thin arms folded over her naked breasts, before him through the thickets toward the camp did Jenny finally turn away, and drift back to the manor.

"And damn me if it wasn't a thing like an iron wash-pot, and no dragon at all!" John leaned forward on the low cushioned divan and gestured earnestly with a handful of fish stew. Lord Ragskar glanced at Lord Ringchin, and then at the three gnomish Wise Ones who completed the circle at the High Table beneath an intricate canopy of pierced and fluted sandstone. All were still, startled, tongs and spoons of inlaid gold poised in their hands. Servants—gnomes all, in liveries of the bright soft silks woven beneath the ground and huge overelaborate jewelry—drew close to listen, and John pitched his voice into tones of deep distress.

"So here I am, sittin' me horse, feelin' a complete ass with all these harpoons and arrows and such—I mean, I'll go after any dragon in the northlands, but how the hell do you fight a wash-pot?—when me son come ridin' out of the gate, and yells, *I'll draw it off, Da',* and goes after the thing with a spear. I shouted at him, but this sort of lid flips up in the thing and an arm comes out, a metal arm like a well-sweep, with iron claws on it, and grabs him, seizes him off his horse, and drags him inside it. And I'm throwing harpoons and firin' the crossbow and none of it's doin' a bloody thing, and the arm comes out again and whacks me silly off me horse, except I snagged me boot in the stirrup and the horse goes tearin' galley-west across the moor with me draggin' along behind . . ."

He saw the two gnome-kings clutch hard at their dignity and their manners and shut their mouths tight to keep from laughing at the image, and knew that he'd destroyed himself as any threat in their eyes. He glanced down at the hunk of pale flesh and sauce dripping in his hand, as if just remembering that he held it, and gulped it down, licking his fingers and then cleaning them fastidiously in the lotus-shaped glass goblet beside his plate. Tongs and spoon lay beside it untouched, the gems on them winking in the glow of lamps that hung on long chains from the ceiling. Clear pale light, far stronger than that of fire: hothwais charged with sunlight, beyond a doubt. John had always found his display of amiable barbarism—his dancing-bear act, as he called it—an effective means of getting people to underestimate him, particularly those who put stock

in table manners. Or, in this case, those who had contempt for all of the
tall men who lived above the ground. They didn't have to know that Aunt
Jane would have worn him out with a birch broom to see him eat with his
hands.

"I've been on this thing's track for three days," he went on after a
time. "Did I say it had wheels? Well, sort of wheels—they were like two
inside another three, and they moved . . ." He gestured vaguely, his hands
trying to describe something that wouldn't tell them anything, really.
He'd seen some fairly bizarre designs in his studies of ancient engineering. The less said the better to the gnomes about dragons, or about mages
who saved their lives in order to enslave them. "Anyroad, the thing I'm
using to track them with—this thing Jen rigged up that will smell out the
magic amulet around Ian's neck—tracked 'em to the Gorm Peaks at the
north of the peninsula here, or maybe to Yarten Isle beyond. I can't tell,
for it's too far, and this device of Jen's needs a thunderstone—a piece of a
star—to work properly. And that's why I'm here."

He wiped his fingers on his plaid, propped his spectacles, and leaned
forward, his face desperate with genuine anxiety and the feigned earnest-
ness of the man he sought to make them think he was: barbarian, brag-
gart, and not terribly bright. "I need magic thingies, y'see," he said.
"Thingies to make this device of Jen's work, and to get close enough to
where this wizard's hidden that I can find him and Ian. You know I've
served your kin in Wyldoom, and served 'em well. And I've come to
ask—I've come to beg—if there's aught I can do that'll get me these
things from you."

Lord Ragskar's pale eyes slid sidelong to touch those of his brother-
king. Lord Ragskar was the smallest gnome John had ever seen, barely
over two feet in height and with a disturbingly babyish, beardless face.
He looked in fact like a child—a wildly overdressed child, with his col-
lars and bracelets of heavy gold and slabs of opal and turquoise, his rings
of jewels faceted as the gnomes knew how to do—until you saw him
move. Lord Ringchin was larger, fatter, and older, but clearly it was
Ragskar who was the brains of the pair.

"In fact, there is." Lord Ragskar set down his tongs and wiped his fingers on a napkin: John had used his to wrap around his hand when he
seized a joint of hot meat. "There is a bandit." He cleared his throat, and
John leaned forward and did his best to look like he believed every word.
"A robber, who . . . er . . . entered the Deep some weeks ago to steal.
Eluding the guards, he took refuge in the mine shafts, but he has attacked
a number of guards—to steal weapons, so he is now well armed—and has
tried several times now to break into the food stores on the Twelfth
Deep."

He nodded to the foremost of the Wise Ones, a hard-looking creature like a densely withered apple, pale gold eyes peeking from beneath brows long enough to braid. "Lord Goffyer here, Lord of the Twelfth Deep, has attempted to scry him out, but Brâk—this is his name—has stolen scry-wards and so protects himself from being found. Moreover, as a human, Brâk is able to move faster than we, particularly where the levels are flooded, and in a narrow way his strength is greater than ours in single combat. We would take it as a great favor if you would deal with this man. Then we can speak of reward."

"I'll do that very thing." John sprang to his feet and managed to knock plate, cup, and three pieces of cutlery off the low stone table as he did so, not bad for a single swipe. "Oops. Sorry." He held out his hand, grasping in turn the tiny, hard, muscular hands of each startled king. "You can count on me. Oh, and accordin' to Cerduces Scrinus' *Principles*, soda-water will take care of that stain."

John did not for a moment believe that any robber in his or her senses would attempt to thieve from the Deeps of the gnomes. In fact, he guessed that his target was the leader of escaped slaves. But simply hav-ing a square meal made him feel better, and afterward the Wise One Goffyer came to the guest chamber and gave him medicaments for his half-healed wounds.

Despite this helpful hospitality, the moment Goffyer was out of sight John went over the chamber very thoroughly, pulling aside wall-hangings and propping what few pieces of furniture there were in front of any part of the delicately hued wall that looked like it might conceal a doorway. He slept with all the lamps of green and gold glass left burning and his satchel of poisons tied around his waist. The Wise One had made two dis-creet attempts to get his hand on it and hadn't taken his eyes from it throughout the visit.

In the morning, after another good meal, John stated his demands: a star-fragment, or thunderstone, which he knew were powerful magic that the gnomes never parted with; a few ounces of ensorcelled quicksilver, something that the gnomes also guarded intently; and incidentally a hoth-wais charged with heat to keep the *Milkweed* afloat. The gnome-kings said they would consider the matter. Then he armed himself in his doublet of iron and grubby leather, his iron cap, dagger, and fighting-sword—his bow would be useless in the inky tunnels—slung the satchel of poisons over his shoulder, and set out for the Twelfth Deep, where the "bandit" had last been reported.

As he'd guessed, though only gnome-servants had been in evidence at dinner last night, at least some of the kitchen staff were human slaves, and they'd reported his presence to their brethren hiding in the deeper tunnels. Even before he left the passageways where the lamps burned bright he sensed himself being watched, though that might have been Goffyer. The Twelfth Deep was where the mine-workings began, both the active seams of silver and the abandoned ones that had been flooded or were infested with some of the more unpleasant creatures that dwelled below ground.

They'd given him a lantern, which burned oil rather than carrying a hothwais, and its light seemed to shrink as he passed into the less and less frequented realms. Somewhere a whiff of foulness breathed from a rock seam: damp stone, then the stink of scalded blood and sulfur. Among the rocks the last lights burned blue and small.

Passing these, he carried his single lantern far into the empty mines, then set down his weapons, and stripped off his doublet and cap. As he'd intended—and hoped—when he walked forward into darkness with his hands upraised, the escapees took him fairly quickly. Invisible hands seized him from the darkness and led him to Brâk, who was perfectly happy to bargain with him for enough soporifics to knock out the guards who prevented the slaves from escaping and a good map of the territory that lay between the Tralchet Peninsula and the first of the King's new garrisons.

"So it's true the King's sent his army again," said Brâk. His voice was deep and musical, with an accent like an educated southerner and a courtier's turn of phrase. "Good news, for everybody except the slave traders and the bandits and these pigs here." John heard him spit. "And what of you, my four-eyed friend? Is it true there's a mad wizard on the loose, raiding the garrisons and stealing horses in a magical iron wash-pot? Or was that just a tale to get old Ragskar to part with a thunderstone? He won't, you know. Those are strong magic, I've heard; strong enough from time to time to break the scry-wards we've surrounded our hideouts with."

"Oh, I knew that," John said cheerfully. "What I need is a hothwais, and a strong one, charged with heat to keep the air hot in my balloons. I had to say somethin', to let them talk me down."

Brâk chuckled, a deep rich sound in the blackness. "We have hoth-wais here among us that will hold heat for two weeks before we have to sneak back up to the forges and replenish their strength. If we win through to the outer air, we'll need them less, once we can be away where the smoke of fires won't show us up. So you're welcome to them, my friend. We'll leave them where you leave the maps, on the north side of Gorm Peak near the rear gate of the mines."

So it was that John returned to the brother-kings and excused himself from further search for their "bandit." "For from what I glimpsed of them in the tunnels—and it was only a glimpse I got—it seems to me there's a lot of 'em, and I'll not work to kill my own people, who're only tryin' to free themselves."

"These are not slaves," said King Ragskar firmly in his strange alto voice. "The bandit is a wicked man who entered our realm with many followers."

"Be that as it may," said John. "I'll not be tricked into workin' for the profit of slave-drivers, no matter what the cost."

That was the only time, in the Deep of the Gnomes, that he genuinely thought he might have to fight his way out, which he knew he was in no shape physically to do. He doubted that even such heroes as Alkmar the Godborn would have been able to fight their way through the corridors and guardrooms that separated him from the main gate, and Brâk had warned him of the kings and especially of Goffyer. "Slaving and treachery is the least of the evils to fear from them, my friend," the deep soft voice had said. "Things we can scarcely guess at are done here. It is best that you get out, and get out quickly. And if you see Goffyer come at you with an opal or a crystal vial in his hand, fight to the death."

But his performance of the night before had had its effect, and he saw it in the contempt in the gnome-king's eyes. No one offered to demonstrate Goffyer's magic opal; they even gave him food before they set him on his way. Regretfully John buried the food without tasting it—*Let's not dig ourselves a grave with our fork, Johnny*—and spent the next several hours and the remainder of the *Milkweed's* lofting power mapping the countryside around the small rear entrance of the Mines of Tralchet and down the vales below Gorm. He left these maps in the cleft of a great gray stand of granite. When he returned to the place on foot the following day, he found a fist-sized pale stone there, and several smaller ones, the air around them shaking with the heat. Written on the granite below were the words, *Thank you. We will not forget,* in the hand and style of the Court of the south.

Alkmar the Godborn would probably have done it differently, John reflected with a sigh. *But we all do what we can.*

On the fifth day after his departure from Alyn Hold, therefore, he lifted off from the rear slopes of Gorm Peak, under heavy ballast, and set forth again to the northwest. By noon he passed the cliffs and glaciers of the hard and terrible peninsula and saw below the green-black water tossing with luminous mountains of ice. Then the land fell behind him, and he was over open sea.

Dark waves flecked with silver lace. White birds winging. Whiter still, icebergs carved and cut and hollowed by the action of the water, and the constant thrumming of the wind. Cold and the smell of the sea. Weariness and silence. Checking the compass and checking it again, and praying the adjustments the gnomes had made to the engines would last until he reached his goal. There seemed no strength left in him now, and he did not know what he would do if anything went wrong.

Sunset, and the dark backs of whales broke through the waves, blowing steamy clouds before they sounded again. The shadow of the *Milkweed* lying on the water for a time, longer and longer, and then twilight and the fairy moon.

Dreams of Jenny. Dreams of Ian.

A dawn of silence and birds.

And after another day of checking the compass, adjusting the engines and the sails and watching the whales and the birds, after another light-filled night, sunrise showed him the rocky fingers of cliffs spiking the sea before him, north and south and stringing away into the west, endless, tiny, dark, and rimmed with white. The new light smote them, seeming to pick glints of silver from the rocks, distant and pure and untouched. And above the twisted cordillera of the Skerries of Light, dragons hung in the air, bright chips of color, like butterflies in the glory of morning.

10

"**M**'am Jenny . . ."

She heard the whispering in her mind, the familiar call of scrying, and let the images of John in his fantastic vehicle fade. He had evidently come unscathed from the fortress of the gnomes, though she had no idea what he had done there.

"M'am Jenny, please . . ."

Balgodorus had attacked again, fire-arrows and catapults and more of Yseult's crude ugly spells of craziness and pain. Food was running low. Scrying the woods, Jenny had seen three more of Rocklys' scouts, hanged or nailed dead to trees. Scraped raw with strain, Jenny understood his strategy, the same strategy he used against the girl who was his slave.

Break her concentration. Wear away her ability to do her part in the manor's defense.

Rocklys is right, Jenny thought. *We do need more mages, trained mages, if we are to defend the Realm.* She reached out to the calling.

Yseult stood in the clearing beside the carven stone. The slanted light of evening brazed the unwashed seaweed tangle of her hair. She held her cloak about her, shivering, and glanced over her thin shoulder again and again. Outside her own window Jenny heard the outcry and cursing of the men on the walls, the bandits attacking—yet again, always again.

"M'am Jenny, please answer me!"

"I'm here." Jenny brushed her hair from her eyes, reached her mind through the scrying-crystal, through the water in the stone. "I'm here, Yseult." Sleepiness gritted on her like millstones; her eyes and skin and soul felt scorched with it.

"Come here and get me!" the girl pleaded desperately. "I'm supposed to be sleeping—he only lets me sleep when I'm not with him, with the men attackin'. I said I felt sick, and I do feel sick. He kicked me and said I better not be ailing. I can't stand it anymore!" She turned, scared, at a sound, eyes huge with terror and guilt. There was a fresh bruise on her chin, and the dark marks of love-bites on her neck.

"M'am Jenny, I'm sorry, I'm so sorry I called him after you!" Her voice was hoarse and shaking. "You got no idea what he's like when he's mad, and he's mad all the time now. Mad that you folks are holding out like you are, and mad because Rocklys be sending patrols and killin' his men, and spoilin' it for him when he tries to take food and slaves and that. M'am Jenny, I know I was bad but I was scared!"

"It's all right," said Jenny, her mind racing. By the noise outside it was a heavy attack, and Pellanor's half-starved defenders were at their last strength. "There's an old house where Grubbies used to live, on the edge of Black Pond, do you know it?" The girl nodded and snuffled, wiping her nose. "Can you get there? Did you take some food with you when you left?"

"A little. I got bread in my pockets."

Probably too frightened to hunt for any, and small blame to her.

"All right. When you get to the house, make these marks at the four corners. Make them slowly, and as you're making them, here are the words to say, and the colors to think about, and the things to hold in your mind . . ."

It was the simplest of ward-spells, the most basic cantrips of There's-Nobody-Here and Don't-You-Have-Pressing-Business-Elsewhere? Still, as Jenny outlined each guardian sigil, repeated the words of Summoning and the focus of power, she wondered despairingly how much of it Yseult's untrained and undisciplined mind would hold. A word said wrong, a sigil misdrawn or misplaced, would invalidate the spell, and Balgodorus' men, who surely knew the location of the ruined house as well as she and Yseult did, would find her. Jenny, worn down from battling the crazy effects of the girl's wild spells, felt a weary urge to slap Yseult senseless, to scream at her for being such a cowardly little fool as to do whatever her master said.

Of course she's a cowardly little fool, thought Jenny tiredly. *If you were unable to defend yourself with your magic two-thirds of the time, if you'd been convinced all your life that you needed a man, any man, to run your life and tell you what to do, how brave would you be?*

Where the hell was she going to get the strength to turn back the bandit attack enough to sneak out? How was she going to drive them away quickly enough that Balgodorus wouldn't find Yseult?

What had John learned, or guessed, or seen, that had sent him north in that crazy contraption to seek the dragons in their lairs on the Skerries of Light?

Ian . . .

She tried not to think about what might have become of Ian.

First things first.

"Mistress Jenny!" Someone pounded at the door of her room. "Mistress Jenny, I'm sorry to wake you, but you must help us!"

Smoke stung her nostrils. Jenny wanted to lay one vast comprehensive death-spell on them all.

First things first. She traced out a power-circle on the floor, shut her mind to the noises, the smoke, the cold tingling of fear under her breastbone. Brought to mind the place and phase of the moon, calling it clear in her heart and memory, circling it with runes. Brought to mind the magics of the three oak trees that lay due north of the manor, and the ash that stood due south, speaking their names and the names of their magics. Called on the silver energies of the stream, positioning it exactly in her mind, aligning it with the deep, still power of standing water, the courtyard well . . .

A little here. A little there.

The stars invisible overhead by day. The granite and serpentine of the rock beneath the ground.

Her bones, and the gold ribbons of dragon-strength that wound around them and through them, legacy of Morkeleb the Black.

The power of the earth and the stars, feeding the dragon-magic.

First things first. Find the girl Yseult and strengthen the wards around her, so that she would not be found—always supposing this was not a trap in the first place. Then redouble the attack against Balgodorus, sure now that her magic would not be counterspelled. It wouldn't be easy, and he'd be searching for Yseult. Too much to hope that Yseult would be strong enough to help them against "her man." Her man forsooth!

At least, without Yseult scrying the woods, a messenger could get through to Rocklys.

Jenny drew a deep breath, the slow fire of power filling her veins. A false glitter, she knew, and one that would take its toll on her later, but later was later. "Mistress . . . !" cried the voices outside, urgent, desperate. Her consciousness, altered by the concentrations of magic, heard them seemingly from a great distance away. Cold, as if, like the dragons, she floated weightless in the air.

She spun a final scrim of gold about herself, a protection and a balancing, a shawl of light. Reaching with her magic, feeling where the other woman's counterspells protected scaling-ladders, weapons, armor, and men. They had been at this game for weeks, shoving and scratching one another like animals in a pen. Counterspells marked the horses' bridles, the axles, triggers, ropes of the catapults.

The spells, thought Jenny, would have to be placed in the ground, or in the air.

This was more difficult, and far more complicated than the usual battle-magic; this was the point at which a mage of lesser strength, but greater lore, could win over a stronger but less skilled opponent. During all the years of knowing herself to be weak, Jenny had learned any number of work-around magics, in the knowledge that even the simplest counterspell could overset the best she could offer. She went back to them in exhaustion, calling images of the battle in her scrying-crystal and placing spells of fire or smoke or temporary blindness in the air where Balgodorus' men would cross them in their rush to attack, rather than on the men or the horses or the tools they used. The spells themselves were weak. Even her calling of power had not yielded much to her spent body and fatigued mind. But in her crystal's heart she saw one of the bandits spring back from the base of the wall as the scaling-ladder burst into flame in his hands; saw another go shrieking and waving his arms into the bloodied, ruin-choked slop of the moat.

She felt no triumph. Poor stupid louts, she thought, and pitied even their chief. To live as they lived, surrounded by brutality and hardship, seemed to her almost punishment enough for being what they were. Many of them had to die, for this would not cease their depredations on the weak; it was all they understood. But her heart ached for the children they had once been.

Not many minutes later Pellanor came to the door of her chamber. He was wounded in the head and blood smeared his armor, but he stopped, looking in silently, and made to silently go. Jenny raised her head from her scrying-stone, "No." Her mouth and face felt numb, as if speech were a great effort through the thick haze of power-spells and concentration. She raised her hand.

The Baron's grizzled eyebrows bunched down over the hatchet of his nose. "Are you all right? Can I fetch you something?"

She shook her head.

"They're wavering," he said. "They've broken, on the south wall. I thought you were spent, you need rest . . ."

"I did," Jenny said thickly. "I do. Not now." She got to her feet. "I must go. Outside."

"Now? Over the wall?"

She nodded, impatient at the flash of disbelief and anxiety in his voice. Did he think that after all this she'd run away? "Yseult," she said, hoping that would explain all this and then realizing that it didn't even come close. If the attackers were wavering before her renewed defenses, it wouldn't be very many minutes before Balgodorus went back to fetch his mistress; wouldn't be many minutes before the hunt was on. She had to reach Yseult and renew the warding-signs before then.

But she couldn't say it, couldn't say anything. Only shook her head and muttered with great effort, "I'll be back."

If Balgodorus even suspected Yseult had taken refuge within the manor, or changed sides to betray him, he would redouble his attacks and would never forgo his vengeance. She barely heard Pellanor's arguments and questions at her heels as she made her way outside. Only once or twice she shook her head and repeated, "I must go. I'll be back."

Men milled about under the south wall. A siege ladder burned in the mud of the ruined moat. Arrows flew back and forth, not nearly as many as there had been earlier; one of the manor children scurried along under the protection of the palisade, pulling out stuck enemy shafts for use tomorrow. Some of those missiles had been back and forth between sides six or eight times. Jenny's spells and Yseult's both marked the feathers. In spite of her weariness Jenny had to smile. John would be amused by that.

"They're breaking." Pellanor looked behind him across the courtyard, to a woman signaling from the opposite wall. "Old Grond Firebeard's decided to give us victory at last. Can you tell me where you're going?"

"Later." Jenny shut her eyes, called to mind the copse of trees just opposite the northeast watchtower and summoned to it a blinding burst of colored light, so sharp that the glare of it penetrated her eyelids even here. She heard the robbers yell—although both she and Yseult had used such diversions on and off for weeks—and opening her eyes, saw them running in that direction. "Now!"

Pellanor dropped the rope. Jenny swung over the sharpened stakes, dragged around her the rags of concealing spells, and let herself down quickly. Someone cried out, and an arrow broke against the stone of the wall near her shoulder. Too much to hope the spells protected her, exhausted as she was. Rather than strengthen them, which wouldn't work anyway as long as she was still in their sight, she called instead the easier illusion that she was an elderly man, low in value in the slave market and running for his life.

Someone shouted, "Don't let him get away!" and a couple of arrows stuck in the earth, wide of their mark. Jenny tightened her grip on her halberd and bolted for the woods.

Nymr sea-blue, violet-crowned . . .
And somehow the turn of that music, medium-swift, trip-foot yet

stately, spoke of the shape of the dragon John saw before him, circling the bare pale spires of the rock near which the *Milkweed* hovered, sixty feet below. Not dark like sapphires, nor yet the color of the sea—not these northern seas at any rate—more was he the color of lobelia or the bluest hearts of blue iris. But he was violet-crowned. The long, curving horns that grew from among the flower-bed mane were striped, white and purple; the ribbon-scales streaming in pennons from the shorter, softer fur gleamed a thousand shades of amethyst and plum. Long antennae swung and bobbed from the whole spiked and rippling cloud, and these were tipped with glowing damson lights. The dragon swung around once and hung motionless on the air like a gull, regarding him. Even at that distance John knew that the eyes, too, were violet, brilliant as handfuls of jewels.

Don't look at his eyes, he thought, bending his head down over the ebon and pearwood hurdy-gurdy, the wind gently rocking the swaying boat. *Don't look at his eyes.*

He played the tune that was Nymr's, fingers moving true with long practice over the ivory keys. A hurdy-gurdy is a street instrument, made to be heard above din and at a great distance in open air. The music curled from the rosined wheel like colored ribbon unspooling: blue and violet.

Nymr hung in the air for a moment longer, then tilted those vast blue butterfly wings and plunged straight down into the sea.

John saw the wings tuck back, cleave water. From overhead, for two days now, he'd watched the movement of the fish in the ocean, seeing down through the creeping waves to the schools of huge seagoing salmon, swordfish, and marlin, pale shapes that flashed briefly into view and sank away again. The gulls and terns, gray and white and black, that wheeled about the cliff-girt promontory scattered and circled, then returned to mew about the balloons. The dragon speared the deep, plunging away in a long spume of silver bubbles. *Creatures of heat and fire,* thought John. *How did they not die in the water's cold?*

Stillness and silence. The waves broke in ruffles of foam on the rocks, without the slightest roll that spoke of shelving shallows anywhere beneath. Rather the rock rose straight out of the water, all cliffs, line behind jagged line. Dwarf juniper, heather, sea-oats furred them with the occasional wind-crippled tree; birds nested among them casually, like chickens on the rafters of a barn. The wind moaned through the rocks and John turned the fans of the *Milkweed* to hold the craft steady. The next island lay ten miles to the northwest. The sea horizon was pricked with them, thumb-tiny in distance. The gulls all opened their mouths and screamed . . .

Then the dragon broke the waves in an upleap of water, purple and flashing in the fountain brilliance directly under the *Milkweed*. John grasped and swung on the rigging, causing the fragile craft to heel, and the tourmaline wing knifed past close enough to douse his face with spray. It had only to spit fire at him and he was done, he thought, swiveling one of the small catapults to bear as the dragon vanished above the air bags. Sixty feet above water, any fight would be a fight to death. Shadow crossed him, light translucent through the stretch of the wings.

Then it was hovering in front of him again, rocking on the air as a boat rocks at anchor.

John stepped back from the weapon, picked up the hurdy-gurdy, and played again the pixilated threnody of the dragon's name.

The swanlike head dipped and angled. The eyes faced front, a predator's eyes. The entire great dripping body, thirty feet from beak-tip to the spiked and barbed pinecone of the tail, drifted closer.

John felt a querying, a touch and a pat, cold and alien as long slender fingers, probing at his mind. He concentrated on the music, wondering if indeed the dragon's name would keep the dragon from killing him. One of Gar's ballads had Selkythar the Golden writing the Crimson Drake Ruilgir's name on his shield, so the dragon's fire rebounded and consumed its creator—not a technique John was eager to put to the test.

Query again, sharper, pricking. He kept himself from looking up, knowing the amethyst eyes sought to capture his.

????, Songweaver.

His heart was beating hard. "I came to work no one's harm," he said, raising his head but keeping his eyes on the lapis claws, the beaded azure enamel of the leg-spines. "I'm here seeking Morkeleb the Black. Does he dwell on these isles?"

The mind slipped aside from his, indifference succeeding a momentary spark of curiosity. Morkeleb the Black had spoken to him mind to mind, in human words or what had felt like human words at the time. All he sensed here was a tumbling surge of images that came and went. For a moment he seemed to see Morkeleb swimming in a thick green sea or flying in thick green air, Morkeleb indefinably different from his memory. Black wings, black mane, black horns; black scales like ebony spikes along back and joints and nape. Black claws reaching out, to slide through a thing that billowed in the water/air before him like a great gelid cloud of poisonous diamond.

Morkeleb in darkness, outlined by the light of stars. Reading the stars, thought John. Weightless in the Night beyond Night and scrying their light, seeing where each star lay and what it was made of.

Then Nymr's mind turned away, with an almost palpable shrug.

"I need to find him," John said and averted his eyes quickly as the dragon floated around to face him, reaching for him with those crystalline mulberry eyes. All that came to him through his mind was a sense of dismissal, contempt:

Tiny, peeping—the image was of a bird-baby in its nest—*nothing. A flower scent passingly pretty. Devoured.*

Nymr floated off. John saw the bird-head cock, rise, and fall on its neck. The star-drake studied the *Milkweed*, air bags and catapults and wheels and flashing fan-blades. He felt the traces and echoes of the dragon's curiosity, as if the creature were trying to fit together pieces of a puzzle. He felt it also when Nymr shrugged it away. Nymr's mind closed, indifferent again. No threat. Nothing that affected him.

Not a thing.

Meaning, as he had heard Morkeleb say, *Not a thing of dragons.*

John leaned on the tiller and put the *Milkweed's* fans over a few degrees, strengthening their beat until the craft moved off around the towering crags, toward the next promontory, many miles away. Nymr hovered for a time, watching him—he was aware of the creature's eyes on his back as he had seldom been aware of anything. Then the dragon plunged down into the ocean again, to emerge a few minutes later with a twelve-foot swordfish struggling in its claws.

Jenny circled the Grubbie house three times before going in. The wards she'd showed Yseult glimmered on the slumped stone and mud of the walls, surprisingly strong. The girl had talent, and a genuine feel for the sources of power, once she had an idea of what they were and how to find them. Casting her awareness through the woods all around, Jenny detected no trace of ambush, no scent of men in the trees, no boot-broken twig or trampled mud. Yseult's tracks, too, had been eradicated where they crossed soft ground, or hidden in the leaves and stones. Crouched in the gathering gloom, Jenny breathed on her crystal and whispered, "Yseult?"

It was a few moments. The girl didn't have a scrying-stone of her own and, by the look of it, was bent over a puddle outside the back door.

"Yseult, I'm here. I'm coming in."

And if it's a trap, thought Jenny, with a twist of wryness to her mouth, *shame on me.*

The house had been looted years ago. The stone walls of the old dwelling, where the family had lived before they'd degenerated into night-creeping scavengers, were charred and smoke-stained. The dirty little hummocks and burrows all around it, where the Grubbies had actually slept and stored their food, appeared undamaged, but Jenny saw that all the entrances had been stopped, imprisoning the inhabitants to starve.

Unlike the Meewinks, who took in travelers, then killed and ate them, Grubbies as a tribe subsisted on garbage, gleanings of the fields and middens, and the occasional pilfered chicken or cow. Yet in their way they were even more despised: inbred, bestial, with neither laws nor lore of any sort. Pellanor, who had begun with intentions of being a ruler to all he found in his part of the Wyrwoods, had ended by simply driving them out.

Jenny saw no sign of Yseult at first. But she waited patiently, showing herself to be alone. After a few moments the girl crawled out from one of the burrows, and stood picking dirt out of her hair. "Don't let him get me," she whispered and glanced around her. "Please." Both her eyes were blackened.

"I promise." Jenny saw by the tilt of the girl's head that *I promise* was something from her childhood, something that meant she was being lied to.

"Just get me away from here." Yseult shivered but made no attempt to escape when Jenny walked over and gave her a gentle hug. It was like putting her arms around a wooden doll. "I don't care if you take me to Rocklys or give me to the demons or what. I just can't be with him no more."

And if he comes back, thought Jenny, looking up into those shadowed eyes, *you'll fly to him again, and you know it.* Yet if she left Pellanor now, to convey this wretched child southwest to Corflyn, there would be only corpses at Palmorgin when she returned. She knew this as clearly as if she saw it in her scrying-stone.

"Can you stay here another night and a day?" she asked. "I can't leave my friends, not until I've made some provision for their safety. Balgodorus will think you've come into the fort with us. I'll make sure he thinks so. He won't be hunting you here. Would you be willing to travel with someone else to Corflyn Hold?"

Yseult looked scared, eyes showing white all around the rims; her blunt childish hands tightened on Jenny's plaid. "Can't I wait for you?" she asked. "If it's not too long? It wouldn't be. Them spells I puts on Balgodorus' armor and weapons and such, I have to put them on just about every day. They wears off that fast."

Of course they would, thought Jenny, with a rush of sympathy for the mind-breaking work of making and remaking all those spells. *She can't source power from one day to the next. She must be on the verge of collapse.*

"Will you be all right here?" she asked. "I'll try to get food to you, but I may not be able to."

Yseult shrugged and wiped her nose. "I been hungry afore."

"Whatever you do," said Jenny, opening her satchel, "don't go out of the circle of these walls. I'm going to strengthen the spells on them, so that Balgodorus' searchers won't see you in here. They won't even see this house or think about the house being here. They'll think they're in another part of the woods entirely. But if you go outside, not only will they be able to see you, but the spells themselves will be broken, and the house will no longer be protection."

"Why's that?" Yseult followed Jenny as she laid out her small packets of powdered herbs and dried wolf-blood, her silver-dust and ochre earth. The girl kept her hands behind her back, watching alertly as Jenny remade the guardians at the corners and began to sketch the power lines to source the magic of sky and stars and earth.

"Because the spells demarcate and stabilize a situation as it is," Jenny replied. "Power moves along the lines, in a flowing circle. Once the lines are broken, the power flows out."

"And you learned all this?" For the first time her expression showed something besides terror or apathy. "And can I learn all this, about witchery? How long did it take?"

"It took many years." Jenny traced a line in the air and saw Yseult's eyes follow. She must see, as the mageborn could, the glowing trace of the spell. "I started learning when I was a little girl. There was an Icerider woman, an Icewitch, living in the Hold . . ."

She hesitated, seeing as if it were yesterday, and not forty years gone, the elongated elegant face, the colorless eyes stony with contempt at Lord Aver's frustrated rage. "Bitch!" he'd screamed at her. "Hagwife!" Jenny couldn't recall what the fight was about, if she ever knew it. Now she understood that John's father had hated this woman because she had given him her body in derision. Because he could not turn away.

Why are you here? she had asked Nightraven once, with a child's frank curiosity. *If you know all this magic, why are you with Lord Aver?* Because even as a five-year-old child, she could see the look in Nightraven's eyes when she regarded her husband/captor, the man who had taken her at the point of his spear. *Why can't you just get away?*

Nightraven had folded those impossibly slender hands. In her height and her slimness, her sinuous bonelessness, she had always seemed almost like a drawing rather than a real woman; her black hair hung braided to her thighs. Her lips were very red, and though they were full and shapely, still they had that sensitive line, that reserve, that marked her son's. *I was cast out by my people, for my failure and my pride,* she had said. *They laid a geas on me, a spell of binding. One day they will send me word that my time of exile is done.*

And so they must have done. For one bitter autumn day when she was eleven Jenny had run from the Hold's kitchens where she slept up to the Lady's rooms and had found her gone, she and her frost-eyed wolf. Gone with no word, only a swirl of snow on the floor, leaving a baffled red-haired toddler motherless and a complex of love-spells on the man who had taken her prisoner such that he had never loved again, nor married any woman to be the stepmother of his child or the rival of Nightraven's memory in his broken heart.

"They's Iceriders with Balgodorus," Yseult ventured timidly, breaking Jenny's long silence. "One or two, that was throwed out of their tribe. They told me about the Icewitches."

"But none of them Icewitches themselves?" *That,* thought Jenny, *would be all we need.*

Yseult shook her head.

"Balgodorus has no other mages in his troop?"

Again the headshake. "Only me. He said . . ." She licked her lips. "He said he needed me." She sounded wistful.

"I daresay." Jenny tried hard to keep the sarcasm from her voice.

"Are there any but you, with Commander Rocklys?"

She sighed and traced the Fourth Guardian, connecting the links save the one through which she must pass when she left. The Sigil of the Rose, which drew the power of the moon, speaking to the others through the silver lines. "No. This would be easier if there were."

"I saw this other," said Yseult, and twisted again her chemise-points around grubby fingers. "Or dreamed about him, bringing a dragon back to life. Are dragons really beautiful, all different colors, with eyes like that? I thought they was green and ugly, and smelled of brimstone."

Jenny's hand froze in the air, and her breath in her lungs.

"He had a boy with him," the girl went on, groping at the recollection. "A wizard-boy, I thought—it was just a dream, I dunno how I knew—and he brought him up to the dragon, and they rode away on it together. I thought in my dream he might have been with Rocklys and was going to feed the wizard-boy to the dragon, and that's why I was afraid when I saw you. That you might do that to me. And there was something else there," she added, frowning. "Something I couldn't see. Something bad."

"Where?" said Jenny. "Did you see where this was? Or where they went? What the man looked like?"

Yseult only shook her head. "I didn't see his face at all. I couldn't. It was almost like he didn't have one. Or like it was a mask, and the eyes in it was a snake's or a dog's. Only the boy, and this dragon. And I was scared. But now I figure, even being fed to a dragon can't be no worse than staying with Balgodorus, if he's going to treat me like this. Can't you . . . Can't you take me not to Rocklys but just away from here? Can't you take me home with you, maybe, and teach me to be a witch and take care of myself? I won't be no trouble. I promise I won't steal from you or anything." And she crossed her heart like a child.

In the dark eaves of the Wyrwoods, Jenny heard the men searching, calling out to one another and cursing as they stepped in mud or on roots. She thought she could hear Balgodorus' voice, a roar of hatred against all things, perhaps women most of all. They'd be launching another attack, she thought. It was time to get back.

"When you meet Rocklys," Jenny said, "I'll let you decide, Yseult. But in the meantime, if there's a wizard out there who's kidnapping boys"—her voice seemed to strangle in her throat—"who's dealing with dragons, I think Rocklys ought to know about it."

11

Not a thing of dragons.

That indifference, John reflected, might just be the saving of him.

The star-drakes were curious but unafraid. Reckoning perhaps that nothing human could do them harm.

God knows that's the truth. He lay on the palm of death like a thistledown on a still day. Like dolphins in the sea, or cows in a pasture, the dragons came to watch.

Two of them picked him up between Nymr's isle and the next, floating, as Nymr had done, weightless as kites above and behind him, following with slow lazy wing-beats above the winking sea. They were too far for him to identify them from the old lists. Likely not all the dragons were on the lists in any case, and only a handful of the tunes had survived. They were multicolored, iridescent as gems: the one to the north striped in yellow and green, to the south a marvelous jumble of reds and golds and blues. Later a third joined them, bronze spotted with blue like a peacock's tail, behind him to the east.

At the second isle he cast anchor, snagging the rocks above a little crescent of beach, and laboriously cranked the *Milkweed* down. This isle was perhaps thrice the size of Nymr's, with freshwater springs around which clustered twisted pines, heather, and hairy-stemmed northland poppies all pale pink and gold. Wild sheep roved here—John had seen them from the air—and birds without number, gulls and terns and pelicans, and some kind of fat gray flightless creature the height of his knee that waddled trustingly up to him as he dropped down over the gunwale and tried to eat the buckles on the sides of his boots.

Killing them would have been embarrassingly easy; so easy in fact that John couldn't bring himself to do it. Never having seen humankind, the mountain sheep would have proved scarcely less challenging targets, but he had no time to hang and smoke that much meat and was loath to waste it. He took his bow and shot gulls and terns; the bronze-dappled dragon flew in close, hovered and circled for some time around the *Milkweed* on its tether. It ignored John completely but reached out its long neck from time to time and bumped the air bags with its beak, like a dog sniffing at a floating bladder. John wondered what would become of him should one of the dragons decide to destroy the craft.

I suppose I'd live on fish and sheep till I'm an old man with a long beard, he thought, bemused by the image though by all rights he supposed he should be stiff with terror. He wondered if the dragons had the imagination to make the experiment, just to see what would happen. Since the dragons would do what they would do, beyond any ability of his to change, and since he had no other enemies in all the northern sea, he stretched out on the beach and slept, grateful not to be setting sail or charting a course or drawing maps or cranking the engine-pulley. He slept deep and did not dream, except for fragments of something about daffodils and Jenny braiding her hair.

When he woke a dragon was there, sitting on the rocks.

It had killed a sheep and was eating it, tearing it open to rip out the meat and entrails but leaving the pelt like a fruit-husk. John had seen such remains before, in the northlands. The dragon was yellow and black and white, with tiny complicated patterns of greens and purples worked along its back and down like a mask over its face. It ate cleanly, licking its paws and whiskers. He felt its mind touch and probe his, though he would not meet its eyes. Its thoughts came like music into his brain.

????—a question as much about the machine as about himself.

"Well, it's too long a way to come in a boat over the sea," pointed out John, sitting up and taking a drink from his water bottle. The dragon tilted its head and settled into a sort of resting crouch, watching him without movement save for the flicker of wind in the soft fuzz around the base of its horns. Gulls settled close to it. A piper ran up over the sand, and the fat gray dummies waddled near and pecked at the sheep's carcass as if they weren't aware of the dragon at all.

In time, keeping a wary eye on his visitor, John set a griddle over the embers of the fire, took a bowl and began to mix barley and water and a little salt, to make bannocks for his dinner. The white slip of the new moon set in the pale sky, the tide retreating from the shallow curve of beach. The world smelled of salt.

"I'm seeking Morkeleb the Black, who's said to be the greatest of the dragons; there's aught I'd learn of him. You lot have to admit it's the fastest way."

The dragon licked his whiskers again and combed them with his claws. John felt the strange-colored alien words tumble in his mind: *Hurrying always hurrying soon to die. Dayfly monkey-making-puzzle, seeking seeking always fiddling always. Learning why learning only to lose it all in the dark so soon?*

"It's just the way of us." John patted the bannocks into shape, dropped them onto the griddle. *And let's not forget and let them burn this time, you git.* "We build cities and tell each other tales, the way sheep climb the crags and birds fly."

Silly peeping. Morkeleb. Morkeleb.

And the thought entered his mind, not of Morkeleb's name but of the music that trailed behind it, and with that music the dragon's dark shape against the limitless stars. Black like the black of night, and misted with light.

Gone away. Gone away. Not a thing of dragons.

"Morkeleb's gone?" His heart sank. He had been prepared for a murderous attack by the black dragon, but not for his absence.

Not a thing of dragons anymore.

"D'you know why? And where he went?"

Indifference, like Nymr's, but tinged with something else. John realized the yellow dragon was afraid of Morkeleb.

Not get too near, not get too near. Always dangerous deep deep, falling into the stars. Black well in a black maze buried under a mountain, thoughts rising into his mind, cold darkness rising, then returning to the well. Shadowdrakes, dragonshadow, birdless isle in the west west west. Not a thing of dragons. This thing is made of what?

The dragon spread its silken wings, leaped skyward like a cat. It circled the *Milkweed,* and John called out the only name he knew—*yellow as the flowers, white and black . . .* "Enismirdal!" And when the dragon checked its flight, backing infinitesimally, he scrambled to his feet and pulled his pennywhistle from his pocket, forming shrill and thin the fifteenth of the dragon-songs, swift and pattering like the rain.

The dragon circled back. Flame and heat haloed its nostrils, and it hung in the air and hissed.

"Enismirdal," called John again, "if that's your name. The dragons themselves may be in peril. I need to find Morkeleb, or one of you who remembers a time when dragons were enslaved and made to serve wizards in the old days."

Peril? Dragons did not laugh, but there was a chiming in the air, like the falling ripple of ten thousand silver discs clashing. Enismirdal flung wide about him the net of his dragon-senses—John could almost see it, like a great cloud of golden spray on the air—and shivered all the defensive spikes of his body, from the horned and spired head down to the cruel mace of tail-tip. *Peril?*

Then it reached from the air with black enameled claws, and like a cat batting an insect in play caught John across the shoulders, lifting him and hurling him down into the sand.

Peril, Flying Man? Peril from that and you to star-drakes of the Skerries of Light?

The silver discords burned the air, needled John's skull. Winded, bleeding, and covered in sand, John rose to his knees in the surf as Enismirdal wheeled toward the *Milkweed,* spitting fire.

"Ye stupid salamander, d'ye think I'd come here in this thing and warn you of it if the peril was from me and from that?" he bellowed. He wiped blood from his face. "Festering hell, I thought you drakes was supposed to be wise!"

Serpentine on flower-bed wings the dragon snapped around in the air, and all about it shimmered the scorch of its anger. *Wise? Wiser than some, who speak thus.*

It hung, a soundless cloud of brilliance above John, shadow lying on him where he knelt in the waves. The acid of its mouth dripped down to burn his face.

"You tell me if Centhwevir has been the same, since he returned from the lands of the east." John's breath rasped in his lungs; he squinted up at the creature. "And then kill me if you will."

The silence was so deep then that the crying of gulls rang loud, and the sough of the waves breaking behind him was a leisurely drum.

Not a thing of dragons, said Enismirdal's voice in his mind. *Others among us, each to his island alone. Centhwevir blue and gold*—and in the dragon's mind there was only the shape of the name, wrought of music—*nothing to me, nothing to me, where he comes or where he goes, and how he abides. Children of the stars, Flying Man; jewels of adamant, not slaves of Time as you. Not you, not me, none to say who we are or what we do.* The silver glitter of the dragon's anger chimed around him. *Being each of us—being. Remember.*

And he spit acid at him, flame hissing in the ocean inches from him, and wheeled in the air, then winged like a thrown spear to the south.

When he was out of sight, John became aware of the smoke from his campfire and the familiar smell of scorching barley. Shaking with shock he got to his feet, holding his arm where the blood ran down and limped up the beach to his camp. *At least,* he thought, shivering as he worked himself out of jacket and doublet and shirt to bind up the cuts the dragon had left on his arm and side, *he didn't destroy the* Milkweed.

But the incident brought home to him again the terrible fragility of his mission. As he packed up his camp—and ate the last of the stale bread he'd pilfered from the gnome-king's table—he found himself scanning again and again the horizons, knowing he was a fool and wondering whether he'd passed the degree of foolishness where it becomes not laughable but fatal. *Long ago, son,* he thought, resigned. *Long ago.*

He wrapped the gull meat in kelp from the beach and threw the burned bannocks to the dummies, who pecked at them once or twice and waddled disgustedly away. Though the sun was dipping toward the sea he unhooked the *Milkweed's* anchor and climbed the ladder as the wind took the silvery air bags, swinging out over the ocean. Once his engine was set he got out his charts again and scanned the sea with his telescope, sketching in the islands of the archipelago. He tried to give each its shape: domed skulls, spiring cliffs, here and there a shallow beach or the bright spangle of a spring. Between the islands the sea plunged blue-black, fathomless. Sometimes he could discern rock ridges joining one island to another: deadly reefs, ship-killers.

Whales sounded and played among the reefs and between the islands, great slate-blue shining backs arching clear of the water. Sometimes with them, and more often swimming alone, he saw other shapes, sinuous and snakelike, but it wasn't until one of these broke the surface with a long swan-neck and swam for some distance beneath the *Milkweed* that he realized these, too, were dragon-kind.

He dropped anchor at a small peak and spent the last of his strength winching the *Milkweed* down between the horns of its cleft. There he ate and in a cave in the rocks slept like a dead man; waking at noon, he brought down the telescope from the vessel and sat on the high cliff with it. Around a cliff-girt island not far off a dozen of the seagoing dragon-kind played. They were luminous dark purples and greens. Only when another dragon, black-figured crimson and gorgeous as a midnight rainbow, appeared in the sky and plunged down into the water with them did John realize that these were the females of the dragon-kind.

He journeyed on, following the Skerries west and north. In the light-drenched northern nights he traveled, searching at sunrise and sunset for the elusive comet Dotys had described. By day he slept, with the *Milkweed* drawn down as close to the rocks as he could force it so their shadows would render the craft less noticeable from a distance. Once he thought, looking through his spyglass at evening, that he saw Centhwevir, and discerned what might have been a man riding on his back. Once, making camp on an islet so isolated that the nearest neighbor was visible only when the *Milkweed* rode high above the crags, he found tracks: a dragon's claws, and a man's boot-prints near the chewed and gull-torn bones of a couple of sheep. There were fragments of what looked like two seashells wrought of blown glass, but finer than any glass he'd ever seen, and near the remains of a fire carefully concealed with brush, a smaller print, a boy's boot with the nail-pattern characteristic of Peg, Alyn Hold's cobbler.

At last he came to the end of the Skerries and set out west over the open sea. For a day he was without any mark at all, as he had been when leaving the peninsula, and swept the horizon with his glass in vain. On the second day he saw peaks in the distance, wind-scoured, tiny, ringed all around with cliffs. When he came nearer, he saw that one of these islets had water, and it was there that he cast the *Milkweed's* anchor and winched the craft down close to the blue-black rocks.

He rested, and ate, and searched until the light grew too dim for safety—the island was all rocks and little of it even flat enough to sit on. Nothing grew there. Not even birds nested on the high crags, though the big and the small islands to the south were alive with them. Only the keening of the wind in the rocks, and the gurgle of the stream, and the slow hammer of the waves broke the silence, and yet it seemed to him that he was never alone. At times this frightened him, at other times he felt he had never been in a place so peaceful in his life. In the morning he saw something like a shadow pass over the water, a gray flickering ghost that circled the rocks where the *Milkweed* was anchored. When he tried to look at it, there was nothing there.

Later he played on his hurdy-gurdy the tune Jenny had taught him, the air of the dragon's name, and the yowling voice of the instrument flung the notes against the cliffs and into the sky. Shadow covered him.

He looked up and saw Morkeleb the Black hanging above him like a nightmare kite.

John set down the hurdy-gurdy and shaded his eyes. The black dragon was not as large as some he had seen: forty feet from the smoking nostrils to the tip of the iron-barbed tail, and wings something close to twice that, outspread in the shining air. Mane, horns, streamers, and fur-tufts, scales above and below—all the things that on other dragons were saturated with color—were black, as if through the endless years the color had wearied him and he had put it aside. His eyes were white and silver, Jenny had said, colorless as diamonds. He was careful not to look at them, or let them meet his.

He said, "Morkeleb," and the dragon reached down with its claws and settled, clinging to the rocks.

Dragonsbane. The voice that spoke in the hollows of his mind was such a voice as might speak omens in dreams. *Has someone paid you with books to seek me here, or with promises of men-at-arms?* As the dragon tilted his head to the side the whole lank rangy frame of him shifted, balanced on the rocks. The half-spread wings folded and tucked themselves against his sides, the long tail wrapped around the spire.

Though there was no particular inflection in the dragon's words—far more clearly articulate as words than any other dragon's John had encountered—he felt the simmer of irony and anger beneath them. The indifference and pride of the dragons, which had protected him thus far, was no protection here.

"No one paid me. I came of me own."

Seeking after knowledge, that you may better slay other dragons?

"Seeking after knowledge, anyroad," replied John. "But then I'm forever doin' that—and there's knowledge and knowledge. What I'm seeking is help." He raised his hand to shade his eyes, his spectacle lenses flashing in the sun.

"Well over a thousand years ago, it says in Juronal's *Moralities*—or anyway I think it's the *Moralities,* I've only got the back half of it—there was this wizard, see, named Isychros saved the life of a dragon. Now savin' a dragon's life involves learnin' its True Name—the true music of it, not the sort of tunes I've learned to play—and with that True Name, that true music, Isychros made the dragon his slave."

I am aware, Dragonsbane, how dragons are enslaved by their names. The anger in the air seemed to thicken, as if it were about to bead on the rocks.

John wet his lips. "Well, it seems Master Isychros didn't let it go at that. He sounds like one of those people that you lend him a horse to ride home on and he butchers it, sells the meat, sells the skin, stuffs a mattress with the hair, sells the mattress, and a year later sends you a silver piece to pay for it all—less interest, of course. This Isychros drove what Juronal calls a glass needle into the back of the dragon's head, which made the dragon Isychros' servant. And Isychros got a couple of pals of his—mages, they were—and ganged up to defeat and enslave other dragons as well, quite a lot of 'em in fact. He ended up with ten or fifteen mages, each of 'em holding sway over a dragon, and the lot of 'em went on to conquer the Kingdom of Ernine. Any of this familiar to you? I know Ernine *was* destroyed, way back in the days, but I don't know how."

What makes you think, Dragonsbane, that I was not there?

"Ah." John scratched his jaw, a scrubby brush of rusty red. "Well, it's good to know I haven't wasted the trip. It did happen, then?"

Silk-fine lids lowered over crystal eyes, and without actual words he felt the assent ripple and shiver in the air.

"And I read—at the end of Juronal's account—that they were defeated in the end, though it doesn't say how. Juronal wrote five centuries after all the shoutin' was over, and maybe all sorts of other stuff got mixed in with the story. But what Juronal says is that the wizards and the dragons all died." His heart was pounding, looking up at the dragon above him on the rocks. "Is that part true?"

That part is true, Dragonsbane.

A wave curled around the rocks below the snip of ledge on which he had slept. The rock feet, exposed by the retreat of the tide, were bearded with weed, alive with silver crabs. Turning his head, the dragon regarded the distance as though to scry the air.

It was not this wizardling's healing that bound Ramasseus and Othronin, Halcarabidar and Idironapirsith and the other star-drakes to the mages who rode on their backs. In his mind John heard the music of the dragons' names, beautiful and archaic as the songs of the stars, and knew without Morkeleb speaking of it that Ramasseus had been dark purple and green, Idironapirsith banded like a coral snake with salmon, yellow, and black.

This Isychros had a mirror, whose surface burned in darkness with a terrible light. Demons lived behind the mirror, and Isychros called them forth and put their power into devices of crystal and quicksilver, which he drove into the dragons' skulls. The demons entered into Isychros and burned out his heart, the core and essence of his being, and dwelled there instead in his flesh. Using his magic as a puppeteer in the marketplaces of men uses a puppet, they drove the souls out of the other mages whom Isychros touched, so that the mirror-demons could enter into their bodies and dwell there in their turn. Thus mage and dragon fused under the power of demons. This is the story of Isychros.

John's throat seemed to close, suffocating him, and he thought *Ian, no. It isn't true.*

His voice sounded like someone else's to him. "This isn't . . . isn't possible, is it? I mean, mages can deal with demons. Jen does. I've seen her."

There are demons and demons, Songweaver, as there are mages and mages. I only know that this was true, in that time and in that place.

"But he was defeated in the end, wasn't he?"

Some of the mages they cut to pieces alive and burned in fire, that the Hellspawn could not use the dead flesh as they had used the living. The mages of the city of Prokep in the desert found magic that would work against demons, withering them where they abode. When the demons were shriveled inside them, the dragons also died. The mirror was destroyed.

John found himself fighting for breath, as if he'd taken a blow to the pit of the stomach. "And was there no saving of any of them? No way to . . . to catch back the souls of those the demons had driven out? Or find them again where they'd been pushed out into the air?"

What is the way to catch back the souls of those that disease drives out, Dragonsbane? Or the violence that you practice against one another for sport?

No. No. No. He pressed his hand to his mouth as if trying to control his breath, or perhaps only to cover it from sight. When he took his hand away and spoke again, his voice was completely steady. "They've taken my son." He told what had happened at Cair Dhû, and what he thought he'd seen; the tracks at Frost Fell, and Rocklys' tale of a wizard with an outlaw band. "Centhwevir was bad hurt and came back here, I think, to recover. I saw Ian's tracks on an island three days' flight east of here, and those of this wizard with his bloody glass needles. There has to be a way to fetch Ian's soul back. I need your help, Morkeleb. I need it bad. And not only me."

And your Wizard-woman? The air rang with his irony and his anger, a cold sound like slips of glass breathed upon by wind.

John said nothing, but it was as if something inside him bled. *Not a thing of dragons anymore,* Enismirdal had said of the black dragon, and looking up at that cut-jet glitter John was suddenly reminded of his mother in her exile, alone on this birdless isle with whatever he had brought with him inside.

All that vast anger, colored by, John thought, years of silence and sea-winds, coalesced in that quiet level voice that spoke in the hollows of his mind.

I told her, when she turned from me, that there was a price for the loving of mortal things. This is that price. Had she remained with me—had she remained a jere-drake . . . John heard and understood the word, a nonbreeding female—*you would not now need to seek me out. Were her son a dragon, there would not be this trouble.*

The dragon's anger was chill as flaying glass. John scratched his beard again, and said, "Well, at the risk of another dunking in the sea, I think you're wrong about that. If it was an accident that Centhwevir chose that time and that place to come raiding, I'll eat me gloves. This bloke in the pretty cap was Johnny on the Spot, waiting for me to do his job. It seems to me it won't be long before dragons'll be having as much of a problem as ever I am."

Dragons look after themselves. Morkeleb shifted his wings again and the early sunlight glistened on the bones of his pelvis, the ebon forest of spikes along joints and spine and skull. *In the days when Isychros formed his corps, we dwelt in the Mountains of the Loom, and in the caves of the mountains they called the Killers of Men; we dwell there no longer.*

Men are weak, Dragonsbane. When a man has been beset by a stronger man, he can run down the street of his smelly village crying, and others will come out of their doors and strike that strong man, for the weaker's sake. This is the way of men, who are always afraid.

John said nothing for a time, hearing on the rocks below him the voice of the surf. Trying to summon what to say that would draw this alien creature; trying with all the desperate knowledge that if he spoke wrongly, Ian was gone indeed. But all he could find to say was, "Don't let your hate for me rob her of the son she loves."

The dark head came swiftly around; John had to look aside fast, to avoid the diamond scintillance of the eyes. *You forget that it is not a man to whom you speak. Hate is not a thing of dragons.*

John said, "Nor is love."

No. With a snap like the strike of lightning the silken wings spread, catching the ocean wind. The dragon uncoiled his tail from the rocks. *It is not.*

A moment before the dragon had perched on his pinnacle, like some great glistening bird. Now it was as if muscle and scale and sinew had become shadow only, with no more weight than a scarf of thinnest silk. The wind lifted him easily, and he rose out of the shadows of the peak and seemed to flash all over with jewels as he came into the sun. John watched him with his whole heart crying out, *No!* The dragon's wings tilted; he swooped low over the waves, then climbed fast and steep, like a falcon rising above his prey. But he did not stoop like a falcon. He gyred again, high, high against the bright air, and flew west, dwindling to a speck and vanishing into the light.

12

I'll *have to tell Jen.*

The thought was almost more than he could bear.

And then: *I'll have to get the* Milkweed *back to land.*

In a kind of blank numbness John refilled every water container on the little craft at the spring, folded his blankets, and scattered the ash of his fire.

Ian was gone.

The demons entered into Isychros and burned out his heart . . . Using his magic as a puppeteer uses a puppet.

John touched the fading ache in his ribs.

Whatever was happening—whyever the demon mage had taken the mageborn boy—it was inevitable that they'd show up somewhere: demons, mages, dragon.

And at the moment, only he, John Aversin, knew.

He checked the *Milkweed's* air bags and found them buoyant still. Scrambling up the ladder and over the withy gunwale as the craft lifted above the shadows of the surrounding cliff, he felt a curious sadness at leaving the birdless isle.

There was little charge in the engine, and he cranked for some time before it grew strong enough to turn the vessel's bow toward the largest of the three Last Islands. His first desire was to head east immediately: If the *Milkweed* came down halfway between the Skerries and the Tralchet peninsula he supposed he could sail her in to the sorry little cluster of huts and ruins on the estuary of the Eld River, but it wasn't anything he wanted to try. Yet his store of food was low. On the largest island he shot gulls and cooked them, gathered eggs to boil, and set forth again in the westering light. Mind and heart felt blank. He wondered if Jenny could see him in these dragon-haunted isles, and if so whether she knew what he did and what he had learned.

Ian was gone.

He closed his eyes and saw his son's boot-track, and the tracks of the man in the embroidered cap.

They were in the islands somewhere. *I could find them . . .*

He thrust the thought away. *They'll turn up,* he thought. *In the Winterlands, in the south, in the air above Cair Corflyn or Bel, spitting smoke and fire . . . They'll turn up.*

He prayed he could reach Commander Rocklys with the warning before they did.

In the pewter twilight of the northern midnight he saw a boy's face desperate with worry, dyed by the firelight and smoke of the lower court of the Hold: *I'm not inexperienced.* Saw a red baby's face no bigger than his own fist, ugly and frowning under a fuzz of silky black hair.

Oh, my son.

Demons.

His heart twisted inside him.

According to Dotys in his *Histories*, and passing references in Gorgonimir, the penalties for trafficking with demons in past times had included being skinned, boned, and burned alive. Gorgonimir listed an elaborate hierarchy of the Hellspawn ranging from simple marsh-wights, Whisperers, gyres, pooks, house-hobs, and erlkings to the dark-wights that bored their way into men's souls. *There are demons and demons,* Morkeleb had said. Reading the ancients, John had gotten the impression that most of them didn't know what they were talking about.

What is the way to catch back the souls of those that disease drives out, Dragonsbane?

He can't be gone. He can't.

Now and then a marsh-wight would take over a child and have to be exorcised. The task left Jenny exhausted and she always treated it with the greatest and most painstaking care, but it wasn't beyond her powers, and sometimes, if it were done quickly enough, the child's soul could be recovered, or part of it anyway. Even the little pooks of the marsh could be deadly of course. John knew that in Far West Riding, near the Boggart Marshes, funeral customs involved binding the corpse to the bier until it could be burned, for fear that demons would inhabit it.

A demon wizard. Demons more powerful than the spells that wizards used to protect themselves.

He shut his eyes, trying to will away the images that crowded and tore in his mind.

He had heard whisperers in the swamps take on the voices of Jenny or Ian, or one of his aunts. They'd call to him to do this or that, or try to lead him away into the marshes. Easy enough, he supposed, for a Hellspawn to speak to a mage through dreams. *Do this rite, speak these words, mix blood and pour it on a heated thunderstone—then you'll have the power you've been seeking* ... Jenny was not the only one to have been taught that the key to more magic was magic. He knew there had been a time when she would have done anything to obtain greater ability in her art.

Only it wasn't power that would hiss up out of the steam.

Through the night and the next day and the night again he flew east over the empty seas, sailing when he could and cranking the springs of the engines taut. He watched the compass, and the spyglass, and consulted the charts he'd made, and betweentimes checked the swivels on the catapults and painted the harpoon-tips with poison. Twice he saw she-dragons, swimming and sporting with the brilliant males in the crests of the waves.

Being each of us, Enismirdal had said. *Being.* Whole galaxies of meanings and shades of meaning attached to *being*: a hot singular purity, like the dense core of a star, from which magic radiated as light. Dragon-magic such as Jenny had absorbed from Morkeleb in her days of dragon-hood, sourced and rooted in adamantine will.

This, too, apparently, the demons could take.

At least I know more than I did, thought John. *At least I can go to Jen—if I make it back alive—and say, There was this wizard named Isychros, see, and he made a bargain with demons* ...

But it was to Rocklys, he thought, that he would have to go first. To tell her that there was a Hellspawn at large wearing a wizard's body and wielding a wizard's power. There was a Hellspawn at large, inhabiting the body and the growing powers of what had been his son.

He was a Dragonsbane. He was the one who understood, as much as any human understood, how to slay star-drakes.

He was the one they would call upon, when that unholy three—demon-haunted mage, demon-haunted slave, demon-haunted dragon—returned from their hiding in the Skerries of Light.

No, he thought, putting the understanding from his mind of what he would in all probability be called upon to do. *No.*

John put the *Milkweed* in at an islet shaped like a court lady's shoe, in the hot glitter of late afternoon, in time to see the bright blink of blue and gold skimming low and fast over the water, and, scrambling to the tip of the peak with his spyglass, discerned the two forms mounted on the dragon's back.

Heart hammering, he followed them with the glass and saw them settle on another isle perhaps twenty miles to the north. His hands were shaking as he pulled out the dozen scraps of parchment from his satchel: It was a C-shaped island with a central lagoon, according to his earlier glimpse, bright with waterfalls, thickly wooded, and populated by sheep.

Build a raft, cross the open sea, and take on the three of them with one fell slash of his mighty blade?

I'll write a ballad about that.

Wait until they'd gone on and then head east as fast as he could and leave his son, or what was left of his son, in the demon's hands?

He closed his eyes, his heart hurting more than he had thought possible.

Ian, forgive me.

Jenny, forgive me.

It was not something, he already knew, that he'd ever be able to forgive himself.

He remained on the peak, waiting, watching, wondering what he'd do if they didn't fly on, if he had to take the *Milkweed* up with them still there, through the fey brittle twilight.

Then in the morning he saw a flash of luminous blue in the sky, and turning his spyglass eastward saw Nymr the Blue circling down toward the waves, where she-dragons dipped and swam in the lagoons among the rocks, sounded in depths a thousand times darker than the light-filled midnight skies.

Exhausted as he was, blinded and aching with grief, John couldn't keep himself from turning the spyglass to watch. Did the females come into season, the way mares and cows did, he wondered. Or were they like women, welcoming this male or that for other reasons more intricate and obscure? Why had he seen no babies, no dragonettes? Dotys—or was it Cerduces?—had said somewhere that the younger dragons were bright-hued but simply patterned, in bars and bands and stripes, like the black and yellow Enismirdal, the patterns becoming more and more intricate over the centuries, and more beautiful as the dragon aged. Morkeleb was black. What did that mean?

And what happened after black?

My son is dead, he thought. *I stand a good chance of coming down in the middle of the ocean halfway back and then if I make it to land walking from Eldsbouch to Cair Corflyn and THEN having to take on a demon mage and a dragon, and here I am wondering about the love-lives of dragons?*

Adric's right. Dad was right. I am frivolous.

Nymr circled over the sea again, wing tips skimming the waves. The air seemed wreathed with the garlands of the dragon's music, filling John's mind, twined with other, stranger airs. Serenading the girls?

But it was not the she-dragons that came.

It was Centhwevir.

Centhwevir dropped on the blue dragon like a stooping falcon, plummeting from the white crystal of the noon sky with wings plastered tight to his blue and golden sides, beak open, claws reaching, eyes blank and terrible. Nymr swung, spinning in the air, whipping clear at the last moment as the blue and gold dragon raked at him; Nymr hissed, slashing back with claws and teeth and tail.

And drove up, striking where Centhwevir was not. Was not, and had never been.

Color and lightning blazed and smote John's eyes, elusive movement and a whirling of the air. Sometimes he could see the two dragons, other times three and four, images of Centhwevir or simply fragments of driving, spinning blue and gold and purple, like the aurora borealis gone mad. They ringed Nymr, who slashed and snapped futilely, furiously, at the air. But out of those planes and whirlwinds of color and lightning fire spewed, spattering Nymr's sides as he rolled in the air, and blood gushed from claw-rakes that appeared in his belly and sides.

The blue dragon fled. Centhwevir pursued, now visible, now veiled in crazy fractures of illusion, above and behind. For a moment, when the blue and gold drake came visible again, John saw then that not one but two figures clung to his back, wedged among the spikes with their feet hooked through a cable of braided leather passed around the dragon's girth.

His heart stopped in his throat, seeing the dark hair, the weather-stained plaid. The two dragons twisted and clutched, light, illusion, magic searing and glittering between them as well as fire and blood and the spray of the waves. They fell, locked together, spikes and fire and thrashing tails, plunging toward the sea. John bit back a cry. They were close to the whirlpools of the twelve rocks, if Ian came off there would be no saving him . . .

There is no saving him, thought John, but still he could not breathe.

Nymr made one final attempt to flee, racing south. Centhwevir fell on him from above and behind, tearing and raking, ripped himself by the great spikes and razors of the other dragon's backbones and wing-joints and neck-frill, and this time Nymr gave a thin hoarse cry—nothing like any sound John had heard from any dragon before—and plunged down into the sea, dragging Centhwevir and his two riders with him.

"Ian!" John stumbled panting to the cliff's beetling edge and knelt among the sea-oats and the poppies. He was shaking all over as he

watched the sea where the two dragons, the wizard and his slave, had all vanished under the chop of the waves. *Too long,* he thought, sickened, unbreathing. *Too long to survive . . .*

Fire flashed in the waves. Centhwevir's head broke the surface, then his glittering back. The telescope showed John the gray-haired mage still clinging to the dragon's back, holding Ian by the collar of his jacket. Ian was gasping, choking, but he did not struggle. The man's face was grim but curiously uncaring, as if he harbored no fear of death. His eyes were fixed on the great blue shape of Nymr, whom Centhwevir had fast by the neck and one wing in teeth and claws.

Driving himself with his tail, Centhwevir made for the round island. Once John thought he saw Nymr struggle and move his other wing. But he was clearly dying as his attacker dragged him up on the beach.

It was hard to see. John looked around desperately, then ran along the cliff-top to a higher rock, thrust precariously out over the night-blue waves three hundred feet below.

Through the lens he saw the dragon-wizard's face clearly: a cold small mouth, and cold small eyes set close. A clean-shaven man, fastidious and rich—a man with a merchant's cold eye. He half-carried Ian from Centhwevir's back and laid him on the sand a little distance away. He didn't even cover him, just turned back to the two dragons, took from his knapsack the silver fire-bowls and the sacks and packets of powders needed for healing spells and began to draw diagrams of power in the sand.

The diagram incorporated Centhwevir, who sat up on his haunches and folded his wings. The blue and gold star-drake seemed unhurt, and settled more still, John thought, than he had seen other dragons sit. When he had accomplished the diagram and completed the sigils of power and of healing, the dragon-wizard—demon-wizard—drew from his knapsack another of the slivers of crystal and, as he had before, drove it into the back of Nymr's head. When Centhwevir turned his head and the wind caught the fur and feathers of his great particolored mane, John saw the blink of crystal there under the horned neck-frill. The dragon-wizard took something—some of the dragon's blood, John thought, but could not be sure—in a cup of gold and nacre, and carried it to where Ian lay. Opening the boy's wrist, he let the blood drip down to mix with that of the dragon, and from out of the cup took a talisman of some kind. It looked to John as if he pressed it to Ian's lips, and then to his own; then unfastened the breast of his robe and slipped the talisman he had made inside. Probably, thought John with a queer cold dispassion, into a locket around his neck, to keep it safe.

Ian lay where he was while the wizard bandaged his wrist. John could not see whether his eyes were open or shut, but as the wizard walked away the boy moved a little, so John knew he lived. The wizard returned to Nymr, this time crossing carelessly over the traced lines of power.

John lowered the telescope from his eye. He was sweating as if he had been struck with some grievous illness, and the only thing in his mind for a time was his son's face and the face of the dragon-wizard—demon-wizard—working over Nymr.

Demon or no, thought John, *he's wounded. Centhwevir's wounded. Ian, or what once had been Ian, is laid up as well.*

If I'm to kill them, now's my chance.

John unloaded the crates and struts and casings from the *Milkweed* through the white mild summer night, though weariness seemed to have settled into his bones. Twice he checked through his spyglass, but the blue dragon and the blue and gold still lay on the beach. Ian remained where he was, covered with a blanket.

Stay there, John whispered desperately. *Just stay there and nap. I'll be along in a bit.*

He didn't let himself think about what would happen then.

He assembled and counted out the various pieces of his second machine on the little level space at the bottom of the cleft that split the island. Toward midnight the twilight there deepened, but overhead the sky still held a milky light, and never did it grow too dark to see what he was doing.

Sometime after the turn of the night he lay down in the warm sand and slept. His dreams were disquieting, dark humped shapes scurrying through them, green pale eyes glistening and the smell of fish, scalded blood, and sulfur everywhere. He thought he saw things like shining lizards creep up out of the surf and dance on the narrow beach of the turtle-shaped island, thought he saw the dragon-wizard sitting in their midst, letting them drink from his cup of gold and pearl.

The old wizard first, he thought, rising from his sleep. He set in the plates of triple-thick crystal, the wheels and gears and the gimballed steering-cage that was the heart and core of the dragon-killing machine. *Maybe that'll end it.*

There was a demon in Ian as well, and he knew that wouldn't end it, but he tried not to think about that. He found himself wishing he'd been able to learn more from Morkeleb about the crystal spikes in the dragons' skulls, the nature of possession when it came to dragons . . .

They were going to strike somewhere, almost certainly before he could make it back to land himself.

Body and bones, his father had said. Body and bones.

He mounted the metal plates to the wooden ribs and transferred all but two of the *Milkweed's* catapults to the Urchin's tough inner hull. It looked indeed like a rolled-up urchin when he was done with it, bristling with spikes as the dragons bristled. If he could not have the maneuverability and speed that a horse would give him, he would need armor and weight and surprise. Common sense told him that he needed to rest, to hunt, to eat. He felt the reserves of his strength trickling away as the moon set and the long summer morning climbed toward noon.

At an hour before noon he wound the gears and springs of the gnome-wrought engine and, in the great wheel of the guidance cage within it, urged it out onto the beach. The Urchin lurched and jolted, then spun in a small circle, refusing to move farther no matter how John swung and pulled his weight. Cursing, he threw over the brake levers, let the tension out of the springs, and dismantled the engine again. Surf beat on the rocks. Gulls cried. Shadows moved. He wondered what was passing on the turtle-shaped island but dared not stop to look.

The second trial worked better. The machine ran smoothly on its wheels, scrunching unsteadily in the soft sand. John had long ago mastered the complicated acrobatics of weight and balance needed in the cage. He turned, swung, swiveled the machine with its spines and its catapults, his half-naked body slick with sweat. *Right. When I build this thing for keeps, it gets vents.* He was gasping for air when he braked again, unlatched the lid and climbed the cage to put his head and shoulders out . . .

And saw, across the spaces of the water, two dragons rising from the island to the south.

Gold and blue they flashed in the light as they turned. Gorgeous as sunlight and flowers they wheeled, dipped low over the surf. Catching up his telescope John followed them, and saw the man with his embroidered cap tied close over his head and the boy with his cowl blown back, his dark hair blowing free.

"No . . ." John was shivering in the sea-wind on his wet shoulders and face. "Don't."

But they were winging away north again, and westward, not even stopping at the island where they'd camped.

"Come back here!" he screamed, dragging himself from the dragon-slaying machine's round belly, watching the great glittering shapes dwindle to hummingbirds. He was alone on his island, with the crabs and the dummies and the sheep. Bowing his head, he beat on the metal side of the Urchin and wept.

13

"**F**ool!" Commander Rocklys slapped the scroll down onto her desk so hard the sealing-wax shattered. "A thousand times a fool! Grond's beard, who the . . . ?" She looked up angrily as the chamberlain stopped short in the doorway, and her face altered when she saw Jenny at the man's slippered heels. "Mistress Waynest!" She sprang to her feet, reminding Jenny of a big tawny puma. "Thank the Twelve you're back safe!" Genuine concern twisted her brow. "Did you find this bandit wizard? Did you bring her here?"

Jenny inclined her head. "And I think you'll find her more than amenable to the idea of a school. Please . . ." She caught the Commander's arm as Rocklys made to stride past her into the anteroom. "She's very young," she said, looking up into Rocklys' face, "and she has been badly used. Be very, very gentle with her."

Rain pounded on the wood shakes of the roof. The parade ground beyond the window was a dreary piebald of rain-pocked gray mud in which the eight surviving members of Rocklys' original twenty-five unloaded their meagre gear. The Commander counted them with a glance, turned back to Jenny with shock and rage in her eyes. "The bandit Balgodorus . . . ?"

"Was gone the third morning after the mage left his forces," said Jenny. "I believe he still had nearly seventy men with him, out of close to three times that at the outset of the siege."

"Siege?" the Commander said sharply.

Jenny nodded. "At Palmorgin. We barely reached the walls before the bandits were upon us."

Rocklys began to speak, outraged, then seemed to see for the first time Jenny's dripping plaids and drawn face. "You're soaked." She laid a hand on Jenny's arm, roughly solicitous. "Gilver . . ." The chamberlain disappeared promptly and came back a moment later with a servant, towels, a blanket, and a pitcher of hot mead. This last he set on the table while Rocklys steered Jenny firmly to the folding chair and brought the brazier over. "This bandit mage . . . she'll serve the Realm?" pressed the Commander, planting one foot on the seat of the chair opposite and leaning her elbow on her knee.

"I think so."

"Good. Good. Another came in yesterday—my cousin may be a fool, but at least he's had the sense to send out word in the south begging those with the inborn power to come forward. The old man kept it secret for years. As if anyone still enforced the old laws against wizards! Bliaud— that's his name, a decent old stiff—has been using magic to keep caterpillars off his roses and prevent himself from losing his hair. Idiots, the lot of them!" She shook her head in disbelief.

"And he came?" Greenhythe was a sleepy backwater of the southern Realm. Jenny couldn't imagine a retired gentleman undertaking the perils and discomforts of the journey.

"He took some persuading, and my cousin sent a decent escort." Rocklys made a face. "His family didn't want him to come—magic 'isn't done' by gentlemen." Her voice flexed with scorn. "Which was why I told Gareth that Cair Corflyn is the only place we could have such a school, away from the prejudices of the south. Can you imagine trying to teach anyone anything of magic with imbeciles like Ector of Sindestray—that's my cousin's treasurer-general—whining like frightened slaves about the old laws?

"The province of Imperteng in full revolt now—and that fool Gareth has taken the King with him to the siege camp at Jotham!—tax revolts in the Marches, upstart merchants in the Isles thinking they're aristocrats, a pardoned traitor, if you'll excuse me saying so, in charge of Halnath . . ." Her fist bunched in exasperation.

Jenny toyed with the idea of objecting to the term *pardoned traitor* in reference to the Master of Halnath, who had revolted against the takeover of the old King's mind by the witch Zyerne. Given Zyerne's abuse of power, in fact, the prejudices of the south were understandable.

Instead she said, as tactfully as she could, "Perhaps Prince Gareth thought his father would be safer with the army at Jotham if there are tax revolts along the Marches. The Marches aren't that far from Bel."

Rocklys' mouth hardened, but she said grudgingly, "Well, it's an argument. More like some fool thought the Twelve Gods wouldn't grant victory if his sacred hoary head wasn't on hand for their silly rites every morning." Her voice twisted with impatience and contempt. "The old man's so fuddled these days all a rebel would have to do is lay hands on him to convince him to oust Gareth from the regency and appoint his captor in his stead."

Behind her, through the open shutters, Jenny watched the red-hooded priests of Grond Firebeard, the Lord of War, process slowly into the camp temple, three and three, with a crowd of men-at-arms in their train. Their candles showed pale in the gloom beneath the colonnade. "All the more reason for us to teach mages to use their powers and use them responsibly, for the betterment of the Realm. Thank the Twelve . . . Yes, what is it?"

The red-robed priest in the doorway discreetly held out to her a beeswax taper, part of the ceremonial crossing the court: Jenny recalled that the Firebeard's altars needed to be kindled by the commander of the company that guarded His temple. Father Hiero had long ago given up trying to get John to perform the chore. Evidently Rocklys' Legalism was as entrenched as John's belief in the Old God, for the Commander simply stuck the wick into the stove.

"Well, mum for all that." The Commander waved the priest brusquely from the room and turned back to Jenny. "You got her here, and you'll be teaching her, and Bliaud . . . What's the girl's name?"

"Yseult."

"Yseult." The Commander dipped her hand into the tribute box, turned its stones over to catch the light. Jenny wondered what merchant she'd pried those gems out of. "If what your man told me was right, if there's a mage abroad who's managed to enslave a dragon to his will, we'll need whatever help we can get."

Jenny listened to Rocklys' account of John's visit with a growing chill in her heart. She had watched John for days in her scrying-stone, in fire and in water, since she had seen him emerge unharmed from the Deep of Tralchet; had watched him turn, not south to Alyn Hold but west across the dark oceans, and guessed at last that he was bound for the Skerries of Light to seek Morkeleb for help or advice. *Dear Goddess, does he think Morkeleb will help him?* she'd wondered desperately. *What had he read that made him think that was the only way?*

Save a dragon, slave a dragon.

A wizard who had used John as a cat's-paw to harm Centhwevir enough that the wizard could then save the dragon's life. Who had enslaved Ian and carried him away.

Rage burned her, prickling at her scalp. Rage and guilt that turned her sick.

And because there was no other help, not even novices here at Corflyn, John had sought Morkeleb.

Morkeleb would kill John on sight.

Ian.

She closed her eyes, the Commander's voice running on past her, willing herself to hear and not to think about the past. Not to think about years spent seeking her own powers, leaving the boys—whom she had never wanted to bear—to be raised by John. The years spent putting her magic before her love of John. *I want your children, Jen,* she heard John's voice. *I want any child I have to be yours. It's only nine months, not long . . .* And her own fears, her hesitations; her unwillingness to take the time, to spare the energy she knew it would demand. She saw herself standing by the hearth at Frost Fell, her back to him, arms folded stubbornly, shaking her head.

Oh, John. My beloved John.

It had been nearly three weeks since she'd last seen him in the heart of the fire, leaning against the mast of that ridiculous flying boat, gazing across the waking sea where dragons circled the spires of the shining islands. After that the dragon-magic foxed and splintered the visions, vouchsafing her only an occasional glance: John alone, patiently cranking his engines; John patting bannocks together beside a fire; John playing the hurdy-gurdy where dawn-tinted water curled to a beach. And once, terrifyingly, John with one knee on the *Milkweed's* railing as a stardrake leaped, blue as lapis, blue as cobalt, blue and violet as the summer sea straight up out of the waves, and dove toward him in a sparkling maelstrom of music and spray.

"—be sending a messenger to Alyn Hold in the morning."

"What?" Jenny jolted back to the present, looked up to see Rocklys standing by her chair. "Oh, I'm . . . I'm sorry, Commander. I . . ."

The general's face, for a moment angry at her inattention, softened. "No. I'm sorry, Lady Jenny. I've been going on as if you weren't soaked to the skin and probably off your feet with fatigue." She flipped a pale green peridot in her fingers, tossed it sparkling back in the strongbox.

"Gilver, show Mistress Waynest to the guest rooms. I hope that man of yours had the sense to take to his bed, and stay in it. If ever I saw a man done up . . ."

"Don't trouble with a messenger," said Jenny, rising and gathering the blanket around her shoulders. "I'll ride out tomorrow morning myself."

"Yourself? Have you seen a mirror? You look like . . ."

"It doesn't matter what I look like." Jenny stood, the blanket drawn around her shoulders. She hesitated for a moment, on the brink of telling Rocklys what she had seen in stone and fire, and then said only, "I've been too long away. Yseult and I can be back . . ."

"Yseult?" Rocklys was shocked. "You can't be thinking of taking her with you! With Balgodorus still at large? Looking for her, belike? If you must go—and I don't like the idea of it at all, though I'll send a guard with you—by all means leave the girl here."

If she'll stay, thought Jenny, wondering how that bruised and abused child would react to being told she must remain, without the woman who had saved her, in an army encampment full of men. She hesitated, trying to decide where the girl would be safest.

"If she elects to stay here," said Jenny, "please promise me this. Keep her safe. Not just from the men in the barracks . . ."

"Of course she'll have her own rooms," protested Rocklys. "In the courtyard with mine. She'll never come near the troops. You can't . . ."

"Not just from the men," said Jenny quietly. "Whoever this dragon-wizard is, if he's kidnapping mages it's for a purpose. It may be we've brought Yseult here just ahead of his seeking her out himself. That goes for your little southern gentleman as well, and his sons. It may be best, until I return . . ."

Rocklys opened her mouth to protest, and Jenny went on over her.

". . . that they don't go beyond the fortress gates at all. I don't want secret messages arriving with Bliaud's sons' signet rings, and maybe their fingers, done up in parcels. With the revolt in Imperteng," she went on, "and the King not in fit mind to rule, I'm very curious about who this dragon-wizard is working for, and what his intentions may be. At the moment I'm the only trained mage in the north, and I'm a little surprised that I haven't been made a target before this. And maybe I have."

"And I sent you out with only twenty-five men. I'll organize a more substantial guard . . ."

Jenny shook her head. "I've traveled the length and breadth of the Winterlands alone all my life. By myself I can go quiet and unseen. An escort would just slow me down and tell Balgodorus, or anyone else, where I am. I should be back within a week, to begin teaching your little fledglings. But right now there's something I need to learn at the Hold."

Though he laded it with every ballast-bag he had, it took all of John's strength to winch the *Milkweed* down to the Urchin and lash the spiked machine to the empty wicker boat. He hunted gulls' eggs and boiled them with rock-anise. *Too long,* he kept thinking, *too long.* The eggs were barely cooked when he pulled them from the water, scuffed out and buried his fire, and, climbing into the wicker boat, dumped ballast and set sail for the west.

The winds were contrary but strong. He was awake, tacking patiently, through the night; he anchored at an islet that was barely a pinnacle sticking straight from the sea, slept an hour and woke to beat his way west again. He dumped ballast at noon and again a few hours later, but the *Milkweed* continued to sag. Then it rained, weeping gray into the empty sea, white bars of lightning leaping between the clouds and the waves, but the wind changed and drove him west through the night, and in the morning his telescope showed him the Last Isles rising through the lashing skirts of the foam.

From the south he saw, too, the dragons coming. Centhwevir and Nymr, flashing like perdition in the newly freed sun.

They must have seen him, but neither turned aside. The wind drove hard out of the northeast. John had to tack again, leaning on the ropes, watching the dragons ahead of him and dizzy with fatigue. He saw them dip and circle the birdless isle, then plunge suddenly down among the rocks. *They'll trap him in a cave,* he thought, almost too tired to think anything, and the *Milkweed* swung in a long sickening arc against the veering wind. *Dragons know what I know—that chances of a kill are stronger if the dragon you're attacking is on the ground.*

He yanked the air valve to bring the *Milkweed* down and cast anchor as close as he could, seeing among the rocks the sunburst and scramble of blue and gold. Nymr and Centhwevir, when he could see them through the blinding aura of lightning and illusion, had their wings folded close, necks striking in long fluid darts, and he could see that their prey was still trapped in its lair. For a moment John glimpsed Morkeleb himself, pressed back among the rocks. Bleeding—the black dragon's neck and face were scored and torn, and the dark gloss of him seemed to have paled, gray as cinder and ash.

He was fighting for his life. John could see that, in every desperate lashing of neck and claws. The two younger drakes seemed to appear and disappear in a chaos of demon-aura, and Morkeleb struck wildly, against air or rock or sand. With a prayer to the Old God, John swiveled one of the catapults and fired a harpoon into Centhwevir's back.

Centhwevir wheeled, mouth gaping, and John fired the second catapult. But the dragon seemed to split and whirl into three green-fire shadows, and the bolt went wild. Acid spattered on the wicker gunwale near John's hand, setting the rail aflame. Without any seeming transition, the crazy burning wildness of the air was all around the *Milkweed,* and through the smolder John had a momentary glimpse of a cold square face and pale eyes somewhere close to him, like an image in a migraine dream. Then Centhwevir screamed, the high metallic shriek of a dragon, and whirled as Morkeleb, slipping past Nymr, seized his flanks with those great black-clawed hands.

Centhwevir reversed direction like a cat, biting and lashing and spattering acid, but Morkeleb had hold of him, and that was not something that could be ensorcelled away. In that moment John flung himself over the *Milkweed's* gunwale and slithered down the ropes to the Urchin, lashing and rocking below. He slashed the ropes and fell with the machine, grabbing the base of the nearest spike to keep from being jolted off; the drop was only a yard or so, but it jarred the bones in his flesh. Nymr and Centhwevir were fully occupied with their victim, whom they drove back against the cliff-face again. John slipped into the Urchin's hatch and slammed it shut, kicked his feet into the braces of the wheel and slapped free the brake lever. The Urchin swiveled; John fired another harpoon, this time catching Nymr in the flank.

He slammed his weight on the wheel to reverse direction but something smote it from the side; a tangled confusion of blue and gold all laced with green flame. He fired another harpoon but in that instant all the crystal ports that surrounded him shattered inward, tearing him with shards, and the pain of cramp and nausea seized limbs and throat and belly, as if he were being bitten by a thousand rats.

Pox-rotted demons . . .

The dragon smashed the Urchin again with his tail, splitting the casing, buckling the struts. John fired again, not letting himself think about where Ian was in this fray or what might happen to him. Panic filled him, as if he were in a nightmare—he seemed to hear his father screaming his name. More demon-magic, the kind of thing Whisperers did, only infinitely more powerful. Another blow flipped the Urchin off its wheels, slammed John hard against the hull. He yanked the last two harpoons free of their catapults and slithered through the broken hatch as Centhwevir seized the Urchin in his claws. The dragon dropped it immediately, and John clung to the edge of the trap for balance. It was impossible to aim— there seemed to be five Centhwevirs coming at him from all directions— but as soon as he was steady he flung the harpoon as the dragon dropped down over him to smash the machine with his tail again. The weapon missed, but Morkeleb, momentarily free from Nymr's attacks, flung himself on Centhwevir's back, raking again at his wings.

Centhwevir writhed free, spitting acid, bleeding now from a dozen wounds. Morkeleb flung himself into the air with a great crack of dark wings, and as the two younger dragons whirled to meet him, wounded and more visible through the flak, John flung his last harpoon, lodging in Nymr's shoulder.

That seemed to decide the dragon-wizard. John heard him cry out an order and, through the splintering firefall, caught a brief glimpse of Ian clinging to Nymr's spiked back. Nymr slipped from beneath Morkeleb's attack and sprang skyward, wings flashing. Golden dragon and blue slashed the air, veering as they caught the wind. Then they were away, dwindling over the sea toward the skerries.

Morkeleb hovered for a moment above the rocks, a floating shadow against the light, while near him the fire on the half-burned *Milkweed* flickered sullenly and went out. John lay in the sand, panting and half-blinded by the blood trickling from his forehead. At least the internal pain was gone. The Urchin resembled nothing so much as a walnut cracked by a child more interested in getting the meat than making a neat job of it.

Three weeks chasing cave-grues at Wyldoom, he reflected, *and dealing with the gnomes into the bargain. This dragon-slaying is getting just too bloody costly. I'll really have to give it up.*

He came to choking, drowning. Ice-cold seawater engulfed him. As he tried to thrash to the surface, he felt the prick of iron claws closing around his body and the next second was dragged gasping into the air.

Hold still or I shall drop you into the sea. I am weary enough.

Though he knew perfectly well the dragon wouldn't let him fall by accident, John hooked one arm around the black wrist nearest him, fitting his hand carefully among the blood-sticky spines. His spectacles had been knocked off: rocks, waves, and the great black dragon himself were blurred as Morkeleb circled back to the island and, stretching down his long hind-legs, settled on his haunches and laid John down on the sand.

They drank my magic. The dragon crouched among the rocks, a movement stirring his bones. Then stillness, and anger like the anger of a star. *They drank the magic from me—ME, Morkeleb the Black, the most ancient and the strongest, Void-Walker, star-rover, destroyer of Elder Droon, and there was nothing I could do against them, no hold upon them that my power could take.*

The word that came into John's mind as *magic* was not what Jenny meant when she spoke of it. It should, he thought, lying numb and dripping on the warm earth, be another word entirely, even as the word *being* that Enismirdal had spoken should have been something else. But he did not know what either of those words should be, and it might be that they were the same.

Like the slow pull of dark tide, Morkeleb's anger flowed through John's mind and, under that anger, fear. Fear of what could not be touched. Fear of singing shadows that killed. The steel-thin hoops of Morkeleb's ribs rose and fell, and the blood that trickled down his mane mingled with the dripping seawater, so the dragon seemed a black island in a lake of gore.

This is a thing of utter abomination, a thing of illness, spreading and eating. This is a thing that swallows the core of magic and fills the empty place with madness and death.

"Help me," said John. He brushed salt-gummed, blood-gummed hair out of his eyes, and every cut and abrasion of him burned with seawater and sand. "I saved your life."

The long birdlike head swung around, and John looked down quickly, lest he be trapped in the crystalline maze of the dragon's eyes. He could feel Morkeleb's fury, the fury of trapped pride and of fear. The fury of scorn, for himself as much as for John; the fury that he should be beholden to anything, much less to a bird-peep of a human meddler who wasn't even mageborn.

The fact was the same. The debt was the same.

Save a dragon . . .

Come then. The black claws reached for him again.

"We need the machine." John sat up painfully. His spectacles lay not far from him in the sand. They'd fallen soft. He brushed the sand from the lenses, but they were too dirty to put on, and in any case his hands were shaking too badly to manipulate them. "I twilkin' near killed meself getting the parts, and we'll need something of the kind."

Morkeleb opened his mouth and hissed with disapproval. *Gather it together then, Songweaver. We must be away.*

14

I saw this other, Yseult had said. *Or dreamed of him, bringing a dragon back to life. He had a wizard-boy with him.*

High summer twilight drenched the sky, though midnight was only an hour off. In that blue clarity even the desolation of Cair Dhû seemed beautiful. Jenny had reached the place to find a band of Iceriders camped among the shattered walls, with their scrubby ponies and their dogs, their silent blue-eyed children and low tents of reindeer hide. She had had to wait until night to send spells into their chieftain's dreams, warning him of terrible disaster coming to that place, and then it had taken them time to drill and shatter the oracle bones, exclaim over the results, break camp, and be on their way.

Nothing was left now of the battle John had fought with Centhwevir, save dark stains on the rocks. But there was no other place to start.

A wizard-boy.

Jenny stood in the place, eyes closed, breathing what had been. Dragons could taste the past, lift from stones and ground and the water under the earth echoes of all that had passed above them. But the echoes were in the form of dragon-senses, difficult for a mortal mind to sort. She felt/smelled/heard the dragon's mind, and John's, even the shrill panic of the warhorse Battlehammer. But there was nothing there of the mind of her son. Only the searing mind-taste of demons.

Jenny's belly curled in on itself. *Demons! Dear God.*

And not little ones either. No Whisperers or swamp-wights here, giggling as they lured travelers into the marshes for the pleasure they could drink from human pain and frustration and fear.

She felt stunned, as if she'd looked unexpectedly into burning light.
Ian. Oh, Ian.

The power of demons was Other. Demons came and went from another plane of existence, where magic was different. Everything was different. And these, she could sense, were more powerful than any she had heard of.

Would she have been able to protect her son, had she remained a dragon? Would she have wanted to?

As a jere-drake she had known intense and passionate desire, and the coupling of dragons was like being transformed into fire made of jewels. But that was not the same as loving, or caring for those one loved.

Patiently, her eyes the eyes of darkness, she searched, and in time she found the place where the dragon-wizard had drawn power out of the earth. At her summons the eroded ghosts of the power lines drifted to the surface once more, but they told her little she did not already know. The dragon-wizard had been trained in the southern traditions—the Line of Erkin, it looked like. But demon-fire had imbued and informed every trace and circle. Every exorcism she had ever performed—and they had been few enough—returned to her, the snaking insinuation of even petty pooks and gyres. The wormlike crawling to get inside a human mind, a human soul; to have a body whose pain the demon could drink. To have the ability to torment and hurt others, to generate more fear and more pain. They would inhabit even corpses, given the chance.

A tiny image came to her, the broken fragment of a memory: a big gray-haired gentleman walking on a beach at dawn. Walking after troubling dreams. Sea-wind lifted his dark scholar's robe to show the clothes of a wealthy merchant beneath. A scholar-dilettante, such as she had met in the Court of Bel. A man with a face too intelligent for the company of money-hoarders and counters-up of bales.

She saw him stop, look down at something—a shell? a piece of glass?—where the waves creamed on the pewter beach. He bent down and took it in his palm.

Oh, John, she thought, as the memory slid away. *Stay away from them.*

She drew her plaids closer about her, trying to still the dreadful hurting of her heart.

In her mind a voice said, *Wizard-woman.*

He was behind her, crouched on the smashed ruin of Cair Dhû's walls. His black bones folded together like a fan of sable silk, and the clear cold silver eyes seemed to emit both light and darkness. Her heart soared at the sight of him as a wave soars when it shatters itself on rock.

Love and wonder.

And as a wave shatters her first words ran away unspoken.

Your heart wept, he said.

They have taken my son. She spoke as dragons speak. *And John was hurt.*

Heat rose off him, and he turned his face aside. Wind shifted the black ribbons of his mane, the tufts of ebon feather. Curving horns striped black on black gleamed as if oiled.

Oh, my friend, she said. *I am so glad to see you.*

So. The heat seemed to spread and widen, but grew calm, like water deepening and deepening, stilling as it deepened. She had a sense of deadliness, of terrible things taking shape far below the surface, things that stared with mad silver eyes into the dark. Then slowly all that rage collected itself and vanished as through a hole in eternity, utterly away from this world.

So, he said again. *It rejoices my heart to see you also, my friend.*

Something in the air around him changed.

She said, *Forgive me.*

Forgiveness is not a thing of dragons. Each deed and each event exists forever in our minds as what it was and is. But what you speak of, when you ask forgiveness, is only a part of what you were and are, Wizard-woman, and what you will be.

He settled himself, a dense black shining shape in the thickening dusk. His eyes were cold twin moons, looking into hers.

Four years now I have dwelt apart from the star-drakes, seeking to understand those things in my heart that were no longer the things of dragons. When we came unto the Skerries of Light, there were Shadow-drakes among us, Dragonshadows, and they lived on the Last Isle. I went there seeking them, for they understand all things, and have in them power greater than that of the greatest among the dragons. They were not there.

For some reason she recalled the stone house on Frost Fell, autumn evenings when rain hissed down the chimney in the fire, when even her harp seemed a violation of the world's sleepy peace.

Yet I stayed in that place, he said. *And in these four years I have tried to do as they anciently taught, hoping that in the achievement of their power I would find relief from my pain. But the pain itself is no less.*

Her heart reached to him in wordless sorrow, but he rippled the dark scales of his back, putting her anguish aside.

It is not as it was, Wizard-woman. You have no need for grief for my sake. In this hour, as I see you, I find that indeed I feel differently than I did, although it was my hope then not to feel at all.

As if jewels shifted, catching a sharp blink of light, she felt his wry humor. *And so my wizardry, and my knowledge, and all the roads of the galaxy that I have walked have led me to this: a black knot that cannot be unraveled, an eyeblink in all the flowing years of time, and yet that I can-not put by. And I do not know whether this knot is a thing of men that came to me from your heart, Wizard-woman, or a thing that lies hid in dragon-kind as the eggs lie hid within the jere-drakes until it is time for them to transform into queens. Perhaps even if I could find the Shadow-drakes I would receive no answer. They do not give answers that make sense except to one another.*

She said, *Perhaps it is a thing that will come clear in time. Time was the thirteenth god, they say, until the other gods cast him out because he was mad. He carries all things in his pockets, but what he will take out, no one knows.*

And as she said it tears came down from her eyes, remembering again all those strange pain-filled gifts the mad Lord of Time had given her.

No one indeed, retorted the dragon. *Least of all did I ever conceive that I, Morkeleb the Black, would come down from the north drawing that silly toy boat of your Songweaver's by a rope, like a dog with a string in its mouth.*

And Jenny laughed, delighted with the shape the dragon put in her mind: the *Milkweed* trailing with half-deflated balloons, its charred gon-dola piled with broken bits of machinery, at the end of a rope whose other end was gripped in the dragon's iron beak. On the heap of debris John sat cross-legged, telescope in one hand and map across his knees, making notes.

My poor Morkeleb! She held out her hand to him. *That was very, very good of you.*

Good is not a thing of dragons. His spikes bristled like Skinny Kitty when routed from a cupboard. *Your Songweaver is in his own walls once more being made much of by his fools of aunts. But it was not for love of you, my Wizard-woman, or for the sake of your brat, that I left the Last Isle.*

Half-rising, he exposed to moonlight the nacre of new-healed flesh on his belly and sides. *They are demons, who eat the souls of dragons and mages alike, as they ate the soul of this southern mage; as they ate the soul of your son. And demons will always seek to open the way for other demons. These have a strength that I have not seen since the Fall of Ernine, a thousand years ago. Whether these are the same demons or others with the same power I know not, but they can devour my magic—I, Morkeleb!—and they can and will devour yours, and anyone else's they so choose.*

Silent, they regarded one another for a time, the dragon black and glistening in the starry night and the woman small in her plaid skirt, her bodice of worn leather. All the old legends warned against meeting a dragon's eyes, but having been a dragon herself Jenny had nothing in her mind or soul that Morkeleb could trap. Rather she saw into his mind, to the will that was core and spine of dragon-magic: the magic at the core of dragon-flesh and dragon-dreams. It was like losing oneself in night sky.

For a moment more their minds touched, his bitterness and her sorrow that each person, each being, has only one future and cannot have two.

Things are as they are, Wizard-woman, he said at last. *Now come away. There is a man who awaits you at that stone hovel you call your home, and two others of your young. And we must speak, you and this Songweaver and I, of demons, and of what must next be done.*

"Where'd you spring from, me lord? And you too, Lady Jenny?" It was the same guard who had admitted John a month ago. He looked past them at the village street, mucky in the cindery dawn, then back, frowning in outrage. "By Cragget's beard, those bandits are getting above theirselves! Were you hurt? Not but that you couldn't take on any bandit in the country, either of you," he added hastily, touching his forehead in salute. "But a band of 'em . . ."

"We took no hurt." Jenny looked around as they stepped under the half-raised portcullis and into the empty parade court. Only a few servants and batmen stirred, though the smell of smoke issued from the bakeries. By the chapel two yellow-hooded priests and a flute player waited for the augur to proclaim the proper moment for them to go in to morning rites.

"Son, I'm a Dragonsbane—and not a very good one—not Alkmar the Godborn." John glanced in the direction of the chapel. "I'd thought the Commander'd be up at rites."

Morkeleb had set them down on the far edge of the hills, after flying most of the night. A day's rest at Alyn Hold had given John at least a chance to shave—he'd resembled some mad, bespectacled hermit two nights ago, when Jenny had run up the stone steps of the Hold to throw herself into his arms—but he still looked desperately thin, face worn down to its bones. His shoulders were pointier than they should have been through the patched linen of his shirt, and his hands bandaged.

Jenny was astonished that he wasn't dead.

"Nay, sir, it's the Iceriders, see." The guard touched his brow in apologetic half-salute. "Not that her La'ship ever puts foot in the Temple, but there! Old Firebeard gives her victory all the same. But yesterday half the garrison rode out, when word of 'em came. They burned out two farms over by the Eldwood . . ."

"There were more at Cair Dhû," Jenny stopped herself just in time from saying, *four days ago.* There was no way, short of riding a dragon, that she could have covered the distance. She concluded with barely an in-taken breath, "a week ago; a woman at the Hold saw them. Is Mistress Yseult still here?"

"Oh, aye. Though not up yet, of course." The guard got a batman to show them to the kitchen, where the cook gave them bread and cheese and mulled cider and John shed his disreputable doublet, pushed up his sleeves, and lent a hand with breakfast porridge for the garrison. Jenny sat quietly in a corner, watching with some amusement his account of being robbed of their horses: " 'Master, master,' says this beggar, 'an entire army of three thousand bandits came down on me farm. They had to take it in turns to sack the house 'cause there wasn't room for more'n twelve inside at a time, and the line of 'em went right down the lane past two other farms. Me neighbor Cob Rushleigh's wife was out sellin' cider to the ones that was waitin' their chance . . . ' "

"They're getting arrogant." Lord Pellanor stepped over to the bench and took a seat beside Jenny, a quarter loaf in one hand and a pitcher of cider to share in the other. "We'll keep a watch for them when we set out for Palmorgin."

"They're miles away." Jenny shook her head. She wondered at the Baron's presence here. He had given no indication of leaving his siege-damaged Keep when she departed it ten days ago. "But thank you just the same. I called their images into the fire as soon as we knew the beasts were gone and set Words to them, so the horses will come back to Alyn Hold, but there's no knowing how long it will take."

The Baron started, then grinned under his gray mustache. "The more fool me, forgetting. Maybe you can come out to Palmorgin again and put a little word on my cattle. Balgodorus hasn't been back, but the small fry are out in the woods. We lose a beast now and then still."

"I'll do that," promised Jenny. "I do it at Alyn. But Come-Back spells on beasts wear off quickly if they don't have an amulet to hold them."

"And of course the amulet's the first thing thieves would get rid of," sighed Pellanor. "Just a thought, my dear."

"Is that the type of thingummy you're going to teach old Papa?" A young man dressed for travel in extravagant yellow joined them—one who was clearly his brother stood drinking cider near the stove and laughing uproariously at John's imitation of himself hunting under rocks and behind bushes for the missing horses. Through the kitchen windows Jenny could see the grooms in the stable court, saddling horses and rop-ing gear onto mules, under the grim eye of a grizzled sergeant, assem-bling the convoy that would take the latest installment of tax money to

Bel in the south. A small, rather fragile-looking old gentleman, bundled in a coat of gray fur fussed around the perimeter of the action, now and then scuttling forward to scribble sigils on the baggage in red chalk—every time he did so the men visibly flinched, and the sergeant had to step in and tactfully draw him back. Bliaud, thought Jenny. Half the sigils were mismade and none of them Sourced or Limited. They would be dangerous if they weren't wholly ineffective.

Jenny laughed. "If he likes. It's just piseog—hedge-magic. I had to put a spell like that on John's spectacles so they wouldn't get lost or broken."

"Strike me purple, it sounds a damned sight more useful than some of those spells in Papa's books." The young man smiled—his name, Jenny recalled hearing somewhere, was Abellus, Bliaud's son. "I always thought them a bit silly myself, and *filthy* dirty and just *centuries* old, but they're nothing to what this fellow Master Caradoc brought in."

"Master Caradoc?" said Jenny. "Did the Commander find still another mage, then?"

"Came two days ago," said Lord Pellanor. "Rode out with her yesterday, after these Iceriders." In the courtyard Master Bliaud made impressive arm-passes over one of the mules, which promptly kicked its groom. The sergeant took the mage by the arm, explaining gently, and behind their backs the head groom bit his thumb and rubbed surreptitiously at the chalked wyrds. "He's from Somanthus Isle, across the gulf from Bel. One of the merchant princes. I think like Master Bliaud he kept quiet out of caution, when the Lady Zyerne was all but ruling in the south. But he and the Commander knew one another at court."

"The Commander said she nearly fell over with surprise when he disclosed himself as a warlock," Abellus laughed, unconsciously using the pejorative variant of the word. Bullion flashed on his glove as he gestured. "Of all the world, she said, he's the *last* she'd have guessed."

"Given that wizards can't hold property in the south, I bet he kept quiet about it." John came over to the table, licking butter off his fingers.

"Stuff." Abellus' younger brother Tundal stepped after him, wiping out his horn cup and hanging it back on his belt. Stout where his brother was willowy, he wore conservative drab, but like his brother expensive and well cut. "Nobody's enforced that wretched law for decades. And besides, what's a wizard? I mean, Papa could go on for days about the vapors of the air and the magical relationships between clouds and the rocks in the earth, but he couldn't so much as charm a wart. At least little Yseult can do that."

"How is Yseult?"

"Oh, she's well, she's well." Tundal impressed Jenny as the kind of young man who always believes others are well, whether that was the case or not.

"She keeps herself to herself," Abellus added, pitching a last scrap of manchet to the kitchen dogs. "I think she's still afraid of that *dreadful* bandit Papa said she was with, and who can blame the poor thing? She hasn't put a foot outside the compound, barely outside her rooms. But she told the Commander yesterday that our convoy needed to leave this morning, else we'd be caught by the most *ghastly* floods crossing the Wildspae. So we're on our merry way. Topping to have glimpsed your lovely countenance again, Mistress Waynest."

He performed an extravagant East Wind in Paradise salaam, and his brother an old-fashioned Greenhythe dip, with knees bent. "Curious," remarked Jenny, as the tall form and the slender made their way from the kitchen, slinging on their travel cloaks. She glanced at Pellanor. "The Wildspae's a good ten days' ride. I didn't think Yseult able to read the weather as far away as Nast Wall, where the river rises. Certainly not what it will be a week from now."

"Well, there's been some sign." Pellanor twisted the ends of his mustache. "I heard Yseult tell the boys that, and Bliaud said as much, too. Maybe this is something Master Caradoc taught them how to do."

"Been teaching 'em already, has he?"

"Some," said the Baron. "The Commander was anxious that he begin, with the news of the Imperteng fighting getting worse. Damned hill-men—I fought them myself twenty years ago and they never seem to learn. She called me here to tell me the Regent wants me in the south. I'm bound back to Palmorgin to get my affairs in order, then I'll be marching out with my men."

John said nothing, but the antic humor that had been on him dropped from him like a wet shirt. Jenny felt his stillness, his silence.

Pellanor felt it, too, for he said, "Well, with the pirates in the Seven Isles and the troop levies coming up short from the Marches, there's folk in the council who say it's madness to keep garrisons here, with so little income from the north."

"Aye." The nimbus of anger around John reminded Jenny strangely of Morkeleb. "Aye, it is that."

"My dear Lord John." Gilver the chamberlain appeared, bowing, in the kitchen doorway. "And my dear Mistress Waynest. I beg a thousand pardons for not greeting you. Breakfast in the kitchen? I am so sorry."

"I'll be off." Pellanor clasped Jenny's hand in his gloved ones, then turned to John. "Don't think ill of me, Aversin. I'm the King's man, as you are."

"Aye." John returned the grip. "Just send me word who they're replacin' you with, so I'll know who I'll be dealin' with; and your people, too."

"I will." Pellanor forced a laugh. "And I'll call on you first thing, if we find we have a dragon to deal with."

"Oh, that'll bring sunshine to me day."

"This is most unexpected." Gilver hurried alongside them as they left the kitchen, crossed the muddy court where Bliaud was bidding an absentminded farewell to his boys. "Your business with Commander Rocklys was urgent?" He looked from John to Jenny, as if asking what could have brought them both away from Alyn Hold.

"Depends on what you think about Icewitches." John hooked his gloved hands through his belt. "We think the band of 'Riders Jenny saw a week ago had a sorceress among 'em."

What an undermanned garrison would make of a rumor about demons, wizards, and dragons, Jenny didn't like to think, especially considering the way the grooms of the convoy regarded Bliaud behind his back. She chimed into John's improvisation with, "There were signs at their camp that I couldn't interpret. I thought perhaps Master Bliaud might have more information, from the books he's read; this Master Caradoc, now, also."

"Ah." Gilver laid a finger beside his red-veined nose. "He's a wise one, Master C. The Commander spoke of you to him, and he wants very much to meet you, my lady. Handsome as ever he was when first he courted her—ten years gone that is now—and just as short-spoken." He chuckled. "And still won't make more of a salaam than a little twitch of his arm, not even to her—barely to the King himself. Flummery, he says. They should be returning tonight—Master Caradoc communicated just lately with Master Bliaud on that head. Shall I have a bath drawn for you? You must be shattered."

As they crossed the small inner court where Rocklys had her rooms, John remarked, "Has that gone bad, then?" A new wooden lid covered the well in the center, and rings had been driven into the stone lip so it could be locked down with a chain.

The chamberlain grimaced. "That was an unpleasant story," he said. "One of the men had a grievance—Dumpet only knows over what—" He named the southern godlet of chaos and anger. "He poured about three buckets of latrine-filth and dead animals into it, the Commander tells me. He's been triced and blistered, of course, but it's taken Master Caradoc these two days to cleanse it. Now, with being called away, he hasn't had a chance to finish the job. The Commander has ordered it be kept covered because some of the servants *will* try to use it still, since it's closer than the kitchen."

John and Jenny exchanged a glance. The wizards lived on this court as well.

Camp servants filled baths in Rocklys' private balneary. The room they were given was beside Bliaud's, on the other side of the chamber in use as a library and schoolroom. Bathed, combed, and refreshed—both turned down Gilver's offer of mulled wine—Jenny and John had a look at the small collection of books Bliaud had brought from Greenhythe and Master Caradoc had carried up from Somanthus Isle.

"Gaw, I never knew Dotys wrote a history of Ernine!" exclaimed John, turning one volume over in his hands. "Not that the old faker knew the first thing of what he's talking about, six hundred years later. Look, he says the kingdom came to ruin because the last monarch didn't worship the Twelve Gods properly and loved concubines to excess. That's what he says about 'em all, you know. And here's a complete copy of Ipycas' *Nature of Minerals*—I didn't think any were still in existence! And copied a treat. Those have to be Carunnus' illuminations—look at the mazework on the borders. D'you know, Jen, that according to Ipycas, or at least the pages I have of Ipycas, King Ebranck Ferrex of Locris used a combination of sulfur and quicksilver as an aphrodisiac and fathered fifty-three children, all on different women?"

"I presume," said Jenny dryly, "that the women had some pressing reason to assure him of the paternity of their offspring?"

"Well, he was gie rich."

"And not particularly bright, it seems."

"Now, Corax, the Master of Halnath, this was back when the Masters ruled Halnath in their own right, had a diamond so big it had been hollowed out into a bottle, like that dew-spoon of yours, and he kept in it what was said to be the tears of a sea monster, because those would dissolve ordinary glass and turn it and themselves into smoke . . . How'd they figure that one out, I wonder?" He perched on the back of a chair, his feet on the seat, lost in the wonder of antique trivia. "Gutheline II, it says, had cages carved for his pet crickets out of chunks of coal . . ."

"Lady Jenny." Yseult stopped in the doorway, startled to see them. She would, Jenny thought, have turned and fled had she been able to do so unseen. "I . . . I'm glad to see you. Did you find your boy?"

"We've found . . . word of him." Jenny drew her breath deep, trying to keep her voice from shaking. The girl looked better than she had a week ago, the food at Corflyn Hold beginning to fill out some of the hollows in her face and body. The dress she wore gave her a curious dignity, green wool embroidered with yellow flowers and quite clearly donated by the wife of a sutler or yeoman. Her oak-colored hair was braided and bound with ribbons of yellow.

But her eyes were downcast, avoiding Jenny's; the wary mouth settled to a neutral line. Jenny frowned a little and put out her hand to raise the girl's face to her; Yseult stepped self-consciously away.

"Are you all right?"

Yseult looked up quickly, the wide brown eyes determinedly smiling, cheerful as she had not been cheerful when Jenny had left. "Yes. 'Course. I'm fine, Lady Jenny."

"Is this Master Caradoc treating you well?"

She nodded, too fast and too many times. "He's good to me, m'am. Good to me, and teaches me everything, everything I always wanted to learn."

Jenny was silent, remembering her own desperate hunger to learn between Kahiera Nightraven's going and Caerdinn's grudging acceptance of her as his student. Remembered the magics she'd tried to invent for herself in those awful years, which almost never worked: the power that would not come. The nights weeping when the patched-together remnants of Nightraven's teachings turned out to be only mumbles of nonsense words.

Even Caerdinn's curses and beatings had been a blessing, then.

Men had called her whore and witch and hag in the streets when they saw her following after Caerdinn, and the children with whom she had once played ran from her. She reached out compassionately and touched Yseult's braided hair. "It isn't easy."

The girl's eyes flickered briefly to hers, then dodged away again. She shrugged and smiled. "You said it weren't going to be easy, m'am. But I've done harder."

"He isn't . . ." There was something very wrong in the too-quick replies, the casual voice. Something evasive in the studiedly averted face. "Are you all right?" she asked again.

"Oh, yes, m'am. Everything's fine." The girl produced a dazzling smile, as if for inspection. "Everyone's so good to me. There's not a thing amiss."

Everything in Jenny screamed at the lie, but she let it go. Quietly, she said, "And yes, we . . . we know what happened to Ian. John saw him." She nodded back to that lithe unlikely form, digging around in a volume titled *Revealed Geometries of the Planetary Movement*. She drew another breath, trying to steady herself against the memory. "Ian was taken—kidnapped—by a mage who appears to be putting together a corps of mages and dragons under the influence of demons. A wizard named Isychros did the same thing a thousand years ago. Has anyone come to you, or to Bliaud, trying to get you away from this Hold?"

"Oh, no, m'am." Yseult retreated a step, shaking her head. "Nothing of that. I stayed in the walls, like you told me to, and I been safe. Master Bliaud, too."

"And no one's sent you dreams, as I did, to try to get you away?"

"No, m'am."

It was on Jenny's lips to ask about the weather witchery, so improbably far in advance, but instead she asked, "Are you happy here, Yseult?"

"Yes, m'am." The girl dropped a quick curtsy. "I maun be going, m'am. 'Cuse me, m'am."

Jenny watched her worriedly as she crossed the courtyard, running a casual hand over the chained cover of the contaminated well, and vanished into one of the three shuttered rooms on its opposite side.

"What the hell are they doin' to the poor chit?"

She looked around. John was still perched on the back of the chair, the book on his knees, but he, too, followed Yseult out of sight with his eyes. "She acts like me cousin Ranny did when her mother's husband was comin' to her bed."

"Yes," murmured Jenny. She folded her arms inside her plaid. "Yes, that's what I thought."

"This old Bliaud bird wouldn't be witchin' her to him on the quiet, would he?" He stepped down from the chair, laid the book aside and came to stand beside her. "Or this Master Caradoc?"

"I'm not sure Bliaud could get the spells right." Jenny's brows pulled together, at the memories of the two or three village girls who'd crept to her cottage in secret, over the years, begging for charms to make "this man I know"—they never would tell names at first—"stop bothering of me." Without exception they pleaded that "this man I know" not be hurt, though Jenny knew perfectly well that those pitiful little cantrips for impotence or "have him be back in love with me mother again" wouldn't put an end to what was going on. "Though you never can tell. And of this Master Caradoc I know nothing."

"Nothing except that Rocklys is in no position to get rid of him, if he's able to teach the others. And that he was a suitor of hers she wouldn't have."

"That wouldn't stop her from sending him about his business."

"You think so?"

Jenny looked up into those sleepy-lidded cynical brown eyes.

"She's first and foremost a military commander, Jen, one of the best I've seen. She lets nothing stand in the way of good order and her objectives, whatever they may be. This school of hers means a lot to her. It may be she just doesn't want to know. If," he added, "that's what's goin' on. It may not be."

"But something is."

"Aye." John scratched the side of his chin. "Somethin' is."

Later in the day word reached Corflyn Hold that Rocklys' forces had been sighted from one of the signal-towers on the Stone Hills and would be at the gates by twilight. John and Jenny had spent most of the afternoon in the library, hunting for further mention of dragons, demons, or the long-forgotten incident of Isychros' Dragon Army, with no success.

"Dependin' on how many dragons this wizard can round up," John said, emerging from a slim and badly corrupted text of the Pseudo-Cerduces, "we're like to need somethin' along the lines of the Urchin. But we'll need to plaster the thing with spells if it's to be the slightest good."

"And I'm not sure ward-spells will work." Jenny laid aside a grimoire. "I have no experience with the magic of the great Spawn, but if dragon-magic won't touch them, I don't know what will."

"Well, they got rid of 'em somehow way back in the days," pointed out John logically. "Morkeleb spoke of desert mages from someplace called Prokep, wherever that was. And with Rocklys behind us we can at least prepare and get word to Gar, and see if there's anything of use in the archives at Bel or Halnath. This Caradoc may have heard somethin', too."

He stood and stretched his back, and walked to the window, where one of the camp washerwomen was crossing the courtyard with an armful of clothes. Fine linen shirts, stiff from drying, and on top a blue robe trimmed with squirrel fur, a southerner's garment for the northern summers. Jenny, looking past John at the bright sun of the court, smiled.

Then she heard the intake of John's breath and saw his shoulders stiffen.

But he waited, silent, until the woman went into the third of the three shuttered chambers and reemerged without her burden. Then he caught Jenny by the wrist. "Come on," he said.

Silently she followed him across the court.

The room assigned to Master Caradoc was small, dim, and filled with half-unpacked boxes and bundles. The laundry lay on the neatly made bed, shirts folded, blue robe carefully spread out. And on top of the blue robe lay an embroidered cap.

Puzzled, Jenny looked at John, who was walking quickly from pack to pack, touching, feeling, manipulating the leather and canvas as if searching. "What is it?"

There weren't many bags. Some appeared to contain blankets, cookpots, and other articles of travel, others books. On the windowsill was what looked like a shell, wrought of thinnest glass and broken at one end.

John twitched aside the knots of one bundle, dug into it like a hound scenting carrion, and straightened up. In his hand was a cup wrought also in the shape of a shell, gold overlying mother-of-pearl as fine as blown glass.

"It's him," he said softly. "It's Caradoc."

Jenny frowned, not understanding.

"The wizard who took Ian. The mage I saw on the isles of the dragons." John raised the cup. "I saw this in his hands."

Jenny opened her mouth to speak, then let her breath out unused. Their eyes met in the shadowy chamber.

John said, "We've got to get out of here."

BOOK TWO
The Burning Mirror

15

Beneath a camouflaging plaid, John and Jenny passed the telescope back and forth and watched Rocklys and her men march into the fort with the setting of the sun.

Mailshirts made a muffled leaden ringing when the drums and pipes fell silent. In the back of her mind Jenny heard Caerdinn's harsh angry voice: *A great gray snake of men, with banners on its spine, they were.* Marching away to the south. Leaving us to our foes, and to poverty and ignorance afterward. Leaving us without law.

Rocklys rode ahead on her big stallion, and the smoky light made her helmet plumes and cloak dark as blood. John touched Jenny's arm and pressed the spyglass into her hand. Through it she saw the man who rode at the Commander's side.

Square-jawed, strong-built, his face was settled into lines of arrogance, the arrogance of money that has always bought unquestioning obedience. A fair match for Rocklys, if she had taken him. *Merchants wanting to be aristocrats,* she said in scorn . . . A maid of the House of Uwanë was perhaps the only thing he couldn't buy. On his hair he wore an embroidered cap; gloves of embroidered leather protected his hands.

The man who'd taken Ian.

Jenny shut her eyes. She should, she knew, feel only pity for the man himself, whatever fragments of his consciousness might still remain. She'd seen what even small wights did to and with those they possessed.

But she could feel no pity. *You arrogant, greedy bastard,* she thought, knowing she was being unjust, for he must have been as hungry for craft as she. *You heard the demon whispering in your dreams, promising power if you just did one simple rite . . .*

Didn't you know? Couldn't you guess?

Or didn't you want to know? Did you think you could control the situation, as you controlled all of your life before?

Her jaw ached and she realized her teeth were clenched.

"There." John nudged her. "Look."

The column was interrupted for a space, where prisoners walked, hands bound up to wooden yokes set over their necks. Women and children mostly, with the alabaster-fair skin, coarse black hair, and low flattened cheekbones of the Iceriders. But nearer the front, where Rocklys and the southerner Caradoc rode side by side, two prisoners rode bound on horses, a boy and a girl. Through the spyglass Jenny saw the silver chains, the sigils and wards that lashed their wrists to the saddlebows.

So John's mother Nightraven must have been brought to Alyn Hold, a prisoner of Lord Aver's spear.

Those, she thought, and not the protection of the farms, were the reason for Rocklys' pursuit of the band.

As Yseult must have been Rocklys' motive in convincing Jenny to seek Balgodorus, while Caradoc took Ian.

To found the Dragon Corps.

Only after the last of the army passed through the thick-planked double gate of the fort, and the gate shut behind it, did the two watchers move. Stealthy as hunters, they wriggled their way down the slope and into the trees, concealed under every ward-spell and guard and Word of Invisibility that Jenny could conjure around them.

"Where are they, anyway?" asked John, as he and Jenny worked their way through the undergrowth toward their camp. "I mean, it's a bit of a trick to hide a full-grown dragon."

"Morkeleb doesn't seem to have any trouble."

Morkeleb awaited them in the deep hollow where they'd hidden the blankets and food they'd taken from Corflyn in departing, though Jenny could see no trace of any living thing. Then something whispered in her mind, and what had been a spiky growth of holly was suddenly revealed, as if by a mere shifting of perception, to be blacker, glossier, harder than holly ever grew. What seemed to be tree branches took on the shape of tall spines and the bristling armory of joints and wing bones and tail. Two flashes of will-o'-the-wisp resolved themselves within a thicket of saplings, and the fireflies that had bobbed there took on the curious unholy glitter of the dragon's jewel-cold antenna lights. The smell of the pines and the water seemed to blow away, though there was no touch of wind, and the acrid, metallic stink they had veiled gleamed through like the blade of a concealed knife.

And so, Wizard-woman. Did you see your son?

"Ian doesn't ride with them. But Rocklys has taken two prisoners,

Icewitches, to add to Bliaud and poor Yseult. That means Caradoc must make slaves of four more dragons or has already done so. I don't think Gareth and all the forces of his father can withstand a corps like that."

Jenny felt the heat of his anger again, rising through the accretions of shadow.

Not of dragons, he said. *And not if they are allied with the Hellspawn.*

"Can you bear us south?" she asked. "Take us to Jotham, where Gareth mounts siege before the fortress of the Prince of Imperteng? From him we can gain access to the archives of the Realm and the University at Halnath. Surely there is something that speaks of demons."

Do not count upon even that to help you, Wizard-woman, said Morkeleb. *Do you not know how it is among the Hellspawn? You, and cats, and whales, and ants, and every other being that has life: You are all beings of flesh in this world. And we, the star-drakes, we are beings of magic, beings unlike your flesh, bone unlike your bone . . . but still of this dimension, this plane of existence. We live and we die, and our magic is drawn from this fact.*

The Hellspawn are Other. Each Hell, each world, each of those separate and several planes from which they come is Other, from ours and from one another as well. All power is sourced from the things that surround us: Moon and Sun, the patterns of the stars and the way trees grow, our very flesh and the beat of our blood. They have Things in their worlds that are not stars. They have Things in their worlds that are not heat or cold, and to strike flint and steel in one of them will not make flame, though in another perhaps it will. There is neither life nor death in some of those Hells, and in some there is, and in some there is something Else that has its own laws. Thus to do the great magic here they must work through humans who have that magic in their flesh, through dragons who are wrought of magic—through those things attuned to the patterns of power in this world.

There was silence. Jenny touched with her mind the kindling in the firepit, calling a small blaze to being. Though the sky would hold light for hours, it was inky-dark under the trees, and the damp close cold of the low ground rose about them. She unpacked the food while John went down to the spring. Morkeleb backed himself still farther into the dark woods, his thin bird-beak laid upon his claws, and it seemed to Jenny that for a time he ceased to be visible at all.

"I don't like it, Jen," said John when he came back. "And I've been fair crippling meself tryin' to find another way. But I think you'll have to go back into Corflyn Hold tonight."

Jenny was silent, gazing into the fire. Thinking of Nightraven standing on the walls of Alyn Hold, gazing away toward the north on nights of

storm. Of the two little Icewitches bound on their horses with silver
chains. Ian running toward her through the poppies that carpeted Frost
Fell in the spring, and John's face in the morning sunlight as he held his
newborn son.

"And do what?" she asked softly.

"See the lie of the land." John set down the dripping water-skin. "And
that only. See who this Caradoc is when he's at home, and how he and
Rocklys get along these days. Any money she's not twigged that it isn't
him anymore? She may have her doubts but not want to know it. It fair
kills me to think Ian was in the fortress when we were there this afternoon, but he must have been. See if there's anythin' about the demon that
would tell us what counterspells to use, always supposing we find counterspells. If there's a book that says, 'Oh, yeah, Muckwort Demons make
their victims turn three times clockwise in a circle before they fall asleep,
and they can be exorcised by dandelion juice,' we're gonna feel like a fair
couple of clots for not countin' how many times Caradoc and Yseult and
Bliaud turned in a circle, and which way they turned.

"I don't know what you're going to do, love," he added softly. "I'd go
meself—since I'm of no use to Caradoc if he does catch me—but he's
sure as check got some kind of magic guard round the place and I'd never
get past it. You can."

"Morkeleb? I'll go, but I will need all the help you can give me, to
pass unseen. Will a demon be aware of me?"

Of you, Wizard-woman? Yes. Wind began to creep through the trees, a
curious icy tugging, and beneath it the frightening undercurrent of heat
that accompanies spells of transformation and change. *They smell blood.
They feel the presence of human minds and human souls through the
roots of their teeth.*

Leaves jerked and threshed on the trees. The fire in the pit leaned,
flattened, stretching yellow fingerlets over the ground as if trying to creep
forth from its prison. Rags of mist and smoke whirled among the tugging
branches of the trees.

*Only a few thousand of us made the journey from our home to this
place, this world, to the Skerries of Light. We can ill spare the wisdom of
their songs, and still less can we risk giving over those songs to those that
dwell on the Other Plane.*

The heat was suffocating, worse than the heat of age that periodically
seized her flesh. The wind ripped at Jenny's hair and clothing, freezing
where it touched, but doing nothing to dispel the brimstone in the air.

*They will be aware of you. It may be that in spite of all that I can do
to turn their thoughts aside, they will be aware of me. Wizard-woman,
stretch out your hand.*

The wind ceased. Fog rose out of the ground, black and impenetrable. Night-sighted, Jenny was barely aware of John's form beside her, and she saw by the way he reached out his hand that he was totally blind. She caught his groping fingers in hers, then extended her other hand, her left, to where Morkeleb's silver eyes had gleamed in the dark.

Something flashed and whirled in the mist, and hard strong claws closed around her wrist, dug into her shoulder. She half-felt, half-saw the dark beat of wings near her face. It seemed no bigger than a peregrine but sinuous and glistening as a snake. Though gripping thorns pricked her wrist, there was no weight on her arm at all.

Give me your name, Wizard-woman, the voice said in her mind, *as once I gave mine to you when in the Deep of Ylferdun you saved my life.*

And she spoke it in her mind. There was a dragon-name, which he had called out of her four years ago, when she had taken on dragon form and flown away with him from Halnath Citadel, but that was not the name she now spoke. Around the spine of that music were woven other memories: Caerdinn cursing her, and John's hand lifting her hair; the lance of pain through her bowels when she bore Ian, and her laughter when lying in her bed in the house at Frost Fell, with her cats and her harp and the sunlight of a hundred summer mornings. The smell of roses. Autumn rain.

Pain in her wrist, then blood-heat on her arm.

Wizard-woman, what do you see?

Her eyes changed. She saw John.

Bent nose, round spectacles silvered over with mist, the alien contours of his face. A different perspective, like a doubled vision . . .

The mists dissolved. Perfect, glistening, deadly as a tiny knife of chipped obsidian and steel, Morkeleb sat on her forearm, no bigger than a hawk, silver eyes infinitely alien in the dark.

His voice was the same as it had always been, speaking in the abyss of her mind. *Open your mind to me,* he said. *Empty your mind to my voice. If I do not return, at least you will have knowledge of what it is that I see.*

He lifted his wings and, releasing her arm, rose like a scarf of black tissue on an updraft, hanging before her face.

What do you think dragons are made of, Wizard-woman? he asked. *Does magic have a shape, or a size? Can the will be bottled in a flask?*

Then he was gone into the dissipating vapors.

Jenny settled herself beside the fire to wait.

She had been a dragon. She knew what Morkeleb meant when he told her to open her mind to his, for it was a thing of dragons: One did not have to look into a dragon's eyes to hear its voice, or see what it saw. She waited, and her thoughts—which had circled a little around Nightraven, and Ian, and the old worn-weary track of her grief—settled, jewel-clear as a dragon's, interested without love or grief. She was aware of John sitting by the fire, drawn sword across his knees. Aware that his face was half-turned away, watching her, but watching also the woods all around.

She was aware of the forest, of the foxes creeping cautiously out, wondering if the dangers of evil heat and evil smell were gone; of the stupid, timid rabbits coming to feed. Of the smell of the pine-mast and the movement of the stars.

She saw Corflyn Hold from above, a quick glimpse of molten amber light cupped in lapis lazuli, and men moving about. Smoke and horses. Then gone.

Stronger to her nostrils came the smells of wood, dust, and mice; water and mold. She became aware of mouse-magic—she hadn't even known such a thing existed—and the darker stench that was the magic of rats. Morkeleb's spells, to keep even rodents from fleeing his approach and so alerting Caradoc.

Dark and mildew.

Firelight. The tawny radiance of pierced clay lamps, and the smell of burning oil. The room lay below her, foreshortened and changed but recognizable as the one in which she and John had been that day. Morkeleb must be lying along a rafter, she thought, with the same detachment she experienced when it crossed her mind to wonder whether John had remembered to put Caradoc's golden cup back exactly as he'd found it. Question and observation simply came and went.

Dragon-sight—mage-sight—showed her three-quarters of the room encircled by a spell-diagram, a vast sigil of power of a kind she had never seen. The glowing lines of it extended up onto the walls and, in a curious way, past the walls, through them, and down through the floor, visible for some distance into the foundations and the earth. Instead of Guardian Wards, thin wisps of greenish light burned at the diagram's five points, reflected in the frightened eyes of the black-haired boy and girl who sat bound in chairs within one of the figure's three circles.

Yseult, Bliaud, and Ian were there, standing behind the young Ice-witches' chairs. It was as if their eyes had been replaced with colored glass. Jenny observed this with a dragon's heart, the only way her own concentration would not be broken by the life-in-death of her son. On the table beside the box of jewels two more glass shells lay, broken and empty. Jenny understood without knowing how that demons wore those shells when they crept into this world through the Gate to their Hell.

Caradoc wore the embroidered cap that the laundress had brought in clean that afternoon. Interlocking circles of satin-work; stylized lilies.

He'd bathed and washed his hair; Jenny could smell the camomile. Rocklys, standing before him, still wore her red military tunic and her riding boots, and her hair was flattened and matted from her helmet.

She said, "What is it that you don't want me to see?"

Caradoc sighed. "We've been through this before, Ro . . . Commander." His voice was a pleasant baritone, but the voice of a man not only used to having his own way but to being always right. "I told you at the outset that the presence of the untrained and uninitiated can completely nullify the effects of a spell."

"And I've heard since then that that isn't the case." Her colorless level brows pinched above her nose. She studied his face. Wondering, as John had said, and not really wanting to know.

"From whom?" His gesture of scornful impatience was, Jenny guessed, a perfect counterfeit of a familiar human mannerism, and one moreover with which Rocklys was well acquainted, for she seemed to relax. "One of the local hedge-witches? The only spells *they're* capable of wouldn't be affected by a brass band and a wrestling-match going on in the room. We're not charming warts here, Roc. We're not casting spells to win some bumpkin's heart. If you want my help, well and good, but you must accept that there is a reason for everything I tell you. There is a reason for every request I make. You don't explain everything to your troops—you can't, nor should you." He used the informal "you," as to a family member, and Rocklys' shoulders stiffened again, this time with familiar annoyance.

"Please understand that my wishes *must* be followed to the letter, else I cannot help you accomplish what you seek to accomplish."

For a time their eyes held, and the part of Jenny's heart that was human still saw the virile impatient merchant, newly come to court, and the granite-hard angry princess he had courted but could not win. It was an old clash of wills, and it served to convince Rocklys, had she in fact harbored doubts, that there was nothing amiss in this man she once knew.

Caradoc held out his hand peremptorily, and after a moment the Commander placed in it two jewels, dark faceted stones. The Icerider boy twisted against the bonds that held him to his chair, bonds twined with spell-riddled chains that glowed faintly to Jenny's mageborn perceptions, and began to weep. The girl, younger, round-faced, and cold-eyed, stared stonily before her, but behind her gag her breath was coming very fast.

"Were these the best you could get?"

"I have to send some taxes to the south, to justify our presence here." Rocklys' voice was cold, angry at being bested. "And I have to pay my men, and feed them, and keep the horses in oats. If word got to that bunch of painted twits the Regent keeps about him that I was purchasing gemstones, do you think"—and the pronoun she used was one of formal usage, of master to servant—"they'd leave me in command?"

"They wouldn't even care." Caradoc, who had glanced up in anger at her choice of address, turned with elaborate unconcern and held one of the jewels up, calling a spot of brilliant light into being, so that lozenges of pale purple were thrown onto his chin and brow.

"No," murmured Rocklys. "No, I think you're right. It would pass unnoticed in their silly quibbling about jurisdiction and whose rights overlay whose."

"So why trouble yourself?" Caradoc shrugged. "Amethysts are all right—these are of good quality and strong color—but if you could get another couple of rubies or emeralds we'd do better. They hold—" He hesitated, trying to answer the question that was in Rocklys' eyes without, it was clear, really telling her anything. "They hold certain spells more strongly. I'm not sure about that peridot—I think you were cheated by the merchant, but we can probably make do with it if we have to. And now, Commander . . ."

He walked to the door, only a step or two, and opened it to look outside and up at the sky. "The timing of these spells is very precise, particularly this close to mid-summer. It's full dark now, and barely time until midnight to do what must be done. Commander," he added, as she nodded brusquely and turned to go.

She turned back. The lintel of the door hid her face from Morkeleb's watching gaze, but every line of her body seemed to radiate discontent.

"Remember what I said about these practices remaining utterly unobserved. Neither of us can risk having one of these wizardlings incompletely given either to my will or to the bonding with the dragon. I tell you, if you or anyone watches what is done in this room or in the courtyard, I cannot promise that you will be able to conquer and hold the south."

The woman nodded and made again to go. Then she looked back. "And I have told you, Sorcerer." Again she addressed him as she would a servant. No wonder, thought Jenny, that wealthy suitor had gone away unwed. "I do not seek to conquer. Nor to wrest control of the Realm from its rightful King for my own pleasure or to satisfy some greed. I only seek to bring order. To make things as they should be."

Caradoc bent his head, and the lamp flames slithered along the embroidered lilies and across his silvery hair. "Of course."

She's lying to herself. The thought floated through Jenny's mind as Rocklys closed the door. *As he to her.*

And the thoughts were gone, put away to be regarded at leisure another time. Morkeleb's dragon-senses followed the Commander's boots across the court, hearing even the opening and shutting of her own door, and the creak of her desk chair as she sat. Aware, but setting the sounds aside.

Caradoc walked carefully through the gate in the magic circle and stood before the two young Icewitches. Morkeleb—and through him, Jenny—could feel the spells that Bliaud, Yseult, and Ian kept over them, spells worked through them, like magics worked through the bones of the dead. Caradoc asked, "Do you understand what I'm saying?"

The boy nodded. The girl said nothing, nor did she move. But she could not control her ice-gray eyes, and the sorcerer nodded briefly, satisfied that she could.

"I'm going to put one of these in each of your mouths." He held up the gemstones, burning purple in the lamplight. "If you swallow them, I'll take a knife and cut them out of your bellies and stuff the cavities with live rats. Do you understand?"

The boy was crying. The girl, bound and ringed and crippled by the spell-wards upon her, flung her hatred at the man, since it was all she had to fling.

Caradoc's broad shoulders tightened. Clearly he hated having his will crossed. "I see we're going to have to do this the hard way." He took the smaller of the two amethysts, a crystal the size of the end of his little finger, and, removing the boy's gag, put it into the boy's mouth, afterward gagging him again. The other stone was perhaps twice the size of the smaller, and a few shades paler in color. Caradoc handed it to Ian, who stood nearest him, as if the boy were no more than a table to hold things. Then he took a scarf of thin silk from his pocket and tied it around the girl's throat, pulling tighter and tighter until her back arched and thin, desperate noises issued from her throat. Leaving only the barest passage for air, he knotted it, then pulled down the gag. Her mouth dropped open, her chest heaving, and he dropped the jewel onto the protruding tongue. The girl moved her head as if in spite of all she would spit it out, but he shoved the gag into place again.

"One thing you will learn," said Caradoc, looking down for a moment into the bulging, frantic eyes and for a clear moment Jenny saw, not the man, but the demon that dwelled inside. "I will be obeyed."

Did he do that to Ian?

Jenny let the thought go.

The rite was surprisingly short. Jenny watched, dispassionately, through the incense-smoke and mists, recognizing more of the gestures and devices than she expected. There was a Summoning of some sort, but the Limitations set carefully around the two chairs seemed wrong to her. They were signs of protection, of the preclusion of demons rather than their calling. The power seemed wrongly centered, drawn in on the two children rather than on the sorcerer.

It was only when, in less time than it would take a loaf of bread to bake, Caradoc brought the rite to a conclusion and walked across the fading lines of the sigil to the young Icewitches again, that Jenny realized what she had seen done. The boy had ceased his tears. The girl, though her eyes followed the blocky form of the man, showed no more hate, no more emotion of any sort, passive and empty.

Empty.

Caradoc removed the gags, took the amethysts from the mouths of each child, then walked to a strongbox. Lamplight flashed on its contents when he opened it, and with Morkeleb's eyes, Jenny saw what it contained.

Two rubies and a sapphire dark as the sea, clear, strongly colored, and without flaw. And in each jewel, it seemed to her, though they lay in the shadows, there burned a tiny, infinitely distant seed of light.

But only when she saw him pick up his cup of crystal and nacre and go to the door, only when she heard the chains of the well-cover clatter back, did realization strike her. She cried out, darkness swallowing the vision, the bridge between her mind and the dragon's collapsing. She cried out again, inarticulate, and felt warm strong hands grasp her arms—

"Jen!"

Her eyes opened and she saw John's face.

"Jen, what is it?"

She was trembling, breathless with shock. Having laid hope aside, she had no idea how painful it would be when it rushed back in; the agony of knowing that there might be something that she could do.

"Ian!" she said.

"Was he there?"

"Ian . . ." She swallowed. "The wizard—Caradoc—he didn't bring the demon into him, to drive out his soul and his mind. John, he took the soul of him—the heart of him—out first, and stored it in a jewel. Then he let the demon in. Ian's still there, John. We can still get him back."

16

"**W**hy would he do it?" John spoke over his shoulder, not looking toward the fire that would dull his night-vision, keeping his eyes turned toward the dark woods. "Why would he want their souls kept around, once he's taken their flesh?"

"I don't know." Jenny glanced up from staring into the fire, from trying to reconnect her spinning mind with Morkeleb's. "It's a thing I never heard of. Usually, according to Caerdinn, anyway, the smaller pooks and wights don't . . . don't completely expel the mind, the soul, of their victim. Sometimes that soul can return when the demon is exorcised, if too much time hasn't passed. With the Great Wights it's different, of course. But this . . ."

She fell silent, remembering the demon blazing in Caradoc's eyes. The hell-light in Ian's.

"It was midnight when he met with the demons before, I think," John said, after a time. Jenny had opened her eyes, unable to find the dragon's mind with her own. "They came up out of the sea, silver and shining. Salamanders I thought they looked like, or toads, creeping out of little glass shells. Water must be one of their Gates."

They come from another place, Caerdinn had muttered to her, when they'd stood together on the edge of the Wraithmire watching the ghostly flicker of the fen-wights in the dark. *Since ancient days there have been men that would open Gates into Hell, in the hopes of finding power for themselves.*

They had been watching, Jenny recalled, for a wight that had seized a simpleminded woman, entering into her mind and dreams and causing her to kill and cut up her husband, children, sister, and father before the villagers had summoned Caerdinn. Together, she and her master had exorcised the woman, but her own mind never returned. Perhaps that, thought Jenny, recalling the silent, bloodied hut, the creeping lines of ants and humming of flies, had been just as well.

Though she knew the presence of wizards in Corflyn Hold would almost certainly make it impossible to scry within its walls, Jenny took the finger-sized sliver of white quartz from her pouch and tried to summon images: the courtyard, Caradoc's chamber, the strongbox in its niche above the bed. But the place was written over with scry-wards, as she had written them everywhere on the manor walls at Palmorgin. All she could see was the dark bulk of the walls themselves, from a great distance off, and she realized from the look of the sky that what she saw was another night, another season, another year. An illusion.

Caradoc was in the courtyard, she thought. Summoning the Hell-spawn from that other plane of existence. Summoning them through that distant Gate, through their medium of water, across whatever space lay between. Summoning them into the emptied minds, the emptied hearts, of those two poor children.

Yseult saying, "Yes, m'am," and "No, m'am," with that evasive, casual brightness, not meeting her eyes.

Yseult sending Bliaud's sons away, lest they see how their father had changed.

Rocklys asking her to stay, demanding that she take an escort.

"So it's been Rocklys all along." She folded her plaid around her shoulders and looked up again at the sky. The red star called the Watcher's Lantern stared back at her. Midnight chimed like cold music on her spine. *All doors open at midnight,* Nightraven had said to her once, separating her hair with a comb of silver and bone and plaiting the power-shadows called to being by that simple act. *All doors open at moments of change: from deepening night to dawning day, from fading winter to the first promises of spring.*

All doors open.

"I should have guessed it." Flames made slabs of fire in John's spectacles as he turned the log.

Jenny looked up, startled. Sometimes it seemed impossible to her that this man was Nightraven's son.

"The Realm as it's constituted drives her mad, you know. Each fief and deme with its own law, most of 'em with their own gods as well, not to speak of measurements. Everybody drivin' in all sorts of directions and not much of anythin' gettin' done, while them at Court make up songs and moon-poems and theological arguments these days, I'm told. Look at the books in Rocklys' library, the ones she keeps by her: Tenantius. Gurgustus. Caecilius' *The Righteous Monarch.* All the Legalists. Of course she's got no patience with Gar trying to do the right thing by old bargains and old promises. Of course she wants to step in and make it all match at the edges."

" 'I only seek to bring order,' " Jenny quoted softly, " 'to make things as they should be.' Gareth has to be warned, John. She has the biggest army, probably, in the Realm right now, even including the one he's taken to Imperteng with him. And whatever he has will be no match against dragons and wizards and demons working in concert."

"What I'm wondering"—John propped up his spectacles with a bandaged forefinger—"is what in the name of God's shoebuckles makes Rocklys think she can control Caradoc? Even given she doesn't know he's possessed by a demon, doesn't this woman *read?*"

"No," said Jenny. "Probably not. All her life she has wielded her own strength successfully, to her own ends. She is used to the struggle for mastery with Caradoc. If he appears to yield to her, do you think it's likely to occur to her that it's a trick? She . . ."

She raised her head, hearing the whisper of vast silken wings. "Here he comes."

And then, realizing that at no time had she ever been able to hear Morkeleb's approach, "The trees!"

At the same instant she hurled a spell of suffocation onto the fire and flung every ounce of strength she had into a great whirling tornado of misdirection and illusion around herself and John as dragons plunged out of the sky.

Lots of dragons.

John shouted, "Fire!" as he grabbed her arm, and claws raked and seared through the canopy of leaves above them. Snakelike heads shot through the branches, mouths snapping; green acid splashed a great charred scar in the pine-mast and Jenny cried out the Word of Fire, hurling it like a weapon at the rustling roof of the trees. The crown of the forest burst into flame, illuminating for a refulgent instant the primitive rainbow colors, glistening scales: pink and green and gold, white and scarlet. One of the dragons screamed as the long scales of its mane caught and the scream was echoed, terribly, from the girl on the other dragon's back, Yseult with her skirts and her hair on fire. Then the two dragons were gone, and John and Jenny were running down the path to the spring, while all around them smoke billowed, flaming twigs and branches rained, and acid splattered in from above.

John dragged them both down into the water, the heat already blistering on their faces. The spring slanted away southeast to join the Black River two or three miles below Cair Corflyn. Jenny shucked off her wet plaids and heavy skirt, pulled her petticoats up high and began to crawl with the sharp stones digging and cutting at her knees and palms. John was behind her, holding his bow awkwardly over his back. Jenny drew the fire after them, Summoned the smoke to lie in a spreading pall over the whole quarter of the forest; it stung and ripped at her lungs, gritted in her eyes.

"Morkeleb will see the fire," she gasped.

"If he's alive." John slipped on a stone and cursed. The water was freezing cold underneath, though it had begun to steam on top. "If he thinks it's worth his while to take on four other dragons . . . Well, three, with the girl out of action . . ."

"He'll come."

Acid splashed into the glaring water in front of them. Through the steam Jenny saw the huge angular shape of a dragon framed in fire, crouched before them in the bed of the stream.

John said, "Fester it."

It stood just beyond the ending of the trees, where the spring ran into a marshy meadow. Wings folded close it bent down, darting its head under the fiery canopy. The flames gilded its scales, blue on blue, an iridescent wonder of lapis, lobelia, peacock; outlined the small shape on its shoulders, among the spines. It opened its mouth to spit again and John, knee-deep in the steaming water, already had his arrow nocked and drawn when Jenny saw the rider's face.

She screamed *"No!"* as John loosed the shaft. *"It's Ian!"* She flung a spell after the arrow, but it was an arrow she had witched herself, months ago. Ian rocked back as the bolt hit him; caught at the spikes around him and slowly crumpled. The dragon backed into the darkness.

"Now!" John grabbed her wrist, dragging her. "There's caves along the river."

"Morkeleb . . ."

"What? You don't think I can take on two dragons by myself?"

And Jenny heard it, the dark dream-voice calling her name.

They stumbled from the burning woods and saw him, a whirl of sliced firelight edging blackness in the air, tearing, snapping, swooping at the gaudy barbaric shapes of the red and white dragon and a sun-yellow splendor that Jenny thought must surely be the dragon Enismirdal. Morkeleb was faster and larger than either, but as the other two rose toward him, fire and darkness seemed to swirl up with them, splintering image and illusion into threes and fours. Jenny narrowed her mind, focused it to a blade of light, and flung that blade toward Morkeleb in spells of perception, of ward.

She saw, for a flashing instant, through his eyes. Saw the other dragons fragment and scatter, now into five or six discrete attacking shapes, now into rainbows of horrific color—maddening, camouflaging—and shot through with splinters of a ghastly and wicked greenish flame. Jenny redoubled her concentration, drawing power from the unchecked rage of the fire, from the granite and dolomite deep beneath the stream's bed. Through the dragon's eyes she saw the shape of an attacker come clear, and Morkeleb struck, black lightning, raking and tearing.

Then the image splintered again, and Jenny gasped at the sudden cold terror that took her, as if a silver worm had suddenly broken through her flesh, creeping and reaching for her heart and her brain. She called on all her power, guarding herself, guarding Morkeleb, but it was as if something within her were bleeding, and the power bleeding away with it. The discipline that Caerdinn had beaten into her took over, systematically calling on the other powers alive in the earth—moonlight, water, the glittering stars—and her eyes seemed to clear. Morkeleb had gotten in another few telling rakes with claws and teeth, driving them back. Blood rained down onto Jenny's face, and droplets of searing acid. The silver hemorrhage within her did not stop.

Morkeleb plunged down, black claws extended. She felt herself seized, ripped up from the earth. Her head snapped back with the shock of the parabola as he swept skyward again, a razoring cloud of wings. Around them both Jenny flung the holed nets of her guardian-spells and felt as her magic locked and melded with his that his power, too, had been drained and drunk away. They were flying east, flying fast, and she was aware of wings storming behind them, of a madness of pursuing color and rage. Rain clouds draped the high bleak shoulders of the Skepping Hills.

Into these Morkeleb drove, and Jenny reached out with her mind, summoning the lightning and drawing around them the warding-spells to prevent their pursuers from doing the same. In the event there was nothing to it: Caught between conflicting powers, the lightning only flickered, sullen glares illuminating the cottony blackness around them.

In time the dragon gyred cautiously to earth.

"John?" Jenny rolled over, wet bodice and petticoat sticking to her limbs. The cave the dragon had brought them to was so low-roofed that only Jenny could have stood upright in it, and narrowed as it ran back into the hill. Rain poured bleakly, steadily down on the slope outside. She could hear the purling of what had to be Clayboggin Beck somewhere close and almost subconsciously identified where they were, and how far they had flown.

Witchlight blinked on glass as John turned his head. She marveled that in the midst of the chaos of fire, blood, and magic, Morkeleb had managed to seize them both.

"I'm sorry about Ian, love."

She drew in a deep breath. "Did you know when you shot?"

"Aye." He sat up cautiously. The tiniest blue threads of light showed her the glint of old metal plated onto his doublet. Behind him, flattened unbelievably, like a bug in a crevice, Morkeleb lay at the back of the cave, a glitter of diamond eyes and spines. "I knew he would be riding Nymr, see."

Jenny turned her face away. The knowledge that Ian was alive, and could be brought back, burned in her: rage, resentment, horror at what John had done.

"Caradoc won't let him die, you know," John went on. "There's too few mages in the world, and he had to pull both of 'em, Nymr and Ian— all three, I should say, if you count whatever goblin's riding 'em—out of the fight, as he pulled Yseult."

"And if your arrow had killed him on the spot?" Her voice was shaky. "We can bring him back, John, but not from the dead."

"If we'd died then," said John softly, "d'you think Ian would ever have been anything but a slave to goblins, a prisoner helpless in that jewel, for as long as his heart kept beating and his lungs kept drawing air? Watchin' what they did, while they lived on his pain? Sometimes an arrow to the heart can be a gift, given in love."

Jenny looked away. He was right, but she hurt so deeply that she had no words for it. John took off his doublet and lay down, pillowing his head on a soggy wad of plaids. His shirt steamed faintly in the heat-spells Morkeleb called to dry their clothing. There was only the sound of breathing in the cave, while the gray light struggled outside. In time Jenny got up and went over to lie beside him, holding his hand.

Given the rugged and heavily wooded terrain of the Fells of Imperteng, and the possibility of rebel guerrillas there, neither John nor Jenny considered it safe to be put down in the dark several miles from the camp of the King's men. Moreover, as John pointed out, there was no telling whether one of the dragons had followed them, waiting to pick him and Jenny up the moment Morkeleb was out of sight.

Thus the dragon flew straight to the camp below the walls of Jotham and circled down from the evening sky on the second day after their escape. Jenny spread out around them a great umbrella of Lousy Aim to deal with the consequences.

It was necessary. Men came running, shouting, from all corners of the camp—camps, for it was clear from above that each of the King's vassals pitched his tents apart, and there was no intermingling of the striped tents of Halnath with the cream-white if grubby shelters of the Men of

Hythe. Jenny saw them clearly, as a dragon sees, the cut and color of their clothing as diverse as the variety and size of their bivouacs. Their voices rose to her, along with the wild neighing from the horses and the frantic bleat of sheep, racing in wild circles in their pens. Arrows soared in a futile cloud. Then spears, brushed aside by Jenny's spells. Then men ran away in all directions as they had run in, pointing and crying out as they saw that the dragon clutched a human being in either claw.

John, being John, waved and blew kisses.

Balancing on his great wings, Morkeleb extended his long hind-legs to earth, then folded himself down to a crouch. By that time two men stood on the edge of the drill-ground where he settled, tall thin young men, the red-haired wearing a black scholar's robe, the fair one's spectacles a note of incongruity against the red military tunic, red breeches, and elaborately stamped and tassled red boots.

It was this bespectacled crimson figure who cried, "Lord John! Lady Jenny!" and strode forward, holding out his hands.

There was a time, Jenny remembered, when he would have run.

She made to curtsy in her ragged petticoat and John's grimy plaids, but he caught her in his arms, bending down his ridiculous height. Then he turned and embraced John, breathless with amazement and pleasure, while Morkeleb folded himself a little more comfortably and regarded the scene with chilly sardonic unhuman eyes. Forty feet seemed to be his true size, larger than which he could not go, but it was difficult for Jenny now to be sure.

"What are you doing here?" demanded Gareth of Magloshal-don, son of—and Regent for—his father the King. Even as he spoke, Uriens of the House of Uwanë appeared, a tall man who in his youth must have looked like the statues of Sarmendes the Sun-God: inlaid golden armor, crimson cloak, his great jeweled sword hurling spangles of light. "It's all right, Father," Gareth said quickly, going to him as the King, seeing Morkeleb, raised his weapon and began to advance.

"Lo, it is the Dragon of Nast Wall!"

"It's all right," Gareth repeated, catching his arm. "He's been conquered. He's here as a . . . a prisoner."

Morkeleb opened his mouth and hissed, but if he said anything Jenny did not perceive it, and Gareth gave no sign.

"He's a dragon." The King frowned, as if there were something there that he could not comprehend. His servants and batmen hurried up around him, tactfully taking him by the arms. "Dragons must be slain. 'Tis the duty of a King . . ."

"No," said Gareth. "Lord Aversin—you remember Lord Aversin?— and Mistress Waynest have taken this dragon prisoner. I'll sing you the

song of it tonight, or . . . or the night after." He turned back to John,
frowning as he saw the burns and blisters of acid-seared flesh. "What
happened?" He looked, too, at Morkeleb, as if knowing that only direst
emergency would bring them to the camp.

"Rocklys is a traitor." John tucked one hand into his sword-belt and
with the other scratched his long nose. "And that's the good news."

Without comment Gareth heard John's tale, though when John spoke
of the Skerries of Light the Regent's eyes glowed with longing and
delight. Sitting quietly between John and the red-haired Polycarp, Master
of Halnath and Doctor of Natural Philosophy—and clothed in an over-
bright and too-long gown lent by an officer's wife—Jenny understood
then that only part of Gareth's obsession with tales of the ancient Dragonsbanes stemmed from more than a gawky boy's craving for heroism
and deeds of courage at arms. What Gareth loved was that they were tales
touching on dragons.

As John, she realized, had come to love dragons as his understanding
of them grew.

"She always looked down on you, you know," Polycarp said to
Gareth. He set aside his note tablets. "She and I spoke two or three times
when she was in command of the troops besieging Halnath. When word
reached her that your father had become . . . ill"—he glanced at the tall
man, seated in the chair of honor at the center of the table—"her first
reaction was horror that you would be ruling the Realm."

"I'm not ill." King Uriens, who had listened to John's recital with the
grave wonderment of a child, sat back a little, frowning. His hair, which
had been the gold of ripe barley, was now nearly white and had grown so
wispy that it had been cropped short. Coming out to slay the dragon earlier, he had worn a flowing golden wig.

Other than that, Jenny thought, he looked hale, with the good healthy
color of a man who eats well and spends part of each day outdoors. Every
time Jenny had seen him, since the death of the sorceress Zyerne who had
drained away so much of his life and spirit, the old King seemed a little
livelier, a little more aware of his surroundings, though he still had a
child's fascination with every flower and button and pulley, as if he had
never seen such things before.

And it was discouraging to reflect that Rocklys had probably been
correct: If Uriens were separated from his son, he could easily be persuaded to forget him and make anyone—Rocklys or the Prince of
Imperteng or John or even Adric—Regent in the young man's stead.

The King went on, "I just get sleepy, but I can still be King even if I get sleepy, can't I?" He turned anxiously to his son, who smiled and laid a hand over the big brown fingers.

"No one better, Father."

"It was mean of her to say that." Uriens turned back to Polycarp. "I wouldn't have thought it of her. She was always such a fine warrior, such a fine fighter. I remember I gave her armor for her thirteenth birthday. You asked for books." He regarded Gareth with mild puzzlement, though with no animosity in his voice.

By the flush that crept up under his thin skin at his father's words, Jenny guessed that his father had had a good deal to say on the subject of boys who asked for books rather than armor.

"Why doesn't she like us anymore?" Uriens said.

"She doesn't like us because she's not getting her own way," said John, with a wry sideways smile, and the King nodded, understanding this.

"Well, that's why she didn't marry that merchant fellow. All for the best, of course."

From outside the plain, dark walls of the tent came the barking of the camp dogs, the caw of rooks about the midden. Very little other noise, thought Jenny. No slap of arms or calling-out of orders. Morkeleb, crouched in the midst of the main parade ground in sinister, glittering silence, seemed to have damped every sound.

What would the spies and scouts of the hill-men make of it, or the Prince of Imperteng, for that matter?

"She told me," said Gareth quietly, "that she hadn't liked the idea of my regency but she was willing to learn different. After that she always treated me with respect."

So maybe even then, Jenny thought, Rocklys had begun to think of taking the throne.

"She spoke out half a dozen times in council against letting the fiefs and the free towns keep their own parliaments and maintain their ancient laws," the young Regent went on. "She said it was foolish and inefficient. But what could I have done? The Princes and Thanes acknowledge me King in part because they are allowed to *have* their own laws, to live the way their ancestors bade them live. A king can't tell his subjects—his *willing* subjects—that he knows more about how they should live than their ancestors did."

"Evidently," John said in a dry voice, "she thought you could."

"As for Caradoc," said Polycarp, long fingers toying with his stylus, "I remember him. About five years ago he came with a dozen copyists and offered me their services in repairing and replacing some of the oldest manuscripts in the library, if I'd grant them permission to make him copies as well. I always thought he was too fortunate in trade to be quite honest."

He glanced over at the King, but His Majesty had become absorbed in contemplating the gold beading around the edge of a plate that held cheeses, sweet breads, and the intricate savories of the south.

John sniffed. "Now we know where he got the fair winds and the good tides from."

"More than that," said Gareth. "In the past two years there have been enough . . . well . . . accidents . . . to shipping in the islands that a motion was made in council to revive the old laws against wizards holding property or office. Only no one knew who the wizard was." He glanced apologetically at Jenny, then went on quickly, "Tell us about your dragon-slaying machine."

John obliged him, keeping the exposition short and businesslike, as he could when need arose. "I've been working on it for owls' years," he said, when he was done. "I got the idea from somethin' in Polyborus—or was it Dotys' *Secret History?*—but most of the actual design came from Heronax of Ernine, except I used the steering cage from Cerduces Scrinus' designs for parade floats." He tapped the drawing he'd sketched in chalk on the tablecloth, surrounded by half-empty goblets.

"And I was trading with the gnomes for pieces for years and driving poor Muffle mad with all the little locks and levers that hold the thing together, so it can be took apart. It's a heavy little bastard."

Gareth and Polycarp exchanged a look. "The Lord of the Deep of Ylferdun would make us more," the Regent said, polishing his spectacles with the tablecloth. "The last thing he or any gnome wants running around loose are dragons."

Four years, Jenny thought, had sobered and quieted him. When she and John had come south two years ago, for the naming-feast of Gareth's daughter, Jenny had seen that the impulsive, sensitive boy who'd come north to beg John's help had settled into a young man well aware of his limitations and willing to ask help, deferring lovingly to the shadow of the warrior king his father had been and granting him every show of royalty and state.

Gareth settled his spectacles back on his nose. "How long do we have, would you say?"

"Depends," replied John. "If Rocklys has all the dragons she wants—and they must take a twilkin' bit of fodder—then we've maybe three weeks. Maybe more, depending on how bad Ian and Yseult were hurt, and how fast Rocklys wants to march her men south. She knows we know of her, and she knows Jen and I got away. My guess is she'll gather her troops and head south as fast as she can"—his eyes narrowed and an edge crept into his voice—"and bugger the bandits and the Iceriders that'll strike the new settlements."

He averted his face to hide his quick anger, but Jenny saw the sudden fisting of his hand, and how his mouth hardened and thinned. Between them, King Uriens had slipped into a doze again.

"I'm sorry," Gareth said quietly. "I'm sorry about this." He straightened the plate and the crumbs before him with embarrassed care, trying not to meet John's eyes. "She . . ."

John shook his head quickly. "She was the best thing going, son, and you'd no reason to doubt she'd keep her trust," he said. "And she's a damn fine commander. I suppose the things that made her good are the very ones that turned her against you: the need to see everything done the way she feels is right. And not hearing excuses for why it can't be done the quickest way. But I tell you," he went on, "and I know, because I've tried doin' both: You can't be a commander and a ruler at the same time. You need to see different things and be two different people. Maybe more. Rocklys would have found that out if she'd ever gotten to try, which we'll make bloody sure she doesn't."

"My lord . . ." A soldier-servant appeared in the doorway of the tent, barely sketching a salaam in the direction of the dozing King. The open flap let through the chill scent of the forest beyond the wooden palisade, and the sound of the River Wildspae roaring through the arches of Cor's Bridge. "My lord, the men are asking all sorts of questions about the . . . the dragon." He lowered his voice as if he feared that Morkeleb might hear, and of course, thought Jenny, he could. The man's mistake was in thinking the star-drake would care.

"They don't like it a bit, and that's a fact, my lord. They say there's witchery in it." He glanced at the King and then at Jenny, and Jenny could almost hear him remembering Uriens a few years before, in his warlike prime. Before the sorceress Zyerne.

"Well, it's good to know your men are up on the obvious, anyway," John said. "You'd better be damn glad that dragon's there, son," he added, addressing the soldier. "And if you'll excuse my sayin' so"—he glanced at Gareth, who nodded, bidding him continue—"if you'll excuse my sayin' so, you're gonna be a whole lot gladder in about three weeks."

17

It was agreed that John would ride east with Polycarp and a small guard to Halnath Citadel, leaving Jenny with Gareth. Rocklys had spoken of the camp as lying "before the walls of Jotham," but Jotham lay in fact in the rough country where the Trammel Fells butted up against Nast Wall. It was impossible to make a camp closer than two miles from the city's gate and thus impossible, too, to mount an effective siege. Here in the flats beside the River Wildspae forage parties had little defense against the tough fell-men and mountaineers who slipped through the forest. Cor's Bridge commanded the road to Belmarie in the south, whence came the army's supplies, and that was something. Now, too, the guards watched the road that led from the north.

The Wildspae was deep here and dangerous. It grew wider farther west, so Rocklys would have to come through here.

Morkeleb remained close, but displayed a surprising facility for being unnoticed. There were times when Jenny, speaking to the servants in the kitchens or the soldiers who worked frantically to dig underground shelters against the coming of dragons, realized that people didn't even remember that he was there.

Does this surprise you, Wizard-woman? The dragon stretched himself along the ridge that shouldered against the camp's eastern wall. Caves were everywhere in these limestone foothills, and without altering his size Morkeleb seemed able to fit, as a rat can, through crevices barely a quarter his apparent girth. The dragon would simply appear among the clumps of hemlock and maple, shake out his mane and resettle his wings.

We are travelers, we star-drakes. When we come to a place where none of us has been before nor glimpsed even in our dreams, we conceal ourselves in the strongest places we can. There we breathe, and sleep, and cast forth our dreams around about us, drinking in the air until it tells us what creatures walk the stones and ride the winds. There are worse beings than dragons in existence—and behind the worst, creatures even more terrible than they.

And his mind brought not only words but images to hers, images that she could little understand: landscapes of black stone under red and swollen suns; worlds of thick, rank mist whose cold carried over thought, where shambling dreadful things roved half unseen among glaciers of purplish ice. She turned her eyes from the digging and building in the camp below and asked him, *Morkeleb, where do the dragons come from?*

And he only said, *Far away.*

Far away. A hole in her awareness of how the world was constituted, infinities of darkness she had never suspected, unimaginable corridors stretching into the night sky and beyond.

Dragons from stars in an empty sky.

Far away.

Is there magic there? she asked. She sat against his shoulder, feeling the heat of him through the enameled iron of his scales. It was unlike the warmth of any other creature, a glowing sense of power. *The place you come from, and all those places that lie between?*

Ah, Wizard-woman, he said, *there is magic everywhere. It breathes from the ground like dew. We drink it; we wrap ourselves in it as if it were a blanket of music; it is of us.*

And having once been a dragon, Jenny understood. And for a moment she ached with the ache of wanting power, power to wield the magic that she knew was abroad in the world. *If I had only been strong enough,* she thought, *Ian would be safe.*

From this hill also they sometimes saw the woodmen or the fell-dwellers in their green jackets and baggy striped trousers, sliding silently through the trees to observe the camp by the river. They were little dark men with thick black hair, and their ancestors had held these fastnesses from time immemorial against the fair-haired race of Belmarie. Twice Jenny watched them attack the men who labored to strengthen the fortifications on Cor's Bridge itself or the redoubts that were being raised to dominate the road beside it; twice saw the warriors of Bel stream from the main camp's gates crying, "Uwanë, Uwanë for Bel!"

The second time, Jenny slipped into the camp as soon as the fighting ceased and made her way to the Regent's tent, knowing that she'd find him curled up on his bed, shaking and sick.

"Were there any way of dealing with them other than subjugation, believe me, I'd try it no matter what Father says—or said—about the honor of the Realm." Gareth dragged in his breath in a shaky sigh and ran a hand through his fair hair—the dyed pink and blue lovelocks thinned almost to nothing and pointy with sweat. Thanks to John's teaching, the young man was capable now of leading men into battle, though he took care to appoint able officers and to stick close to them and to their advice.

"I take it they're less than pleasant neighbors?" Jenny fetched a basin of hot water from the pavilion's outer chamber. She'd seen the King in the battle also, leading the soldiers with a ferocity startling to one used to seeing him as only a smiling elderly man.

He was the Lord of the House of Uwanë, raised to war; Gareth had only to tell him which way to ride. The men followed him gladly, crying out his name, and told themselves afterward that he was himself again or nearly so.

Gareth shook his head. The greenish pallor was fading a little from his cheeks. "There's always border raiding going on," he said. "Prince Tinán claims his lands stretch all the way down to Choggin, though they never were farmed by anybody before our people started to settle there. It's been owned by the Thanes of Choggin and their people for more generations than you can count. And of course now everything's complicated by blood-feuds. No, just the tunic," he added, as Jenny brought fresh clothing from the press. "And the mantlings—those green ones—and the hood. I have to change and get out there for the victory celebration."

"That was victory?" It had not had the look of victory to her.

"We have to call it one." Gareth pulled off his tunic, spattered with gore, and reached for the fresh one. He flinched as he handled the soiled cloth, fingers avoiding the blood. "Thank you," he added, as she gave him a cloth to wash with. "Dear King of the Gods, I wish I didn't have to do this. I wish I could just . . . just lie down." He swallowed hard. "Father's the Pontifex of the Realm, but I have to be there because he forgets. And truly, if there isn't some show of strength against them, the fell-men only push harder. It isn't . . ."

He hesitated, his thin height drooping over her, gray eyes blinking nakedly, for it does not do for a commander to appear in spectacles before the assembled armies of his Realm. His shoulders, under the purple wool of the tunic, had lost some of the weediness Jenny had first known, and his arms had strengthened from diligent sword practice, but there was a terrible sadness in his face. "I wish it wasn't like this," he said softly. Then he turned away and made a business of fastening his sword-belt, stamped in gold and set with cabochon emeralds; of adjusting the elaborately dagged and ribboned mantlings that spread like a butterfly's plumage over his back and made his shoulders seem wider. "I wish it was all as easy as it was when we only had to defeat and drive out a dragon. Like all the ballads, about Alkmar and the other heroes of old. I wish . . ."

He half-turned back to her, gloves of bullion and velvet and agate in his hands, and she saw what he wished in the weary grief of his eyes. She smiled, as she would have smiled at Ian, encouraging him to go on when the road was difficult.

"I'm glad you're here." He put his arm around her again in a bony hug. "I've missed you."

But as Gareth passed through the tent doorway for the procession to the altar of the Red God of War, Jenny sat on the bed again, the memory of her son piercing her heart.

He was alive. Trapped in a jewel, as this boy was trapped in the gem of kingship, his will no longer his own.

She pressed her hand to her mouth to stop her tears.

"Shall I bring you gold?" she asked Morkeleb later. She lay against the curve of the dragon's foreleg, a harp she had borrowed from Gareth resting on her shoulder. In its music, and in the magics the star-drake had shown her, she was able for a time to rest from the nightmare of Ian's enslavement, to put from her mind Caradoc's grim little smile as he thrust the jewel into the strangling Icewitch's mouth. "There is gold in the camp. I can get Gareth to contribute a few golden plates and cups, so you can have the music of the gold."

I am aware, said Morkeleb's dark slow voice above her, *of the gold in the camp, Wizard-woman.* He arched his long neck, and the night-breeze that trailed down from Nast Wall stirred the gleaming ribbons of his mane. *There are days when I am aware of little else. I saw what gold could do to me four years ago, when the sorceress Zyerne trapped me through the gold in the gnomes' deep. Sometimes it seems to me that if I accept even a cup or a chain, or a single coin, the longing for gold would conquer me, and I would not stop until I had devastated these lands.*

The glowing bobs of his antennae drew fireflies from the twilight woods, and the voice that spoke in her mind had a strangeness to it, as a man's would have, did that man grope for words. But Morkeleb never groped for words.

Gold laces the rocks of the Skerries of Light, Wizard-woman. Those of us who dwell there breathe our magic into that gold and bask and revel in the wonder that chimes forth. As we travel from world to world, gold is not the only thing we seek, but it is one of the things. When we come to a place that has gold, we remain a long while.

On the Last Isle, there is no gold. I find that I think differently away from its presence, and meditations become possible to me that were not even conceivable before. This was something that the Shadow-drakes told me, years ago. They said that to become one of them one must put gold aside. I did not see why it was necessary that I should, and so I did not. But after Zyerne and the Stone in the heart of Ylferdun Deep made me a slave, I thought again.

He fell silent, the run of his thoughts sinking down below words, like the heartbeat of the sea.

Finally he said, *The Shadow-drakes said also that they gave up their magic, as well as gold. This I do not understand. Magic IS the thing of dragons. Without magic, what would I be?*

Each night, and many times during each day, Jenny scried for sight of John. Frequently she saw him in the great library of Halnath, a maze of chambers and shelves that had been a temple of the Gray God lifetimes ago. Sometimes she saw the Dragonsbane with the Master of Halnath in the Master's private study, a round chamber whose walls were lined with books and with lamps of pierced work, scrolls and tablets and books and bundles of pages spread out between them on the table. But sometimes, late in the night, she saw him alone, sitting on the floor, surrounded by volumes or scattered handfuls of notes in unreadable old courthand. Candles stood fixed in winding-sheets of drippings on the shelves or the floor, their light outlining his gleaming spectacles and making shadows in the quiet set of his mouth. Once she saw him press thumb and forefinger to the sides of his beaky nose, eyes closed and face still, as if even in solitude he would show no one what he felt.

In the daytimes more often John and the Master were with the gnomes of Ylferdun Deep, who had for centuries maintained close ties with the Master and the university. Occasionally these glimpses were fragmented or obscured by scry-wards, for the exquisite stone chambers in the Deep of Ylferdun were guarded like those of Tralchet. She recognized Balgub, Sevacandrozardus the Lord of the Deep of Ylferdun; and others, too, of the gnome-kind, engineers by the way they looked at the drawings and diagrams John unrolled before them. They shook their heads and fingered their heavy, polished stone jewelry, and John hurled his diagram on the floor and stormed from the room. Later, she saw him half-naked and covered with grime in a deserted courtyard of Halnath Citadel, checking over the metal shell of a half-built Urchin. So they must, she thought, have come to a compromise. They guarded alloys and engines and secrets jealously, but dragons were dragons.

One of the engineers was with him now, a tiny gnome-wife whose vast cloud of smoke-green hair was pinned up in spikes tipped with opal and sardonyx. She pointed out something in the coldly glittering engine and touched a crank. John shook his head. He asked about something, and held up his fingers to demonstrate an item the size of a gull's egg. A hothwais, Jenny guessed, charged with some form of energy. The engineer glanced at the two gnomes with them—lords of high rank, whose jewels were even more ostentatious than hers—and all shook their heads again.

John gave up, disgusted, and climbed into the interlocking double wheels of the steering cage. He hooked his feet into position and grasped the steering bars, and said something, gesturing, to the gnomes. The engineer patted the air reassuringly with her little white hands.

John yanked off the brake.

If it was power John was concerned about, he could rest easy on that score. The Urchin, which had a dozen small wheels instead of the four of the original design, leaped away like a racehorse from the starting-post, John clinging to the steering-bars with an expression of startled horror and the gnomes racing behind.

John caught at a lever. By the way it simply gave, Jenny guessed at a serious design flaw. The Urchin whirled like a mad bull for the courtyard wall, and John twisted at the steering bars, sending it smashing into the gate instead. The gate crashed open in splintering gusts of wood; the Urchin rolled down the ramp beyond into the dairy yard, milkmaids and cows and chickens scattering in all directions. It crashed through the wooden water trough, hit a dropped dung fork just right, and sent it pinwheeling through the air; John flung his weight against the steering cage in time to avoid a barrow full of milk buckets and then, with the Urchin headed full-bore for the dairy-house itself, wrenched the cage with all his strength as if to turn.

The Urchin rolled, flipped up on its back with its twelve wheels spinning crazily in the air, and slid into the midden piles, with John hanging upside-down in the cage. Even after the thing came to a stop, half-buried in dung and soiled straw, the wheels continued to churn.

John calmly unhooked his feet from the straps and turned in a slow somersault from the bent steering cage to sink knee-deep in muck. The gnomes ran up to join the ring of children, dogs, dairymaids, scullery help, and guards and the still enthusiastically whirring Urchin. John wiped the slime off his face and adjusted his spectacles.

Jenny could read his lips as he said, "You're right; works fine. Fix the brake, though."

"Which is as well," she said, when she told Morkeleb of it later. Another evening, after another day of waiting, another day of scrying landmarks to the north and finding that she still could see them, which would be impossible when Rocklys' legions approached. Though she would not use her magic against the soldiers of Imperteng—and indeed, Gareth never asked it of her—she did this for him and also laid spell-wards and guards on the new fortifications his men were building on Cor's Bridge and the dugouts.

With the coming of evening Jenny's anxiety for Ian always grew. To assuage it she had climbed the hogback ridge behind the camp and sat gazing out over the slow-slanting smoke of the cookfires into the light-drenched distance of fading woodlands and shining streams, her fingers finding almost unthinking solace in the ancient tunes summoned from Gareth's harp. Old ballads and old tears, the laments of ladies long dead for lords whose names were forgotten. Pain and sweetness rolled together like a southern candy. Darkness filled with the promise of light. In time, the dragon had come.

"Spells of some kind must be laid on the Urchins," she said at the conclusion of her tale, "if they're to withstand the magic of the demon mages. The magic of the gnomes is different from that of humankind. It may serve . . ."

It is not different. The dragon shifted his hindquarters and scratched like a dog at the cable of braided leather he had begun to wear about his body, just forward of the wings. *Different to you, yes, as an ass differs from a horse, or a chicken from a hummingbird. But to a demon they are the same. And such a demon as I think these are will breathe them aside, as a child breathes away the flame of a candle.*

Sometimes she watched the affairs of Alyn Hold through her crystal; called the images of Adric and Mag while the boy trained in weapons and the girl plagued her nurse and John's aunts half to death, slipping out to be with her friends or to rig elaborate experiments with pulleys and pendulums in the hay barns. At such times the pain was the worst, for the children were deep embedded in the pattern of her life, and it was hard to be away from them. Ian she tried and tried to see, using all the methods that Morkeleb could teach her. She knew that if she succeeded it would only hurt her worse, but still she made the attempt. Nor would she put it by with failure, but spent weary nights at it, until she fell asleep to the dawn-callings of the birds.

Then one evening she summoned John's image in the crystal and saw that he'd tied a red ribbon through the epaulet of his disreputable old doublet. She said to Gareth, "I have to go. He must have found something."

"I thought these all were burned." Polycarp of Halnath unlocked the inner door of his study, revealing a secret chamber, furnished only with a chair, a small table over which a lamp hung, and two shelves of books, each volume chained to a ring in the wall. He cast a nervous glance at Morkeleb, who had reduced himself in size and perched like a jet gargoyle on Jenny's shoulder. Morkeleb turned his snakelike head and returned his gaze: the Master quickly averted his eyes.

"I came across them in a volume of Clivy." John crossed to the table and lowered the lamp on its counterweighted chain. "Clivy's the world's prize idiot on the subject of farming and from what I read of this book he knew even less about women—it's called *Why the Female Sex Must Be Inferior to the Male*—but it was one I'd never read before. These were stuck in the middle."

Four sheets of papyrus lay on the table, tobacco-colored with age and cracked down the center where they had been folded.

"As far as I can guess from the date of the handwriting," said Polycarp, closing the door behind them, "those have to have been written by Lyth the Demon-caller. He was a priest of the Gray God here at the time of the Kin-wars. The Master at the time had him carved up alive for trafficking with demons, and all his books and notes were thrown into the same fire with the pieces. According to the catalogs that particular volume of Clivy was one of the original manuscripts in the library, so it would have been there then."

"There was any amount of dust on it," added John, and perched on a corner of the table. "No surprise, considerin'. If I had incriminating notes about me, Clivy's where I'd stick 'em."

"And did this Lyth traffic with demons?" Jenny touched a corner of the papyrus. Caerdinn had taught her three or four styles of writing, including the runes of the gnomes as they were used in Wyldoom and in Ylferdun, but the old man's own scholarship had been grievously limited. A word or two of the jagged script leaped clear to Jenny's perusal— "gate" and "key" she knew, and "erlking," a word sometimes used for the Hellspawn in the Marches. But more than those, she felt the paper itself imbued with a darkness, as if it had been in a room thick with the smoke of scorching blood.

She drew her hand back, her question answered.

"They kept the matter quiet because of the upheavals," said Polycarp. "But yes. There were two gyre-killings here in the Citadel, and two recorded during that same time in Ylferdun Deep. One of those was after Lyth was taken prisoner, but when the Master's men went through and smashed or burned everything in Lyth's house, there were no more."

"So he used something in his house as a gate," said Jenny.

"By what it says here"—John nodded to the four sheets of paper—"it seems to have been a glass ball floating in a basin of blood, though God knows what the neighbors said about the flies. Not that they'd say much to his face, I don't suppose. But he says as how there were other demon gates, and that one of 'em lay in a sea-cave on the Isle of Urrate . . ."

"Urrate?" Jenny looked up sharply. "That's the sunken island—"

"Just north of Somanthus," finished John. "Somanthus, as in where Caradoc hails from. Lyth—if it is Lyth—says that particular gate was blocked when Urrate sank in an earthquake, but it accounts for the things I saw comin' out of the sea in me dream, and out of the well in Corflyn's court. Anythin' that'd hold water could be sorcelled into a gate."

Morkeleb had crept down Jenny's arm and now crouched on his haunches on the tabletop, his head weaving above the papers like a serpent's, the diamond reflections of his antennae making firefly spots in the ochre gloom. He hissed, like a cat, and like a cat his tail moved here and there, independent of the stillness of his body.

"Sea-wights, Lyth calls them in his notes," Polycarp said. "He doesn't describe them—they weren't the things that came to him out of the glass ball and the blood. And this is the only other mention I've ever seen of the Dragons of Ernine."

"It doesn't give Isychros' name," said John. "But it says here that 'an ancient mage' enslaved dragons—no mention of wizards—by a bargain he struck with demons he summoned out from behind a mirror. But this is the most interestin' thing." He propped up his spectacles again and hunted through the manuscript. "Here we go: *Demons are ever at war with one another, for the demons of one Hell will torment and devour the demons of another Hell, even as they torment and devour men. Thus the magic of the Hellspawn can be used, one against another.*"

He looked across at Morkeleb. "Had you ever heard that before?"

I had heard it, the dark voice of the dragon murmured in Jenny's mind. *The Hellspawn seek always to find ways into this world, for the hearts and the bodies of the living are to them as gold is to dragons, the medium of an art that gives them pleasure. They drink pain, as the dragons drink the music that dwells in gold. And I had heard also that the demons of one kind can—and do—drink the pain of the demons of another kind.*

"Then that may be what the mages of Prokep did, to defeat the dragon corps. Not used human magic at all, but made a bargain with . . ."

The dragon's antennae flicked forward, and his eyes were tiny opals, terrible in the gloom.

Do not think, Songweaver, to ride to the ruins of Ernine and seek behind the mirror of Isychros. It is a bad business to have any dealings whatever with the darkling-kind. They give no help without the payment of a teind in return, and the teinds they require imperil not only those who bargain but everyone whose lives they touch.

"Ernine?" Polycarp turned his head sharply. "No one knows where Ernine lay. The records speak of it, but—"

After the fall of the city to the dragons, it was destroyed, said Morkeleb. *But later another city rose on its ruins. It was called Syn after the god that was worshiped there.*

"Syn? You mean Sine, the ruins where the Gelspring runs out of the hills?" Eagerness charged the Master's voice. "That was Ernine? You're sure?"

Morkeleb swung his head around, and again Polycarp had to look aside quickly, lest he meet the dragon's eyes. Jenny saw the ember-glare of Morkeleb's nostrils and felt the heat of his anger pass like desert wind through her mind. *This is what comes,* said the dragon, *of making myself the size of a ratting dog; grubs whose memories barely compass a single round of the moon's long dance with the sun ask if I am sure of cities that I saw founded, and laid waste, and founded and laid waste again. Pah!*

Thoroughly embarrassed, Polycarp apologized, but Jenny barely heard. She had barely heard anything, beyond the words *the magic of the Hellspawn can be used, one against another.* Her breathing seemed to her to have stilled, and her heart turned cold in her chest.

Ian.

Quietly, John laid a hand on her arm. His voice was a murmur in her ear. "He's right, love."

She looked up at him quickly.

"Whatever we do to deal with Caradoc and his wrigglies, playin' one tribe of demons off against another will only make it worse, for us and for everyone who comes after."

She looked aside. "I know."

But through supper and into the night, reading the scrolls and tablets and books of the library of Halnath, she could not dismiss those words from her mind, nor the thought of Ian, a prisoner in his own body and in a sapphire in Caradoc's strongbox. When she slept, the thought of him, the image of him, followed her down into her dreams.

18

In her dreams Jenny came to Ernine, the yellow city where the Gel-spring ran out of the mountains, where orchards flowered in the fertile lands of the river's loop. In her dreams she saw it as it was in the time of the mage Isychros and the heroes Alkmar the Godborn and Öontes of the singing lyre. She passed through the market that lay before the citadel hill and climbed the curved path to the palace of sandstone and marble, where the Queen's ladies with their gold-braided hair wove cloth among the pillars.

It seemed to her that someone who walked at her heels asked her, "Did you ever wonder who this Isychros was, Pretty Lady? Where he lived, and what kind of a man he was? He was a prince of the royal house, you know. And his eyes were like bright emeralds that catch the sun."

When she turned to see who spoke there was no one there. Nevertheless, as she hurried on, Jenny felt a hand brush her arm.

She was afraid then and wanted John. But John lay asleep beside her, far away in their borrowed bed in Halnath Citadel, and she was here in Ernine, a thousand years ago, alone.

She passed down shallow steps and saw the plastered stone blocks of the walls give way to the raw hill's bones. Gazelles were painted on the plaster, the big black Royal gazelles with six-foot back-curving horns, the kind that were never seen close to Nast Wall anymore. Somehow she knew that herds of them roved within a few miles of the city walls. Close by, someone played the harp, a gentle tune that made her want to weep. As the hotness welled behind her eyes she heard a soft chuckle behind her, laughter at her weakness, and something more. She put the tears away.

A corridor was cut in the rock, constellations painted on its ceiling. A comet hung among the stars, trailing its harlot's hair. Curtains covered the corridor's entrance, and others blocked it a few feet farther on; still more covered the door at the end, layer on layer. The round chamber beyond was draped with them, all save the ceiling, where the night sky again was painted, and the comet, brighter and colder than before.

The mirror was in the chamber. It was bigger than she'd thought it would be, five feet tall at least. It was wrought of the curious blue-pink opaline glass that one found in the oldest ruins of cities in the south, and what it was backed with she did not know. Whatever it was, it seemed to burn through the glass, so threads of steam rose from the surface, though when she came near there was no feeling of heat. The mirror's sides were framed in soapy-looking silver-gray metal—it had a disturbing sheen in the dark. Curves and angles drew the eye in an unfamiliar fashion, as if to darkness previously unseen.

The flamelets of the bronze lamp that hung from the ceiling's center doubled in the burning depths. Beneath them she saw reflected the table under the lamp, and the chair that faced the mirror across the table, and Jenny herself in her borrowed red and blue dress. Though she heard the chuckle of laughter again, close to her ear, the mirror reflected no one else.

But someone said—or she thought someone said—*Put out the lamps, Jenny. You know mirrors turn back light and blind those who look in them to all but themselves and what they think they know.*

She reached with her mind and put out the lamps.

Then she saw, in the darkness, what crowded against the glass on the other side. Watching, and smiling, and knowing her name.

She awoke screaming, or trying to scream, muffled incoherent whimpers, and John shook her, pulled her out of her terror and her dreams. She clung to him in the darkness, smelling the comforting scent of his bare flesh and hearing his voice say softly, over and over, "It's all right, Jen. It's all right," as his hand stroked her cheek.

But she knew that it wasn't all right.

In the morning, after scrying deep and long in crystal, water, wind, and smoke for any sign of Rocklys' army advancing beyond the Wildspae, she flew with Morkeleb south to the Seven Islands. Because they passed over the heart of the Realm, Jenny cloaked herself and the dragon in spells of inconspicuousness, something humans were better at than dragons; Gareth had problems enough. In the Wildspae Valley, and the green lands of Belmarie, where the Wildspae and the Clae joined, the farms were rich and the harvest ripening, and Jenny compared them to the Winterlands with bitterness in her heart. Then they passed over the sea to the six fertile islands that constituted the greatest wealth of the Realm, and the spine of gray rocks that marked what had been Urrate.

Morkeleb lighted among the broken pillars of a shrine, all that was left of Urrate's acropolis. Waves crashed barely a dozen yards below. Seabirds wheeled and yarked about their heads, and perched again on the lichen-cloaked shoulders of the Great God's statue. Poppies and sea grass swayed in the wind. Jenny could see the gleam of marble for some distance under the dark of the sea, white as old bones.

The dragon rocked on his tall haunches, swaying his head back and forth above the waves, balancing with wings and tail. Jenny kicked her feet free of the cable around his body, slid from his back, and settled herself in the chill sunlight. She closed her eyes, listening with the deep perceptions of the dragon-mind beneath the surge of the waters. Feeling, scenting, following Morkeleb's mind deeper and deeper, among the waving leathery kelp forests and the shards of the city's drowned temples and walls. Scenting for the stink of infection.

But there was nothing. Above her she heard Morkeleb singing, stretching luminous blue music into the abyss where the sunshafts faded, and in time she heard music answer him. Pipings and hoonings, deep echoing throbs. With Morkeleb's mind she saw shapes rising, black-backed, white-bellied, wise ancient eyes glittering in pockets of leathery flesh. Great fins stroked the water, guiding as Morkeleb used his wings to guide; great tails that could smash a boat thrust and drove. They all breached at once, fourteen slate-dark backs curving out of the sea, fourteen plumes of steam blown glittering in the sun. Then they rested on the surface, rolling a little, loving the warmth after the cold currents below, perhaps thirty feet from the rocks where the dragon sat, and the eldest of them asked Morkeleb why he had called.

Demons—Morkeleb framed them in his mind. Jenny, watching and listening, absorbed the images and the way the black dragon arranged them: different, very different from the dark voice that spoke to her in her mind. Long slow images of ugliness and hate, of bitter green magic like poison spreading in the water. Sickness, pain, blindness, death. Soul-drowning as a trapped porpoise drowns among the deep kelp. Dark rocks far down under the isle? Heat without light? Steam pulsing out into the sea?

The calves of the abyss replied. Not on Urrate but under Somanthus, far down where the western side of the isle fell away into a great deep: There was the burning gate. Dreams of wisdom for the taking. Dreams of power to summon at will the great warm shrimp-tides, and promise of new stories to tell, rich new songs beautiful and strange. Dreams rising to the men of Somanthus. A man used to walk on the shore to study the waves, or to learn the ways of the dolphins, or with a little sky-tube gaze at the stars. The whalemage Squidslayer did not know what to do, but it was clear, he said, that something must be done, lest greater ill befall.

Will you come, Wizard-woman, and see these things?

She surrounded herself with a Summoning of Air and clung to the leather cable around his body as he slid from the rocks. The water was colder than she'd expected. Her hair floated behind her like the kelp, and the whalemages surrounded them, not ponderous at all in their element but weightless as milkweed and swift as birds. They passed through the avenues of the sunken city, where weeds reached up through windows of toppled houses and the marble door-guardians gazed sadly through masks of barnacles and snails. The deeps beyond were icy, and very dark.

They did not go too near the abyss where the demons dwelled. Jenny could smell them nevertheless, feel them through the water, and her flesh crept on her bones with loathing and terror. Far down the endless cliff-face a kind of greenish light played around the rocks. On rock-ledges all the way down she could see the little glass shells that the sea-wights shed, and she thought she could see things moving, bloated and spiky, very different from the shapes they took in the upper world.

Chewing through the rocks, she heard Squidslayer's thoughts in her mind, like slow silvery bubbles. *All the underpinnings of Urrate, cut, eroded, dissolved. Years on years on years. Island falling, shutting dark within. Vast ecstatic sobbing of sea-wights at the deaths.*

And Jenny felt its echo, through the whalemages' minds, the thunderclap of pleasure at devouring such terror and pain.

Morkeleb turned beneath her like an eel. Surrounded by the whales they gained the surface again, and the wind dried her clothing as they flew through gathering dusk to Jotham. Neither spoke. That night Jenny dreamed again of the vault below ruined Ernine, seeing the things that watched from the other side of the burning mirror. Waking alone and cold with sweat in her little tent, she rose and climbed the hill behind the camp in the warm summer darkness, until against the blue-black sky a blacker shape loomed. She lay down between his great claws and slept, and the dreams of the things behind the mirror left her in peace.

John came into camp two mornings later, driving a flatbed wagon drawn by ten mules with the first two Urchins. He was accompanied by the little green-haired engineer Jenny had seen in her scrying-stone—Miss Tee was her name among humankind—and by the gnome-witch Taseldwyn, called Miss Mab among men. Gareth's treasurer, Ector of Sindestray, accompanied them, bearing documents any courier could have delivered, and also a very young warrior of Polycarp's guard who'd been trained, more or less, to operate an Urchin.

From the edges of the woods the warriors of Imperteng watched with suspicion as John and Miss Tee and Elayne the Halnath guard demonstrated the Urchins to Gareth. *Probably still believing,* Jenny thought, *that these things concern them.* The horses snorted and pulled at their tethers as the squat, spiked oval whirred and clicked around the parade ground, firing harpoons in all directions: Gareth flinched and ducked down beside Jenny in the shelter of the heavily fortified earthwork, then emerged to touch the tip of the harpoon. It had pierced two layers of target planking, thicker than the length of Jenny's finger.

"Ingenious, of course," approved Lord Ector temperately, "but expensive." He was a small man, stout and dark, and younger than his defeated hairline led one to think at first, and he wore a courtier's blue and white mantlings even in the camp's dirt. There was about him, though, none of Gareth's air of loving display for its own foolish gorgeousness. He was one, thought Jenny, who sought by the courtier's garb to establish birth and rights beyond all possible questionings of lesser men.

"Cheap at the price, though." John swung himself out of the Urchin's hatch and slithered rather gingerly to the ground among the spikes. "Long as we can keep the things wound, we're fine." After him came the young Halnath archer. At Polycarp's suggestion, the Urchins had been made large enough to accommodate a second person, both to fire the harpoons and, if necessary, to crank the engine. "And you can just hike the taxes on the Winterlands a little higher for 'em, can't you?" he added maliciously and flicked Ector's mantlings.

Ector glared.

"We have people working on poisons for the harpoons," said Gareth rather quickly, nodding back toward the camp. "I've sent two messages to Prince Tinán, warning him about an attack by wizards and dragons, and offering a truce in exchange for help, but I've heard nothing."

"Stubborn bumpkins," said Ector.

"Have they been lured into traps before?" John smote the dust from his patched sleeves, and the Thane of Sindestray fanned irritably at the billowing dirt with a circle of stiffened silk. "You have to admit that with garrisons from everyplace in the Realm on the march for here, professions of friendship don't have much of a true ring."

"It wasn't me who went back on the last truce," blurted Gareth, flushing. "That was—"

"And it wasn't Tinán, probably, who burned out the farms that got his dad killed," John pointed out. "In my experience, anyway, that's how these things work, son. Jen," he went on, "can you and Mab lay death-spells on that many harpoons?"

Jenny nodded, cringing inside at the thought.

Like Gareth, she thought—like Ian, like John—she, too, was trapped in this jewel of necessity.

She drew a deep breath. "This morning when I scried the fords of the Catrack River I saw nothing: fog, broken images, the woods ten miles away. They are close. And she'll send the dragons ahead." Ector looked skyward as if expecting to see it filled with fire-spitting foes.

"You'd better send for all the Urchins Polycarp has in readiness."

While Gareth dealt patiently with the council's messages, Jenny drew circles of power around the Urchins themselves in the parade ground, under the distrustful and disapproving eye of the troops. She summoned what power she could from the earth, and from the pattern of the waters below—from river's currents and the exact combinations of rocks in the hills—from the turning of the unseen stars. These spells she imbued meticulously in the stubby little machines. Her spells of human and dragon power she braided with the gnomish wyrds of Miss Mab, both on the machines themselves and then on the fierce barbed points of the poisoned harpoons.

"I always hate the death-spells," said Jenny, straightening her aching back and brushing aside the tendrils of her hair. Sunset turned the air to copper around them and the poison smoke burned her nostrils; the anger of the sullen soldiers who brought up wood for that endless boiling muttered at the back of her mind like the pull of an unseen stream. "And it seems like the older I get the more I hate them. And yet"—she gestured wearily at the pile of iron bolts—"and yet here I am working them again."

Her hands trembled as she spoke. She had returned twice in the last hour to the sanded flat behind Gareth's dugout to remake her own circles of power and draw into herself, and into her spells, more of the strength and magic she needed. Mab had worked her magic all afternoon without pause. Jenny couldn't imagine how she was doing it.

The gnome-witch, seated on a firkin, tilted her head a little, looking up at the woman with one round hand shading her pale-blue eyes. "It is because thou lovest," she said simply. Her hand was smaller even than Jenny's, smaller than Adric's, but thick and heavy as a miner's. Both women had shed all jewelry, braided up their long hair, and changed for the work into coarse linsey-woolsey shifts that could afterward be burned. Beneath the hem the gnome-woman's bare dangling feet were like lumps of muscled rock.

"The more years thou see, the greater grows thy love: for this John, for thy children, for Gareth; for thy sister and her family and for all the world. And as thy love grows, so grows it for every woman and man, for gnomes and whales and mice and even for the dragons." Miss Mab set aside the harpoon she had held on her knees and reached for another. They were stacked all around the two women like corn, tips and edges black with the sludge of the poison dip.

Jenny's voice was unsteady, remembering John between walls of fire, the black horn bow steady in his hands. Aiming at their son. "Is there another way?"

Mab's wide mouth flexed in what might have been a smile. "Child, there is," she said. "But not for a woman of bare five-and-forty, standing at this crossroad. Time is long," she said. "Love is long." And looking up, she smiled and waved as John strode across the sanded death-field in his shirtsleeves, a clay pot of lemonade in his hands.

The dragons dropped from the sky in the dead of the night.

Knowing that mages and dragons both could see in darkness, Gareth kept the men standing to in shifts through the night. Bending sweat-soaked over the reeking harpoons, Jenny heard in the dark of her mind Morkeleb's voice: *Wizard-woman, they come,* and a moment later saw the black soaring shape of him against the stars.

"They're coming," she said, her tone perfectly calm. Miss Mab looked up. Jenny was already turning to the nearest wood-bearer. "They're coming. The dragons. Now. Tell His Highness to alert the camp."

The boy stared at her, openmouthed. "What?"

"Tell His Highness—*now.* I'm going up."

"What?" Then he swung around, fist to his mouth in shock and horror, "Beard of Grond!"

Morkeleb hung, a nightmare of firelit bones, above the smoke-wreaths.

"Uwanë!" The young soldier snatched at the nearest harpoon—Mab yanked it impatiently out of his hand.

"Not that dragon!"

"Get His Highness!" repeated Jenny and gave the youth a shove. "Now! Run!"

Wordlessly Mab gave her the harpoon and caught up two others in a leather sling. Men were already running about, crying and snatching up weapons; the cry of "Dragons! Dragons!" and *"Uwanë!"* fractured the black air. At least, thought Jenny, Morkeleb's appearance would rouse the camp.

Then the dark claw reached from the darkness, closed around her waist.

See, to the northeast, said Morkeleb as they rose, and the hot circle of smoke and fire around the cauldrons shrank to the red heart of a burning flower, ringed with circles of tinier lights. *Along the rim of the Wall.*

And Jenny saw.

There were seven of them, seven dragons, hugging close to the shape of the mountains, taking advantage of shadows. With the far clear sight of the dragons she saw them, even in darkness knowing their colors and the music of their names: Centhwevir blue and golden, Nymr blue upon blue, Enismirdal yellow as buttercups, Hagginarshildim green and pink. The other three were too young to have their names in the lists, but she recognized the white and crimson jere-drake Bliaud had ridden to attack the camp in the Wyrwoods. The other two, younger still, were marked by gorgeous rainbow hues, not yet having begun to shape and alter the colors of their scales to chime with the inner music of their hearts. It seemed to her, even miles away, that she could see their eyes, and their eyes were dark, like filmed and broken glass.

Ian was riding Nymr. The knowledge went through her heart like a spear.

Do not think the boy on the Blue One's back is your son, Wizard-woman, said Morkeleb. *It is only a demon that wears his flesh.*

If the house is burned, said Jenny, with her harpoon resting upright on her thigh and the other two heavy on her shoulder, *the traveler will have no home to return to.*

There was no time for further words or further thought. She locked her mind and heart together with the dragon's, fusing the iron and the gold of their joined powers, and so fused, they attacked.

Jenny flung about them both the spells of concealment, of remaining unnoticed and unseen. But Centhwevir and the others split and fell upon Morkeleb from all directions, clearly able to see. The young fry hung back—Jenny wondered what wizard Rocklys had found to give to Caradoc as the seventh rider—letting the larger and stronger drakes, Centhwevir, Nymr, and Enismirdal, take on Morkeleb. Centhwevir was larger than the black dragon, but Morkeleb much the swifter and more agile. Morkeleb spat fire at the riders, forcing the star-drakes to back and veer to protect them, himself looping and diving to rip and tear at their underbellies, where no spikes protected the shining scales.

Clinging among the spikes herself with her feet hooked through the leather cable, burned by the acid of the other dragons, Jenny watched and waited, drawing power around herself and trying to use it as a shield and a blind. But every spell of evasion and concealment she used slid away like water, as if she only threw handfuls of leaves and dirt at the other dragons. Through Morkeleb's eyes she saw the dragons fragment into whirling flames of color, arcs of burning motion that were now here, now there, impossible to see. With Jenny concentrating, drawing on all her power, she resolved them now and then into their true shapes, allowing Morkeleb to attack, but he was only fending them off and falling back.

Behind them, below them, the camp was arming. Men's voices cried
out, tiny as insects' on the walls. How long had it been? And how long
would they need? Time dissolved and fractured, whirled like the attacking dragons.

And she felt in her mind, gripping and scratching, the strange wailing
strength of the sea-wights, drawing at her, tearing at her thoughts. Wanting her. Knowing her.

And the worst of it was that in the depths of her bones, she knew
them, too.

She called on her power, summoning it from her heart and marrow-
bones. But the magic only seemed to feed that need, and the demon songs
grew all the sweeter, waves of sleepy strength. Brilliant wings sheared out
of the blackness, claws raked down. Once she saw a pink dripping mouth
snatching at her and thrust a harpoon into it with all her strength, but as if
a veil dropped over her head she did not see whether she wounded the
dragon or not. She only knew she was still alive afterward, and the harpoon gone from her hand.

The camp was under them. Fire and men shouting, arrows flying up,
falling back spent. Her mind burned with the effort of calling up power,
drawing on her own strength, on Morkeleb's strength, all the magic of
their joined souls a wall of holed and acid-eaten bronze. The world swung
sickeningly, and she clutched tight at the cable. Wheeling stars, smoke
and the reek of death-spells biting at her lungs. She glimpsed the Urchins
below, saw their harpoons slam upward as the dragons descended on the
camp—saw by the way the harpoons went that the men inside the
machines struggled too against demon-glamors and spells of ruin.

Blue on blue, drenched and dyed with firelight, firelight reflected in
dead golden eyes. Wings hammering, claws descending, then the still
white face, black hair like her own flying, blue dead eyes in which a single frantic spark remained.

His heart was locked in the dragon's heart, his mind in the dragon's
mind. And with her dragon mind Jenny called out to him, *Ian!* Desperately willing that he hear. *Ian!*

And like hooks in her mind she felt the demons catch her. Through
all her wardings, through all her defenses, as if they had not been there.
Like nothing she had expected, nothing she had prepared for even in her
craziest dreams, a power sourced from something she did not understand.
Like nothing she had ever heard spoken of.

As love had been.

That was what they never told you about demons.

In her flesh. In her mind. Drinking her magic and Morkeleb's magic
like maniac glutting swine. Without pain.

No one had ever told her, no account had ever hinted, how deep the pleasure of it went. How utterly right it felt.

Somewhere she heard Morkeleb cry, *Let go! Jenny, let go!*

And she felt his magic vanish. It dissolved and dispersed like smoke, leaving him defenseless—*Without my magic,* he had asked, *what am I?* As the magic swirled away it was as if he turned first to smoke and glass, and then winked utterly from sight.

She cried out again, *Ian!* Reached with all her magic, all her strength, all her will. Trying to grasp and hold the boy's mind and drag it to her, to safety.

And the demons inhaled her strength like smoke, swallowing it away. The last thing she heard with her own thoughts was their laughter.

Pretty Lady, he said. *I am Amayon.* And he possessed her, in spite of herself, for there was nothing that she could touch or thrust from her. Those who saw her later described the rips and scratches where she had tried to gouge and dig the thing she felt spreading through her flesh, but of course she could not. She could no more excise it thus than she could have picked one drop of her blood away from another drop. It was a heat devouring her. All she knew was that flame overwhelmed her body as if she burned with fever, and when the flame reached a certain hotness, silvery explosions of what she could not identify as either pleasure or pain: the intensity of sensation on that borderline where the two fuse. And Amayon, like the odor of brimstone and lilies.

She was aware, later, of being with Ian, beside him with the wind slashing and streaming through her hair. She felt wild and light and mad, like the young girl she had never truly been allowed to be, watching hilariously as men below poured out of a burning bunker. The white and scarlet dragon Yrsgendl slashed at them with his iron-spiked tail as they stumbled and fell. One of the spiny Urchins raced and trundled toward the dragon, firing its harpoons, silly as a toy. The air seemed colored to Jenny's eyes, rich greens and purples, luminous, everything edged with colored flame. She could see her own spells woven around the Urchin, a net of dancing light. Pain rose from below, a shiveringly glorious song: music and warmth and love and well-being and power, heady beyond any joy she had ever known.

"I'll bet they'd run if we pulled those spells away," she laughed, and Ian joined in her laughter. His eyes were no longer dead, but aglow with lively fire, more alive than she'd ever seen him before. She sensed his forgiveness for all the years of her neglect, sensed his admiration, his approval, his love.

"How about it, Nymr?" he called down to the dragon, and the

dragon—both were mounted on the same one, Jenny didn't remember how—stooped like a falcon. Snatching away the net of spells was as easy, and as fun, as whipping a string away from a cat. The gnome-wardings tangled in the spellwork raveled away as well, and with a whoop of glee Bliaud—or Bliaud's demon, mounted on Yrsgendl—tossed a Word of Heat at the lumbering machine.

It lurched to a stop, whirled, and rocked comically as smoke poured from every vent and crack. Jenny, clinging to her son's shoulders, hooted with laughter, mirth that was echoed from the others: Bliaud, Yseult, Werecat, and Summer . . . A man tried to get out, and Yseult drove Hagginarshildim in close, spitting fire at him as he was caught in the hatch. It was like tormenting a snail, distant and ridiculous in its futile tininess: "Whoa, that'll cook his cockles for him!" whooped Ian, and Jenny laughed until she ached. Firelight flashed on the man's harpoon-tip and spectacles as he struggled to get free.

The second Urchin was flipped on its side, wheels spinning helplessly. Enismirdal and Centhwevir had ripped the earthen roofs from the bunkers, the men inside churning about like maggots doused in salt, terror and agony billowing up like the bouquet of a summer garden. Laughing, calling out to one another, the raiders spiraled upward into the night, gaudy leaves borne by the updraft of fire.

"We'll be back!" yelled Yseult, at the confusion of the camp. "Don't go anywhere!"

And pleasure washed over Jenny, deep caressing waves that penetrated the most secret caves of her body and her mind: contentment, belonging, the promise of reward and the drunken hilarity of power. Power and pain. This, truly, was life. The men in the broken camp raced madly here and there, funny as ants when the nest drowns, trying to put out fires or pulling vainly at the arms and legs of the injured. Dozens more of them simply fled toward the hills— "Do they think the fell-men are going to let them through?" shouted Bliaud, his long gray curls whipping. "I'd like to be there when they try!"

One man, the man who had wrenched himself free from the burning Urchin, got slowly to his feet, leaning on his broken harpoon. Jenny was aware of him watching the dragons as they swirled triumphantly away into the night.

19

They gave her a young girl, all for her own; probably one of the camp servants or whores. By being judicious in her applications of pain and terror, Jenny managed to keep her alive most of the night.

Deep inside, Jenny was aware of her own horror, aghast, disgusted, sickened at what she saw herself doing to the weeping child. But she was aware that Amayon supped and munched and reveled in her emotions, her revulsion and pity, as much as in the victim's uncomprehending agony. And Amayon—as is the way of demons—routed his pleasure and delight back into Jenny's body and mind. Riven and battered, Jenny tried to find some way to fight, but it seemed to her that she could only watch herself performing upon the girl a violent parody of what Caerdinn had done to her when she was that age; watch herself as if she were someone else.

But you're not someone else, whispered Amayon. *That's you, Pretty Lady, my dearest Jenny dear. I don't make anything from whole cloth. No demon does. Admit it. Ever since Caerdinn beat you and harried you and demanded of you that you do what you couldn't do—*

"What do you want from me?" the girl was crying, blood coursing down her face. "What do you want?"

—you've wondered how it would feel to have that kind of power. You wanted to be him then. And now you are.

I'm not! screamed Jenny desperately, her voice tiny as the peep of a cricket in a crack. *I'm not, I'm not, I'm not!*

And the demon drank up her tears, mixed with the little whore's blood, and smacked his lips in delight.

The girl died toward dawn. The sensation was beyond description, a ringing climax of physical pleasure and emotional satisfaction that left

Jenny shattered, confused, wrung out like a rag washed up on an unknown beach.

The dragon-mages had tents set a little apart from the rest of Rocklys' forces, in the camp where the Wildspae curved through the bare gray hills. Lying on the soaked carpets of the tent floor, breathing in the thick blood-odor that permeated them, Jenny—the tiny part of Jenny that huddled weeping like a ghost still clinging to her own flesh—wondered what else had gone on in the mages' compound, what rewards they had been given for their nights' work. What Ian had done.

The blue and yellow curtain rippled back. Bland and fresh-bathed, Caradoc stood in the opening, his hard mouth relaxed a little as if even he had been pleased and sated in the night. He went for a minute to the body of the girl, turning it over with the goblin-curved tip of his staff. Jenny heard Amayon—or maybe it was herself—chuckle, and sat up, aware that her face wore the smile of a woman yawning tousled in the bed of a hated rival's husband or son.

"*What* a little spit-cat she was." She stretched luxuriously and shook back her matted hair. "Have they got the balneary set up? I'm absolutely sticky."

Caradoc grinned with the side of that grim mouth, and impure fire flickered in his eyes. It crossed Jenny's mind, Jenny's own ousted and terrified mind, to wonder how long the real Caradoc had lasted, held by slow-dissolving ghostly bonds to his own flesh and screaming with horror that this wasn't what he'd meant when he asked the demons to give him power.

Or maybe it was. Maybe after enough time passed you could no longer tell the difference.

He chucked Jenny under the chin, as a man would a whore in a tavern. "How'd you like it?"

Monster, Monster! she screamed at him, or maybe at herself, desperate and tiny and unheard. Except, of course, by Amayon, who giggled in sated delight that she was still capable of emotion, and savored her horror like a piquant dessert. The demon in her laughed for answer to Caradoc's question, and Jenny's hand stroked down her own body in a caressing expression of total satisfaction. Somewhere she heard Amayon reply to the demon—its name was Folcalor, she somehow knew, a bloated thing in which struggled the half-digested whimpering remains of a dozen other imps—that lived behind Caradoc's eyes. *You know how delicious it is, to bring a new one to it for the first time.*

And Caradoc—Folcalor—laughed appreciatively. "Roc's getting on the road soon," he said. "We'll hit them again tonight." Something changed, shifted in his expression, and with a casual air he took from his pocket a green gem, a polished peridot the size of a quail's egg, which he held out to her like a sweet to a child.

Bastards, bastards! Jenny cried, trying to summon even a fingerhold of power over her own body, trying to thrust Amayon out of her self, her heart, her mind. Though she knew that without this she, the Jenny part of herself, would die, long before anyone could exorcise Amayon, if in fact anyone could do such a thing, still terror gripped her at the thought of being forever their prisoner.

Amayon did something to her, almost thoughtlessly, as a man would strike a child to hush it, something that left her gasping with pain. *And what's this?* he asked, eyeing Folcalor, eyeing the jewel.

"I have my reasons," the dragon-mage replied, and flipped the jewel in his palm.

All the teasing, playful cruelty vanished, and Amayon was suddenly cold and deadly as a cobra. *Reasons that the Lord of Hell knows about?*

The demon-light changed and flickered in Caradoc's dead eyes. "My dear Amayon . . ." The voice was a tiger's purr in her mind, velvet sheathing the threat of razor-clawed violence. "You don't think I'd do anything here without Lord Adromelech's knowledge? He is my lord, as he is yours—and if he hasn't opened his mind and his plans to you, he has at least to me. Adromelech has his plans. Now here, precious"—he held out the stone to Jenny again—"have a little sweet."

Jenny blew a kiss at him (*Filth!* she screamed at him, at them both, at them all), opened her mouth to receive the stone, and sat smiling and making little faces and playing with it with her tongue while the dragon-mage made magic circles around her, and drew together the curves of power. Inside herself Jenny wept, with what last strength was in her, trying to call together enough power to resist.

She felt herself go into the stone.

Rocklys' army broke camp with the coming of full light and marched through the day under the wood of Imperteng's somber boughs. Caradoc, and Jenny, and the other mages summoned an unseasonable fog to cover the land to the foot of Nast Wall. Through this the dragon-mages glided silent as shadow, just above the trees, gray cold wetness hemming them in. Through the latticed structure of the jewel Jenny felt the touch of magic trying to disperse the fog, and she and the others renewed their spells, drawing the vapors thick. When the dragon she rode, a lovely green and gold youngling named Mellyn, descended, Jenny could see with her demon eyes the Commander herself, riding fully armored on her sleek bay stallion, with Caradoc at her side. Now and then they spoke,

Caradoc explaining matters in the smooth comforting voice that Rocklys had known for all those years, little realizing that it was the demon Folcalor who actually did the talking.

"This is the way many wizards are, Commander." The moonstone flashed softly on his goblin-carved staff. "You have to humor them if you want their help. Of course I'm as appalled as you are, but . . ."

Two or three times in the course of that morning Jenny was troubled by something, some watchfulness she felt turned upon them; she didn't know what. Scanning the fogs around her, with the magic of the demons that now filled her heart and body, she detected nothing. Yet in that separated part of her, that heart imprisoned within the pale-green crystal in the flat silver bottle that hung around Caradoc's neck, she knew, and whispered the name.

Morkeleb.

He was there. Somewhere. She had seen him vanish, dissolve into smoke, even as her knees and thighs had still felt his scales and spines.

And her imprisoned heart, looking out through her own eyes in the fog as she had once looked out through Morkeleb's, knew something else as well: the jewel in which she was imprisoned was flawed.

Through the long day she grew to know that jewel as intimately as she knew her own body. In a sense, this was now what it was. She remembered seeing it in the strongbox in Rocklys' chamber at Corflyn, and she familiarized herself with every molecule of carbon, every milky impurity, every fracture line and energy fault. Knew them and hated them. *These were the best you could do?* Caradoc had complained to Rocklys. And, *I think you were cheated . . .*

Caradoc was right. Rocklys was a warrior, not a mage. Faced with the need to conserve money for her soldiers' pay, faced with a clever gem merchant and a handful of brilliant stones, she wouldn't have known how to check each jewel.

Jenny could not have said exactly why a diamond or a ruby was better for the imprisonment of a disembodied spirit than a topaz or a peridot. Nor could she have explained to a layperson why magic must be worked with pure metals and flawless gems in order to be itself flawless. But within her crystalline prison she was able to move a little, and carefully— gently—she begin to draw power through the stone's threadlike fault.

And all the while she was aware of herself, and Amayon, riding the green and gold jere-drake overhead, braiding and gathering spells. Half-seen in the misty world below, the army crept, drenched, as the drifting shapes of the other dragons about her were drenched, in the feral sparkle of demon fire. She was aware that her spells—the demon's spells—made her beautiful, and being forty-five years old and never a pretty woman, she reveled in that beauty and that power. She rejoiced in the pert breasts and silky skin, in the sudden absence of any need at all to fight migraines, hot flashes, aches, indigestion. She was young and could do whatever she pleased, for none could touch her. And she smiled at the thought of that haughty bitch Rocklys' surprise, when the time came for the demons to take their pay.

The ground below them sloped gradually toward the river. Above the soft-rolling grayness of the fogs, the sun stood high.

All together, demons, mages, dragons spoke a word, and the fog sank into the ground like translucent dust. Gareth's camp—blotched with the burns of acid and the soaked blood of the men killed last night—lay naked under the dragons' shadows.

The army of Bel was ready for them at the outlying defenses of the bridge. The spikes of the gutted Urchins had been laid over the two main bunkers of the camp, and from these, harpoons slashed upward from a dozen salvaged catapult slings. Two wounded the little rainbow-drakes ridden by Werecat and Miss Enk—that semi-trained gnome adept Rocklys had brought in at the last minute from the Deep of Wyldoom—before all the demons, all the wizards pulled about themselves the spells of illusion and confusion, the fractioning of colors, images, shapes. At the same moment there was a great sounding of horns and drums on the northward road, and Rocklys' mighty voice roaring her battle-cry, "Firebeard! Firebeard!" The paean shook the air as they attacked the redoubts of the bridge, while the dragons struck at the defenders as they tried to rush from the main camp.

The battle was short, for the clouds that had lain on the mountain flanks stirred and swirled, and cold winds blew them down above the river and the camp. Thunder roared, lightning striking at the dragons, and rain streamed down in torrents. *Gnome-magic,* Jenny heard Folcalor say in her mind, with a curse. *They can't keep it up long.* She was hard put to turn aside the lightning bolts that struck at Mellyn's wings, and she felt her own rage rise, that squatty ugly creatures like the gnomes should dare defy them: *We will make them pay for this,* she said.

Wind howled and twisted at her long black hair, and below by the river fortifications she saw Rocklys' troops struggling against mud and rain. Rocklys stood at the top of a siege-ladder, sword in hand, waterfalls of rain hammering in her eyes. Wind swept away her shouted commands, and rage and pride came off her in such waves that Jenny laughed.

Behind her she heard a hissing and a shriek. One of the rainbow-drakes writhed, twisted in the air. Its rider, the Icerider boy Werecat, was thrown clear, dangling by one leg caught in the leather cable hundreds of feet above the ground. Jenny thought the young dragon must have been struck by lightning, for blood poured from its opened belly and sides; she could hear the cursing of its demon from where she sat. Dragon and boy fell, the dragon already dead, the demons drawing back to savor the desperate terror of the youth, imprisoned in his crystal, watching his last hopeless hope of freedom plunge away. The young dragon sprawled wrecked and bleeding on the earth, and she thought it bore less the marks of lightning than of attack by another dragon. But she had seen nothing.

Yet in her jewel, in her heart, in the part of her that was still Jenny, she knew.

They can't keep up the storm forever, she heard Folcalor say in her mind again. He was a big demon, and an old one, swollen with the hearts and lives of other demons he'd devoured; his mind was like a cesspool, stinking as he spoke. *And when they tire, we'll still be here.* He added, *Gnome-bitch.*

The troops retreated from the defense-works, back beneath the eaves of the woods, and made camp in the rain. Above the trees the lightning continued to flash in a sky turned to night. Rocklys deployed her forces around the wall of Gareth's camp. The demons settled in to amuse themselves, asking for soldiers or camp-slaves or the captives Rocklys had taken. Pain sometimes, or lust, or terror, usually all three: It was an art form, rendered the more entertaining by the echoed outcry from the imprisoned hearts of their hosts.

The demons grew drunk with delight.

You can't say you don't enjoy it, Amayon whispered to Jenny when she tried to look away, to will her awareness away from what was being done with her senses and her power and her body. *An ugly little thing like you never wanted to have all the men you could manage? To have them worship at your feet and beg for your favors? To have them see you as beautiful, as desirable—and then to punish them for it? To make them weep?*

Locked in the heart of the jewel, Jenny could only plead, *Let me alone.*

Your son's a better student of these arts than you are. The demon was disgusted. *Would you like to get him in here? Would that be fun?* And he laughed at the pleasure he made her feel.

The soldiers wore out, and left, or passed out drunk on the fouled carpets of the tent floor. Jenny lay for a time in the tangle of silks and furs on the tent's divan, drinking straight brandy and savoring the afterglow. Ian, the demon part of her knew, was still engaged in his own practices, but it would be good to go over there in time. It had been Ian's idea to weave the illusion that Bliaud's sons had been taken in the onslaught and tortured to death and to send this illusion to Bliaud where the old man was trapped in his ensorcelled gem. They had all laughed fit to split their sides at the father's pitiful weeping. She stretched, rolling her head in the sable pillows of her hair.

And turning her head, saw there was another man in the tent.

For a moment she recognized him only as the warrior who'd been trapped half-in, half-out of the burning Urchin, a lithe tallish man with brown hair rain-lank to his shoulders. Wet leather, wet plaids, polishing the rain from his spectacles with his torn shirttail. She was smiling, holding out an inviting hand, when she realized it was John.

She turned her face away, hand pressed to her mouth in shame and horror, and with her other hand drew up the sheet to cover herself. For a moment her throat locked shut, her whole body twisted with the pain. Then she heard Amayon laugh and the thought came to her that it would be entertaining beyond words to bring John to her—her magic would easily overcome his revulsion, but it might be more amusing to simply use a spell to bring him against his will—and then call for the guards while he lay in her bed.

Stop it! she screamed. *Stop it, stop it, stop it!*

And the demon roared with laughter. So loud did it ring in her mind that for a time she wasn't aware of how silent the tent was.

Her face still averted, she said, "Leave here, John."

"Am I talking to you, Jen?" he asked. "Or to the demon? Not that I'd get a truthful answer from whatever took possession of you."

Jenny faced him, and as the strength of the demon closed hard on her soul and her mind she forced it back with all the power she could draw through the flawed prison of the crystal, all she could still numbly wield. She trembled and could not speak, but she saw the hard wariness in John's eyes change. He stepped forward, as if he would have taken her hand, and she drew back.

He looked around at the soldiers sleeping on the floor, and the two snoring grossly beside her on the divan. His voice was very steady. "I understand it wasn't you, Jen."

She fought back the throaty chuckle, the words, *Then you can't have known me well, all these years,* and, *You should go over to the next tent and have a look at our son.* Fought them back so hard her jaws ached. And felt the sudden furious stab of Amayon's anger in her bowels.

Her hand drew back from his reach again, and she huddled the sheet around her, "It isn't that." The words were like gagging dry stones from her throat as she reached through to take fumbling hold on her flesh. "I—know—I pray—you understand."

The pain redoubled, twisted and dragged at her; pain worse than any she had known. She dug her nails into the back of her hand until blood came, to hold control against Amayon's terrible strength. "I can't—keep the demon—at bay. Go now."

"Not without you."

"You can't help."

"Mab, and Morkeleb . . ."

"Stay away!" Fire flared in the air between them as he stepped forward, driving him back. She had to back away again, put the divan between them, to keep herself from hurting him, from sending the second flash of demon-fire into his body. Agony ripped her and she half-doubled over, clinging to the head of the divan. Morkeleb's magic, all that was left of her own, burned her like a poison as she turned it against the thing inside her body, the thing that was fighting now like a tiger to take her over again.

Her breath came in gasps and she brought the words out quickly: "John, get out of here. Trust me. Don't try to help me and whatever you do don't try to find Ian, just get out . . ."

Her voice choked off as one of the soldiers on the divan sat up, eyes staring madly: "Spy!" he roared, and lunged at John.

John stepped back, tripped and elbowed him, sending him sprawling to the carpets, but the damage was done. The other men lurched to their feet, grabbing swords and knives. There was an outcry from beyond the tent wall, and the clashing of metal. John sprang over the divan, catching up the tawny fur coverlet and throwing it around Jenny's body, muffling her arms, lifting her from her feet. Jenny twisted, mute as a snake, kicking and butting with her head. John set her down at the back of the tent, drew his sword and turned to face the soldiers closing in around him. In Jenny's mind Amayon's laughter grew louder and louder, drowning thought, drown-ing resistance.

What kind of a ballad does he think he's in? Folcalor, Gothpys, come here, you have to see this!

John hacked, gutted one man, kicked another in the belly and sent him sprawling into three more, then turned and sliced open the back wall of the tent. He swung back around to catch the blades of those who'd come in from outside—armored, these warriors, and two of them had pikes—twisting, cutting, dodging, backing toward the spilling rain of the outside.

He was here, you know, Jenny; he saw you with the soldiers. You really think he doesn't think it was you?

A man fell near her, flopped and gasped and tried to close up the gaping sword-slash in his breast with his hands; his sword lay at Jenny's feet. Pain clawed her, the terror that she would die if she didn't pick it up, drive it to the hilt in John's back . . .

She kicked it from her with all her strength and with everything left in her, called a slamming burst of lightning down on the attacking soldiers, and darkness that swallowed the lamps. *"Run!"* Handfuls of wet leather, bloody plaids, the familiar scent of them ripping her heart . . .

"Run!" She thrust him through the slit in the tent, whirled back and flung fire at the men coming through the flap. Ian, Caradoc, Yseult naked and wine-soaked . . . A blast of light, darkness, power throwing them back, then she fell to her knees, balled tight on the squishing rugs, sobbing, emptied, pain and more pain through which the unconsciousness she prayed for never came . . .

Stop it, said Folcalor harshly.

Amayon's reply was beyond words, beyond even the concept of words. Raw violent hatred at being defied. A beast lifting a bloody mouth from its prey.

STOP IT. You'll kill her.

She's safe in your hellfestering little jewel. Only it wasn't words, just a river of poison poured over the raw pulp of her soul. *She can't die.*

Don't think it, snapped the other.

Doesn't matter, laughed Gothpys wearing Ian's body as he returned through the slit in the tent. There was a spear in his hand running with rainwater and blood. *He's dead.*

And Jenny saw the scene in her mind. John kneeling in the soup of rain-thinned blood where they'd hamstrung him, trying to fend off their pikes and swords and harpoons with his hands. Wet hair hung down over his broken spectacles and he tried once more to get to his feet, tried to crawl away; looked up, and saw Ian with a spear in his hands, rain sluicing down his black hair, looking down at him with smiling hell-blue eyes.

Jenny's heart seemed to shut in white blank horror. *You're lying!* she screamed at them. *You're lying! Like you lied to Bliaud!* Her grip over her body slithered away again as the last flame of her resistance died.

On the third night after that, two horses picked their way through the bracken-choked rubble and inexplicable gashes of darkness that filled in the cup-shaped valley on the eastern rim of Nast Wall's foothills. Feathers and fragments of blue-white light drifted along the ground, and now and then showed up, among the skeins of wild grape and ivy, a startling white stone hand or incised lintel. High thin cloud hid the pale fingernail of the slow-waxing moon.

The rider of the smaller horse, a coarse-maned mountain pony, drew rein where fallen pillars marked the gate of what had been a path to the citadel on the hill: "Art determined to do this thing, man?"

Aversin's voice was weary, beaten with three nights of broken sleep and foul dreams. "Show me any other way and I'll do it, Mab. I swear to you I'll do it."

She sat silent, night wind lifting the ghostly cloud of her hair.

"The penalties are terrible for those that seek the spawn of Hell."

"More terrible than havin' seven wizards possessed? Seven dragons at their beck?"

She said nothing for a time. Then, "Understand that my spells may not protect thee beyond the Gate of Hell."

His spectacles flashed as he bent his head, rubbed his forehead with a gloved hand. The horses fidgeted, uneasy at the smells in this place. At length he said, "No spells protected Jen, did they?"

"Never since the Fall of Ernine have demons so strong entered into our world." The gnome-wife's deep voice was troubled. "No lore I have studied touches upon the case. Yet the dragon says it was through her magic that they entered her soul."

"The dragon wouldn't bloody well get his whiskers singed to take his own child out of the fire," John retorted viciously. "The dragon's got no bloody room to talk. He wouldn't even bring me past the spell-bounds set around Rocklys' camp . . ."

"The dragon is right," Mab said quietly. "And the dragon did save thy life." In the flickering witchlight the shapes of the hillocks altered, and one could see in them the echoes of temples, palaces, market-halls long crumbled.

"Then it looks like I'm a fool, doesn't it?" John swung down from his horse and knotted the rein angrily around a sapling. "Only since I'd sooner be dead than live without her, I haven't got a lot to lose now, have I?"

Mab sighed. The will-o'-the-wisp coalesced into a glowing ball, shining in the air before John's knees. It illuminated a face drawn with exhaustion, eyes bruised with weariness and flaming with anger. Beyond them the gnome-witch evidently saw something else, for her voice gentled. "Thou hast no knowing, man, of what it is thou stand to lose. Still, for her sake I will do for you what I can."

She dismounted and held out her hand. After a moment John knelt before her. "No spell of this world can touch the Spawn of Hell themselves," she said, "nor yet turn aside the illusions and the ills they send within their own Hells. They are of a nature that we do not understand, and it seems that now they have found some new power besides to grant them greater might. Yet can I strengthen thine eyes against the blindness that is one of their entertainments. Greater discernment I can give to thy mind, that thou might find thy way back to the Gate that I shall make in the burning mirror; and give that thy heart beat stronger, that thou remember thy love for Jenny, and put aside the desire to remain in Hell forever. I can strengthen thy flesh, that it will not die behind the mirror unless thou so wish. But remember, man, if thou diest, thy soul shall remain there a prisoner, unable to travel on to where the souls of men return."

While she spoke, she touched his eyelids with her thick little thumb and marked rune signs on his temples and breast. John thought he should have felt something, some warmth or strength or increase of power, but he felt nothing, not even the lessening of his fear.

Don't do this, Johnny . . . He could almost hear Muffle screaming the words at him. *Don't do this . . .*

"These signs and this strength will not hold long in the world behind the mirror," said Mab's voice. He looked up at her, hoping his terror didn't show in his eyes. "Beware of what thou sayst there, and beware more than all else what promises thou make to them. They shall try to hold thee in their world and make thee their servant; departing, they shall try to put thee in debt to them, owing a teind of your loyalty and all you possess, to serve them here in this one. This above all things thou must not permit. My blessings go with thee." Her hard hand ruffled his hair. "Good luck."

He rose. "Does 'good luck' mean that I find the place or that I don't?"

Unwillingly, the old wrinkled face returned the smile. "In Ernine of old," she said, "they worshiped the Lord of Time, who saw forward and backward, and knew answers to such things. But it is the nature of mortals, of gnomes and of men, that they could not abide this knowledge, so they turned instead to the worship of the Twelve. Even the Twelve ask no questions of the Lord of Time."

Leaving the gnome-wife standing like moonlit rock, John followed the path Jenny had described to him, when she'd waked moaning from the horrors of her dream. A second palace, and a third, had been built over the Citadel of Ernine since the days of the heroes, but once past the gates there was only one way to go. Under knee-deep ivy and grapevines the very sandstone of the stairway was grooved and smoothed by water and the feet of long-dead servants and kings. In the courtyard where the queen's ladies had worked their looms, a fountain still gurgled from the broken basin. Mab's pale guide-light drifted and flickered over the dark laurel, thorn-bristling roses, and wisteria grown monstrous with age that perfumed the night.

Shallow steps led him down. Under faded and fallen plaster, blacker shadows seemed to take the shapes of great-horned gazelles, and beyond an archway that had once been filled in with layer on layer of brick and mortar the witchlight showed him a rock-cut corridor whose ceiling still bore constellations of stars and a comet with trailing hair.

The door at the corridor's end had been closed with bricks also. But shifting in the earth had cracked them, and water and age had done the rest. *The Lord of Time strikes again,* thought John, regarding the crevice.

The witchlight flowed through ahead of him. He saw something silver in the dark.

He found the circular room Jenny had described. The witchlight shone on the mirror's tall frame, cold and strange in the light. Thunderstone, he thought, and written with runes against the mirror's breaking, for instead of destroying the thing, someone had covered over the glass with what appeared to be black enamel, hard and shiny as Morkeleb's scales. Steam rose off it, drifting in the light.

From the breast of his doublet John took the square of parchment Mab had given him, written with a sigil that could have been either an eye or a door. His mouth felt dry and his hands icy. He remembered again how Jenny had waked in the night, crying and clinging to him. But that memory brought him another, her eyes in the lamplight of her tent in Rocklys' camp, her hair pointed and sticky with blood and wine. She had told him not to look for Ian, not knowing he had already seen his son—or the demon that lived in his son's flesh.

I'd sooner be dead than live without her, he had said to Mab. But it wasn't the whole truth. If the recollection of what he had seen in the camp—of Jenny a vicious whore, and Ian . . . He shook away the thought. If that memory was going to be part of his life, together with the knowledge that they were possessed, forever subject to the demons that made them do those things, death looked good.

Only, he thought, as he spit on the back of the parchment and stuck it to the mirror's enameled face, *it might not be death.*

That was the tricky part.

He didn't know how the tiny sigil was big enough to admit his body, but it was.

He closed his eyes, said a prayer to the Old God, and stepped through.

20

They were waiting for him, right behind the glass.

Well, there's a brave one, said the Demon Queen, and took his face between her hands. Her hands were cold as marble in winter. Her lips, when they forced his open—tonguing, nipping, tasting—were icy, too. A dead woman's lips. Her tongue a serpent's probing tongue.

But heat burned under the chill. Heat flowed into his palms, though he felt how cold her flesh was under the clinging silk—if it was silk. The dark of the place was the purple dark of nightmares, where flesh glowed strangely and all things were outlined in fire. Scents and noises hammered and whispered in his brain, as if sound and odor were in fact designed for other organs of sensation than those he possessed. For a time he struggled only to adjust his awareness, and it came to him that the Demon Queen's blinding, blood-pounding kiss was a way of making sure he didn't adjust.

He caught her wrists, pushed her back, though she was tremendously strong. "Say, you aren't married, are you, love?" he asked her, and it took her by surprise. He fished through his pockets. "I had a ring . . . Here it is." He produced a cheap bronze bearing that had gone into the Urchin's engines and caught the Demon Queen's hand. "You'd have to talk to me man of business about the dowry—we're that set on dowries where I come from—but you and me together, we'll talk him down to not more than half a dozen feather beds and a set of pots. Can you make lamb and prune pie? The last lady I thought to marry was a tall bonny girl like yourself, only couldn't find her way about the kitchen with a map of the place and one of the scullery boys for a guide. She ended up cookin' a horsehead in mistake for a turkey-poult, stuffed with oats, for a Yule feast, and I had to call off the match . . ."

You're a fool! The Demon Queen stepped back from him and pulled her hand from his attempt to slip the bronze ring onto her finger.

"That's what they all said," agreed John, "when I spoke of coming here." He was careful to put the ring back in his pocket.

She looked like a woman to him, a tall woman, slim as a catkin but for the lush upstanding heaviness of her breasts. Luminous white skin seemed to shine through the garment she wore, smoke-blue shot through with fire when she moved; winds that he could not feel rippled and lifted and turned the fabric, as it rippled her hair. Black hair drawn up and back, strands and braids and swags of it falling around her face, down her back, glittering with gems as the manes of the dragons glittered. Her eyes were a goat's eyes.

And why did you come here?

He'd made her angry, breaking the falseness of her welcome; he saw that falseness return as she took him by the hands. He saw now they were in an enormous chamber: smokes, and lights, and portions of the floor that flowed like glimmering water. He could not tell whether he was hot or cold—both together, it seemed, and both unbearable—and it was difficult to breathe. Difficult, too, to decide whether the smells that freighted the air were sweet or nauseating. The Queen's courtiers who ringed in behind him had the appearance of men and women until he took his eyes off them. He knew they changed then and almost saw them at it.

He sensed them following as the Queen led him down corridors and stairs, through arcaded terraces where it was sometimes day and sometimes night, past windows where snow fell, or rain, or slow flakes of fire.

"Gie nice furniture," he remarked and paused to trace a line of porcelain flowers set in the C-curved ebony of a chair-leg. "I saw stuff like this in the palace at Bel two years ago, though how they got the wood to bend like this was more than I could learn. Still it's all the newest fashion, they say. How'd you come by it, if you've been locked up behind a covered mirror for the past thousand years?"

You are a fool, she said again, but this time there were a thousand undertones of other things in her voice. Her hand on his arm was the stroking of feathers on bare flesh, and he had to look aside from her lips and her breasts. The room was filled with pale mist and scented with applewood and burnt sugar. Oddly, through the mists, he could still see Miss Mab's sigil, burning like a distant lamp.

Lamps surrounded a divan, haloing it and seeming to hold the mists at bay. The floor was green marble, scattered with almond flowers.

"Why did you come?" She spoke as humans speak, through those blood-ruby lips, and her long ivory-pale face was sad.

"To ask your help, love."

"Alas." She drew him onto the divan beside her. Her voice was deep, and the note of it was like a warm hand curled around his manhood. "Would that we could offer it. But as you see, we cannot help even ourselves. That I, Aohila, should have been betrayed and imprisoned so, for things that were none of our doing."

A grave-faced child emerged from the fog, wearing nothing more than a garland of roses and bearing an enameled tray. Glass vessels on it held wine, clear as the last slant of afternoon light, dates, figs, cherries, and a pomegranate.

"You're hungry," said Aohila. "You've ridden a long way."

John shook his head. Mab had warned him about this, if he hadn't already encountered it in a hundred legends and songs. On that, at least, they all agreed, if on little else. "Narh. I had a meat-pie in me saddlebags, and the last time I took wine I made a fair disgrace of meself, dancin' on the table at me aunt Tillie's wedding and making that free with the bridesmaids. Aunt Tillie was like to die of mortification." He took the cup that she raised to his lips and emptied it out onto the floor. "But thank you all the same, love. And you really ought to get some socks on that page. She'll catch her death, runnin' about on the stone floor. Who was it covered your mirror over in black like that?"

Her eyes changed, losing the faint illusion of humanity, and green flame wickered and threaded through her hair. She said nothing.

"Not humans?" he asked.

The red lip lifted a little from her teeth, and he felt the blood start, where her nails cut into the flesh of his arm.

"These wizards of the desert are supposed to have done it, but it was other demons, wasn't it?"

It was like entering the cave of a poisonous serpent, naked and with bound hands. Hearing the movement of dry silken coils in the dark.

What do you know of it?

"Not much." His heart pounded. The fog behind him stirred, but he dared not turn his head; he caught the movement of light, and shapes within the light, from the corner of his eye. "I think I know which of the Nightspawned Kin it was, though."

She pressed him back on the cushions of the divan, and her fingers closed around the back of his neck, strong and cold, like a metal garrote. He realized she was strong far beyond the strength of the strongest of men. *Why are you here?*

"Because the sea-wights from the foundations of the Seven Isles are doin' exactly what you tried to do here, a thousand years ago," said John. "They've tempted a mage to his fall and are using him to manipulate a pretender to the local throne. They've got up a corps of dragons and mages, the same way you did for Isychros. Only instead of tryin' to set themselves up, they've got some poor sap of a human to rule for them, while they hang back and kill and fornicate and torture. I think that's been in their minds for a thousand years, since they helped the Lords of Syn to close you off in here."

What do you know, whispered her sulfurous voice in the hollows of his mind, *of the minds of the seaspawn?* Her nails dug into his flesh and he could feel the others behind him, a wall of slow-burning bones. Coming closer, smelling his blood. *And how do you know it was they who closed our door into the world of men?*

"It's not somethin' I can discuss."

Her body stretched out on top of his, fingers cold through his hair. Her lips were cold, too, brushing his, but they kindled a fire in him, like a drug. What had been fog seemed now to be enclosing walls, bright with frescoes and the light of a few candles, and she drew the jeweled pins from her hair, and from the knots of silk that held her robe. *What is your business, then?*

Her breasts were round as melons where they pressed his flesh, silk-soft and heavy, and again he was conscious of the underlying warmth, not of her flesh, but of some core of flame deep within. The scent of her intoxicated him. His hands closed hard over hers, stopping their caress. "To do a bargain with you, Lady," he said, his voice husky and dry. "Nothing more. I'm an old married man with children."

If he took her, he knew, it would give her power over him, as surely as if he had eaten or drunk in the realm of the demons. But it was hard to speak, difficult even to think, with his need for her blinding and burning and hammering in his blood.

"I came to ask help of you against the seaspawn, lest they do to you what they do to us."

She twisted her wrists from his grasp—it was like trying to hold on to the foreleg of a maddened horse—and reared above him, black hair swirling around her and the gold and crimson silk of her dress falling around her hips.

Bargain? BARGAIN? With US?

He saw when the red lips lifted back from her mouth that her teeth were fangs; and in any case he knew she didn't look like a woman when he closed his eyes. Still the desire to seize her, to crush her beneath him, to force her mouth and her thighs apart, overwhelmed him, so that he rolled swiftly off the divan and stood, shaking, behind its head.

"It's a fair bargain," he said. "Bein' your servant isn't in it."

Their eyes met and locked, and he saw that he'd guessed truly: that it was less the blow to her pride that a man would bargain with her than that he acted as a free agent, unswayed by her will. Her mouth pulled back in a snarl again, and for a moment he saw her as she was.

Then the demons seized him from behind: pain, and cold, and the breath ripped from his lungs. Black blindness, and the roaring agony of fire.

If I die in this realm, thought John, *it's here I'll remain, forever.* Mab's spells had strengthened his flesh, but according to Gantering Pellus, demons seldom or never killed those who went to their realms, though how the encyclopedist had obtained that information wasn't mentioned. Chained naked between pillars of red-hot iron, his flesh being cut slowly to pieces by the whips of the demons, John didn't take much comfort in the *Encyclopedia's* assertion even if it was true. If he couldn't die, he couldn't faint either, and the servants of the Demon Queen were ingenious in how they used the razor-edged whalebone and leather. Dotys, or was it Heronax of Ernine?—he forced his mind to pursue the reference— wrote that sages of the old Kingdom of Choray had used certain incantations to keep pain at bay, but John was forced to conclude that this was probably a lie.

All you need to do is ask, whispered the Queen in the screaming core of his mind. *All you need to do is ask.*

Ask my mercy. Ask my favor. Ask my love.

He was lying, it seemed, in the open, under a white dimpled horror of sky. Chains held his wrists and ankles to what felt, under his bare back, like a circle of stone, though beyond his outstretched fingers he saw thin gray grasses moving in windless alien wind.

Silk blew over his face. He turned his head back, squinted up—he could not remember what had become of his spectacles—and saw Aohila standing just behind his head. He knew that what was going to happen next would be worse than the previous illusion. He said, "You know they'd never have sent me to bargain if there'd been any question of opening the mirror again. There isn't. It can't be done."

She was holding a golden cup. She dipped her fingers into it, brought them out wet. "Why then should we help you?"

She dripped the liquid from her fingers onto his body. Where it struck it was deathly cold, then at once began to itch, and slowly, to smoke and to burn.

"Because what you're doing to me, the seaspawn can do to you, and for the same reasons. Maybe the pain of demons is tastier than the pain of men. I'll look it up when I get back—it's probably in Gantering Pellus, or maybe Curillius, though Curillius isn't even accurate about how many horses you need to go on a quest across the Marches. But if they take over the southern kingdom, they'll be able to get at your mirror, you know."

She dipped out a handful of liquid from the cup and dribbled it down over his face. He jerked his head aside and got the splash of it down his cheek and neck, burning away the flesh, eating deeper and deeper.

"You don't think we can take care of ourselves?"

"I think you can." He had to fight to keep his voice steady, to keep the terror of more pain from dissolving his thoughts. "But I think there'll be evil and horror if a demon war is fought in the lands of men. I'm bargaining not so that you can get out, but so that you'll at least be left in peace."

"It isn't peace that we want, man." She squatted behind his head and, reaching over, pulled his chin back, setting the rim of the cup to his lips. "It's revenge on those who imprisoned us here." She pinched his nostrils shut, forced his mouth open and poured the poison in, so that he choked, gagged, swallowed. "All we need is one servant in the realm of humankind to start with. And it need not be unpleasant." She smiled and dipped her finger into the cup. Slowly, sensuously, she drew spells on his body, lines of fire and pain that ate into the flesh until his mind blotted with agony that never quite swallowed up his ability to feel. Then she emptied the remainder of the cup on the stone beside him, and rising, walked leisurely away across the endless gray grass.

He came to lying on her divan again. Raw inside and out, as if all that illusion had been done to him in fact. With his eyes closed he was aware of the other demons crowding around, whispering, but when he heard the dry friction of her silks and her hair beside him, and opened his eyes, it was only she. The mists were gone and the room had frescoes of deer and fishes on the walls; its windows opened into a darkness of jasmine and orange-trees.

She asked him again, "What do you want?"

What he wanted most was a drink of water, but he stopped himself from saying so. Not having drunk the poison willingly he supposed it didn't count, if it hadn't in fact been illusion. He sat up and coughed, the pain of just that was excruciating, as if he were all scar tissue inside.

"I want a spell that will defend machines against the magic of the sea-wights," he said. He rubbed his wrists, felt the raw galls of shackles, though the skin was unmarked. "We've built a number of 'em— machines, that is—and we need to protect 'em all."

"Done." From the folds of her gown she produced a vial of red-black glass, like something carved out of ancient blood.

John grinned shakily, "Surely you don't have pockets in that frock, now, do you, love?" and was rewarded with a stab of pain, as if she'd driven a sword into his belly and twisted it.

No sense of humor, he thought, sweating, as soon as he could breathe again. *It'd never work out between us.*

He blinked up at her nearsightedly and almost asked for his spectacles back. She'd probably count that as one of the traditional three requests—*why was it always three?*—and anyway, oddly enough, he could still see Mab's sigil shining somewhere beyond the wall. Maybe the wall didn't really exist. "I want a spell that will free both mages and dragons from the thrall of the sea-wights and restore their own minds and wills to them again."

The goatish eyes narrowed, under the jeweled swanks of hair. But she said, "Done." She produced a seal cut of crystal, cold and tiny and greenish-white, and laid it beside the vial on the cushions.

A wight the size of a chicken ran up to the divan and leaping up, caught John's wrist and drove its proboscis into the flesh. With a curse he shook it off, feeling the blood hot on his arm, but not daring to take his eyes from the Queen's. The wight lunged at him again; the Queen caught it by the neck, casually, and bringing it to her mouth bit through its throat, her head jerking aside and back like a dog's, to rip and kill.

With blood on her face, on her breasts and garments, she asked him, "Is there anything else?"

"And I want a spell that will heal them of any damage they've taken."

"Well." Her red lips curved in scorn. The dead thing in her hand had ceased to twitch, but the blood still ran out of it over her fingers. "Done." She dropped the dead wight to the floor, and something ran out from under the divan and began to gnaw it with thick little ripping sounds. With sticky hands she produced a blue stone box, soapy to the feel and heavier than it should have been as he took it in his hand. "Now let us talk of the teind you will pay me in return."

His hands closed around the box, the seal, the vial; he could not stop them shaking. He got to his feet and backed from her, and she lay back along the divan and smiled.

"I'll even let you out of here, for as long as it takes for you to take my revenge on the sea-wights," she said.

"Thank you," he said.

"Afterward . . ."

"No afterward," said John. "I'll pay whatever price you ask of me, but I won't be your servant in my own world. I hired my sword to the gnomes for a price, but when that price was paid I went my way. Sooner than that I'll remain here."

She sat up, angry, her lip raised a little to show a fang. He saw now that things lived in her hair—or maybe they were a part of the hair: eyeless, darting, toothed. *I don't think you've thought about what that will be like, o my beloved.*

Sweat stood cold on his face, because like the dragons her mind spoke in images and sensations, and he could see what it would be: agonizing and without any end. Ever. He made himself meet her eyes, and though the runes and sigils she'd traced on his flesh began to burn with the memory of the poison, he did not look away.

God of Time, don't let her take me up on it, he pleaded, in the deepest hollows of his heart. *I don't think I could do it . . .*

They faced one another for some minutes in silence.

Very well, she said softly. *We shall speak of terms, then.*

The walls behind her shifted, and he could see the Hellspawn through them, like fish in murky water. He recognized the two with the whips. Others held bits and pieces of a man's body—entrails, a hand, a foot. A long hank of bloodied brown hair with a faded red ribbon braided into it. A pair of spectacles. He looked back at the Demon Queen's eyes and saw lazy amusement in them, and something else that frightened him badly.

Since you will not be my servant, in exchange I will ask that you bring us rare and precious things.

His mouth felt like flesh long dead. "Name 'em."

Her smile widened, as if he had walked into a trap. "Even so. You're a scholar, Aversin. You found the mirror here; you make machines that will slay dragons or fly with them across the skies. Therefore I name as your bond that you bring here a piece of a star, a dragon's tears . . . and a gift given to you freely by one who hates you. That is your teind. If you do not redeem it by the last full moon of the summer, the one they used to call the King's Moon, then you will return to this place and come through the mirror again, to become my bondsman indeed."

Bugger. Dizziness swept him, and the knowledge of what she was asking, of what she would do. *Dragons don't shed tears. Not a thing of dragons, Morkeleb would say . . .*

"And if I don't come?"

She got to her feet. He could not tell if she were clothed or naked, but only sheathed in moving light. He had backed to the wall and felt behind him sometimes plaster, sometimes picking, bony hands that caught his wrists when he tried to sidestep her languid advance. She had a jewel in her hand, small and coldly sparkling, he could not tell its color. He tried to flinch aside but could not move in the grip of the things behind him, only turned his face away. For a moment he felt it burning in the pit of his throat. Then it was gone.

Her hand crept down the side of his face, along his throat, and he felt the scratch of her nails on his breast.

"If you don't come," she said softly, "we will assume that it is not your intention to redeem your bond. Then we will take you, wherever you are. Your flesh will be our gate. Living or dead."

His mouth was dry. He felt Mab's spells fading, colder and colder in his flesh. His breath dragged in his lungs. Too soon, he thought desperately, too soon . . .

He only said, "Done," forcing his voice to remain as level and calm as he could. Turning, he reached over and took the spectacles from the demon that held them. There was blood on them, and from the thing's mouth dangled strings of sinew and part of a hand whose scarred fingers he refused to recognize. "Now I've taken up enough of your time . . ."

It was getting hard for him to see, his vision tunneling to gray. In the mists that parted before him he saw black glass, and tiny in its midst the inverted silvery sigil of the door. "Until the King's Moon, then." The Demon Queen drew him back to her and pressed herself to him, kissing his lips. The desire to stay with her, to throw her to the iron earth and take her then, rushed back onto him, consuming him like a flame.

To hell with Jenny, to hell with Ian, to hell with the outer world . . .

He thrust her from him and walked toward the sigil, with the wailing sweetness of her singing in his ears.

"Better than your little brother, aren't I?" whispered Jenny into the ear of the man who grunted on top of her and laughed as she felt his body tense, chill in horror as he reared back from her, whiskered face aghast. How she knew about the incident she didn't know—the distant, locked-up part of her assumed it to be some knowledge of Amayon's—but she saw that the clear tiny incident was in fact true. The guilt of it had driven this poor soldier all his life, and lived, cruel as a snake in his vitals, even after all these years.

"What was it he said to you?" she purred, as the man tried to throw himself from her couch. "*Bultie*—he did call you Bultie, didn't he? *Bultie, don't hurt me anymore, don't hurt me . . .*" Her mimickry was flawless; it was as if the seven-year-old's voice flowed out of her throat as she held onto Bultie with iron strength.

"Whore bitch!" he yelled at her, struggling, and Jenny laughed again at the comical revulsion and nausea that contorted his face.

"What, can't take it?" She shook back her hair, lovely and thick as a cat's pelt. All around the canvas walls the camp echoed with men's voices, jesting and laughing over the latest triumph, and saying *it won't be long now*. The dragons had burned the Regent's camp and scattered most of his men into the woods. The Regent himself, and his father, and a small remnant held out in the devastated fort. In celebration Rocklys had distributed an extra rum ration to the men. Jenny hadn't found it difficult to entice them one after another to her tent. Stupid fools.

"You know what happened to him, to little Enwr, after you were done? When he ran to your papa and tried to tell on you? Oh, don't worry, Bultie, your papa didn't believe him—"

"Stop it, whore!"

She raised her perfect eyebrows mockingly. "What, didn't you pick Enwr because you knew your papa wouldn't believe him?" Her perfect fingers toyed with the silver collar about her throat, a silver and crystal dew-spoon hanging like a gem below. "After your papa beat him—"

"Stop it!"

"—little Enwr ran away—"

"Be silent or I'll kill you!"

"—and met some bandits in the road . . ."

With an inarticulate cry the man dragged his hand from her, bloodied from the grip of her nails, and stumbled toward the door, sobbing. He didn't make it, but fell to his knees vomiting wine onto the carpets, cursing weakly and weeping while Jenny crooned in little Enwr's voice, *"Oh, Bultie, that hurts! Oh, it hurts!"*

She nearly rolled off the divan, laughing, as Bultie crawled out of the tent. And turning her head, saw a man standing nearby, half in shadow.

She knew him. She'd never seen him before, but she knew him.

She held out her hand—Amayon held out her hand—and said, "What, you've never seen a woman before, handsome?"

For he was handsome, in a curious thin-boned way. Long gray hair framed a narrow face marked with fresh cuts, as if he'd seen recent battle. Shadow concealed his eyes, but in the dark under those brows she thought there were stars shining far off. His long thin hands were folded under a cloak like a black silk wing. He said, "You can call fire with your mind, Wizard-woman, and salt with your mind. Call them through the flaw in the jewel and ring the flaw with them, to guard you as you reach through it, and to sustain you there."

She heard Amayon scream, felt the stab of pain, the flush of heat, rising and rising . . .

"You are dragon as much as you are woman," said the stranger, and his voice was dark echoes in her mind. "There is a dragon within you . . ."

"Pig! Bastard! Catamite!" It was Amayon screaming, Amayon who flung Jenny's body against the stranger, clawing, biting, gouging.

But the stranger was strong, astonishingly so. He caught her wrists, held her hands from his eyes, eyes that, she saw now, were white as stars. "You are dragon," he repeated, and the words shone through the flaw in the jewel, through into her heart. "You have no shape, no body of this world. Slip through that flaw as water slips through the crack in a jar."

Nausea gripped her, wrenched her; nausea and pain, pain that took her breath. She—Amayon—began to scream at the top of her lungs: "Rape! Murder! Help! Save me!" And outside the tent men cried out, running.

The stranger flung his cloak around her, dragged her through the tent's postern door. Frenzied, Jenny sought to break his hold on her, flung out a wailing, desperate cry for Mellyn, for Folcalor, for anyone to help her . . . And at the same time, gasping in pain, deep in the lightless jewel's heart, Jenny gathered the dragon-strength, drew and drew at the essences of fire and salt. Though the pain hammered her, she formed them in her mind, and they whispered through the flaw in the jewel, real, as she was real, only without physical body, as she had no physical body . . .

The strength of a dragon stirred in her, reached out to fight Amayon . . .

Water, whispered the voice in her mind. *Become water, Wizard-woman. Do not fight him but flow away. Turn to steam and let the wind take you.*

Men ran from the tents to drive them back from the camp's palisade. Jenny saw with her wizard's sight the rope that hung down against the logs. The soldiers didn't. Laboriously, as if gathering seeds of millet with hands stiffened by cold, she formed spells of Look-Over-There, spells of Kill-Fire that doused the torches among the tents, spells of clumsiness, of inattention, of trailing bootlaces and dropped weapons. Smoke from the snuffed campfires mingled with white wet unseasonable fog that lifted from the river . . .

And she felt Folcalor's spells. The demon-spells of the gross, great thing that rode Caradoc like a dying horse, the thing that she had come to hate in these past five days only slightly less than she hated Amayon—that she loved with Amayon's bizarre and carnal passion. Spells dispersing the fogs and the smokes, illuminating cold flares of marshlight around them.

"Stop them!" Rocklys pounded out among her men, her great black-horned bow in her hands and Caradoc at her heels. Soldiers fell on them, soldiers whom Jenny had taken into her bed for four nights now. The gray-haired stranger was armed with a staff; he used it to fell the first man, and Jenny caught up the soldier's fallen halberd and dagger. Spells tangled like glowing wool around her, and she fought them off; opened one man's face from brow to chin, reversed the halberd and broke the jaw of another, clearing the path to the wall.

Overhead she heard the soft deadly beating of wings and knew the dragons were coming.

Up the rope, said the voice within her mind.

Kill him! screamed Amayon, and the muscles of her arm cramped with the effort not to drive a blade into the stranger's back. Arrows thudded into the wall. Mellyn's voice cried *Jenny!* despairingly as Jenny groped through the flaw in the peridot, grasped the rope, the silk cloak whirling about her as she climbed. Her rescuer struck and slashed with his staff, and looking down, she bent her aching concentration against his enemies. He would, she knew, have to turn his back on them to climb.

She stayed her climb, sweating, shaking, forming in her mind all the limitations, all the power lines, all the runes of a spell of fire and lightning. She felt the demons drag and drink at the magic, tearing at the spells even as she formed them; saw Caradoc, on the edge of the phosphor-lit clearing among the tents, raise his hand.

Unarmed men, she thought; *if not unarmed, at least not ready for magic . . .*

Still she flung her power down on the circle of soldiers around her rescuer, and even with Folcalor's power fighting hers, even with Amayon dragging and tearing at her mind, fire exploded from the air. Men screamed and fell back, dropping their weapons to claw at their burning clothes. The gray-haired man leapt for the rope, and Jenny saw him climb behind her, bony and lean as if his body had no weight at all. Rocklys' black-feathered arrow slammed into his shoulder, hurling him hard into the wall. Jenny reached down, grasped his hand, and dragged him up beside her to the top of the wall. Wind slashed and tore at her hair, at the swirling black silk cloak, and she barely dodged aside as a greenish gout of acid splattered on the wall, the wood hissing as it began to burn. Another arrow struck inches from her knee, and Mellyn's voice cried to her mind in music that ripped her with grief.

"Jump!" Jenny said.

But the stranger caught her around the waist and threw himself not down from the wall but up. And up, wings cracking open, bones melting and changing. The hands that held her turned to claws. Above her Jenny saw the black glister of scales, the swirl of stars and darkness, mane and spines and iron-barbed tail.

The campfires fell away. They plunged up and still up, into the lightning-pregnant clouds, arrowing away to the east.

21

It was like being pregnant with some carnivorous thing that gnawed at her womb, seeking to eat its way out.

It was like standing guard on some rocky place alone in the freezing rain, on the second night without sleep, knowing there would be no relief.

It was like lying in bed with a lover in the hot flush of first youth, knowing that to embrace him would be death.

Amayon knew her very well. He had had time to familiarize himself with every flaw in the imprisoning jewel that was Jenny's heart and body, and it was only a matter of time, she knew, before he triumphed.

The Lord of Time was her enemy, as he was of all men. He was the demons' friend.

Thunder ringed the citadel of Halnath. Jenny felt in the rain that sluiced her face the Summonings of wizards and welcomed the protection of the lightning and the storm. As Morkeleb descended to the wet slates of the topmost court through the flaring glower of morning, the soldiers around the wall looked askance, but they raised their spears in salute as she walked past them. Someone gave her a cloak, for she wore only the silken rags of her nightgown.

The Master waited in his study. "Jenny—" He held out his hand. He wore battered mail over a black scholar's robe and didn't look as if he'd slept the previous night.

She gestured him back. The wet wool cloak stuck to her bare flesh underneath, and her wet hair to her face. She must, she knew, look every day of her forty-five years and more, haggard and puffy-lipped with debauchery, weary, soiled. It was hard to bring out the words. "The demon is still in me," she said. "Don't trust me. Don't trust what I say."

"It takes one to know one, love."

She turned, startled, at the voice, and fought to maintain the uncaring dragon-calm that did not release its hold on power for anything. *Don't let yourself feel,* she commanded, but it was the hardest thing she had ever done. *Amayon is there waiting for you . . .*

John went on, "I'll know if it's you talking, or him." He sat slumped in a chair by the hearth. He looked more tired than she had ever seen him, even more weary than when he returned from the Skerries of Light. The skin at his throat was marked, as if hot metal had been laid there, and deep slits and scratches etched his hands and neck. But it was in his eyes themselves, half-hidden by his straggling hair, that the real damage showed.

They lightened and brightened when they met hers, however; the old gay madness, and the trust of love. He was glad to see her, and it made her want to weep with shame and joy.

"They told me you were dead." She did not add that it was Ian who had said so. She thought about the way she had dealt with that grief, losing her mind to the demon, uncaring.

Then, "You went to the ruins." She didn't know how she knew it.

"I couldn't think what else to do, love." He got to his feet and came to her, carefully, not trusting himself nor wanting to break her concentration. His fingers shook as they touched hers. She knew her own were cold, after the long flight over the bitter mountains, but his were icy against them.

She thought about the things she'd seen, gathered behind the mirror in her dreams. Thought about what she'd read of demons in his books.

"He lay unconscious in the mirror chamber for many hours." Miss Mab rose from her little tussock before the fire, her thick exquisite jewelry flashing like a dragon's scales. "Barely was the spell I laid upon him sufficient to bring him forth again." She glanced back at Polycarp, who looked quickly away.

"I made the best bargain I could." John propped up his spectacles. "I never was any damn good at the market—you remember that time I bought the stone nutmegs from that feller with the monkey?—but I did try. Miss Mab's been tellin' me what exactly I've got myself into, and all I've got to say is, that Demon Queen ought to be ashamed of herself."

He turned away from her, fumbling with the battered pouch at his belt. When he turned back, he had something that looked like a seal in his hand, wrought of crystal or glass. At the same moment Miss Mab came from the other side to take Jenny by the wrist.

It was well she did. Within her jewel-bound mind Jenny felt Amayon drag and lurch at her arm, and she was overwhelmed with the desire to flee the room, to hide, to use her will and her magic and never be found.

She twisted, pulled away, and other hands caught her from the other side. She had a glimpse of the gray-haired stranger's pale face, the eyes that were nothing but shadow and starshine: Morkeleb in his human guise, stepping through the terrace doors.

She understood—Amayon understood—what the crystal seal John held was.

Hatred, treachery, poison, murder, pain . . .

The demon's voice screamed in her, and like a dragon, she sheathed her mind in diamond and steel.

Leave you, leave you, leave you . . .

Waves of unbearable pleasure, indescribable pain, swept her. She clutched at John's arm, at the corner of the table, as she doubled over, sweating, nauseated.

"Hold on, love." His hand touched her chin, raising her head; she saw he had a white shell in his hand, a common one from the beaches of Bel, and Amayon's voice within her rose to a shriek.

DON'T LET HIM . . .

A child within her. A desperate, terrified lover-child . . .

Her mind shut hard, Jenny opened her mouth as the shell was put against her lips. Closed her eyes on the sight of Polycarp, holding a candle to an ensorcelled stick of crimson sealing-wax. Held out her hand obediently, for Mab to slash her palm and smear the crystal seal with blood. The little gnome-witch had to step up onto a chair to press the blooded sigil to Jenny's forehead.

THEY WILL TORTURE ME THROUGH ETERNITY!

Jenny remembered the nights of her own torment and replied calmly, *Good.*

And Amayon was gone.

Desolation swept her. She was barely aware of Mab taking the shell from her mouth. Jenny turned away and put her hands over her face, brokenhearted, and wept.

"The demons have asked of Aversin that he bring them certain things." Miss Mab sat forward in the Master's big chair, and Polycarp, seated on the floor beside her, brought up a footstool again.

Nearly twenty-four hours had passed. The gnome-witch wore silk slippers of an astonishing shade of blue, emblazoned with rosettes of lapis and gold and bearing on their toes little golden bells. They jingled when she crossed her ankles. "That was the price he paid for these."

On the study table the crystal seal lay, cold greenish-white, as if wrought from ice. Indeed, by the frost upon it, in which any human touch left a print, it might have been so. The vial beside it had a slippery feel,

and Jenny could see that it had burned rings in the tabletop. Now it rested
on a saucer of glass. The blue stone box between them, though more prosaic, seemed somehow darker and heavier than any stone of the world she
knew, and it was difficult to look at it for long at a time. Dark marks
crusted it. Blood, she thought.

The white shell should be there, too, Jenny thought. *Amayon's prison.*
She was ashamed of her desire to see it. To know if he were comfortable.

Absurd, she thought, burning with embarrassment. *Absurd.* As if
John were not in desperate peril, as if Ian were not still a demon's
slave . . .

After leaving the study last night she had slept and wakened to find
John lying beside her. He had cupped her cheek in his hand and touched
his lips to hers, and it was as if all the filthiness and cruelty and lust
Amayon had dragged her through were washed from her body and her
mind. She wasn't beautiful—she knew this and had always known it—
but she saw her beauty in his eyes, and that was enough.

Her mind still felt detached, as it had when she saw Cair Corflyn
through Morkeleb's eyes. She dwelt still, she knew, within the ensorcelled peridot, and that jewel lay in the silver bottle around Caradoc's
neck. Her hold on her flesh, she sensed, even without Amayon in occupa-
tion, was tenuous. The difference was that no demon dwelt in her abandoned flesh, and she could operate herself, like one of John's machines,
through the flaw in the jewel. The relief was greater than anything she
had known.

Later they'd slept again, but John still looked tired. There was a
haunted look in his eyes, as if he glanced always over his shoulder for
something he expected but never saw.

"There shouldn't be much of a trouble about the first." Sitting on the
floor at Jenny's feet, John squeezed her hand. "There'll be thunderstones
in the treasuries of the Deep, won't there, M'am?" He glanced over at
Miss Mab. "I've heard as how the gnomes treasure 'em up. I reckon me
credit's good enough with old Balgub after this that he'd sell me one for
not much more than a couple pounds of me flesh."

He spoke with a quick grin, but the gnome-witch looked away. Jenny
felt John's sudden stillness through her knees against his back.

"No thunderstones lie in the Deep of Ylferdun," said Miss Mab and
looked away from his eyes.

"Don't be daft, M'am," said John. "Your old pal Dromar spoke of
'em to me, four years ago . . ."

"He was mistaken," said the gnome-witch. "All have been sent to
Wyldoom, in payment for a debt. And such things are far less common

than rumor makes them. And in any case," she added, as John drew in his breath to speak, "none would they surrender to thee for this matter."

Her old pale eyes met John's squarely. Silence fell like a single water drop in a dream that spreads out to form a pond, and then a lake, and then an ocean that swallows the world.

"It is from the metal of the thunderstones, you see," she said, "that the Demon Gates are wrought. The metal from the stars holds spells as no other can, to render the Gates impervious to harm."

"As for a dragon's tears," said Polycarp, "I think that's simply fanciful, for dragons do not weep."

Did Mellyn weep, Jenny wondered, *when I escaped from Rocklys' camp?*

And from that her mind turned again to Amayon, and she averted her face, ashamed that the others would see her own eyes fill.

The silence in the small library was like crystal poison in a cup. The pierced lamps salted the Master's foxy, pointed face, the old gnome-witch's wrinkled one, with patterns of topaz flecks.

John took a deep breath. "I see." His voice was deadly level. "I'd thought to pay the third part of the teind with me own hair and nails, they bein' the gift of me mother, who, barrin' Rocklys herself, probably hated me most in the world. Everybody always tells me I have me mother's nose but I need it meself to keep me specs on. Or do you plan to take that away from me as well?" His glance cut to Polycarp.

The Master met his eyes squarely. "If we have to."

"Thy hair and nails will confirm the Demon Queen's hold upon thee, Aversin," said Miss Mab, turning the rings on her stubby fingers. "She counted upon just such a reading of the riddle, I think, divining as demons do in the shadows of thy mind the hatred thy mother bore thy father's son. Of them could she fashion a fetch, to send into this world in thy stead. Perhaps use them to control thy heart and thy mind as well."

"Ah." Jenny felt the tension in all of John's muscles. Anger first, and then fear.

"Was that somethin' you knew, when you made me the spells to pass into the world behind the mirror?" he asked at last. "What they were likely to ask of me? Or that nobody here had the slightest intention of helping me pay this teind?"

"I told thee they would trick thee, John Aversin," Miss Mab said steadily. "And that it was not likely that thou wouldst leave the mirror with thy life."

"But you didn't bother mentionin' that all anyone would say about it was, *Oh, sorry, son, can't pay your teind, bit on the steep side.*" He stood, dragonlike himself in his spiked rusty doublet. *"But we'll take the protection and the freedom and the healin' nonetheless, thanks ever so, and we'll see to it that your name lives forever. So just lay right down there and wait while I get the ax."*

He swung angrily to face the Master. "Tell me one thing. Those guards who've been hangin' about every time I turn around today—they're to make sure I don't leave this place, aren't they?"

Polycarp looked away.

Face rigid, John looked down at Jenny, who had half-risen in shock and horror and rage. He bent to take her hands, his fingers like ice, and kissed her lips. To her he said, "Well, and they're right, love." There was a scathe of bitter rage in his voice. "Can't let the demons into this world, but somebody's got to go in and get the things to fight them with, for the sake of the King, and for Gar, and for the Law and all me friends. But it was for you, love. It was all for you."

He strode from the chamber, and the blue wool curtains lifted and swung with his passing. Polycarp rose at once and went to the door, and Jenny, reaching with her mind, heard him say to the men outside, "Go after him. You know what to do, but be quiet about it."

The Master caught Jenny by the wrist as she tried to follow. For a moment they looked into one another's eyes, bright blue into blue, understanding and not wanting to understand. "They won't hurt him," said Polycarp. "Just escort him to his room. Please understand, Lady Jenny. We cannot let him go free. No one who has had dealings with the Hellspawn, who owes a teind to any of that kind, can go free."

She jerked her arm against his grip, but he did not let go. Furious, she demanded, "Or me either?"

His blue eyes were sad. "Or you either, Lady Jenny. Think about it."

She pulled away and stood in the lamplit study, trembling.

"The Law holds harmless those who have been possessed," said Polycarp, "because in any case they seldom survive. But those who go willingly to the Hellspawn and bargain with them cannot be trusted, nor let to live. It is the bravest thing I've ever seen a man do, but it remains that he owes them a teind he cannot pay, and in the end he must be theirs. That we cannot allow. Not in life, and not in death."

Jenny looked back helplessly at Miss Mab, but the gnome-witch met her eyes with calm pity and grief. "Thou knowst it for truth, Lady. I helped him, that they would have one less mage within their thrall, knowing that you, as mage, would understand. With the King's Moon he is theirs; when the breath goes out of his ribs he is theirs; and by the demons that seized thee, the demons that hold thy son, thou knowst that he cannot pay them what it is they ask. This is how demons work, child. Through terror, and love, and fear to let the worst come to pass."

"There has to be a way."

The last New Moon of summer had set almost three hours ago. Even so far to the south the sky held a lingering indigo luminosity in which each star, like a dragon, sang its own name in music undecipherable to the human heart. From the battlements Jenny looked up at them in a kind of horror, and then beside her, into the white eyes of the gray-haired man who had come silently to her side.

Her voice sounded steady, detached, unreal to her own ears. "John tells me that the King's Moon was what they called the season when the King of the Long Strand, where Greenhythe is now, and the lords of the little realms of Somanthus and Silver and Urrate Isles were killed to pay a teind to the gods for harvest."

I know. The dragon tilted his head a little to one side, a characteristic movement. She could almost see the glowing bobs of his antennae. *I was there.* His gestures were not human, nor was there anything resembling humanity in the structure of the narrow, odd-boned face. It was curious to see him as a man, though no stranger, she thought, than the days she had passed in the form of a dragon. If he could transform himself into a dragon no larger than a peregrine, surely this matter was little to him.

Yet still it gave her a strange feeling, looking into those diamond-crystal eyes, alien and without pity.

She repeated, "There has to be a way."

It would be ill done, Wizard-woman, to cheat the demons, as though we were petty gamesters plying ruses with fake gems in the marketplace. Morkeleb laid his long white hands on the stone of the parapet. Only his nails were unhuman, black curving claws like enameled steel. His shoulders seemed stick-thin, like a doll wrought of bird-bone.

Honor is honor, whether one bargains with the honorable or the dishonorable. This is what the Shadow-drakes said. Once I did not think so. But to take freedom and healing, and return to them only charred bones; this is theft. Moreover, I do not think demons would be deceived even by the slyest of illusion.

Sometimes, Jenny, there is no way.

"Easy words," she cried, thinking of the means by which demon-callers were killed. And her mind formed the shape, if not the words: *You do not love.*

The white eyes regarded her, and hers fell before them.

It is true that loving is not a thing of dragons. Yet sometimes we do not only because we do not know how. I would not have entered the Hell behind the mirror, Jenny, because I know the hopelessness of it. Yet he, too, knew, and here you stand in the hope of being freed. I could never have done such, for I did not—I do not—know how to perform acts of such foolishness. Yet I am grateful to him that he did what I, Morkeleb the Black, the Destroyer of the Elder Droon and the greatest of the star-drakes, what I could not and would not have done because it is not a thing of dragons.

He turned his eyes from her, to the velvet gulfs of Nast Wall and the thin red flicker of John's comet burning low above its ridges. His brows pinched above the thin birdlike nose.

Now I am not even a thing of dragons, for I surrendered my will—surrendered my magic—that the demons should not trap me through it, and I do not understand now what it is that I am.

Morkeleb, my friend . . . She touched his shoulder, and he regarded her with eyes that were no longer a crystalline labyrinth, but a straight road infinitely distant, vanishing into colorless air.

Morkeleb, my friend, you are what you are. I treasure you as you are, always. Whatever you do and are, or whatever you become, I will be your friend. Maybe not what you wanted, once on a time, but the best that is in me to give.

Not once on a time, he said, *and not always.* And she saw on his face the cold crystal track of tears. *For you will die, Wizard-woman, as humans die, and I will become what I will become, and what will exist of what lay between us?*

He looked away, unwilling that any should see his tears or his heart. He had loved gold with a deep and terrible covetousness, and he had loved power and the knowledge that power opened to him. She sensed in him the grief of knowing, as she did, that there was no going back to what he had been.

She put up her hand to brush away his tears, and he stayed it with his long cold-taloned grip.

Touch them not, Wizard-woman; they would burn your hand.

So she took the crystal dew-spoon from around her neck and caught the tears in its bowl, and set it aside on the parapet.

What exists of the worlds that once you visited? she asked him, and gestured to the darkness and the stars. *They are still there, living in your heart.*

The hearts of dragons are not as the hearts of men. They are of a different composition, like their tears. I can return unto those worlds whensoever I choose. But you will be lost to me in the dark oceans of time, and there will be no calling you back. It was for this reason that I sought the Birdless Isle, and for this reason that I remained.

Nothing is ever lost, said Jenny. *Nor ever forgotten. And who knows what lies in the hearts and the dreams of the Dragonshadows? When the Twelve Gods drove the Lord of Time away from them into exile, it was because they had forgotten that they were only things that he had himself dreamed. Nevertheless he let them drive him away and surrendered his godhood to them. He knew that they would always have existence in his heart for as long as it mattered either to him or to them.*

He said nothing for a time, but wept, and she stood silent beside him, holding his hand, and now and then gathering his tears in the crystal spoon. And it was true what he had said, that they blackened the silver handle where they touched it, as if, though the body he wore was that of a man, it was like his dragon-shape, formed of elements unknown on the planet of oceans and trees.

In time he looked at her with a glint of his old amused irony and said, *Vixen, that you turn even my grief into a present for your husband's sake,* and she heard under his wryness a new understanding of what it is to be human.

She picked up the spoon, which had a pool of tears in the bowl perhaps the volume of the first joint of her thumb. *I will throw this over the parapet, then,* she said, willing in her heart that she would have the strength to do as she said. *I would not rob you of your grief, my friend.*

Nor I rob you of your husband, he said, *my friend.* And he took the spoon from her hand and laid it carefully down on the stone once more. *Nor yet would I rob my friend of his wife, for whom he did what I have neither the courage nor the foolishness—love, as you term it—to know how to do.* He touched her cheek and her hair, as John did, and looked into her eyes with eyes that were not human and had never been. *I understand now why we star-treaders do not take the semblance of humankind more often.*

She shook her head, not understanding, and he drew her to him and kissed her lips.

Because it is not a semblance, he said. *And we are not fools. There. Now I have done.* He reached up one hand with its long black nails and touched aside the tears that ran down her own face. *Is this why the God of Women is also the Queen of the Sea? Because tears are as the ocean is, salt?*

She smiled a little. *I do not know. Maybe because they are as the ocean is, endless.*

As is all human grief that waters the roots of loving. And his words in her mind encompassed the great stretches of time he had seen, before her birth or her mother's birth, and long after she and John and Ian would be dead. He nodded toward the spoon with its thin, glimmering pool. "If you will send that to the Demon Queen, look that the vial you choose is wrought of crystal, not glass." He spoke now as men speak, though in her mind she still felt the moving currents of his thought. "The tears of dragons are dangerous things. They will consume ordinary glass. Even crystal they will burn away in time."

She had been reaching toward the spoon but now stayed her hand. In Morkeleb's star-dark eyes she saw the echo of her own thought. And because she had lived many years with a naturalist who tinkered with flying machines and chemicals and clockspring toys, she asked, "Exactly how much time?"

22

"**M**y only love," breathed the Demon Queen, and her mouth, like a black blood-ruby, touched and traced John's lips, the shape of his nose and the oval scar in the pit of his throat. "My servant and my love." Her hand slipped down his arm, his flank; her skin under his answering caress was pale pink as the hearts of lilies, flawless as that of a young girl, and scented of sweet-olive and jasmine. Her hair was a coiled ocean of sable silk.

She had the look, Jenny realized, of Kahiera Nightraven.

Her body laid over John's in the ember-cave of red velvet and candle flame, sinuous as a snake's. Jenny tried to shut her eyes and look away. Warm arms embraced her, and Amayon's voice breathed in her ear, *I had to show you this, my darling. For your own good I had to show you. He turned from you, the moment he entered her realm.*

You are lying. Jenny tried to call to her memory the image of John dying in the rain, run through by Ian's spear. She couldn't. It had never happened and the lie had never been told.

You are lying.

But her body ached with the memory of Amayon's pleasure-heat within her, with the gold-stained glory of domination and power. She struggled to wake but sank into memories of other embraces, delicious and degrading, and through them heard Amayon's voice calling her name. Calling from the white shell where he was imprisoned, as her own heart was imprisoned in the flawed jewel in Caradoc's silver bottle.

I can still come back to you. I can still love you, as he never loved you. How could he love you, he who never understood?

"Love?" came John's voice softly through the haze of the dream. "Love?"

She woke up with tears on her face and a desperate urge to know where exactly Amayon's white shell was being kept. John was bending over her. And her first thought, swiftly shoved aside, was rage that John was there to keep her from going to search.

His finger brushed her face. "You're crying."

I'm crying because you lay with the Demon Queen!

But that had been her dream, not his. Or maybe not his. Or she could not prove it had been his.

She drew a shaky breath and wiped her face, which was indeed wet with tears. John had kindled the lamp beside his narrow bed, but the heavily latticed square of the chamber window—he was not yet being kept in a barred cell—was cinder-gray with dawn. "I'm beginning to understand why dealing with demonkind is always an ill thing," she said. "They don't leave you alone. Not in sleep, not in waking, not in death."

His jaw tightened, and she saw the oval scar where the Demon Queen had marked him. Last night, after he had fallen asleep, she had turned back the blankets, and it had seemed to her that his body was marked with half-visible silvery traces that disappeared when she leaned close to look. The marks of the Queen's lovemaking. The lines of possession.

"We'll get through this." He cupped the side of her face in his palm.

But in her heart she thought—or perhaps Amayon whispered to her, sometimes it was not possible to tell—*They're only waiting for you to leave, to get out the acid and the ax.*

"Miss Mab's outside," John said softly. "She says she's sorry it's so early, but she's got word calling her back into the Deep."

Jenny pulled a voluminous robe over her head and sat up as the gnome-witch came in, followed by a servant. The servant bore a tray of braided breads, honey, clotted cream, and apples. "You lads all right out there?" John put his head out through the door to address the guards in the gallery. "Gaw, Polycarp should at least send you what I get in here," he added, inspecting the bowls of porridge the men had before them. He went back and fetched a couple of apples from the tray.

"No, thank you, sir," said one of the soldiers, studying the fruit with a wary eye.

John stood for a moment, the apple in his hand; Jenny saw the change in his eyes.

Demon-caller. Trafficker with the Spawn. Helltreader.

"Aye, well, then," he said. And then, "I'm not their servant yet, y'know."

"No, sir," said the man stolidly.

John returned quietly to the room and bit into the apple himself.

Miss Mab had opened the blue stone box. It contained white powder, which she touched with her spit-dampened finger and used to mark Jenny's wrists, eyelids, and tongue. "How well this may work I know not," said the gnome-witch, brushing back Jenny's hair to peer into her eyes. "Thy heart is still prisoner within the talisman jewel, and it may be that nothing can be cured until it be freed."

Jenny nodded. She didn't think she could endure another night of Amayon whispering to her in her dreams. Of the knife-crystal visions that had visited her: her own drunkenness, cruelty, and rut; Ian grosser, more sarcastic, more filthy of mind and more ingenious at the giving of pain to people and to animals as each day passed. Ian trapped in a jewel as she was still trapped, weeping in agony and humiliation, begging his demon to let him die.

John in the arms of the Demon Queen.

She shut her teeth on the pain and made herself nod.

"Perhaps you can apply it again tomorrow," she said. "With some spells I've found repeated applications to have effect when a single occasion has not the strength."

"Indeed I have so found," replied the old gnome, carefully closing up the box. "I shall try again at sunset, if thou feel no better through the day. I should return from the Deep by that time. And in my home warren I shall try to weave other spells for your comfort, until such time as the healing takes hold. The Talking River beneath the ground is a stream of power, and its power grows as it flows deeper into the earth. By the time it passes singing over the Five Falls on the ninth level, where my warren lies, its influence can be woven into wreaths and braids, and such I will bring to you, to help you sleep without dreams, and Aversin also."

Jenny glanced quickly at those wise old pale eyes, praying that the gnome-witch could not read those dreams, but she could not interpret what she saw in Miss Mab's wrinkled face.

A guard came to fetch John, for the half-made Urchins were being brought into the courtyard. Jenny, who had dressed by that time in a plain brown and yellow dress such as servants wore, gathered her magic within her, to witch the senses of the guards that none might see her pass. But as she did so she felt Amayon's mind, the strength of his will, redouble within her, in response to her calling of power. She felt, too, that curious dislocation, as if all things were seen through a fragment of glass— through the green crystal of the imprisoning jewel.

Morkeleb had spoken of the Shadow-drakes putting aside their magic. It was hard to do. She simply walked as quietly as she could from the room in John's wake, and the guards, having had no instructions concerning her, let her pass.

*   *   *

It was said in the north that everything that could be bought and sold, was bought and sold in the Undermarket beneath Halnath Citadel, where the Marches of the Realm met Ylferdun Deep. The giant cavern, cut into the cliff on which the citadel stood, was the gate-court of the gnomes. Legend said they could seal that opening with a stone wall in the space of a night. The gates at the inner side of the huge chamber were certainly solid, closed fast night and day and guarded from four turrets. As she entered the Undermarket, Jenny could see in the stone floor the metal tracks on which the little gnome carts ran to carry goods in and out of the cavern.

The gnomes mostly sold silver and gold, gems and objects wrought of rare alloys, or ingenious machines produced by their incomparable skill. In exchange, merchants brought spices and herbs, rare chemicals and salts. There was silk from the Seven Islands and the stiffer, drier silks of Gath and Nim; rare birds and the feathers of birds completely unknown in the north; jade and porcelain and musk. In another part of the market oxen, pigs, and sheep were penned. These the gnomes bought with silver and copper, for they were fond of meat and in their caverns had only white cave-fish and mushrooms.

The merchants set up tables in long rows, their wares laid out on blankets or bright cloths. Some erected booths or pavilions of wood, with flowers or bundles of fresh greens tied on the posts. Others put up tents, and near the front of the cavern, where the wind drew off the smoke, hawkers fried sausages and river fish or steamed sweet dumplings and custards. Thus the whole vast gloomy space smelled of hot fat and fresh flowers, of crushed greens, spices, sweat, stone, lamp oil, animals, dung, and blood. The noise in the vaulted space was terrific.

Jenny walked from dealer to dealer in vessels of stone and glass, and finally settled on a snuff-bottle of alabaster as thin and brittle as paper— "So fine you can tell whether it contains nut-brown or betel, my lady!" enthused the huckster. Then she found a worker in colored glass who, after turning the bottle over in her calloused fingers, nodded and said, "Aye, I can enclose it in a vial, though the work of it's so fine t'were a shame to hide it."

"It's a riddle," said Jenny. "Designed for one who is clever enough to remove the glass without damaging the alabaster inside."

She paid for it in silver that Miss Mab had given her—neither she nor John had a penny of their own—and promised to return the following day for the finished vessel. Then she ascended the endless wearying flights of stairs, pausing to rest on the frequent landings where benches were set and vendors of lemonade and felafel plied their wares. At the citadel again she sought out the courtyard where John and Miss Tee, the gnome engineer, were instructing several dozen of the Master's warriors in the use of the dragon-slaying Urchin machines.

"It doesn't need a deal of strength to haul the cage around," John was saying. He stood on the wheeled engine platform surmounted only by the steering cage itself, stripped like his audience to singlet and breeches. Miss Tee—Ordagazedgwyn was her name among her own folk—worked among the craftsmen at the side of the court, assembling the other machines.

"Keep your arms and legs soft—it'll gie kill you if you go heavin' about with all your might when you don't have to. Just swing your body's weight, and harden up at the end, like this . . ." He moved, the characteristic shift of weight necessary to guide the cage, and as he positioned each soldier, made sure they understood the balance necessary, the peculiar use of momentum.

Watching him, Jenny's soul seemed to knot itself behind her breastbone. He bore the demon's mark in the pit of his throat, and the knowledge in his heart of what humankind would do to him before the ripening of the moon. But he was making sure these children—in their youth they seemed no more—understood enough about the machines that they'd stand a chance against dragons and magic.

Jenny crossed to him, through the dust and clanging of hammers. She was half the courtyard away when he turned his head, his eyes seeking hers. It was as if his whole face grew light. "Jen." He stepped down and took her hands and kissed her. "Miss Mab was out here before daybreak, Miss Tee tells me, markin' each of our Urchins with magic chicken-tracks in whatever was in that red vial." He gestured toward the dusty confusion of machinery. "She left the vial with me, for you to finish up. We've gie little time."

He glanced past her at the two bodyguards, leaning stolidly against the wall. Polycarp himself stood in the colonnade, blue eyes bright and filled with envy. Jenny felt it when John's gaze crossed that of the Master. For a moment it seemed to her that she could see, with the thin slip of the waxing day-moon over his shoulder, the marks of the Demon Queen's patterns down his arms and across his shoulders: Runes spelling out words that she could almost read. They faded the next instant, but his face looked as if he had not slept.

But he asked her only, "How is it with you?"

"Well." She made herself smile.

Shadow fell over the court; soundless dark wings. The students looked up, crying out and reaching for swords that no longer hung at their belts. Someone made a move for one of the catapults set up nearby, and

John said, "Don't shoot at your dancing-master, son; y'know how far in advance I had to book us the lesson?" He swung up into the unprotected cage and settled his feet into the straps. "You, Blondie. Up here with me, and hold tight. We'll make the lot of you Dragonsbanes before the full moon."

Morkeleb circled high once, then dropped, striking and snatching. John whipped and jerked on the steering cage, spinning the platform clear of the blow. "You got to watch for his tail," he called to the students who scattered in a wide, fascinated ring. "Head and tail, like right fist and left fist. Don't waste your shots on his sides." Morkeleb dove and snatched, slashed and hissed, and beside her, Jenny felt Polycarp shiver with awe and delight.

It was, as John had said, a dancing lesson, a game of cat-and-mouse: graceful, deadly, and astonishingly agile and swift. Once Morkeleb got his claws under the platform and flipped it; John kicked his feet free, swung his weight on and under the cage, and with a lurch and a jerk got the platform on its wheels again. *They must have counterweighted it,* thought Jenny, *after the battle at Cor's Bridge.* "Watch how the dragon moves," panted John, waiting while the tall blond girl scrambled back onto the platform. "They have no weight, but they use their wings to balance and turn, see? When they shift, that's when to try to get a shot off under the wing." Only Jenny felt the steaming mental ripple of Morkeleb's ire and felt in her mind the unspoken words that he did not send to John:

Beware, little Songweaver. I teach you that the demons' hold may be broken, but I learn from you, too.

She remembered his human face in the starlight, the lonely grief in his labyrinthine eyes. And it seemed to her that as the dragon passed before the afternoon sun, bone and muscle and sinew were momentarily only a trick of the light. She seemed to see not the black steel and enamel of muscle and bone, but only smoke shot with starlight, half-visible.

Not human, she thought, and now not of dragons either. But he understands. *Sometimes there is no way . . .*

Only trust in the mad Lord of Time to sort it all out.

Oh, my friend, she thought. *Oh, my friend.*

"Up you get." John slapped the blond girl's flank. "Feet in the straps. Grab the handles—one of you, get up here and let me show you how to crank the engine. They need a deal of that. There. Now. Off we go."

Polycarp crossed to where Jenny stood, slipping the black robe from his shoulders to stand in his singlet and hose. "I have to learn this," he said, breathless with delight. "I have to try."

His young soldiers applauded wildly when they saw him coming, laughed and called out. Spread-eagled motionless in the Urchin's cage against the pale sky, John regarded him in silence, then tilted his head a little and said, "You've your nerve."

The Master of Halnath looked away. The two bodyguards glanced at one another, started to speak, and then stopped. There was a silence, too, among the young warriors. Obviously none of them knew that John stood under sentence of burning alive the hour before the teind came due.

Polycarp looked up again. "Do you understand?"

"Aye. I understand." John stepped from the cage and handed the Master up onto the platform, to the soldiers' renewed cheers. Only afterward, when Jenny was examining the spell-wards Miss Mab had laid on the other Urchins, did John come over and take her aside. Morkeleb was patiently working with another pair of students, slowing his slashes and feints; Jenny could hear the rumble of his thoughts in the back of her mind, like a wolf-killer hound grumbling about being put to watch pups. The liquid in the Demon Queen's vial, like the vial itself, was dark red, shiny, and thick. Miss Tee told her it had been thinned with water and painted on the frames with a doghair writing-brush, but the liquid did not thin. Rather, it seemed to convert the water into itself. It was as if the runes of safeguard and countermagic, traced up the ribs and across the spiked plates of the Urchins, were drawn in blood.

"Are you all right, love?" John took off his spectacles and with the back of his arm wiped the sweaty dust from his face. "Listen. Don't be angry at the Master—about those two blokes, I mean." He jerked his head at the bodyguards. "And don't . . ." He hesitated. "Spells or no spells, they're going to need all the help they can against Rocklys and her dragons." His eyes met hers, peering and naked without the protective lenses; made as if to flinch away and then returned. Knowing she knew. "It'd be good if you went with them."

Don't fight him, she saw in them, behind the fear of what he knew would happen when she left the citadel. *Don't widen the gap, for demons to come into the world. Don't leave yourself open to them by craving power or revenge.*

"It was stupid of me, bargaining with the Demon Queen. It's not like I hadn't read a thousand books and scrolls and legends sayin' *This is a bad idea.* I"—he swallowed hard—"I'll pay this teind somehow. I won't go back and be her servant, you know."

"No," Jenny said, "and I think I've found the way."

While they ate supper in John's chamber and waited for Miss Mab, Jenny told John of what Morkeleb had said the previous night, and what she had purchased that day. "According to Morkeleb, a dragon's tears are corrosive. They combine with glass, volatilizing both, so neither the glass nor the tears remain. The alabaster they'll eat through in, I calculate, about thirteen days—the time that lies between now and the full moon. We can . . ."

There was a scratching at the shutters of the chamber's single window. Jenny went to open it; Morkeleb slipped through. Strangely, Jenny found the sight of him in miniature more disturbing than at his true size, like jeweler's work come alive. He spread his wings and floated to the back of her abandoned chair, wrapped his long tail about one of the back-supports and cocked his glittering head.

Victorious in your seeking, Wizard-woman?

"I was. The glassmaker should have it ready tomorrow. Is there something that can destroy a thunderstone in the same fashion, minutes after we render it over to them? Before they can use it for their own purposes? What destroys iron?"

Water, said Morkeleb in her mind. *Rust. Time.*

"It always comes back to time." John picked out a fragment of pork from the stew and offered it to Morkeleb with his fingers. "If the Lord of Time were to return with a bag of the stuff for sale he'd make a bloody fortune."

Only among men, replied the dragon. *It is said the Shadow-drakes play with it, make music from it, as we make music from gold. Keep your scorched and lifeless pap, Dreamweaver; it is not a thing of dragons to eat such stuff.*

"Polycarp's cook'll slit his wrists with grief if he hears." John popped the meat into his own mouth. "Is it true thunderstones are bits of stars?"

They are pieces of what men call Falling Stars, the dragon replied. *No more true stars than this comet you have been seeking. In truth, they are balls and fragments of rock that float in the dark between worlds. Thus human magic cannot weave spells to destroy or change them, for you do not know the world whereof they come. Most are covered with ice; between worlds it is very cold. They drift in great shoals, like north-sea pack-ice in the spring. The young sport among them.*

Into Jenny's mind came the image of drifting chunks and towers and fortresses of ice, glimmering in the starlight, and the rainbow shadows of dragons flickering among them, no bigger, it seemed, than dragonflies. In the void between worlds the dragons did not have the same shape that they wore in the world of ocean and trees, and this, too, she found troubling.

Stars themselves are not what they appear. They consist solely of fire, and heat, and the light they emit. There is no "fragment" of a star.

"Aye, well," said John softly, "she didn't say 'fragment,' now, did she? She said 'piece.' Which could mean the star's light itself, couldn't it? Gathered in a hothwais, like the fire's heat that kept the old *Milkweed* in the air, or like the air the gnomes use when they go into the levels where the air is foul."

They looked at each other, with uncertainty and hope. "Miss Mab will know," said Jenny. "It would take the magic of the gnomes to prepare one. No line of human wizardry ever understood how to source magic to alter stone. What about the gift from an enemy?"

"Well," said John softly. "I've had a thought or two about that. And I'm afraid you're going to have to break me out of here so I can collect that one meself."

The moon had long sunk below the citadel walls when Jenny emerged from John's room. She nodded to the guards and felt their eyes on her the length of the battlement: *the Demon-trafficker's woman. Maybe a trafficker in demons herself. Like that woman a year ago in Haylbont Isle who cut her children to pieces.*

Jenny found herself praying that Miss Mab had returned with the spells against dreaming. The prospect of another night like the last made her frightened and sick.

The narrow stair at the end of the gallery—the dark arched doors of the empty Scriptorium, then down the winding servants' ways. Storerooms and kitchen wings. Gnomes never liked to be housed in towers. There was a small courtyard at the citadel's lowest level, near the bronze doors that led to the Deep stairs. From the cobbled pavement Jenny descended a further half-dozen steps to an area barely larger than a closet, from which several doors let into a suite of subterranean rooms. She saw no light in the round window she knew was Miss Mab's, but this meant nothing. Mageborn and a gnome, Miss Mab could read in the dark if she chose. When Jenny tapped at the door and spoke the gnome-wife's name, however, she received no reply, and the door gave inward with her touch.

"Miss Mab?" She stepped through, looking around at the darkened room. "Taseldwyn?"

The cupboard stood open and empty; the blankets had been stripped from the bed. Where Miss Mab's enormous jewel box had stood on the end of the table there was nothing, no combs or brushes, no blue satin slippers. Puzzled, Jenny stepped out into the areaway.

"What is it? Who comes?" Light flared topaz behind the glass of another door. The door opened wider and revealed the wrinkled face of Miss Tee. "Ah, the magewife!" The door opened wider. The engineer was dressed for bed, in tucked and embroidered linen. Her pale-green hair lay braided on her thick breasts, and she had removed all her many earrings for the night. "Didst come for Arawan-Taseldwyn, dear? She has gone."

"Gone?"

Miss Tee nodded. "The Lord of the Deep sent this morn, bidding her return to Ylferdun. Word of this traffic of demons reached him, I think. She has gone to be tested by the other Wise Ones of the Deep." She clicked her tongue disapprovingly and shook her head. "Fools. As if any would think Taseldwyn would have aught to do with such, or that I wouldn't know of it, I wouldn't see it in her eyes."

"Tested?" Jenny's heart turned chill. "You mean she's a prisoner?"

"They're all fools." Miss Tee shrugged. "And so they'll find, the Wise Ones, Utubarziphan and Rolmeodraches and the rest of the mages, but only after they've wasted a year . . ."

"A year?"

The green eyes blinked up at her. They were the color of peridot, a stone Jenny had come to hate. "This is the length of time, they say, in which a demon's influence will show itself." She set down the lamp she carried and took and patted Jenny's hand in her own hard muscular ones. "Worry not on this, child. She is only held in her own warrens on the Ninth level, under guard to be sure, but she will be well treated. Thou canst be sure of that. She is of the Howteth-Arawan, and they are powerful in all the Deeps of the Delver-Folk. Their Patriarch will never let the council condemn one of theirs. Even for humans a year can't be that long. Sevacandrozardus, Lord of the Deep, is a fool and a twitterer on the subject of demons. Dost know he wished even to have the doors to the citadel shut, because of that vial, and the seal, and the box? Because thou who wert possessed of a demon still walked unhindered? Yes, great ill came of the demons in times past, but just because man or woman touched an object that was touched by Hellspawn does not mean they will become corrupt themselves."

Climbing the stair to the citadel's upper levels, Jenny wasn't so sure of that. Throughout the day, the reminiscence of Amayon had returned to her, over and over again, like an itch that could be neither scratched nor salved. It came back now, the frantic desire to know at least where the shell had been bestowed.

She put it aside. It would do no good, she thought. She was reminded of her sister, when Sparrow suspected her husband of carrying on an affair with Mol Bucket: Sparrow had followed Trem one night and had seen him go into the bold-eyed cowherd's house. There were some things it was better not to know.

Miss Mab in prison. Even in her own chambers a year would be a long time. Would the Lord of the Deep or the gnome sorcerers whose magic was the true heart of the Deep permit Jenny to see Miss Mab? Would they even let her into the Deep?

At the dark archways of the Scriptorium she paused. Jenny could see a line of brightness framing the door of Polycarp's study. On impulse she hurried across the cold tiles. A thunderstone that could be used to form a demon-gate was one matter. A hothwais, which, for all the understanding of the nature of stone that lay at its creation, was at bottom a low-level spell, was another. Even if it retained within it the light of the stars, it could not be used by the demons for any purpose whatever.

When she reached the door, she found it open a little, the lamp inside sending a slice of yellow light across the octagonal tiles. Jenny touched the door, pushing it farther ajar. Within she saw Polycarp seated at the pickled oak table where she had so often scried him in conference with John. The fire burned low in the round hearth, mingling its glow with that of the pierced lamps to thread the Master's mop of curls with amber, edge the bony arch of the nose, and tip the lashes of his shadowed eyes with brightness.

His arms were stretched out on the table and cupped in his palms he held a small white conch-shell, mottled with pink and stoppered with crimson wax. He bent his head, as if listening to a voice whispering almost too low to be understood. His eyes were half-shut, concentrating on everything that was being said.

Jenny stepped back, cloaking herself automatically in darkness and glamour. She almost threw up with shock. *No,* she thought. *Polycarp, no. Put it down. Put it away.*

She thought, *No wonder the Lord of the Deep suspects Miss Mab as well. No wonder he speaks of having the Deep locked.*

No wonder they want to kill John.

Morkeleb spoke truly. This is an infection spreading poison to whatever it touches.

The Master's thin fingers stroked the shell delicately. Then his mouth flinched in revulsion, and he put the thing on the table and pushed it away. He rose so suddenly that he nearly overset his chair, and stood for a time, breathing hard and shivering in every limb. With convulsive speed he snatched up the shell and carried it to the black iron cupboard on the wall. He thrust the shell inside and slammed the door with a clank. His fingers fumbled with the key, the brass glinting fiery in the lamplight. He twisted it hard and crossed the room in two strides to his desk, flipping open a box of carved black oak, as if he would put the key into it.

But he didn't. He put it in his pocket.

Jenny melted into the shadows and fled to John's room with cold dread beating in her heart.

23

"**D**estroy her."

It was Ian's voice.

He lounged in a camp chair in Caradoc's tent, though Jenny couldn't see the rest of the tent; it was as though the wicked ur-light shone sickly only around the table where the boy and Caradoc sat. His long black hair was oily and unwashed, and his face was not the face of a child.

"And find another wizard where?" Caradoc's shirt was open and the silver bottle that he carried around his neck now lay on the table. Eight jewels were scattered across the table. Each flickered in the wasted light.

"We can't risk it."

"Scared?"

Ian's eyes narrowed. He turned his head and looked through the wall of green crystal that separated them from Jenny. The jewels on the table seemed more alive than his eyes. "Concerned," he temporized, and through the double and treble meanings in his voice Jenny sensed—felt—remembered from Amayon's mind the shape and terror and darkness of the Hell from which they'd come, a cold place where soft things shifted and mutated, feeding upon one another and living in fear of the formless awfulness in the Hell's heart.

"Don't be." Caradoc held up a bright green jewel and, with it in his hand, walked over to the crystal wall behind which Jenny crouched, naked and shivering.

He smiled, his broad, clean-shaven face curved with contempt. She saw again, through the human arrogance, the face of the demon Folcalor: more intelligent than the others of his kind, sly and greedy and watchful. "It's this easy." He raised his staff with its moonstone head.

Jenny cried, *Don't! No!*

He struck the wall, struck it on the great fire-rimmed flaw that ran from the floor to lose itself in the darkness above Jenny's head, and at the blow she felt faint, as if she were bleeding.

John! she screamed, but John was asleep—she could see him sleeping far off. Her own body lay curled at his side, the body she could no longer reach, no longer touch. Though the moon had set early, Jenny could see, as if by its pallid light, the patterns that traced his flesh like the slime-track of some unspeakable thing; the pale mark left in the pit of his throat. As she watched John turned his face away, his expression taut with pleasure: *Aohila,* he said.

Help me!

He reached out, and she heard the Demon Queen laugh.

"Mother?" For a quick second she saw through the crack the bright summer night in the Winterlands, and Adric's stocky form against the backdrop of battlements and stars. "Mother, is that you?"

Then Caradoc's staff smote the crack in the wall like an ore-crusher's hammer, and Jenny staggered back and fell. Blood from a hundred painless cuts was sticky on her hands. She tried to crawl away from the wall, but the demon loomed there in the darkness, striking the crack again and again. Splinters burst and flew from his knotted staff and from the wall itself, like chips of glass. Rage contorted his face; when he opened his mouth, green light came out, and curls of smoke. Unable to breathe, Jenny crept toward the farthest wall, but her own flesh was too much for her to endure. She sank to the floor in her own blood, covered her head with her arms, and waited.

She woke sometime after, exhausted.

Caradoc was gone. The circles he had drawn glowed faintly still in the darkness. Something told her that it was mid-morning in the world outside, the world most people knew as real.

Aching with weakness, she dragged herself to the flaw in the jewel and through it poured her consciousness into her distant body again.

There was a very old spell Jenny had learned from Nightraven—not that Nightraven had ever used such a cantrip herself. But the women of the Iceriders sometimes used it, in the places where their magic feathers told them their lovers were meeting with younger and better-favored girls. It was a spell that could be worked with very slight power.

Exhaustion weighed her down, beyond anything she had felt in the hard days at Palmorgin. Food lay ready on a tray for her: John had used the bread, the boiled eggs, the fruits, and the salt fish to create a dumpy little lady all stuck together with jam, "I love you" squiggled in honey around the rim. But though she laughed, she was barely able to eat, and the bitter memory returned, of John whispering the Demon Queen's name, oblivious to Jenny's cries for help.

She washed and dressed and collected what she would need for Nightraven's spell: a curtain weight for a spindle and a basketful of weed-fibers, dust, lint, and the combings of her own hair. These she carried down to the Undermarket. Spreading her cloak in a corner behind the booth of a woman selling gourds—cut and glazed and painted as bottles and dippers—she began to spin thread, and with every turn of the spindle, with every twist of her fingers, she daubed a little magic into the air.

Morkeleb joined her, guised as a gray-haired man. Jenny did not know when. Maybe some spell of unseeing cloaked him; she did not know. But none spoke to either of them, and when the town merchants packed up their goods and the market wardens came around the hall making sure the last stragglers departed, they passed them by as if they were not there.

Once the hall was cleared, the bronze doors at its inner end opened. From the hall beyond those doors, carts were trundled out and loaded. Jenny used little magic, but only sat and spun and watched. And in time it was obvious that no one was looking at the end cart of the line, so she gathered her spinning into her basket and slipped into that cart, covering herself with her cloak.

She didn't know where Morkeleb hid, but after the carts had all been rolled into the inner hall and the doors closed and locked for the night, the dragon was there. Guards sat at a little table playing dominoes near the outer doors. The click of the dominoes sounded very loud, and the smell of the cocoa they drank filled the dark: rank, sweet, spicy. There were few lamps in the hall, and they hung on chains dozens of feet from the high stone ceiling. The night below the ground lay heavy on most of the chamber, among the looming shadows of the neatly packed carts. It did not take much magic to collect it a little thicker about herself as she crossed to the doors that led into the Deep.

Morkeleb met her there. He seemed uneasy, drawn in on himself: *It is troubling to me,* he said, *to become of humankind. The things of humans speak loudly in my flesh and my mind, anger and envy, sloth and fear— above all other things, fear. I ask myself things I would never ask: What if we cannot leave this place? What if I do not recall the turnings of the passageways and stairs? What if we are found, or my magic fails me, or we return to discover that this Master of Halnath has indeed listened to the demon in the shell and freed it to take over his flesh? Do men and women truly live in such fear?*

Most do, said Jenny. *And most of the ills and griefs of humankind arise out of it. And at the bottom of all fears is the knowledge that all will one day end.*

Morkeleb said, *Ah,* and fell silent for a time. At the foot of the stair they crossed a bridge, lacy stone grown in a thousand turrets and columns. Water thundered far below them in darkness. *And magic is the anodyne to those fears? The way to braid and weave air and fate and time? Or to give oneself the illusion that one does so?*

I suppose it is, said Jenny, startled. *I had not thought of it before, but yes. Magic is the weapon we wield against chance and time.*

And does it succeed? asked the dragon.

She said, *I do not know.*

The world beneath Nast Wall was crossed and woven with rivers, gorges, and bridges where lamps of silver burned. Everywhere, as they descended deeper, Jenny saw latticework windows looking out into those gorges, or opening from smaller dwelling-caverns into larger. Each passageway, each stair, each road was dimly illumined with globes and tall thin chimneys of colored glass, and by the light they shed the gnomes passed by on their business, their long ghostly hair wound up in jeweled sticks and combs and frames, or else left to trail over their bowed shoulders like clouds. None spoke to Morkeleb and Jenny, or seemed to see them. The dragon's cold hand, with its long claws, held Jenny's, and he led her unerringly through the ways that he had traversed with his mind and his dreams, when four years ago he had lain in the upper reaches of the Deep on the far side of the mountains, whispering music to be whispered in turn from the gnomes' gold.

There is too much gold here, he said, pausing to get his bearings at the head of a road through a cavern where the very stones sparkled. *The Shadow-drakes were right. I find now that its mere presence is a taste in my heart, a sweetness remembered, and it is difficult.*

Do any legends speak of where the Dragonshadows might have gone? asked Jenny, to distract him. To distract herself maybe, from the memories of her fear and her dream. *Could they have departed entirely from this world?*

I think . . . The dragon began and stopped, and Jenny could feel the currents of his thought check and swirl, like water around rocks. His profile shifted slightly as he looked at her sidelong. She saw in her mind what John had told her of, the Birdless Isle under the crystal brilliance of new morning, heard the slow heartbeat of the sea and the breathing of the wind. Felt their presence as a core of peace that plumbed the foundations of the world.

I do not think they would have departed this world, said the dragon, a new thought naked as a bird-peep, *without telling us.*

He led her between sparkling mountains of sinter and great pools that stretched like glass. In time they came to a place where a small river fell singing over five ledges of corrugated white limestone, overlooked by balconies cut and fretted into cavern wall. *They will be watching her,* said Morkeleb. *The Wise Ones of the gnomes.*

She said once that she comes forth often on her balcony, said Jenny. *We will wait.*

The dragon looked at her sidelong again, as if he sensed her weariness and hunger, but he said nothing. While they waited, a little to Jenny's surprise, he told her stories after the fashion of dragons, by speaking in music and images and scents in her mind, as if he would distract her as she had him. She saw a mingled wonderment of violet suns and gray oceans beating endlessly on lifeless shores, felt the different forms of magic, sourced from all those different stones and suns and those different patterns of stars. He told of worlds where livid-colored plants fought and devoured one another, of raindrop and seagull and the creeping life of the tide pools on the Last Isle. He spoke of the Dragonshadows he had known long ago, their deep power, their wisdom, their peace.

They are like the wind and the air, he said. *And yet now that I look back I see that they loved us, all of us who thought we chose our own way here.*

His hand, white and thin with its long black curving claws, lay on hers, and looking at his face she could not tell whether she saw a man's face or a dragon's.

In time Miss Mab came out on her balcony, clothed in a red robe. Morkeleb and Jenny climbed up to her, quietly, through the soft murmuring of the water and the smooth snow-and-salmon curves of the rock.

"A hothwais," she said thoughtfully, curling her short legs under her robe and looking from woman to dragon and back.

"Would this be safe?" asked Jenny. "Could demons turn a hothwais to harm, were one given them?"

"The very grasses of the field can demons turn to harm, child. I am not sure but that they cannot turn to harm the starlight thou wilt give them, in this hothwais, though I know not any way they can do so. And indeed, anything will be of lesser harm than what they might do with a true thunderstone. Is it true," she asked, turning her wise pale eyes on Morkeleb, "that stars be as thou sayest, vast storms of light and fire, not solid anywhere? This be a marvelous thing."

"Would it not be possible," asked Morkeleb after a time, "to place a Limitation on the hothwais itself, that its essence, its nature, fades with the fading of the starlight it holds? Thus the Demon Queen would be left with only a stone, of which one presumes, even in the realm of Hell, they have sufficient for their needs."

Miss Mab was silent for a long time, turning her huge, heavy rings on stubby fingers. Below the balcony the waterfalls gurgled a kind of endless, ever-varying music. As she had said, there was great power in the stream, power that Jenny felt even sitting on the terrace. Close-by someone played a harp, very different from the gnomish zither, and a woman's voice, unmistakably human, lifted in a sad and wistful song.

Here, too, thought Jenny, *they keep human slaves.*

"It should be so," Miss Mab replied slowly. "The nature of hothwais is permanence, not evanescence, so such is not commonly done. Yet I know of no reason why it could not be done. Let me see what I can do. I will send thee word, Jenny Waynest, at Halnath."

"I misdoubt this will be possible." Morkeleb spoke up quietly. "With Mistress Waynest's absence overnight, I think she may not return openly to the citadel. The fear of the Hellspawn is very strong, and she bears their mark."

Jenny looked, startled, at the dragon, and he returned her gaze with strange galactic eyes.

"It is true," said Miss Mab, "that mine own people have imprisoned me for a year and a day for even entering the Mirror chamber in the ruins of Ernine."

"Then send this thing to the camp at Cor's Bridge," said Morkeleb. "For there under the Regent's protection we will surely be."

Upon those words Miss Mab returned to her chamber and brought out honey-bread and curdled cream, strong-tasting white cheese and fruit, and light woolen blankets, for the air in the caverns was clammy and chill. Jenny slept uneasily, and woke, it seemed to her, more weary than when she had lain down. Morkeleb she did not think slept at all.

The dragon's prediction about Jenny's absence overnight turned out to be alarmingly true. When she slipped out of the merchandise cart into the Undermarket shortly before dawn, it was to find the citadel's soldiers searching the corners of the great cavern—perfunctorily, it was true, as if they truly did not expect to find anyone there. "What would a witch possessed of a demon be doing sleeping here anyway?" demanded one warrior of another, disgustedly pushing back his visor. "She's probably in Bel by now. And anyway, would we be able to see her?"

Probably, thought Jenny, settling into the darkest corner she could find and freezing. Despite Miss Mab's spells of dreamless rest the demon Folcalor had returned to her in the night, drawing circles of violation around the jewel that housed her true self, and the effort to keep his power at bay had sapped her strength badly. Still she managed to remain unseen until the guards had gone, then slipped out of the market cavern on their heels and up to the citadel again.

She did not know when Morkeleb left her. It was less magic than simply quiet and remaining unnoticed that got her through the service quarters, down the guarded passageway ("I've a bit of food from his Lordship the Master for Master John," she said to the guards, displaying a pot of honey and several rolls on a glazed tray borrowed from the kitchen) to the cell where she guessed, even without reaching forth her mageborn senses, they would be holding him chained.

She was right. Morkeleb was right. The chains were long enough that he could lie down, and the cell dry and provided with a pallet, but it was heavily guarded. The chains themselves were wyrd-written to render them proof against all but the most powerful spells. Weary as she was, spent as she was, it took Jenny nearly three-quarters of an hour to fashion a tiny cantrip that would send the guard outside to the privy, where she was able to abstract his keys when he set aside his belt.

"Jen!" John sat up, startled, as she entered his cell. He'd been sitting on his pallet, his back against the wall, reading—Polycarp had left him an enormous pile of books, but because of the manacles on his wrists he had to prop his hands and the book with his knees. "I was afraid some guard hereabouts took it into his head to kill you out of hand. They said you'd been missing overnight."

"I was in the Deep. They have Miss Mab a prisoner—"

"Gah!"

"They're afraid of the demons, John, and they've every right to be so." She was unlocking the ring of iron around his neck, the spancels on his wrists, as she spoke. The Demon Queen's mark stood out like a wound. She forced herself not to think about her dream, about the visions of him in those white serpent arms. "Miss Mab is going to make a hothwais to hold the light of a star. A harmless gift for the Demon Queen. But as to the third part of the teind . . ."

"I'll settle that." John stood up, hesitating with the book in his hand, clearly loath to abandon it. Then he shrugged and stuffed it into the front of his doublet, adding for good measure another one. "But to do it we'll have to go to Jotham."

The camp at the bridge bore every mark of hard usage under the bitter gray downpour of guardian storms. Its palisade protected the stone span but was black with fire, save where new wood gleamed yellow under the wet. And yet the banners of the House of Uwanë flew over the charred dugouts. As Morkeleb swept in low from the cloud-choked canyons, Jenny saw that few tents remained standing. The blackened ground within the defensive work was gashed with trenches, the earth above them giving them the look of long, twisted graves.

John, held in the dragon's claws, waved a white sheet taken from the citadel laundry at the men who came running from the trenches, crying out and pointing their arrows skyward. Only when Jenny saw one man, taller than all the rest and thinner, spectacles flashing in the pale day, emerge from underground at a run and wave his arms at the men did she say softly, "That's him. We can go in."

It is a trusting Wizard-woman.

"Even so," said Jenny. She felt the wave of Morkeleb's cynicism pass over her, as if he'd plunged through a wall of dark water, but he spread wide his wings for balance and drifted toward the ground. The men below jockeyed for position, but Gareth gestured again. A sweep of fugitive sunlight riffled his hair. The storms were definitely breaking. Flying through the passes, Jenny had felt it—the clouds dissolving, the magic that held them failing at last.

Morkeleb stretched out his hind-legs and settled on the earth.

"My lord, really!" Ector of Sindestray exclaimed angrily as Gareth walked forward, his hands outstretched.

"Jenny. John."

"Polycarp get in touch with you?" John asked jauntily.

"My lord, this man is under sentence of death . . . !"

"One of his pigeons came in this morning." Gareth's eyes flicked to the demon mark, then away. He looked unhappy. "He said Jenny had vanished. He said he was putting you under guard—"

"Ah. You haven't had the one about us stealing the vial and the seal and the box, then? You'll get that one tomorrow."

As he spoke Jenny touched the satchel she had tied around her body, the satchel Morkeleb had given her just before he resumed the form of the dragon. *I think it best we have charge of these, instead of Master Polycarp,* he had said. *They are, after all, Aversin's, purchased with the costliest of all currency.*

"This is outrageous!" insisted Lord Ector. He still wore court mantlings—Jenny couldn't imagine how he kept them properly folded. "My lord, you're aware of how demons influence men's minds! How they take over men's bodies! You can't pretend you trust these . . . people."

Gareth reached out, then drew his hand back without touching the satchel. "Polycarp wrote of these things," he said. "And of what you did to achieve them." Ector cleared his throat significantly but Gareth would not meet his eyes. Wind flicked the pink and blue ends of his hair. He had a fresh wound on his cheek, and his thick spectacles had been broken and mended, and there was a hardness to his face, a grim set to his mouth.

"It wasn't you by any chance who told him to chain me up?"

There was long a dreadful silence. Gareth shuffled—*No ballad of old Dragonsbanes,* thought Jenny, *provided guidance on situations like this*—then at length said quietly, "No. But you yourself know all the legends, the histories, involving demons. Polycarp isn't the only one who favors invoking the penalty, you know."

John glanced at Ector and said nothing. Gareth flushed.

"I've told Polycarp, and others on the council, to wait. That I trusted you."

John bowed his head, but his mouth was wry. "Thank you. But you really shouldn't. If it weren't me, you shouldn't. And with Jen vanishing as she did I can't blame him, I suppose, for lockin' me up. Mind you, I'm not ettlin' to walk into the rest of it, but I'm workin' on that." He propped his spectacles on his nose. "Poly'll be here . . . when?"

"Tomorrow," said Gareth. "They're taking the Urchins through the Deep of Ylferdun today. Reinforcements from Bel have been sighted—the rain that protected us slowed them down." Another sweep of sunlight sparkled on the soaked and puddled earth of the camp, and Gareth and every warrior there looked uneasily at the sky.

"Played hob with your harvest, too, I'll bet." John shoved back the long hair from his eyes. "They'll be on us tonight, you know—Rocklys and her lot, I mean."

"I know. They have to, if they're to take the bridge. I'm having the men stand to . . ."

"Nah." John shook his head. "Let 'em eat their dinners and catch a bit of kip. Nuthin'll happen till . . . eighth hour of the night, I'd say. Halfway till dawn."

"Why halfway?"

"Because that's when men who've been standing to since the eighth hour of the afternoon slack their guard and figure nothing's going to happen till dawn. That's when they take a bit of a doze or sneak off to the privy, or start lookin' about the camp to see who else is on watch they can talk to."

Lord Ector opened his mouth in indignant protest as Gareth and John brushed past him, side by side. "Have you got flares built up, ready to burn? They can see in the dark as well as in daylight, so the bigger the pyres you can torch the better."

Gareth nodded. "We've kept the wood dry as best we can, and we got oil in yesterday's convoy. When the clouds clear, we'll need the light. The moon won't rise until mid-morning tomorrow, and anyway it's only three days old."

"Son," sighed John, "I can tell you to three-quarters of an inch how far the moon's waxed since I rode to Ernine. Now show me where you've got the Urchins from the first attack. Are they put back together? Good. Jen, d'you feel up to a bit of magic?"

True to John's prediction, the dragons attacked between midnight and morning. Jenny was dozing in John's arms in the dugout of Gareth and his father the King, reveling in the peace of being left alone by Caradoc and his spells of intrusion and domination. Curled in the heart of her jewel, she was aware that Folcalor had other fish to fry and assumed her, probably, to be still in Halnath Citadel.

Dimly, very dimly, she seemed to see Caradoc himself, the man who had truly once loved Rocklys, who had sought learning and power and walked along Somanthus' northwestern strand: a broken, white-haired man sleeping, dazed, in the heart of some far-off jewel.

But she felt no pity. Now and then she would reach out through the crystal's flaw to her body, to feel more closely the warmth of John's arms, and the tickle of his breath in her hair. Time seemed to her very fragile then, very precious—later she would look back on those moments with an aching longing, as a traveler lost on the winter barrens dreams of warmth. She knew the sentence of death to be a reasonable one, having seen Polycarp alone in the dimly lit study with Amayon's prisoning shell. She knew, too, that even the manner of death prescribed was necessary, given the power demons could wield over the dead.

But not John, she thought, closing her hand tight over his. *Not John.*

Then in her mind Morkeleb's voice said, *Jenny. It is now.*

She flowed through the fault in the jewel like water. Flowed into her flesh, her bones, her mind.

John was already sitting up, hair in his eyes and groping around for his spectacles. "Here we go, love," he said, and slung around his neck the frosted crystal of the Demon Queen's seal and a little stone knife to draw the blood for freeing. He gathered her to him, his hands cupping her face, collecting together the night of her hair, and kissed her lips. "You know what to do?"

"I know." There were crossbows stacked in the corner of the room, horn reinforced with steel. The poisoned bolts were so long and heavy she could barely lift the weapons. John slung three of them over his own back, and two over hers. She felt the touch of his hands adjusting the straps; his heart and hers already armored, drawn apart into the fight.

Not good-bye, she thought. *Not good-bye.*

Above, at ground level, men were shouting, boots pounding by the dugout's opening. The orange glare of torches flashed and juddered along the wall. The King sat up and called out a woman's name, confused; Gareth was holding his hands and talking to him gently, telling him that all things were well. "Use them carefully," John said to her, "but if you get the chance, don't hesitate for anything. Understand?"

He was talking about Ian. She thought about the drunken, slack-mouthed boy fumbling at the bound bodies of camp whores, tied up for his pleasure; thought about the sickened, weeping child she had sometimes glimpsed, a prisoner as she was a prisoner, in her dreams.

"I won't."

"Good lass." He slapped her flank and followed her up the ladder to the slit under the earth-heaped roof. As they made to part he caught her hand; already, against the darkness, the black skeletal shape of Morkeleb had risen. "You haven't . . . There isn't some spell you can lay on me, to keep me from . . ." He hesitated, then said, without change of expression, "If I die in the fighting, I'm theirs, y'see."

Jenny hesitated a long time, weighing what she knew of her waning strength against her love for this man. She knew that though destroying his body afterward would prevent his returning as a fetch, if he died in the fighting there would be no way of retrieving his naked soul from the Demon Queen's hands.

She said, "I can't. Not and lay the spells I'll need for the battle." She didn't even know if she'd be able to summon sufficient power to protect herself and Morkeleb against the magic of the other dragons. Weaving the wards would take all she had, after laying spells upon the Urchins and these crossbows in the afternoon.

"Aye, well," he sighed. "I'll just have to manage to not get meself killed, then." He kissed her again. "You don't get yourself killed either, love."

John caught a soldier outside the trench and handed him the three crossbows, to follow Jenny. They parted in the firelight, John to the squat glittering ball of the Urchin, and Jenny to the smoky shadow of the waiting dragon.

24

Jenny wove the wards of protection around them, listening for the first beating of dragon wings in the dark.

Put all of your magic into it, whispered Morkeleb's voice in her mind. *Leave none for yourself, none in your flesh, your bones, your heart. It will do you no good in any case, and the demons will take you again through it. That is the secret of the Shadow-drakes.*

Jenny said, *I can't. We'll be in danger . . .*

Trust, said Morkeleb. *The whalemages have laid on us spells of warding as well, as good as yours or mine.*

Jenny's hands shook, and the circles of power and energy and Limitation with which she had surrounded herself and him waned in the jumping torchflare. The crossbows hung on their straps from the cable that ringed the dragon's body, the spiked and terrible shape of them blending with his spines. She tried to call on the dragon within her soul, but since her escape from Rocklys' camp, it seemed to her that that portion had been left behind. *I can't.*

Trust.

She thought she saw the flares and torches through his body, as if he were insubstantial, wrought of smoke himself. His eyes, and the bobs on the ends of his antennae, were a glitter of stars in the darkness that thinned away like smoked glass.

But his voice remained strong in her mind. *Trust.*

She surrendered the last of her magic, pouring it into the spells that would guard them both from delusion and panic. Without it she felt empty, cold, and naked as she climbed onto his back.

His wings unfurled without a sound. He lifted as the fire showed them the first of the attackers. It was Yrsgendl, white and scarlet, with

Bliaud on his back. Silently they rose, higher and higher, fading into the dark.

Jenny saw the dragons winging from Rocklys' camp: pink and green, gold and green, yellow, rainbow . . . blue. *Oh my son,* she thought, as she hooked her feet hard through the cable and slung the first of the heavy crossbows into the cradle of her arms. *Oh my son.* Only the discipline of having studied magic let her close her mind.

Yrsgendl plunged, spitting fire and acid onto the camp. From all around the redoubt, from every trench and dugout, arrows spired up, fell back . . . And a single black heavy javelin slammed up straight and hard from the trundling Urchin that suddenly swung to life, pinning the dragon through the left wing.

It was a lucky shot, taking him through the widest portion of his silhouette against the dark. Morkeleb plunged from above, and Jenny swung the crossbow to her shoulder and fired downward, and that arrow pierced the younger dragon's back among the spines. Yrsgendl whipped around, mouth opening in a furious hiss, and Jenny felt/saw the demon illusions shiver and spatter around the wardings laid by the Demon Queen's vial. She fired again, driving the red dragon down, and a second harpoon from the Urchin knifed upward, burying itself in Yrsgendl's breast.

Yrsgendl wheeled, heading for the darkness, and again Morkeleb drove him down. Spitting, hissing, Enismirdal and Nymr plunged out of the sky above Morkeleb, but he slithered unseen from beneath their attacks, snapped and fastened on Yrsgendl's wing, dragging him back. Yrsgendl flapped and fluttered, weakening, and the Urchin, breaking through the damaged redoubt, trundled with surprising speed toward where the injured dragon would fall. Hagginarshildim, green and pink, and the surviving rainbow drake swooped on the machine, but John whipped and dodged, ducking from under the lashing tails, and the rainbow drake tore its own flesh open on the Urchin's spines. When Hagginarshildim attacked a second time, she received a harpoon in her foreleg; Morkeleb drove her down, too, forcing her to remain at the scene of the action.

Yrsgendl was on the ground, sick with the effects of the drug on the harpoon's tip. This, Jenny knew, was the tricky part, for the harpoons were tipped not with poison but with a powerful serum of poppy, and the dragons would be able to shake it off quickly. The rainbow drake spat fire at John as he rolled free of the Urchin, dived across the intervening ground to where the red and alabaster shape lay. Jenny saw firelight flash in the crystal seal that John pulled from his doublet.

Then Nymr was attacking, and Morkeleb whipped around to evade, and Jenny saw nothing of what passed below. But a moment later, as her own drugged crossbow bolt sank into the flesh of the blue dragon's neck, she saw from the corner of her eye a slither of dark-red flame, and as Nymr lashed at Morkeleb, teeth and tail gleaming, Yrsgendl whirled up from below and sank his teeth into the blue dragon's tail, wrenching and tearing at the flesh.

Jenny heard a dim shrieking in her mind, the cursing and wailing of a demon disembodied, but could not spare a thought to the matter. Nymr was a big dragon, too big to be easily driven into range of the Urchin's bolts. As he fought, Yrsgendl released him, only to circle and plunge on him from above as Morkeleb held him in combat. By the glinting torch-light Jenny saw who rode the white and scarlet dragon, and her heart stood still. Had she had any magic remaining she would have stretched it forth—

Don't do it! she thought wildly. *Don't do it!*

John unhooked his feet from the braided cable around Yrsgendl's body, and as the younger dragon fastened for a third time on the spiky ridge of Nymr's spine, he slid down and caught his footing among the bristling spears.

John . . . !

Ian swung around, the thin hollows of his face transformed by exhaustion into a man's. The blank blue eyes widened as he raised his hand, but John was quick and very strong. He caught the boy's wrist, and Jenny saw, lashed to his palm by a thong, the pale cold seal of the Demon Queen.

Ian screamed and gasped, his head falling back; Nymr gave a great frenzied thrash in the air, and John grabbed the cable, hooked his arm through it as he swung free and fell. Below them whirled darkness, flares, and the spinning shapes of dragons: Morkeleb said, *Stay where you are, Wizard-woman! I'll catch him should he fall.*

But John didn't fall. Entangled in his two captors, Nymr could only thrash, and Ian reached down, grabbing his father's arm, dragging him back onto the blue dragon's back. He moved clumsily, for it took far greater effort for him to reach out from an unflawed crystal, but he managed at least to hang on. Dimly, Jenny could hear Morkeleb calling out instructions to Yrsgendl, or rather using the younger dragon as another limb of himself, so powerful were the wordless impulses of his mind. Morkeleb's teeth shifted from Nymr's foreleg to his neck, and held the bigger dragon immobilized while John worked his way, hand over hand, to Nymr's head. In her mind Jenny could hear the screaming of demons, furious, dispossessed, thick as whirling leaves in the air: Gothpys, and Bliaud's demon Zimimar, and the one that had held sway over Yrsgendl.

Among the torrents of cobalt and peacock Jenny glimpsed silver, like a ball of glass, and this ball John seized and drew out, dripping with the dragon's blood.

Then he flung his other arm around Nymr's neck, pressed his face into the swirling ribbons of the mane, and held on, as Morkeleb and Yrsgendl released their hold and floated back, and the blue dragon began to circle, slowly and carefully, to the earth.

Jenny could hear Ian crying out, "Father! Father!" Desperate, terrified, but with enough sense to simply hold fast to the cable and let Nymr bring them both to ground.

John and Ian were clinging together, the boy weeping, John stroking black handfuls of his son's hair, when Morkeleb lit nearby and Jenny all but fell from his back. "It's all right," John whispered to the boy's frantic sobbing, "it's all right, you're all right now," as Jenny threw her arms around them both.

"It's all right," she said—foolish, she thought, but the only thing she could say, "Ian, the demon is gone . . ."

"You saw," he whispered, choked. "Mother, you saw . . . I . . . I . . ."

And he had seen her.

Above! cried Morkeleb, and Nymr and Yrsgendl launched themselves skyward again, as the rainbow drake and the surviving Icerider gyred down on them, spitting and slashing.

Jenny flung herself back to Morkeleb, a barely visible star-wraith in the smoke and dark, and John dragged his dazed son to the protection of the Urchin, half-lifting him through the hatch. Then the Shadow-dragon leaped skyward again, with Jenny slinging to her shoulder another of the double-weight crossbows, and Nymr and Yrsgendl sweeping out under Morkeleb's command to gather in the next dragon to be driven into the Urchin's line of drugged fire.

Together they drove down Mellyn, numbed with poppy. The screams of the demons echoed in Jenny's mind when she heard a hissing shriek above her and, turning, saw Caradoc himself and the golden drake Centhwevir streaking down on them like aureate lightning. Below her, from every ravine of the hills, rose the throbbing of drums and the braying of Rocklys' trumpets as her forces advanced.

They had, Jenny thought, intended to hold off their attack till dawn, when the dragons would have reduced Uriens' camp to confusion. But with the dragons slipping out of her grasp, it was now or never, and she threw her forces toward the fortress wall. As the other dragons closed protectively around Morkeleb's flickering shape, Jenny heard the deep battle-cry, "Uwanë! Uwanë!" and knew that Gareth had been ready, waiting for this.

John, get Ian out of there! It occurred to her to wonder where Bli-aud—as clumsy at working from his prison as Ian—had hidden himself, and if they could get themselves out from between the hammer and the anvil in time.

Then dragons closed around Centhwevir, catching and dragging at him, trying to force him to earth. The rainbow drake was down, twitching faintly on the ground—Jenny got the barest glimpse of him as Haggi-narshildim, green and pink, circled back from spreading havoc on the camp, and Enismirdal winged out of the passes of the mountains at Caradoc's call. Jenny wasted two of her three remaining shots trying to hit Centhwevir but buried the third bolt in Enismirdal's primrose neck. In the vast rout of slashing wings and snapping teeth that followed, she saw the yellow dragon veer and falter as the drug took its effect. Dimly she could hear Folcalor calling on his forces, trying to rally the remaining dragons and wizards, while the furious shouting of men in battle rose from beneath them.

A heaving sea of forms struggled blindly in darkness below. Blood on steel, and now and then pale faces contorted in pain. Flares threw some light, but mostly it was primal chaos, the confusion as legend said had reigned upon the waters of the ocean before the Old God sang sea and sky apart. On a hill above the road a ring of fire had been estab-lished, and in its golden crown she glimpsed Rocklys on her horse, her standard-bearers around her signaling the corps commanders to their positions. Then the rainbow drake rose, with more crossbows, more heavy drugged bolts, and two of the great dragon-killing harpoons in her claws.

An outcry from below made Jenny look down again. Through the striving knots of warriors the Urchin was moving, cutting down all in its path with its spikes, and Jenny saw it was heading straight for the lighted knoll where Rocklys sat. The Commander turned her head. She said something to an aide, who handed her her bow, and the men afoot closed up around her with their spears. Still the Urchin advanced, and there were soldiers running behind it, slipstreaming through the carnage where none dared stand in its way. Jenny was aware of Caradoc hurling spells at it, spells that glanced off the Demon Queen's wards.

Bolts shot from the Urchin's forward ports, striking among Rocklys' guards. Still she remained where she was, watching it come, mechanical and strange. She had chosen rocky ground, too steep for the Urchin to climb readily, though Jenny thought later that it could have done so.

But it stopped. The hatch flipped open, and John emerged, his bow held in hands bloody from Nymr's spines. He nocked an arrow, but he was slow—exhausted, Jenny thought.

And Rocklys was not slow. She never was.

Her arrow took John in the chest, the impact of it jarring him back, out of the Urchin's hatchway. He fumbled, caught at the spines behind him, trying to get down unhurt. Jenny saw the blood, saw the fire gleam on his spectacles.

Then he fell. With a roar of rage, the men who had run behind the Urchin surged up around it, cutting and slashing their way through Rocklys' guard.

Centhwevir wheeled and fled.

Take him! Jenny cried. *Follow him! Stop him! He has the prison-jewels!*

But the other dragons—Yrsgendl and Nymr and the young rainbow drake—circled and turned to the business of driving to ground Enismirdal and Hagginarshildim; Jenny thought she heard a voice in her mind say something about Time. *Time. Follow and time.*

The prison-jewels, the talismans! Folcalor can still use them!

Ian, and Bliaud, and the other mages—and she herself—were still prisoners.

But Morkeleb was streaking after, leaving the battle behind in the night.

We can't let him land! How long, she wondered, could Ian maintain the connection between his imprisoned self and his body? Could his demon retake him before it was trapped, as Amayon had been trapped? Could another demon step into its place?

Would he be strong enough to use magic to save his father's life?

John falling with an arrow in his heart . . .

She thrust the thought aside.

The demons would not have John's body—Lord Ector would certainly make sure it was burned before it could be put to demon service—but his mind, his consciousness, would be forever behind the mirror, the prey of the vengeful Demon Queen.

But of course, she seemed to hear Amayon saying it, of course, she herself could save him, if she turned back.

Centhwevir winged on into the night, with Morkeleb and Jenny hard on his track. They passed over the wood of Imperteng and the Wildspae's ebon curve; passed over the formless lands of Hythe and Magloshaldon and the farms of Belmarie. *The sea,* Jenny thought. *They are going to the sea.* To the Gate of Hell that lay below Somanthus Isle. She was desperate, terrified, when she felt the alien consciousness of Squidslayer and the other mages of the deep, rise out of that blue-black abyss.

Rims of silver on the black waves and rocks. Centhwevir striking water, gold and blue shining for a moment. Then gone, and a moment later Morkeleb, plunging from the sky like invisible lightning, and the cold living impact with the sea.

The spells of the whalemages enveloped her in air. She saw Centhwevir, wings and legs folded flat, a vast sea serpent lashing sideways as he dove.

Frantic with horror, Jenny saw the Gate, the green glow deep within the rocks; saw herself, prisoned in the talisman jewel. All of them—Ian, Bliaud, Yseult . . . And deep in her mind the memory rose of the half-glimpsed horrors of that lightless watery Hell, of the thing the other demons called Adromelech, a silent, terrible darkness at its core. . . .

Jenny sensed the whalemages following but afraid to reach forth with their magic lest they be taken, too. Green things, vile and deformed, floated in the water or reached from holes in the rocks: endlessly long tendrils of seaweed that finished in grasping hands, fish with glowing mouths and twisted, vestigial wings. These swarmed around Morkeleb, biting at him, tearing at Jenny's shoulders and arms.

Among the rocks, a hundred yards above the Gate, Morkeleb cornered Centhwevir, cutting him off from the sicklied glow beyond.

The blue and gold dragon belched fire—not the acid of true dragons but demon-fire that enveloped witch and dragon in a searing cloud. Morkeleb rocked back, then attacked again, lashing and snapping, quicker than the larger drake and more able to slither through the holes and canyons. The deformed fish of the deeper trenches near the Gate rose up, but the whalemages and the dolphins formed a protective ring around the struggling dragons, driving the infected monsters back.

Jenny fired her crossbow bolts into Centhwevir's breast and neck, but the bubbles in the threshing water spoiled her aim, and the water itself slowed the missiles. At last she kicked her feet free of the cable, and with one harpoon in hand and the other slung on her back she launched herself across the black space toward the dragon and the demon-ridden mage.

Caradoc saw her coming. She felt the burning weight of the spells that for three nights had dragged her strength. His shirt was torn, and his cap gone; the silver bottle floated behind him on its ribbon, and his gray hair lifted like seaweed in the swirling water. His eyes opened wide, and there was in them nothing but greenish light; his mouth opened, and like the dragon he blew fire out of it, transforming the water around her to searing steam.

Illusion, pain, death, like the illusions of a dream. The demon Folcalor reached into her and tore at the roots and stumps of her magic for a handhold, but these she let go of, dragon and human alike, trusting only in the whalemages' spells. With vicious demon wisdom it snatched at her dreams, the ancient longings and fears, and these, too, she released,

letting them go. There was nothing in her mind, and only a clear whiteness in her heart, as she drove the harpoon with all her strength into
Caradoc's body, pinning him to the rocks against which Morkeleb had
forced Centhwevir. Then, while Caradoc thrashed and picked at the harpoon and blood poured from his working mouth, she turned like a fish in
the water and plunged her hands into the waving particolored glory of
Centhwevir's mane.

As she drew out the crystal spike, the demon behind her hurled lightning, power, blasting her body away and against the rocks, driving the
breath from her lungs. Cold claimed her, heat and cold together, and then
falling darkness that seemed to stretch to the abyss beneath the world.

25

She came to herself with the sounding of the ocean in her ears. She lay on a bed of something soft and damp and smelling of fish; morning sun sparkled in her eyes.

Is it well with you, Jenny?

Well? asked a number of other voices in her mind. *Well?*

She sat up, and something rolled off her chest and plopped onto the stuff on which she lay—seaweed, she saw. When she reached down for it, she saw that her hand was crinkled and shiny, red with the scarring of burns. Though the pain was suppressed by spells of healing and of nepenthe, she was aware of it, as if her very bones had been cored with a red-hot rod.

Everywhere that the rags of her burned clothing did not cover, her skin was the same, wrinkled and stiff with scars.

Her hair was gone.

So was her magic.

Morkeleb asked again, *Is it well with you?*

She could barely make her stiff fingers undo the stopper of the silver bottle still clutched in her hand. From it she poured seven jewels into her palm: two rubies, two amethysts, a topaz that had clearly been pried out of another setting, a sapphire, and a flawed peridot. As if in a dream she put the peridot into her mouth and felt herself flow through the flaw and into her body again. Her pain redoubled at once, so she bent over, gasping. Her hands trembled as she spat out the jewel and cast it into the sea.

She said, *It is well.* And she wept.

All around her on the rocks the dragons perched, like winged jewels themselves, gorgeous in the morning sun. The air was filled with their music, music that had been silent the whole of the time Jenny had seen them at Rocklys' camp, the whole of the battle. It whispered on the air, like the sea breeze or the salt smell of the ocean. Seven dragons, and there was a sort of glitter over the sea, a smoky darkening of the air that Jenny knew was Morkeleb.

Nymr bent his azure head, *Tears/distress/thing of men?* He had a voice like distant wind in trees.

And Morkeleb formed a thought, a silver crystal of loss and necessity and the ongoing tread of time, which Jenny saw that Nymr did not understand. And patiently, Morkeleb explained, *Thing of men.*

Save a dragon, slave a dragon, said Centhwevir's sweet voice in her mind. *Debt.*

My magic, said Jenny, raising her scarred face from her ruined hands. *Dragon-magic.*

It is only possible, said Morkeleb, *if you will become a dragon; for in your human self there is nothing now that magic can fasten on. It is all burned away.*

And John's life with it, she wondered, if the mages back at the camp can't save him?

She said, *I free you then, all of you. Morkeleb, take me back.*

The music circled her round, and she saw how all the airs and threads of those so-different melodies were in truth part of a single enormous singing. She didn't know why she hadn't been aware of it before.

Dragon-friend, said Centhwevir, the soft clashing of a universe of golden chimes. *Dragon-friend.*

Then he spread his wings, a field of lupine and daffodils, and let the wind lift him. They all lifted afterward, pink and green, white and crimson, blue on blue on blue . . . Lifted, and spun like a drift of leaves over the ocean where the whales rolled and spouted, and swirled away to the north.

Morkeleb said, *The whalemages sent fishes to tear Caradoc's body to pieces, that the sea-wights could make no use of it. Likewise they have heaped stones before the demon Gate. There is nothing further for us here, Jenny. I will take you back.*

"Some general she was." John grinned weakly as Jenny came into the infirmary tent. "Couldn't hit a man in the heart at less than fifty feet? The country's well rid of her." And he held out his hands to her. "Ah, love, don't cry."

He gathered her gently to him and hesitantly ("Does this hurt too bad, love?") cradled her scarred and hairless head to his shoulder. "Don't cry."

But she could not stop. And neither he nor Ian, who came out of the shadows to awkwardly pat her back—he had grown, she saw, two inches in his time with Caradoc—could ease the pain that encompassed all her being.

Rocklys was dead. "When the reinforcements arrived, we called on her to surrender," said Gareth, who came in, battered and blood-streaked, some time later, in attendance on his father. Uriens, resplendent in his golden wig and armored and cloaked as befit a King, walked among the wounded who had bled for his sake. Now and then he would bend down and speak to this man or that. Once he held the surgeon's implements when a dirty wound was cleansed and stitched; when Pellanor of Palmorgin was carried in, bleeding from wounds he'd taken fighting at Rocklys' side, he took his hands and sat beside him until the Lord of Palmorgin whispered, "Forgive me," and died. Men reached from their beds to touch the King's cloak, and Ector of Sindestray, walking in his wake, made nervous approving noises in his throat and tried to get him to finish up and leave.

Cringing with shyness, Gareth brought up a stool and sat, barely noticed, beside John's cot. He fished out his bent and broken pair of spare spectacles and perched them on his nose, taking care around a place where a blow had opened the side of his face.

"She called for her sword and rode straight into the thick of the enemy," he went on unhappily. "I wouldn't have executed her, you know."

"She would have executed you." Polycarp, who had come in just after him, gingerly eased his left arm, which he wore in a sling. His red hair was sweaty and flattened from a war-helm, but looking up into the Master's eyes, Jenny could see no trace of the demon. In any case she would have known it, had Amayon gone into another. Would have known and died of jealous grief.

"That doesn't mean I'd have . . ."

"No," said the Master. "I mean that she knew what she would have done to you and expected the same."

A shadow fell across the lamplight. "Why is this man here?" King Uriens stood looking down at John.

Gareth stood, tangling the stool in his military cloak and knocking it over. "Father, you remember Lord Aversin." He scrabbled awkwardly to pick it up. "He defeated the dragon . . ."

"He didn't kill it." Uriens folded his hands before the ruby buckle of his sword-belt and frowned. "He's a trafficker with demons. Ector said so. I think the demons must have helped him drive the dragon away the first time, and now it's come back."

"That's right, your Majesty." The Lord of Sindestray appeared at his elbow again like an overweight blue-and-white butterfly. "And the woman, too."

John's eyes blazed dangerously. "Now wait a bloody minute! I hadn't so much as heard about the demons four years ago when I . . ."

"He'll have to be locked up." Uriens spoke with the self-evident logic of a child. "If he's trafficked with demons, he'll have to be done away with. He'll try to destroy the Realm. They all do."

"Father . . ." Gareth straightened protestingly.

"I'm sorry, my son. I know he's your playmate but he'll try to destroy the Realm."

"And the woman," Ector reminded.

"He's a Dragonsbane! He fought the dragon for the sake of the Realm . . ."

"Of course we know how Prince Gareth feels about Dragonsbanes," Ector said smoothly. "Naturally, any demon who wanted to gain influence with him has only to . . ."

"If you say one more word about how I've sold me soul to demons," began John, half-rising, then sinking back with a quick intake of breath. Guards in the white and azure of the Lord of Sindestray stepped out of the shadows. Jenny raised her hand, furious, conjuring in her mind the Word of Fire and Blindness . . .

And it was only a word. A cast dry chiten in her mind. Dead leaves falling from her hand.

A guard took her by the arm. Jenny whirled, yanking free, but there were other guards, coming from all directions. John somehow had Polycarp's dagger in his hand, sitting up again with blood staining the bandages on his chest, and Gareth stepped forward and caught his wrist.

"John . . ." He turned his head and caught Polycarp's eye.

The Master looked aside. Jenny couldn't find it in her heart to blame him; he knew, too well now, the strength of the demon whispers, the terrible temptation of those promises.

Gareth's eyes met John's. Desperate, pleading . . . *Trust me.*
Trust me.

John glanced at Jenny. Then he opened his hand and let the knife be taken from him.

Guards brought a litter: "Take him to the dugout His Majesty slept in last night," instructed Ector, for the King had wandered away.

"You mean the one he doesn't have to sleep in now?" demanded John sarcastically. "Because the dragons have all been sent on their way and the wizards who rode them cured?" His voice was shaking with anger.

"I will not be drawn into controversy with a demon," Lord Ector said primly. "It is well known they twist any argument to their advantage."

John looked at Gareth, who averted his gaze. Jenny watched as John was lifted onto the litter; while Ector's attention was on that she stepped back into the shadows. Gareth was right, she thought, in not forcing an issue. She would be of more use free than if Ector remembered her presence and persuaded the King to have her imprisoned as well. But John's face, still as marble, struck in her heart like a dagger of accusation, and the torchlight made a dark patch of the Demon Queen's mark on his throat.

As the curtain fell behind Ector and the guards, Jenny saw Gareth return soundlessly and slide his hand under the pillows. He took out a piece of iron, an arrowhead, she thought. This he slipped into the breast of his tunic, out of sight.

That night the surviving mages came to the Regent's tent. Bliaud seemed the most alive, the most sure of himself, but even he was vague; Miss Enk and Summer the Icerider girl were little more than sleepwalkers until the talisman jewels were put in their mouths and their souls returned to them. And then, because Jenny was keenly aware of Gothpys and Zimimar and the other demons lingering and whispering outside the tent, all the mages joined together in using the Demon Queen's seal to draw the disabled demons back through the bodies to which they had once been linked and imprisoned them in shells and pebbles and snuffbottles.

Afterward they went out, by the flickering witchlight summoned by Yseult, and cast the emptied talisman gems into the River Wildspae, where the current roared strong over the rocks. The amethyst that held the soul of the Icerider boy Werecat, his sister Summer smashed to pieces with a hammer, her face void of expression. Polycarp did the same with the topaz that was among the talismans, which they guessed contained the soul of Caradoc himself. Jenny made herself hope that the merchant prince's soul would find peace.

Her magic did not return. Bliaud and Yseult both treated Jenny with the Demon Queen's powder, but it had no effect. She remembered the demon Folcalor biting and chewing and ripping like a maddened rat at her mind; remembered releasing into the ocean anything that he might have seized to draw her into his power.

There was nothing inside her.

Only an aching longing that slowly crystallized: a longing for Amayon. For the fire and color, the power and joy, of the demon within her.

This was insanity, and she knew it, yet the longing did not go away. In her emptiness it glowed like a gentle comfort, and it seemed to her that even John's love was a pallid thing beside the wisdom and understanding of the demon who knew her so well.

She nursed John in the days that followed, in the guarded dugout under the eyes of Uriens' and Ector's warriors, and it tormented her soul to see Ian and Yseult and Bliaud able to work the magic of healing on him. Tormented her, too, to imagine them looking aside from her while she performed the humbler tasks, fetching water and grinding herbs. Pitying her. The world turned to poison around her, and she found herself thinking—against all reason and experience—that Amayon alone would care and understand.

The moon burgeoned fatter and fatter in the afternoon skies, like a white flaccid creature drawing nearer each day to be glutted on the flesh of dying kings; Ector's men built a pyre on the other side of the bridge. One hot afternoon Jenny could smell the oil they soaked it with. Ector glared at the mages whenever he passed them, for the laws in the south had been made with the understanding that those who had been possessed against their wills by demons, once exorcised, never really returned to their right minds. There was no legal provision for mages who had been taken against their will, for at no time in the history of Bel had demons appeared strong enough to do so. All this Jenny glimpsed through the curtain of obsession, of weariness, of pain.

That night Jenny met Gareth and Ian beside the dugout prison and took the keys from the sleeping guards. The silence of that enchanted sleep lay over the whole camp as Gareth descended the ladder and came up again with John leaning heavily on his shoulder.

"I'm sorry I couldn't . . . couldn't stand up for you," said the young man. "I did everything I could to get Father to change the sentence. It's abominable after what you've done for the Realm!"

"It's good sense." John had shaved that morning for the first time since the battle, and looked haggard and thin. The burn on his throat stood out dark where his doublet and shirt were unlaced; the blazing moonlight seemed to pick out threads of silver where the Demon Queen's other marks crossed his collarbone and neck. "Meself, I wouldn't trust a soul who'd gone and made deals with demons. For you to do it, Regent as you are for your dad, you'd have every lord in the land in revolt, and me among 'em. Have you got it?" he added, and Gareth handed him the piece of iron he'd taken from the cot the day John had been placed under arrest.

"Ian?" John held out his hand to his son. But Ian turned away without speaking. He'd worked quietly, steadily, to heal his father's wounds, and

with Yseult had put spells of healing likewise on Jenny's burned and crippled hands. Yseult had even done what she could to alleviate the
migraines, the hot flashes, the aches and griefs that flooded back to Jenny
once the magic that held them at bay had gone.

But through it all Ian had been silent and avoided his mother, pitying
her, she thought—or worse, repulsed by what he had seen in the days
when both had been the slaves of their demons.

Jenny could not watch when Gareth handed John a satchel containing the shells and bottles and pebbles, stopped and marked with sealing-
wax, that contained the souls of the demons. She'd spent a week trying
not to give in to the desire to scour the camp for them. Under her linen
sleeves her scarred arms were welted with the marks of her own fingernails, when the pain of wanting to search grew too bad. For three nights
now Amayon had shown her in dreams what would be done to him
through all eternity once he was sent behind the mirror, and it was nothing she would have done to her worst enemy—not even to the Demon
Queen, whose name she had heard John murmur longingly in his
dreams. Some of it she hadn't conceived of any sentient being doing to
anyone or anything.

Let me out. Let me out. Let me out before they send me there.

She must not free the demon into this world. She knew that—digging
her nails once again into her own flesh she knew it—and knew, too, that
there was no chance of sending him back to his own *(Yes, there is! I
promise I'll go back there!).* And he had done terrible things to her,
degraded her in ways she sometimes found it difficult to recall. *(When
I'm gone, you'll remember them! In every detail in your dreams forever!
Unless you set me free . . .)*

But still . . .

The worst of it was that the aching hollow where her magic had been
left her desperate for something to fill it. Amayon's presence had been
comforting. With him occupying her, she had never been alone.

*If you take me back, Pretty Lady, my adorable one, you will have your
magic again.*

Be silent. Be silent. Be silent.

"What was that he gave you," she asked John, as they drifted to
where Morkeleb waited for them at the edge of the camp. "The first thing,
the arrowhead?"

"This?" He drew it from the pocket where he had also concealed the
hothwais of starlight and the glass and alabaster bottle of the dragon's
tears. He held it up, a savagely barbed war-point with an inch or so of
shaft still attached.

"A gift from Rocklys," he said. "Maybe the last one she ever gave—

anyway the most wholehearted. Unless there's a way you can draw off some of the pain I'm in and put it in a vial to throw in for good measure. I count that as her gift as well."

"No." Jenny looked away, hating him suddenly for reminding her of her loss. For speaking so casually of her pain. Amayon, she thought, would never have harmed her so. "That's not something I can do now."

26

On the last night before the King's Moon, two shadows made their way down the painted corridors of the old temple of Syn, in what had been the city of Ernine. Their lantern threw swaying light over the painted gazelles and brought the stars depicted overhead into alternating brightness and obscurity; the comet seemed to wink and follow them through the corridor and into the round room. Along with the hothwais of starlight, Miss Mab had smuggled to Jenny a diagram to follow and the correct powder of mingled silver and blood: *It'll never work,* whispered Amayon in her mind. *Not without my help. Nothing you do will ever work again.*

What would I be, Morkeleb had asked, *without magic?*

That was different. He was a dragon—whatever, she thought, a dragon was. She was only a woman, left with nothing.

She wondered how she could face life without magic. How she could face life, face John, face her children, with the memory of what she had done. And of what she had lost.

Somehow she made herself draw the sigils of power on the floor. Her twisted fingers trembled as she arranged within it the bottle of glass and alabaster, the softly glowing hothwais of starlight, the arrowhead. Behind them in a semicircle she set out the seven demon prisons and the seven spikes of glass and mercury that had been extracted from the heads of the dragons, grimly sealing her mind to the far-off howling of the spirits imprisoned within.

The dreams of their upcoming torment were fresh as a new brand on her: agony, nausea, shame. How could she turn Amayon over to that?

It took her some time to realize that it was John that she'd saved from it.

Still, she couldn't set down the white shell. He'd been difficult, yes. But at other times he'd been so good to her, so considerate. The pleasure he had given her could never be duplicated. It wasn't something she'd turn to often, of course, but to know it was there, now and then when things were bad . . .

A warm hand closed over her scarred one. "Better leave it, love."

He was right, but she pulled her hand away from his, slapped the shell into it, hating him. "You do it, then," she said. "You'll be glad to see it, won't you?"

He looked for a long time into her eyes. "That I will," he said gently. "That I will."

She turned away, shaking all over, and would not look. It was John who completed the sigil and spoke to the seal still printed on the mirror's burning darkness.

"It's the Moon of Sacrifice, love," he said, "and here I am. And here's all the rare and precious things you asked me for: a piece of a star, a true star, caught in the stone of the gnomes; and a dragon's tears." He smiled. "And the arrowhead was given to me gie hard by one who wished me ill, and if you like I'll show you the hole to prove it. And to show you I've no ill will, you can have a baker's dozen and one of the rest of 'em, to serve as you served me; and as they'd have served you."

Jenny heard the voices of the things behind the mirror. The slurping of their tongues, and the long, thick breath.

Then the Demon Queen said, "And you, beloved?" Her voice was roses and smoke, amber and the whisper of the summer sea. "Will you not leave that scarred dwarf you've been tupping all these years and come, too? She's protected you for the last time—dried up now, and bitter. Think carefully, my love. In another year she'll be a screaming hag-wife, if she isn't one now. You may not find it pleasant to live with what the sea-wights left behind."

Jenny turned and left the chamber, fumbled her way through the anteroom, and along the painted hallway in the dark. She stumbled out into the thick liquid warmth of the night and crumpled on the step, her shoulder against the stained marble, the strange sweetness of the Marches swamps filling her lungs and her mind. She doubled over, trembling, hurting inside and knowing what the Demon Queen said was true. Seeing what she would be, what she would become, without magic, without music . . . without Amayon. She buried her face in her crippled hands.

Jenny, don't! Go back there! Stop him, beloved, enchanted one! Amayon's voice screamed all the more clearly in her mind. *Pretty Lady! Heart of my hearts! Do you know what they'll do to me? Do you know*

*what demons do to other Hellspawn, when they get hold of them? I'm
immortal, enchanted one, I can't die, but I can feel—I can feel . . .*

She closed her mind, dug her nails into the papery scabs on her wrist,
and his voice went on, desperate, frantic, like a fist beating at a door.

*Don't let him! He's jealous, jealous because he cannot give you what
I gave! You think he'll want you in his bed, knowing what you were to me?*

Don't answer, Morkeleb had said—and so she did not. But the memory of the pleasure was a torment in her flesh, rising to drown her.

Jenny! JENNY!

She knew when the Demon Queen reached out and claimed him—
claimed them all. All the payment of John's teind. The screaming rose to
a crescendo in her mind, so she crushed her head between her slick
scarred hands and closed her eyes, trying not to hear, trying not to know.
Trying not to call out his name.

Amayon . . .

And he was gone. The desolation was worse than when his hold over
her had been broken.

She wrapped her arms around herself, shivering and trying to
breathe, and was still shuddering when she heard behind her the slow
drag of John's staff; the sliding thud when he fell. She knew she should
get up to help him, but she could not. The black hollow within her was
too deep.

In time she heard him crawl to his feet again.

"Why'd you leave?" His voice was very quiet behind her.

She didn't look up, scarred head bowed, scarred hands folded on her
breast. "Because I couldn't stay."

She heard his breathing, saw her own shadow thrown by the lantern,
a distorted rumple on the worn sandstone steps.

"Aye, well, then," he said in time. "We'd better go."

Morkeleb bore them back to a vale not far from the Jotham camp.
Gareth and Ian were waiting for them in the cold glimmer of moonset and
dawn, with horses and mules laden for the journey north.

"Yseult hanged herself," said Gareth, when John and Jenny came
near enough to him to speak. "And Summer, the Icerider girl." He glanced
at Ian, seated silent and alone on a fallen tree, and the boy looked neither
at him nor at his parents. "About midnight."

Jenny remembered Amayon's scream, still bleeding in her heart. The
gods knew what Ian's demon had said to him, promised him, pleaded
with him to stop John from ridding the world of them. From sending
them behind the mirror. The gods knew what Ian had been going through,
while she, Jenny, longed for and hurt for Amayon—did he want his own
demon's return as desperately?

He couldn't, she thought. He has his magic to comfort him. Her jaw ached from clenching and she put her hands before her mouth.

John said nothing. Armored in his silence, he helped Jenny onto the mare Gareth had provided, swung to the saddle of a gray warhorse, and bent to clasp the young Regent's hands. "Thank you," he said.

"I've arranged for Master Bliaud to go quietly back to Greenhythe," Gareth said. "He has estates there, away from his family, where Lord Ector won't find him if he decides to make trouble. Once you and Jenny are north of the Wildspae I don't think you need have any fear of . . . of my father's sentence against you, or of Lord Ector and the council. What Rocklys left of the garrison at Corflyn won't have the strength to go against you, and when I replenish it I'll speak to the new commander."

"So you're going to replenish it, are you?" John tilted his head a little, expressionless, suspicious.

Gareth looked shocked. "Of course I am. As soon as the men can be organized to march."

John inclined his head and bent from the saddle to kiss his lord's ring. "Then I thank you again. For all."

But all these things Jenny saw only from a distance, as if through a thousand layers of dark glass. Amayon's absence was a blackness and a weariness, the leaden loss of everything that had made the world magical and colorful and wild. Her head ached, her burns throbbed, and the hollow from where her magic had disappeared was a chasm in her soul.

In all the ballads, evil was vanquished, order was restored, and the shining hero prince wed his lady, both beautiful and young. Neither, apparently, had nightmares afterward or dreamed of what they had lost. All wounds healed cleanly and no souls were broken by longings or obsessions or mistrust.

Jenny dreamed about the Mirror of Isychros. Saw again the sigils drawn on the stone floor in blood and silver: the bottle of tears and the softly glowing hothwais of starlight, the arrowhead stained with John's blood. Amayon's voice screamed in her mind again, but beneath it, in the still quiet part of herself, she thought, *I missed something.*

Something important.

She looked back at the scene again.

Amayon's white shell seemed to drag her attention to it, to be the only thing she could see. She forced herself to look beyond: There was a snuff-bottle holding Bliaud's demon Zimimar, a pebble that prisoned Gothpys. Miss Enk's demon had been trapped in a perfume vessel, and Summer's in another shell. Yseult's demon was in another perfume bottle, that one of alabaster.

Six demons. Eight cold silver spikes.

Better leave it, love.

You'll be glad to see it.

That I will.

And Amayon screaming, screaming as he was thrust into the Hell of those who hated him, who would torture him beyond the imaginings of humankind, forever.

Six demons. Eight silver spikes.

Caradoc and Ian sitting at a table, eight jewels scattered between them. *Destroy the jewel,* Ian said, and Caradoc shook his head.

I have my reasons . . .

What reasons? Jenny asked.

Pretty Lady! Heart of my hearts! She heard Amayon's voice again in her soul, drowning out all thought. *Do you know what they'll do to me? He's jealous . . . He's jealous . . .*

John turning his face away from her as he whispered Aohila's name.

It will pass, Morkeleb said.

Jenny leaned her head on his shoulder, where the steel scales were smooth as glass.

How can you be sure?

His warmth came through ironclad bony angles, comforting in the thin autumn chill. Predawn mists filtered both the night's dark and the light of the breakfast fire, where John was mechanically burning bannocks. Jenny supposed she should care, for Ian's sake, but Ian had eaten almost nothing for three days that she knew about and almost certainly for longer than that . . .

And that, too, she found hard to care about, to think about.

It was difficult to think about anything but her loss and her pain.

She had dreamed last night, something, she couldn't remember what, and upon waking had felt only bitterness and despair. She knew she was behaving like an insane woman, that her longings for Amayon, her obsession with her demon, was disastrous, blinding her to something only she could remember . . . Something she dreamed, she thought, back at Halnath perhaps, but it was beyond her power to wrest herself free. Ian was silent, drawn in on himself and more so every day that passed. And John . . .

She found she could no longer think very clearly about John.

All things pass, Jenny, the dragon said. *That is the one fact about all things.*

As my magic passed? She threw the words bitterly at him, though she told herself daily that she must accept it and make an end of self-pity. But when John had lashed at her to do so, only a few minutes ago, she had snapped, *I'll stop pitying myself when you stop dreaming about the Demon Queen!*

The days without her magic had been torture, redoubled by the shame she felt when resentment scalded her at the sight of Ian kindling the campfire with a gesture or healing his father's wounds. Last night, seeking respite, she had attempted to play the harp Gareth had given Ian, but her crippled hands were slow to respond despite Ian's healing, and when her son had reached to touch her she had stiffened, so he shrank away.

Morkeleb said nothing. In the darkness he seemed a thing of flesh still, ebony and jet. With the coming of dawnlight, she knew she would be able to see through him, a strange beautiful clearness that held within it both darkness and light.

He had guided them now for three days, scouting through the tangled ravines and thick woods where the men of Imperteng still made war on the Realm. Only an hour ago he had returned to tell them that the road to the north was clear and that he himself would take his departure for the Skerries of Light.

Now he said, *It is only magic, Jenny. One thing among a thousand things of life.*

Her head jerked up and she hated him, hated him as she hated John and all other things, and her painful stiff little hands tried unsuccessfully to ball into fists to strike him. *So he says,* she lashed at him, *he who never tasted it, never knew it! Easy for you, who gave it up and got wisdom in return, or the illusion of wisdom! It was the core of my bones, the heart of my mind, and I do not know if I can live without it!*

Without it? he asked. *Or without the demon?*

She tried to draw back within herself, where everything gaped and bled. Where everything daily, hourly, spoke Amayon's name.

Amayon was not the only one, she realized, who knew her well.

Go to him! John had screamed at her as she fled the camp. *Become a dragon-wife if you're going to leave me, but leave me or return for good! You go and you come back and I don't know if you're going to stay next time or not!*

Tears ran down her face, a river like the blood of pain in her mind. She said, *There is nothing for me, when I gave everything to save him. To save them.*

And he, said the dragon softly, *to save you.*

But she could only close her eyes and rest her head on the strength of his bones. She thought that something touched her hair, though whether it was a dragon's claw or the semblance of a man's hand she could not tell;

only that it brought her comfort, and peace such as John had said that he had felt on the Birdless Isle.

What would you, then? he asked.

The words fell into the hot aching blackness of her soul like glowing diamonds, stilling the roil of her thoughts. It seemed to her that whatever she asked—to go with him to the Skerries of Light, to find peace and healing, to simply be turned to stone until all this had been worn away by a thousand years of rains—whatever she asked he would do.

Peace seemed to come into her mind. She drew breath, and sat up, and ran her hands over her bare, scarred scalp. *Once before you asked me that,* she said. *You gave me a choice: to become a dragon, and to live forever in magic. It would be easy, I think, to do that now.*

He sat still, like a great cat, his forepaws crossed and his diamond eyes glimmering from the transparencies of dawn. Smoke from John's campfire momentarily delineated him, becoming for an instant the curve of the horns, the riffle of the beribboned mane, then dissolving to a skeletal ghost.

Maybe I've been with John too long for my peace, she went on. *It will be hard to go back, now, as I am. To be pitied by those who knew me when I had power. To see Ian in pain, and John ...* She shook the thoughts away. *And I'm not ... able, really, to cope with what I think may lie ahead.*

Because Folcalor didn't die, Morkeleb. Folcalor wasn't one of the demons we imprisoned and sent behind the Mirror of Isychros. And Folcalor is more intelligent than the other demons; slyer and more patient. He had some plan, some intention, beyond the dragons and the mages whose bodies he enslaved: something that involved the mages' souls. If I went with you now, if I sought peace now, I would not be in the Winterlands when he comes again.

Morkeleb said, *Ah.*

Do you understand?

It is not a thing of dragons, said Morkeleb, *to serve, and to risk, and to bleed for others. It may be that I, too, have associated too long with your Songweaver, my friend. Because I understand. Will you be able to endure?*

Jenny looked down at her scarred hands. Thought about Yseult, and Summer, whose despair at losing the sweet poison of their demons had cost them their lives.

Thought about John.

I will endure, she said. *I will trust the Lord of Time, as humans must, who cannot will pain away by magic, nor seek relief either in illusion or immortality. This is what I am.*

Even so, said the dragon. *I have lived for many years and have seen those things that humans receive, who trust the Lord of Time. And whether those things are bitter or sweet, or whether they are all only illusion—this I cannot tell. I would that I could heal you, my friend, but this is not possible: I, who destroyed the Elder Droon and brought down the gnomes of Ylferdun to ruin, I cannot make so much as a single flower prosper when frost has set its touch upon it.*

His warmth surrounded her, velvet against her wasted flesh and peace-filled as the sunlight on the Skerries of the north. *Therefore I can only say, Live however best you can. Watch for these evils, and seek healing for yourself, even when the darkness and the pain seem unending. I will come back to you, my friend, to your help or to your rescue or only to sit on the hillside and gossip, as friends do.*

She smiled as he spread his ghostly wings and lifted from the ground as mist lifts, an unearthly glitter of starlight and bones. *I will be there when you come, Dragonshadow.*

He thinned away into the silver morning and was gone . . .

To be continued in
The Knight of the Demon Queen

ABOUT THE AUTHOR

At various times in her life, BARBARA HAMBLY has been a high-school teacher, a model, a waitress, a technical editor, a professional graduate student, an all-night clerk at a liquor store, and a karate instructor. Born in San Diego, she grew up in Southern California, with the exception of one high-school semester spent in New South Wales, Australia. Her interest in fantasy began with reading *The Wizard of Oz* at an early age and has continued ever since.

She attended the University of California, Riverside, specializing in medieval history. She spent a year at the University of Bordeaux in the south of France and worked as a teaching and research assistant at UC Riverside, eventually earning a master's degree in the subject. She now lives in Los Angeles.